The Bear and
the Nightingale

The Bear and the Nightingale

BOOK ONE OF
The Winternight Trilogy

A NOVEL

Katherine Arden

DEL REY · NEW YORK

Published in the United States by Del Rey, an imprint of Random House, a division of Penguin Random House LLC, New York.

DEL REY and the HOUSE colophon are registered trademarks of Penguin Random House LLC.

LIBRARY OF CONGRESS CATALOGING-IN-PUBLICATION DATA
NAMES: Arden, Katherine, author.
TITLE: The bear and the nightingale: a novel / Katherine Arden.
DESCRIPTION: New York: Del Rey, 2017.
IDENTIFIERS: LCCN 2016011345 (print) | LCCN 2016022241 (ebook) |
ISBN 9781101885932 (hardback) | ISBN 9781101885949 (ebook)
SUBJECTS: LCSH: Young women—Fiction. | Villages—Fiction. | Good and
evil—Fiction. | Spirits—Fiction. | Magic—Fiction. | Russia—Fiction. |
BISAC: FICTION / Fantasy / General. | FICTION /
Literary. | GSAFD: Fantasy fiction.
CLASSIFICATION: LCC PS3601.R42 B43 2017 (print) | LCC PS3601.
R42 (ebook) | DDC 813/.6—dc23 LC record available at
https://lccn.loc.gov/2016011345

Hardcover ISBN 978-1-1018-8593-2
International edition ISBN 978-0-3995-9328-4
Ebook ISBN 978-1-1018-8594-9

Printed in the United States of America on acid-free paper

randomhousebooks.com

6897

Book design by Barbara M. Bachman

To my mother
with love

By the shore of the sea stands a green oak tree;
Upon the tree is a golden chain:
And day and night a learned cat
Walks around and around on the chain;
When he goes to the right he sings a song,
When he goes to the left he tells a tale.

—A. S. PUSHKIN

Part One

ꝼROST

I T WAS LATE WINTER IN NORTHERN RUS', THE AIR SULLEN WITH wet that was neither rain nor snow. The brilliant February landscape had given way to the dreary gray of March, and the household of Pyotr Vladimirovich were all sniffling from the damp and thin from six weeks' fasting on black bread and fermented cabbage. But no one was thinking of chilblains or runny noses, or even, wistfully, of porridge and roast meats, for Dunya was to tell a story.

That evening, the old lady sat in the best place for talking: in the kitchen, on the wooden bench beside the oven. This oven was a massive affair built of fired clay, taller than a man and large enough that all four of Pyotr Vladimirovich's children could have fit easily inside. The flat top served as a sleeping platform; its innards cooked their food, heated their kitchen, and made steam-baths for the sick.

"What tale will you have tonight?" Dunya inquired, enjoying the fire at her back. Pyotr's children sat before her, perched on stools. They all loved stories, even the second son, Sasha, who was a self-consciously devout child, and would have insisted—had anyone asked him—that he preferred to pass the evening in prayer. But the church was cold, the sleet outside unrelenting. Sasha had thrust his head out-of-doors, gotten a faceful of wet, and retired, vanquished, to a stool a little apart from the others, where he sat affecting an expression of pious indifference.

The others set up a clamor on hearing Dunya's question:

"Finist the Falcon!"

"Ivan and the Gray Wolf!"

"Firebird! Firebird!"

Little Alyosha stood on his stool and waved his arms, the better to be heard over his bigger siblings, and Pyotr's boarhound raised its big, scarred head at the commotion.

But before Dunya could answer, the outer door clattered open and there came a roar from the storm without. A woman appeared in the doorway, shaking the wet from her long hair. Her face glowed with the chill, but she was thinner than even her children; the fire cast shadows in the hollows of cheek and throat and temple. Her deep-set eyes threw back the firelight. She stooped and seized Alyosha in her arms.

The child squealed in delight. "Mother!" he cried. "Matyushka!"

Marina Ivanovna sank onto her stool, drawing it nearer the blaze. Alyosha, still clasped in her arms, wound both fists around her braid. She trembled, though it was not obvious under her heavy clothes. "Pray the wretched ewe delivers tonight," she said. "Otherwise I fear we shall never see your father again. Are you telling stories, Dunya?"

"If we might have quiet," said the old lady tartly. She had been Marina's nurse, too, long ago.

"I'll have a story," said Marina at once. Her tone was light, but her eyes were dark. Dunya gave her a sharp glance. The wind sobbed outside. "Tell the story of Frost, Dunyashka. Tell us of the frost-demon, the winter-king Karachun. He is abroad tonight, and angry at the thaw."

Dunya hesitated. The elder children looked at each other. In Russian, Frost was called Morozko, the demon of winter. But long ago, the people called him Karachun, the death-god. Under that name, he was king of black midwinter who came for bad children and froze them in the night. It was an ill-omened word, and unlucky to speak it while he still held the land in his grip. Marina was holding her son very tightly. Alyosha squirmed and tugged his mother's braid.

"Very well," said Dunya after a moment's hesitation. "I shall tell the story of Morozko, of his kindness and his cruelty." She put a slight emphasis on this name: the safe name that could not bring them ill luck. Marina smiled sardonically and untangled her son's hands. None of the others made any protest, though the story of Frost was an old tale, and they had all heard it many times before. In Dunya's rich, precise voice it could not fail to delight.

"In a certain princedom—" began Dunya. She paused and fixed a quelling eye upon Alyosha, who was squealing like a bat and bouncing in his mother's arms.

"Hush," said Marina, and handed him the end of her braid again to play with.

"In a certain princedom," the old lady repeated, with dignity, "there lived a peasant who had a beautiful daughter."

"Whasser name?" mumbled Alyosha. He was old enough to test the authenticity of fairy tales by seeking precise details from the tellers.

"Her name was Marfa," said the old lady. "Little Marfa. And she was beautiful as sunshine in June, and brave and good-hearted besides. But Marfa had no mother; her own had died when she was an infant. Although her father had remarried, Marfa was still as motherless as any orphan could be. For while Marfa's stepmother was quite a handsome woman, they say, and she made delicious cakes, wove fine cloth, and brewed rich kvas, her heart was cold and cruel. She hated Marfa for the girl's beauty and goodness, favoring instead her own ugly, lazy daughter in all things. First the woman tried to make Marfa ugly in turn by giving her all the hardest work in the house, so that her hands would be twisted, her back bent, and her face lined. But Marfa was a strong girl, and perhaps possessed a bit of magic, for she did all her work uncomplainingly and went on growing lovelier and lovelier as the years passed.

"So the stepmother—" seeing Alyosha's open mouth, Dunya

added, "—Darya Nikolaevna was her name—finding she could not make Marfa hard or ugly, schemed to rid herself of the girl once and for all. Thus, one day at midwinter, Darya turned to her husband and said, 'Husband, I believe it is time for our Marfa to be wed.'

"Marfa was in the izba cooking pancakes. She looked at her step-mother with astonished joy, for the lady had never taken an interest in her, except to find fault. But her delight quickly turned to dismay.

"'—And I have just the husband for her. Load her into the sledge and take her into the forest. We shall wed her to Morozko, the lord of winter. Can any maiden ask for a finer or richer bridegroom? Why, he is master of the white snow, the black firs, and the silver frost!'

"The husband—his name was Boris Borisovich—stared in horror at his wife. Boris loved his daughter, after all, and the cold embrace of the winter god is not for mortal maidens. But perhaps Darya had a bit of magic of her own, for her husband could refuse her nothing. Weep-ing, he loaded his daughter into the sledge, drove her deep into the forest, and left her at the foot of a fir tree.

"Long the girl sat alone, and she shivered and shook and grew colder and colder. At length, she heard a great clattering and snapping. She looked up to behold Frost himself coming toward her, leaping among the trees and snapping his fingers."

"But what did he look like?" Olga demanded.

Dunya shrugged. "As to that, no two tellers agree. Some say he is naught but a cold, crackling breeze whispering among the firs. Others say he is an old man in a sledge, with bright eyes and cold hands. Others say he is like a warrior in his prime, but robed all in white, with weap-ons of ice. No one knows. But something came to Marfa as she sat there; an icy blast whipped around her face, and she grew colder than ever. And then Frost spoke to her, in the voice of the winter wind and the falling snow:

"'Are you quite warm, my beauty?'

"Marfa was a well-brought-up girl who bore her troubles uncom-plainingly, so she replied, 'Quite warm, thank you, dear Lord Frost.' At this, the demon laughed, and as he did, the wind blew harder than ever. All the trees groaned above their heads. Frost asked again, 'And now? Warm enough, sweetheart?' Marfa, though she could barely speak from the cold, again replied, 'Warm, I am warm, thank you.' Now it was a storm that raged overhead; the wind howled and gnashed its teeth until poor Marfa was certain it would tear the skin from her bones. But Frost was not laughing now, and when he asked a third time: 'Warm, my darling?' she answered, forcing the words between frozen lips as blackness danced before her eyes, 'Yes . . . warm. I am warm, my Lord Frost.'

"Then he was filled with admiration for her courage and took pity on her plight. He wrapped her in his own robe of blue brocade and laid her in his sledge. When he drove out of the forest and left the girl by her own front door, she was still wrapped in the magnificent robe and bore also a chest of gems and gold and silver ornaments. Marfa's father wept with joy to see the girl once more, but Darya and her daughter were furious to see Marfa so richly clad and radiant, with a prince's ransom at her side. So Darya turned to her husband and said, 'Husband, quickly! Take my daughter Liza up in your sledge. The gifts that Frost has given Marfa are nothing to what he will give *my* girl!'

"Though in his heart Boris protested all this folly, he took Liza up in his sledge. The girl was wearing her finest gown and wrapped in heavy fur robes. Her father took her deep into the woods and left her beneath the same fir tree. Liza in turn sat a long time. She had begun to grow very cold, despite her furs, when at last Frost came through the trees, cracking his fingers and laughing to himself. He danced right up to Liza and breathed into her face, and his breath was the wind out of the north that freezes skin to bone. He smiled and asked, 'Warm enough, darling?' Liza, shuddering, answered, 'Of course not, you fool! Can you not see that I am near perished with cold?'

"The wind blew harder than ever, howling about them in great, tearing gusts. Over the din he asked, 'And now? Quite warm?' The girl shrieked back, 'But no, idiot! I am frozen! I have never been colder in my life! I am waiting for my bridegroom Frost, but the oaf hasn't come.' Hearing this, Frost's eyes grew hard as adamant; he laid his fingers on her throat, leaned forward, and whispered into the girl's ear, 'Warm now, my pigeon?' But the girl could not answer, for she had died when he touched her and lay frozen in the snow.

"At home, Darya waited, pacing back and forth. 'Two chests of gold at least,' she said, rubbing her hands. 'A wedding-dress of silk velvet and bridal-blankets of the finest wool.' Her husband said nothing. The shadows began to lengthen and there was still no sign of her daughter. At length, Darya sent her husband out to retrieve the girl, admonishing him to have care with the chests of treasure. But when Boris reached the tree where he had left his daughter that morning, there was no treasure at all: only the girl herself, lying dead in the snow.

"With a heavy heart, the man lifted her in his arms and bore her back home. The mother ran out to meet them. 'Liza,' she called. 'My love!'

"Then she saw the corpse of her child, huddled up in the bottom of the sledge. At that moment, the finger of Frost touched Darya's heart, too, and she fell dead on the spot."

There was a small, appreciative silence.

Then Olga spoke up plaintively. "But what happened to Marfa? Did she marry him? King Frost?"

"Cold embrace, indeed," Kolya muttered to no one in particular, grinning.

Dunya gave him an austere look, but did not deign to reply.

"Well, no, Olya," she said to the girl. "I shouldn't think so. What use does Winter have for a mortal maiden? More likely she married a rich peasant, and brought him the largest dowry in all Rus'."

Olga looked ready to protest this unromantic conclusion, but Dunya had already risen with a creaking of bones, eager to retire. The top of the oven was large as a great bed, and the old and the young and the sick slept upon it. Dunya made her bed there with Alyosha.

The others kissed their mother and slipped away. At last Marina herself rose. Despite her winter clothes, Dunya saw anew how thin she had grown, and it smote the old lady's heart. *It will soon be spring,* she comforted herself. *The woods will turn green and the beasts give rich milk. I will make her pie with eggs and curds and pheasant, and the sun will make her well again.*

But the look in Marina's eyes filled the old nurse with foreboding.

2.

THE WITCH-WOMAN'S GRANDDAUGHTER

THE LAMB CAME FORTH AT LAST, DRAGGLED AND SPINDLY, BLACK as a dead tree in the rain. The ewe began licking the little thing in a peremptory way, and before long the tiny creature stood, swaying on minute hooves. "Molodets," said Pyotr Vladimirovich to the ewe, and stood up himself. His aching back protested when he drew it straight. "But you could have chosen a better night." The wind outside ground its teeth. The sheep flapped her tail nonchalantly. Pyotr grinned and left them. A fine ram, born in the jaws of a late-winter storm. It was a good omen.

Pyotr Vladimirovich was a great lord: a boyar, with rich lands and many men to do his bidding. It was only by choice that he passed his nights with his laboring stock. But always he was present when a new creature came to enrich his herds, and often he drew it to the light with his own bloody hands.

The sleet had stopped and the night was clearing. A few valiant stars showed between the clouds when Pyotr came into the dooryard and pulled the barn door shut behind him. Despite the wet, his house was buried nearly to the eaves in a winter's worth of snow. Only the pitched roof and chimneys had escaped, and the space around the door, which the men of Pyotr's household laboriously kept clear.

The summer half of the great house had wide windows and an open hearth. But that wing was shut when winter came, and it had a deserted look now, entombed in snow and sealed up in frost. The winter half of the house boasted huge ovens and small, high windows. A perpetual smoke trickled from its chimneys, and at the first hard freeze, Pyotr fitted its window-frames with slabs of ice, to block the cold but let in the light. Now firelight from his wife's room threw a flickering bar of gold onto the snow.

Pyotr thought of his wife and hurried on. Marina would be pleased about the lamb.

The walks between the outbuildings were roofed and floored with logs, defense against rain and snow and mud. But the sleet had come with the dawn, and the slanting wet had soaked the wood and frozen solid. The footing was treacherous, and the damp drifts loomed head-high, pockmarked with sleet. But Pyotr's felt-and-fur boots were sure on the ice. He paused in the drowsing kitchen to ladle water over his slimy hands. Atop the oven, Alyosha turned over and whimpered in his sleep.

His wife's room was small—in deference to the frost—but it was bright, and by the standards of the north, luxurious. Swaths of woven fabric covered the wooden walls. The beautiful carpet—part of Marina's dowry—had come by long and circuitous roads from Tsargrad itself. Fantastic carving adorned the wooden stools, and blankets of wolf and rabbit skin lay scattered in downy heaps.

The small stove in the corner threw off a fiery glow. Marina had not gone to bed; she sat near the fire, wrapped in a robe of white wool, combing her hair. Even after four children, her hair was still thick and dark and fell nearly to her knee. In the forgiving firelight, she looked very like the bride that Pyotr had brought to his house so long ago.

"Is it done?" asked Marina. She laid her comb aside and began to plait her hair. Her eyes never left the oven.

"Yes," said Pyotr, distractedly. He was stripping off his kaftan in the grateful warmth. "A handsome ram. And its mother is well, too— a good omen."

Marina smiled.

"I am glad of it, for we shall need one," she said. "I am with child."

Pyotr started, caught with his shirt half off. He opened his mouth and closed it again. It was, of course, possible. She was old for it, though, and she had grown so thin that winter . . .

"Another one?" he asked. He straightened up and put his shirt aside.

Marina heard the distress in his tone, and a sad smile touched her mouth. She bound the end of her hair with a leather cord before replying. "Yes," she said, flicking the plait over her shoulder. "A girl. She will be born in the autumn."

"Marina . . ."

His wife heard the silent question. "I wanted her," she said. "I want her still." And then, lower: "I want a daughter like my mother was."

Pyotr frowned. Marina never spoke of her mother. Dunya, who had been with Marina in Moscow, referred to her only rarely.

In the reign of Ivan I, or so said the stories, a ragged girl rode through the kremlin-gates, alone except for her tall gray horse. Despite filth and hunger and weariness, rumors dogged her footsteps. She had such grace, the people said, and eyes like the swan-maiden in a fairy tale. At length, the rumors reached the ear of the Grand Prince. "Bring her to me," Ivan said, thinly amused. "I have never seen a swan-maiden."

Ivan Kalita was a hard prince, eaten with ambition, cold and clever and grasping. He would not have survived otherwise: Moscow killed her princes quickly. And yet, the boyars said afterward, when Ivan first saw this girl, he sat unmoving for a full ten minutes. Some of the more fanciful swore that his eyes were wet when he went to her and took her hand.

Ivan was twice widowed by then, his eldest son older than his young lover, and yet a year later he married the mysterious girl. However, even the Grand Prince of Moscow could not silence the whispers. The princess would not say where she had come from: not then and not ever. The serving-women muttered that she could tame animals, dream the future, and summon rain.

※

PYOTR COLLECTED HIS OUTER CLOTHES and hung them near the oven. A practical man, he had always shrugged at rumors. But his wife sat so very still, looking into the fire. Only the flames moved, gilding her hand and throat. She made Pyotr uneasy. He paced the wooden floor.

Rus' had been Christian ever since Vladimir baptized all of Kiev in the Dneiper and dragged the old gods through the streets. Still, the land was vast and changed slowly. Five hundred years after the monks came to Kiev, Rus' still teemed with unknown powers, and some of them had lain reflected in the strange princess's knowing eyes. The Church did not like it. At the bishops' insistence, Marina, her only child, was married off to a boyar in the howling wilderness, many days' travel from Moscow.

Pyotr often blessed his good fortune. His wife was wise as she was beautiful; he loved her and she him. But Marina never talked about her mother. Pyotr never asked. Their daughter, Olga, was an ordinary girl, pretty and obliging. They had no need for another, certainly not an heir to the rumored powers of a strange grandmother.

"You are sure you have the strength for it?" Pyotr said finally. "Even Alyosha was a surprise, and that was three years ago."

"Yes," said Marina, turning to look at him. Her hand clenched slowly into a fist, but he did not see. "I will see her born."

There was a pause.

"Marina, what your mother was . . ."

His wife took his hand and stood. He wound an arm around her waist and felt her stiff under his touch.

"I do not know," said Marina. "She had gifts that I have not; I remember how in Moscow the noblewomen whispered. But power is a birthright to the women of her bloodline. Olga is your daughter more than mine, but this one"—Marina's free hand slipped up, shaping a cradle to hold a baby—"this one will be different."

Pyotr drew his wife closer. She clung to him, suddenly fierce. Her heart beat against his breast. She was warm in his arms. He smelled the scent of her hair, washed clean in the bathhouse. *It is late,* Pyotr thought. *Why borrow trouble?* The work of women was to bear children. His wife had already given him four, but surely she would manage another. If the infant proved strange in some way—well, that bridge could be crossed when necessary.

"Bear her in good health, then, Marina Ivanovna," he said. His wife smiled. Her back was to the fire, so he did not see her eyelashes wet. He tilted her chin up and kissed her. Her pulse beat in her throat. But she was so thin, fragile as a bird beneath her heavy robe. "Come to bed," he said. "There will be milk tomorrow; the ewe can spare a little. Dunya will bake it for you. You must think of the babe."

Marina pressed her body to his. He picked her up as in the days of their courting and spun her around. She laughed and wound her arms around his neck. But her eyes looked an instant past him, staring into the fire as though she could read the future in the flames.

❧

"GET RID OF IT," said Dunya the next day. "I don't care if you're carrying a girl or a prince or a prophet of old." The sleet had crept back with the dawn and thundered again without. The two women huddled near the oven, for warmth and for its light on their mending. Dunya stabbed her needle home with particular vehemence. "The sooner the better. You've neither the weight nor the strength to carry a child, and if by a miracle you did, the bearing would kill you. You've given three sons to your husband, and you have your girl—what need of another?" Dunya had been Marina's nurse in Moscow, had followed her to her husband's house and nursed all of her four children in turn. She spoke as she pleased.

Marina smiled with a hint of mockery. "Such talk, Dunyashka," she said. "What would Father Semyon say?"

"Father Semyon is not likely to die in childbed, is he? Whereas you, Marushka . . ."

Marina looked down at her work and said nothing. But when she met her nurse's narrowed eyes, her face was pale as water, so that Dunya fancied she could see the blood creeping down her throat. Dunya felt a chill. "Child, what have you seen?"

"It doesn't matter," said Marina.

"Get rid of it," said Dunya, almost pleading.

"Dunya, I must have this one; she will be like my mother."

"Your mother! The ragged maiden who rode alone out of the forest? Who faded to a dim shadow of herself because she could not bear to live her life behind Byzantine screens? Have you forgotten that gray crone she became? Stumbling veiled to church? Hiding in her rooms, eating until she was round and greasy with her eyes all blank? Your mother. Would you wish that on any child of yours?"

Dunya's voice creaked like a calling raven, for she remembered, to her grief, the girl who had come to Ivan Kalita's halls, lost and frail and achingly beautiful, trailing miracles behind her. Ivan was besotted. The princess—well, perhaps she had found peace with him, at least for a little. But they housed her in the women's quarters, dressed her in heavy brocades, gave her icons and servants and rich meats. Little by little that fiery glow, the light to take one's breath, had faded. Dunya had mourned her passing long before they put her in the ground.

Marina smiled bitterly and shook her head. "No. But remember before? You used to tell me stories."

"A lot of good magic or miracles did her," growled Dunya.

"I have only a little of her gift," Marina went on, ignoring her old nurse. Dunya knew her lady well enough to hear the regret. "But my daughter will have more."

"And that is reason enough to leave the other four motherless?"

Marina looked at her lap. "I—no. Yes. If need be." Her voice was barely audible. "But I might live." She raised her head. "You will give me your word to care for them, will you not?"

"Marushka, I am old. I can give my promise, but when I die . . ."

"They will be all right. They—they will have to be. Dunya, I cannot see the future, but I will live to see her born."

Dunya crossed herself and said no more.

3.

THE BEGGAR AND
THE STRANGER

THE FIRST SCREAMING WINDS OF NOVEMBER RATTLED THE BARE trees on the day Marina's pains came on her, and the child's first cry mingled with their howl. Marina laughed to see her daughter born. "Her name is Vasilisa," she said to Pyotr. "My Vasya."

The wind dropped at dawn. In the silence, Marina breathed out once, gently, and died.

The snow hurried down like tears the day a stone-faced Pyotr laid his wife in the earth. His infant daughter screamed all through the funeral: a demon wail like the absent wind.

All that winter, the house echoed with the child's cries. More than once, Dunya and Olga despaired of her, for she was a scrawny, pallid infant, all eyes and flailing limbs. More than once Kolya threatened, half in earnest, to pitch her out of the house.

But the winter passed and the child lived. She ceased screaming and throve on the milk of peasant women.

The years slipped by like leaves.

On a day much like the one that brought her into the world, on the steely cusp of winter, Marina's black-haired girl-child crept into the winter kitchen. She put her hands on the hearthstone and craned to see over the edge. Her eyes glistened. Dunya was scooping cakes from the ashes. The whole house smelled of honey. "Are the cakes ready, Dun-yashka?" she said, poking her head into the oven.

"Nearly," said Dunya, hauling the child back before she could set her hair on fire. "If you will sit quiet on your stool, Vasochka, and mend your blouse, then you will have one all to yourself."

Vasya, thinking of cakes, went meekly to her stool. There was a heap of them already cooling on the table, brown on the outside and flecked with ash. A corner of one cake crumbled as the child watched. Its insides were midsummer-gold, and a little curl of steam rose up. Vasya swallowed. Her morning porridge seemed a year ago.

Dunya shot her a warning look. Vasya pursed her lips virtuously and set to sewing. But the rip in her blouse was large, her hunger vast, and her patience negligible even under better circumstances. Her stitches grew larger and larger, like gaps in an old man's teeth. At last Vasya could stand it no more. She put the blouse aside and crept nearer that steaming plate, on the table just out of reach. Dunya had her back to it, stooping over the oven.

Closer still the girl crept, stealthy as a kitten after grasshoppers. Then she pounced. Three cakes vanished into her linen sleeve. Dunya spun round, caught a glimpse of the child's face. "Vasya—" she began sternly, but Vasya, frightened and laughing all at once, was already over the threshold and out into the sullen day.

The season was just turning, the drab fields full of shaved stubble and dusted with snow. Vasya, chewing her honeycake and contemplat-ing hiding-places, ran across the dooryard, down among the peasants' huts, and thence through the palisade-gate. It was cold, but Vasya did not think of it. She had been born to cold.

Vasilisa Petrovna was an ugly little girl: skinny as a reed-stem with long-fingered hands and enormous feet. Her eyes and mouth were too big for the rest of her. Olga called her frog, and thought nothing of it. But the child's eyes were the color of the forest during a summer thun-derstorm, and her wide mouth was sweet. She could be sensible when she wished—and clever—so much so that her family looked at each other, bewildered, each time she abandoned sense and took yet another madcap idea into her head.

A mound of disturbed earth showed raw against the patchy snow, just at the edge of the harvested rye-field. It had not been there the day before. Vasya went to investigate. She smelled the wind as she scampered and knew it would snow in the night. The clouds lay like wet wool above the trees.

A small boy, nine years old and Pyotr Vladimirovich in miniature, stood at the bottom of a respectable hole, digging at the frosty earth. Vasya came to the edge and peered down.

"What's that, Lyoshka?" she said, around a mouthful.

Her brother leaned on his spade, squinting up at her. "What's it to you?" Alyosha quite liked Vasya, who was up for anything—nearly as good as a younger brother—but he was almost three years older and had to keep her in her place.

"Don't know," said Vasya, chewing. "Cake?" She held out half of her last one with a little regret; it was the fattest and least ashy.

"Give," said Alyosha, dropping his shovel and holding out a filthy hand. But Vasya put herself out of range.

"Tell me what you're doing," she said. Alyosha glared, but Vasya narrowed her eyes and made to eat the cake. Her brother relented.

"It's a fort to live in," he said. "For when the Tatars come. So I can hide in here and shoot them full of arrows."

Vasya had never seen a Tatar, and she did not have a clear notion of what size fort would be required to protect oneself from one. Nonetheless she looked doubtfully at the hole. "It's not very big."

Alyosha rolled his eyes. "That's why I'm digging, you rabbit," he said. "To make it bigger. Now will you give?"

Vasya started to hold out the honeycake but then she hesitated. "I want to dig the hole and shoot the Tatars, too."

"Well, you can't. You don't have a bow or a shovel."

Vasya scowled. Alyosha had gotten his own knife and a bow for his seventh name-day, but a year's worth of pleading had borne no fruit as far as weapons for her were concerned. "It doesn't matter," she said. "I can dig with a stick, and Father will give me a bow later."

"No, he won't." But Alyosha made no objection when Vasya handed over half the cake and went to find a stick. They worked for some minutes in companionable silence.

But digging with a stick soon palls, even if one is jumping up every few moments to look about for the wicked Tatars. Vasya was beginning to wonder whether Alyosha might be persuaded to leave off fort-building and go climb trees, when suddenly a shadow loomed over them both: their sister, Olga, breathless and furious, roused from a place by the fire to uncover her truant siblings. She glared down at them. "Mud to the eyebrows, what *will* Dunya say? And Father—" Here Olga broke off to make a fortuitous lunge, seizing the clumsier Alyosha by the back of his jacket just as the children broke cover like a pair of frightened quail.

Vasilisa was long-limbed for a girl, quick in her movements, and it was well worth a scolding to eat her last crumbs in peace. So she did not look back but ran like a hare over the empty field, dodging stumps with whoops of glee, until she was swallowed by the afternoon forest. Olga was left panting, holding on to Alyosha by his collar.

"Why don't you ever catch *her*?" said Alyosha, with some resentment, as Olga towed him back to the house. "She's only six."

"Because I am not Kaschei the Deathless," said Olga with some asperity. "And I have no horse to outrun the wind."

They stepped into the kitchen. Olga deposited Alyosha beside the oven. "I couldn't catch Vasya," she said to Dunya. The old lady raised her eyes heavenward. Vasya was extremely hard to catch when she did not wish to be caught. Only Sasha could do it with any regularity. Dunya turned her wrath on a shrinking Alyosha. She stripped the child beside the oven, sponged him with a cloth that, thought Alyosha, must have been made of nettles, and dressed him in a clean shirt.

"Such goings-on," muttered Dunya while she scrubbed. "I'll tell your father, you know, next time. He'll have you carting and chopping and mucking for the rest of the winter. *Such* goings-on. Filth and digging holes—"

But she was interrupted in her tirade. Alyosha's two tall brothers came stamping into the winter kitchen, smelling of smoke and livestock. Unlike Vasya, they did not resort to subterfuge; they made straight for the cakes, and each shoved one whole into his mouth. "A wind from the south," said Nikolai Petrovich—called Kolya—the eldest, to his sister, his voice indistinct from chewing. Olga had regained her wonted composure and sat knitting beside the oven. "It will snow in the night. A good job the beasts are in and the roof is finished." Kolya dropped his sopping winter boots near the fire and flung himself onto a stool, seizing another cake in passing.

Olga and Dunya eyed the boots with identical expressions of disapproval. Frozen mud had spattered the clean hearth. Olga crossed herself. "If the weather is changing, then half the village will be ill tomorrow," she said. "I hope Father comes in before the snow." She frowned as she counted stitches.

The second young man did not speak, but deposited his armload of firewood, swallowed his cake, and went to kneel before the icons in the corner opposite the door. Now he crossed himself, stood, and kissed the image of the Virgin. "Praying again, Sasha?" said Kolya with cheerful malice. "Pray the snow comes gently, and Father not catch cold."

The young man shrugged slim shoulders. He had wide, grave eyes, thick-lashed as a girl's. "I do pray, Kolya," he said. "You might try it yourself." He padded to the oven and peeled off his damp stockings. The pungent stink of wet wool joined the general smell of mud and cabbage and animals. Sasha had spent his day with the horses. Olga wrinkled her nose.

Kolya did not rise to the jab. He was examining one of his sopping winter boots, where the fur had separated at the stitching. He grunted with disgust and let it drop next to its fellow. Both boots began to steam. The oven towered over the four of them. Dunya had already put in the stew for dinner, and Alyosha watched the pot like a cat at a mouse-hole.

"What goings-on, Dunya?" Sasha inquired. He had come into the kitchen in time to hear the tirade.

"Vasya," said Olga succinctly, and told the story of the honeycakes and her sister's escape into the forest. As she talked, she knitted. The faintest of rueful smiles dimpled her mouth. She was still fat with summer's bounty, round-faced and lovely.

Sasha laughed. "Well, Vasya will come back when she gets hungry," he said, and turned to more important matters. "Is that pike in the stew, Dunya?"

"Tench," said Dunya shortly. "Oleg brought four at dawn. But that strange sister of yours is too small to linger in the woods."

Sasha and Olga looked at each other, shrugged, and said nothing. Vasya had been disappearing into the forest ever since she could walk. She would come back in time for dinner, as always, bearing a handful of pine-nuts in apology, flushed and repentant, catlike on her booted feet.

But in this case they were wrong. The brittle sun slipped across the sky, and the shadows of the trees stretched monstrously long. At last Pyotr Vladimirovich himself came into the house, bearing a hen-pheasant by its broken neck. Still Vasya had not come back.

※

THE FOREST WAS QUIET on the cusp of winter, the snow thicker between the trees. Vasilisa Petrovna, half-ashamed and half-pleased with her freedom, ate her last half honeycake stretched out on the cold limb of a tree, listening to the soft noises of the drowsing forest. "I know you sleep when the snow comes," she said aloud. "But couldn't you wake up? See, I have cakes."

She held out the evidence, now little more than crumbs, and paused as though expecting a reply. But none came, beyond a soft, rattling wind that stirred all the trees together.

So Vasya shrugged, dabbed up the crumbs of her honeycake, and ran about the wood awhile, looking for pine-nuts. The squirrels had eaten them all, though, and the forest was cold, even to a girl born to it. At last, Vasya brushed the ice and bark from her clothes and set her feet for home, finally feeling the pricking of conscience. The forest was thick with shade; the shortening days slid rapidly to night, and she hurried. She would get a thundering scold, but Dunya would have dinner waiting.

On and on she went, and then paused, frowning. Left at the gray alder, round the wicked old elm, and then she would see her father's fields. She had walked that path a thousand times. But now there was no alder and no elm, only a cluster of black-needled spruces and a little snowy meadow. Vasya swung round, tried a new direction. No, here were slender beeches, standing white as maidens, naked with winter and trembling. Vasya was suddenly uneasy. She could not be lost; she was never lost. Might as well be lost in her own house as lost in the woods. A wind picked up that set all the trees to shaking, but now they were trees she did not know.

Lost, Vasya thought. She was lost in the dusk on the cusp of winter and it was going to snow. She turned again, tried another direction. But in that wavering wood, there was not one tree she knew. The tears welled suddenly in her eyes. *Lost, I am lost.* She wanted Olya or Dunya; she wanted her father and Sasha. She wanted her soup and her blanket and even her mending.

An oak-tree loomed in her way. The child stopped. This tree was not like the others. It was bigger and blacker and gnarled like a wicked old woman. The wind shook its great black branches.

Vasya, beginning to shiver, crept toward it. She laid a hand on the bark. It was like any other tree, rough and cold even through the fur of her mitten. Vasya stepped around it, craning up at the branches. Then she looked down and nearly tripped.

A man lay curled like a beast at the foot of this tree, fast asleep. She could not see his face; it was hidden between his arms. Through rents in his clothes, she glimpsed cold white skin. He did not stir at her approach.

Well, he could not lie there sleeping, not with snow coming out of the south. He would die. And perhaps he knew where her father's house lay. Vasya reached out to shake him awake but thought better of it. Instead, she said, "Grandfather, wake up! There will be snow before moonrise. *Wake up!*"

For long moments, the man did not stir. But just when Vasya was nerving herself to lay a hand on his shoulder, there came a snuffling grunt, and the man raised his face and blinked one eye at her.

The child recoiled. One side of his face was fair, in a rough-hewn way. One eye was gray. But the other eye was missing, the socket sewn shut, and that side of his face a mass of bluish scars.

The good eye blinked sulkily at the girl, and the man sat back on his haunches as though to see her better. He was a thin creature, ragged and filthy. Vasya could see his ribs through the rents in his shirt. But when he spoke, his voice was strong and deep.

"Well," he said. "It is a long time since I have seen a Russian girl."

Vasya did not understand. "Do you know where we are?" she said. "I am lost. My father is Pyotr Vladimirovich. If you can take me home, he will see you fed, and give you a place beside the oven. It is going to snow."

The one-eyed man smiled suddenly. He had two dog-teeth, longer than the rest, that dented his lip when he smiled. He came to his feet, and Vasya saw that he was a tall man with big, crude bones. "Do I know where we are?" he said. "Well, of course, devochka, little maiden. I'll take you home. But you must come here and help me."

Vasya, spoiled since she could remember, had no particular reason to be untrusting. Yet she did not stir.

The gray eye narrowed. "What manner of girl-child comes here, all alone?" And then, softer, "Such eyes. Almost I remember . . . Well, come here." He made his voice coaxing. "Your father will be worried."

He bent his gray eye upon her. Vasya, frowning, took a small step toward him. Then another. He put out a hand.

Suddenly there came the crunch of hooves in the snow, and the snorting breaths of a horse. The one-eyed man recoiled. The child stumbled backward, away from his outstretched hand, and the man fell to the earth, cringing. A horse and rider stepped into the clearing. The horse was white and strong; when her rider slid to the ground, Vasya saw that he was slender and bold-boned, the skin drawn tight over cheek and throat. He wore a rich robe of heavy fur, and his eyes gleamed blue.

"What is this?" he said.

The ragged man cringed. "No concern of yours," he said. "She came to me—she is mine."

The newcomer turned a clear, cold look on him. His voice filled the clearing. "Is she? Sleep, Medved, for it is winter."

And even as the sleeper protested, he sank once more to his place between the oak-roots. The gray eye filmed over.

The rider turned on Vasya. The child edged backward, poised on the edge of flight. "How came you here, devochka?" said this man. He spoke with swift authority.

Tears of confusion spilled down Vasya's cheeks. The one-eyed man's avid face had frightened her, and this man's fierce urgency frightened her, too. But something in his glance silenced her weeping. She lifted her eyes to his face. "I am Vasilisa Petrovna," she said. "My father is lord of Lesnaya Zemlya."

They looked at each other for a moment. And then Vasya's brief courage was gone; she spun and bolted. The stranger made no attempt to follow. But he did turn to his horse when the mare came up beside him. The two exchanged a long look.

"He is getting stronger," said the man.

The mare flicked an ear.

Her rider did not speak again, but glanced once more in the direction the child had taken.

⚜

OUT FROM THE SHADOW of the oak, Vasya was startled by how fast night had fallen. Beneath the tree, it had been indeterminate dusk, but now it was night, woolly night on the cusp of snow, the air all dour with it. The wood was full of torches and the desperate shouts of men. Vasya cared nothing for them; she recognized the trees again, and she wanted only Olga's arms, and Dunya's.

A horse came galloping out of the night, whose rider bore no torch. The mare saw the child an instant before her rider did, and skidded to a halt, rearing. Vasya tumbled to one side, skinning her hand. She thrust a fist into her mouth to muffle her cry. The rider muttered imprecations in a voice she knew, and the next instant, she was caught up in her brother's arms. "Sashka," sobbed Vasya, burying her face against his neck. "I was lost. There was a man in the forest. Two men. And a white horse, and a black tree, and I was afraid."

"What men?" demanded Sasha. "Where, child? Are you hurt?" He put her away from him and felt her over.

"No," quavered Vasya. "No—I am only cold."

Sasha said nothing; she could tell he was angry, though he was gentle when he put her on his mare. He swung up behind and wrapped her in a fold of his cloak. Vasya, safe, with her cheek against the well-tended leather of his sword-belt, slowly ceased her weeping.

Ordinarily Sasha tolerated his small sister following him about, trying to lift his sword or pluck the string of his bow. He indulged her, even, giving her a stump of candle, or a handful of hazelnuts. But now fear had made him furious and he did not speak to her as they rode.

He shouted left and right, and slowly word of Vasya's rescue passed among the men. If she had not been found before the snow came, she would have died in the night, and only been discovered when the spring came to loosen her shroud—if she was found at all.

"Dura," growled Sasha at last, when he had done shouting, "little fool, what possessed you? Running from Olga, hiding in the woods? Did you think yourself a wood-sprite, or forget the season?"

Vasya shook her head. She was shivering in hard spurts now. Her teeth clattered together. "I wanted to eat my cake," she said. "But I got lost. I couldn't find the elm-stump. I met a man at the oak-tree. Two men. And a horse. And then it was dark."

Sasha frowned over her head. "Tell me of this oak-tree," he said.

"An old one," said Vasya. "With roots about its knees. And one-eyed. The man, not the tree." She shivered harder than ever.

"Well, do not think of it now," said Sasha, and urged on his tired horse.

Olga and Dunya met him at the threshold. The good old lady had tears all over her face and Olga was white as a frost-maiden in a fairy tale. They had raked all the coals out of the oven, and they poured water on the hot stones to make steam. Vasya found herself unceremoniously stripped and shoved into the oven-mouth to warm.

The scolding began as soon as she was out.

"Stealing cakes," said Dunya. "Running away from your sister. How could you frighten us so, Vasochka?" She wept as she said it.

Vasya, heavy-eyed and repentant, murmured, "I'm sorry, Dunya. Sorry, sorry."

She was rubbed with horrible mustard-seed, and beaten with quick, whisking birch-branches, to liven her blood. They wrapped her in wool, bandaged her skinned hand, and poured soup down her throat.

"It was very wicked, Vasya," Olga said. She smoothed her sister's hair and cradled her on her lap. Vasya was already asleep.

"Enough for tonight, Dunya," Olga added. "Tomorrow is soon enough for more talk."

Vasya was put to bed atop the oven, and Dunya lay down beside her.

When at last her sister slept, Olga sank down limp beside the fire. Her father and brothers sat spooning up their stew in a corner, wearing identical thunderous expressions. "She'll be all right," said Olga. "I do not think she'll take a chill."

"But any man might, who was called from his hearth to look for her," snapped Pyotr.

"Or *I* might," said Kolya. "A man wants his dinner after a day of mending his father's roof, not a night's ride by torchlight. I'll belt her tomorrow."

"And so?" retorted Sasha coolly. "She's been belted before. It is not the task of men to manage girl-children. It wants a woman. Dunya is old. Olya will marry soon, and then the old lady will be left alone to raise the child."

Pyotr said nothing. Six years since he put his wife in the earth, and he had not thought of another, though there were many who would have heard his suit. But his daughter had frightened him.

When Kolya had sought his bed, and he and Sasha sat together in the dark, watching the candle burn low before the icon, Pyotr said, "Would you see your mother forgotten?"

"Vasya never knew her," rejoined Sasha. "But a woman of sense— not a sister or a kindly old nurse—would do her good. She will soon be unmanageable, Father."

A long pause.

"It is not Vasya's fault Mother died," added Sasha, lower.

Pyotr said nothing, and Sasha rose, bowed to his father, and blew out the candle.

THE GRAND PRINCE
OF MUSCOVY

PYOTR THRASHED HIS DAUGHTER THE NEXT DAY, AND SHE WEPT, though he was not cruel. She was forbidden to leave the village, but for once, that was no hardship. She had taken the threatened chill, and she had nightmares in which she revisited a one-eyed man, a horse, and a stranger in a clearing in the woods.

Sasha, though he told no one, ranged the forest to the west, looking for this one-eyed man, or an oak-tree with roots about its knees. But never man nor tree did he find, and then the snow fell for three days, straight and hard, so that none went out.

Their lives drew in, as always in the winter, a round of food and sleep and small drowsy chores. The snow mounded up outside, and on a bitter evening Pyotr sat on his own stool, smoothing a straight piece of ash for an ax-handle. His face was set like stone, for he was remembering what he had pleased to forget. *Take care of her,* Marina had said, so many years ago, as the tinge of mortal illness spread over her lovely face. *I chose her, she is important. Petya, promise me.*

Pyotr, grieving, had promised. But then his wife had let go his hand, had lain back in her bed, and her eyes had looked beyond him. She smiled once, soft and joyful, but Pyotr did not think the look was for him. She did not speak again and died in the gray hour before dawn.

And then, Pyotr thought. *They made ready a hole to receive her, and I bellowed at the women who tried to bar me from the death-chamber. I myself—I wrapped her cold flesh, that stank still of blood, and with my own two hands put her in the ground.*

All that winter his infant daughter had screamed, and he could not bear to look the baby in the face, because her mother had chosen the child and not him.

Well, now he must make amends.

Pyotr squinted at his ax-handle. "I am going to Moscow when the rivers freeze," he said into the silence.

The room erupted in exclamations. Vasya, who had been drowsing, heavy with fever and hot honey-wine, squeaked and poked her head over the side of the oven.

"To Moscow, Father?" asked Kolya. "Again?"

Pyotr's lips thinned. He had gone to Moscow in that first, bitter winter after Marina's death. Ivan Ivanovich, Marina's half brother, was Grand Prince, and for his family's sake, Pyotr had salvaged what he could of their connection. But he had taken no woman, then or later.

"You mean to marry this time," said Sasha.

Pyotr nodded curtly, feeling the weight of his family's stare. There were women enough in the provinces, but a Muscovite lady would bring alliances and money. Ivan's indulgence for the husband of his dead sister would not last forever. And, for his small daughter's sake, he needed a new wife. But . . . *Marina, what a fool I am, to think I cannot bear it.*

"Sasha and Kolya, you will come with me," Pyotr said.

Delight quite overspread the censure on his sons' faces. "To Moscow, Father?" asked Kolya.

"It is two weeks' riding if all goes well," said Pyotr. "I will need you on the road. And you have never been to court. The Grand Prince ought to know your faces."

There was chaos in the kitchen then, as the boys exchanged delighted exclamations. Vasya and Alyosha both clamored to go. Olga begged for jewels and good cloth. The elder boys retorted gloatingly, and in arguing, pleading, and speculation, the evening passed.

༄༅

THE SNOW FELL THRICE, deep and solid, after midwinter, and after the last snowfall came a great blue frost, when men felt their breath stop in their nostrils and weak things grew apt to die in the night. That meant the sledge-roads were open, the roads that ran down snow-covered rivers smooth as glass and sparkled over dirt tracks that in summer were a misery of ruts and broken axles. The boys watched the sky and felt of the frost and took to pacing the house, oiling their greasy boots and scraping the hair-fine edges of their spears.

At last the day came. Pyotr and his sons rose in the dark and spilled into the dooryard as soon as it grew light. The men were gathered already. The keen dawn reddened their faces; their beasts stamped and snorted clouds of steam. A man had saddled Buran, Pyotr's evil-tempered Mongol stallion, and was clinging, white-knuckled, to the beast's headstall. Pyotr slapped his waiting mount, dodged the snapping teeth, and swung into the saddle. His grateful attendant fell back, gasping.

Pyotr kept half an eye on his unpredictable stallion; the rest was for the seeming chaos around him.

The stable-yard seethed with bodies, with beasts, with sledges. Furs lay mounded beside boxes of beeswax and candles. The jars of mead and honey jostled for room with bundles of dried provisions. Kolya was directing the loading of the last sledge, his nose red in the morning chill. He had his mother's black eyes; the serving-girls giggled as he passed.

A basket fell with a thud and a puff of dry snow, almost under the feet of a sledge-horse. The beast shied forward and sideways. Kolya sprang out of the way, and Pyotr started forward, but Sasha was before them. He was off his mare like a cat, and next instant had caught the horse by its headstall, talking into its ear. The horse stilled, looking abashed. Pyotr watched as Sasha pointed, said something. The men hurried to take the horse's rein and seize the offending basket. Sasha said something else, grinning, and they all laughed. The boy remounted his mare. His seat was better than his brother's; he had an affinity for horses, and he bore his sword with grace. *A warrior born,* thought Pyotr, *and a leader of men; Marina, I am fortunate in my sons.*

Olga ran out the kitchen door, Vasya trotting in her footsteps. The girls' embroidered sarafans stood out against the snow. Olga held her apron in both hands; piled within were dark, tender loaves, hot from the oven. Kolya and Sasha were already converging. Vasya tugged on her second brother's cloak while he ate his loaf. "But why may I not come, Sashka?" she said. "I will cook your supper for you. Dunya showed me how. I can ride your horse with you; I am small enough." She clung to his cloak with both hands.

"Not this year, little frog," Sasha said. "You *are* small—too small." Seeing her eyes sad, he knelt in the snow beside her and pressed the remainder of his bread into her hand. "Eat and grow strong, little sister," he said, "so that you are fitted for journeys. God keep you." He put a hand on her head, then sprang again to the back of his brown Mysh. "Sashka!" cried Vasya, but he was away, calling swift orders to the men loading the last wagon.

Olga took her sister's hand and tugged. "Come on, Vasochka," she said when the child dragged her feet. The girls ran up to Pyotr. The last loaf was cooling in Olga's hand.

"Safe journey, Father," Olga said.

How little my Olya is like her mother, Pyotr thought, *for all she has her face. Just as well—Marina was like a hawk in a cage. Olga is gentler. I will make her a fine marriage.* He smiled down at his daughters. "God keep you both," he said. "Perhaps I will bring you a husband, Olya." Vasya made a sound like a muted growl. Olga blushed and laughed, and almost dropped the bread. Pyotr stooped in time to seize it and was glad he had; she had slit the crust and spooned honey inside, to melt in the heat. He tore off a great hunk—his teeth were still good—and paused, blissfully chewing.

"And you, Vasya," he added, stern. "Mind your sister, and stay near the house."

"Yes, Father," said Vasya, but she looked longingly at the riding-horses.

Pyotr wiped his mouth with the back of his hand. The mob had come to something resembling order. "Farewell, my daughters," he said. "We are going; mind the sledges." Olga nodded, a little wistful. Vasya did not nod at all; she looked mutinous. There was a chorus of shouting, the cracking of whips, and then they were away.

Behind them Olga and Vasilisa stood alone in the dooryard, listening to the bells on the wagons until they were swallowed up by the morning.

⧉

TWO WEEKS AFTER SETTING OUT, with plenty of delay but no disas-ter, Pyotr and his sons passed the outer rings of Moscow, that seething, jumped-up trading post on a hill beside the Moskva River. They smelled the city long before they saw it, hazed as it was with the smoke of ten thousand fires, and then the brilliant domes—green and scarlet and cobalt—showed dimly through the vapor. At last they saw the city it-self, lusty and squalid, like a fair woman with feet caked in filth. The high golden towers rose proudly above the desperate poor, and the gold-fretted icons watched, inscrutable, while princes and farmers' wives came to kiss their stiff faces and pray.

The streets were all snowy mud, churned by innumerable feet. Beg-gars, their noses winter-blackened, clutched at the boys' stirrups. Kolya kicked them off, but Sasha clasped their grimy hands. The red winter sun was tilting west when at last they came, weary and mud-splattered, to a massive wooden gate, bound in bronze and topped with towers. A dozen spearmen watched the road, with archers on the wall.

They looked coldly at Pyotr, his sledges and his sons, but Pyotr passed their captain a jar of good mead, and instantly the hard faces softened. Pyotr bowed, first to the captain and then to his men, and the guards waved them through in a chorus of compliments.

The kremlin was a town in itself: palaces, huts, stables, smithies, and countless half-built churches. Though the original walls had been built with a double thickness of oak, the years had rotted the timber to matchwood. Marina's half brother, the Grand Prince Ivan Ivanovich, had commissioned their replacement with walls more massive still. The air reeked of the clay that had been caked on the timber, meager protection against fire. Everywhere carpenters called back and forth, shaking sawdust from their beards. Servants, priests, boyars, guardsmen, and merchants milled about, bickering. Tatars riding fine horses rubbed shoulders with Russian merchants directing laden sledges. Each broke out shouting at the other on the slightest pretext. Kolya gawked at the crush, masking nervousness with a high head. His horse jerked at its rider's touch on the reins.

Pyotr had been to Moscow before. A few peremptory words unearthed stabling for their horses and a place for their wagons. "See to the horses," he said to Oleg, the steadiest of his men. "Do not leave them." There were idle servants on all sides, narrow-eyed merchants, and boyars in barbaric finery. A horse would disappear in an instant and be forever lost. Oleg nodded, and one rough fingertip grazed the hilt of his long knife.

They had sent word of their coming. Their messenger met them outside the stable. "You are summoned, my lord," he said to Pyotr. "The Grand Prince is at table, and greets his brother from the north."

The road from Lesnaya Zemlya had been long; Pyotr was grimed, bruised, cold, and weary. "Very well," he said curtly. "We are coming. Leave that." The last was to Sasha, who was digging balled-up ice out of his horse's hoof.

They splashed frigid water on their grimy faces, drew on kaftans of thick wool and hats of shining sable, and laid aside their swords. The fortress-town was a warren of churches and wooden palaces, the ground churned to muck, the air smarting with smoke. Pyotr followed the messenger with a quick step. Behind him Sasha gazed narrow-eyed at the gilded domes and painted towers. Kolya was scarcely less circumspect, though he stared more at the fine horses and the weapons of the men who rode them.

They came to a double door of oak that opened onto a hall packed full of men and crawling with dogs. The great tables groaned with good things. On the far end of the hall, on a high carven seat, sat a man with bright hair, eating slices off the joint that lay dripping before him.

Ivan II was styled Ivan Krasnii, or Ivan the Fair. He was no longer young—perhaps thirty. His elder brother Semyon had ruled before him, but Semyon and his issue had all died of plague in one bitter summer.

The Grand Prince of Moscow was indeed very fair. His hair gleamed like palest honey. Women swarmed around this prince's golden beauty. He was also a skilled hunter and a master of hounds and horses. His table creaked under a great roast boar, crusted with herbs.

Pyotr's sons swallowed. They were all hungry after two weeks on the wintry road.

Pyotr strode across the vast hall, his sons behind. The prince did not look up from his dinner, though calculating or merely curious stares assailed them from all sides. A fireplace large enough to roast an ox burned behind the prince's dais, throwing Ivan's face into shadow and gilding the faces of guests. Pyotr and his sons came before the dais, halted, and bowed.

Ivan speared a gobbet of pork with the tip of his knife. Blood stained his yellow beard. "Pyotr Vladimirovich, is it not?" he said slowly, chewing. His shadowed gaze swept them from hat to boots. "The one that married my half sister?" He took a swallow of honey-wine and added, "May she rest in peace."

"Yes, Ivan Ivanovich," said Pyotr.

"Well met, brother," said the prince. He tossed a bone to the cur beneath his chair. "What brings you so far?"

"I wished to present you my sons, gosudar," said Pyotr. "Your nephews. They are men soon to wed. And if God wills, I desire also to find a woman of my own, so my youngest children need no longer go motherless."

"A worthy aim," said Ivan. "Are these your sons?" His gaze flicked out to the boys behind Pyotr.

"Yes—Nikolai Petrovich, my eldest, and my second son, Aleksandr." Kolya and Sasha stepped forward.

The Grand Prince gave them the same sweeping look he'd given Pyotr. His glance lingered on Sasha. The boy had the merest scrapings of a beard and the jutting bones of a boy half-grown. But he was light on his feet and the gray eyes did not waver.

"We are well met, kinsmen," said Ivan, not taking his eyes off Pyotr's younger son. "You, boy—you are like your mother." Sasha, taken aback, bowed and said nothing. There was a moment's silence. Then, louder, Ivan added, "Pyotr Vladimirovich, you are welcome in my house, and at my table, until your business is done."

The prince inclined his head abruptly and returned to his roast. Dismissed, the three were left to take three hastily cleared places at the high table. Kolya needed no encouragement; hot juices were still running down the roast pig's sides. The pie oozed with cheese and dried mushrooms. The round guest-loaf lay in the middle of the table, beside the prince's good gray salt. Kolya fell to at once, but Sasha paused. "Such a look the Grand Prince gave me, Father," he said. "As though he knew my thoughts better than I do."

"They are all like that, the princes that live," said Pyotr. He took a steaming slice of pie. "They all have too many brothers, and all are eager for the next city, the richer prize. Either they are good judges of men, or they are dead. Go wary of the living ones, synok, because they are dangerous." Then he gave his full attention to the pastry.

Sasha furrowed his brow, but he let his plate be filled. Their journey had been an endless round of strange stews and hard flat cakes, broken once or twice by their neighbors' hospitality. The Grand Prince kept a good table, and they all feasted until they could hold no more.

After, the party was given three rooms for their use: chilly and crawling with vermin, but they were too tired to care. Pyotr saw to the settling of the wagons, and of his men for the night, then collapsed on the high bed and surrendered to a dreamless sleep.

THE HOLY MAN OF
MAKOVETS HILL

"FATHER," said Sasha, vibrating with excitement. "The priest says there is a holy man north of Moscow, on Makovets Hill. He has founded a monastery and gathered already eleven disciples. They say he talks with angels. Every day many go to seek his blessing."

Pyotr grunted. He had been in Moscow a week already, enduring the business of currying favor. His latest effort—only just concluded—had been a visit to the Tatar emissary, the baskak. No man from Sarai, that jewel-box city built by the conquering Horde, would deign to be impressed by the paltry offerings of a northern lord, but Pyotr had doggedly pressed furs upon him. Heaps of fox and ermine, rabbit and sable passed beneath the emissary's calculating gaze until at last he looked less condescending and thanked Pyotr with every appearance of goodwill. Such furs fetched much gold in the court of the Khan, and further south, among the princes of Byzantium. *It was worth it,* thought Pyotr. *I might be glad one day, to have a friend among the conquerors.*

Pyotr was weary and sweating in his gold-threaded finery. But he could not rest, for here was his second son on fire with eagerness, bearing a tale of holy men and miracles.

"There are always holy men," Pyotr said to Sasha. He knew a sudden longing for quiet and for plain food; the Muscovites were fond of

Byzantine cookery, and the resulting collision with Russian ingredients did his stomach no favors. Tonight there was to be more feasting—and more intrigue; he still sought a wife for himself, and a husband for Olga.

"Father," said Sasha, "I should like to go to this monastery, if I may."

"Sashka, you cannot cast a stone without hitting a church in this city," said Pyotr. "Why waste three days' riding on another?"

Sasha's lip curled. "In Moscow, priests are in love with their standing. They eat fat meat and preach poverty to the miserable."

This was true. But Pyotr, though a good lord to his people, lacked an abstract sense of justice. He shrugged. "Your holy man might be the same."

"Nonetheless, I should like to see. Please, Father." Sasha, though gray-eyed, had his mother's jet brows and long lashes. They swept down, oddly delicate against his thin face.

Pyotr considered. Roads were dangerous, but the well-traveled road running north from Moscow was not markedly so. He had no desire to raise a timid son. "Take five men. And two dozen candles—that should ensure your reception."

A light came into the boy's face. Pyotr's mouth tightened. Marina was bone in the unyielding earth, but he had seen her look just that way, when her soul lit her face like firelight.

"Thank you, Father," the boy said. He dashed out the door and away, lithe as a weasel. Pyotr heard him in the dvor before the palace, calling the men, calling for his horse.

"Marina," said Pyotr, low, "thank you for my sons."

⁂

THE TRINITY LAVRA HAD been carved out of the wilderness. Though the feet of passing pilgrims had beaten a path through the snowy forest, the trees still pressed close on either side, dwarfing the bell-tower of the plain wooden church. Sasha was reminded of his own village at

Lesnaya Zemlya. A sturdy palisade surrounded the monastery, which was composed mostly of small, wooden buildings. The air smelled of smoke and baking bread.

Oleg had ridden with him, the head of his attendants. "We can't all go in," said Sasha, reining his horse.

Oleg nodded. The whole party dismounted, bits jingling. "You, and you," Oleg said. "Watch the road."

The men chosen settled beside the path, loosened the horses' girths, and began searching for firewood. The others passed between the two uprights of a narrow unbarred gate. Great trees threw sooty shadows onto the raw wood of the little church.

A slim man ducked out of a doorway, wiping floury hands. He was not very tall, and not very old. His broad nose was set between large, liquid eyes, the green-brown of a forest pool. He wore the coarse robe of a monk, splattered with flour.

Sasha knew him. The monk might have been wearing the rags of a beggar or the robes of a bishop and Sasha would still have known him. The boy dropped to his knees in the snow.

The monk pulled up short. "What brings you here, my son?"

Sasha could barely bring himself to look up. "I would ask your blessing, Batyushka," he managed.

The monk raised a brow. "You needn't call me so; I am not ordained. We are all children of God."

"We brought candles for the altar," Sasha stammered, still on his knees.

A thin, brown, work-hardened hand thrust itself under Sasha's elbow and raised him to his feet. The two were nearly of a height, though the boy was broader of shoulder and not yet full-grown, gangly as a colt. "We kneel to God alone here," said the monk. He studied Sasha's face a moment. "I am making the altar-bread for services tonight," he added abruptly. "Come and help me."

Sasha nodded, wordless, and waved his men off.

The kitchen was rude, and hot from the oven. The flour and water and salt lay to hand, to be mixed, kneaded, and baked in the ashes. The two worked in silence for a time, but it was an easy silence. Peace lay thick on that place. The monk's questions were so mild that the boy hardly noticed he was being questioned, but, a little clumsy with the unaccustomed task, he rolled out dough and related his history: his father's rank, his mother's death, their journey to Moscow.

"And you came here," the monk finished for him. "What are you seeking, my son?"

Sasha opened his mouth and closed it again. "I—I do not know," he admitted, shamefaced. "Something."

To his surprise, the monk laughed. "Do you wish to stay, then?"

Sasha could only stare.

"It is a hard life we lead here," the monk went on more seriously. "You would build your own cell, plant your garden, bake your bread, aid your brothers as necessary. But there is peace here, peace beyond anything. I see you have felt it." Seeing Sasha still dumbfounded, he said, "Yes, yes, many pilgrims come here, and many of them ask to stay. But we take only the seekers who do not know what they are looking for."

"Yes," Sasha said at last, slowly. "Yes, I would like to stay, very much."

"Very well," said Sergei Radonezhsky, and turned back to his baking.

❦

THEY PRESSED THE HORSES hard on the road back to Moscow. Oleg mistrusted the fiery look on his young lord's face. He rode close to Sasha's stirrup and resolved to speak to Pyotr. But the young lord reached his father first.

They rode into the city in the midst of the brief, burning sunset, with the towers of church and palace silhouetted against a violet sky. Sasha left his horse steaming in the dvor and ran at once up the stairs to his father's rooms. He found both father and brother dressing.

"Well met, little brother," said Kolya when Sasha came in. "Have you done with churches yet?" He threw Sasha a quick, tolerant glance and returned his attention to his clothes. Tongue between his lips, he settled a hat of black sable rakishly on his black hair. "Well, you are in good time. Wash off the stink. We are feasting tonight, and it may be the family will show us the woman Father is to marry. She has all her teeth—I have it on good authority—and a pleasant . . . *what*, Sasha?"

"Sergei Radonezhsky has asked me to join his monastery on Makovets Hill," repeated Sasha, louder.

Kolya looked blank.

"I wish to be a monk," Sasha said. That got their attention. Pyotr was drawing on his red-heeled boots. He slewed round to stare at his son and nearly tripped.

"*Why?*" cried Kolya, in tones of deep horror. Sasha clamped his teeth on several uncharitable remarks; his brother had already cut a large swath through the palace serving-women.

"To dedicate my life to God," he informed Kolya, with a touch of superiority.

"I see your holy man made quite an impression," Pyotr said, before the astonished Kolya had recovered. He had regained his balance and was drawing his second boot on, with perhaps a bit more vim than necessary.

"I—yes, he did, Father."

"Very well, you may," said Pyotr.

Kolya gaped. Pyotr put his foot down and stood. His kaftan was ocher and rust; the gold rings on his hands caught the candlelight. His hair and beard had been combed with scented oil; he looked both imposing and uncomfortable.

Sasha, who had been expecting a drawn-out battle, stared at his father.

"On two conditions," Pyotr added.

"What are they?"

"One, you may not visit this holy man again until you go to join his order. That will only be after next year's harvest, when you will have had a year to reflect. Two, you must remember that as a monk, your inheritance will go to your brothers, and you will have naught but your prayers to sustain you."

Sasha swallowed hard.

"But, Father, if I might only see him again——"

"No." Pyotr cut him off in a tone that brooked no argument. "You may turn monk if you will, but you will do it with your eyes open, not enthralled by the words of a hermit."

Sasha nodded reluctantly.

"Very well, Father," he said.

Pyotr, his face a little grimmer than usual, turned without another word and strode down the stairs to where the horses waited, drowsing in the faded evening light.

6.

DEMONS

Ivan Krasnii had only one son: the small blond wildcat Dmitrii Ivanovich. Aleksei, Metropolitan of Moscow, the highest prelate in Rus', ordained by the Patriarch of Constantinople himself, was charged with teaching the boy letters and statecraft. Some days, Aleksei thought the job was beyond anyone short of a wonder-worker.

Three hours already the boys had labored over the birchbark: Dmitrii with his elder cousin, Vladimir Andreevich, the young Prince of Serpukhov. They scuffled; they spilled things. *Might as well ask the palace cats,* thought Aleksei, despairing, *to sit and attend.*

"Father!" cried Dmitrii. "Father!"

Ivan Ivanovich came through the door. Both boys sprang off their stools and bowed, pushing each other. "Get you gone, my sons," said Ivan. "I would speak with the holy father."

The boys disappeared on the instant. Aleksei sank into a chair by the oven and poured out a large measure of mead.

"How is my son?" said Ivan, drawing up the chair opposite. The prince and the Metropolitan had known each other a long time. Aleksei had been loyal even before the death of Semyon assured Ivan the throne.

"Bold, fair, charming, flighty as a butterfly," said Aleksei. "He will be a good prince, if he lives so long. Why have you come to me, Ivan Ivanovich?"

"Anna," said Ivan succinctly.

The Metropolitan frowned. "Is she getting worse?"

"No, but she'll never be any better. She is growing too old to lurk around the palace and make folk nervous." Anna Ivanovna was the only child of Ivan's first marriage. The girl's mother was dead, and her stepmother hated the sight of her. The people muttered when she passed, and crossed themselves.

"There are convents enough," returned Aleksei. "It is a simple matter."

"No convent in Moscow," said Ivan. "My wife won't have it. She says the girl will cause talk if she stays near. Madness is a shameful thing in a line of princes. She must be sent away."

"I will arrange it if you like," said Aleksei, wearily. Already he arranged many things for this prince. "She can go south. Give an abbess enough gold, and she will take Anna and hide her lineage in the bargain."

"My thanks, Father," said Ivan, and poured more wine.

"However, I think you have a larger problem," added Aleksei.

"Numerous ones," said the Grand Prince, gulping his wine. He wiped his mouth with the back of his hand. "Which were you referring to?"

The Metropolitan jerked his chin in the direction of the door, where the two princes had gone. "Young Vladimir Andreevich," he said. "The Prince of Serpukhov. His family wants him married."

Ivan was unimpressed. "Plenty of time for that; he is only thirteen."

Aleksei shook his head. "They have a princess of Litva in mind— the duke's second daughter. Remember, Vladimir is also a grandson of Ivan Kalita, and he is older than your Dmitrii. Well-married and full-grown he would have a better claim to Moscow than your own son, should you die untimely."

Ivan grew pale with anger. "They dare not. I am the Grand Prince and Dmitrii is my son."

"And so?" said Aleksei, unmoved. "The Khan heeds the claims of princes only as long as they suit his ends. The strongest prince gets the patent; that is how the Horde assures peace in its territories."

Ivan reflected. "What then?"

"See Vladimir wed to another woman," said Aleksei at once. "Not a princess, but not one so lowborn as to cause insult. If she is beautiful, the boy is young enough to swallow it."

Ivan reflected, sipping his wine and biting his fingers.

"Pyotr Vladimirovich is lord of rich lands," he said at last. "His daughter is my own niece and she will have a great dowry. She cannot fail to be a beauty. My sister was very beautiful, and *her* mother charmed my father into marriage, though she came to Moscow a beggar."

Aleksei's eyes sparked. He tugged his brown beard. "Yes," he said. "I had heard that Pyotr Vladimirovich was in Moscow in search of a wife for himself as well."

"Yes," said Ivan. "He surprised everyone. It is seven years since my sister died. No one thought he would marry again."

"Well, then," said Aleksei. "If he is looking for a wife, what if you gave him your daughter?"

Ivan put down his cup in some surprise.

"Anna will be well hidden in the northern woods," Aleksei continued. "And will Vladimir Andreevich dare refuse Pyotr's daughter then? A girl so closely connected to the throne? It would be an insult to you."

Ivan frowned. "Anna wants, most particularly, to go to a convent."

Aleksei shrugged. "And so? Pyotr Vladimirovich is not a cruel man. She will be happy enough. Think of your son, Ivan Ivanovich."

ॐ

A DEMON SAT SEWING in the corner, and she was the only one who saw. Anna Ivanovna clutched at the cross between her breasts. Eyes shut, she whispered, "Go away, go away, *please* go away."

She opened her eyes. The demon was still there, but now two of her women were staring at her. Everyone else was looking with studied interest at the sewing in their laps. Anna tried not to let her eyes dart again to the corner, but she couldn't help it. The demon sat on its stool, oblivious. Anna shuddered. The heavy linen shirt lay on her lap like a dead thing. She thrust her hands into its sleek folds to hide her trembling.

A serving-woman slipped into the room. Anna hastily took up her needle and was surprised when the worn bast shoes stopped in front of her. "Anna Ivanovna, you are summoned to your father."

Anna stared. Her father had not summoned her for the better part of a year. She sat a moment bewildered, then jumped to her feet. Swiftly she changed her plain sarafan to one of crimson and ocher, drawing it over her grimy skin, trying to ignore the stink of her long chestnut braid.

The Rus' liked to be clean. In winter, scarce a week went by when her half sisters did not visit the bathhouses, but there was a little potbellied devil in there that grinned at them through the steam. Anna tried to point him out, but her sisters saw nothing. At first they took it for her imagination, later for foolishness, and at last just looked at her sideways and didn't say anything at all. So Anna had learned not to mention the eyes in the bathhouse, just as she never mentioned the bald creature sewing in the corner. But she would look sometimes; she couldn't help it, and she never went to the bathhouse unless her stepmother dragged or shamed her into it.

Anna unraveled and replaited her greasy hair and touched the cross over her breast. She was the most devout of all her sisters. Everyone said so. What they didn't know was that in church there were only the unearthly faces of the icons. No demons haunted her there, and she'd have *lived* in a church if she could, shielded by incense and painted eyes.

The oven was hot in her stepmother's workroom, and the Grand Prince stood beside it, sweating in winter finery. He wore his usual acerbic expression, though his eyes sparkled. His wife sat beside the fire, her thin plait straggling out from beneath her high headdress. Her needles lay forgotten in her lap. Anna halted a few paces away and bent her head. Husband and wife looked her over in silence. Finally her father spoke to her stepmother:

"Glory of God, woman," he said, sounding annoyed. "Can you not get the girl to bathe? She looks as though she's been living with pigs."

"It doesn't matter," her mother replied, "if she is already promised."

Anna had been staring at her toes like a well-bred maiden, but now her head shot up. "Promised?" she whispered, hating the way her voice rose and squeaked.

"You are to be married," her father said. "To Pyotr Vladimirovich, one of those northern boyars. He is a rich man, and he will be kind to you."

"Married? But I thought—I hoped—I meant to go to a convent. I would—I would pray for your soul, Father. I wish that above all things." Anna twisted her hands together.

"Nonsense," said Ivan, brisk. "You will like having sons, and Pyotr Vladimirovich is a good man. A convent is a cold place for a girl."

Cold? No, a convent was safe. Safe, blessed, a respite from her madness. Since she could remember, Anna had wanted to take vows. Now her skin blanched in terror; she flung herself forward and caught her father's feet. "No, Father!" she cried. "No please! I don't want to marry."

Ivan picked her up, not unkindly, and set her on her feet. "Enough of that," he said. "I have decided, and it is for the best. You will be well dowered, of course, and you will make me strong grandsons."

Anna was small and scrawny, and her stepmother's expression indicated doubt on that score.

"But—please," whispered Anna. "What is he like?"

"Ask your women," said Ivan indulgently. "I'm sure they'll have rumors. Wife, see that her things are in order, and for God's sake make her bathe before the wedding."

Dismissed, Anna trudged back to her sewing, biting back sobs. Married! Not to retreat, but to be the mistress of a lord's domain; not to be safe in a convent, but to live as some lord's breeding sow. And the northern boyars were lusty men, the serving-girls said, who dressed in skins and had hundreds of children. They were rough and warlike and—some liked to say—spurned Christ and worshiped the devil.

Anna pulled her pretty sarafan off over her head, shivering. If her sinful imagination conjured demons in the relative security of Moscow, what would it be like alone on the estate of a wild lord? The northern forests were haunted, the women said, and the winter lasted eight months in twelve. It did not bear thinking of. When the girl sat down again to her sewing, her hands trembled so that she could not set her stitches straight, and for all her efforts, the linen was blotched with si-lent tears.

7.

THE MEETING IN
THE MARKETPLACE

Pyotr Vladimirovich, unaware that his future had been agreed upon between the Grand Prince and the Metropolitan of Moscow, rose early the next morning and went to the market in Moscow's main square. His mouth tasted of old mushrooms, and his head throbbed with talk and drink. And—*foolish old man to let the boy run wild*—his son wished to turn monk. Pyotr had high hopes for Sasha. The boy was cooler-headed and cleverer than his older brother, better with horses, defter with weapons. Pyotr could imagine no greater waste than to have him disappear into a hovel, to cultivate a garden to the glory of God.

Well, he consoled himself. *Fifteen is very young.* Sasha would come round. Piety was one thing, quite another to give up family and inheritance for deprivation and a cold bed.

The din of many voices penetrated his reverie. Pyotr shook himself. The cold air reeked of horses and fires, soot and honey-wine. Men with mugs dangling from their belts proclaimed the virtues of the latter beside their sticky barrels. The pasty-sellers were out with their steaming trays, and the sellers of cloth and gems, wax and rare wood, honey and copper, worked bronze and golden trinkets jostled for room. Their voices thundered up to fright the morning sun.

And Moscow has only a little market, Pyotr thought.

Sarai was the seat of the Khan. It was there the great merchants went, to sell marvels to a court jaded by three hundred years of plunder. Even the markets further south, in Vladimir, or west, in Novgorod, were bigger than the one in Moscow. But merchants still trickled north from Byzantium and further east, tempted by the prices their wares fetched among the barbarians—and tempted even more by the prices the princes paid in Tsargrad for furs from the north.

Pyotr could not go home empty-handed. Olga's gift was easy enough; he bought her a headdress of pearl-strewn silk, to glow against her dark hair. For his three sons he bought daggers, short but heavy, with inlaid hilts. However, try as he might, he could find nothing to give Vasilisa. She was not a girl for trinkets, for beads or headdresses. But he could not very well give her a dagger. Frowning, Pyotr persevered, and was testing the heft of gold brooches when he caught sight of a strange man.

Pyotr could not have said, exactly, what about this man was strange, except that he had a sort of—stillness, striking amid the bustle. His clothes were fit for a prince, his boots richly embroidered. A knife hung at his belt, white gems sparkling at the hilt. His black curls were uncovered, odd for any man, and more so as it was white winter—brilliant sky and snow groaning underfoot. He was clean-shaven—something all but unheard-of among the Rus'—and Pyotr, from a distance, could not tell if he was old or young.

Pyotr realized he was staring, and turned away. But he was curious. The jewel-merchant said confidingly:

"You are curious about that man? You are not alone. He comes sometimes, to the market, but no one knows who his people are."

Pyotr was skeptical. The merchant smirked. "Truly, gospodin. He is never seen in church, and the bishop wants him stoned for idolatry. But he is rich, and he always brings the most marvelous things to trade. So the prince keeps the Church quiet, and the man comes and goes away again. Perhaps he is a devil." This was tossed off, half-laughing, but then the merchant frowned. "Never once have I seen him in the springtime. Always, always he comes in winter, at the turning of the year."

Pyotr grunted. He himself was quite open to the possibility of devils, but he was not convinced that they would stroll about markets—summer or winter—dressed in princely raiment. He shook his head, indicated a bracelet, and said, "This is rotten stuff; already the silver is green round the edges." The merchant protested, and the two settled to chaffering in earnest, forgetting all about the black-haired stranger.

※

THE STRANGER IN QUESTION halted before a market-stall, not more than ten paces from where Pyotr stood. He ran thin fingers over a heap of silk brocade. His hands alone could tell him the quality of the wares; he paid only cursory attention to the cloth before him. His pale eyes flicked here and there, about the crowded market.

The cloth-seller watched the stranger with a sort of obsequious wariness. The merchants knew him; a few thought he was one of them. He had brought marvels to Moscow before: weapons from Byzantium, porcelain light as morning air. The merchants remembered. But this time the stranger had another purpose; else he'd never have come south. He did not like cities, and it was a risk to cross the Volga.

The flashing colors and voluptuous weight of the fabric suddenly seemed tedious, and after a moment, the stranger abandoned the cloth and strode across the square. His horse stood on the south side, chewing wisps of hay. A rheumy old man stood at her head, pale and thin and oddly insubstantial, though the white mare was magnificent as a rearing mountain, and her harness was tooled and chased with silver. Men stared at her with admiration as they passed. She flicked her ears like a coquette, drawing a faint smile from her rider.

But suddenly a big man with cracked fingernails appeared out of the crowd and snatched the horse's rein. Her rider's face darkened.

Though his pace did not quicken—there was no need—a cold wind rippled across the square. Men snatched for hats and loosened garments. The would-be thief flung himself into the mare's saddle and dug in his heels.

But the mare did not move. Neither did her groom, oddly enough; he neither shouted nor raised a hand. He merely watched, an unreadable look in his sunken eyes.

The thief lashed the mare's shoulder. She did not stir a hoof, only swished her tail. The thief hesitated a bewildered instant, and then it was too late. The mare's rider strode up and wrenched him out of the saddle. The thief might have screamed, but found his throat frozen. Gasping, he groped for the wooden cross at his throat.

The other smiled, without humor. "You have trespassed on what is mine; do you think faith will save you?"

"Gosudar," the thief stammered, "I did not know—I thought—"

"That such as I do not walk in the places of men? Well, I go where I will."

"Please," choked the thief. "Gosudar, I beg—"

"Don't mewl," said the stranger, with cool humor. "And I will leave you awhile, to walk free in the sun. However"—the quiet voice dropped lower and the laughter drained out of it like water from a smashed cup—"you are marked, you are mine, and one day I shall touch you again. You will die." The thief choked out a sobbing breath, then found himself suddenly alone, a stinging like fire in his arm and throat.

Already in the saddle, though no one had seen him mount, the stranger wheeled and sent his horse through the crush. The horse's groom bowed once and melted into the crowd.

The mare was light and swift and sure. Her rider's anger quieted as he rode.

"The signs led me here," said the man to his horse. "Here, to this stinking city, when I should not have left my own lands." He had been in Moscow a month already, searching, tireless, face after face. "Well, signs are not infallible," he said. "The witch's daughter is hidden from me, and her child is long gone. The hour might have passed; the hour might never come."

The mare slanted an ear back at her rider. His lips firmed. "No," he said. "Am I so easily defeated?"

The mare went on at a steady canter. The man shook his head. He was not yet beaten; he held the magic trembling in his throat, in the hollow of his hand, ready. His answer lay somewhere in this miserable wooden city, and he would find it.

He turned the mare west, urging her into a long-striding gallop. The coolness among the trees would clear his head. He was not defeated.

Not yet.

❦

THE REEK OF MEAD and dogs, dust and humanity, greeted the stranger when he arrived at the Grand Prince's feast. Ivan's boyars were big men used to battle, and to carving life out of the land of frost. The stranger was not so large as even the smallest. But no one, not even the bravest—or the drunkest—could meet his eyes, and no one offered him challenge. The stranger took a place at the high table and drank his honey-wine unmolested. The silver embroidery on his kaftan shone in the torchlight. One of the princess's waiting-women sat beside him, gazing up through her long lashes.

Lent was near and the feasting was raucous. But—*It is all the same here*, thought the stranger. *All these dim, busy faces.* Sitting amid the din and the stink, he felt, for the first time—not despair, perhaps, but the beginning of resignation.

It was then that a man walked into the hall with two grown boys. The three took places at the high table. The older man was quite ordinary, his clothes of good quality. His elder son swaggered and the younger walked softly, his glance cool and grave. Perfectly ordinary.

And yet.

The stranger's gaze shifted. With the three came a curling breath of wind, a wind out of the north. In the space between one breath and the next, the wind told him a tale: of life and death together, of a child born with the failing year.

"The blood holds, brother," he whispered. "She lives, and I was not mistaken." His face was triumphant. He returned to the table (though indeed he had never moved), and smiled with sudden delight into the eyes of the woman beside him.

PYOTR HAD ALL BUT forgotten the stranger in the market. But when he came that night to the Grand Prince's table, he was quickly reminded, for the same stranger was sitting among the boyars, beside one of the princess's waiting-women. She was staring up at him, her painted eyelids trembling like wounded birds.

Pyotr, Sasha, and Kolya found themselves sitting to the left of the lady. Though she was one Kolya himself had been courting, she did not so much as glance in his direction. Furious, the young man neglected eating in favor of glaring (ignored), fingering his belt-knife (likewise), and declaiming to his brother the beauties of a certain merchant's daughter (which the entranced lady did not hear). Sasha remained as expressionless as possible, as though feigning deafness would make the impious talk go away.

There came a cough from behind. Pyotr looked up from this interesting scene to find a servant at his elbow. "The Grand Prince would speak to you."

Pyotr frowned and nodded. He had barely seen his erstwhile brother-in-law since that first night. He had talked with innumerable dvoryanye, dispensed his bribes liberally, and had in return been assured that—so long as he paid tribute—he would go unmolested by the tax collectors. Furthermore, he was deep in negotiations for the hand of a modest, decent woman who would tend his household and mother his children. All was proceeding in order. So what could the prince want?

Pyotr made his way along the table, catching the gleam of teeth in the firelight from the dogs at Ivan's feet. The prince was not slow in coming to the point. "My young nephew, Vladimir Andreevich of Serpukhov, wishes to take your daughter to wife," he said.

Had the prince informed him that his nephew wished to become a minstrel and wander the streets playing a guzla, Pyotr could not have been more astonished. His eyes flicked sideways to the prince in question, who sat drinking, a few places down the table. Ivan's nephew was thirteen years old, a boy on the cusp of manhood, loose-limbed and spotty. He was also the grandson of Ivan Kalita, the old Grand Prince. Surely he could aspire to a more exalted match? All the ambitious families at court were pushing their virgin daughters at him, under the blithe assumption that one must eventually stick. Why waste the position on the daughter of a man, even a rich man, of modest lineage, a girl whom the boy had never seen and who moreover lived at a considerable distance from Moscow?

Oh. Pyotr shook off his surprise. Olga came from far away. Ivan would be wary of girls who came armed with tribes of relations; an alliance between great families tended to give the descendants royal ambitions. Young Dmitrii's claim was not much stronger than his cousin's, and Vladimir was three years older than the heir. Princes inherited at the Khan's pleasure. Pyotr's daughter would have a large dowry, but that was all. Ivan was doing his best to muzzle the Muscovite boyars, to Pyotr's benefit.

Pyotr was pleased. "Ivan Ivanovich," he began.

But the prince was not finished. "If you will yield up your daughter to my cousin, I am prepared to give you my own daughter, Anna Ivanovna, in marriage. She is a fine girl, yielding as a dove, and can surely give you more sons."

Pyotr was startled for the second time, and somewhat less pleased.

He had three boys already, among whom he must divide his property, and was in no need of more. Why would the prince waste a virginal daughter on a man of no enormous consequence who wanted only a woman of sense to run his house?

The prince raised an eyebrow. Still Pyotr hesitated.

Well, she was Marina's niece, a Grand Prince's daughter, cousin to his own children, and he could not very well ask what was wrong with her. Even if she were diseased, a drunkard, or a harlot, or—well, even so, the benefit of accepting the match would be considerable. "How could I refuse, Ivan Ivanovich?" Pyotr said.

The prince nodded gravely. "A man will come to you tomorrow to negotiate the bridal contract," he said, turning back to his goblet and his dogs.

Pyotr, dismissed, was left to make his way back to his place at the long table and tell his sons the news. He found Kolya sulking into his cup. The dark-haired stranger had left, and the woman was staring in the direction he had gone, with a look of such terror and agonized longing on her pale face that Pyotr, for all his troubles, found his hand darting almost involuntarily for the sword he was not wearing.

8.

THE WORD OF
PYOTR VLADIMIROVICH

PYOTR VLADIMIROVICH TOOK HIS BRIDE'S COLD HAND, SQUINTED
at her small, clenched face, and wondered if he could have been mistaken. It had taken a headlong week to negotiate the details of his marriage (so that it might be celebrated before Lent began). Kolya had
spent the interval dallying with half the serving-women in the kremlin,
looking for word on his father's prospective bride. Consensus eluded
him. Some said she was pretty. Others said that she had a wart on her
chin and only half her teeth. They said that her father kept her locked
up, or that she hid in her rooms and never came out. They said she was
ill, or mad, or sorrowful, or merely timid, and at last Pyotr decided that
whatever the problem was, it was worse than he had feared.

But now, facing his unveiled bride, he wondered. She was very
small, about the same age as Kolya, though her demeanor made her
seem younger. Her voice was soft and breathless, her manner submis-
sive, her lips pleasingly full. There was nothing in her of Marina,
though they had the same grandfather, and for that Pyotr was grateful.
A warm chestnut braid framed her round face. Seen up close, there was
also a suggestion of tightness about her eyes, as though her face would
fall into lines like a closed fist as she got older. She wore a cross that she
fingered constantly, and she kept her eyes lowered, even when Pyotr

sought to look her in the face. Try as he might, Pyotr could not see anything manifestly wrong with her, except perhaps incipient ill temper. She certainly did not seem drunk, or leprous, or mad. Perhaps the girl was just shy and retiring. Perhaps the prince really did propose this marriage as a mark of favor.

Pyotr touched the sweet outline of his bride's lips and wished he could believe it.

They feasted in her father's hall after the wedding. The table groaned under the weight of fish and bread, pie and cheeses. Pyotr's men shouted and sang and drank his health. The Grand Prince and his family smiled, more or less sincerely, and wished them many children. Kolya and Sasha said little and looked with some resentment at their new stepmother, a cousin scarce older than they.

Pyotr plied his wife with mead and tried to set her at ease. He did his best not to think of Marina, sixteen when he married her, who had stared him full in the face as she said her vows, and laughed and sung and eaten heartily at her wedding feast, tossing him sidewise glances as though daring him to frighten her. Pyotr had taken her to bed half-crazed with desire, and kissed her until defiance turned to passion; they had risen the next morning drunk with languor and shared delight. But this creature did not seem capable of defiance, perhaps not even of passion. She drooped under her headdress, answering his questions in monosyllables and shredding a bit of bread in her fingers. Finally, Pyotr turned away from her, sighing, and let his thoughts race along the winding track through the winter-dark forest, to the snows of Lesnaya Zemlya and the simplicities of hunting and mending, away from this city of smiling enemies and barbed favors.

☙❧

SIX WEEKS LATER, PYOTR and his retinue prepared to take their leave. The days were lengthening, and the snow in the capital had begun to soften. Pyotr and his sons eyed the snow and hastened their preparations. If the ice thinned before they crossed the Volga, they must exchange their sledges for wagons and wait an eternity before the river was passable by raft.

Pyotr was worried for his lands and eager to get back to his hunting and husbandry. He also thought, vaguely, that the clean northern air might calm whatever was frightening his wife. Anna, though quiet and compliant, never stopped gazing around her, wide-eyed, fingering the cross between her breasts. Sometimes she muttered disconcertingly into empty corners. Pyotr had taken her to bed every night since their wedding, more for duty than for pleasure, true, but she had yet to look him in the face. He heard her weeping when she thought he slept.

The party's numbers had increased significantly with the addition of Anna Ivanovna's belongings and retinue. Their sledges filled the courtyard, and many of the servants had packhorses on leading reins. Both Pyotr's sons were mounted. Sasha's mare picked up one foot, then another, and flung her dark head. Kolya's horse stood still and Kolya himself drooped in the saddle, bloodshot eyes slitted against the morning sun. Kolya had known great success among the boyars' sons in Moscow. He'd bested them all at wrestling and many of them at archery; he had drunk nearly all of them under the table; and he had dallied with any number of palace women. He had, in short, enjoyed himself, and he was not relishing the prospect of a long journey, with nothing but hard labor at the end of it.

For his part, Pyotr was satisfied with their expedition. Olga was betrothed to a man—well, boy—of far more consequence than he would have dreamed. He himself had remarried, and if the lady was rather strange, at least she was not promiscuous, or diseased, and she was another Grand Prince's daughter. So it was with high good humor that Pyotr saw all in readiness for their departure. He looked around for his gray stallion, that they might mount and be gone.

A stranger was standing at his horse's head: the man from the market, who had also supped in the Grand Prince's hall. Pyotr had forgotten the stranger in the haste surrounding his wedding, but now there he was, stroking Buran's nose and looking at the stallion appraisingly.

Pyotr waited—not without a certain anticipation—for the stranger to have his hand bitten off, for Buran did not suffer familiarities, but after a moment he realized with astonishment that the horse was standing perfectly still, ears drooping, like a peasant's old donkey.

Baffled and annoyed, Pyotr took a long step toward them, but Kolya was before him. The boy had found a target upon which to vent his wrath, headache, and general dissatisfaction. Spurring his gelding, he pulled up not more than a long step away from the stranger, near enough for his horse's hooves to splatter filthy snow all over the man's blue robe. The gelding curvetted, eyes rolling. A sweat broke out on its brown flanks.

"What are you doing here?" Kolya demanded, curbing the gelding with hard hands. "How dare you touch my father's horse?"

The stranger wiped a splatter off one cheek. "He is a very fine horse," he replied, tranquil. "I thought to buy him."

"Well, you can't." Kolya sprang to the ground. Pyotr's eldest son was as broad and heavily built as a Siberian ox. The other, who was both shorter and more slender, ought to have looked frail beside him, but he didn't. Perhaps it was the look in his eyes. With a thrill of unease, Pyotr quickened his pace. Kolya was maybe still drunk, maybe just unwary, but he mistook the stranger's mildness for yielding. "And how do you propose to manage a horse like that, little man?" he added scornfully. "Run back to your lover and leave riding war-horses to men of strength!" He pressed forward until the two were nose to nose, fingering his dagger.

The stranger smiled, with a wry, self-deprecating twist of the lips. Pyotr wanted to shout a warning, but the words froze in his throat. For a moment the stranger was perfectly still.

And then he moved.

At least, Pyotr assumed that he moved. He did not see it. He saw nothing but a flicker, like light on a bird's wing. Kolya cried out, clutching his wrist, and then the man stood behind him, an arm around his neck and a dagger pressed to his throat. It had happened so fast even the horses hadn't had time to startle. Pyotr sprang forward, hand on his sword, but stopped when the man looked up. The stranger had the oddest eyes Pyotr had ever seen, a pale, pale blue, like a clear sky on a cold day. His hands were supple and steady.

"Your son has insulted me, Pyotr Vladimirovich," he said. "Shall I demand his life?" The knife moved, just the tiniest motion. A thin line of red opened on Kolya's neck, soaking his new beard. The boy drew a sobbing breath. Pyotr did not spare him a glance.

"It is your right," he said. "But I beg you—allow my son to make amends."

The man threw Kolya a scornful glance. "A drunken boy," he said, and tightened his hand again on the knife.

"No!" rasped Pyotr. "Perhaps I might make amends. We have some gold. Or—if you wish—my horse." Pyotr did his best not to glance at his beautiful gray stallion. A faint—very faint—amusement appeared in the stranger's frozen eyes.

"Generous," he said drily. "But no. I will give you your son's life, Pyotr Vladimirovich, in exchange for a service."

"What service?"

"Have you daughters?"

That was unexpected.

"Yes," Pyotr answered warily, "But . . ." The stranger's look of amusement deepened.

"No, I will not take one as a concubine or ravish her in a snowbank. You are bringing gifts for your children, are you not? Well, I have a gift for your younger daughter. You shall make her swear to keep it by her always. You shall also swear never to recount to any living soul the circumstances of our meeting. Under these, and only these, conditions will I spare your son his life."

Pyotr considered for an instant. *A gift? What gift must be given with threats to my son?* "I will not put my daughter in danger," he said. "Even for my son. Vasya is a only a little girl-child, my wife's lastborn." But he swallowed hard. Kolya's blood was seeping down in a slow scarlet stream.

The man looked at Pyotr through narrowed eyes, and for a long moment there was silence. Then the stranger said, "No harm will come to her. I swear it. On the ice and the snow and a thousand lives of men."

"What is this gift, then?" said Pyotr.

The stranger let go of Kolya, who stood like a sleepwalker, his eyes curiously blank. The stranger strode over to Pyotr and withdrew an object from a belt-pouch.

In his wildest imaginings, never would Pyotr have dreamed of the bauble the man held out to him: a single jewel, of a brilliant silver-blue, nestled in tangle of pale metal, like a star or a snowflake and dangling from a chain as fine as silk thread.

Pyotr looked up, questions on his lips, but the stranger forestalled him. "There it is," he said. "A trinket, no more. Now, your promise. You will give that to your daughter, and you will tell no one of our meeting. If you break your word, I shall come and kill your son."

Pyotr looked to his men. They stood blank-eyed; even Sasha on his horse nodded a heavy head. Pyotr's blood chilled. He feared no man, but this uncanny stranger had bewitched his folk; even his brave sons stood helpless. The necklace hung icy cold and heavy in his hand.

"I swear it," Pyotr said in his turn. The man nodded once, turned, and strode away across the muddy yard. As soon as he was out of sight, Pyotr's men stirred around him. Pyotr hastily thrust the shining object into his belt-pouch.

"Father?" said Kolya. "Father, what is wrong? Everything is ready; it wants only your word and we shall go." Pyotr, staring incredulously at his son, was silent, for the bloodstains had gone and Kolya blinked at him with a placid bloodshot gaze unclouded by his recent encounter.

"But . . ." he began, and then hesitated, remembering his promise.

"Father, what is wrong?"

"Nothing," said Pyotr.

He strode over to Buran, mounted, and urged the horse forward, resolving to put the strange meeting out of his mind. But two circumstances conspired against him. For one, when they made camp that night, Kolya found five white oblong marks on his throat, as though he had taken frostbite, though his beard was heavy, his throat well wrapped. For another, listen as he might, Pyotr heard not a single word of discussion among his servants about the strange events in the courtyard and was forced, reluctantly, to conclude that he was the only one who remembered them at all.

9.

THE MADWOMAN
IN THE CHURCH

THE ROAD HOME SEEMED LONGER THAN IT HAD WHEN THEY SET out. Anna was unused to travel, and they went at little more than foot pace, with frequent halts for rest. Despite their slowness, the journey was not as tedious as it might have been; they had left Moscow heavy-laden with provisions, and took also the hospitality of villages and boyars' houses, as they came upon them.

Once they were out of the city, Pyotr went to his wife's bed with renewed eagerness, remembering her soft mouth and the silky grip of her young body. But each time she met him—not with anger or laments, which he might have managed—but with baffling silent weeping, tears sliding down her round cheeks. A week of this drove Pyotr away, half angry and half bewildered. He began to range further during the day, hunting on foot or taking Buran deep into the woods, until man and horse returned scratched and weary, and Pyotr was tired enough to think only of his bed. Even sleep was no respite, though, for in his dreams he saw a sapphire necklace and spidery white fingers against the neck of his firstborn. He would wake in the dark calling for Kolya to run.

He itched to be home, but they could not hurry. For all his efforts, Anna grew pale and feeble with journeying, and would beg them to halt earlier and earlier in the day, to set up tents and braziers, that the servants might serve her hot soup and warm her numb hands.

But they crossed the river at last. When Pyotr judged the party less than a day away from Lesnaya Zemlya, he set Buran's feet on the snowy track and gave the stallion his head. The bulk of his men would follow with the sledges, but he and Kolya flew home like windblown ghosts. It was with inexpressible relief that Pyotr broke from the cover of the trees and saw his own house standing silvery and unharmed in the clear winter daylight.

※

EVERY DAY SINCE PYOTR and Sasha and Kolya had gone away, Vasya had slipped from the house whenever she could contrive it and run to climb her favorite tree: the one that stretched a great limb over the road to the south of Lesnaya Zemlya. Alyosha went with her sometimes, but he was heavier than she, and a clumsier climber. So Vasya was alone on the day she saw the flashing of hooves and harness. She slid down her tree like a cat and bolted on her short legs. By the time she reached the palisade-gate, she was shouting, "Father, Father, it is Father!"

By then it was no great news, for the two riders, coming on much faster than one small girl, were already crossing the fields at a great pace, and the villagers, from their little rise, could see them plainly. The people looked at each other, wondering where the others were, fearing for their kin. And then Pyotr and Kolya (Sasha had stayed with the sledges) swept into the village and reined their stamping horses. Dunya attempted to seize Vasya, who had stolen Alyosha's clothes to climb her tree and was grubby to boot, but Vasya wriggled away and ran into the dooryard. "Father!" she cried. "Kolya!" and laughed when each caught her up in turn. "Father, you are back!"

"I have brought a mother for you, Vasochka," said Pyotr, looking her over with a raised eyebrow. She was covered in bits of tree. "Though I did not tell her she was getting a wood-sprite instead of a little girl." But he kissed her grubby cheek and she giggled.

"Oh—then where is Sasha?" cried Vasya, looking about her in sudden fear. "Where are the sledge-horses?"

"Never fear, they are on the road behind us," said Pyotr, and he added louder, so all the assembled people could hear, "They will be here before nightfall; we must be ready to receive them. And you," he added lower to Vasya, "get you into the kitchen and bid Dunya dress you. All else equal, I'd rather present a daughter to her stepmother and not a wood-sprite." He put her down with a little push, and Olga hauled her sister into the kitchen.

The sledges came with the westering sun. They made their weary way over the fields and up through the village gate. The people cheered and exclaimed at the fine closed sleigh that contained the new wife of Pyotr Vladimirovich. Most of the village assembled to see her.

Anna Ivanovna came out of the sleigh tottering, stiff, pale as ice. Vasya thought that she looked scarcely older than Olya, and not nearly so old as her father. *Well, all the better,* the child thought. *Perhaps she will play with me.* She smiled her best smile. But Anna did not answer, by word or sign. She cringed at all the stares, and Pyotr remembered belatedly that women in Moscow lived apart from the men. "I am tired," Anna Ivanovna whispered, and crept into the house clinging to Olga's arm.

The people looked at each other, nonplussed. "Well, it was a long journey," they said at last. "She will be well in time. She is a Grand Prince's daughter, as Marina Ivanovna was." And they were proud that such a woman had come to live among them. They returned to their huts to build up their fires against the dark and eat their watery soup.

But in the house of Pyotr Vladimirovich, they all feasted as best they could with Lent upon them and winter grown old and bony. They made decent shrift of it, with fish and porridge. Afterward, Pyotr and his sons told the tale of their journey while Alyosha leaped about, threatening the fingers of servants with his splendid new dagger.

Pyotr himself set the headdress on Olga's black hair, and said, "I hope you will wear it on your wedding day, Olya." Olga blushed and paled, while Vasya, wordless, turned her vast eyes onto her father. Pyotr raised his voice, so the room at large could hear. "She will be the Princess of Serpukhov," he said. "The Grand Prince himself betrothed her." And he kissed his daughter. Olga smiled with half-frightened delight. In the tumult of congratulation, Vasya's thin, forlorn cry went unheard.

But the feast wound down, and Anna sought her bed early. Olga went to help her, and Vasya trotted after. Slowly the kitchen emptied.

Dusk deepened to night. The fire crumbled on a glowing core and the air in the kitchen chilled and sank. At last the winter kitchen was empty but for Pyotr and Dunya. The old lady sat weeping in her place near the fire. "I knew it must come, Pyotr Vladimirovich," she said. "And if ever there was a girl who ought to be a princess, it is my Olya. But it is a hard thing. She will live in a palace in Moscow, like her grandmother, and I will never see her again. I am too old for journeys."

Pyotr sat before the fire, fingering the jewel in his pocket. "It comes to all women," he said.

Dunya said nothing.

"Here, Dunyashka," said Pyotr, and his voice was so strange that the old nurse turned quickly to look at him. "I have a gift for Vasya." He had already given her a length of fine green cloth, to make a good sarafan. Dunya frowned. "Another, Pyotr Vladimirovich?" she said. "She will be spoiled."

"Even so," said Pyotr. Dunya squinted at him in the dark, puzzled by the look on his face. Pyotr thrust the necklace at Dunya as though eager to be rid of it. "Give it to her yourself. You must see she keeps it always by her. Make her promise, Dunya."

Dunya looked more puzzled than ever, but she took the cold blue thing and squinted at it.

Pyotr frowned more terribly than ever; he reached out as though to take it back. But his fist closed on itself, and the motion died unfinished. Abruptly he turned on his heel and sought his bed. Dunya, alone in the dim kitchen, stared down at the pendant. She turned it this way and that, muttering to herself.

"Well, Pyotr Vladimirovich," she murmured, "and where in Moscow does a man get such a jewel?" Shaking her head, Dunya slipped it into her pocket, resolving to keep it safe until the little girl was old enough to be trusted with the glittering thing.

Three nights later, the old nurse dreamed.

In her dream she was a maiden again, walking alone in the winter woods. The bright sound of sleigh bells rang out on the road. She loved sledging, and spun to see a white horse trotting toward her. Its driver was a man with black hair. He did not slow when he came up alongside, but caught her arm and pulled her roughly onto the sledge. His gaze did not leave the white road. Air like the iciest of January blasts eddied around him despite the winter sunshine.

Dunya was suddenly afraid.

"You have taken something that was not given to you," he said. Dunya shuddered at the whine of storm winds in his voice. "Why?" Her teeth were chattering so hard she could barely form words, and the man whirled on her in a blaze of thin winter light. "That necklace was not meant for you," he hissed. "Why have you taken it?"

"Her father brought it for Vasilisa, but she is only a child. I saw it and I knew it was a talisman," stammered Dunya. "I have not stolen it, I have not . . . but I am afraid for the girl. Please, she is too young—too young for sorcery or the favor of the old gods."

The man laughed. Dunya heard a grinding bitterness in the sound. "Gods? There is but one God now, child, and I am no more than a wind through bare branches." He was silent, and Dunya, trembling, tasted blood where she'd bitten into her lip.

At last he nodded. "Very well, keep it for her, then, until she is grown—but no longer. I think I need not tell you what will happen if you play me false."

Dunya found herself nodding vigorously, shaking harder than ever. The man cracked his whip. The horse raced off, running ever faster over the snow. Dunya felt her grip on the seat slipping; frantically she clutched at it but she was falling, falling over backward . . .

She woke with a gasp, on her own pallet in the kitchen. She lay in the dark, shivering, and it was a long time before she could get warm.

§◊§

ANNA CAME RELUCTANTLY AWAKE, blinking dreams from her eyes. It had been a pleasant dream, the last; there had been warm bread in it and someone with a soft voice. But even as she reached for it, the dream slipped away, and she was left empty, clutching blankets around her to ward off the dawn chill.

She heard a rustling and craned her head around. A demon sat on her own stool, mending one of Pyotr's shirts. The gray light of a winter morning threw bars of shadow over the gnarled thing. She shuddered. Her husband snored beside her, oblivious, and Anna tried to ignore the specter, as she had every day in the seven since she first awoke in this horrible place. She turned away and burrowed into the coverlet. But she could not get warm. Her husband had thrown off the blanket, but she was always cold here. When she asked that the fire be built up, the serving-women just stared at her, politely perplexed. She thought about creeping closer, to share her husband's warmth, but he might decide he wanted her again. Though he tried to be gentle, he was insistent, and most of the time she wanted to be left alone.

She risked a look back at the stool. The thing was staring straight at her.

Anna could stand it no more. She slipped to the floor, pulled on garments at random, and wrapped a scarf round her half-raveled braids. Darting through the kitchen and out the kitchen door, she earned a startled look from Dunya, who always rose early to set the bread baking. The gray morning light was giving way to rose; the ground glittered as though gem-studded, but Anna didn't notice the snow. All she saw was the little wooden church not twenty paces from the house. Heedless, she ran toward it, yanked open the door, and slid inside. She wanted to weep, but she clenched her teeth and her fists and silenced her tears. She did altogether too much weeping.

Her madness was worse here in the north—far, far worse. Pyotr's house was alive with devils. A creature with eyes like coals hid in the oven. A little man in the bathhouse winked at her through the steam. A demon like a heap of sticks slouched around the dooryard.

In Moscow, her devils had never looked at her, never spared her a glance, but here they were always *staring*. Some even came quite close, as though they would speak, and each time Anna had to flee, hating the puzzled stares of her husband and stepchildren. She saw them all the time, everywhere—except here in the church.

The blessed, quiet church. It was nothing, really, compared to the churches in Moscow. There was no gold or gilt, and only one priest to give service. The icons were small and ill-painted. But here she saw nothing but floor and walls and icons and candles. There were no faces in the shadows.

She stayed and stayed, by turns praying and staring into space. It was well past dawn when she crept back to the house. The kitchen was crowded, the fire roaring. The baking and stewing and cleaning and drying went on without cease, from dark to dark. The women did not react when Anna crept in; no one so much as turned her head. Anna took that, above all, as a comment on her weakness.

Olga looked up first. "Would you like some bread, Anna Ivanovna?" she asked. Olga could not like the poor creature that had taken her mother's place, though she was a kind girl and pitied her.

Anna was hungry, but there was a tiny, grizzled creature sitting just inside the mouth of the oven. Its beard glowed with the heat as it gnawed a blackened crust.

Anna Ivanovna's mouth worked, but she could make no answer. The little creature looked up from its bread and cocked its head. There was curiosity in its bright eyes. "No," Anna whispered. "No—I don't want any bread." She turned and fled to the dubious safety of her own room, while the women in the kitchen looked at each other and slowly shook their heads.

10.

THE PRINCESS OF SERPUKHOV

THE FOLLOWING AUTUMN, KOLYA WAS MARRIED TO THE DAUGH-
ter of a neighboring boyar. She was a fat, strapping, yellow-haired girl,
and Pyotr built them a little house of their own, with a good clay oven.

But it was the great wedding the people awaited, when Olga Petrovna would become the Princess of Serpukhov. That had taken almost a year to negotiate. The gifts began coming from Moscow before
the mud closed the roads, but the details took longer. The way from
Lesnaya Zemlya to Moscow was a hard one; messengers were delayed
or disappeared; they broke their skulls, were robbed, or lamed their
horses. But it was settled at last. The young Prince of Serpukhov was to
come himself, with his retinue, to marry Olga and take her back to his
house in Moscow.

"It is better for her to be married before she travels," said the messenger. "She will not be so frightened." And, the messenger might have
added, Aleksei, Metropolitan of Moscow, wanted the marriage accomplished and consummated before Olga came to the city.

The prince arrived just as pale spring became dazzling summer,
with a tender, capricious sky and the fading flowers buried in a wash
of summer grass. A year had ripened him. The spots had faded, though

he was still no beauty; and he hid his shyness with boisterous good temper.

With the Prince of Serpukhov came his cousin, the blond Dmitrii Ivanovich, calling out greetings. The princes had come with hawks and hounds and horses, with women in carved wooden carts, and they brought many gifts. The boys came also with a guardian: a clear-eyed monk, not very old, silent more often than speaking. The cavalcade raised a great noise and dust and clamor. The whole village came to gawk, and many to offer the hospitality of their huts to the men and pasture for the weary horses. The boy-prince Vladimir shyly slipped a sparkling green beryl onto Olga's finger, and the whole house gave itself to mirth, as it had not since Marina breathed her last.

⚜

"THE BOY IS KIND, at least," said Dunya to Olga in a rare quiet moment. They sat together beside the wide window in the summer kitchen. Vasya sat at Olga's feet, listening and poking at her mending.

"Yes," said Olga. "And Sasha is coming with me to Moscow. He will see me to my husband's house before he joins his monastery. He has promised." The beryl ring blazed on her finger. Her betrothed had also hung her throat with raw amber and given her a bolt of marvelous cloth, fiery as poppies. Dunya was hemming it for a sarafan. Vasya was only pretending to sew; her small hands were clenched in her lap.

"You will do very well," said Dunya firmly, biting the end of a thread. "Vladimir Andreevich is rich, and young enough to take the advice of his wife. It was generous of him to come and marry you here, in your own house."

"He came because the Metropolitan made him," Olga interjected.

"And he stands high in the Grand Prince's favor. He is young Dmitrii's dearest friend, that is plain. He will have a high place when Ivan Krasnii is dead. You will be a great lady. You could not do better, my Olya."

"Ye—es," said Olga again, slowly. At her feet, Vasya's dark head drooped. Olga bent to stroke her sister's hair. "I suppose he is kind. But I . . ."

Dunya smiled sardonically. "Were you hoping that a raven-prince would come, like the bird in the fairy tale that came for Prince Ivan's sister?"

Olga blushed and laughed, but she did not reply. Instead she picked up Vasilisa, though she was a great girl to be held like a child, and rocked her back and forth. Vasya curled rigid in her sister's arms. "Hush, little frog," said Olga, as though Vasya were a baby. "It will be all right."

"Olga Petrovna," said Dunya, "my Olya, fairy tales are for children, but you are a woman, and soon you will be a wife. To wed a decent man and be safe in his house, to worship God and bear strong sons—that is real and right. It is time to put aside dreaming. Fairy tales are sweet on winter nights, nothing more." Dunya thought suddenly of pale cold eyes, and an even colder hand. *Very well, until she is grown, but no longer.* She shivered and added, lower, looking at Vasya, "Even the maidens of fairy tales do not always end happily. Alenushka was turned into a duck and watched the wicked witch butcher her duck-children." And seeing Olga still downcast, smoothing Vasya's hair, she added, a little harshly, "Child, it is the lot of women. I do not think you wish to be a nun. You might grow to love him. Your mother did not know Pyotr Vladimirovich before her wedding, and I remember her afraid, though your mother was brave enough to face down Baba Yaga herself. But they loved each other from the first night."

"Mother is dead," said Olga in a flat voice. "Another has her place. And I am going away forever."

Against her shoulder, Vasya let out a muffled wail.

"She will never die," retorted Dunya firmly. "Because you are alive, and you are as beautiful as she was, and you will be the mother of princes. Be brave. Moscow is a fair city, and your brothers will come to see you."

THAT NIGHT, VASYA CAME to bed with Olga and said urgently, "Don't go, Olya. I'll never be bad again. I'll never even climb trees." She looked up at her sister, owl-like and trembling. Olga could not forbear a laugh, though it broke a little at the end. "I must, little frog," she said. "He is a prince and he is rich and kind, as Dunya says. I must marry him or go to a convent. And I want children of my own, ten little frogs just like you."

"But you have me, Olya," Vasya said.

Olya pulled her close. "But you will grow up yourself one day and not be a child anymore. And what use will you have then for your tottering old sister?"

"Always!" Vasya burst out passionately. "Always! Let's run away and live in the woods."

"I'm not sure you'd like to live in the woods," said Olga. "Baba Yaga might eat us."

"No," said Vasya, with perfect assurance. "There is only the one-eyed man. If we stay away from the oak-tree he will never find us."

Olya did not know what to make of this.

"We will have an izba among the trees," said Vasya. "And I will bring you nuts and mushrooms."

"I have a better idea," said Olya. "You are a great girl already, and it will not be too many years before you are a woman. I will send for you from Moscow when you are grown. We will be two princesses in a palace together, and you will have a prince for yourself. How would you like that?"

"But I am grown now, Olya!" cried Vasya immediately, swallowing her tears and sitting up. "Look, I am much bigger."

"Not yet, I think, little sister," said Olga gently. "But be patient and mind Dunya and eat plenty of porridge. When Father says you are grown, then will I send for you."

"I will ask Father," said Vasya confidently. "Perhaps he will say I am grown already."

⬥

SASHA HAD RECOGNIZED THE monk the moment he strode into the yard. In the confusion of welcome and bride-gifts, with a feast in the making among the green summer birches, he ran forward, seized the monk's hand, and kissed it. "Father, you came," he said.

"As you see, my son," said the monk, smiling.

"But it is so far."

"Indeed not. When I was younger, I wandered the length and breadth of Rus', and the Word was my path and my shield, my bread and my salt. Now I am old, and I stay in the Lavra. But the world is fair to me still, especially the north of the world in summertime. I am glad to see you."

What he did not say—at least not then—was that the Grand Prince was ill, and that Vladimir Andreevich's marriage was all the more urgent in consequence. Dmitrii was barely eleven, freckled and spoiled. His mother kept him in her sight and slept beside his bed. Small heirs of princes were wont to disappear when their fathers died untimely.

That spring, Aleksei had summoned the holy man Sergei Radonezhsky to his palace in the kremlin. Sergei and Aleksei had known each other a long time. "I am sending Vladimir Andreevich north to be married," Aleksei had said. "As soon as may be. He must be wed before Ivan dies. Young Dmitrii will go with the bridal party. It will keep him out of harm's way; his mother fears for the child's life if he remains in Moscow."

The hermit and the Metropolitan were drinking honey-wine, much watered. They sat together on a wooden seat in the kitchen garden. "Is Ivan Ivanovich so very ill, then?" said Sergei.

"He is gray and yellow together; he sweats and stinks, and his eyes are filmy," said the Metropolitan. "God willing, he lives, but I will be ready if he does not. I cannot leave the city. Dmitrii is so young. I would ask you to go with the bridal party to watch over him and see Vladimir wed."

"Vladimir is to marry Pyotr Vladimirovich's daughter, is he not?" said Sergei. "I have met Pyotr's son. Sasha, they call him. He came to me at the Lavra. Such eyes as I have never seen. He will be a monk or a saint or a hero. A year ago he wished to take vows. Would that he still does. The Lavra could use a brother like that."

"Well, go and see," said Aleksei. "Persuade Pyotr's son to come back to the Lavra with you. Dmitrii must live in your monastery for his minority. All the better if he has Aleksandr Petrovich, a man of his blood, one dedicated to God, to be his companion. If Dmitrii is crowned, he will want every ally ingenuity can yield him."

"So will you," said Sergei. The bees droned about them. The northern flowers made up in heady scents for their brief, doomed days. Hesitantly, Sergei added, "Will you be his regent, then? Regents do not live long either, if their boy-princes are slain."

"Am I such a faintheart that I would not put myself between that boy and assassins?" said Aleksei. "I would, though it cost me my life. God is with us. But you must be Metropolitan when I die."

Sergei laughed. "I will see the face of God, and be blinded by glory, before I come to Moscow to try and manage your bishops, Brother. But I will go north with the Prince of Serpukhov. It is long since I traveled, and I would see the high forests again."

❦

PYOTR SAW THE MONK among the riders, and his face grew grim. But he spoke only courtesies until the evening after their arrival. That night, they all feasted together in the twilight, and when the laughter and torches of full-fed people slipped away toward the village, Pyotr came in the dusk and caught Sergei by the shoulder. The two faced each other beside the running stream.

"And so you came, man of God, to steal my son from me?" Pyotr said to Sergei.

"Your son is not a horse, to be stolen."

"No," snapped Pyotr. "He is worse. A horse will listen to reason."

"He is a warrior born, and a man of God," said Sergei. His voice was mild as ever, and Pyotr's anger burned hotter, so that he choked on his words and said nothing.

The monk frowned, as though making a decision. Then he said, "Listen, Pyotr Vladimirovich. Ivan Ivanovich is dying. By now, perhaps he is dead."

This Pyotr had not known. He started and drew back.

"His son Dmitrii is a guest in your house," Sergei continued. "When the boy leaves here, he will go straight to my own monastery, there to be hidden. There are claimants to the throne for whom the life of one small boy is as nothing. A prince needs men of his own blood to teach him, and to guard him. Your son is Dmitrii's cousin."

Pyotr was silent in his surprise. The bats were coming out. In his youth, Pyotr's nights had been full of their cries, but now they flittered silent as the encroaching dusk.

"We do not just bake altar-bread and chant, my folk and I," added Sergei. "You are safe here, in this forest that could swallow an army, but there are few who can say as much. We bake our bread for the hungry and wield swords in their defense. It is a noble calling."

"My son will wield a sword for his family, serpent," snapped Pyotr, reflexively, angrier now because he was uncertain.

"Indeed he will," said Sergei. "For his own cousin: a boy that will one day have all Muscovy in his charge."

Pyotr again was silent, but his anger was broken.

Sergei saw Pyotr's grief and bowed his head. "I am sorry," he said. "It is a hard thing. I will pray for you." He slipped away between the trees, the sound of his going swallowed by the stream.

Pyotr did not stir. There was a full moon; the edge of its silver disc rose over the treetops. "You would have known what to say," he whispered. "For myself, I do not. Help me, Marina. Even for the Grand Prince's heir, I would not lose my son."

༄

"I WAS ANGRY WHEN I heard you had sold my sister so far away," said Sasha to his father. He spoke rather jerkily; he was training a young horse. Pyotr rode Buran, and the gray stallion, no plow-horse, was looking with some wonder at the young beast curvetting beside him. "But Vladimir is a decent enough man, though he is so young. He is kind to his horses."

"I am glad of it, for Olya's sake. But even if he was a drunken lecher and old to boot, I could do nothing else," said Pyotr. "The Grand Prince did not *ask*."

Sasha thought suddenly of his stepmother, a woman that his father would never have chosen, with her easy tears, her praying, her starts and terrors. "You could not choose either, Father," he said.

I must be old, Pyotr thought to himself, *if my son is being kind to me.* "It matters not," he said. The light slanted gold between the slender beeches, and all the silver leaves shivered together. Sasha's horse took exception to the shimmer and reared up. Sasha checked him midleap and set him back on his haunches. Buran came up beside them, as though showing the colt how a real horse behaved.

"You have heard what the monk has to say," said Pyotr slowly. "The Grand Prince and his son are our kin. But, Sasha, I would ask you to think better of it. It is a harsh life, that of a monk—always alone, poverty and prayers and a cold bed. You are needed here."

Sasha looked sideways at his father. His sun-browned face seemed suddenly much younger. "I have brothers," he said. "I must go and try myself, against the world. Here, the trees hem me in. I will go forth and fight for God. I was born to it, Father. Besides, the prince—my cousin Dmitrii—he has need of me."

"It is a bitter thing," growled Pyotr, "to be a father whose sons abandon him. Or to be a man with no sons to mourn his passing."

"I will have brothers in Christ to mourn me," Sasha rejoined. "And you have Kolya and Alyosha."

"You will take nothing with you, Sasha, if you go," snapped Pyotr. "The clothes on your back, your sword, and that mad horse you think to ride—but you will not be my son."

Sasha looked younger than ever. His face showed white under the tan. "I must go, Father," he said. "Do not hate me for going."

Pyotr did not answer; he set Buran for home with such a vengeance that Sasha's colt was left far behind.

⚜

VASYA CREPT INTO THE STABLE that evening when Sasha was looking over a tall young gelding. "Mysh is sad," said Vasya. "She wants to go with you." The brown mare was hanging her head over her stall.

Sasha smiled at his sister. "She is growing old for journeys, that mare," he said, reaching out to stroke her neck. "Besides, there is little use for a broodmare in a monastery. This one will serve me well." He slapped the gelding, who flicked his pointed ears.

"I can be a monk," said Vasya, and Sasha saw that she had stolen her brother's clothes again and stood with a small skin bag in one hand.

"I have no doubt," said Sasha. "But monks are usually bigger."

"I am always too small!" cried Vasya in great disgust. "I will get bigger. Don't go yet, Sashka. Another year."

"Have you forgotten Olya?" said Sasha. "I promised I'd see her to her husband's house. And then I am called to God, Vasochka; there is no gainsaying."

Vasya thought a moment. "If I promised to see Olya to her husband's house, could I go, too?"

Sasha said nothing. She looked down at her feet, scraping a toe in the dust. "Anna Ivanovna would let me go," she said all in a rush. "She wants me to go. She hates me. I am too small and too dirty."

"Give her time," said Sasha. "She is city-bred; she is not used to the woods."

Vasya scowled. "She's been here forever already. I wish *she'd* go back to Moscow."

"Here, little sister," said Sasha, looking at her pale face. "Come and ride." Vasya, when she was smaller, had loved nothing more than riding on his saddlebow, her face in the wind, safe in the curve of his arm. Her face lit, and Sasha put her on the gelding. When they came into the dvor, he sprang up behind. Vasya leaned forward, breath quickening, and then they were off, galloping with a swift thunder of hooves.

Vasya leaned gleefully forward. "More, more!" she cried when Sasha eased off the horse and turned him for home. "Let's go to Sarai, Sashka!" She turned to look at him. "Or Tsargrad, or Buyan, where the sea-king lives with his daughter the swan-maiden. It is not too far. East of the sun, west of the moon." She squinted up as though to make sure of their direction.

"A bit far for a night's gallop," said Sasha. "You must be brave, little frog, and listen to Dunya. I'll come back one day."

"Will it be soon, Sasha?" whispered Vasya. "Soon?"

Sasha did not answer, but then he did not have to. They had ridden up to the house. He reined in the gelding and put his sister down in the stable-yard.

II.

DOMOVOI

AFTER SASHA AND OLGA WENT AWAY, DUNYA NOTICED A CHANGE in Vasya. For one thing, she disappeared more than ever. For another, she talked much less. And sometimes when she did talk, folk were startled. The girl was growing too big for childish babble, and yet . . .

"Dunya," Vasya asked one day, not long after Olga's wedding, when the heat lay like a hand over the woods and fields, "what lives in the river?" She was drinking sap; she took a great draught, eyed her nurse expectantly.

"Fish, Vasochka, and if you will only behave yourself until tomorrow, we shall have some caught fresh with new herbs and cream."

Vasya loved fish, but she shook her head. "No, Dunya, what else lives in the river? Something with eyes like a frog and hair like waterweed and mud dripping down its nose."

Dunya shot the child a sharp glance, but Vasya was occupied with the last bits of cabbage in the bottom of her bowl and did not see. "Have you been listening to peasants' stories, Vasya?" asked Dunya. "That is the vodianoy, the river-king, who is always looking for little maidens to take to his castle under the riverbank."

Vasya was scraping the bottom of her bowl with a distracted air.

"Not a castle," she said, licking broth off her fingers. "Just a hole in the riverbank. But I never knew what he was called before."

"Vasya . . ." began Dunya, looking into the child's bright eyes.

"Mmmm?" said Vasya, putting down her empty bowl and clambering to her feet. It was on the tip of Dunya's tongue to warn her explicitly against—what? Talking of fairy tales? Dunya bit the words back and thrust a cloth-covered basket at Vasya.

"Here," said Dunya. "Take this to Father Semyon; he's been ill."

Vasya nodded. The priest's room was part of the house, but it could be entered through a separate door on the south wall. She seized a dumpling, stuffed it into her mouth before Dunya could object, and slipped out of the kitchen, humming loud and off-key, as her father was once wont to do.

Slowly, as though against her will, Dunya's hand plunged into a pocket sewn inside her skirt. The star around the blue jewel gleamed, perfect as a snowflake, and the stone was icy cold to her touch, though she had labored over the oven all that sweltering morning.

"Not yet," she whispered. "She's still a little girl—oh, please, not yet." The gem lay gleaming against her withered palm. Dunya thrust it angrily back into her pocket and turned to stir the soup with a vindictiveness most unlike her, so that the clear broth sloshed over the sides and hissed on the oven's hot stones.

⊱♦⊰

SOME TIME LATER, KOLYA saw his sister peering out from a clump of tall grass. He pursed his lips. No one in ten villages, he was sure, could contrive to be always underfoot, as Vasya was.

"Shouldn't you be in the kitchen, Vasya?" he asked, an edge to his voice. The day was hot, his sweating wife irritable. His newborn son was teething and shrieked without pause. At last Kolya, gritting his teeth, had snatched line and basket and made for the river. But now here was his sister come to trouble his peace.

Vasya poked her head further out of the weeds but did not quite leave her hiding-place. "I could not help it, brother," she said coaxingly. "Anna Ivanovna and Dunya were screeching at each other, and Irina was crying *again*." Irina was their new baby half sister, born a little before Kolya's own son. "I can't sew when Anna Ivanovna's about anyway. I forget how."

Kolya snorted.

Vasya shifted in her hiding-place. "Can I help you fish?" she asked, hopefully.

"No."

"Can I *watch* you fish?"

Kolya opened his mouth to refuse, and then reconsidered. If she was sitting on the riverbank, she wouldn't be getting in trouble somewhere else. "Very well," he said. "If you sit over there. *Quietly.* Don't cast your shadow over the water." Vasya crept meekly to the indicated spot. Kolya paid her no more attention, concentrating on the water and the feel of the line in his fingers.

An hour later, Vasya was still sitting as instructed, and Kolya had six fine fish in his basket. Perhaps his wife would forgive his disappearance, he thought, glancing at his sister and wondering how she'd managed to sit still for so long. She was looking at the water with a rapt expression that made him uneasy. What was she seeing to make her stare so? The water whispered over its bed as it always had, beds of cress swaying in the current on either bank.

There came a sharp tug on his line, and he forgot Vasya as he drew it in. But before the fish cleared the bank, the wooden hook snapped. Kolya swore. He coiled his line impatiently and replaced the hook. Preparing to cast again, he looked around. His basket was no longer in its place. He swore again, louder, and looked at Vasya. But she was sitting on a rock ten paces away.

"What happened?" she asked.

"My fish are gone! Some durak from the village must have come and . . ."

But Vasya was not listening. She had run to the very brink of the river.

"It's not yours!" she shouted. "Give it back!" Kolya thought he heard an odd note in the splash of the water, as though it was making a reply. Vasya stamped her foot. "Now! Catch your own fish!" A deep groan came up from the depths, as of rocks grinding together, and then the basket came flying out of nowhere to hit Vasya in the chest and knock her backward. Instinctively, she clutched it, and turned a grin on her brother.

"Here they are!" she said. "The greedy old thing just wanted . . ." But she stopped short at the sight of her brother's face. Wordless, she held out the basket.

Kolya would have liked to make for the village and leave both his basket and his peculiar sister to themselves. But he was a man and a boyar's son, and so he stalked forward, stiff-legged, to seize his catch. He might have wished to speak; certainly his mouth worked once or twice—rather like a fish himself, Vasya thought—but then he turned on his heel without a word, and strode away.

৪৩

FALL CAME AT LAST TO LAY cool fingers on the summer-dry grass; the light went from gold to gray and the clouds grew damp and soft. If Vasya still wept for her brother and sister, she did not do it where her family could see her, and she stopped asking her father every day if she was big enough to go to Moscow. But she ate her porridge with wolflike intensity and asked Dunya often if she had grown any bigger. She avoided her sewing and her stepmother both. Anna stamped and gave shrill orders, but Vasya defied them.

That summer she rambled the woods, while the light lasted and into the night. There was no Sasha now to catch her when she fled, and she fled often, despite Dunya's scolding. But the days drew in, the weather worsened, and on the short, blustery afternoons, Vasya would sometimes sit indoors on her stool. There, she would eat her bread and talk to the domovoi.

The domovoi was small and squat and brown. He had a long beard and brilliant eyes. At night he crept out of the oven to wipe the plates and scour away the soot. He used to do mending, too, when people left it out, but Anna would shriek if she saw a stray shirt, and few of the servants would risk her anger. Before Vasya's stepmother arrived, they had left offerings for him: a bowl of milk or a bit of bread. But Anna shrieked then, too. Dunya and the serving-maids had begun hiding their offerings in odd corners where Anna rarely came.

Vasya talked between bites, kicking her feet against the legs of her stool. The domovoi was stitching—she had furtively handed him her mending. His tiny fingers flicked fast as gnats on a summer day. Their conversation was, as always, rather one-sided.

"Where do you come from?" Vasya asked him, her mouth full. She had asked this question before, but sometimes his answer changed.

The domovoi did not look up or pause in his work. "Here," he said.

"You mean there are more of you?" inquired the girl, peering about. The notion seemed to disconcert the domovoi. "No."

"But if you're the only one, then where do you come from?"

Philosophical conversation was not the domovoi's strong suit. His seamed brow furrowed, and there was a suggestion of hesitation in his hands. "I am here because the house is here. If the house weren't here, I wouldn't be, either."

Vasilisa could not make head or tail of his answer. "So," she tried again, "if the house is burned by Tatars, you'll die?"

The domovoi looked as though he were struggling with an unfathomable concept. "No."

"But you just said that—"

The domovoi intimated at this point, with a certain brusqueness in his hands, that he did not care for any more talk. Vasya had finished her bread, anyway. Puzzling to herself, she slid from her stool in a scatter of crumbs. The domovoi gave her a tight-lipped glare. Guiltily, she brushed at the crumbs, scattering them further. Finally she gave up and fled, only to trip on a loose board and carom into Anna Ivanovna, who stood in the doorway staring with her mouth half open.

In her defense, Vasya did not mean to send her stepmother reeling against the doorframe, but she was strong and rawboned for her age and could scamper very fast. Vasya looked up in quick apology but stopped, arrested. Anna was white as salt, with a little color burning in each cheek. Her breast heaved. Vasya took a step backward.

"Vasya," Anna began, sounding strangled. "Who were you talking to?"

Vasya, taken aback, said nothing.

"Answer me, child! Who were you talking to?"

Vasya, disconcerted, settled on the safest answer. "No one."

Anna's glance darted from Vasya to the room behind. Abruptly she reached out and slapped Vasya across the face.

Vasya put her hand to her cheek, pale with astonished fury. The tears sprang to her eyes a moment later. Her father beat her often enough, but with a grave application of justice. She had never been struck in anger in her life.

"I won't ask again," said Anna.

"It's only the domovoi," Vasya whispered. Her eyes were huge. "Just the domovoi."

"And what manner of devil," demanded Anna, shrilly, "is the domovoi?"

Vasya, bewildered and trying not to cry, said nothing.

Anna raised a hand to slap her again.

"He helps clean the house," Vasya stammered hastily. "He does no harm."

Anna's eyes darted, blazing, into the room and her face flushed dully red. "Go away, you!" she screeched. The domovoi looked up in aggrieved confusion. Anna rounded back on Vasilisa. "Domovoi?" Anna hissed, advancing on her stepdaughter. "Domovoi? There is no such thing as a *domovoi!*"

Vasya, furious, bewildered, opened her mouth to contradict, caught her stepmother's expression, and closed it with a snap. She'd never seen anyone look so frightened.

"Get out of here," cried Anna. "Get out, get *out*!" The last word was a screech, and Vasya turned and fled.

⁓

THE ANIMALS' HEAT STRUCK up from below and warmed the sweet-smelling loft. Vasya buried herself in a heap of straw, chilly, bruised, and baffled.

There was no such thing as a domovoi? Of course there was. They saw him every day. He'd been right there.

But *did* they see him? Vasya couldn't recall anyone except herself talking to the domovoi. But—of course Anna Ivanovna saw him: *Go away,* she had said. Hadn't she? Maybe—maybe there *wasn't* such a thing as a domovoi. Perhaps she was mad. Maybe she was destined to be a Holy Fool and wander begging among the villages. But no, Holy Fools were protected by Christ; they would not be nearly as wicked as her.

Vasya's head hurt with thinking. If the domovoi wasn't real, then what about the others? The vodianoy in the river, the twig-man in the trees? The rusalka, the polevik, the dvorovoi? Had she imagined them all? Was she mad? Was Anna Ivanovna? She wished she could ask Olya or Sasha. They would know, and neither of them would ever strike her. But they were far away.

Vasya buried her head in her arms. She wasn't sure how long she lay there. The shadows drifted across the dim stable. She dozed a bit in the manner of tired children, and when she awoke, the light in the hayloft was gray and she was furiously hungry.

Stiffly, Vasya uncurled herself, opened her eyes—and found herself looking straight into the eyes of a strange little person. Vasya gave a moan of dismay and curled up again, pressing her fists into her eye sockets.

But when she looked again, the eyes were still there, still large, brown, and tranquil, and attached to a broad face, a red nose, and a wagging white beard. The creature was quite small, no larger than Vasya herself, and he sat in a pile of hay, watching her with an expression of curious sympathy. Unlike the domovoi in his neat robe, this creature wore a collection of tattered oddments, and his feet were bare.

So much Vasya saw before she squeezed her eyes shut again. But she could not sit buried in the hay forever; at last she screwed up her courage, opened her eyes once more, and said tremulously:

"Are you a devil?"

There was a small pause.

"I don't know. Maybe. What is a devil?" The little creature had a voice like the whicker of a kindly horse.

Vasya reflected. "A great black creature with a beard of flame and a forked tail that wishes to possess my soul and drag me off to be tortured in a pit of fire."

She eyed the little man again.

Whatever he was, he did not seem to fit this description. His beard was quite reassuringly white and solid and he was turning round and examining the seat of his trousers as though to confirm the absence of a tail.

"No," he answered at length. "I do not think that I am a devil."

"Are you really here?" Vasya asked.

"Sometimes," answered the little man tranquilly.

Vasya was not greatly reassured, but after a moment's reflection she decided that "sometimes" was preferable to "never." "Oh," she said, mollified. "What are you, then?"

"I look after the horses."

Vasya nodded wisely. If there was a little creature to look after the house, well, then, there should be another for the stables. But the girl had learned caution.

"Can—can everyone see you? Do they know you're here?"

"The grooms know I'm here; at least, they leave offerings on cold nights. But no, no one can see me. Except you. And the one other, but she never comes." He sketched a small bow in her direction.

Vasya eyed him in growing consternation. "And the domovoi? No one can see him either, can they?"

"I do not know what is a domovoi," the little creature replied equably. "I am of the stables and of the beasts that live here. I do not venture outside except to exercise the horses."

Vasya opened her mouth to ask how he did so. He was no taller than she, and all of the horses had backs several handspans above her head. But at that moment she became aware of Dunya's cracked voice calling. She jumped up.

"I must go," she said. "Will I see you again?"

"If you like," the other returned. "I have never talked with anyone before."

"I am called Vasilisa Petrovna. What is your name?"

The little creature thought for a moment. "I have never had to name myself before," he said. He thought again.

"I am—the vazila, the spirit of horses," he said finally. "I suppose that you may call me so."

Vasya nodded once, respectfully.

"Thank you," she said. Then she rolled over and scurried for the hayloft ladder, trailing straw from her hair.

⚜

THE DAYS WORE AWAY, and the seasons. Vasya grew older, and she learned caution. She made sure never to speak to anyone but other people unless she was alone. She determined to shout less, run less, worry Dunya less, and above all, avoid Anna Ivanovna.

She even succeeded somewhat, for almost seven years passed in peace. If Vasya heard voices on the wind, or saw faces in the leaves, she ignored them. Mostly. The vazila became the exception.

He was a very simple creature. Like all household-spirits, he said, he had come into being when the stables were built and remembered nothing before. But he had the generous simplicity of horses, and under her impishness Vasilisa had a steadiness that—though she did not know it—appealed to the little stable-spirit.

Whenever she could, Vasya disappeared into the barn. She could watch the vazila for hours. His movements were inhumanly light and deft, and he would clamber all over the horses' backs like a squirrel. Even Buran stood like a stone while he did so. After a while, it seemed only natural that Vasya take up knife and comb and assist him.

At first the vazila's lessons were in craft only: in grooming, and doctoring, and mending. But Vasya was very eager, and soon enough he was teaching her stranger things.

He taught her to talk to horses.

It was a language of eye and body, sound and gesture. Vasya was young enough to learn quickly. Soon enough she was creeping into the barn not only for the comfort of hay and warm bodies, but for the horses' talk. She would sit in the stalls by the hour, listening.

The grooms might have sent her out had they caught her, but they managed to find her surprisingly seldom. Sometimes it worried Vasya that they never found her. All she had to do was flatten herself against the side of a stall and then duck around the horse and flee, and the groom would never even look up.

Part Two

THE PRIEST WITH
THE GOLDEN HAIR

IN THE YEAR THAT VASILISA PETROVNA TURNED FOURTEEN, THE
Metropolitan Aleksei made his plans for the accession of Prince Dmitrii
Ivanovich. For seven years the Metropolitan had held the regency of
Moscow; he schemed and skirmished, made alliances and broke them,
called men to battle and sent them home again. But when Dmitrii came
to manhood, Aleksei, seeing him bold and keen and steady in judgment, said, "Well, a good colt must not be left in pasture," and began
making plans for a coronation. The robes were stitched, the furs and
jewels bought, the boy himself sent to Sarai to beg the Khan's indulgence.

And Aleksei continued, as ever, to look quietly about him for those
who might be in a position to oppose the prince's succession. It was
thus that he learned of a priest named Father Konstantin Nikonovich.

Konstantin was quite a young man, true, but the fortunate (or unfortunate) possessor of a terrible beauty: old-gold hair and eyes like
blue water. He was renowned throughout Muscovy for his piety, and
despite his youth he had traveled far—south even to Tsargrad and west
to Hellas. He read Greek and could argue obscure points of theology.
Moreover he chanted with a voice like an angel, so that the people wept
to hear him and lifted up their eyes to God.

But most of all, Konstantin Nikonovich was a painter of icons. Such icons, said the people, as had never been seen in Muscovy; they must have come from the finger of God to bless the wicked world. Already his icons were copied throughout the monasteries of northern Rus', and Aleksei's spies brought him tales of rapturous, rioting crowds, of women weeping when they kissed the painted faces.

These rumors troubled the Metropolitan. "Well, and I will rid Moscow of this golden-haired priest," he said to himself. "If he is so beloved, his voice, should he choose, could turn the people against the prince."

He fell to considering this means or that.

While he deliberated, a messenger came from the house of Pyotr Vladimirovich.

The Metropolitan sent for the man at once. The messenger arrived in due course, still in his dust and weary, awed by his glittering surroundings. But he stood steadily enough and said, "Father, bless," with only a little stammer.

"God be with you," said Aleksei, sketching the sign of the cross. "Tell me what brings you so far, my son."

"The priest of Lesnaya Zemlya has died," explained the messenger, gulping. He had expected to explain his errand to a less exalted personage. "Good fat Father Semyon has gone to God, and we are adrift, says the mistress. She begs you send us another, to hold us fast in the wilderness."

"Well," said the Metropolitan immediately. "Give thanks, for your salvation is just at hand."

Metropolitan Aleksei dismissed the messenger and sent for Konstantin Nikonovich.

The young man came into the prelate's presence, tall and pale and burning. His robe of dark stuff set off the beauty of his hair and eyes.

"Father Konstantin," said Aleksei, "you are called to a task by God."

Father Konstantin said nothing.

"A woman," the Metropolitan continued, "the Grand Prince's own sister, has sent a messenger begging our help. Her village flock is without a shepherd."

The young man's face did not change.

"You are the very man to go and minister to the lady and her family," Aleksei finished, smiling with an air of studied benevolence.

"Batyushka," said Father Konstantin. His voice was so deep it was startling. The servant at Aleksei's elbow squeaked. The Metropolitan narrowed his eyes. "I am honored. But already I have my work among the people of Moscow. And my icons, that I have painted for the glory of God, they are here."

"There are many of us to tend to the people of Moscow," replied the Metropolitan. The young priest's voice was soothing and unnerving at the same time, and Aleksei watched him warily. "And no one at all for those poor lost souls in the wilderness. No, no, it really must be you. You will leave in three weeks."

Pyotr Vladimirovich is a sensible man, thought Aleksei. *Three seasons in the north will kill this upstart, or at least fade that oh-so-dangerous loveliness. Better than killing him now, lest the people take his flesh for relics and make him a martyr.*

Father Konstantin opened his mouth. But he caught the Metropolitan's eye, which was hard as flint. The guards waited at every hand, and more in the anteroom, with long scarlet pikes. Konstantin bit back whatever he had wanted to say.

"I am sure," said Aleksei softly, "that you have much to do before your departure. God be with you, my son."

Konstantin, white-faced and biting his red lip, bent his head stiffly and turned on his heel. His heavy robe rippled and snapped behind him as he left the room.

"Good riddance," muttered Aleksei, though he was uneasy still. He dashed kvas into a cup and tossed it cold down his throat.

AT HIGH SUMMER, the roads were grass-grown and dry. The mild sun loved the sweet-smelling earth, and soft rains scattered flowers in the forest. But Father Konstantin saw none of it; he rode beside Anna's messenger in a white-lipped rage. His fingers ached for his brushes, for his pigments and wood panels, for his cool, quiet cell. Most of all he ached for the people, for their love and hunger and half-frightened rapture, for the way their hands stretched out to his. Devils take the meddling Metropolitan. And now he was exiled, for no other reason than that people preferred him.

Well. He'd train some village boy, see him ordained, and then be free to return to Moscow. Or perhaps go farther south, to Kiev, or west to Novgorod. The world was wide, and Konstantin Nikonovich would not be left to rot on some farm in the woods.

Konstantin spent a week fuming, and then natural curiosity took over. The trees grew steadily larger as they rode deeper into the wild lands: oaks of giant girth and pines tall as the domes of churches. The bright meadows grew sparser as the forest drew in on either side; the light was green and gray and purple, and the shadows lay thick as velvet.

"What is it like, the land of Pyotr Vladimirovich?" Konstantin asked his companion one morning. The messenger started. They had been riding a week, and the handsome priest had hardly opened his lips except to eat his meals.

"Very beautiful, Batyushka," the man replied respectfully. "Trees fine as cathedrals, and bright streams on all sides. Flowers in summer, fruit in autumn. Cold in winter, though."

"And your master and mistress?" asked Konstantin, curious despite himself.

"A good man is Pyotr Vladimirovich," said the man, warmth creeping into his voice. "Hard sometimes, but fair, and his folk never go wanting."

"And your mistress?"

"Oh, a good woman; a good woman. Not like the mistress that was, but a good woman all the same. I know no harm of her." He shot Konstantin a furtive glance as he spoke, and Father Konstantin wondered what it was that the messenger had not said.

৪৩১৪

THE DAY THE PRIEST ARRIVED, Vasya was sitting in a tree talking to a rusalka. Once, Vasya had found such conversations disconcerting, but now she had gotten used to the woman's green-skinned nakedness and the constant drip of water from her pale, weedy hair. The sprite was sitting on a thick limb with catlike nonchalance, steadily combing her long tresses. Her comb was the rusalka's greatest treasure, for if her hair dried, she would die; but the comb could conjure water anywhere. When she looked closely, Vasya could see the water flowing from the comb's teeth. The rusalka had an appetite for flesh; she would snatch fawns drinking in her lake at dawn, and sometimes the young men who swam there at midsummer. But she liked Vasilisa.

It was late afternoon, and the light of the long northern days shone down on the two, bringing out the radiance in Vasya's hair and fading the rusalka to a greenish, woman-shaped ghost. The water-spirit was old as the lake itself, and sometimes she looked wonderingly on Vasya, the brash child of a newer world.

They had become friends under strange circumstances. The rusalka had stolen a village boy. Vasya, seeing the youth vanish, gurgling, and the flash of green fingers, had dived into the lake after him. Child though she was, she blazed with the strength of her own mortality and was a match for any rusalka. She seized the boy and dragged him back into daylight. They made it safe to shore, the boy bruised and spitting water, staring at Vasya with equal parts gratitude and terror. He tore away from her and ran for the village as soon as he felt the earth under his feet.

Vasya had shrugged and followed, wringing the water from her braid. She wanted her soup. But late in the long spring twilight, when each leaf and blade of grass stood out black against the blue-tinged air, Vasya had returned to the lake. She sat down on the verge, toes in the water.

"Did you wish to eat him?" she asked the water conversationally. "Can you not find other meat?"

There was a small leaf-filled silence.

Then—"No," said a rippling voice. Vasya sprang to her feet, eyes flicking through the foliage. It was luck more than anything else that her glance lit on the sinuous outlines of a naked woman. The rusalka crouched on a limb, a glimmering white thing clutched in one hand.

"Not meat," the creature had said with a shudder, hair scudding like wavelets over her skin. "Fear—and desire—not that *you* know anything of either. It flavors the water and nourishes me. Dying, they know me for who I am. Otherwise I'd be no more than lake and tree and waterweed."

"But you kill them!" said Vasya.

"Everything dies."

"I will not let you slay my people."

"Then I will disappear," replied the rusalka, without inflection.

Vasya thought for a moment. "I know you're here. I can see you. I am not dying, and I am not afraid—but—I can see you. I could be your friend. Is that enough?"

The rusalka was looking at her curiously. "Perhaps."

And true to her word, Vasya would come looking for the water-spirit, and in spring she threw flowers into the lake, and the rusalka did not die.

In return, the rusalka taught Vasya to swim as very few could, and to climb trees like a cat, and so it was that the two found themselves together, lounging on a limb overlooking the road, as Father Konstantin approached Lesnaya Zemlya.

The rusalka saw the priest first. Her eyes gleamed. "Here comes one who would be good eating."

Vasya peered down the road and saw a man with dusty golden hair and the dark robes of a priest. "Why?"

"He is full of desire. Desire and fear. He does not know what he desires, and he does not admit his fear. But he feels both, strong enough to strangle." The man was coming closer. It was indeed a hungry face. High, protruding cheekbones cast gray shadows over his hollow cheeks; he had deep-set blue eyes and soft, full lips, though set sternly as though to hide the softness. One of her father's men rode beside him, and both horses were dusty and tired.

Vasya's face lit. "I'm going home," she said. "If he is come from Moscow, he will have news of my brother and sister."

The rusalka was not looking at her, but down the path the man had taken, a hungry light in her eyes.

"You promised you wouldn't," said Vasya sharply.

The rusalka smiled, sharp teeth gleaming between greenish lips. "Perhaps he desires death," she said. "If so—I can help him."

⁂

THE DOORYARD BEFORE THE HOUSE churned like an ant pile, washed in gold by the afternoon light. A man was unsaddling the weary horses, but the priest was nowhere to be seen. Vasya ran for the kitchen door. Dunya, who met her at the threshold, hissed at the twigs in her hair and the stains on her cut-down dress. "Vasya, where—?" she said, then, "Never mind. Come on, hurry." She hustled the girl off to have her hair combed and her dirty clothes exchanged for a blouse and embroidered sarafan.

Flushed and smarting, but more or less presentable, Vasya emerged from the room she shared with Irina. Alyosha was waiting for her. He grinned at her appearance. "Maybe they will manage to marry you off after all, Vasochka."

"Anna Ivanovna says not," Vasya replied composedly. "Too tall, skinny as a weasel, feet and face like a frog." She clasped her hands and raised her eyes. "Alas, only princes in fairy tales take frog-wives. And they can do magic and become beautiful on command. I fear I will have no prince, Lyoshka."

Alyosha snorted. "I'd pity the prince. But do not take Anna Ivanovna to heart; she does not want you to be beautiful."

Vasya said nothing, and a quick shadow darkened her face.

"Well, so there is a new priest," Alyosha added hastily. "Curious, are you, little sister?"

The two slipped outside and circled the house.

The look she gave him was limpid as a child's. "Aren't you?" she said. "He is come from Moscow; perhaps he will have news."

⊱⊰

PYOTR AND THE PRIEST sat together on the cool summer grass drinking kvas. Pyotr turned when he heard his children approach, and his eyes narrowed when he saw his second daughter.

She is nearly a woman, he thought. *It is too long since I looked at her truly. She is so like and so unlike her mother.*

In truth, Vasya was still awkward, but she had begun growing into her face. The bones were still rough-hewn and overlarge, her mouth still too wide and full-lipped for the rest of her. But she was compelling: the moods passed like clouds over the clear green water of her gaze, and something about her movements, the line of her neck and braided hair, caught the eye and held it. When the light struck her black hair it did not gleam bronze as Marina's had, but dark red, like garnets caught in the silky strands.

Father Konstantin was regarding Vasya with raised eyebrows and a slight frown. *And no wonder,* Pyotr thought. There was something feral about her, for all her neat gown and properly braided hair. She looked like a wild thing new-caught and just barely groomed into submission.

"My son," Pyotr said hastily, "Aleksei Petrovich. And this is my daughter, Vasilisa Petrovna."

Alyosha bowed, both to the priest and to his father. Vasya was looking at Konstantin with transparent eagerness. Alyosha elbowed her, hard.

"Oh!" said Vasya. "You are welcome here, Batyushka." And then she added, all in a rush, "Have you news of our brother and sister? My brother rode away seven years ago to take his vows at the Trinity Lavra. And my sister is the Princess of Serpukhov. Tell me you have seen them!"

Her mother should take her in hand, Konstantin thought darkly. A soft voice and a bent head were more fitting when a woman addressed a priest. This girl stared him brazenly in the face with fey green eyes.

"Enough, Vasya," said Pyotr, stern. "He has had a long journey."

Konstantin was spared any reply. There came a rustle of feet in the summer grass. Anna Ivanovna swept breathlessly into view, dressed in her finest. Her small daughter, Irina, followed her, spotless as always and pretty as a doll. Anna bowed. Irina sucked her finger and stared round-eyed at the newcomer. "Batyushka," said Anna. "You are most welcome."

The priest nodded back. At least these two were proper women. The mother had a scarf wrapped round her hair, and the little girl was neat and small and reverent. But, despite himself, Konstantin's glance slid sideways and caught the other daughter's interested stare.

⁂

"Colors?" said Pyotr, frowning.

"Colors, Pyotr Vladimirovich," said Father Konstantin, trying not to betray his eagerness.

Pyotr was not sure he'd heard the priest aright.

Dinner in the summer kitchen was a raucous affair. The forest was kind, in the golden months, and the kitchen garden overflowed. Dunya outdid herself with delicate stews. "And then we ran like hares," said Alyosha, from the other side of the hearth. Beside him, Vasya blushed and covered her face. The kitchen rang with laughter.

"Dyes, you mean?" said Pyotr to the priest, his face clearing. "Well, you need have no fear on that score; the women will dye whatever you like." He grinned, feeling benevolent. Pyotr was content with life. His crops grew tall and green beneath a clear, fair sun. His wife wept and shrieked and hid less since this fair-haired priest had come.

"We can," Anna interjected breathlessly. She was neglecting her stew. "Anything you like. Are you still hungry, Batyushka?"

"Colors," said Konstantin. "Not for dyes. I wish to make paints."

Pyotr was offended. The house was painted under the eaves, scarlet and blue. But the paintwork was bright and well-kept, and if this man thought he needed to meddle . . .

Konstantin pointed to the icon corner opposite the door. "For the painting of icons," he said very distinctly. "For the glory of God. I know what I need. But I do not know where to find it, here in your forest."

For the painting of icons. Pyotr eyed Konstantin with renewed respect.

"Like ours?" he said. He squinted at the smoke-dimmed, indifferently painted Virgin in her corner, with the candle-stub set before her. He had brought the family icons from Moscow, but he'd never seen an icon-painter. Monks painted icons.

Konstantin opened his mouth, closed it, smoothed his features, and said, "Yes. A little like them. But I must have paints. Colors. Some I brought with me, but . . ."

Icons were holy. Men would honor his house when they knew he harbored a painter of icons. "Of course, Batyushka," said Pyotr. "Icons—the painting of icons—well, we'll get you your paints." Pyotr raised his voice. "Vasya!"

On the other side of the hearth, Alyosha said something and laughed. Vasya was laughing, too. The sunlight shone through her hair and lit the freckles adorning the bridge of her nose.

Gawky, Konstantin thought. *Clumsy, half-grown. But half the house watches to see what she will do next.* "Vasya!" Pyotr called again, more sharply.

She left off whispering and came toward them. She wore a green dress. Her hair had loosened at the temples and curled a little about her brows, beneath her red and yellow kerchief. *She is ugly,* thought Konstantin, and then wondered at himself. What was it to him if a girl was ugly?

"Father?" said Vasya.

"Father Konstantin wishes to go into the wood," said Pyotr. "He is looking for colors. You will go with him. You will show him where the dye-plants grow."

The look she threw the priest was not the simper or shy glance of a maiden; it was transparent as sunlight, bright and curious. "Yes, Father," she said. And, to Konstantin: "At dawn tomorrow, I think, Batyushka. It is best to harvest before full light."

Anna Ivanovna took the moment to ladle more stew into Konstantin's bowl. "By your leave," she said.

He did not take his eyes off Vasya. Why couldn't some man of the village help him find his pigments? Why the green-eyed witch? Abruptly he realized he was glaring. The brightness had faded from the girl's face. Konstantin recalled himself. "My thanks, devushka." He sketched the sign of the cross in the air between them.

Vasya smiled suddenly. "Tomorrow, then," she said.

"Run along, Vasya," said Anna, a little shrill. "The holy father can have no more need of you."

⊹

THERE WAS A MIST on the ground the next morning. The light of the rising sun turned it to fire and smoke, striped with the shadows of trees. The girl greeted Konstantin with a wary, glowing face. She was like a spirit in the haze.

The forest of Lesnaya Zemlya was not like the forest around Moscow. It was wilder and crueler and fairer. The vast trees whispered together overhead, and all around, Konstantin seemed to feel eyes. *Eyes . . . nonsense.*

"I know where the wild mint grows," said Vasya as they followed a thin dirt track. The trees made a cathedral-arch above their heads. The girl's bare feet were delicate in the dust. She had a skin bag slung across her back. "And there will be elderberries if we are fortunate, and blackberries. Alder for yellow. But that is not enough for the face of a saint. You will paint us icons, Batyushka?"

"I have the red earth, the powdered stones, the black metal. I even have the lapis-dust to make the Virgin's veil. But I have no green or yellow or violet," said Konstantin. Belatedly he heard the eagerness in his own voice.

"Those we can find," said Vasya. She skipped like a child. "I have never seen an icon painted. Neither has anyone else. We will all come and beg you for prayers, that we might stare as you work."

He had known folk to do just that. In Moscow, they thronged about his icons . . .

"You are human after all," said Vasya, watching the thoughts cross his face. "I wondered. You are like an icon yourself sometimes."

He did not know what she'd seen on his face and was angry at himself. "You wonder too much, Vasilisa Petrovna. Better to stay quiet at home with your little sister."

"You are not the first to tell me that," said Vasya without rancor. "But if I did, who would go with you at dawn to find bits of leaves? Here—"

They stopped for birch, and again for wild mustard. The girl was deft with her small knife. The sun rose higher, burning away the mist.

"I asked you a question yesterday when I should not," said Vasya, when the lacy mustard-greens were tucked in her bag. "But I will ask again today, and you will please forgive a girl's eagerness, Batyushka. I love my brother and my sister. It is long since we have had news of either. My brother is called Brother Aleksandr now."

The priest's mouth narrowed. "I know of him," he said, after a brief hesitation. "There was a scandal when he took his vows under the name of his birth."

Vasya half-smiled. "Our mother chose that name for him, and my brother was always stubborn."

Rumors of Brother Aleksandr's impious intransigence on the matter had spread throughout Muscovy. But, Konstantin reminded himself, monastic vows were not a subject for maidens. The girl had fastened her great eyes on his face. Konstantin began to feel uncomfortable. "Brother Aleksandr came to Moscow for the coronation of Dmitrii Ivanovich. It is said he has gained a certain renown for his ministry in the villages," the priest added stiffly.

"And my sister?" said Vasya.

"The Princess of Serpukhov is honored for her piety and for her strong children," Konstantin said, wishing an end to the conversation.

Vasya spun around with a little whoop of satisfaction. "I worry for them," she said. "Father does, too, though he pretends not. Thank you, Batyushka." And she turned on him a face all lit from within, so that Konstantin was startled and unwillingly fascinated. His expression grew colder. There was a small silence. The path widened and they walked abreast.

"My father said you have been to the ends of the earth," said Vasya. "To Tsargrad, and the palace of a thousand kings. To the Church of Holy Wisdom."

"Yes," said Konstantin.

"Will you tell me of it?" she said. "Father says that at dusk the angels sing. And that the Tsar rules all men of God, as though he were God himself. That he has roomfuls of gems and a thousand servants."

Her question took him aback. "Not angels," Konstantin said slowly. "Men only, but men with voices that would not shame angels. At nightfall they light a hundred thousand candles, and everywhere there is gold and music . . ."

He stopped abruptly.

"It must be like heaven," Vasya said.

"Yes," said Konstantin. Memory had him by the throat: gold and silver, music, learned men and freedom. The forest seemed to choke him. "It is not a fit subject for girls," he added.

Vasya lifted a brow. They came upon a blackberry bush. Vasya plucked a handful. "You did not want to come here, did you?" she said, around the blackberries. "We have no music or lights, and precious few people. Can you not go away again?"

"I go where God sends me," Konstantin said, coldly. "If my work is here, then I will stay here."

"And what is your work, Batyushka?" said Vasya. She had stopped eating blackberries. For an instant, her glance darted to the trees overhead.

Konstantin followed her eyes, but there was nothing there. An odd feeling crept up his spine. "To save souls," he said. He could count the freckles on her nose. If ever a girl needed saving, it was this one. The blackberries had stained her lips and her hands.

Vasya half-smiled. "Are you going to save us, then?"

"If God gives me strength, I will save you."

"I am only a country girl," said Vasya. She reached again into the blackberry bush, wary of thorns. "I have never seen Tsargrad, or angels, or heard the voice of God. But I think you should be careful, Batyushka, that God does not speak in the voice of your own wishing. We have never needed saving before."

Konstantin stared at her. She only smiled at him, more child than woman, tall and thin and stained with blackberry juice. "Hurry," she said. "It will be full light soon."

⁊◊⁊

THAT NIGHT, FATHER KONSTANTIN lay on his narrow cot and shivered and could not sleep. In the north, the wind had teeth that bit after sunset, even in summer.

He had placed his icons, as was right, in the corner opposite the door. The Mother of God hung in the central place, with the Trinity just below. At nightfall, the lady of the house, shy and officious, had given him a fat beeswax candle to set before the icons. Konstantin lit it at dusk and enjoyed the golden light. But in the moonlight, the candle cast sinister shadows over the Virgin's face and set strange figures dancing wildly among the three parts of the Almighty. There was something hostile about the nighttime house. Almost, it seemed to breathe . . .

What foolishness, thought Konstantin. Annoyed with himself, he rose, intending to blow out the candle. But as he crossed the room, he heard the distinct click of a door closing. Without thinking, he veered to the window.

A woman darted across the space before the house, muffled in a heavy shawl. Plump she looked, and shapeless under the wrapper. Father Konstantin could not tell who she might be. The figure came to the church door and paused. She set a hand on the bronze ring, dragged the door open, and disappeared inside.

Konstantin stared at the place where she'd vanished. Of course there was nothing to prevent someone going to pray in the dead of night, but the house had its own icons. One might easily pray before them without braving the dark and the damp night air. And there had been something furtive—almost guilty—in the woman's manner.

Growing more curious and irritated—and wakeful—by the moment, Konstantin turned from the window and drew on his dark robe. His room had its own outer door. He slid noiselessly through, not bothering with shoes, and made his way across the grass to the church.

⚶

ANNA IVANOVNA KNELT IN the dark before the icon-screen and tried to think of nothing. The scent of dust and paint, beeswax and old wood, wrapped around her like a balm, while the sweat of yet another nightmare dried in the chill. She had been walking in the midnight woods this time, black shadows on all sides. Strange voices had risen around her.

"Mistress," they cried. "Mistress, please. See us. Know us, lest your hearth go undefended. Please, Mistress." But she would not look. She walked on and on while the voices tore at her. At last, desperate, she began to run, hurting her feet on rocks and roots. A great cry of lamentation rose up. Suddenly her path ended. She ran on into nothingness and fell back into her skin, gasping and dripping sweat.

A dream, nothing more. But her face and feet stung, and even awake, Anna could hear those voices. At last she bolted for the church and huddled at the foot of the icon-screen. She could stay in the church and creep back at first light. She had done it before. Her husband was a tolerant man, though all-night disappearances were awkward to explain.

The soft creak of hinges slipped thieflike to her ears. Anna lurched upright and spun around. A black-robed figure, silhouetted by the risen moon, passed softly through the doorway and came toward her. Anna was too frightened to move. She stood frozen until the shadow came close enough for her to catch the gleam of old-gold hair.

"Anna Ivanovna," Konstantin said. "Is all well with you?"

She gaped at the priest. All her life, folk had asked her angry questions and exasperated questions. "What are you doing?" they said, and "What is wrong with you?" But no one had ever asked her how she did in that tone of mild inquiry. The moonlight played over the hollows of his face.

Anna stuttered into speech: "I—of course, Batyushka, I am well, I just—forgive me, I . . ." The sob in her throat choked her. Shaking, unable to meet his eyes, she turned away, crossed herself, and knelt again before the icon-screen. Father Konstantin stood over her for a moment, wordless, then turned, very precisely, to cross himself and kneel at the other end of the iconostasis, before the tranquil face of the Mother of God. His voice as he prayed came faintly to Anna's ears: a slow, resonant murmur, though she could not catch the words. At last the whine of her breathing quieted.

She kissed the icon of Christ and slanted a glance at Father Konstantin. He was contemplating the dim images before him, hands clasped. His voice, when it came, was deep and quiet and unexpected.

"Tell me," he said, "what brings you to seek solace at such an hour."

"They have not told you that I am mad?" Anna replied bitterly, surprising herself.

"No," the priest said. "Are you?"

Her chin dipped in the barest fraction of a nod.

"Why?"

Her eyes flew up to meet his. "Why am I mad?" Her voice came out a hoarse whisper.

"No," Konstantin answered patiently. "Why do you believe that you are?"

"I see—things. Demons, devils. Everywhere. All the time." She felt as though she stood beyond herself. Something had taken control of her tongue and was shaping her answers. She'd never told anyone before. Half the time she refused to admit it to herself, even when she muttered at corners and the women whispered behind their hands. Even kind, drunk, clumsy Father Semyon, who had prayed with her more times than she could count, had never wrung this confession from her.

"But why should that mean you are mad? The Church teaches that demons walk among us. Do you deny the teachings of the Church?"

"No! But . . ." Anna felt hot and cold at once. She wanted to look into his face again but did not dare. She looked at the floor instead and saw the faint shadow of his foot, incongruously bare beneath the heavy robe. At last she managed a whisper:

"But they aren't—*can't*—be real. No one else sees . . . I am mad; I know I am mad." She trailed off, then added slowly: "Except sometimes I think—my stepdaughter Vasilisa. But she's only a child who hears too many stories."

Father Konstantin's gaze sharpened.

"She speaks of it, does she?"

"Not—not recently. But when she was a little girl sometimes I thought . . . Her eyes . . ."

"And you did nothing?" Konstantin's voice was supple as a snake and well-tuned as any singer's. Anna quailed under his tone of incredulous contempt.

"I beat her when I could and forbade her to talk of it. I thought, maybe, that if I caught her young enough, the madness wouldn't take hold."

"Is that all you thought? Madness? Did you never fear for her soul?"

Anna opened her mouth, closed it again, and stared at the priest, bewildered. He stalked toward the center of the iconostasis where a second Christ sat enthroned, surrounded by apostles. The moonlight turned his gold hair to gray-silver, and his shadow crawled black across the floor.

"Demons can be exorcised, Anna Ivanovna," he said, not taking his eyes from the icon.

"Ex—exorcised?" she squeaked.

"Naturally."

"How?" She felt as though she were thinking through mud. All her life she had borne her curse. That it might just go away—her mind wouldn't compass the notion.

"Rites of the Church. And much prayer."

There was a small silence.

"Oh," Anna breathed. "Oh please. Make it go away. Make them go away."

He might have smiled, but she couldn't be sure in the moonlight.

"I will pray and think on it. Go back and go to sleep, Anna Ivanovna." She stared at him with big stunned eyes, then whirled and blundered toward the door, feet clumsy on the bare wood.

Father Konstantin prostrated himself before the iconostasis. He did not sleep at all the rest of the night.

The next day was Sunday. In the green-gray dawn, Konstantin returned to his own room. Heavy-eyed, he flung cold water over his head and washed his hands. Soon he must give service. He was weary, but calm. During the long hours of his vigil, God had given him the answer. He knew what evil lay upon this land. It was in the sun-symbols on the nurse's apron, in that stupid woman's terror, in the fey, feral eyes of Pyotr's elder daughter. The place was infested with demons: the chyerti of the old religion. These foolish, wild people worshipped God by day and the old gods in secret; they tried to walk both paths at once and made themselves base in the sight of the Father. No wonder evil had come to work its mischief.

Excitement rolled through his veins. He'd thought to molder here, in the back of beyond. But here was battle indeed, a battle for mastery of the souls of men and women, with evil on one side and him as God's messenger on the other.

The people were gathering. He could almost feel their eager curiosity. It was not yet like Moscow, where people snatched hungrily at his words and loved him with their frightened eyes. Not yet.

But it would be.

✤

VASYA TWITCHED A SHOULDER and wished she could take off her headdress. Because they were in church, Dunya had added a veil to the heavy contrivance of cloth and wood and semiprecious stones. It itched. But she was nothing compared to Anna, who was dressed as though for a feast-day, a jeweled cross round her neck and rings on each finger. Dunya had taken one look at her mistress and muttered under her breath about piety and gold hair. Even Pyotr raised an eyebrow at his wife, but he held his peace. Vasya followed her brothers into church, scratching her scalp.

Women stood on the left of the nave, before the Virgin, while men stood on the right, in front of the Christ. Vasya had always wished she could stand next to Alyosha so they could poke and fidget during the service; Irina was so small and sweet that poking was not rewarding, and anyway Anna always saw. Vasya locked her fingers behind her back.

The doors at the center of the iconostasis opened, and the priest came out. The murmurs of the assembled village drifted into silence, punctuated by a girl's giggle.

The church was small, and Father Konstantin seemed to fill it. His golden hair drew the eye as even Anna's jewels could not. His blue gaze pierced the throng like knives, one at a time. He did not speak at once. A breathless hush spread like sound among the people, so that Vasya found herself straining to hear their soft, eager breathing.

"Blessed is the kingdom," said Konstantin at last, his voice washing over them, "of the Father, and of the Son, and of the Holy Spirit now and ever and unto ages of ages."

He didn't *sound* like Father Semyon, thought Vasya, though the words of the liturgy were the same. His voice was like thunder, yet he placed each syllable like Dunya setting stitches. Under his touch, the words came alive. His voice was deep as rivers in spring. He spoke to them of life and death, of God and of sin. He spoke of things they did not know, of devils and torments and temptation. He called it up before their eyes so that they saw themselves submitting to the judgment of God, and saw themselves damned and flung down.

As he chanted, Konstantin pulled the crowd to him until they echoed his words in a daze of fascinated terror. He drove them on and on with the supple lash of his voice until their answering voices broke and they listened like children frightened during a thunderstorm. Just as they were on the verge of panic—or rapture—his voice gentled.

"Have mercy on us and save us, for He is good and the Lover of mankind."

A heavy silence fell. In the stillness, Konstantin raised his right hand and blessed the crowd.

They trickled out of the church like sleepwalkers, clutching one another. Anna had a look of exalted terror that Vasya couldn't understand. The others looked dazed, even exhausted, the trailing ends of fearful rapture in their eyes.

"Lyoshka!" Vasya called, darting over to her brother. But when he turned to her, he was pale like the others, and his gaze seemed to meet hers from a long way away. She slapped him, frightened to see his eyes blank. Abruptly Alyosha came back to himself and gave her a shove that should have put her in the dust, but she was quick as a squirrel and wearing a new gown. So she writhed backward and kept her feet, and then the two were glaring at each other, chests heaving and fists clenched.

They both recovered their senses at the same time. They laughed, and Alyosha said, "Is it true then, Vasya? Demons among us and torments in store if we do not cast them out? But the chyerti—is he talking about the chyerti? The women have always left bread for the domovoi. What care has God for that?"

"Stories or no, why should we cast out the household-spirits on the word of some old priest from Moscow?" snapped Vasya. "We have always left them bread and salt and water, and God was not angry."

"We have not starved," said Alyosha hesitantly. "And there have been no fires or sickness. But perhaps God is waiting for us to die so that our punishment might never end."

"For heaven's sake, Lyoshka," Vasya began, but she was interrupted by Dunya calling. Anna had decreed a meal of special magnificence, and Vasya must roll dumplings and stir the soup.

They dined outside, on eggs and kasha and summer greens, bread and cheese and honey. The usual cheerful muddle was subdued. The young peasant women stood in knots and whispered.

Konstantin, chewing meditatively, wore a glow of satisfaction. Pyotr, frowning, swung his head here and there like the bull that scents danger but has not yet seen the wolves in the grass. *Father understands wild beasts and raiders,* thought Vasya. *But sin and damnation cannot be fought.*

The others gazed at the priest with terror and a hungry admiration. Anna Ivanovna glowed with a kind of hesitant joy. Their fervor seemed to lift Konstantin and carry him, like a galloping horse. Vasya did not know it, but in the silence of the nave after all the people had gone, the priest had thrown that feeling into his exorcism, thrown it all, until even a man without the sight would swear he could hear devils crying out and running for their lives, out of Pyotr's walls and far away.

⁂

THAT SUMMER, KONSTANTIN WENT among the people and listened to their woes. He blessed the dying and he blessed the newborn. He listened when spoken to, and when his deep voice rang out, the people fell silent to hear him. "Repent," he told them, "lest you burn. The fire is very near. It is waiting for you and for your children, each time you lie down to sleep. Give your fruits to God and God alone. It is your only salvation."

The people murmured together, and their murmurs grew more and more fearful.

Konstantin ate at Pyotr's table every night. His voice set their honey-wine rippling and rattled their wooden spoons. Irina took to putting her spoon against her cup, giggling to hear them click together. Vasya abetted her in this; the child's gaiety was a relief. Talk of damnation did not frighten Irina; she was too young.

But Vasya was frightened.

Not of the priest, and not of devils, nor of pits of fire. She had seen their devils. She saw them every day. Some were wicked, and some were kind, and some were mischievous. All were as human in their way as the folk they guarded.

No, Vasya was frightened of her own people. They did not joke on the way to church anymore; they listened to Father Konstantin in heavy, hungry silence. And even when they were not in church, the people made excuses to visit his room.

Konstantin had begged beeswax from Pyotr, which he would melt and mix with his pigments. When the daylight shone into his cell, he would take up brushes and open phials of crushed powders. And then he would paint. Saint Peter took form under his brush. The saint's beard was curly, his robe yellow and umber, his strange, long-fingered hand raised in benediction.

Lesnaya Zemlya could talk of nothing else.

One Sunday, desperate, Vasya smuggled a handful of crickets into the church and dropped them among the worshippers. Their chirping made an amusing counterpoint to Father Konstantin's deep voice. But no one laughed; they cringed and whispered of evil omens. Anna Ivanovna had not seen, but she did suspect who was behind it. After the service, she called Vasya to her.

Vasya came unwillingly to her stepmother's chamber. A length of willow lay ready in Anna's hand. The priest sat by the open window, grinding a scrap of blue stone to powder. He did not seem to listen while Anna questioned her stepdaughter, but Vasya knew the questions were for the priest's benefit, to show her stepmother righteous and mistress in her own house.

The questioning went on and on.

"I would do it again," snapped Vasya at last, exasperated beyond caution. "Did not God make all creatures? Why should we alone be allowed to raise our voices in praise? Crickets worship with songs as much as we."

Konstantin's blue glance flicked toward her, though she could not read his expression.

"Insolence!" shrieked Anna. "Sacrilege!"

Vasya, chin high, kept silence even as her stepmother's willow switch whistled down. Konstantin watched, grave and inscrutable. Vasya met his eyes and refused to look away.

Anna saw the girl and the priest, their steady mutual regard, and her furious face turned redder than ever. She put all the strength of her arm into the sharp willow. Vasya stood still for it, biting her lip bloody. But the tears welled, despite her best efforts, and hurried down her cheeks.

Behind Anna, Konstantin watched, wordless.

Vasya cried out once toward the end, as much in humiliation as in pain. But then it was over; Alyosha, white-lipped, had gone to find their father. Pyotr saw the blood and his daughter's white face and seized Anna's arm.

Vasya said no word to her father or to anyone else; she stumbled away at once, though her brother tried to call her back, and hid in the wood like a wounded thing. If she wept, only the rusalka heard.

"That will teach her the price of sin," said Anna proudly, when Pyotr reproved her for brutality. "Better she learn now than burn later, Pyotr Vladimirovich."

Konstantin said nothing. What he thought he did not say.

After her cuts healed, Vasya walked more softly and held her tongue more readily. She spent more time with the horses, and concocted wild plans to dress as a boy and go to join Sasha in his monastery, or send a secret messenger to Olga.

Alyosha, though he did not tell her, began to mark her comings and goings, so that she was never alone with their stepmother.

All this while, Konstantin condemned the people's offerings—bread or honey-wine—that they made to their hearth-spirits. "Give it to God," he said. "Forget your demons, lest you burn." The people listened. Even Dunya was half convinced; she muttered to herself, shook her old head, and picked the sun-symbols from aprons and kerchiefs.

Vasya did not see it; she hid in the wood or in the stable. But the domovoi regretted her absence more than anyone else, because for him now there was nothing but crumbs.

13.

WOLVES

FALL CAME IN A BURST OF GLORY THAT QUICKLY FADED TO GRAY. The silence of the waning year lay like a haze over the lands of Pyotr Vladimirovich while the icons multiplied under Father Konstantin's hand. The men of the village labored over a new icon-screen to hold them: Saint Peter and Saint Paul, the Virgin and the Christ. The people lingered about Konstantin's room and gazed with awe at the finished icons, at their shapes and shining faces. Konstantin was making a whole iconostasis, one image at a time.

"You owe your salvation to God," said Konstantin. "Look on His face and be saved." They had never seen anything like his Christ's great eyes, the pale flesh, and the long, thin hands. They looked and knelt and sometimes cried.

What is a domovoi, they said, *but a tale for bad children? We are sorry, Batyushka, we repent.*

Almost no one made offerings, even at the autumn equinox. The domovoi grew feeble and listless. The vazila grew thin and haggard and wild-eyed; the straw lay thick in his tangled beard. He stole rye and barley stored for the horses. The horses themselves began stamping in their stalls and shying at breezes. Tempers in the village grew short.

"WELL, IT WASN'T ME, boy, and it wasn't a horse or a cat or a ghost,"
snarled Pyotr to the stable boy one bitter morning. More barley had
vanished in the night, and Pyotr, already on edge, was furious.

"I didn't see!" cried the boy, sniffling. "I would never——"

The air smarted, those mornings in November, and the earth seemed
to ring underfoot, brittle with frost. Pyotr stood nose to nose with the
youth and answered his denials with a clenched fist. There was a thud
and a howl of pain. "Never steal from me again," Pyotr said.

Vasya, just slipping through the stable-door, frowned. Her father
was never short-tempered. He never even beat Anna Ivanovna. *What
is happening to us?* Vasya ducked out of sight and climbed into the hayloft. It took her a moment to locate the vazila, who was curled in on
himself and half-buried in straw. She shivered at the look in his eyes.

"Why are you eating the barley?" she asked, gathering her courage.

"Because there have been no offerings." The vazila's eyes glowed
disconcertingly black.

"Are you frightening the horses?"

"Their moods are mine and mine theirs."

"You are very angry, then?" the girl whispered. "But my people do
not mean it. They are only frightened. The priest will go away one day.
Things will not always be so."

The vazila's eyes gleamed darkly, but Vasya thought she saw sorrow
in them as well as anger.

"I am hungry," he said.

Vasya felt a rush of sympathy. She had often been hungry. "I can
bring you bread," she said stoutly. "*I* am not frightened."

The vazila's eyelids flickered. "I need little," he said. "Bread. Apples."

Vasya tried not to think too hard about giving away part of her
meals. Food was never plentiful after midwinter; soon she would be
grudging every crumb. But— "I will bring them to you. I swear it," she
said, looking earnestly into the demon's round, brown eyes.

"My thanks," returned the vazila. "Keep your pledge and I will leave the grain alone."

Vasya kept her pledge. It was never much. A withered apple. A gnawed crust. A drip of honey-wine, carried on her fingers, or in her mouth. But the vazila came for it eagerly, and when he ate, the horses quieted. The days darkened and drew in; the snow fell as though to seal them up in whiteness. But the vazila grew pink and content; the winter-time stable grew drowsy as of old.

Just as well. The season was a long one, and in January the cold deepened until even Dunya could remember nothing like it.

The remorseless winter dusk drove folk indoors. Pyotr had plenty of time to suffer the sight of his family's pinched faces. They huddled by the fire, chewing at bread and strips of dried meat, taking turns adding wood to the blaze. Even by night, they did not dare let it burn low. The older folk murmured that their firewood burned too fast, that it took three logs to keep the flames high, where before they had needed one. Pyotr and Kolya decried that as nonsense. But their woodpiles dwindled.

Midwinter had come and gone; the days lengthened once more, but the cold only worsened. It killed sheep and rabbits and blackened the fingers of the unwary. Firewood they must have in such cold, come what may, and so as their stocks ran low, the people dared the silent forest under the glare of the winter sun. It was Vasya and Alyosha, out with a pony, a sledge, and short-hafted axes, who saw the paw prints in the snow.

"Ought we go after them, Father?" Kolya asked that night. "Kill some, take their skins, and drive the rest away?" He was mending a scythe, squinting in the oven-light. His son Seryozha, stiff and silent, huddled against his mother.

Vasya had given the enormous basket of sewing a dispirited look and seized her ax and a whetstone. Alyosha shot her an amused look over the haft of his own ax.

"See?" said Father Konstantin to Anna. "Look around you. In God's grace is your deliverance." Anna's eyes were fastened on his face; her sewing lay forgotten on her lap.

Pyotr wondered at his wife. She had never seemed so much at ease, though this was the bitterest winter in memory.

"I think not," said Pyotr, in answer to his son's question. He was inspecting his boots; in winter, holes could cost a man a foot. He put one down near the fire and picked up the other. "They are bigger than boarhounds, the wolves from the high north; it has been twenty years since they came so near." Pyotr reached down and caressed Pyos's gaunt head; the dog gave him a dispirited lick. "That they do so now means they are desperate, that they would hunt children if they could, or slaughter sheep under our noses. The men together might take on a pack, but it is too cold for bows; it would be spear-work, and not everyone would come back. No, we must look to our children and our livestock, and only go into the forest in daylight."

"We might set snares," put in Vasya, over the scrape of her whetstone.

Anna gave her a dark look.

"No," Pyotr said. "Wolves are not rabbits; they would smell you on the trap, and *no one* will risk the forest on such a small chance of gain."

"Yes, Father," Vasya said, meekly.

That night was deadly cold. They all huddled together on top of the oven, packed like salted fish and covered with every blanket they possessed. Vasya slept badly; her father snored, and Irina's small, sharp knees dug into her back. She tossed and turned, tried not to kick Alyosha, and at last, near midnight, fell into a shallow sleep. She dreamed of wolves howling, of winter stars swallowed up by warm clouds, of a man with red hair, a woman on horseback, and last of a pale, heavy-jawed man with a look of hunger and malice, who leered and winked his single good eye. She woke up gasping, in the bitter hour before dawn, and saw a figure cross the room, outlined by the light of the banked oven-fire.

It is nothing, she thought: *a dream, the kitchen cat.* But then the figure paused, as though it sensed her regard. It turned a fraction. Vasya hardly dared to breathe, for she saw its face, a pale scrawl in the dim light. The eyes were the color of winter ice. She drew breath—to speak or to scream—but then the figure was gone. Daylight was filtering in round the kitchen door and from the village there came a wailing cry.

"It is Timofei," said Pyotr, naming a village boy. Pyotr had risen before dawn to see to his stock. Now he came briskly through the door, stamping snow from his boots and brushing away the ice that had formed in his beard. He was hollow-eyed from cold and sleeplessness. "He died in the night." The kitchen filled with exclamations. Vasya, half-awake on the oven, remembered the figure that had passed in the darkness. Dunya said nothing at all, but went about her baking, lips set. Her glance flicked often and worriedly from Vasya to Irina. Winter was cruel to the young.

At midmorning, the women gathered in the bathhouse to wrap his wasted body. Vasya, spilling into the hut behind her stepmother, caught a glimpse of Timofei's face: he was glassy-eyed, the tears frozen on his thin cheeks. His mother clutched the stiffening body to her, whispering to him, ignoring her neighbors. Neither patience nor reason would draw the child from her, and when the women tugged him forcibly from her arms, she began to scream.

The room dissolved into chaos. The mother flew at her neighbors, crying for her son. Most of the women had children themselves; they quailed at the look in her eyes. The mother clawed blindly, scrabbling. The room was too small. Vasya thrust Irina out of harm's way and seized the reaching arms. She was strong, but slender, and the mother was wild with grief. Vasya clung and tried to speak. "Let go of me, witch!" screamed the woman. "Let go!" Vasya, disconcerted, loosened her grip and an elbow caught her across the face. She saw stars, and her arms fell away.

In that moment, Father Konstantin appeared in the doorway. His nose was red, his face as raw as anyone's, but he absorbed the scene in an instant, took two strides across the tiny hut, and caught the mother's groping fingers. The woman gave one desperate wrench and then stilled, trembling.

"He is gone, Yasna," Konstantin said, stern.

"No," she croaked. "I held him in my arms, all last night I held him, as the fire burned low—he cannot, he *will* not leave if I hold him. Give him back to me!"

"He belongs to God," said Konstantin. "As do we all."

"He is my son! My only son. Mine—"

"Be still," he said. "Sit down. This is unseemly. Come, the women will lay him before the fire and heat water for washing." His deep voice was soft and even. Yasna allowed him to lead her to the oven and sank down beside it.

All that morning—indeed, all that brief dull winter day—Konstantin talked, and Yasna stared at him like a swimmer caught in a riptide, while the women stripped Timofei's body, and washed it, and wrapped it in cold linen. The priest was still there when Vasya came back from another bitter day searching for firewood; she saw him standing before the door of the bathhouse, gulping the cold air as though it were water.

"Would you like some mead, Batyushka?" she said.

Konstantin jerked in surprise. Vasya made no noise walking, and her gray furs mingled with the falling night. But after a pause he said, "I would, Vasilisa Petrovna." His beautiful voice was little more than a thread, the resonance gone. Gravely she handed him her little skin of honey-wine. He gulped it with desperate eagerness. Wiping his mouth with the back of his hand, he handed the skin back to her, only to find her studying him, a furrow between her brows.

"Will you keep vigil tonight?" she asked.

"It is my place," he replied with a hint of hauteur; the question was impertinent.

She saw his annoyance and smiled; he frowned. "I honor you for it, Batyushka," she said.

She turned toward the great house, melting into the shadows. Konstantin watched her go, lips pressed together. The taste of mead was heavy in his mouth.

The priest kept that night's vigil by the body. His gaunt face was set, and his lips moved in prayer. Vasya, who had returned in the small hours to keep her own vigil, could not help but admire his steady purpose, though the air had never echoed so with sobs and prayers as it had since his coming.

It was far too cold to linger over the boy's tiny grave, hacked with much labor out of the iron-hard earth. As soon as decency permitted, the people scattered back to their huts, leaving the poor thing alone in his icy cradle, with Father Konstantin hindmost, half-dragging the bereaved mother.

People began cramming into fewer and fewer izby, with extended families sharing one oven to save firewood. But the wood disappeared so quickly—as though some ill wish made it burn. So they went into the woods regardless of paw prints, the women goaded by the sight of Timofei's marble face and the dreadful look in his mother's eyes. It was inevitable that someone would not come back.

Oleg's son Danil was only bones when they found him, scattered widely over a stretch of trampled and bloody snow. His father brought the gnawed bone-ends to Pyotr and, wordless, laid them before him.

Pyotr looked down at them and said nothing.

"Pyotr Vladimirovich—" Oleg began, croaking, but Pyotr shook his head.

"Bury your son," he said, his glance lingering on his own children. "I shall summon the men tomorrow."

Alyosha spent the long night checking the haft of his boar-spear and sharpening his hunting-knife. A little color showed in his beardless cheeks. Vasya watched him work. Part of her itched to take up a spear herself, to go and brave dangers in the winter wood. The other part wanted to crack her brother over the head for his heedless excitement.

"I will bring you a wolfskin, Vasya," Alyosha said, laying his weapons aside.

"Keep your wolfskin," Vasya retorted, "if you can only promise to bring your own skin back without freezing your toes off."

Her brother grinned, his eyes glittering. "Worried, little sister?"

The two sat apart from the mob near the oven, but Vasya still lowered her voice. "I don't like this. Do you think I *want* to have to chop your frozen toes off? Or your fingers?"

"But there's no help for it, Vasochka," said Alyosha, putting down his boot. "Wood we must have. Better to go out and fight than freeze to death in our houses."

Vasya pursed her lips but made no answer. She thought suddenly of the vazila, black-eyed with wrath. She thought of the crusts she brought him to quiet his anger. *Is there another who is angry?* Such a one could only be in the wood, where the cold winds blew and the wolves howled.

Don't even think it, Vasya, said the sensible voice in her skull. But Vasya glanced at her family. She saw her father's grim face, her brothers' suppressed excitement.

Well, I can but try. If Alyosha is hurt tomorrow, I will hate myself forever if I did not try. Without pausing to think longer, Vasya went for her boots and winter cloak.

No one bothered asking where she was going. The truth would not have occurred to anyone.

Vasya climbed the palisade, hampered by her mittens. The stars were few and faint; the moon cast a blaze of light over the hard-frozen snow. Vasya passed the eave of the wood, from moonlight into darkness. She walked briskly. It was dreadfully cold. The snow squeaked under her feet. Somewhere, a wolf howled. Vasya tried not to think of the yellow eyes. Her teeth would surely rattle out of her head from shivering.

Suddenly Vasya stumbled to a halt. She thought she'd heard a voice. Slowing her breath, she listened. No—only the wind.

But what was that there? It looked like a great tree: one she half-remembered, with an odd sly memory, that slid in and out of her mind. No—it was only a shadow, cast by the moon.

A bone-chilling wind played in the branches high above.

Out of the hiss and clatter, Vasya suddenly thought she heard words. *Are you warm, child?* said the wind, half-laughing.

In fact, Vasya felt her bones would splinter like frost-killed branches, but she replied steadily, "Who are you? Are you sending the frost?"

There was a very long silence. Vasya wondered if she had imagined the voice. Then it seemed she heard, mockingly, *And why not? I, too, am angry.* The voice seemed to throw echoes, so that the whole wood took up the cry.

"That is no answer," retorted the girl. The sensible part of her pointed out that perhaps a little meekness was in order when dealing with half-heard voices in the dead of night. But the cold was making her sleepy; she fought it with every scrap of will and had none left over for meekness.

I bring the frost, said the voice. Suddenly it was curling icy, loving fingers about her face and throat. A cold touch like fingertips slipped beneath her clothes and wrapped round her heart.

"Then will you stop?" Vasya whispered, fighting fear. Her heart beat as though against another's hand. "I speak for my people; they are afraid; they are sorry. Soon it will be as it always was: our churches and our chyerti together and no more fear or talk of demons."

It will be too late, said the wind, and the forest took it up: *too late, too late.* Then, *Besides, it is not my frost you should fear, devushka. It is the fires. Tell me, do your fires burn too fast?*

"It is only the cold that makes them burn so."

Nay, it is the coming storm. The first sign is fear. The second is always fire. Your people are afraid, and now the fires burn.

"Turn the storm aside then, I beg you," said Vasya. "Here, I brought a gift." She put a hand into her sleeve.

It was nothing much, just a scrap of dry bread and a pinch of salt, but when she held it out, the wind died.

In the silence, Vasya heard the wolf howl again, very near now, and answered in a chorus. But in the same instant a white mare stepped out from between two trees, and Vasya forgot the wolves. The mare's long mane fell like icicles, and her snorting breath made a plume in the night.

Vasya caught her breath. "Oh, you are beautiful," she said, and even she could hear the longing in her voice. "Are you bringing the frost?"

Did the white mare have a rider? Vasya could not tell. One instant it seemed she did, and then the mare twitched her skin and the shape on her back was only a trick of the light.

The white horse put her small ears forward, toward the bread and salt. Vasya held out her hand. She felt the horse's warm breath on her face and stared into her dark eye. Suddenly she felt warmer. Even the wind felt warmer where it twined around her face.

I bring the frost, said the voice. Vasya did not think it was the mare. *It is my wrath and my warning. But you are brave, devushka, and I relent. For the sake of an offering.* A small pause. *But the fear is not mine, and neither are the fires. The storm is coming, and the frost will be as nothing beside it. Courage will save you. If your people are afraid, then they are lost.*

"What storm?" whispered Vasya.

Beware the turning seasons, she thought the wind sighed. *Beware . . .* and the voice was gone. But the wind remained. Harder and harder it blew, wordless, flinging clouds across the moon, and the wind smelled, blessedly, of snow. The deep frost could not last while it snowed.

When Vasya stumbled back through the door of her own house, the flakes that covered her hood and caught in her eyelashes effectively silenced her family's clamor. Alyosha seized her in speechless delight, and Irina went laughing outside to catch a handful of the falling whiteness.

That night the cold indeed broke. It snowed for a week. When the snow finally stopped, it took them three more days to dig themselves out. By then the wolves had taken advantage of the relative warmth to feast on stringy rabbits and move deeper into the forest. No one ever saw them again. Only Alyosha seemed disappointed.

⟐

DUNYA SLEPT BADLY THOSE late-winter nights, and it was not only because of the cold and aching of her bones, nor yet her worry over Irina's cough or Vasya's pale face.

"It is time," said the frost-demon.

There was no sledge in Dunya's dream this time, no sunshine or crisp winter air. She stood in a gloomy and muttering forest. It seemed that a greater shadow lurked somewhere in the dark. Waiting. The winter-demon's pale features were drawn fine as etching, his eyes drained of color. "It must be now," he said. "She is a woman, and stronger than even she knows. I can perhaps keep evil from you, but I must have that girl."

"She is a child," protested Dunya. *Demon,* she thought. *Tempter. Liar.* "A child still—she teases me for honeycakes even when she knows there are none—and she has grown so pale this winter, all eyes and bones. How can I give her up now?"

The demon's face was cold. "My brother is waking; every day his prison weakens. That child, all unknowing, has done what she can to protect you, with crusts and courage and the sight. But my brother laughs at such things; she must have the jewel."

The dark seemed to press closer, hissing. The frost-demon spoke sharply, in words Dunya did not know. A bright wind filtered around the clearing, and the shadows drew back. The moon came out and set the snow to glowing.

"Please, winter-king," Dunya said humbly, clenching her hands together. "Another year. One more sun-season; she will grow strong with rain and sunlight. I will not—I cannot—give my girl to Winter now."

Laughter suddenly boomed from the undergrowth: old, slow laughter. Suddenly it seemed to Dunya that the moonlight shone through the frost-demon, that he was nothing but a trick of light and shadow.

But then he was a real man again, with weight and shape and form. His head was turned away, scanning the undergrowth. When he turned back to Dunya, his face was grim.

"You know her best," he said. "I cannot take her unready; she will die. Another year, then. Against my judgment."

14.

THE MOUSE AND
THE MAIDEN

ANNA IVANOVNA SUFFERED WITH THE OTHERS THAT WINTER. Her hands swelled and stiffened; her teeth ached. She dreamed of cheese and eggs and cresses, all the while eating sour cabbage and black bread and smoked fish. Irina, never strong, faded to a listless shadow of herself, and Anna, terrified for her child, found a strange kinship with Dunya in coaxing broths and honey down the child's throat and keeping her warm.

But at least she saw no demons. The little bearded creature did not creep about the house; the twiggy brown beggar did not creep about the dvor. Anna saw only men and women, and endured only the ordinary troubles of a crowded house in a bad winter. And Father Konstantin was there: a man like an angel, such as she had never imagined a man to be, with his shining voice and tender mouth and the blessed icons that took shape under his strong hands. She saw him every day that winter, when they were all cooped up indoors. It was meat and drink to her to bask in his presence, and she desired nothing more. Her mind was at ease; she could even bring herself to smile at her stepsons and endure Vasilisa.

But when the snow came and the cold broke, Anna's peace was shattered.

A gray noontide, with little snow flurries out of a leaden sky, found Anna running to find Konstantin in his cell. "The demons are still here, Batyushka," she cried. "They came back; they were only hiding before. They are sly; they are liars. How have I sinned? Father, what must I do?" She was weeping, shivering. Only that morning, the domovoi had crept, stubborn and smoldering, out of the oven and taken up Dunya's basket of mending.

Konstantin did not answer at once. His fingers were blue and white where they gripped the brush—he had retreated to his room to paint. Anna had brought him soup. It sloshed in her trembling hands. *Cabbage,* Konstantin noted with disgust. He was mortally weary of cabbage. Anna put the bowl down beside him, but she did not go.

"Patience, Anna Ivanovna," the priest replied, when it became clear she was waiting for him to speak. He did not turn around, nor slow his quick, dabbing brushstrokes. It was weeks since he had painted. "It is an infestation of long standing, fed by the straying of many. Only wait, and I will bring them back to God."

"Yes, Batyushka," Anna said. "But today I saw—"

He hissed between his teeth, "Anna Ivanovna, you will never be rid of devils if you creep around looking for them. What good Christian woman behaves so? You would do better to fear God and pass your time in prayer. Much prayer." He glanced pointedly toward the door.

But Anna did not go. "You have done wonders already. I am—do not think me ungrateful, Batyushka." She swayed toward him, trembling. Her hand dropped onto his shoulder.

Konstantin shot her an impatient glance. She jerked back as though burned, and a dull flush crept up her face. "Give thanks to God, Anna Ivanovna," Konstantin said. "Leave me to my work."

She stood a moment, wordless, and then fled.

Konstantin seized his soup and swallowed it at a gulp. He wiped his mouth and tried again to find the calm needful for painting. But the lady's words scratched at him. *Demons. Devils. How have I sinned?* Konstantin's mind wandered. He had filled these people with the fear of

God, and they were on the path to salvation. They needed him—loved and feared him in equal measure. Rightly, for he was God's messenger. They worshipped his icons. All that he could contrive with words and fierce looks, of obedience to God's will and spirit of humility, he had done. He felt the effect.

And yet.

Unwillingly, Konstantin thought of Pyotr's second daughter. He had watched her that winter, her childish grace, her laughter, her care-less impudence, the secret sadness that sometimes crossed her face. He remembered how once she had emerged out of the dusk, at home in the cold and the falling night. He himself had taken mead from her hand, not thinking beyond his gratitude that he might slake his thirst.

She is not afraid, Konstantin thought dourly. *She does not fear God; she fears nothing.* He saw it in her silences, her fey glance, the long hours she spent in the forest. In any case, no good Christian maid ever had eyes like that, or walked with such grace in the dark.

For her soul, and for the souls of all in this desolate place, thought Konstantin, he must have her humility. She must see what she was and fear it. Save her, and he would save them all. Failing that . . . Konstantin paid no mind to his fingers; he painted in a haze while his mind worried away at the problem. At last he swam back to consciousness and his eyes took in what he had painted.

Wild green eyes stared back at him, that he had meant to make only a gentle blue. The woman's long veil could just as easily have been a curtain of red-black hair. She seemed to laugh at him, caught in the wood and forever free. Konstantin shouted and flung the board away. It thudded to the floor, splattering paint.

⚭

THAT SPRING WAS TOO WET, and too cold. Irina, who loved flowers, wept, for the snowdrops never bloomed. The fields were plowed under torrents of unseasonable rain, and for weeks nothing would dry, in-doors or out. Vasya, in desperation, tried putting their stockings in the oven with the fire pushed to one corner. She withdrew them considerably warmer, but no drier. Half the village was coughing, and she looked her brother over frowningly as he came to dress.

"As your experiments go, this one could have been worse," said Alyosha, eying his slightly charred stockings. His eyes were red, his voice hoarse. He made a face as he pulled the warm, damp wool over his foot.

"Yes," said Vasya, drawing on her own stockings. "I could have cooked the lot." She eyed him again. "There will be something hot for dinner tonight. Don't die before the rain stops, little brother."

"No promises, little sister," said Alyosha darkly, coughing. He straightened his hat and slipped outside.

With the rain and the damp, Father Konstantin took to making his brushes and grinding his stone in the winter kitchen. It was considerably warmer and somewhat drier than his room, though much noisier, with dogs and children and the feeblest of their goats underfoot. Vasya regretted the change. He never once spoke to her, though he commended Irina and instructed Anna Ivanovna often enough. But, even in the uproar, Vasya could feel his eyes on her. While she joked with Dunya, kneaded their poor thin bread, and plied her distaff, Vasya was always aware of the priest's steady stare.

Better to tell me my fault to my face, Batyushka.

She hid in the stable whenever she could. Her forays into the crowded house meant rounds of unremitting work while Anna screeched and prayed by turns. And always, there was the priest's silence and his grave regard.

Vasya never told anyone where she'd gone that bitter night in January. Afterward, she sometimes thought she had dreamed it: the voice on the wind and the white horse. With Konstantin watching, she was careful to address no remarks to the domovoi. But the priest watched her all the same. It was, she thought, almost despairing, simply a matter of time before she got herself into trouble and he pounced. But the days ran together, and the priest kept his silence.

April came, and Vasya found herself in the horse-pasture stitching up Mysh, Sasha's old horse, now a broodmare who had borne seven foals. Though no longer young, the mare was still strong and sound, and her wise old eyes missed nothing. The most valuable horses—Mysh among them—spent the winter in the stable and went out to pasture with the others as soon as the grass showed through the snow. Certain disagreements always arose in consequence, and Mysh had a hoof-shaped gash on her flank. Vasya plied her needle more deftly in flesh than she did in cloth. The scarlet slash grew steadily smaller. The horse stood still, only shivering from time to time.

"Summer summer summer," sang Vasya. The sun shone warm again, and the rain had stopped long enough to give the barley a chance. Measuring herself against the horse, Vasya found she had grown even taller over the winter. *Well,* she thought ruefully, *we can't all be small as Irina.*

Tiny Irina was already hailed as a beauty. Vasya tried not to think of it.

Mysh broke into the girl's reverie. *We would like to offer you a gift,* she said. She put down her head to nibble at the new grass.

Vasya's hands faltered. "A gift?"

You brought us bread this winter. We are in your debt.

"Us? But the vazila—"

Is all of us together, replied the mare. *Something more as well, but mostly he is us.*

"Oh," said Vasya, perplexed. "Well, I thank you."

Best not be grateful for the grass until you've eaten it, the mare said with a snort. *Our gift is this: we wish to teach you to ride.*

This time Vasya really did freeze, except the blood came rushing into her heart. She could ride—on a fat gray pony she shared with Irina—but . . . "Truly?" she whispered.

Yes, said the mare, *though it may prove a mixed blessing. Such a gift could drive you apart from your people.*

"My people," said Vasya, very low. *They wept before the icons while* the domovoi starved. *I do not know them. They have changed and I have not.* Aloud she said, "I am not afraid."

Good, said the mare. *We shall begin when the mud dries.*

⁂

VASYA HALF-FORGOT THE MARE'S promise in the weeks that followed. Spring meant weeks of numbing labor, and at each day's close, Vasya ate the poor bread from the previous year's barley, with soft white cheese and tender new herbs, then flung herself onto the oven and slept like a child.

But suddenly it was May, and the mud disappeared under new grass. Dandelions shone like stars amid the deep green. The horses threw long shadows and the sickle moon stood alone in the sky, on the day that Vasya, sweating, scratched and exhausted, stopped in the horse-pasture on her way back from the barley-field.

Come here, said Mysh. *Get on my back.*

Vasya was almost too tired to reply; she gazed stupidly at the horse and said, "I've no saddle."

Mysh snorted. *Nor will you. You must learn to manage without. I will carry you, but I am not your servant.*

Vasya met the mare's eye. A flicker of humor showed in the brown depths. "Does your leg not pain you?" she asked, feebly, nodding at the half-healed gash on the mare's flank.

No, Mysh replied. *Mount.*

Vasya thought of her hot supper, of her stool by the oven. Then she gritted her teeth, backed up, ran, and flung herself belly-down onto the mare's back. A bit of squirming, and Vasya settled herself uncomfortably just behind the hard withers.

The mare's ears eased back at the scrabbling. *You will need practice.*

Vasya could never remember where they went that day. They rode, of necessity, deep in the woods. But the riding was painful; that, Vasya always remembered. They jogged along until Vasya's back and legs trembled. *Be still,* said the mare. *It is as if there are three of you instead of one.* Vasya tried, slipping this way and that. At last, exasperated, Mysh pulled up sharply. Vasya rolled over the mare's shoulder and landed, blinking, on the loamy forest floor.

Get up, said the horse. *Be more careful.*

When they returned to the pasture, Vasya was filthy, bruised, and certain that walking was beyond her. She had also missed her supper and earned a scolding. But the next evening she did it again. And again. It was not always with Mysh; the horses took turns teaching her to ride. She could not go every day. In spring she worked incessantly—they all did—to put the crops in the earth.

But Vasya went often enough, and slowly her back and thighs and stomach began to hurt less. Finally the day came when they did not hurt at all. And in the meantime, she learned to keep her balance, to vault to a horse's back, to spin and start and stop and leap until she could no longer tell where the horse ended and she began.

The sky seemed bigger that midsummer, clouds scudding across it like swans. The barley rippled green in the fields, though it was stunted and Pyotr shook his head over it. Vasya, her basket over her arm, disappeared into the forest every day. Dunya would sometimes look askance at the girl's offerings—birchbark, mostly, or buckthorn for making dye, and rarely in sufficient quantities. However, Vasya was golden and shining with happiness, so Dunya just harrumphed and said nothing.

But all the while, the heat deepened until it was honey-thick: too hot. For all the people's prayers, fires broke out in the tinder-dry forest, and the barley grew but slowly.

A white-hot day in August saw Vasya making her way to the lake, trying not to limp. Buran had taken Vasya riding. The gray stallion— white now—was still the biggest of the riding horses, and he had the wickedest sense of humor. Vasya had bruises to prove it.

The lake dazzled in the sunlight. As Vasya drew nearer, she thought she heard rustling in the trees that fringed the water. But when she looked up, she saw no flash of green skin. After a few moments' fruitless search, Vasya gave up, stripped, and slid into the lake. The water was purest snowmelt, cold even at midsummer. It drove the air from her lungs, and Vasya bit back a yelp. She dove at once, the icy water startling life from her weary limbs. She cavorted about underwater, peering here and there. But there was no rusalka. Vaguely uneasy, Vasya paddled to the bank, pulled her clothes into the water, and pounded them clean on rocks. Finally she hung them, dripping, on a nearby limb and climbed the tree herself, stretching catlike along a branch to dry in the sun.

Perhaps an hour later, Vasya roused herself from an exhausted stupor and eyed her half-dry clothes. The sun had passed its zenith and begun to tilt west, which meant, in the long days of midsummer, that the afternoon was well advanced. By now Anna would be seething, and even Dunya would give her a tight-lipped glare when she slunk in the door. Irina was no doubt crouched over the sweltering oven or wearing out her fingers with mending. Feeling guilty, Vasya crept down to a lower limb—and froze.

Father Konstantin was sitting in the grass. He might have been a handsome farmer and not a priest at all. He had traded his robe for a linen shirt and loose trousers, studded with bits of barley-stem, and his uncovered hair blazed in the afternoon sun. He was looking out at the lake. *What is he doing here?* Vasya was still screened by the tree's foliage; she hooked her knees around the branch, let herself down, and snatched her clothes, quick as a squirrel. Perching awkwardly on an upper limb, trying not to fall and break an arm, she slipped into her shirt and leggings—stolen from Alyosha—and used her fingers to wrestle some order into her hair. Finally she flicked the end of a lumpy braid behind her, caught the tree-limb, and swung to the ground. *Maybe if I creep away very quietly . . .*

Then Vasya saw the rusalka. She was standing in the water. Her hair floated around her, half-masking her bare breasts. She smiled, just a little, at Father Konstantin. The priest, entranced, stood up and swayed toward her. Without thinking, Vasya darted at him and caught his hand. But he shoved her off, almost casually, stronger than he looked.

Vasya turned to the rusalka. "Leave him alone!"

"He will kill us all," the rusalka replied, voice soft, eyes never leaving her prey. "Already it has begun. If he goes on as he has, all the guardians of the deep forest will disappear; the storm will come and the land will go undefended. Have you not seen it? Fear is first, then fire, then famine. He made your people afraid. And then the fires burned, and now the sun scorches. You will be hungry when the cold comes. The winter-king is weak, and his brother very near. He will come if the wards fail. Better anything than that." Her voice shook with passion. "Better I take this one now."

Father Konstantin took another step. The water welled up around his boots. He was on the very brink of the lake.

Vasya shook her head, trying to clear it. "You must not."

"Why not? Is his life worth everyone else's? And I say to you surely that if he lives now, many will die."

Vasya hesitated a long moment. She remembered, unwillingly, the priest praying beside Timofei's stiffening corpse, mouthing the words long after his voice had gone. She remembered him holding the boy's mother upright when she would have fallen weeping to the snow. The girl set her teeth and shook her head.

The rusalka threw back her head and shrieked. And then she wasn't there at all; there was only sun on the water, weeds, and tree-shadows. Vasya caught the priest's hand and yanked him away from the edge. He looked down at her and awareness came back to his eyes.

※

KONSTANTIN'S FEET WERE COLD, and he felt strangely bereft. Cold because he was standing in six inches of water on the very brink of the lake, but he wondered at the stab of loneliness. He never felt lonely. A face was swimming into focus. Before he could put a name to it, the person caught his hand and dragged him stumbling back to dry land. The light glanced red off the black braid and suddenly he knew her. "Vasilisa Petrovna."

She dropped his hand, turned and looked at him. "Batyushka."

He felt his wet feet, remembered the woman in the lake, and felt the beginnings of fear. "What are you doing?" he demanded.

"Saving your life," she replied. "The lake is a danger to you."

"Demons . . ."

Vasya shrugged. "Or the guardian of the lake. Call her what you will."

He made as though to turn back to the water, fumbling at his cross with one hand.

She reached forward and seized it, breaking the thong that held it around his neck. "Leave it, and her," the girl said fiercely, holding the cross out of reach. "You've done enough damage; can you not let them be?"

"I want to save you, Vasilisa Petrovna," he said. "I will save you all. There are dark forces that you do not understand."

To his surprise, and perhaps to hers, she laughed. Amusement smoothed the angles of her face. Caught, he stared at her in unwilling admiration.

"It seems to me, Batyushka, that it is you who do not understand, as it was your life that needed saving. Go back to the work in the barley-fields and leave the lake alone." She turned without waiting to see if he followed, feet noiseless on the moss and pine needles. Konstantin fell in beside her. She still held his wooden cross between her two fingers.

"Vasilisa Petrovna," he tried again, cursing his clumsiness. Always he knew what to say. But this girl turned her clear gaze on him, and all his certainty grew vague and foolish. "You must leave your barbaric ways. You must return to God in fear and true repentance. You are the daughter of a good Christian lord. Your mother will run mad if we do not exorcise the demons from her hearth. Vasilisa Petrovna, turn. Repent."

"I go to church, Father," she replied. "Anna Ivanovna is not my mother, nor is her madness my business. Just as my soul is not yours. And it seems to me we did very well before you came; for if we prayed less, we also wept less."

She had walked swiftly. Through the tree-trunks he could see the palisade of the village.

"Mark me, Batyushka," she said. "Pray for the dead, comfort the sick, and comfort my stepmother. But leave me alone, or next time one of them comes for you, I shall not lift a finger to stop it." She did not wait for a reply but thrust his cross back into his hand and strode off toward the village.

It was warm from her hand, and his fingers curled reluctantly around it.

THEY ONLY COME FOR
THE WILD MAIDEN

THE BLINDING AFTERNOON SUNLIGHT GAVE WAY TO HONEY-GOLD, and at last to amber and rust. A faint half moon showed just above a line of pale yellow sky. The heat of the day went with the light, and the men in the barley-field shivered in their cooling sweat. Konstantin put his scythe over his shoulder. Bloody blisters had blossomed beneath the hardened skin of his palms. He balanced the scythe with his fingertips and avoided Pyotr Vladimirovich. Longing closed his throat and wrath stole his voice. *It was a demon. It was your imagination. You did not cast her out; you crawled toward her.*

God, he wanted to go back to Moscow—or Kiev—or further yet. To eat bread hot and plentiful instead of starving half the year, to leave the plowing to farmers, to speak before thousands, and never lie awake, wondering.

No. God had given him a task. He could not lay it aside half-finished. *Oh, if I could but finish.*

His jaw set. He would. He must. And before he died he would live again in a world where girls did not defy him and demons did not walk in Christian daylight.

Konstantin passed the mown barley and skirted the horse-pasture. The edge of the wood threw hungry shadows. He turned his face away, toward Pyotr's herds grazing in the long twilight. A flash of brightness showed among the grays and chestnuts. Konstantin narrowed his eyes. One horse—Pyotr's war-stallion—stood still, his head up. A slender figure stood at the beast's shoulder, silhouetted against the sunset. Konstantin knew her at once. The stallion curved its wicked head around to nibble at her braid, and she laughed like a child.

Konstantin had never seen Vasya so. In the house, she was grave and wary, careless and charming by turn, all eyes and bones and soundless feet. But alone, under the sky, she was beautiful as a yearling filly, or a new-flown hawk.

Konstantin forced his face to coldness. Her people offered him beeswax and honey, begged him for counsel and prayers. They kissed his hand; their faces lit when they saw him. But that girl avoided his glance and his footstep, yet a *horse*—a dumb beast—could charm that light from her. The light should have been for him—for God—for him as God's messenger. She was as Anna Ivanovna named her: hard-hearted, undutiful, unmaidenly. She conversed with demons and dared to boast that she'd saved his life.

But his fingers itched for wood and wax and brushes, to capture the love and loneliness, the pride and half-blossomed womanhood written in the lines of the girl's body. *She saved your life, Konstantin Nikonovich.*

Savagely, he quelled both thought and impulse. Painting was for the glory of God, not to glorify the frailty of transient flesh. *She summoned a devil; it was the finger of God that saved my life.* But when he tore himself away, the scene was burned on the backs of his eyelids.

⚘

IT WAS VIOLET EVENTIDE when Vasya came into the kitchen, still flushed with the day's sun. She seized her bowl and spoon, claimed a portion for herself, and took it to the window. The twilight greened her eyes. She tore into her food, pausing from time to time to glance out into the long summer dusk. With stiff, deliberate steps, Konstantin placed himself beside her. Her hair smelled of earth and sun and lake-water. She did not look away from the window. The village was starry with well-tended fires; a faint half moon soared in a cloud-fretted sky. The silence between them stretched out, amid the bustle of the crowded kitchen. It was the priest that broke it. "I am a man of God," Konstantin said, low. "But I would have been sorry to die."

Vasya gave him a swift, startled glance. A ghost of a smile showed in the corner of her mouth. "I don't believe it, Batyushka," she said. "Did I not rob you of your quick ascent to heaven?"

"I thank you for my life," Konstantin went on, stiffly. "But God is not mocked." His hand was suddenly warm on hers. The smile left her face. "Remember," he said. He slipped an object between her fingers. His hand, roughened with the scythe, slid over her knuckles. He did not speak. Suddenly Vasya understood why the women all begged him for prayers; understood, too, that his warm hand, the strong bones of his face, were a weapon, to use where the weapons of speech had failed. He would get her obedience thus, with his rough hand, his beautiful eyes.

Am I as great a fool as Anna Ivanovna? Vasya threw her head back and pulled away. He let her go. She did not see his hand tremble. His shadow wavered on the wall when he walked away.

Anna was stitching linens on her stool by the hearth. The cloth slipped to her knees and, when she stood, fell unheeded to the floor. "What did he give you?" she hissed. *"What was it?"* Every spot and line stood out on her face.

Vasya had no idea, but she lifted the thing for her stepmother to see. It was his wooden cross, with the two reaching arms, carved of silky pine-wood. Vasya gazed at it in some wonder. *What is this, priest? A warning? An apology? A challenge?*

"A cross," she said.

But Anna had seized it. "It's mine," she said. "He meant it for me. Get out!"

There were several things Vasya might have said, but she settled on the safest: "I am sure he did." But she did not go; she took her bowl to the hearth, to charm more stew out of Dunya and steal a heel of bread from her unwary sister. In a few minutes Vasya was dabbing her bowl with the crust and laughing at Irina's bewildered face.

Anna did not speak again, but neither did she take up her sewing. Vasya, for all her laughter, could feel her stepmother's burning stare.

***

ANNA DID NOT SLEEP that night, but paced from her bed to the church. When a deep, clear dawn replaced the blue summer midnight, she went to her husband and shook him awake.

Never once, in nine years, had Anna come to Pyotr of her own will. Pyotr seized his wife in a very businesslike choke before he realized who it was. Anna's hair straggled, gray-brown, about her face, and her kerchief hung askew. Her eyes were like two stones. "My love," she said, gasping and massaging her throat.

"What is wrong?" Pyotr demanded. He slipped from his warm bed and hurried into his clothes. "Is it Irina?"

Anna smoothed her hair, straightened her kerchief. "No—no."

Pyotr dragged a shirt over his head and did up his sash. "Then what?" he said in no very pleasant tones. She had startled him, badly.

Anna trembled, her eyelids downswept. "Have you noticed that your daughter Vasilisa is much grown since last summer?"

Pyotr's movements faltered. The infant day threw lines of pale gold across his floor. Anna had never taken an interest in Vasya. "Has she?" he said, bewildered now.

"And that she is grown quite passably attractive?"

Pyotr blinked and frowned. "She is a child."

"A woman," snapped Anna. Pyotr was taken aback. She had never contradicted him before. "A hoyden, all arms and legs and eyes. But she will have a good dowry. Better to see her married now, husband. If she loses what looks she has, she might not marry at all."

"She will not lose her looks in the next year," said Pyotr curtly.

"And certainly not in the next hour. Why rouse me, wife?" He left the room. The nutty tang of baking bread gladdened the house, and he was hungry.

"Your daughter Olga was married at fourteen." Anna followed him breathlessly. Olga had prospered since her marriage; she was become a great lady, a fat matron with two children. Her husband was high in the Grand Prince's favor.

Pyotr seized a new loaf and broke it open. "I will consider the matter," he said, to silence her. He took a great ball of the steaming insides and filled his mouth. His teeth ached sometimes; the softness was not unwelcome. *You are an old man,* Pyotr thought. He shut his eyes and tried to drown his wife's voice with the sound of chewing.

⁑

THE MEN WENT TO the barley-fields at daybreak. All morning, they scythed the rippling grass with great howling strokes, and then they spread the stalks to dry. Their rakes went to and fro with a monotonous hiss. The sun was a live thing, throwing its hot arms over their necks. Their feeble shadows hid at their feet, their faces glowed with sweat and sunburn. Pyotr and his sons worked alongside the peasants; everyone worked at harvest-time. Pyotr was jealous of every kernel. The barley had not grown so tall as it ought, and the heads were thin and poor.

Alyosha straightened his aching back and shielded his eyes with a dirty hand. His face lit. A rider was coming down from the village, galloping on a brown horse. "Finally," he said. He put two fingers in his mouth. A long whistle split the midday stillness. All across the field, men put aside their rakes, rubbed grass-ends from their faces, and made for the river. The deep green banks and the chuckling water gave a little relief from the heat.

Pyotr leaned on his rake and pushed the wet, grizzled hair from his brow. But he did not leave the barley-field. The rider was coming nearer, galloping on a neat-footed mare. Pyotr squinted. He could make out his second daughter's black braid, streaming behind her. But she was not riding her own quiet pony. Mysh's white feet flashed in the dust. Vasya saw her father and swung an arm in salute. Pyotr waited, scowling, to reprove his daughter when she came nearer. *She will break her neck one day, that mad thing.*

But how well she sat the horse. The mare vaulted a ditch and came on at a gallop, her rider motionless except for the flying hair. The two came to a halt at the edge of the wood. Vasya had a reed basket balanced before her. In the bright sunlight, Pyotr could not make out her features, but it struck him how tall she had grown. "Are you not hungry, Father?" she called. The mare stood still, poised. And bridleless—she wore nothing at all, not so much as a rope halter. Vasya rode with both hands on her basket.

"I am coming, Vasya," he said, feeling unaccountably grim. He set his rake on his shoulder.

The sun glanced off a golden head; Konstantin Nikonovich had not quit the barley-field, but stood watching the slender rider until the trees hid her. *My daughter rides like a steppe boy. What must he think of her, our virtuous priest?*

The men were flinging the cold water over their heads and drinking it in great handfuls. When Pyotr came to the creek, Vasya was off her horse and among them, passing a skin bag full of kvas. Dunya had made an enormous pasty in the oven, lumpy with grain and cheese and summer vegetables. The men gathered round and sawed off wedges. Grease mixed with the sweat on their faces.

It struck Pyotr how strange Vasya looked among the big, coarse men, with her long bones and her slenderness, her great eyes set so wide apart. *I want a daughter like my mother was,* Marina had said. Well, there she was, a falcon among cows.

The men did not speak to her; they ate their pie quickly, heads down, and went back to the scorching fields. Alyosha tugged his sister's braid and grinned at her in passing. But Pyotr saw the men throwing her backward glances as they went. "Witch," one of them murmured, though Pyotr did not hear. "She has charmed the horse. The priest says—"

The pasty was gone, and the men with it, but Vasya lingered. She set the skin of kvas aside and went to dip her hands in the stream. She walked like a child. *Well, of course she does. She is a girl still: my little frog.* And yet she had a wild thing's heedless grace. Vasya left the stream and came toward him, gathering up her basket on the way. Pyotr had a shock when he looked her in the face, which is perhaps why he frowned so blackly. Her smile faded. "Here, Father," she said, and handed him the skin of kvas.

Oh, savior, he thought. *Perhaps Anna Ivanovna did not speak so wrong. If she is not a woman, she will be soon.* Father Konstantin's gaze, Pyotr saw, lingered again on his daughter.

"Vasya," Pyotr said, rougher than he meant. "What is the meaning of this, taking the mare, and riding her so, without saddle or bridle? You'll break an arm or your foolish neck."

Vasya flushed. "Dunya bid me take the basket and make haste. Mysh was the nearest horse, and it was only a little way, too short to trouble with a saddle."

"Or a halter, dochka?" said Pyotr with some asperity.

Vasya's blush deepened. "I did not come to harm, Father."

Pyotr looked her over in silence. If she'd been a boy, he'd have been applauding that display of horsemanship. But she was a girl, a hoydenish girl, on the cusp of womanhood. Pyotr remembered again the young priest's stare.

"We'll talk of this later," said Pyotr. "Go home to Dunya. And do not ride so fast."

"Yes, Father," said Vasya meekly. But there was pride in the way she vaulted to the horse's back, and pride also in the control with which she turned the mare and sent her cantering, neck arched, back in the direction of the house.

THE DAY WOUND ON to dusk and past, so that the only light was the pale glow of summer that lit the nights like morning. "Dunya," said Pyotr. "How long has Vasya been a woman?" They sat alone in the summer kitchen. All around them the household slept. But for Pyotr, the daylit nights banished sleep, and the question of his daughter bit at him. Dunya's limbs ached, and she was not eager to lie down on her hard pallet. She twirled her distaff, but slowly. It struck Pyotr how thin she was.

Dunya gave Pyotr a hard glance. "Half a year. It came on her near Easter."

"She is a handsome girl," said Pyotr. "Though a savage. She needs a husband; it would steady her." But as he spoke, an image came to him of his wild girl wedded and bedded, sweating over an oven. The image filled him with a strange regret, and he shook it away.

Dunya put aside her distaff and said slowly, "She has not thought of love yet, Pyotr Vladimirovich."

"And so? She will do as she is told."

Dunya laughed. "Will she? Have you forgotten Vasya's mother?"

Pyotr was silent.

"I would counsel you to wait," said Dunya. "Except . . ."

All the summer, Dunya had watched Vasya disappear at dawn and return at twilight. She had watched the wildness grow in Marina's daughter and a—remoteness—that was new, as though the girl was only half-living in her family's world of crops and stock and mending. Dunya had watched and worried and struggled with herself. Now she made a decision. She plunged her hand into her pocket. When she withdrew it, the blue jewel lay nestled upon her palm, incongruous against the worn skin. "Do you remember, Pyotr Vladimirovich?"

"It was a gift for Vasya," said Pyotr harshly. "Is this treachery? I bade you give it her." He eyed the pendant as though it were a serpent.

"I have kept it for her," replied Dunya. "I begged, and the winter-king said I might. It was too great a burden for a child."

"Winter-king?" said Pyotr angrily. "Are you a child, to believe in fairy tales? There is no winter-king."

"Fairy tales?" returned Dunya, an answering anger in her voice. "Am I so wicked that I would invent such a lie? I, too, am a Christian, Pyotr Vladimirovich, but I believe what I see. Whence came this jewel, fit for a khan, that you brought for your little daughter?"

Pyotr, throat working, was silent.

"Who gave it to you?" Dunya continued. "You brought it from Moscow, but I never asked further."

"It is a necklace," said Pyotr, but the anger had gone from his voice. Pyotr had tried to forget the pale-eyed man, the blood on Kolya's throat, his men standing insensible. *Was that he, the winter-king?* Now he remembered how quickly he had agreed to give the stranger's trinket to his daughter. *Ancient magic,* it seemed he heard Marina say. *A daughter of my mother's bloodline.* And then, softer: *Protect her, Petya. I chose her; she is important. Promise me.*

"Not just a necklace," said Dunya harshly. "It is a talisman, may God forgive me. I have seen the winter-king. The necklace is his, and he will come for her."

"You have seen him?" Pyotr was on his feet.

Dunya nodded.

"Where did you see him? Where?"

"Dreaming," said Dunya. "Only dreaming. But he sends the dreams and they are true. I am to give her the necklace, he says. He will come for her at midwinter. She is no longer a child. But he is deceitful—all his kind are." The words came out in a rush. "I love Vasya like my own daughter. She is too brave for her own good. I am afraid for her."

Pyotr paced toward the great window and turned back toward Dunya. "Are you telling me the truth, Avdotya Mikhailovna? On my wife's head, do not lie to me."

"I have seen him," said Dunya again. "And you, I think, have seen him, too. He has black hair, curling. Pale eyes, paler than the sky at midwinter. He has no beard, and he is dressed all in blue."

"I will not give my daughter to a demon. She is a Christian maid." The raw fear in Pyotr's voice was new, born of Konstantin's sermons.

"Then she must have a husband," said Dunya simply. "The sooner the better. Frost-demons have no interest in mortal girls wed to mortal men. In the stories, the bird-prince and the wicked sorcerer—they only come for the wild maiden."

⬡

"VASYA?" SAID ALYOSHA. "MARRIED? That rabbit?" He laughed. The dry barley-stalks rustled; he was raking beside his father. There were straws in his brown curls. He had been singing to break the afternoon stillness. "She's a girl still, Father; I knocked down a peasant that watched her overlong, but she noticed nothing. Not even when the oaf went about for a week with his face all bruised." He had knocked down a peasant that called her witch-woman as well, but he did not tell his father that.

"She has not met a man that caught her fancy, that is all," said Pyotr. "But I mean that to change." Pyotr was brisk, his mind made up. "Kyril Artamonovich is my friend's son; he has a great inheritance, and his father is dead. Vasya is young and healthy, and her dowry is very fine. She will be gone before the snow." Pyotr bent once more to his raking.

Alyosha did not join him. "She will not take kindly to it, Father."

"Kindly or not, she will do as she's told," said Pyotr.

Alyosha snorted. "Vasya?" he said. "I'd like to see it."

⬡

"YOU ARE GOING TO BE MARRIED," said Irina to Vasya, enviously. "And have a fine dowry and go live in a big wooden house and have many children." She stood beside the rough post-and-rail fence but did not lean upon it, so as not to smudge her sarafan. Her long chestnut braid was wrapped in a bright kerchief and her small hand lay delicate on the wood. Vasya was trimming Buran's hoof, muttering dire threats to the stallion should he choose to move. He looked as though he was debating which part of her to bite. Irina was rather frightened.

Vasya put the hoof down and glanced at her small sister. "I am not going to be married," she said.

Irina's mouth creased in half-envious disapproval when Vasya vaulted the fence. "Yes, you are," she said. "A lord is coming; Kolya has gone to bring him. I heard Father say it to Mother."

Vasya's brow wrinkled. "Well—I suppose I must marry—someday," she said. She tilted her sister a sideways grin. "But how am I to catch a man's eye with you about, little bird?"

Irina smiled shyly. Already her beauty was talked of between the villages of their father's domain. But then— "You will not go into the woods, Vasya? It is nearly suppertime. You are all-over filth."

The rusalka was sitting above them, a green shadow along an oak-branch. She beckoned. The water dripped down her streaming hair. "I'll be along presently," said Vasya.

"But father says . . ."

Vasya leaped for a limb, one foot on the trunk, catching the branch overhead in her strong hands. She hooked a knee over it, dangling head-down. "I'll not be late for supper. Don't worry, Irinka." The next instant she had disappeared among the leaves.

⚬

THE RUSALKA WAS GAUNT and shivering. "What are you doing?" Vasya said. "What is wrong?" The rusalka shivered harder than ever. "Are you cold?" It hardly seemed possible; the earth gave back the day's heat, and the breeze was scant.

"No," said the rusalka. Her lank hair hid her face. "Little girls get cold, not chyerti. What is that child saying, Vasilisa Petrovna? Will you leave the forest?"

It came to Vasya that the rusalka was afraid, though it was not easy to know; the inflections of her voice were not like a woman's.

Vasya had never thought in those terms before. "One day I will," she said slowly. "Someday. I must marry and go to my husband's house. But I did not think it would be so soon." How faint the rusalka was. The rustling leaves showed through her gaunt face.

"You cannot," said the rusalka. Her lips peeled back from her green teeth. The hand that combed her hair jerked, so that the water falling down ran from her nose and chin. "We will not survive the winter. You did not let me kill the hungry man, and your wards are failing. You are only a child; your bits of bread and honey-wine cannot sustain the household-spirits. Not forever. The Bear is awake."

"What bear?"

"The shadow on the wall," said the rusalka, breathing quickly. "The voice in the dark." Her face did not move like a human face, but the pupils of her eyes swelled black. "Beware the dead. You must heed me, Vasya, for I will not come again. Not as myself. He will call me, and I will answer; he will have my allegiance and I will turn against you. I cannot do otherwise. The leaves are falling. Do not leave the forest."

"What do you mean, beware the dead? How will you turn against us?"

But the rusalka only reached out a hand, with such force that her damp, cloudy fingers felt like flesh, locked around Vasya's arm. "The winter-king will help you as you can," she said. "He promised. We all heard it. He is very old, and the enemy of your enemy. But you must not trust him."

Questions crowded Vasya's lips so fast they choked her silent. Her eyes met the rusalka's. The water-sprite's shining hair fell around her naked body. "I trust you," Vasya managed. "You are my friend."

"Be of good heart, Vasilisa Petrovna," said the rusalka, sadly, and then there was only a tree, with stormy silver leaves. As though she'd never been. *Perhaps I am mad, in truth,* thought Vasya. She caught the limb beneath her and dropped to the ground. She was soft on her feet as she ran home through the glorious late-summer twilight. All around her the forest seemed to whisper. *The shadow on the wall. You cannot trust him. Beware the dead. Beware the dead.*

⚜

"MARRIED, FATHER?" THE CLEAR green dusk breathed coolness onto the parched and gasping earth, so that the oven-fire comforted and did not torment. At noon they had eaten bread only, with curds or pickled mushrooms, for there was no time to spare from the fields. But that night there was stew and pie, roasted fowl and green things dipped in a little precious salt.

"If anyone can be brought to have you," said Pyotr, none too kindly, putting aside his bowl. Sapphires and pale eyes, threats and half-understood promises, thrashed unpleasantly in his skull. Vasya had come into the kitchen with a wet face, and there were distinct signs that she had tried to clean the dirt beneath her nails. But the water had only smeared the grime. She was dressed like a peasant girl in a thin dress of undyed linen, her black hair uncovered and curling. Her eyes were huge and wild and troubled. *It would be much easier to see her married,* Pyotr thought irritably, *if she would contrive to look more like a woman and less like a peasant child—or a wood-sprite.*

Pyotr watched the successive objections rise to her lips and fall away. All girls married, unless they became nuns. She knew that as well as anyone. "Married," she said again, striving for words. "Now?"

Again, Pyotr knew a pang. He saw her heavy with child, bowed over an oven, sitting before a loom, the grace gone . . .

Don't be a fool, Pyotr Vladimirovich. It is the lot of women. Pyotr remembered Marina warm and pliant in his arms. But he also remembered her slipping away into the forest, light as a ghost, that same wild look in her eyes.

"Who am I to marry, Father?"

My son was right, Pyotr thought. Vasya was indeed angry. Her pupils had swelled and her head was flung back like a filly that will not take the bit. He rubbed his face. Girls were happy to be married. Olga had glowed when her husband put a jewel on her finger and took her away. Maybe Vasya was jealous of her elder sister. But this daughter would never find a husband in Moscow. Might as well put a hawk in a dovecote.

"Kyril Artamonovich," said Pyotr. "My friend Artamon was rich, and his only son inherited. They are great breeders of horses."

Her eyes took up half her face. Pyotr scowled. It was a good match; she had no business looking stricken. "Where?" she whispered. "When?"

"A week to the east, on a good horse," said Pyotr. "He will come after the harvest."

Vasya's face stilled and set; she turned away. Pyotr added, coaxing, "He is coming here himself. I have sent Kolya to him. He will make you a good husband and give you children."

"Why such haste?" Vasya snapped.

The bitterness in her voice struck him raw. "Enough, Vasya," he said coldly. "You are a woman and he is a rich man. If you wanted a prince like Olga, well, they like their women fatter and less insolent."

He saw the quick stab of hurt before she masked it. "Olya promised she would send for me when I was grown," she said. "She said we would live in a palace together."

"Better you are married now, Vasya," said Pyotr at once. "You can go to your sister after your first son is born."

Vasya bit her lip and stalked away. Pyotr found himself wondering uneasily what Kyril Artamonovich would make of his daughter.

"He is not old, Vasya," said Dunya, when Vasya flung herself down by the hearth. "He is renowned for his skill in the chase. He will give you strong children."

"What is Father not telling me?" retorted Vasya. "It is too sudden. I could have waited a year. Olya promised to send for me."

"Nonsense, Vasya," said Dunya, perhaps over-briskly. "You are a woman; you are better off with a husband. I am sure Kyril Artamonovich will allow you to go visit your sister."

The green eyes flew up, narrowed. "You know Father's reason. Why this haste?"

"I—I cannot say, Vasya," said Dunya. She looked suddenly small and shrunken.

Vasya said nothing. "It is for the best," said her nurse. "Try to understand." She sank onto the oven-bench as though her strength deserted her, and Vasya felt a pang of remorse.

"Yes," she said. "I am sorry, Dunyashka." She laid a hand on her nurse's arm. But she did not speak again. When she had swallowed her porridge, she slipped away like a ghost through the door and out into the night.

⁂

THE MOON WAS LITTLE thicker than a crescent, the light a glitter of blue. Vasya ran, with a panic she could not understand. The life she led made her strong. She bolted and let the cool wind wash the taste of fear from her mouth. But she had not gone far; the firelight of her family's hearth still beat upon her back when she heard someone call her name.

"Vasilisa Petrovna."

She almost ran on and let the night swallow her. But where was there to go? She halted. The priest stood in the shadow of the church. It was dark; she would not have known him by his face. But she could not mistake the voice. She did not say anything. She tasted salt and realized there were tears drying on her lips.

Konstantin was just leaving the church. He had not seen Vasya leave the house, but he could not mistake her flying shadow. He called before he knew, and cursed himself when she stopped. But the sight of her face shook him. "What is it?" he said roughly. "Why are you crying?"

If his voice had been cool and commanding, Vasya would not have answered. But as it was, she said wearily, "I am going to be married."

Konstantin frowned. He saw all at once, as Pyotr had seen, the wild thing brought indoors, busy and breathless, a woman like other women. Like Pyotr, he felt a strange sorrow and shook it away. He stepped closer without thinking, so that he might read her face, and saw with astonishment that she was afraid.

"And so?" he said. "Is he a cruel man?"

"No," Vasya said. "No, I don't think so."

It is for the best was on the tip of the priest's tongue. But he thought again of years, of childbearing and exhaustion. The wildness gone, the hawk's grace chained up . . . He swallowed. *It is for the best.* The wildness was sinful.

But even though he knew the answer, he found himself asking, "Why are you frightened, Vasilisa Petrovna?"

"Do not you know, Batyushka?" she said. Her laugh was soft and desperate. "You were frightened when they sent you here. You felt the forest closing about you like a fist; I could see it in your eyes. But you may leave if you will. There is a whole wide world waiting for a man of God, and already you have drunk the water of Tsargrad and seen the sun on the sea. While I . . ." He could see the panic rising in her again, and so he strode forward and seized her arm.

"Hush," he said. "Do not be a fool; you are making yourself frightened."

She laughed again. "You are right," she said. "I am foolish. I was born for a cage, after all: convent or house, what else is there?"

"You are a woman," said Konstantin. He was still holding her arm; she stepped back and he let her go. "You will accept it in time," he said. "You will be happy." She could barely see his face, but there was a note in his voice that she did not understand. It sounded as though he was trying to convince himself.

"No," Vasya said hoarsely. "Pray for me if you will, Batyushka, but I must . . ." And then she was running again, between the houses. Konstantin was left swallowing the urge to call her back. His palm burned where he had touched her.

It is for the best, he thought. *It is for the best.*

16.

THE DEVIL BY CANDLELIGHT

IT WAS AN AUTUMN OF GRAY SKIES AND YELLOW LEAVES, OF SUD-
den rain and unexpected shafts of livid sunlight. The boyar's son came
with Kolya after their harvest had been put away safe, in cellars and
lofts. Kolya sent a messenger ahead of them on the muddy track, and on
the day of the lord's coming, Vasya and Irina spent the morning in the
bathhouse. The bannik, the bathhouse-spirit, was a potbellied creature
with eyes like two currants. He leered good-naturedly at the girls.
"Can't you hide under a bench?" said Vasya, low, when Irina was in the
outer room. "My stepmother will see you; she'll scream."

The bannik grinned. Steam drifted between his teeth. He was barely
taller than her knee. "As you like. But do not forget me this winter,
Vasilisa Petrovna. Every season I am less. I do not want to disappear.
The old eater is waking; this would not be a good winter to lose your
old bannik."

Vasya hesitated, caught. *But I am going to be married. I am going
away. Beware the dead.* Her lips firmed. "I will not forget."

His smile widened. The steam wreathed his body until she could not
tell mist from flesh. A red light heated the backs of his eyes, the color of
hot stones. "A prophecy then, vedma."

"Why do you call me that?" she whispered.

The bannik drifted up to the bench beside her. His beard was the curling steam. "Because you have your great-grandmother's eyes. Now hear me. Before the end, you will pluck snowdrops at midwinter, die by your own choosing, and weep for a nightingale."

Vasya felt cold despite the steam. "Why would I choose to die?"

"It is easy to die," replied the bannik. "Harder to live. Do not forget me, Vasilisa Petrovna." And there was only vapor where he had been. *Holy Mother,* Vasya thought, *I've had enough of their mad warnings.*

The two girls sat and sweated until they were flushed and shining, beat each other with birch-branches, and ladled cold water over their steaming heads. When they were clean, Dunya came with Anna to comb and braid their long hair. "It is a shame you are so like a boy, Vasya," said Anna, running a comb of scented wood through Irina's long chestnut curls. "I hope your husband will not be too disappointed." She looked sideways at her stepdaughter. Vasya flushed and bit her tongue.

"But such hair," said Dunya tartly. "The finest hair in Rus', Vasochka." And indeed it was longer and thicker than Irina's, deep black with soft red lights.

Vasya managed a smile for her nurse. Irina had been told from babyhood that she was lovely as a princess. Vasya had been an ugly child, often and unfavorably compared with her delicate half sister. Recently, though, long hours on horseback—where her long limbs were useful—had put Vasya in better charity with herself, and in any case, she was not much given to contemplating her own reflection. The only mirror in the house was a bronze oval belonging to her stepmother.

Now though, every woman in the house seemed to be staring at her, assessing as though she were a goat fattening for market. It occurred to Vasya to wonder if there was something in being beautiful.

The two girls were dressed at last. Vasya's head was wrapped in a maiden's headdress, the silver wire hanging down to frame her face. Anna would never let Vasya outshine her own daughter, even if Vasya was the one being married, and so Irina's headdress and sleeves were embroidered in seed pearls, her little sarafan of pale blue trimmed in white. Vasya wore green and deep blue, no pearls, and a bare hint of white embroidery. The plainness was her own fault; she had left much of the sewing to Dunya. But simplicity suited her. Anna's face soured when she saw her stepdaughter dressed.

The two girls emerged into the dvor. The dooryard was mud to the ankles; rain misted gently down. Irina kept close to her mother. Pyotr waited in the dvor already, stiff in fine fur and embroidered boots. Kolya's wife had come with her children; Vasya's small nephew Seryozha ran around shouting. A great stain already marred his linen shirt. Father Konstantin stood by, silent.

"It is a strange time for a wedding," said Alyosha low to Vasya, coming up beside her. "A dry summer and a small harvest." His brown hair was clean, his short beard combed with scented oil. His blue-embroidered shirt matched the sash round his waist. "You are very lovely, Vasya."

"Don't make me laugh," his sister rejoined. More seriously, she added, "Yes—and Father feels it." Indeed, though Pyotr looked jovial, the line between his brows showed clear. "He looks like someone bound to an unpleasant duty. He must be quite desperate to send me away."

She tried to make a joke of it, but Alyosha looked at her with quick understanding. "He is trying to keep you safe."

"He loved our mother, and I killed her."

Alyosha was silent a moment. "As you say. But, truly, Vasochka, he is trying to keep you safe. The horses have coats like duckdown, and the squirrels are still out, eating as though their lives depend on it. It will be a hard winter."

A rider came through the palisade gate and galloped toward the house. The mud flew in great arcs from beneath his horse's feet. He came to a skidding halt and sprang from the saddle: a man in his middle years, not tall but broadly built, weathered and brown-bearded. A hint of irrepressible youth lurked about his mouth. He had all his teeth, and his smile was bright as a boy's. He bowed to Pyotr. "I am not late, I hope, Pyotr Vladimirovich?" he asked, laughing. The two men clasped forearms.

No wonder he outstripped Kolya, Vasya thought. Kyril Artamonovich was riding the most magnificent young horse she had ever seen. Even Buran, a prince among horses, looked rough-hewn next to the sinewy perfection of the roan stallion. She wanted to run her hands over the colt's legs, feel the quality of his bone and muscle.

"I told Father this was a bad idea," said Alyosha in her ear.

"What? And why?" said Vasya, preoccupied by the horse.

"To marry you off so soon. Because blushing maidens are supposed to look covetously upon the lords that vie for their hands, not upon the lords' fine horses."

Vasya laughed. Kyril was bowing to tiny Irina with exaggerated courtesy. "A rough setting, Pyotr Vladimirovich, to find such a jewel," he said. "Little snowdrop, you ought to go south and bloom among our flowers." He smiled, and Irina blushed. Anna looked at her daughter with some complacency.

Kyril turned toward Vasya, the easy smile still on his lips. It died away quite when he saw her. Vasya thought he must be displeased with her appearance; she raised her chin a defiant fraction. *All the better. Find another wife if I displease you.* But Alyosha understood his darkening eyes very well. Vasya looked you full in the face: she was more like a warrior unblooded than a house-bred girl, and Kyril was staring in fascination. He bowed to her, the smile once more playing about his lips, but it was not the smile he'd given Irina. "Vasilisa Petrovna," he said. "Your brother said you were beautiful. You are not." She stiffened, and his smile deepened. "You are magnificent." His eyes swept her from headdress to slippered feet.

Beside her, Alyosha's hand clenched into a fist. "Are you mad?" hissed Vasya. "He has the right; we are betrothed."

Alyosha was eyeing Kyril very coldly. "This is my brother," said Vasya hurriedly. "Aleksei Petrovich."

"Well met," said Kyril, looking amused. He was nearly ten years the elder. His eyes swept Vasya once more, leisurely. Her skin prickled under her clothes. She could hear Alyosha grinding his teeth.

At that moment there came a snort, a shriek, and a splash. They all spun around. Seryozha, Vasya's nephew, had crept to the off-side of Kyril's red stallion and tried to clamber into the saddle. Vasya could sympathize—already she wanted to ride the red colt—but the unexpected weight had left the young stallion rearing and wild-eyed. Kyril ran to seize his horse's bridle. Pyotr heaved his grandson from the mud and clouted him across the ear. At that moment, Kolya came galloping into the dvor, and his arrival put a cap on the confusion. Seryozha's mother carried the boy away, howling. Far down the road, the first wagon of the rest of the party appeared, vivid against the gray autumn forest. The women hastily went into the house to dish up the noon meal.

"It is only natural that he preferred Irina, Vasya," said Anna, while they wrestled an immense stew-pot. "A mongrel dog will never equal a purebred. At least your mother is dead—all the easier to forget your unfortunate ancestry. You're strong as a horse; that counts for something."

The domovoi crept out of the oven, wavering but determined. Vasya had surreptitiously spilled some mead for him. "Look, stepmother," said Vasya. "Is that the cat?"

Anna looked, and her face turned the color of clay. She swayed where she stood. The domovoi frowned at her, and she promptly swooned. Vasya dodged, clutching the scalding pot. She saved the stew. But the same could not be said for Anna Ivanovna. Her knees buckled and she hit the hearthstones with a satisfying crack.

§♥§

"Did you like him, Vasya?" asked Irina in bed that night.

Vasya was half-asleep; she and Irina had been up before the sun to ready themselves, and the feasting that night had gone late. Kyril Artamonovich had sat beside Vasya and drunk from her cup. Her betrothed had fleshy hands and a trick of laughing so that the walls seemed to shake. She liked the size of him, but not the insolence. "He is a goodly man," Vasya said, but she wished to all the saints that he would disappear.

"He is handsome," agreed Irina. "His smile is kind."

Vasya rolled over, frowning. In Moscow, girls were not allowed to mingle with suitors, but things were freer in the north. "His smile might be kind," she said, "but his horse is afraid of him." When the feast wound down, she had slipped away to the barn. Kyril's colt, Ogon, had been put in a stall; he could not be trusted in pasture.

Irina laughed. "How do you know what a horse thinks?"

"I know," said Vasya. "Besides, he is old, little bird. Dunya says he is nearly thirty."

"But he is rich; you will have jewels, and meat every day."

"You marry him, then," said Vasya tolerantly, poking her sister in the stomach. "And you will be as fat as a squirrel and sit all day sewing atop the oven."

Irina giggled. "Maybe we will see each other when we are married. If our husbands do not live far apart."

"I'm sure they won't," said Vasya. "You can save some of your fat meats for me, when I come begging with my beggar-husband while you are married to a great lord."

Irina giggled again. "But it is you who are marrying a great lord, Vasya."

Vasya did not answer; she did not speak again. At length, Irina gave up; she curled up against her sister and fell asleep. But Vasya lay long awake. *He has charmed my family, but his horse fears his hand. Beware the dead. It will be a hard winter. You must not leave the forest.* The thoughts raced like water, and she was borne on the current. But she was young and weary, and eventually she, too, rolled over and slept.

※

THE DAYS PASSED IN a round of games and feasting. Kyril Artamonovich filled Vasya's bowl at supper and teased her through the kitchen door. His body gave off an animal heat. Vasya was angry to find herself blushing beneath his gaze. At night she lay awake, wondering how all that warmth would feel between her hands. But his laughter did not reach his eyes. Fear rose at odd moments to seize her by the throat.

The days wore by, and Vasya could not understand herself. *You must marry,* the women scolded. *All girls marry. At least he is not old, and he is well-favored besides. Why then be afraid?* But afraid she was, and she avoided her betrothed whenever she could, pacing back and forth, a bird in a shrinking cage.

"Why, Father?" said Alyosha to Pyotr, not for the first time, at the start of yet another raucous supper. The long, dim room reeked of furs and mead, roast meats, pottage, and sweating humanity. The kasha went round in a great bowl; the mead was dipped out and tossed back. Their neighbors packed the room. The house overflowed now, and visitors crammed the peasants' huts.

"Three days until she is married; we must honor our guest," said Pyotr.

"Why is she getting married now?" retorted his son. "Can she not wait a year? Why after a hard winter and a hard summer must we waste food and drink on these?" His gesture took in the long room where their guests busily demolished the fruit of a summer's labor.

"Because it must be," Pyotr snapped. "If you want to make yourself useful, convince your mad sister not to geld her husband on their wedding night."

"He is a bull, that Kyril," said Alyosha shortly. "He has got five children on peasant girls, and he thinks nothing of flirting with the farmers' wives, while he stays in your house, no less. If my sister sees fit to geld her husband, Father, she would have reason, and I would not dissuade her."

As if by some unspoken accord, they looked to where the couple in question sat side by side. Kyril was talking to Vasya, his gestures broad and imprecise. Vasya was eyeing him with an expression that made both Pyotr and Alyosha nervous. Kyril did not seem to notice.

"And there I was alone," Kyril said to Vasya. He refilled their cup, sloshing a bit. His lips left a ring of grease round the rim. "My back was to a rock and the boar was charging. My men had scattered, save for the dead one, with the great red hole in him."

This was not the first narrative featuring the heroics of Kyril Artamonovich. Vasya's mind had begun to wander. *Where is the priest?* Father Konstantin had not come to the feast, and it was unlike him to keep to himself.

"The boar came for me," said Kyril. "Its hooves shook the earth. I commended my soul to God—"

And died there with blood in your mouth, Vasya thought in disgust. *I should have been so fortunate.*

She laid a hand on his arm and looked up at him with an expression she hoped was piteous. "No more—I cannot bear it."

Kyril eyed her, puzzled. Vasya shuddered all over. "I cannot bear to know the rest. I fear I will faint, Kyril Artamonovich."

Kyril looked nonplussed.

"Dunya has much stronger nerves than I," said Vasya. "I think you should finish the story in her hearing." There was nothing wrong with Dunya's ears (or Vasya's nerves, for that matter); the old lady glanced resignedly heavenward and shot Vasya a warning look. But Vasya had the bit between her teeth, and even her father's glare from down the table would not turn her. "Now"—Vasya rose with theatrical grace and seized a loaf from the table—"now, if you will forgive me, I must fulfill a pious duty."

Kyril opened his mouth to protest, but Vasya made a hasty reverence, slipped the loaf into her sleeve, and bolted. Outside the packed hall, the house was cool and quiet. She stood in the dvor for a long moment, breathing.

Then she went and scratched upon the priest's door.

"Come in," said Konstantin, after a chilly pause. The whole room seemed to quiver with candlelight. He was painting by the glow. A rat had gnawed the crust that lay untouched beside him. The priest did not turn when Vasya opened the door.

"Father, bless," she said. "I have brought you bread."

Konstantin stiffened. "Vasilisa Petrovna." He put down his brush and made the sign of the cross. "May the Lord bless you."

"Are you ill, that you do not feast with us?" asked Vasya.

"I fast."

"Better to eat. There will not be food like this all winter."

Konstantin said nothing. Vasya replaced the gnawed crust with the new loaf. The silence stretched out, but she did not go.

"Why did you give me your cross?" asked Vasya abruptly. "After we met at the lake?"

His jaw set, but he did not at once reply. In truth, he hardly knew. Because she had moved him. Because he hoped the symbol could reach her when he could not. Because he had wanted to touch her hand and look her in the face, disquiet her, perhaps see her fidget and simper like other girls. Help him forget his wicked fascination.

Because he could never look at his cross again without seeing her hand around it.

"The Holy Cross will make your way straight," said Konstantin at last.

"Will it?"

The priest was silent. At night now he dreamed of the woman in the lake. He could never make out her face. But in his dreams her hair was black; it snapped and slid against her naked flesh. Awake, Konstantin spent long hours in prayer, trying to carve the image from his mind. But he could not, for every time he saw Vasya, he knew the woman in his dream had her eyes. He was haunted, ashamed. Her fault for tempting him. But in three days she would be gone.

"Why are you here, Vasilisa Petrovna?" His voice came out loud and ragged, and he was angry with himself.

The storm is coming, Vasya thought. *Beware the dead. Fear first, then fire, then famine. Your fault. We had faith in God before you came, and faith in our house-spirits also, and all was well.*

If the priest left, then perhaps her people would be safe once more.

"Why do you stay here?" Vasya said. "You hate the fields and the forest and the silence. You hate our rude bare church. Yet you are still here. No one would fault you for going."

A dull flush crept across Konstantin's cheekbones. His hand fumbled among his paints. "I have a task, Vasilisa Petrovna. I must save you from yourselves. God has punishments for those who stray."

"A self-appointed task," said Vasya, "in service of your own pride. Why is it for you to say what God wants? The people would never revere you so, if you had not made them afraid."

"You are an ignorant country maid; what do you know?" snapped Konstantin.

"I believe the evidence of my eyes," Vasya said. "I have seen you speak. I have *seen* my people afraid. And you know what I say is true; you are shaking." He had picked up a bowl of half-mixed color. The warm wax within shivered. Konstantin let it go abruptly.

She came nearer, and nearer yet. The candlelight brought out the flecks of gold in her eyes. His glance strayed to her mouth. *Demon, get you gone.* But her voice was a young girl's, with a soft note of pleading. "Why not go back? To Moscow or Vladimir or Suzdal? Why linger here? The world is wide, and our corner so very small."

"God gave me a task." He bit off each word, almost spitting.

"We are men and women," she retorted. "We are not a *task*. Go back to Moscow and save folk there."

She was standing too near. His hand shot out; he struck her across the face. She stumbled back, cradling her cheek. He took two quick steps forward, so that he was looking down at her, but she stood her ground. His hand was raised to strike again, but he drew breath and forbore. It was beneath him to strike her. He wanted to seize her, kiss her, hurt her, he did not know what. *Demon.*

"Get out, Vasilisa Petrovna," he said through gritted teeth. "Don't presume to lecture me. And don't come here again."

She retreated to the door. But she turned back with one hand on the latch. Her braid followed the line of her throat. The scarlet handprint stood out livid on her cheek. "As you wish," she said. "It is a cruel task, to frighten people in God's name. I leave it to you." She hesitated and added, very softly, "However, Batyushka, I am not afraid."

⚜

AFTER SHE LEFT, KONSTANTIN paced to and fro. His shadow leaped before him, and the hand that had struck her burned. Fury closed his throat. *She will be gone before the snow. Gone and long gone: my shame and my failure. But better than having her here.*

The candle guttered where it stood before his icons, and the flame threw ragged shadows.

She will be gone. She must be gone.

The voice came from the earth, from the candlelight, from his own breast. It was soft and clear and shining. "Peace be with you," it said. "Though I see you are troubled."

Konstantin stopped dead. "Who is that?"

"—Wanting despite yourself, and hating where you love." The voice sighed. "Oh, you are beautiful."

"Who is speaking?" snapped Konstantin. "Do you mock me?"

"I do not mock," came the ready reply. "I am a friend. A master. A savior." The voice throbbed with compassion.

The priest spun, seeking. "Come out," he said. He forced himself to stand still. "Show yourself."

"What is this?" The voice held a hint now of anger. "Doubts, my servant? Don't you know who I am?"

The room was bare, except for the bed and the icons, and the shadows collected in the corners. Konstantin stared into these, until his eyes smarted. There—what was that? A shadow that did not move with the firelight. No, that was just his own shadow, cast by the candle. There was no one outside, there was no one behind the door. Then who . . . ?

Konstantin's glance sought his icons. He looked deep into their strange solemn faces. His own face changed. "Father," he whispered. "Lord. Angels. After all your silence, do you speak to me at last?" He shook in every limb. He strained all his senses, willing the voice to speak again.

"Can you doubt it, my child?" said the voice, gentle again. "You have always been my loyal servant."

The priest began to weep, open-eyed, soundless. He fell to his knees.

"I have watched you long, Konstantin Nikonovich," continued the voice. "You have labored bravely on my behalf. But now there is this girl who tempts and defies you."

Konstantin clasped his hands together. "My shame," he said feverishly. "I cannot save her alone. She is possessed; she is a she-devil. I pray that in your wisdom you will show her light."

"She will learn many lessons," replied the voice. "Many—many. Have no fear. I stand with you, and you will never again be alone. The world will fall to your feet, and know my wonders through your lips, because you have been loyal."

It seemed that trumpets must play when that voice spoke. Konstantin shuddered with pleasure, the tears still falling. "Only never leave me, Lord," he said. "I have always been faithful." He clenched his fists so tightly his nails made furrows in the skin of his hands.

"Be faithful," said the voice, "and I will never leave you."

17.

A HORSE CALLED FIRE

KYRIL ARTAMONOVICH LOVED ABOVE ALL TO HUNT THE LONG-tusked northern boars, swifter than horses. The day before his wedding, he called for a boar-hunt. "It will while away the time," he said to Pyotr, with a wink at Vasya, who said nothing. But Pyotr made no objection. Kyril Artamonovich was a famous hunter, and pig-meat in the autumn was a fine thing, fattened on chestnut-mast. A good haunch would grace the wedding-feast and bring color to his daughter's pale face.

The whole household rose before dawn. The boar-spears lay already in a shining heap. The dogs had heard the sound of sharpening, and paced their kennels all night, whining.

Vasya was up before anyone else. She did not take food, but went to the stable, where the horses pawed anxiously at the noise from the dogs outside. Kyril's young roan stallion trembled with each new sound. Vasya went to him and found the vazila there, perched on the colt's back. Vasya smiled at the little creature. The stallion snorted at her and pinned his ears.

"You have bad manners," Vasya told him. "But I suppose Kyril Artamonovich drags you around by the mouth."

The colt put his ears forward. *You do not look like a horse.*

Vasya grinned. "Thank God. Do you not wish to go hunting?"

The horse considered. *I like running. But the pig smells foul, and the man will strike me if I am afraid. I'd rather graze in a field.* Vasya laid a comforting hand on the horse's neck. Kyril was going to ruin the beautiful colt—little more than a foal—if he kept on. The colt bumped her chest with his nose. Water and greenish slime dribbled onto her dress.

"Now I'm more of a scarecrow than usual," Vasya remarked, to no one in particular. "Anna Ivanovna will be delighted."

"The pig won't hurt you if you're quick," she added to Ogon. "And you are the quickest thing in the world, my beauty. You need not fear."

The colt said nothing, but put his head in her arms. Vasya rubbed his silky ears and sighed. She would have liked nothing better than a wild ride through autumn forest, preferably on the long-legged Ogon, who looked as though he could outrun a hare in an open field. Instead, she was to go to the kitchen, knead bread, and listen to the gossip of a bevy of visiting women. All this while Irina showed off her many perfections and Vasya tried not to burn anything.

"Ordinarily I would curse a maid for a fool that got so near my horse," said a voice from behind her. Ogon threw his head up, nearly breaking Vasya's nose. "But you have a hand with beasts, Vasilisa Petrovna." Kyril Artamonovich came toward them, smiling. He caught the colt by his rope halter.

"Hush, mad thing," he said. The colt rolled his eyes but stood, shivering.

"You are abroad early, my lord," said Vasya, recovering.

"As are you, Vasilisa Petrovna." Their breath made clouds; the stable was chilly.

"There is much to do," said Vasya. "The women will ride to meet you after the kill, if the day is fine. And tonight we are feasting."

He grinned. "No need to excuse yourself, devushka. I think it a fine thing in a girl to rise early, and to interest herself in a man's stock." He had a dimple on one side of his mouth. "I'll not tell your father that I found you here."

Vasya regained her composure. "Tell him if you will," she said.

He smiled. "I like your spirit."

She shrugged.

"Your sister is prettier than you," he added musingly. "She will be an easy wife in a few years' time: a little flower. Not a girl to trouble a man's nights. But you——" Kyril reached out, pulled her to him, and ran a hand down her back, in an assessing sort of way. "Too many bones," he said, "but I like a strong girl. And you will not die in childbed." He handled her confidently, with the expectation of being obeyed. "Will you like making me sons?" He kissed her before she knew, while she was still bewildered by the strength in his hands. His kiss was like his touch: firm, with a sort of proficient enjoyment. Vasya shoved at him, to little effect. He tilted her face up, digging his fingers into the soft place behind her jaw. Her head swam. He smelled of musk and mead and horses. His hand was very large, splayed against her back. His other hand slid over her shoulder and breast and hip.

Whatever he found seemed to please him. When he let her go, his chest heaved, and his nostrils flared like a stallion's. Vasya stood still, swallowing her nausea. She looked up into his face. *I am a mare to him,* she thought suddenly and clearly. *And if a mare will not yield to harness, well, he will break her.*

Kyril's smile slipped a fraction. She could not know how much he had seen of her pride and scorn. His eyes strayed again to her mouth, the shape of her body, and she knew he saw her fear as well. The brief unease left his face. He reached for her again, but Vasya was quicker. She struck his hand aside, ran from the stable, and did not look back. When she reached the kitchen, she was so pale that Dunya made her sit by the fire and drink hot wine until a little color came back into her face.

❧

ALL THAT DAY, A COLD mist rose from the earth, winding itself about the trees. The hunt made a kill near midday. Vasya, wielding a bread paddle with grim competence, heard, faintly, the shriek of the dying animal. It matched her mood.

The women left the house at gray noontide, with men to lead the laden packhorses. Konstantin rode out with them, his face pale and exalted in the autumn light. Men and women watched him with reverence and furtive admiration. Vasya, avoiding the priest, stayed with Irina near the back of the cavalcade, shortening her mare's long stride to match Irina's pony.

The mist crept over the earth. The women complained of chill and drew their cloaks about them.

Suddenly Mysh reared. Even Irina's placid beast shied, so that the child gave a stifled scream and clutched her reins. Vasya hastily brought the mare down and caught the pony's bridle. She followed Mysh's ears with her eyes. A white-skinned creature stood between two tall birch trunks. He was man-shaped and light-eyed. His hair was the tangled undergrowth of the forest. He cast no shadow. "It's all right," Vasya said to Mysh. "That does not eat horses. Only foolish travelers."

The mare swiveled her ears but, hesitantly, began to walk again.

"Leshy, lesovik," murmured Vasya as they rode past. She bowed from the waist. He was the wood-guard—the leshy—and he seldom came so close to men.

"I would speak with you, Vasilisa Petrovna." The wood-guard's voice was the whisper of branches at dawn.

"Presently," she said, mastering her surprise.

Beside her, Irina squeaked, "Who are you talking to, Vasya?"

"No one," said Vasya. "Myself."

Irina was quiet. Vasya sighed inwardly—Irina would tell her mother.

They found the hunters a little way into the forest, taking their ease under a great tree. They had already hung the pig, a sow, by her hocks from a massive limb. Her slit throat drained blood into a bucket. The wood rang with laughter and boasting.

Seryozha, who considered himself quite grown, had only with difficulty been persuaded to ride with the women. Now he leaped from his pony and darted over to stare, round-eyed, at the hanging pig. Vasya slid from Mysh's back and gave the reins into a servant's hand.

"A fine beast we have taken, is it not, Vasilisa Petrovna?" The voice came from her elbow. She whirled round. The blood had caked in the lines of Kyril's palms, but his boyish smile was undimmed.

"The meat will be welcome," said Vasya.

"I will save the liver for you." His glance was speculative. "You could use fattening."

"You are generous," said Vasya. She bowed her head and slipped away, like a maiden too modest for speech. The women were extracting a cold meal from laden bundles. Carefully, Vasya worked herself closer and closer to a little grove of birch, then slipped among the trees and disappeared.

She did not see Kyril smile to himself and follow.

LESHIYE WERE DANGEROUS. WHEN they wished, they could lead travelers in circles until they collapsed. Sometimes the travelers were wise enough to put their clothes on backward for protection—but not often; they mostly died.

Vasya found him at the center of a little copse of birch. The leshy looked down at her with glittering eyes.

"What news?" said Vasya.

The leshy made a grinding sound of displeasure. "Your people come with clamor to fright my woods and kill my creatures. They would have asked my leave once."

"We ask your leave again," said Vasya quickly. They had trouble enough without angering the wood-guard. She untied her embroidered kerchief and laid it in his hand. He turned it over in his long, twiggy fingers.

"Forgive us," said Vasya. "And—do not forget me."

"I would ask the same," said the wood-guard, mollified. "We are fading, Vasilisa Petrovna. Even I, who watched these trees grow from saplings. Your people waver, and so the chyerti wither. If the Bear comes now you are unprotected. There will be a reckoning. Beware the dead."

"What does it mean, 'beware the dead'?"

The leshy bowed his hoary head. "Three signs, and the dead are fourth," he said. Then he disappeared, and all she heard were the birds singing in the rustling wood.

"Enough of this," Vasya muttered, not really expecting a reply. "Why can none of you speak plainly? What are you afraid of?"

Kyril Artamonovich emerged from between the trees.

Vasya stiffened her spine. "Are you lost, my lord?"

He snorted. "No more than you, Vasilisa Petrovna. I have never seen a girl walk so light in the woods. But you should not go unprotected."

She said nothing.

"Walk with me," he said.

There was no way to refuse. They walked side by side through the thick wet loam, while the leaves drifted down around them. "You will like my lands, Vasilisa Petrovna," Kyril said. "The horses run across fields larger than the eye can tell, and merchants bring us jewels from Vladimir, the city of the Mother of God."

A vision seized Vasya then, not of a lord's fine house, but of herself on a galloping horse, in a land unbounded by forest. She stood a moment, frozen and far away. Kyril lifted and smoothed her long braid where it lay over her breast. Startled back to herself, she flicked it out of his grip. He caught her hair, smiling, in a fist, and drew her nearer. "Come, none of that." She backed up, but he followed her, wrapping her braid round his hand. "I will teach you to want me." His mouth sought hers.

A piercing shriek split the midafternoon silence.

Kyril let her go. There was a brown flash between the trees, and

Vasya took off running, cursing her skirts. But even hampered, she was lighter than the big man behind her. She darted round a holly bush and skidded to a horrified halt. Seryozha was clinging to Mysh's neck, and the brown mare bucked and spun like a yearling colt. A ring of white showed all around her frantic eye.

Vasya could not understand it; the boy had ridden the mare before, and Mysh was very sensible. But now she jumped as though three devils sat her back. Irina was pressed up against a tree at the edge of the clearing, both hands over her mouth. "I told him!" she wailed. "I told him he was being bad, but he said he was grown—that he could do as he liked. He wanted to race the horses. He wouldn't listen."

The alder clearing was full of shadows, too big for the noon light. One of them seemed to lurch forward. For a second, Vasya could have sworn she saw a madman's grin, and a single, winking eye.

"Mysh, be still," she said to the horse. The mare came plunging to a stop, ears pricked. There was a split second of stillness.

"Seryozha," said Vasya. "Now—"

Kyril came crashing through the undergrowth. In the same instant, the shadows seemed to spring from three places at once. The mare's nerve broke again; she wheeled and bolted. Her long legs dug into the forest track and she almost scraped her rider off in her wild career between tree-trunks. Seryozha screamed, but he was still in the saddle, clinging to the horse's neck.

Somewhere, someone was laughing.

Vasya ran for the other horses, seizing her belt-knife. Kyril was behind her, but she was faster. She flashed past her astonished father and reached Ogon first. "What are you doing?" shouted Kyril. Vasya did not answer. The colt was tied, but a stroke split the rope, and a vault saw her settled onto his bare back, fingers wound into the red mane.

The horse bolted in pursuit. Kyril was left with his mouth hanging open. Vasya leaned forward, catching the stallion's rhythm, feet locked around his barrel. She wished she'd had time to untangle her layers of skirt. They swept through the trees like a thunderstorm. Vasya bent low over the horse's neck. A fallen log loomed in their way. Vasya took a deep breath. Ogon cleared the barrier, surefooted as a stag.

They burst out of the forest and into a muddy field scarce ten horse-lengths behind the runaway. Miraculously, Seryozha was still clinging to Mysh's neck. He did not have much choice; a fall at speed would be fatal, the going made treacherous by hundreds of half-hidden stumps. Ogon gained steadily; he was much the faster horse, and the mare was racing in panicked zigzags, twisting in an effort to throw the child from her back. Vasya shouted at Mysh to stop, but the mare did not hear, or she did not heed. Vasya cried encouragement to Seryozha, but the wind snatched the words away. She and Ogon slowly closed the gap. Foam flew back from the horses' lips. There was a ditch coming up at the far side of the field, dug to drain rainwater off the barley. Even if Mysh could jump it, Seryozha would never stay on her back. Vasya screamed at Ogon. A series of powerful leaps brought him level with the run-away. The ditch was coming up fast. Vasya reached out, one-armed, for her nephew.

"Let go, let *go*!" she shouted, grabbing a fistful of his shirt. Seryozha had time for one panic-stricken glance, then Vasya yanked him clear and slung him facedown over Ogon's red withers. The boy had a hand-ful of black mane clutched in each fist. Simultaneously, Vasya shifted her weight, urging the colt to turn before the looming edge. Somehow the stallion managed, gathering his hindquarters and lunging sideways on a course that took him parallel to the ditch. He came to a sliding, slithering halt a few paces later, trembling all over. Mysh was not so lucky; in her panic she blundered into the ditch and now lay thrashing at the bottom.

Vasya slid from Ogon's back, staggering as her legs tried to buckle beneath her. She pulled her sobbing nephew down and looked him over quickly. His nose and lip were bloody from the stallion's iron-hard shoulder. "Seryozha," she said. "Sergei Nikolaevich. You're all right. Hush." Her nephew was sobbing and trembling and giggling all at once. Vasya slapped him across his bloody face. He shuddered and fell silent, and she hugged him tight. Behind them came the sound of a horse struggling.

"Ogon," said Vasya. The stallion was behind her, flecked with foam. "Stay here."

The horse twitched an assenting ear. Vasya let her nephew go and half-ran, half-slid to the bottom of the ditch. Mysh lay in a foot of water, but Vasya ignored it. She knelt beside the mare's foam-streaked head. Miraculously, the horse's legs weren't broken. "You're all right," Vasya whispered. "You're all right." She matched the mare's breathing once, and again. Suddenly Mysh lay quiet under her burning hand. Vasya stood up and drew away.

The mare collected herself, clumsy as a foal, and came spraddle-legged to her feet. Vasya, shaking now with reaction, wrapped her arms around the horse's neck. "Fool," she whispered. "What possessed you?"

I saw a shadow, said the mare. *And it had teeth.* There was no time for more. A confusion of voices came from the top of the ditch. A small avalanche of rocks heralded the appearance of Kyril Artamonovich. Mysh shied. Kyril was staring.

Vasya's face burned. "The mare's had a fright," the girl said hurriedly, catching hold of Mysh's bridle. "You smell of blood, Kyril Artamonovich; best you stay up there."

Kyril had no intention of sliding down into the mud and water, but even so Vasya's words did not sweeten him. "You stole my horse."

Vasya had the grace to look abashed.

"Who taught you to ride like that?"

Vasya swallowed, measuring his horrified expression. "My father taught me," she said.

Her betrothed looked gratifyingly shocked.

She scrambled out of the ditch. The mare followed her like a kitten. The girl paused at the top. Kyril gave her a stony stare. "Perhaps I can ride all your horses, when we are married," Vasya said innocently.

Kyril did not answer.

Vasya shrugged—and only then realized how tired she was. Her legs were weak as reed-stems, and her left shoulder—the arm she had used to yank Seryozha over Ogon's back—ached.

A cluster of riders was racing across the ragged field. Pyotr led them on sure-footed Buran. Vasya's brothers rode at his heel. Kolya was first off his horse; he leaped down and ran to his son, who was weeping still. "Seryozha, are you all right?" he demanded. "Synok, what happened? Seryozha!" The child did not answer. Kolya turned on Vasya. "What happened?"

Vasya did not know what to say. She stammered something. Her father and Alyosha dismounted in Kolya's wake. Pyotr's urgent glance darted from her, to Seryozha, to Ogon and Mysh. "Are you all right, Vasya?" he said.

"Yes," Vasya managed. She flushed. Their neighbors—all men—were galloping up now. They stared. Vasya was suddenly, flinchingly aware of her bare head and torn skirts, her dirty face. Her father stepped across to murmur a quiet word to Kolya, who was holding his weeping son.

Vasya had let fall her cloak in her wild charge; now Alyosha slid off his horse and put his own about her. "Come on, fool," he said, while she fastened his cloak gratefully. "Best get you out of view."

Vasya recalled her pride and lifted her chin a stubborn fraction. "I am not ashamed. Better to have done *something* than see Seryozha dead of a cracked skull."

Pyotr heard her. "Go with your brother," he growled, rounding on her unexpectedly. "*Now*, Vasya."

Vasya stared at her father, and then, without a word, let Alyosha boost her into the saddle. Muttering swelled among their neighbors. They were all gazing avidly. Vasya clenched her fists, and refused to drop her eyes.

But their neighbors did not have much time to gape. Alyosha swung on behind her, spurred his beast and galloped away. "Are *you* ashamed,

Lyoshka?" asked Vasya, with heavy scorn. "Will you lock me in the cellar now? Better our nephew dead than I bring shame on the family?"

"Don't be an idiot," said Alyosha shortly. "This will blow over faster if they don't have your torn dress to stare at."

Vasya said nothing.

More gently, her brother added, "I'm taking you to Dunya. You looked ready to fold up where you stood."

"I won't deny it." Her voice had softened.

Alyosha hesitated. "Vasochka, what did you *do*? I knew you could ride, but . . . like that? On that mad red colt?"

"The horses taught me," Vasya said, after a pause. "I used to take them out of the pasture."

She didn't elaborate. Her brother was silent a long time. "We would be bringing our nephew back dead or broken if you hadn't rescued him," he said, slowly. "I know it, and I am grateful for it. Father, too, surely."

"Thank you," Vasya whispered.

"But," he added, in tones of light irony, "I fear you are for a hut in the woods, if you don't want to take the veil or marry a farmer. Your warrior's ways have quite put off our neighbor. Kyril was humiliated when you took his horse."

Vasya laughed, but there was a hard note in it. "I am glad," she said. "I am saved from running away before my wedding. I'd have married a peasant before that Kyril Artamonovich. But Father is angry."

Just as the house came in sight, Pyotr rode up beside them. He looked grateful and exasperated and angry and something darker. It might have been worry. He cleared his throat. "You aren't hurt, Vasochka?"

Vasya hadn't heard that endearment from him since she was small. "No," she said. "But I am sorry to have shamed you, Father."

Pyotr shook his head, but did not speak. There was a long pause.

"Thank you," Pyotr said at last. "For my grandson."

Vasya smiled. "We should be grateful to Ogon," she said, feeling more cheerful. "And that Seryozha had the presence of mind to hold on as long as he did."

They rode home in silence. Vasya quickly took herself off to hide in the bathhouse and steam her aching limbs.

But Kyril went to Pyotr that evening at dinner. "I thought I was getting a well-bred maiden, not a wild creature."

"Vasya is a good girl," said Pyotr. "Headstrong, but that can be—"

Kyril snorted. "Black magic might have held that girl on my horse's back, but no mortal art."

"Strength only, and wildness," said Pyotr, a little desperately. "She will give you strong sons."

"At what price?" said Kyril Artamonovich, darkly. "I want a woman in my house, not a witch or a wood-sprite. Besides, she shamed me before all your company."

And though Pyotr tried to reason with him, he would not be swayed.

Pyotr rarely beat his children. But when Kyril broke off his betrothal, he thrashed Vasya all the same, mostly to assuage his own fear for her. *Can she not do as she's told for once in her life?*

They only come for the wild maiden.

Vasya bore it dry-eyed and gave him only a look of reproach before she walked stiffly away. He did not see her weeping afterward, curled between Mysh's forefeet.

But there was no wedding. At dawn, Kyril Artamonovich rode away.

18.

A GUEST FOR THE
WANING YEAR

WHEN KYRIL HAD GONE, ANNA IVANOVNA WENT AGAIN TO HER husband. Already the long nights hemmed in the autumn days; the household rose in the dark and supped by firelight. That night, Pyotr sat wakeful before the oven. His children had sought their beds, but sleep eluded him. The embers of the banked fire filled the room with red. Pyotr stared into the shimmering maw and thought of his daughter.

Anna had her mending on her lap, but she was not sewing. Pyotr never looked up, and so he did not see his wife's face, hard and bloodless. "So Vasilisa will not marry," she said.

Pyotr started. His wife spoke with authority; she reminded him, for the first time, of her father. And her words echoed his thought.

"No man of good birth will have her," she continued. "Will you give her to a peasant?"

Pyotr was silent. He had been turning the question over in his mind. It went against his pride, to give his daughter to a baseborn man. But ever in his ear rang Dunya's warning: *Better anything than a frost-demon.*

Marina, thought Pyotr. *You left me this mad girl, and I love her well.*

She is braver and wilder than any of my sons. But what good is that in a woman? I swore I'd keep her safe, but how can I save her from herself?

"She must go to a convent," Anna said. "The sooner the better. What other choice is there? No man of decent birth will have her. She is possessed. She steals horses, she made a horse go mad, she risked her nephew's life for sport."

Pyotr, staring in astonishment at his wife, found her almost beautiful in her steady purpose. "A convent?" said Pyotr. "Vasya?" He wondered, briefly, why he was so surprised. Unmarriageable daughters went to convents every day. But a more unlikely nun than Vasya he had never seen.

Anna clenched her hands. Her eyes seized and held him. "A life among holy sisters might save her immortal soul."

Pyotr remembered again the face of the stranger in Moscow. Talisman or no, a frost-demon could not very well come for a girl vowed to God.

But still he hesitated. Vasya would never go willingly.

Father Konstantin sat in the shadows beside Anna. His face was drawn, his eyes dark as sloes.

"What say you, Batyushka?" Pyotr said. "My daughter has frightened her suitors. Shall I send her to a convent?"

"You have little choice, Pyotr Vladimirovich," Konstantin said. His voice was slow and hoarse. "She will not fear God, and she will not listen to reason. The Ascension is a convent for highborn maidens within the walls of the Moscow kremlin. The sisters there would take her."

Anna's mouth tightened. Once, long ago, she had dreamed of entering that convent.

Pyotr hesitated.

"The walls of the kremlin are strong," added Konstantin. "She would be safe and she would not go hungry."

"Well, I will think on it," said Pyotr, torn. She could go with the sledges, when he sent his tribute forth. But what man could he send to give warning of her coming? His daughter could not be delivered like an unwanted parcel, and it was late in the year for messengers.

Olya, he could send her to Olya, and she would arrange it. But no . . . Vasya must be wed or behind convent walls before midwinter. *At midwinter he will come for her.*

Vasya . . . Vasya in a convent? A veil over her black hair, a virgin until she died?

But her soul—above all there was her soul. She would have peace and plenty. She would pray for her family. And she would be safe from demons.

But she will not go willingly. It would grieve her so.

Konstantin watched Pyotr struggle, and was silent. He knew that God was on his side. Pyotr would be persuaded and means would be found. And indeed the priest was right.

Three nights later, Vasya brought home a wet and sneezing monk whom she had found lost in the woods.

⚬

SHE DRAGGED HIM IN a little before sundown, in the midst of a downpour. Dunya was telling a story. "Their father fell sick with longing," she said. "So Prince Aleksei and Prince Dmitrii set out to find the bright-winged firebird. Long they rode, over three times nine kingdoms, until they came to a place where the road split. Beside the way lay a stone carved with words."

The outer door thundered open and Vasya strode into the room, holding a big, young, bedraggled monk by the sleeve. "This is Brother Rodion," she said. "He was lost in the forest. He is come from Moscow. Sasha sent him to us."

Instantly the startled house sprang into motion. The monk must be dried and fed, a new robe found, mead put in his hand. Dunya, in all the hurry, still had time to make a protesting Vasya change her wet clothes and sit near the fire to dry her sopping hair. All the while, the monk was pelted with questions: of the weather in Moscow, the jewels the court women wore to church, the horses of Tatar warlords. Above all they asked him about the Princess of Serpukhov and Brother Aleksandr. The questions flew so thick the monk could hardly answer.

Pyotr intervened at last; he pushed his children aside. "Peace, all of you," he said. "Let him eat."

The kitchen slowly quieted. Dunya took up her distaff, Irina her needle. Brother Rodion applied himself single-mindedly to his supper. Vasya took up a mortar and pestle and began to pound dried herbs. Dunya resumed her story.

"Beside the way lay a stone carved with words.

> *"Who rides straight forward shall meet both hunger and cold.*
> *Who rides to the right shall live though his horse shall die.*
> *Who rides to the left shall die though his horse shall live.*

"None of these sounded at all pleasant. So the two brothers turned aside, pitched their tents in a green wood, and whiled away the time, forgetting why they had come."

Prince Ivan rode to the right, Vasya thought. She had heard the story a thousand times. *The gray wolf killed his horse. He wept to see it slain. But the stories never say what awaited him had he gone straight. Or left.*

Pyotr sat in close conversation with Brother Rodion on the other side of the kitchen. Vasya wished she could hear what they were saying, but the rain still thudded on the roof.

She had gone out foraging at first light. Anything, even a drenching, for a few hours in the clean air. The house oppressed her. Anna Ivanovna and Konstantin and even her father watched her with looks she could not read. The villagers muttered when she passed. No one had forgotten the incident with Kyril's horse.

She had found the young monk riding in circles on his strong white mule.

Odd, Vasya thought, that she had found him alive. In her wandering, the girl had come across bones, but never a living man. The forest was perilous to travelers. The leshy would lead them in circles until they collapsed, or the vodianoy, peering with his cold fish-eyes, would pull them into the river. But this large, good-natured creature had blundered in, and yet he lived.

The rusalka's warning sprang to Vasya's mind. *What are the chyerti afraid of?*

"YOU ARE FORTUNATE THAT my foolhardy daughter went out foraging in such weather, and that she found you," said Pyotr.

Brother Rodion, his first hunger satisfied, risked a quick glance at the hearth. The daughter in question was grinding herbs; the firelight limned her slim body in gold. At first sight, he had thought her ugly, and even now he did not think her beautiful. But the more he looked, the harder it was to look away.

"I am glad she did, Pyotr Vladimirovich," Rodion said hastily, seeing Pyotr's raised eyebrow. "I have a message from Brother Aleksandr."

"Sasha?" asked Pyotr, sharply. "What news?"

"Brother Aleksandr is adviser to the Grand Prince," returned the novice, with dignity. "He has earned fame for good deeds and defense of the small. He is renowned for his wisdom in judgment."

"As if I wished to hear of prowess Sasha might have put to better use as master of his own lands," said Pyotr. But Rodion heard the pride in his voice. "Get to the point. Such tidings would not bring you here so late in the year."

Rodion looked Pyotr in the eye. "Has your tribute to the Khan gone forth yet, Pyotr Vladimirovich?"

"It will go with the snow," growled Pyotr. The harvest had been scanty, the game thin. Pyotr grudged every grain and every pelt. They would slaughter what sheep they might, and his sons wore themselves to shadows hunting. The women went out foraging in all weathers.

"Pyotr Vladimirovich, what if you did not need to pay such tribute?" Rodion pursued.

Pyotr did not like leading questions, and said so.

"Very well," said the young man steadily. "The prince and his councilors have asked themselves why we should pay tribute anymore, or bend the knee to a pagan king. The last Khan was murdered, and his heirs cannot sit a twelvemonth on their thrones before they, too, are slain. They are all in disarray. Why should they be masters of good Christians? Brother Aleksandr has gone to Sarai, to judge their quality, and he has sent me to ask your help, should the Grand Prince choose to fight."

Vasya saw her father's face change and wondered what the young monk had said.

"War," said Pyotr.

"Freedom," Rodion rejoined.

"We wear the yoke lightly, here in the north," said Pyotr.

"And yet you wear it."

"Better a yoke than the fist of the Golden Horde," said Pyotr. "They need not meet us in open battle, only send men in the night. Ten firearrows would burn Moscow to the ground, and my house is also made of wood."

"Pyotr Vladimirovich, Brother Aleksandr bid me say—"

"Forgive me," said Pyotr, rising abruptly, "but I have heard enough. I hope you will forgive me."

Rodion had perforce to nod, and turn his attention to his mead.

༄

"WHY SHOULD WE NOT FIGHT, FATHER?" Kolya demanded. Two dead rabbits dangled by the ears from his fist. Father and son were taking advantage of a break in the downpour to walk a trapline.

"Because I foresee little good in it, and much harm," Pyotr replied, not for the first time. Neither of his sons had given him any peace since the monk had turned their heads with stories of their brother's renown. "Your sister lives in Moscow; would you have her caught in a city under siege? When the Tatars invest a city, they do not leave survivors."

Kolya dismissed the possibility with a wave, the rabbits jerking grotesquely at the end of his arm. "Of course we would meet them in battle well before the gates of Moscow."

Pyotr bent to check the next snare, which was empty.

"And think, Father," Kolya went on, warming to his theme, "we might send goods south in trade, not tribute. My cousin would kneel to no one: a prince in truth. Your great-grandchildren might be Grand Princes themselves."

"I'd rather my sons living, and my daughters safe, than a chance at glory for unborn descendants." Seeing his son's mouth open on another protest, Pyotr added, more gently, "Synok, you know that Sasha left sorely against my will. I will not stoop to tying my own son to the door-post; if you wish to fight, you may go as well, but I will not bless a fool's war, and no scrap of cloth or silver or horseflesh will I give you. Sasha, you remember, might be rich in renown, but he must beg his bread and tend the herbs in his own garden."

Whatever Kolya might have replied was drowned by an exclamation of satisfaction, for yet another rabbit hung in a snare, its mottled autumn coat streaked with dirt. While his son bent to extricate it, Pyotr raised his head and went suddenly still. The air smelled of new death. Pyos, Pyotr's boarhound, shrank against his master's shins, whining like a puppy.

"Kolya," said Pyotr. Something in his father's tone sent the young man to his feet, a flash in his black eyes.

"I smell it," he said, after a moment's pause. "What ails the dog?" For Pyos whined and trembled and looked eagerly back toward the village. Pyotr shook his head; he was casting from side to side, almost like a scenthound himself.

He said no word, but pointed: a splash of blood in the leaf-litter around their feet, not the rabbit's. Pyotr gestured peremptorily at the dog; the boarhound whined and slunk forward. Kolya hung a little to the left, owl-silent as his father. They came cautiously round a stand of trees, into a small, scrubby clearing, grim with decaying leaves.

It had been a buck. A haunch lay almost at Pyotr's feet, trailing blood and tendon. The main part of the carcass lay a little way off, the entrails burst and spreading, stinking even in the cold.

The gore gave neither man pause, though the buck's horned head lolled near their feet, tongue dangling. But they exchanged a speaking glance, for nothing in those woods could so mutilate a creature. And what beast would kill a fat autumn buck but leave the meat?

Pyotr squatted in the mud, eyes skimming the ground.

"The buck ran and the hunter gave chase; the buck had been running hard, and was favoring a foreleg. He bounded into the clearing—here." Pyotr was moving as he spoke, half-crouched, "One leap, two—and then a blow from the side struck him down." Pyotr paused. Pyos crouched on his belly at the very edge of the clearing, never taking his eyes off his master.

"But what struck the blow?" he muttered.

Kolya had read a similar tale in the mud. "No tracks," he said. His long knife hissed as it slid free of its scabbard. "None. Nor any signs that someone tried to sweep them away."

"Look to the dog," said Pyotr. Pyos had risen from his crouch and was staring at a gap between the trees. Every hair on his rough-coated spine stood on end, and he was growling low between bared teeth. As one, both men spun, Pyotr's knife in his hand almost before he willed it. Briefly he thought he saw movement, a darker shadow in the gloom, but then it was gone. Pyos barked once, high and sharp: a sound of fearful defiance.

Pyotr snapped his fingers at his dog. Kolya turned with him. They crossed the blood-smeared leaf-mold and made for the village without a word.

⸙

A DAY LATER, WHEN Rodion knocked on Konstantin's door, the priest was inspecting his paints by candlelight. The ends and dribbles of mixed color turned to mold in the damp. There was daylight outside, but the priest's windows were small and the roar of the rain held back the sun. The room would have been dim if not for the candles. *Too many candles*, Rodion thought. *A terrible waste.*

"Father, bless," said Rodion.

"God be with you," said Konstantin. The room was cold; the priest had wrapped a blanket round his thin shoulders. He did not offer Rodion one.

"Pyotr Vladimirovich and his sons have gone hunting," said Rodion. "But they will not speak of their quarry. Said they nothing in your hearing?"

"Not in my hearing, no," replied Konstantin.

The rain poured down without.

Rodion frowned. "I cannot imagine what they would bring their boar-spears for, while leaving the dogs behind. And this is cruel weather for riding."

Konstantin said nothing.

"Well, God grant them success, whatever it is," Rodion persevered. "I must leave in two days, and I do not care to meet whatever put that look in Pyotr Vladimirovich's eye."

"I will pray for your safety on the road," said Konstantin curtly.

"God keep you," replied Rodion, ignoring the dismissal. "I know you do not like your reflections disturbed. But I would ask your counsel, Brother."

"Ask," said Konstantin.

"Pyotr Vladimirovich wishes his daughter to take vows," said Rodion. "He has charged me, with words and money, that I might go to Moscow, to the Ascension, and prepare them for her coming. He says she will be sent with the tribute-goods, as soon as there is enough snow for sledges."

"A pious duty, Brother," said Konstantin. But he had looked up from his paints. "What need of counsel?"

"Because she is not a girl formed for convents," said Rodion. "A blind man could see it."

Konstantin set his jaw, and Rodion saw with surprise the priest's face ablaze with anger. "She cannot marry," said Konstantin. "Only sin awaits her in this world; better she retire. She will pray for her father's soul. Pyotr Vladimirovich is an old man, he will be glad of her prayers when he goes to God."

This was all very well. Nonetheless Rodion knew a pang of conscience. Pyotr's second daughter reminded him of Brother Aleksandr. Though Sasha was a monk, he had never stayed long at the Lavra. He rode the breadth of Rus' on his good war-horse, tricking and charming and fighting by turns. He wore a sword on his back and was adviser to princes. But such a life was not possible for a woman who took the veil.

"Well, I will do it," said Rodion reluctantly. "Pyotr Vladimirovich has been my host, and I can hardly do less. But, Brother, I wish you would change his mind. Someone surely can be persuaded to marry Vasilisa Petrovna. I do not think she will last long in a convent. Wild birds die in cages."

"And so?" snapped Konstantin. "Blessed are those who linger only a little in this mire of wickedness before going into the presence of God. I only hope her soul is prepared when the meeting comes. Now, Brother, I would like to pray."

Without a word, Rodion crossed himself and slipped out the door, blinking in the feeble daylight. *Well, I am sorry for the girl,* he thought.

And then, uneasily, *How thick the shadows lie in that room.*

※

PYOTR AND KOLYA TOOK their men hunting not once but several times before the snow. The rain would not cease, though it grew steadily colder, and their strength faltered in the long, wet days. But try as they might, they never found so much as a trace of the thing that had torn the buck to pieces. The men began to mutter, and at last to protest. Weariness vied with loyalty, and no one was sorry when the frost put an end to the hunting.

But that was when the first dog disappeared.

She was a tall bitch: a good whelper and fearless before the boar, but they found her near the palisade, headless and bloody in the snow. The only tracks near her frozen body were her own running paw prints.

Folk took to going into the woods in twos, with axes in their belts.

But then a pony disappeared, while it stood tied to a sled for hauling firewood. Its owner's son, returning with an armful of logs, saw the empty traces and a great swath of scarlet splashed across the muddy earth. He dropped his logs, even his ax, and ran for the village.

Dread settled over the village: a clinging, muttering dread, tenacious as cobwebs.

19.

NIGHTMARES

NOVEMBER ROARED IN WITH BLACK LEAVES AND GRAY SNOW. On a morning like dirty glass, Father Konstantin stood beside his window, tracing with his brush the slim foreleg of Saint George's white stallion. His work absorbed him, and all was still. But somehow the silence listened. Konstantin found himself straining to hear. *Lord, will you not speak to me?*

When someone scratched at his door, Konstantin's hand jerked and almost smeared the paint. "Come in," he snarled, flinging his brush aside. Anna Ivanovna it was, surely, with baked milk and adoring, tedious eyes.

But it was not Anna Ivanovna.

"Father, bless," said Agafya, the serving-girl.

Konstantin made the sign of the cross. "God be with you." But he was angry.

"Do not take offense, Batyushka," the girl whispered, wringing her work-hardened hands. She hovered at the doorway. "If I may have only a moment."

The priest pressed his lips together. Before him, Saint George bestrode the world on an oaken panel. His steed had only three legs. The fourth, as yet unpainted, would be raised in an elegant curve to trample a serpent's head.

"What do you wish to say to me?" Konstantin tried to make his voice gentle. He did not entirely succeed; she paled and shrank away. But she did not go.

"We have been true Christians, Batyushka," she stammered. "We take the sacrament and venerate the icons. But it has never gone so hard with us. Our gardens drowned in the summer rain; we will be hungry before the season turns."

She paused, and licked her lips.

"I wondered—I cannot help but wonder—have we offended the old ones? Chernobog, perhaps, who loves blood? My grandmother always said it would come to disaster, if ever he turned against us. And I fear now for my son." She looked at him in mute supplication.

"Better to be afraid," growled Konstantin. His fingers itched for his brush; he fought for patience. "It shows your true repentance. This is the time of trial, when God will know his loyal servants. You must hold fast, and you shall see kingdoms presently, the like of which you do not imagine. The things you speak of are false: illusions to tempt the unwary. Hold to truth and all will be well."

He turned away, reaching for his paints. But her voice came again.

"But I don't need a kingdom, Batyushka, just enough to feed my son through the winter. Marina Ivanovna kept the old ways and our children never starved."

Konstantin's face assumed an expression not unlike that of the spear-wielding saint before him. Agafya stumbled against the doorframe. "And now God will have his reckoning," he hissed. His voice flowed like black water with a rime of ice. "Think you that just because it was delayed two years, or ten, that God was not wroth at such blasphemy? The wheel grinds slowly."

Agafya quivered like a netted bird. "Please," she whispered. She seized his hand, kissed the spattered fingers. "Will you beg forgiveness for us, then? Not for my own sake, but for my son."

"As I can," he said more gently, putting a hand on her bowed head. "But you must first ask it yourself."

"Yes—yes, Batyushka," she said, looking up with a face full of gratitude.

When at last she hurried out into the gray afternoon and the door clicked shut behind her, the shadows on the wall seemed to stretch like waking cats.

"Well done." The voice echoed in Konstantin's bones. The priest froze, every nerve alight. "Above all they must fear me, so that they can be saved."

Konstantin flung his brush aside and knelt. "I wish only to please you, Lord."

"I am pleased," said the voice.

"I have tried to set these people on the path of righteousness," said Konstantin. "I would only ask, Lord . . . That is, I have wanted to ask . . ."

The voice was infinitely gentle. "What would you ask?"

"Please," said Konstantin, "let me see my task here finished. I would carry your word to the ends of the earth, if only you asked it. But the forest is so small."

He bowed his head, waiting.

But the voice laughed in loving delight, so that Konstantin thought his soul would flee his body in joy. "Of course you shall go," it said. "One more winter. Only sacrifice and be faithful. Then you shall show the world my glory, and I will be with you forever."

"Only tell me what I must do," said Konstantin. "I will be faithful."

"I desire you to invoke my presence when you speak," said the voice. Another man would have heard the eagerness in it. "And when you pray. Call me with every breath and call me by name. I am the bringer of storms. I would be present among you, and give you grace."

"It shall be done," said Konstantin fervently. "Just as you say, it shall be done. Only never leave me again."

All the candles wavered with something very like a long sigh of satisfaction. "Obey me always," returned the voice. "And I will never leave you."

THE NEXT DAY THE SUN drowned in sodden clouds and cast ghostly light over a world stripped of color. It began to snow at daybreak. Pyotr's household went shivering to the little church and huddled together inside. The church was dark except for the candles. Almost, thought Vasya, she could hear the snow outside, burying them until spring. It shut off the light, but the candles lit the priest. The bones of his face cast elegant shadows. He wore a look more remote than his icons, and he had never been so beautiful.

The icon-screen was finished. The risen Christ, the final icon, was enthroned above the door. He sat in judgment above a stormy earth with an expression that Vasya could not read. "I invoke Thee," said Konstantin, low and clear. "God who has called me up to be his servant. The voice out of darkness, lover of storms. Be Thou present among us."

And then, louder, he began the service. "Blessed be God," Konstantin said. His eyes were great dark hollows, but his voice seemed to flicker with fire. The service went on and on. When he spoke, the people forgot the icy damp and the grinning specter of starvation. Earthly troubles were as nothing when that voice touched them. The Christ above the doors seemed to raise his hand in benediction.

"Listen," said Konstantin. His voice dropped so that they had to strain to hear. "There is evil among us." The congregation looked at each other. "It creeps into our souls in the night, in the silence. It is waiting for the unwary." Irina crept closer to Vasya, and Vasya put an arm around her.

"Only faith," Konstantin continued, "only prayer, only *God*, can save you." His voice rose on each word. "Fear God, and repent. It is your only escape from damnation. Otherwise you will burn—you will burn!"

Anna screamed. Her scream echoed the length of the little church; her eyes bulged beneath the bluish lids. "No!" she screamed. "Oh, God, not here! *Not here!*"

Her voice seemed to split the walls and multiply so that there were a hundred women shrieking.

In the instant before the room fell into chaos, Vasya followed her stepmother's pointing finger. The risen Christ over the door was smiling at them now, when before he had been solemn. His two dog-teeth dented his lower lip. But instead of his two eyes, he had only one. The other side of his face was seamed with blue scars, and the eye was a socket, crudely sewn.

Somewhere, Vasya thought, fighting the fear that closed her throat, she had seen that face before.

But she had no time to think. The folk on either side of her clapped their hands to their ears, flung themselves facedown, or shoved their way toward the safety of the narthex. Anna was left standing alone. She laughed and wept, clawing the air. No one would touch her. Her screams echoed off the walls. Konstantin shoved his way to her side and struck her across the face. She subsided, choking, but the noise seemed to echo on and on, as though the icons themselves were screaming.

Vasya seized Irina in the first moil of chaos, to keep her from being swept off her feet. An instant later, Alyosha appeared and wrapped strong arms around Dunya, who was small as a child, fragile as November leaves. The four clung together. The people milled and shouted. "I must go to Mother," said Irina, squirming.

"Wait, little bird," said Vasya. "You would only be trampled."

"Mother of God," Alyosha said. "If anyone learns Irina's mother takes such fits, no one will ever marry her."

"No one will know," snapped Vasya. Her sister had turned very pale. She glared at her brother as the crowd pushed them against the wall. She and Alyosha shielded Dunya and Irina with their bodies.

Vasya looked again at the iconostasis. Now it was as it had always been. Christ sat in his throne above the world, his hand raised to bless. Had she imagined the other face? But if she had, why had Anna screamed?

"Silence!"

Konstantin's voice rang like a dozen bells. Everyone froze. He stood before the iconostasis and raised a hand, a living echo of the image of Christ above his head. "Fools!" he thundered. "Are you children to be afraid of a woman screaming? Get up, all of you. Be silent. God will protect us."

They crept together like chastened children. What Pyotr's bellowing had not accomplished, the voice of the priest did. They swayed nearer him. Anna stood shuddering, weeping, ashen as the sky at dawn. The only face paler in that church belonged to the priest himself. The candlelight filled the nave with strange shadows. There—again—one flung across the iconostasis that was not the shadow of a man.

God, thought Vasya, when the service haltingly renewed. *Here? Chyerti cannot come into churches; they are creatures of this world, and church is for the next.*

Yet she had seen the shadow.

✢

PYOTR LED HIS WIFE home as soon as could be managed. Her daughter undressed her and put her to bed. But Anna cried and retched and cried, and would not stop.

At last, Irina, desperate, went back to the church. She found Father Konstantin kneeling alone before the icon-screen. After the service that day, the people had kissed his hand and begged him to save them. He looked at peace then. Even triumphant. But now Irina thought he looked like the loneliest person in the world.

"Will you come to my mother?" she whispered.

Konstantin jerked to his knees, looked around.

"She is weeping," said Irina. "She will not stop."

Konstantin did not speak; he was straining all his senses. After the people left the church, God had come to him in the smoke of extinguished candles.

"Beautiful." The whisper sent the smoke curling in little eddies along the floor. "They were so frightened." The voice sounded almost gleeful. Konstantin was silent. For an instant he wondered if he was a madman and the voice had come crawling out of his own heart. But—*no, of course not. It is only your wickedness that doubts, Konstantin Nikonovich.*

"I am glad you came among us," murmured Konstantin under his breath. "To lead your people in righteousness."

But the voice had not answered, and now the church was still.

Louder, Konstantin said to Irina, "Yes, I will come."

※

"HERE IS FATHER KONSTANTIN," said Irina, drawing the priest into her mother's room. "He will comfort you. I will get supper; Vasya is burning the milk already." She ran out.

"The church, Batyushka?" sobbed Anna Ivanovna when the two were alone. She lay in her bed, wrapped in furs. "The church—never the church."

"What foolishness you talk," said Konstantin. "The church is protected by God. God alone makes his dwelling in the church, and his saints and his angels."

"But I saw—"

"You saw nothing!" Konstantin laid a hand on her cheek. She shivered. His voice dropped lower, hypnotic. He touched her lips with a forefinger. "You saw nothing, Anna Ivanovna."

She raised one trembling hand and touched his. "I will see nothing, if you tell me so, Batyushka." She blushed like a girl. Her hair was dark with sweat.

"Then see nothing," Konstantin said. He pulled his hand away.

"I see you," she said. It was barely a breath. "You are all I see, sometimes. In this horrible place, with the cold and the monsters and the starving. You are a light to me." She caught at his hand again; she propped herself on one elbow. Her eyes swam with tears. "Please, Batyushka," she said. "I want only to be close."

"You are mad," he said. He pushed her hands down and drew away.

She was soft and old, rotted with fear and disappointed hopes. "You are married. I have given myself to God."

"Not that!" she cried in despair. "Never that. I want you to see me." Her throat worked, and she stammered. "To *see* me. You see my step-daughter. You watch her. As I have watched you—I watch you. Why not me? Why not *me*?" Her voice rose to a wail.

"Hush." He laid a hand on the door. "I see you. But, Anna Iva-novna, there is little to see."

The door was heavy. When closed, it muffled the sound of her weeping.

⚜

THAT DAY THE PEOPLE stayed near their ovens while the snow flur-ried down. But Vasya slipped away to see to the horses. *He is coming,* said Mysh, rolling a wild eye.

Vasya went to her father.

"We must bring the horses inside the palisade," she said. "Tonight, before dusk."

"Why are you here to burden us, Vasya?" snapped Pyotr. The snow was falling thickly, catching on their hats and shoulders. "You ought to have been gone. Long gone and safe. But you frightened your suitor and now you are here and it is winter."

Vasya did not reply. Indeed she could not, for she saw suddenly and clearly that her father was afraid. She had never known her father afraid. She wanted to hide in the oven like a child. "Forgive me, Fa-ther," she said, mastering herself. "This winter will pass, as others have passed. But I think that now, at night, we should bring the horses in."

Pyotr drew a deep breath. "You are right, daughter," he said. "You are right. Come, I will help you."

The horses settled a little when the gate was shut behind them. Vasya took Mysh and Buran into the stable itself, while the less prized horses milled in the dooryard. The little vazila put his hand in hers. "Do not leave us, Vasya."

"I must get my soup," said Vasya. "Dunya is calling. But I will come back."

She ate her soup curled in the back of Mysh's narrow stall and fed the mare her bread. Afterward, Vasya wrapped herself in a horse-blanket and counted the shadows on the stable wall. The vazila sat beside her. "Do not go, Vasya," he said. "When you stay, I remember my strength, and I remember that I am not afraid."

So Vasya stayed, shivering despite the straw and her horse-blanket. The night was very cold. She thought she would never sleep.

But she must have, for after moonset she awoke, freezing. The stable was dark. Even Vasya, cat-eyed, could barely make out Mysh standing above her. For a moment all was still. Then, from without, came a soft chuckle. Mysh snorted and backed, tossing her head. The white showed in a ring around her eye.

Vasya rose in silence, letting her blanket fall. The cold air sank fangs into her flesh. She crept to the stable door. There was no moon, and fat clouds smothered the stars. The snow was still falling.

Creeping over the snow, silent as the flakes, was a man. He darted from shadow to shadow. When he let out his breath, he laughed deep in his throat. Vasya crept closer. She could not see a face, only ragged clothes and a thatch of coarse hair.

The man drew near the house and put a hand on the door. Vasya shouted aloud just as the man flung himself into the kitchen. There was no sound of flesh on wood; he passed through the door like smoke.

Vasya ran across the dvor. The yard glittered with virgin snow. The ragged man had left no footprints. The snow was thick and soft; Vasya's limbs felt heavy. Still she ran, shouting, but before she could come to the house, the man had leaped back into the dooryard, landing animal-lithe on all fours. He was laughing. "Oh," he said, "it has been so long. How sweet are the houses of men, and oh, how she screamed—"

He caught sight of Vasya then, and the girl stumbled. She knew the scars, the single gray eye. It was the face on the icon, the face . . . *the face of the sleeper in the woods, years ago. How can that be?*

"Well, what is this?" the man said. He paused. She saw memory cross his face. "I remember a little girl with your eyes. But now you are a woman." His eye fastened on hers as though he meant to strip a secret from her soul. "You are the little witch who tempts my servant. But I did not see . . ." He came nearer and nearer.

Vasya tried to flee, but her feet would not obey. His breath reeked of hot blood, he blew it in waves over her face. She gathered her courage. "I am no one," she said. "Get out, leave us be."

His humid fingers flicked out and lifted her chin. "Who are you, girl?" And then, lower, "Look at me." In his eye lay madness. Vasya would not look—knew she must not—but his fingers were like an iron trap and in a moment she would . . .

But then an icy hand seized her, pulled her away. She smelled cold water and crushed pine. Over her head a voice was speaking. "Not yet, brother," it said. "Go back."

Vasya could see nothing of the speaker except a curving line of black cloak, but she could see the other, the one-eyed man. He was grinning and cringing and laughing all at once.

"Not yet? But it is done, brother," he said. "It is done." He winked his good eye at Vasya and was gone. The black cloak around Vasya became the whole world. She was cold, and a horse was neighing, and far away someone was screaming.

Then Vasya awoke, stiff and shivering on the floor in the stable. Mysh pressed her warm nose to the girl's face. But though Vasya was awake, the cry could still be heard. It went on and on. Vasya sprang to her feet, shaking away her nightmare. The horses in stalls whinnied and kicked, splintering the stable walls. The horses in the freezing dvor milled in panic. There was no ragged one-eyed figure. *A dream*, Vasya thought. *Only a dream.* She darted among the horses, dodging the heaving bodies.

The kitchen was churning like a nest of angry wasps. Her brothers bulled their way in, half-awake and armed; Irina and Anna Ivanovna crowded into the opposite doorway. The servants milled here and there, crossing themselves or praying or clutching one another.

And then her father came, big and steady, his sword in one hand. He forced his way, cursing, between clusters of terrified servants. "Hush," he said to the milling people. Father Konstantin burst in on his heels.

It was little Agafya, the maidservant, who was screaming. She sat bolt upright on her pallet. Her white-knuckled hands clutched the wool of her blanket. She had bitten into her lower lip so that the blood bloomed on her chin, and a ring of white showed around her unblinking eyes. The screams sliced the air, like icicles falling from the eaves outside.

Vasya pushed her way through the frightened people. She seized the girl by the shoulders. "Agafya, listen to me," she said. "Listen—it's all right. You are safe. All is well. Hush now. Hush." She held the girl tightly, and after a moment Agafya moaned and fell silent. Her wide eyes slowly focused on Vasya's face. Her throat worked. She tried to speak. Vasya strained to hear. "He came for my sins," she choked. "He . . ." She heaved for breath.

A small boy crawled through the crowd. "Mother," he cried. "Mother!" He flung himself on her, but she did not heed.

Irina was suddenly there, her small face grave. "She has fainted," the child said seriously. "She needs air and water."

"It is only a nightmare," said Father Konstantin to Pyotr. "Best to leave her to the women."

Pyotr might have replied, but no one heard, for Vasya cried out then in shock and sudden fury. The entire room convulsed in new fright.

Vasya was staring at the window.

Then—"No," she said, visibly gathering herself. "Forgive me. I— nothing. It was nothing." Pyotr frowned. The servants looked at her with open suspicion and murmured among themselves.

Dunya shuffled to Vasya, her breath rustling hollow in her chest. "Girls always have nightmares when the weather changes," Dunya wheezed, loud enough for the room to hear. "Go on, child, fetch water and honey-wine." She gave Vasya a hard look.

Vasya said nothing. Her glance strayed once more to the window. For an instant she could have sworn she'd seen a face. But it could not be, for it was the face out of her dream, blue-scarred and one-eyed. It had grinned and winked at her through the wavering ice.

⟨◇⟩

AS SOON AS IT was light the next morning, Vasya went looking for the domovoi. She searched until the watery sun was high, and into the brief afternoon, shirking her work. The sun was tilting west when she managed to drag the creature surreptitiously out of the oven. His beard was smoldering around the edges. He was thin and bent, his clothes shabby, his manner defeated.

"Last night," Vasya said without preamble, cradling a burnt hand, "I dreamed of a face and then I saw it at the window. It had one eye and it was smiling. Who was it?"

"Madness," mumbled the domovoi. "Appetite. The sleeper, the eater. I could not keep it out."

"You must try harder," snapped Vasya.

But the domovoi's gaze wandered, and his mouth drooped open. "I am weak," he slurred. "And the wood-guard is weak. Our enemy has loosened his chain. Soon he will be free. I cannot keep him out."

"*Who is the enemy?*"

"Appetite," said the domovoi again. "Madness. Terror. He wants to eat the world."

"How can I defeat it?" said Vasya urgently. "How may the house be protected?"

"Offerings," muttered the domovoi. "Bread and milk will strengthen me—and perhaps blood. But you are only one girl alone, and I cannot take my life from you. I will fade. The eater will come again."

Vasya seized the domovoi and shook him so that his jaws clacked together. His dull eyes cleared, and he looked momentarily astonished. "You will *not* fade," Vasya snapped. "You can take your life from me. You *will*. The one-eyed man—the eater—he will not get in again. He will not."

There was no milk, but Vasya stole bread and shoved it into the domovoi's hand. She did it that night, and every night thereafter, scanting her own meals. She cut her hand and smeared the blood on sills and before the oven. She pressed her bloody hand to the domovoi's mouth. Her ribs started through her skin, her eyes grew hollow, and nightmares dogged her sleeping. But the nights slipped past—one, two, a dozen—and no one else screamed at something that was not there. The wavering domovoi held, and she poured her strength into him.

But little Agafya never spoke sense again. Sometimes she would plead with things that no one could see: saints and angels and a one-eyed bear. Later she raved of a man and a white horse. One night she ran out of the house, collapsed blue-lipped in the snow, and died.

The women prepared the body with as much haste as was seemly. Father Konstantin kept vigil beside her, white to the lips, head bent, with a face no one could read. Though he knelt for hours at her side, he never once prayed aloud. The words seemed to catch in his straining throat.

They buried Agafya in the brief winter daylight while the forest groaned around them. In the swift-falling twilight, they hurried to huddle before their ovens. Agafya's child cried for his mother; his wailing hung like mist over the silent village.

◦◊◦

THE NIGHT AFTER THE FUNERAL, a dream seized Dunya like sickness, like the jaws of a hunting creature. She was standing in a dead forest strewn with the stumps of blackened trees. An oily smoke veiled the flinching stars; firelight flickered against the snow. The frost-demon's face was a skull-mask with the skin drawn tight. His soft voice frightened Dunya worse than shouting.

"Why have you delayed?"

Dunya gathered all her force. "I love her," she said. "She is like my own daughter. You are winter, Morozko. You are death; you are cold. You cannot have her. She will give her life to God."

The frost-demon laughed bitterly. "She will die in the dark. Every day my brother's power waxes. And she saw him when she should not have. Now he knows what she is. He will slay her if he can, and take her for his own. Then you well may talk of damnation." Morozko's voice softened, a very little. "I can save her," he said. "I can save you all. But she must have that jewel. Otherwise . . ."

And Dunya saw that the flickering firelight was her own village burning. The forest filled with creeping things whose faces she knew. Greatest among them was a grinning one-eyed man, and beside him stood another shape, tall and slender, corpse-pale, lank-haired. "You let me die," the specter said in Vasya's voice, and her teeth gleamed between bloody lips.

Dunya found herself seizing the necklace and holding it out. It made a tiny scrap of brightness in a world formless and dark.

"I did not know," Dunya stammered. She reached for the dead girl, the necklace swinging from her fist. "Vasya, take it. Vasya!" But the one-eyed man only laughed, and the girl made no sign.

Then the frost-demon put himself between her and horror, seized her shoulders with hard, icy hands. "You have no time, Avdotya Mikhailovna," he said. "Next time you see me, I will beckon and you will follow." His voice was the voice of the wood; it seemed to echo in her bones, vibrate in her throat. Dunya felt her guts twist with fear and with certainty. "But you can save her before you go," he went on. "You must save her. Give her the necklace. Save them all."

"I will," whispered Dunya. "It will be as you say. I swear it. I swear . . ."

And then her own voice woke her.

But the chill of that burnt forest, of the frost-demon's touch, lingered. Dunya's bones shook until it seemed they would shake through her skin. All she could see was the frost-demon, intent and despairing, and the laughing face of his brother, the one-eyed creature. The two faces blurred into one. The blue stone in her pocket seemed to drip icy flame. Her skin cracked and blackened when her hand closed tight around it.

20.

A GIFT FROM A STRANGER

VASYA WENT TO THE HORSES EVERY MORNING AT FIRST LIGHT during those clipped, metallic days, only a little after her father. They had a kinship in this, to fear so passionately for the animals. At night, the horses were put in the dvor, safe behind the palisade, and as many as would fit were sheltered in the sturdy stable. But during the day they were turned loose to fend for themselves, roaming the gray pastures and digging grass from beneath the snow.

One bright, bitter morning, not long before midwinter, Vasya ran the horses into the field, whooping, riding the bareback Mysh. But once the horses were settled, the girl dismounted and looked the mare over frowning. Her ribs were beginning to show through her brown coat, not from want, but from waiting.

He will come again, the mare said. *Can you smell it?*

Vasya had not the nose of a horse, but she turned into the wind. For an instant, the smell of rotting leaves and pestilence closed her throat. "Yes," she said grimly, coughing. "The dogs smell it, too. They whine when the men set them loose, and run for their kennels. But I will not let him hurt you."

She began her round, going from horse to horse with withered apple cores, poultices, and soft words. Mysh followed her like a dog. At the edge of the herd, Buran scraped the ground with a forehoof and bugled a challenge to the waiting wood.

"Be easy," said Vasya. She came alongside the stallion and put a hand on his hot crest.

He was furious as a stallion that sees a rival among his mares, and he almost kicked her before he got hold of himself. *Let him come!* He reared, lashing out with his forefeet. *This time I will kill him.*

Vasya dodged the flying hooves, pressing her body to his. "Wait," she said into his ear.

The horse spun, snapping his teeth, but she clung close and he could not reach her. She kept her voice quiet. "Keep your strength."

Stallions obey mares; Buran put his head down.

"You must be strong and calm when it comes," said Vasya.

Your brother, said Mysh. Vasya turned to see Alyosha, hatless, running toward her out the palisade-gate.

In an instant, Vasya had her forearm behind Mysh's withers, and then she was on the horse's back. The mare galloped across the field, kicking up the frozen glaze. The sturdy pasture fence loomed, but Mysh cleared the barrier and ran on.

Vasya met Alyosha just outside the palisade. "It is Dunya," said Alyosha "She will not wake. She is saying your name."

"Come on," said Vasya, and Alyosha sprang up behind her.

❧

THE KITCHEN WAS HOT; the oven roared and gaped like a mouth. Dunya lay atop the oven, open-eyed and unseeing, still except for her twitching hands. She muttered to herself now and again. Her brittle skin stretched over her bones, so tight that Vasya thought she could see the ebbing blood. She climbed quickly atop the oven. "Dunya," she said. "Dunya, wake up. It is I. It is Vasya."

The open eyes blinked once, but that was all. Vasya felt a moment of panic; she forced it down. Irina and Anna knelt side by side before the icon-corner, praying. The tears slid down Irina's face; she wasn't pretty when she cried.

"Hot water," snapped Vasya, turning round. "Irina, for God's sake, praying will not keep her warm. Make soup." Anna looked up with venomous eyes, but Irina, with surprising quickness, got to her feet and filled a pot.

All that day, Vasya sat at Dunya's side, hunched atop the oven. She packed blankets around her nurse's shriveled body and tried to coax broth down her throat. But the liquid dribbled out of her mouth, and she would not wake. All that long day the clouds drifted in, and the daylight darkened.

In the late afternoon, Dunya sucked in a breath as though she meant to swallow the world, and caught at Vasya's hands. Vasya jerked back in surprise. The strength in her old nurse's grip astonished her. "Dunya," she said.

The old lady's eyes wandered. "I did not know," she whispered. "I did not see."

"You will be all right," said Vasya.

"He has one eye. No, he has blue eyes. They are the same. They are brothers. Vasya, remember . . ." And then her hand fell away and she lay still, mumbling to herself.

Vasya spooned more hot drinks down Dunya's throat. Irina kept the fire roaring. But the old lady's pulse faded with the daylight. She ceased to mutter and lay open-eyed. "Not yet," she said to the empty corner, and sometimes she cried. "Please," she said then. "Please."

The feeble day flickered, and a hush fell over house and village. Alyosha went out for firewood; Irina went to tend to her peevish mother.

When Konstantin's voice broke the silence, Vasya nearly leaped out of her skin.

"Does she live?" he said. The shadows lay across him like a woven mantle.

"Yes," Vasya said.

"I will pray with her," he said.

"You will not," snapped Vasya, too weary and frightened for courtesy. "She is not going to die."

Konstantin came nearer. "I can ease her pain."

"No," Vasya repeated. She was going to cry. "She is not going to die. As you love God, I beg you, go."

"She is *dying*, Vasilisa Petrovna. This is my place."

"She is *not*!" Vasya's voice came wrenching from her throat. "She is not dying. I am going to save her."

"She will be dead by morning."

"You want my people to love you, so you made them afraid." Vasya was pale with fury. "I will not have Dunya afraid. *Get out*."

Konstantin opened his mouth, then closed it again. Abruptly he turned and left the kitchen.

Vasya forgot him at once. Dunya had not wakened. She lay still, her pulse a thread, her breathing barely felt on Vasya's unsteady hand.

Night fell. Alyosha and Irina returned; the kitchen filled briefly with a subdued bustle as the evening meal was served. Vasya could not eat. The hour drew on and the kitchen emptied once more until it was only they four, Dunya and Vasya, Irina and Alyosha. The latter two dozed on the oven. Vasya was nodding herself.

"Vasya," said Dunya.

Vasya jerked awake with a sob. Dunya's voice was feeble, but lucid. "You're all right, Dunyashka. I knew you would be."

Dunya smiled toothlessly. "Yes," she said. "He is waiting."

"Who is waiting?"

Dunya did not answer. She was struggling for breath. "Vasochka," she said. "I have something your father gave me to keep for you. I must give it to you now."

"Later, Dunyashka," said Vasya. "You must rest now."

But Dunya was already fumbling for her skirt pocket with one stiff hand. Vasya opened the pocket for her and withdrew something hard, wrapped in a scrap of soft cloth.

"Open it," whispered Dunya. Vasya obeyed. The necklace was made of some pale, glittering metal, brighter than silver, and shaped like a snowflake, or a many-rayed star. A jewel of silver-blue burned in the center. Anna had no jewels to equal it; Vasya had never seen anything so fine. "But what is it?" she asked, bewildered.

"A talisman," said Dunya, struggling for breath. "There is power in it. Keep it hidden. Do not speak of it. If your father asks, tell him you know nothing of it."

Madness. A line formed between Vasya's brows, but she slipped the chain over her head. It swung between her breasts, invisible under her clothes. Suddenly Dunya went rigid, her dry fingers scrabbling at Vasya's arm. "His brother," she hissed. "He is angry that you have the jewel. Vasya, Vasya, you must . . ." She choked and fell silent.

From without, there came a long, savage chuckle.

Vasya froze, heart hammering. *Again? Last time, I was dreaming.* Then came a scrape: the soft sound of a dragging foot. Another and another. Vasya swallowed. Noiseless, she slid off the oven. The domovoi was crouching at the oven-mouth, frail and intent. "It cannot get in," said the domovoi, fierce. "I will not let it. I will not."

Vasya laid a hand on his head and crept to the door. In winter, nothing smells of rot outdoors, but on the threshold, she caught a whiff of decay that turned her empty stomach. There came a flare of burning cold where the jewel lay over her breastbone. She made a low sound of pain. Wake Alyosha? Wake the house? But what was it? *The domovoi says he will not let it in.*

I will go and see, Vasya thought. *I am not afraid.* She slipped out the kitchen door.

"No," breathed Dunya from the oven. "Vasya, no." She turned her head a little. "Save her," she whispered to the empty air. "Save her, and I care not if your brother comes for me."

WHATEVER IT WAS, IT stank like nothing else: death and pestilence and hot metal. Vasya followed the track of the dragging footsteps. There—a quick movement, in the shadow of the house. She saw a thing like a woman, hunched down small, wearing a white wrapper that trailed in the snow. It moved crabwise, as though it had too many joints.

Vasya gathered her courage and crept nearer. The thing darted from window to window, pausing at each, sometimes reaching out a flinching hand, never touching the sill. But at the last window—that of the priest—it went taut. Its eyes gleamed red.

Vasya ran forward. *The domovoi said it could not get in.* But a swipe of a bloodless fist ripped the ice from its mooring in the window-frame. Vasya saw a flash of gray skin in the moonlight. The trailing white garment was a winding-sheet, and the creature was naked beneath.

Dead, Vasya thought. *That thing is dead.*

The grayish, weeping hands seized the high sill of Konstantin's window, and it—*she,* for Vasya caught a glimpse of long, matted hair—flung itself into the room. Vasya paused beneath the window, then followed the thing up and over. She pulled herself through with brute strength. It was pitch-black inside. The thing crouched, snarling, over a thrashing figure on the bed.

The shadows on the wall seemed to swell, as though they would burst out of the wood. Vasya thought she heard a voice. *The girl! Leave him—he's mine already. Take the girl, take her . . .*

A pain in her breastbone goaded her; the jewel was burning with a fiery cold. Without thinking, Vasya raised a hand and shouted. The creature on the bed whirled, face black with blood.

Take her! snarled the shadow-voice again. The dead thing's white teeth caught the moonlight as it gathered itself to spring.

Suddenly Vasya realized that there was someone else beside her—not a dead woman nor a voice made of shadows, but a man in a dark cloak. She could not see his face in the darkness. Whoever this other was, he seized her hand and dug his fingers into her palm. Vasya swallowed a cry.

You are dead, said the newcomer to the creature. *And I am still master. Go.* His voice was like snow at midnight.

The dead thing on the bed cowered back, wailing. The shadows on the wall seemed to rise up in clamorous fury, growling, *No, ignore him; he is nothing. I am master. Take her, take*—

Vasya felt the skin of her hand split and blood drip to the floor. She knew a fierce exultation. "Go," she said to the dead thing, as though she had always known the words. "By my blood you are barred from this place." She curled her hand round the hand that held hers, felt it slick with her blood. For an instant the other hand felt real, cold and hard. She shuddered and turned to look, but there was no one there.

The shadows on the wall seemed suddenly to shrink, quivering, crying out, and the dead creature's lips writhed back over long, thin teeth. It shrieked at Vasya, turned, and made for the window. It gained the sill, dropped into the snow, and bounded for the woods, faster than a running horse, the tangled, filthy hair streaming out behind.

Vasya did not see it go. She was already at the bed, pulling away the filthy blankets, looking for the wound on the priest's naked throat.

❧

THE VOICE OF GOD had not spoken to Konstantin Nikonovich that evening. The priest had prayed alone, hour after hour. But his thoughts would not settle on the well-worn words. *Vasilisa is wrong,* Konstantin had thought. *What is a little fear if it saves their souls?*

He'd almost gone back to the kitchen to tell her so. But he was weary and stayed in his room, kneeling, even after it grew too dark to see the peeling gold on the icon.

Just before moonrise, he went to bed and dreamed.

In his dream, the gentle-eyed virgin stepped down from her wooden panel. An unearthly light was in her face. She smiled. More than anything, he wanted to feel her hand on his face, to have her blessing. She bent over him, but it was not her hand he felt. Her mouth grazed his forehead, touched his eyes. Then she put a finger under his chin, and her mouth found his. She kissed him again and again. Even dreaming, shame warred with desire; feebly, he tried to push her away. But the blue robes were heavy; her body was like a coal against his. At last he yielded, turning his face to hers with a groan of despair. She smiled against his mouth, as though his anguish pleased her. Her mouth darted down to his throat with the speed of a stooping hawk.

Then she shrieked and Konstantin jerked awake, pinned beneath a quivering weight.

The priest took a full breath and gagged. The woman hissed and rolled off him. He caught a glimpse of matted hair that half-hid eyes like rubies. The creature made for the window. He saw two other figures in his room, one limned in blue, the other dark. The blue shape reached for him. Weakly, Konstantin groped for the cross about his neck. But the blue-lit face was Vasilisa Petrovna's: an icon in itself, all hard angles and huge eyes. Their eyes met for a moment, his wide with shock, and then her hands went to his throat and he fainted.

⚜

He was not hurt; his throat and arm and breast were unmarked. So much Vasya felt, groping in the dark, and then a hammering came on the door. Vasya sprang for the window and half-fell into the dvor. The moon shone over the snowy yard. She dropped to earth and crouched in the shadow of the house, shaking with cold and the aftermath of terror.

She heard men burst into the room and pull up short. Clinging with both hands, Vasya was just tall enough to peer over Konstantin's sill. The room stank of decay. The priest sat bolt upright, clutching his neck. Vasya's father stood over him holding a lantern.

"Are you all right, Batyushka?" Pyotr said. "We heard a cry."

"Yes," replied Konstantin, faltering, wild-eyed. "Yes, forgive me. I must have cried out in my sleep." The men in the doorway looked at each other. "The ice broke," said Konstantin. He climbed out of bed and staggered as he found his feet. "The cold gave me bad dreams."

Vasya ducked hastily as their pale faces turned toward her hiding-place. She crouched in the shadow of the house beneath the window, trying not to breathe.

She heard her father grunt and stride across to the broken casement, where the whole block of ice had fallen away. The shadow of his head and shoulders fell over her as he leaned warily into the dvor. Blessedly, he did not look down. Nothing moved in the dooryard. Then Pyotr drew the shutters closed and placed a wedge between.

But Vasya did not hear it. The instant the shutters closed, she was sprinting silently for the winter kitchen.

THE KITCHEN WAS WARM and dark, womblike. Vasya slipped softly through the door. She ached in every limb.

"Vasya?" Alyosha said.

Vasya clambered atop the oven. Alyosha knelt up beside her. "It's all right, Dunya," said Vasya, taking her nurse's hands. "You will be all right now. We are safe."

Dunya opened her eyes. A smile touched her shrunken mouth. "Marina will be proud, my Vasochka," she said. "I will tell her when I see her."

"You will do nothing of the kind," said Vasya. She tried to smile, though her eyes blurred with tears. "You are going to get well again."

At that, the old lady lifted a cold hand and, with surprising firmness, pushed Vasya away. "No, I am not," she said, with a little of her old tartness. "I have lived to see all of my little ones grown, and I want nothing more than to die with my last three children on either side." Irina was awake now, too, and Dunya's other hand reached out and found hers.

Alyosha laid his hand over them all. He spoke up before Vasya could protest. "Vasya, she's right," he said. "You must let her go. It will be a cruel winter, and she is weary."

Vasya shook her head, but her hand wavered.

"Please, my darling," whispered the old lady. "I am so tired."

Vasya hesitated for a frozen moment, then tipped her head in a tiny nod.

The old lady laboriously freed her other hand and clasped Vasya's in both of hers. "Your mother blessed you at her parting, and now I do the same. Be at peace." She paused as though listening. "You must remember the old stories. Make a stake of rowan-wood. Vasya, be wary. Be brave."

Her hand fell away and she lay silent. Irina and Alyosha and Vasya were left to pick up her cold hands, straining to hear the sound of her breathing. Finally Dunya roused herself and spoke again, so low that they had to lean close to catch the words.

"Lyoshka," she whispered. "Will you sing for me?"

"Of course," whispered Alyosha. He hesitated, then drew a deep breath.

> *There was a time, not long ago*
> *When flowers grew all year*
> *When days were long*
> *And nights star-strewn*
> *And men lived free from fear*

Dunya smiled. Her eyes glowed like a child's, and in her smile, Vasya saw the shadow of the girl she had been.

> *But seasons turn and seasons change*
> *The wind blows from the south*
> *The fires come, the storms, the spears*
> *The sorrow and the dark*

A wind was rising without, the cold wind that portends snow. But the three atop the oven sat insensible. Dunya listened, open-eyed, her gaze fixed on something that even Vasya could not see.

> But far away there is a place
> Where yellow flowers grow
> Where rising sun
> Lights stony shore
> And gilds the flying foam
> Where all must end
> And all—

Alyosha was cut off. The wind slammed the kitchen door open and tore shrieking through the room. Irina gave a little scream. With the wind came a black-cloaked figure, though no one saw it but Vasya. The girl caught her breath. She had seen it before. The figure gave her a single lingering look, then reached out to lay long fingers on Dunya's throat.

The old lady smiled. "I am not afraid anymore," she said.

Next moment, the shadow came. It fell between the black-cloaked figure and Dunya as an ax cleaves wood.

"Oh, brother," said the shadow-voice. "So unwary?" The shadow smiled, a great black gaping smile, and seemed to reach out and seize Dunya with two vast arms. The peace on Dunya's face turned to terror. Her eyes started from her head, bulging, and her face turned scarlet. Vasya found herself on her knees, frightened, bewildered, shuddering with sobs. "What are you doing?" she shouted. "No—let her go!" The wind roared again through the room, first a wind of winter, and then the humid crackling wind that runs before a summer storm.

But the wind died quick as it had risen, taking with it both the shadow and the black-cloaked man.

"Vasya," said Alyosha into the silence. "Vasya." Pyotr and Konstantin rushed in, the men of the household on their heels. Pyotr was flushed with cold; he had not gone to bed after the incident in the priest's room but set his men to patrol the sleeping village. They had all heard Vasya shouting.

Vasya looked down at Dunya. Dunya was dead. Blood suffused her face and a little foam flecked the corners of her mouth. Her eyes bulged, the dark swimming in pools of red.

"She died afraid," Vasya said, very softly, shaking. "She died afraid."

"Come on, Vasochka," said Alyosha. "Come down." He had tried to close Dunya's eyes, but they bulged too much. The last thing Vasya saw before she climbed off the oven was the look of horror on Dunya's dead face.

21.

THE HARD-HEARTED CHILD

THEY LAID DUNYA IN THE BATHHOUSE, AND AT DAWN THE WOMEN came loud as hens cackling. They bathed Dunya's withered body; they wrapped her in linen and sat vigil beside her. Irina knelt weeping, her head in her mother's lap. Father Konstantin knelt, too, but it did not seem that he prayed. His face was white as the linen. Again and again, his trembling hand felt at his unmarked throat.

Vasya was not there. When the women looked for her, she was not to be found.

"She has always been a hoyden," muttered one to another. "But I never thought her so bad as this."

Her friend nodded darkly, mouth pinched small. Dunya had been as a mother to Vasilisa when Marina Ivanovna died. "It is in the blood," she said. "You can see it in her face. She has a witch's eyes."

⚜

AT FIRST LIGHT, VASYA crept outside, a shovel over her shoulder. Her face was set. She made a few preparations, then went to find her brother. Alyosha was chopping firewood. His ax whistled down so hard that the logs burst apart and lay strewn in the snow at his feet.

"Lyoshka," said Vasya. "I need your help."

Alyosha blinked at his sister. He had been weeping; the ice-crystals glinted in his brown beard. It was very cold. "What, Vasya?"

"Dunya gave us a task."

The young man's jaw tightened. "This is hardly the time," he said. "Why are you here? The women are keeping vigil; you should be with them."

"Last night," said Vasya urgently. "There was a dead thing. In the house. An upyr, like in Dunya's stories. It came as she was dying."

Alyosha was silent. Vasya met his gaze. His knuckles showed white when he drove the ax down again. "Ran the monster off, did you?" he said with some sarcasm, between chops. "My little sister, all by herself?"

"Dunya told me," Vasya said. "She said to remember the stories. Make a stake of birch-wood, she said. Remember? Please, brother."

Alyosha paused in his chopping. "What are you suggesting?"

"We must get rid of it." Vasya took a deep breath. "We need to look for disturbed graves."

Alyosha frowned. Vasya was white to the lips, her eyes great dark holes. "Well, we will see," Alyosha said, with the barest edge of irony. "Let's go dig up the cemetery. Truly, it has been too long since Father beat me."

He stacked his wood and hoisted his ax.

It had snowed in the hour before dawn. There was nothing to be seen in the graveyard but vague hummocks beneath the sparkling drifts. Alyosha glanced at his sister. "What now?"

Vasya's mouth twitched despite herself. "Dunya always said that male virgins are best for finding the undead. You walk in circles until you trip over the right grave. Care to lead, brother?"

"You're out of luck, I'm afraid, Vasochka," said Alyosha with some asperity, "and have been for some time. Do we need to kidnap a peasant boy?"

Vasya assumed a righteous expression. "Where greater virtue fails, the lesser must do its poor best," she informed him, and clambered first among the glittering graves.

In honesty, she doubted that virtue had much to do with it. The smell hung like evil rain over the graveyard, and it was not long before Vasya stopped, choking, in a familiar corner. She and Alyosha looked at each other, and her brother began to dig. The earth ought to have been stiff with frost, but it was moist and fresh-tumbled. As Alyosha cleared away the snow, the smell struck up with such force that he turned away, gagging. But, lips tight, he drove his shovel into the earth. In a surprisingly short time they had uncovered the head and torso of a figure, wrapped in a winding-sheet. Vasya drew out a small knife and cut the cloth away.

"Mother of God," said Alyosha, and turned away.

Vasya said nothing. Little Agafya's skin was the grayish-white of a corpse, but her lips were berry-red, full and tender, as they had never been in life. Her eyelashes cast lacy shadows on her wasted cheeks. She might have been asleep, at peace in a bed of earth.

"What do we do?" Alyosha asked, very pale and breathing as little as possible.

"A stake through the mouth," said Vasya. "I made a stake this morning."

Alyosha shuddered, but knelt. Vasya knelt beside him, hands trembling. The stake was crudely shaped but sharp, and she hefted a large rock to do the hammering.

"Well, brother," said Vasya, "Will you hold its head or drive in the stake?"

He was white as the snowdrifts, but he said, "I'm stronger than you."

"True enough," said Vasya. She handed over stake and rock and pried open the thing's jaws. The teeth, sharp as a cat's, gleamed like bone needles.

The sight of them shook Alyosha out of his stupor. Gritting his teeth, he thrust the stake between the red lips and slammed the rock down. Blood spurted, welling out of the mouth and over the gray chin. The eyes flew open, huge and horrible, though the body did not stir.

Alyosha's hand jerked; he missed the stake and Vasya snatched her fingers away just in time. There was a nasty crunch as the stone shattered the right cheekbone. The thing let out a thin scream, though still it did not move.

To Vasya, it seemed that a roar of fury came faintly from the woods. "Hurry," she said. "Hurry, hurry."

Alyosha bit his tongue and resettled his grip. The rock had made a shapeless ruin of the face. He struck the stake again and again, sweating despite the cold. At last the tip of the stake grated against bone, and a final, ferocious strike sent the stake out through the other side of the skull. The light went out of the corpse's open eyes, and the stone fell from Alyosha's nerveless fingers. He flung himself away, gasping. Vasya's hands dripped blood, and worse things, but she let go of Agafya almost absently. She was staring into the forest.

"Vasya, what is it?" Alyosha asked.

"I thought I saw something," Vasya whispered. "Look there." She was on her feet. A white horse and a dark rider were cantering away, swallowed almost instantly in the loom of the trees. Beyond them, it seemed she saw another figure, like a great shadow, watching.

"There is no one here but us, Vasya," said Alyosha. "Here, help me bury her and smooth the snow. Hurry. The women will be looking for you."

Vasya nodded and hefted the shovel. She was still frowning. "I have seen the horse before," she said to herself. "And her rider, who wears a black cloak. He has blue eyes."

༺༻

VASYA DID NOT GO BACK to the house after the upyr was buried. She washed the earth and blood from her hands, went to the stable, and curled up in Mysh's stall. Mysh nuzzled the top of her head. The vazila sat beside her.

Vasya sat there a long time and tried to cry. For Dunya's face as she died, for the bloody ruin of Agafya. Even for Father Konstantin. But though she sat a long time, the tears would not come. There was only a hollow place inside her, and a great silence.

When the sun was westering, the girl joined the women in the bath-house.

All the women turned on her together. *Heedless,* they said. *Wild. Hard-hearted.* Softer, she heard, *Witch-woman. Like her mother.*

"You're an ungrateful little thing, Vasya," gloated Anna Ivanovna. "But I expected nothing better." That evening, she bent Vasya over a stool and plied her birch switch hard, though Vasya was too old for beatings. Only Irina was silent, but she looked at her sister with a red-eyed reproach that was worse than the women's words.

Vasya bore it all, but she could not summon speech in her defense.

They buried Dunya at the close of day. The people whispered among themselves all through the quick, freezing funeral. Her father was haggard and gray; she had never seen him look so old.

"Dunya loved you like her daughter, Vasya," he said, later. "Of all the days to play truant."

Vasya did not speak, but she thought of her wounded hand, of the bitter, star-strewn night, of the jewel at her throat, of the upyr in the dark.

⚬◈⚬

"FATHER," SHE SAID THAT NIGHT. The peasants had gone back to their huts. She drew her stool up beside Pyotr's. The flames in the oven leaped red, and there was an empty space at their hearth where Dunya had been. Pyotr was making a new hilt for a hunting-knife. He scraped away a little curl of wood and glanced at his daughter. In the firelight, her face was drawn. "Father," she said. "I would not have disappeared without need." She spoke so soft that in the crowded kitchen only they two heard.

"What need, then, Vasya?" Pyotr laid aside his knife.

He looked as though he feared her answer, Vasya realized; she bit back the jumbled confession quivering in her throat. *The upyr is dead,* she thought. *I will not burden him more, not to salve my own pride. He must be strong for all of us.*

"I—went to Mother's grave," she said hastily. "Dunya bid me go and pray for them both. She is with Mother now. It was—easier to pray there. In the silence."

Her father looked wearier than she had ever seen him. "Very well, Vasya," he said, turning back to his hunting-knife. "But it was ill-done, to go alone and with no word. It has made talk among the people." There was a small silence. Vasya twisted her hands together. "I am sorry, child," he added more gently. "I know Dunya was as a mother to you. Did she give you anything before she died? A token? A trinket?"

Vasya hesitated, caught. *Dunya said I must not tell him. But it is his gift.* She opened her mouth . . .

There came a great thundering knock on the door, and a man burst through and fell, half-frozen, at their feet. Pyotr was on his feet in an instant, and the moment was lost. The winter kitchen filled with cries of astonishment. The man's beard rattled with the ice of his breathing; his eyes stared out over mottled cheeks. He lay shivering on the floor.

Pyotr knew him. "What is it?" he demanded, stooping and catching the shuddering man by the shoulder. "What has happened, Nikolai Matfeevich?"

The man said nothing; only lay curled on the floor. When they drew off his mittens, his frozen hands were like claws.

"We'll need hot water," Vasya said.

"Get him to speak as soon as you can," said Pyotr. "His village is two days distant. I cannot think what disaster would bring him here at midwinter."

Vasya and Irina spent an hour rubbing the man's hands and feet and pouring hot broth down his throat. Even when his strength returned, all he would do was huddle by the oven, gasping. Finally he took food, gulping it down scalding-hot. Pyotr bit back his impatience. At last the messenger wiped his mouth and looked fearfully at his liege lord.

"What brings you here, Nikolai Matfeevich?" demanded Pyotr.

"Pyotr Vladimirovich," the man whispered, "we are going to die."
Pyotr's face darkened.

"Two nights since, our village caught fire," said Nikolai. "There is nothing left. If you do not take pity, we are all going to die. Many of us have died already."

"Fire?" said Alyosha.

"Yes," said Nikolai. "A spark fell from an oven, and the whole village went up. An ill wind was blowing, and such a wind—too warm for midwinter. We could do nothing. I left as soon as we had dug the living from the ashes. I heard them scream when the snow touched their skin—better perhaps if they had died. I walked all day and all night—such a night—with terrible voices in the wood. It seemed the screams followed me. I did not dare to stop, for fear of the frost."

"It was bravely done," said Pyotr.

"Will you help us, Pyotr Vladimirovich?"

There was a long silence. *He cannot go,* thought Vasya. *Not now.* But she knew what her father would say. These were his lands, and he was their lord.

"My son and I will ride back with you tomorrow," said Pyotr heavily, "with such men and beasts as can be spared."

The messenger nodded. His eyes were far away. "Thank you, Pyotr Vladimirovich."

⚬

THE NEXT DAY DAWNED in a dazzle of blue and white. Pyotr ordered the horses saddled at first light. The men who would not ride laced snowshoes to their feet. The winter sun shone coldly down. Great white plumes curled from the horses' nostrils like the breath of serpents, and icicles dangled from their whiskery chins. Pyotr took Buran's rein from the servant. The horse stretched out his lip and shook his head, the ice rattling in his whiskers.

Kolya crouched in the snow, eye to eye with Seryozha. "Let me come with you, Father," pleaded the child. His hair fell into his eyes. He had come out leading his brown pony and wearing every garment he possessed. "I am big enough."

"You are not big enough," said Kolya, looking harried.

Irina hurried out of the house. "Come," she said, taking the child by the shoulder. "Your papa is going; come away."

"You're only a girl," said Seryozha. "What do you know? Please, Papa."

"Go back to the house," said Kolya, stern now. "Put your pony away and listen to your aunt."

But Seryozha did not; instead he howled and bolted, startling the horses, and disappeared behind the stable. Kolya rubbed his face. "He'll come back when he's hungry." He heaved himself onto his own horse's back.

"God be with you, brother," said Irina.

"And you, sister," said Kolya. He clasped her hand and turned away.

Cold leather creaked as the men put up the horses' girths and checked the bindings of their snowshoes. Their steaming breath thickened the icy bristles in their beards. Alyosha stood at the edge of the dvor, a look of thunder on his good-natured face. "You must stay," Pyotr had said to him. "Someone must look after your sisters."

"You will need me, Father," he had said.

Pyotr shook his head. "I will sleep easier if you are guarding my girls. Vasya is rash and Irina is fragile. And Lyoshka, you must keep Vasya at home. For her own sake. There is an ugly mood in the village. Please, my son."

Alyosha shook his head, wordless. But he did not ask again.

"Father," said Vasya. "Father." She appeared at Buran's head, face strained, her hair very black against the pale fur of her hood. "You must not go. Not now."

"I must, Vasochka," Pyotr said, wearily. She had begged the night before. "It is my place, and they are my people. Try to understand."

"I understand," she said. "But there is evil in the wood."

"These are evil times," said Pyotr. "But I am their lord."

"There are dead things in the wood—the dead are walking. Father, the woods are dangerous."

"Nonsense, Vasya," snapped Pyotr. *Mother of God*. If she started spreading such stories about the village . . .

"Dead," said Vasya again. "Father, you must not go."

Pyotr seized her shoulder, hard enough to make her flinch. All about him, his men were clustered and waiting. "You are too old for fairy tales," he growled, trying to make her see.

"Fairy tales!" said Vasya. It came out a strangled cry. Buran threw his head up. Pyotr got a better grip on the stallion's rein and settled the horse. Vasya flung her father's hand aside. "You saw Father Konstantin's broken window," she said "You cannot leave the village. Father, *please.*"

The men could not hear everything, but they heard enough. Their faces showed pale beneath the beards. They stared at Pyotr's daughter. More than one glanced toward his wife or his children, standing small and valiant against the snow. There would be no ruling them, Pyotr thought, if his foolish daughter kept on. "You are not a child, Vasya, to take fright at tales," Pyotr snapped. He spoke calmly and crisply, to reassure the men. "Alyosha, take your sister in hand. Do not be afraid, dochka," he said, lower and more gently. "We shall win a brave victory; this winter will pass like the others. Kolya and I will come back to you. Be kind to Anna Ivanovna."

"But, Father—"

Pyotr sprang to Buran's back. Vasya's hand closed on the horse's headstall. Anyone else would have been yanked off his feet and trampled, but the stallion pricked his ears at the girl and stood.

"Let go, Vasya," said Alyosha, coming up beside her. She didn't move. He laid a hand on hers where it wrapped round the bridle, and bent to whisper in her ear: "Now is not the time. The men will break. They are afraid for their houses and they are afraid of demons. Besides, if Father heeds you, they will say he was ruled by his maiden daughter."

Vasya sucked a breath between her teeth, but she let go of Buran's bridle. "Better to believe me," she muttered.

Released, the brave, aging stallion reared up. The subdued men fell in behind Pyotr. Kolya saluted his brother and sister as the party trotted out into the white world, leaving the two alone in the stable-yard.

THE VILLAGE SEEMED VERY QUIET when the riders had left. The icy sun shone gaily down. "I believe you, Vasya," said Alyosha.

"You drove the stake in with your own hand; of course you believe me, fool." Vasya paced like a wolf in a cage. "I should have told Father everything."

"But we slew the upyr," said Alyosha.

Vasya shook her head helplessly. She remembered the rusalka's warning, and the leshy's. "It is not over," she said. "I was warned: beware the dead."

"Who warned you, Vasya?"

Vasya halted in her pacing and saw her brother's face cold with faint suspicion. She knew a twist of despair so strong she laughed. "You, too, Lyoshka?" she said. "True friends, old and wise, warned me. Do you believe the priest? Am I a witch?"

"You are my sister," said Alyosha, very firmly. "And our mother's daughter. But you should stay out of the village until Father returns."

THE HOUSE FELL GRADUALLY silent that night, as though the hush crept in with the nighttime chill. Pyotr's household huddled by the oven, to sew or carve or mend in the firelight.

"What is that sound?" said Vasya suddenly.

One by one, her family fell silent.

Someone outside was crying.

It was little more than a choked whimper, barely audible. But at length there could be no doubt—they heard the muffled sound of a woman weeping.

Vasya and Alyosha looked at each other. Vasya half-rose. "No," Alyosha said. He went himself to the door, opened it, and looked long into the night. At last he came back, shaking his head. "There is nothing there."

But the crying went on. Twice, and then three times, Alyosha went to the door. At last Vasya went herself. She thought she saw a white glimmer, flitting between the peasants' huts. Then she blinked, and there was nothing.

Vasya went to the oven and peered into its shining maw. The domovoi was there, hiding in the hot ash. "She cannot get in," he breathed in a crackle of flames. "I swear it, she cannot. I will not let her."

"That is what you said before, but it got in then," said Vasya, under her breath.

"The fearful man's room is different," whispered the domovoi. "That I cannot protect. He has denied me. But here, now—that one cannot get in." The domovoi clenched his hands. "She will not get in."

At length the moon set, and they all sought their beds. Vasya and Irina huddled close together, wrapped in furs, breathing the black dark.

Suddenly, the sound of crying came again, very near. Both girls froze.

There was a scratching at their window.

Vasya glanced at Irina, who lay open-eyed and rigid beside her. "It sounds like . . ."

"Oh, don't say it," pleaded Irina. *"Don't."*

Vasya rolled out of bed. Unconsciously, her hand sought the pendant between her breasts. The cold of it burned her flinching hand. The window was set high in the wall; Vasya clambered up and wrestled with the shutters. The ice in the window distorted her view of the dvor.

But there was a face behind the ice. Vasya saw the eyes and mouth— great dark holes—and a bony hand pressed to the frozen pane. The thing was sobbing. "Let me in," it gasped. There was a thin screeching noise, nails on ice.

Irina whimpered.

"Let me in," hissed the thing. "I am cold."

Vasya lost her hold on the windowsill, fell, and landed sprawling. "No. No . . ." She scrambled to regain the window. But all was empty now and still; the moon shone untroubled over the empty dvor.

"What was it?" whispered Irina.

"Nothing, Irinka," snapped Vasya. "Go to sleep."

She had begun to cry, but Irina could not see her.

Vasya crawled back into bed and wound her arms around her sister. Irina did not speak again but lay long awake shivering. At last she drifted off, and Vasya put aside her sister's arms. Her tears had dried; her face was set. She went to the kitchen.

"I think we will all die if you are gone," she said to the domovoi. "The dead are walking."

The domovoi put his weary head out of the oven. "I will hold them off as long as I can," he said. "Watch with me tonight. When you are here, I am stronger."

⁜

FOR THREE NIGHTS PYOTR did not come back, and Vasya stayed in the house and kept watch with the domovoi. On the first night, she thought she heard weeping, but nothing came near the house. On the second night, there was perfect silence, and Vasya thought she would die of wishing to sleep.

On the third day she resolved to ask Alyosha to watch with her. That evening a bloody dusk flamed up and died, leaving blue shadows and silence.

The family lingered in the kitchen—the bedchambers seemed very cold and remote. Alyosha sharpened his boar-spear by oven-light. The leaf-shaped blade threw little dazzles onto the hearth.

The fire had burned low, and the kitchen was full of red shade, when a long, low wail sounded without. Irina huddled beside the oven. Anna knitted, but all could see she was clammy and shivering. Father Konstantin's eyes were so wide that the white showed in a ring; he whispered prayers under his breath.

There came the sound of dragging footsteps. Nearer they came, nearer. Then a voice rattled the window.

"It is dark," said the voice. "I am cold. Open the door. Open it." Then—*Tap. Tap. Tap* on the door.

Vasya rose to her feet.

Alyosha's hands locked around the haft of his spear.

Vasya went to the door. Her heart hammered in her throat. The domovoi was at her side, teeth clenched.

"No," Vasya managed, though her lips were numb. She dug her fingers into the wound on her hand and laid her bloody palm flat against the door. "I am sorry. The house is for the living."

The thing on the other side wailed. Irina buried her face in her mother's lap. Alyosha stumbled to his feet, spear in hand. But the shuffling footsteps started up, faded into nothing. They all drew breath and looked at each other.

Then came the squealing of terrified horses.

Without thinking, Vasya wrenched open the door, even as four voices cried out.

"Demon!" shrieked Anna. "She will let it in!"

Vasya had already run out into the night. A white shape darted among the horses, scattering them like chaff. But one horse was slower than the others. The white shape attached itself to the animal's throat and bore it down. Vasya shouted, running, forgetting fear. The dead thing looked up, hissing, and a bar of moonlight fell across its face.

"No," said Vasya, stumbling to a halt. "Oh, no, please. Dunya. Dunya . . ."

"Vasya," lisped the thing. The voice was a corpse's cracked wheeze, but it was Dunya's voice. "Vasya."

It was she, and it was not. The bones were there; the shape and form and grave-clothes. But the nose drooped; the lips had fallen in. The eyes were blazing holes, the mouth a blackened pit. Blood caked in the lines of chin and nose and cheeks.

Vasya wrenched together her courage. The necklace burned coldly against her breast and she wrapped her free hand round it. The night smelled of hot blood and grave-mold. She thought a dark figure stood beside her, but she did not look round to see.

"Dunya," Vasya said. She fought to keep her voice steady. "Get you gone. You have done enough evil here."

Dunya pressed a hand to her mouth. The tears sprang to her empty eyes even as she bared her teeth. She swayed, quivered, chewed her lip. Almost it seemed she wished to speak. She started forward, snarling, and Vasya backed up, already feeling the teeth in her throat. And then the upyr screeched, flung herself backward, and ran like a dog toward the woods.

Vasya watched her until she was lost in the moonlight.

There came a rasping breath from the horse at Vasya's feet. He was Mysh's youngest, little more than a foal. She fell to her knees beside him. The colt's throat was laid open. Vasya pressed her hands to the torn place, but the black tide ran carelessly away. She felt the death as a sinking in her belly. From the stable, she heard the vazila's anguished cry.

"No," Vasya said. "Please."

But the colt lay still. The black tide slowed and stopped.

A white mare stepped out of the darkness and laid her nose very gently against the dead horse. Vasya felt the mare's warm breath against her neck, but when she turned to look, there was only a little trickle of starlight.

Despair and weariness were a black tide, like the horse's blood on her hands, and they swallowed Vasya whole. She held the stiffening, blood-streaked head in her arms and wept.

THE HOUR HAD GROWN OLD, and they should have long since gone to bed, when Alyosha came back into the winter kitchen. He was gray-faced, his clothes all spattered with blood. "One of the horses is dead," he said heavily. "Its throat was torn away. Vasya is staying in the stable tonight. She will not be dissuaded."

"But she will freeze. She will die!" cried Irina.

Alyosha smiled faintly. "Not Vasya. You try arguing with her, Irinka."

Irina pressed her lips together, laid aside her mending, and went to heat a clay pot in the oven. No one was quite sure what she was about until she dished up milk, baked hard, with old porridge, picked it up, and made for the door.

"Irinka, come back!" cried Anna.

Irina, to Alyosha's certain knowledge, had never in her life defied her mother. But this time, the girl disappeared over the threshold without a word. Alyosha cursed and went after her. *Father was right,* he thought darkly. *My sisters cannot be left alone.*

It was very cold, and the dvor smelled of blood. The colt lay where he had fallen. The corpse would freeze overnight, and tomorrow was soon enough to bring the men to butcher it. The stable seemed empty when Alyosha and Irina went inside. "Vasya," called Alyosha. Sudden fear seized him. What if . . . ?

"Here, Lyoshka," said Vasya. She emerged from Mysh's stall, soft-footed as a cat. Irina squeaked and nearly dropped her pot. "Are you all right, Vasochka?" she managed, tremulously.

They could not see Vasya's face, only a pale blur beneath the darkness of her hair. "Well enough, little bird," she replied, hoarse.

"Lyoshka says you are staying in the stable tonight," said Irina.

"Yes," said Vasya, visibly gathering herself. "I must—the vazila is afraid." Her hands were black with blood.

"If you must," said Irina, very gently, as though to a beloved lunatic. "I brought you porridge." Clumsily, she thrust the pot at her sister. Vasya took it. The weight and the warmth seemed to steady her. "You would do better to come in and eat it by the fire, though," said Irina. "The people will talk if you stay here."

Vasya shook her head. "It doesn't matter now."

Irina's lips firmed. "Come along," she said. "This way is better."

Alyosha watched in astonishment as Vasya let herself be led back to the house, put into her own place by the oven, and fed.

"Go to bed, Irinka," said Vasya at last. A little color had come back into her face. "Sleep on the oven; Alyosha and I will watch tonight." The priest had gone. Anna was already snoring in her own chamber. Irina, who was drooping heavily, did not hesitate long.

When Irina was asleep, Vasya and Alyosha looked at each other. Vasya was white as salt, with circles beneath her eyes. Her dress was streaked with the horse's blood. But food and fire had steadied her.

"What now?" said Alyosha, low.

"We must watch tonight," said Vasya. "And we must try the cemetery at dawn, and do what we can in daylight. May God be merciful."

⁂

KONSTANTIN WENT TO THE CHURCH at sunrise. He dashed across the dvor as though the angel of death followed, barred the door to the nave, and flung himself down before the icon-screen. When the sun rose and sent gray light crawling across the floor, he did not heed it. He prayed for forgiveness. He prayed the voice would come back and remove all his doubting. But all that long day the silence held perfect.

It was only in the sad twilight, when there was more shadow than light on the floor of the church, that there came a voice.

"Fallen so far, my poor creature?" it said. "Twice now the she-demons have come for you, Konstantin Nikonovich. They break your window; they knock at the door."

"Yes," groaned Konstantin. Waking and sleeping now he saw the she-demon's face, felt her teeth in his throat. "They know I am fallen, and so they pursue me. Have mercy. Save me, I beg. Forgive me. Take this sin from me." Konstantin's hands clenched together and he bowed his face to the floor.

"Very well," said the voice mildly. "Such a little thing to ask of me, man of God. See, I am merciful. I will save you. You need not weep."

Konstantin pressed his hands to his wet face.

"But," said the voice, "I would ask something in return."

Konstantin looked up. "Anything," he said. "I am your poor servant."

"The girl," said the voice. "The witch. All this is her fault. The people know it. They whisper among themselves. They see your eyes follow her. They say she has tempted you from grace."

Konstantin said nothing. *Her fault. Her fault.*

"I desire greatly," said the voice, "that she retire from the world. It must be sooner, not later. She has brought evil upon this house, and there can be no remedy while she is here."

"She will go south with the sledges," said Konstantin. "She will go before midwinter. Pyotr Vladimirovich has said it."

"Sooner," said the voice. "It must be sooner. There are fires and torments in store for this place. But send her away and you can save yourself, Konstantin Nikonovich. Send her away, and you can save them all."

Konstantin hesitated. The dark seemed to breathe out a long soft sigh.

"It will be as you say," whispered Konstantin. "I swear it."

Then the voice was gone. Konstantin was left empty, rapturous and cold, alone on the church floor.

⚘

THAT VERY AFTERNOON, KONSTANTIN went to Anna Ivanovna. She had taken to her bed, and her daughter brought her broth.

"You must send Vasya away now," said Konstantin. There was sweat on his brow; his hands trembled. "Pyotr Vladimirovich is too soft-hearted; perhaps she will sway him. But for all our sakes, the girl must go. The demons come because of her. Did you see how she ran out into the night? She summoned them; she is not afraid. It may be that your own daughter, the little Irina, will be the next to die. Demons have appetite for more than horses."

"Irina?" Anna whispered. "You think Irina is in danger?" She quivered with love and fear.

"I know it," said Konstantin.

"Give Vasya to the people," said Anna at once. "They will stone her if you ask it. Pyotr Vladimirovich is not here to stop them."

"Better she go to a convent," said Konstantin after the briefest hesitation. "I would not have her meet God without the chance of repentance."

Anna pursed her lips. "The sledges are not ready. Better she dies. I will not see my Irina hurt."

"The first two sledges are ready," replied Konstantin. "There are men enough. A few would be more than willing to take her away from here. I will arrange it. Pyotr can go see his daughter, if he wishes, after she is safe in Moscow. He will not be angry when he knows the whole of it. All will be well. Do you be quiet and pray."

"You know best, Batyushka," said Anna peevishly. *Such care,* she thought. *And all for that green-eyed demon's spawn. But he is wise; he knows she cannot stay, corrupting good Christians.* "You are merciful. But I will see the girl dead before my Irina is put in danger."

⚘

IT WAS ALL ARRANGED. Oleg, rough and old, would drive the sledge, and Timofei's parents, their hearths empty without their dead son, would be Vasya's servants and guards.

"Of course we will do it, Batyushka," said Yasna, Timofei's mother. "God has turned his face from us, and that demon-child is the reason. If she had been sent away sooner, I would never have lost my child."

"Here is rope," said Konstantin. "Bind her hands lest she forget herself."

In his mind he saw the hart brought down in the hunt, feet tied, the eye bewildered, trailing blood in the snow. He knew a twist of lust and shame and satisfied pride. Tomorrow. On the morrow she would go, half a moon's turning before midwinter.

22.

SNOWDROPS

THAT NIGHT ANNA IVANOVNA CALLED VASYA TO HER.

"Vasochka!" Anna shrilled, making the girl jump. "Vasochka, come here!"

Vasya glanced up, haggard in the firelight. She and Alyosha had gone to the cemetery at sunrise. But when they dug flinchingly into Dunya's grave, they found it empty. They had stared at each other across the bare cold earth, Alyosha shocked, Vasya grimly unsurprised.

"This cannot be," said Alyosha.

Vasya had taken a deep breath. "But it is," she said. "Come. We must protect the house."

Cold and exhausted, they smoothed the snow, and came home. The women cut up the colt to stew his flesh in their ovens and eat it with withered carrots, and Vasya hid herself, vomiting until there was nothing left in her stomach. Now it was the cusp of night, and Dunya would come again to torment them with sobbing. Father was still gone, and Vasya was sick with dread.

She went reluctantly to where Anna sat. A small wooden chest bound with strips of bronze sat beside her. "Open it," Anna urged.

Vasya looked a question at her brother. Alyosha shrugged. She knelt before the chest and lifted the lid. Inside lay—fabric. A great folded length of handsome undyed linen.

"Linen," said Vasya, bewildered. "Linen enough for a dozen shirts. Do you intend for me to sew all winter, Anna Ivanovna?"

Anna smiled despite herself. "Of course not. It is an altar cloth; you will hem it and present it to your abbess." Seeing Vasya still puzzled, she added, smiling more widely still, "You are going south to a convent in the morning."

For a moment Vasya was light-headed, and blackness darted before her eyes. She stumbled to her feet. "Does Father know?"

"Oh, yes," said Anna. "You were to be sent away with the tribute-goods. But we have had enough of you summoning devils. You will go at dawn. The men are ready, and a woman to see to your virtue." Anna smirked. "Pyotr Vladimirovich would have it so. Perhaps the holy sisters can make you obey where I could not."

Irina looked troubled and said nothing.

Vasya was trembling all over. "Stepmother, no."

Anna's smile slipped. "Defy me? It is done, and you will be bound with ropes if you do not care to walk."

"Come," Alyosha broke in. "What madness is this? Father is from home and he would never countenance—"

"Would he not?" said Konstantin. Now, as ever, his soft, deep voice caught and held the room. It filled the walls and the dark space near the rafters. Everyone fell silent. Vasya saw the domovoi cowering, deep in the oven. "He has given it his countenance. A life among holy sisters might save her soul. She is not safe in this village where she has wronged so many. They call you witch, Vasilisa Petrovna, don't you know? They call you demon. You will be stoned before this evil winter ends, if you do not go."

Even Alyosha was silent.

But Vasya spoke, hoarse as a raven. "No," she said. "Not now and not ever. I have wronged no one. I will never set foot in a convent. Not if I have to live in the forest, and beg work from Baba Yaga."

"This is not a fairy tale, Vasya," Anna broke in, shrilly. "No one is asking your opinion. It is for your own good."

Vasya thought of the wavering domovoi, of the dead things creeping about the house, of disaster narrowly averted. "But what have I done?" she demanded. She was horrified to find tears in her eyes. "I have hurt no one. I have tried to save you! Father—" she turned to Konstantin "—I saved you from the rusalka, when she would have had you by the lake. I drove off the dead, or I tried . . ." She stopped, choking, fighting for air.

"You?" breathed Anna. "Drive them off? You invited your demon cohort in! You have brought all our misfortunes upon us. *You think I haven't seen?"*

Alyosha opened his mouth, but Vasya was before him: "If I am sent away this winter, you will all die."

Anna drew in a gasping breath. "How dare you threaten us?"

"I do not threaten," said Vasya desperately. "It is the truth."

"Truth? Truth, you little liar, there is no truth in you!"

"I will not go," said Vasya, and so fierce was her voice that even the crackling fire seemed to waver.

"Will you not?" said Anna. Her eyes were wild, but something in her bearing reminded Vasya that her father was a Grand Prince. "Very well, Vasilisa Petrovna. I will give you a choice." Her eyes darted around the room and fastened on the white flowers adorning Irina's kerchief. "*My* daughter, my true, fair, and obedient daughter, is weary in all this snow for the sight of green things. You, ugly witch of a girl, will do her a service. Go out into the woods and bring her back a basket of snowdrops. If you do, you will be free to do as you like hereafter."

Irina gaped. Konstantin had his mouth open in alarmed protest.

Vasya stared blankly at her stepmother. "Anna Ivanovna, it is midwinter."

"Go!" screeched Anna, laughing wildly. "Out of my sight! Bring me flowers or go to the convent! Now get you gone!"

Vasya looked from face to face: Anna triumphant, Irina frightened,

Alyosha furious, Konstantin inscrutable. The walls seemed to shrink again; the fire burned up all the air, so that no matter how her lungs heaved, she could not draw breath. Terror overtook her, the terror of the wild thing in the trap. She turned and ran from the kitchen.

Alyosha caught her at the outer door. She had yanked on her boots and mittens, wrapped a cloak about her and a shawl about her head. He seized her with both hands, turned her around.

"Have you gone mad, Vasya?"

"Let me go! You heard Anna Ivanovna. I'd rather take my chances in the forest than be locked up forever." She was shaking, wild-eyed.

"All that is nonsense. Wait for Father to return."

"Father has agreed to it!" Vasya swallowed back the tears, but still they crept down her cheeks. "Anna would not have dared otherwise. People say our misfortunes are my fault. Do you think I have not heard? I will be stoned as a witch if I stay. Perhaps Father *is* trying to protect me. But I'd rather die in the forest than in a convent." Her voice broke. "I will never be a nun—do you hear me? Never!" She yanked away from him, but Alyosha held her tightly.

"I will guard you until Father returns. I will make him see sense."

"You cannot protect me if every man of the village turns on us. Do you think I have not heard their whispers, brother?"

"So you mean to go into the woods and die?" snapped Alyosha. "A noble sacrifice? How will that help anyone?"

"I have helped all I can, and earned the people's hatred," retorted Vasya. "If this is the last decision I can ever make, at least it is *my* decision. Let me go, Alyosha. I am not afraid."

"But I am, you stupid girl! Do you think I want to lose you to this folly? I won't let you go." Surely he would leave fingermarks on her shoulders where he held her.

"You as well, brother?" said Vasya furiously. "Am I a child? Always someone else must decide for me. But this I will decide for myself."

"If Father or Kolya went mad, I wouldn't let him decide things for himself, either."

"Let me go, Alyosha."

He shook his head.

Her voice softened. "Perhaps there is magic in the forest, enough for me to defy Anna Ivanovna; did you think of that?"

Alyosha laughed shortly. "You are too old for fairy tales."

"Am I?" said Vasya. She smiled at him, though her lips trembled.

Alyosha remembered suddenly all the times her eyes had moved, following things that he could not see. His arms fell away. They looked at each other.

"Vasya—promise me I will see you again."

"Give bread to the domovoi," said Vasya. "Watch by the oven at night. Courage might save you. I have done what I can. Farewell, brother. I—I will try to come back."

"*Vasya—*"

But she had slipped out the kitchen door.

Father Konstantin was waiting for her beside the door of the church. "Are you mad, Vasilisa Petrovna?"

Her green eyes flew up to his, mocking now. The tears had dried; she was cold and steady. "But Batyushka, I must obey my stepmother."

"Then go take your vows."

Vasya laughed. "She will see me gone; dead, or vowed; she doesn't care. Well, I will please myself and her as well."

"Forget your mad folly. You will be vowed. It will be as God wills, and he has willed it so."

"Has he?" said Vasya. "And you are the voice of God, I presume. Well, I was given a choice and I am taking it." She turned toward the wood.

"You are not," said Konstantin, and something in his voice had Vasya spinning round. Two men stepped out of the shadows.

"Put her in the church tonight, and bind her hands," said Konstantin, never taking his eyes from Vasya. "She will leave at dawn."

Vasya was already running. But she had only three strides' head start and they were very strong. One of them reached out, and his hand snagged on the hem of her cloak. She tripped and sprawled, rolling, striking out, panicked. The man flung himself on her, held her down. The snow was cold on her neck. She felt the scrape of icy rope on her wrists.

She forced herself to go limp, as though she had fainted in her fright. The man was more used to tying dead beasts for carrying; his grip relaxed while he fumbled with the rope. Vasya heard the footsteps as the priest and the other man approached.

Then she flung herself up, shrieking a wordless cry, jabbing her fingers at her captor's eyes. He recoiled; she wrenched sideways, rolled to her feet, and ran as she had never run in her life. Behind her she heard shouts, panting, footsteps. But she would not be caught again. Never.

She ran on and did not stop until she was swallowed by the shadow of the trees.

§◇§

THE CLEAR NIGHT LIT the snow, which lay firm underfoot. Vasya ran into the woods, bruised and panting. Her loosened cloak flapped about her. She heard shouting from the village. Her tracks showed clear in the virgin snow, so that her only hope was speed. She darted headlong from shadow to shadow, until the shouting grew fainter and at last died away. *They dare not follow,* thought Vasya. *They fear the forest after dark.* And then, darkly: *They are wise.*

Her breathing slowed. She walked deeper into the wood, pushing loss and fear into the back of her mind. She listened; she called aloud. But all was still. The leshy did not answer. The rusalka slept, dreaming of summertime. The wind did not stir the trees.

Time passed; she was not sure how much. The wood thickened and blotted out the stars. The moon rose higher and cast shadows, then the clouds came and threw the forest into darkness. Vasya walked until she began to grow sleepy, and then the terror of sleep forced her awake again. She turned north and east and south again.

The night drew on, and Vasya shivered as she walked. Her teeth clacked together. Her toes grew numb despite her heavy boots. A small part of her had thought—hoped—that there would be some help in the woods. Some destiny—some magic. She had hoped the firebird would come, or the Horse with the Golden Mane, or the raven who was really a prince . . . *foolish girl to believe in fairy tales.* The winter wood was indifferent to men and women; the chyerti slept in winter, and there was no such thing as a raven-prince.

Well, die then. It is better than a convent.

But Vasya could not quite believe it. She was young; her blood ran hot. She could not bring herself to lie down in the snow.

On she stumbled, but she was growing weaker. She feared her flagging strength; she feared her stiffening hands, her cold lips.

In the blackest part of the night, Vasya stopped and looked back. Anna Ivanovna would mock her if she returned. She would be bound like a hart, locked in the church, and sent to a convent. But she did not want to die, and she was very cold.

Then Vasya took in the trees on either side and realized that she did not know where she was.

No matter. She could follow her own trail back the way she had come. She looked behind again.

Her tracks were gone.

Vasya quelled a surge of panic. She was not lost. She could not be lost. She turned north. Her weary feet crunched dully in the snow. Once more, the ground began to look inviting. Surely she could lie down. Just for a moment . . .

A dark shape loomed before her: a tree, all twisted, bigger than any tree Vasya knew. Memory stirred, breaking through her fog. She remembered a lost child, a great oak, a sleeper with one eye. She remembered an old nightmare. The tree filled her sight. *Go nearer? Run away?* She was too cold to turn back.

Then she heard the sound of weeping.

Vasya halted, scarcely breathing. When she stopped, the sound stopped as well. But when she moved again, the sound followed her. The sickly moon came out and made strange patterns on the snow.

There—a white flicker—between two trees. Vasya walked faster, clumsy on her numb feet. There was no house to run back to, no vazila to offer her strength. Her courage flickered like a guttering candle. The tree seemed to fill the world. *Come here,* breathed a soft, snarling voice. *Closer.*

Crunch. Behind her, a step that was not hers. Vasya spun. Nothing. But when she walked, the other feet kept pace.

She was twenty paces from the twisted oak. The footsteps drew nearer. It grew difficult to think. The tree seemed to fill the world. *Closer.* Like a child in a nightmare, Vasya did not dare look back.

The feet behind broke into a run, and there came a shrill, desiccated scream. Vasya ran as well, spending her last strength. A ragged figure appeared before her, standing beneath the tree, a hand outstretched. Its single eye gleamed with greedy triumph. *I have found you first.*

Then Vasya heard a new sound: the smack of galloping hooves. The figure by the tree cried to her furiously: *Faster!* The tree was before her, the wheezing creature behind—but to her left a white mare came galloping, swift as fire. Blind, terrified, Vasya turned toward the horse. Out of the corner of her eye she saw the upyr lunge, teeth shining in the old, dead face.

In that instant, the white mare came up alongside. The horse's rider reached out a hand. Vasya seized it and was flung bodily across the mare's withers. The upyr landed in the snow where she'd been. The horse tore away. Behind them came twin cries: one of pain and one of fury.

The mare's rider did not speak. Vasya, panting, had only a moment to be grateful for the reprieve. She hung head-down over the mare's withers, and so they rode. The girl felt as though her guts would come through her skin with each strike of the mare's hooves, yet on and on they galloped. She couldn't feel her face or her feet. The strong hand that had seized her out of the snow held her still, but the rider did not speak. The mare smelled unlike any horse Vasya had ever known, like strange flowers and warm stone, incongruous in the bitter night.

They ran until Vasya could not stand the pain or the cold anymore. "Please," she gasped. "Please."

Abruptly, bone-jarringly, they came to a halt. Vasya slid backward off the horse and fell, doubled over in the snow, numb, retching, clinging to her bruised ribs. The mare stood still. Vasya did not hear the mare's rider dismount, but suddenly he was standing in the snow. Vasya stumbled upright on feet she could no longer feel. Her head was bare to the night. It was snowing; the snowflakes tangled in her braid. She had gone beyond shivering; she felt heavy and dull.

The man looked down at her, and she up at him.

His eyes were pale as water, or winter ice.

"Please," whispered Vasya. "I am cold."

"Everything is cold here," he replied.

"Where am I?"

He shrugged. "Back of the north wind. The end of the world. Nowhere at all."

Vasya swayed suddenly and would have fallen, but the man caught her. "Tell me your name, devushka." His voice raised strange echoes in the wood around them.

Vasya shook her head. His flesh was icy. She pulled away, stumbling. "Who are you?"

The snowflakes caught in his dark curls; his head was bare as hers. He smiled and said nothing.

"I have seen you before," she said.

"I come with the snow," he said. "I come when men are dying."

She knew him. She had known him the instant his hand seized hers. "Am I dying?"

"Perhaps." He put a cold hand beneath her jaw. Vasya felt her heart throbbing against his fingers. Then, all at once, pain struck. Her breath came short; she sank to her knees. Shards of crystal seemed to form in her blood. He knelt with her. *Karachun*, Vasya thought. *Morozko the frost-demon. Death, this is death. They will find me frozen in the snow, like the girl in the story.*

She took a breath and felt that the frost had spread to her lungs. "Let go," she whispered. Her lips and tongue were too cold to obey. "You would not have saved me at the tree if you meant to kill me."

The demon's hand dropped. She fell back into the snow, gasping, doubled over.

He got to his feet. "Would I not, fool?" he said, his voice thin with anger. "What madness brought you into the forest tonight?"

Vasya forced herself to stand. "I am not here by choice." The white mare came up behind her, blew warm breath on her cheek. Vasya buried her cold fingers in the long mane. "My stepmother was going to send me to a convent."

His voice was alive with scorn. "And so you ran? Easier to escape a convent than the Bear."

Vasya met his eyes. "I did not run. Well, I did run, but only . . ."

She could manage no more. She clung to the horse, at the end of her strength. Her head swam. The horse curved her neck around. The smell of stone and flowers revived Vasya a little; she straightened and firmed her lips.

The frost-demon came nearer. Vasya put out one hand, instinctively, to keep him back. But he caught her mittened hand in both of his. "Come then," he said. "Look at me." He pulled the mitten away and set his palm to hers.

Her whole body tensed, dreading the pain, but it did not come. His hand was hard and cool as river ice; it was even gentle, against her frozen fingers.

"Tell me who you are." His voice sent a shiver of bitter air across her face.

"I . . . am Vasilisa Petrovna," she said.

His eyes seemed to bore into her skull. She bit her tongue and did not look away.

"Well met, then," said the demon. He let go and stepped back. His blue eyes threw sparks. Vasya thought she had imagined the look of triumph on his face. "Now tell me again, Vasilisa Petrovna," he added, half-mockingly, "what are you doing wandering the black forest? This is my hour and mine alone."

"I was to be sent to the convent at dawn," said Vasya. "But my stepmother said I needn't go if I brought her the white flowers of spring, the podsnezhniki."

The frost-demon stared, and then he laughed. Vasya gazed at him in astonishment, then continued, "The men tried to stop me. But I got away. I ran into the forest. I was so frightened I couldn't think. I meant to turn back, but I got lost. I saw the twisted oak-tree. And then I heard footsteps."

"Folly," the frost-demon said drily. "I am not the only power in these woods. You should not have left your hearth."

"I had to," Vasya rejoined. Blackness darted suddenly before her eyes. Her brief flare of strength was fading fast. "They were going to send me to a *convent*. I decided I would rather freeze in a snowbank." Her skin shivered all over. "Well, that was before I began to freeze in a snowbank. It hurts."

"Yes," said Morozko. "Yes, it does."

"The dead are walking," Vasya whispered. "The domovoi will disappear if I am gone. My family will die if they send me away. I don't know what to do."

The frost-demon said nothing.

"I must go home now," Vasya managed. "But I do not know where it is."

The white mare stamped and shook her mane. Vasya's legs suddenly buckled, as though she were a newborn foal.

"East of the sun, west of the moon," said Morozko. "Beyond the next tree."

Vasya did not answer. Her eyelids fluttered closed.

"Come, then," Morozko added. "It is cold." He caught Vasya as she was falling. Beside them stood a grove of old firs with interlaced branches. He picked the girl up. Her head and hand hung limp; her heart stirred feebly.

That was a near-run thing, said the mare to her rider, blowing a cloud of steaming breath into the girl's face.

"Yes," replied Morozko. "She is stronger than I dared hope. Another would have died."

The mare snorted. *You did not need to test her. The Bear has done that already. Another instant and he'd have had her first.*

"Well, he did not, and we must be grateful."

Will you tell her? asked the mare.

"Everything?" the demon said. "Of bears and sorcerers, spells made of sapphire and a witch that lost her daughter? No, of course not. I shall tell her as little as possible. And hope that it is enough."

The mare shook her mane and her ears eased back, but the frost-demon did not see. He strode into the fir trees, the girl in his arms. The mare sighed out a breath and followed.

Part Three

23.

THE HOUSE THAT
WAS NOT THERE

SOME HOURS LATER, VASYA OPENED HER EYES TO FIND HERSELF lying in the loveliest bed anyone had ever dreamed of. The coverlets were white wool, heavy and soft as snow. Pale blues and yellows drifted through the weave, like a sunny day in January. The bed-frame and posts were carved to look like the trunks of living trees, and over it hung a great canopy of branches.

Vasya struggled to get her bearings. The last thing she remembered: *flowers,* she had been looking for flowers. Why? It was December. But she had to get flowers.

Gasping, Vasya heaved herself upright, floundering in the drifts of blanket.

She saw the room and fell back, shuddering.

The room—well, if the bed was magnificent, the room was simply strange. At first Vasya thought she was lying in a grove of great trees. High above hung a vault of pale sky. But the next moment, she seemed to be indoors, in a wooden house whose ceiling was painted a thin sky-blue. But she had no idea which was real, and trying to decide made her dizzy.

At last Vasya buried her face in a blanket and decided she would go back to sleep. Surely she'd wake up at home, with Dunya by her side asking if she'd had a nightmare. No, that was wrong—Dunya was dead. Dunya was wandering the woods wrapped in the cloth they'd buried her in.

Vasya's brain whirled. But she couldn't remember . . . and then she did. The men, the priest, the convent. The snow, the frost-demon, his fingers on her throat, the cold, a white horse. He had meant to kill her. He'd saved her life.

She struggled again to sit up, but only managed to kneel among the blankets. She squinted desperately, but failed to make the room stay still. Finally she shut her eyes, and discovered the edge of the bed by tumbling over it. Her shoulder struck the floor. She thought she felt a brush of wetness, as though she had fallen into a snowdrift. No—now the ground was smooth and warm, like well-planed wood near a hearth. She thought she heard a fire crackling. She stood up, unsteadily. Some-one had taken off her boots and stockings. She had frozen her feet; she saw her toes white and bloodless.

She could not look at anything in the house. It was a room; it was a fir-grove under the open sky, and she could not decide which was which. She shut her eyes tight, stumbling on her injured feet.

"What do you see?" said a clear, strange voice.

Vasya turned toward the voice, not daring to open her eyes. "A house," she croaked. "A fir-grove. Both together."

"Very well," said the voice. "Open your eyes."

Flinching, Vasya did so. The cold man—the frost-demon—stood in the center of the room, and at least she could look at him. His dark, unruly hair hung to his shoulders. The sardonic face might have be-longed to a youth of twenty or a warrior of fifty. Unlike every other man Vasya had ever seen, he was clean-shaven—perhaps that was what gave his face the odd note of youthfulness. Certainly his eyes were old. When she looked into them, she thought, *I did not know anything could be that old and live.* The thought made her afraid.

But stronger than fear was her resolve.

"Please," she said. "I must go home."

His pale stare swept her up and down. "They cast you out," he said. "They will send you to a convent. And yet you will go home?"

She bit down hard on her lip. "The domovoi will disappear if I am not there. Perhaps my father has returned by now and I can make him understand."

The frost-demon studied her a moment. "Perhaps," he said at length. "But you are wounded. You are weary. Your presence will do the domovoi little good."

"I must try. My family is in danger. How long was I asleep?"

He shook his head. A faint dry humor curled his mouth. "Here there is only today. No yesterday and no tomorrow. You may stay a year and be home just after you left. It does not matter how long you slept."

Vasya was silent, absorbing this. At last she said, in a lower voice, "Where am I?"

The night in the snow had blurred in her memory, but she thought she remembered indifference in his face, a hint of malice and a hint of sorrow. Now he looked only amused. "My house," he said. "As far as I have one."

That is not helpful. Vasya bit back the words before they could escape, but they must have shown on her face.

"I fear," he added gravely, though there was a glint in his eye, "that you are gifted—or cursed—with what your folk might call the second sight. My house is a fir-grove, and this fir-grove is my house, and you see both at once."

"And what do I do about that?" Vasya hissed between clenched teeth, quite unable to strive for politeness—in another moment she would be sick on the floor at his feet.

"Look at me," he said. His voice compelled her; it seemed to echo in her skull. "Look only at me." She raised her eyes to his. "You are in my house. Believe it is so."

Hesitantly, Vasya repeated this to herself. The walls seemed to solidify as she looked. She was in a rough, roomy dwelling, with worn carvings on its crosstrees, and a ceiling the color of the noon sky. A large oven at one end of the room radiated heat. The walls were hung with woven pictures: wolves in the snow, a hibernating bear, a dark-haired warrior driving a sledge.

She tore her eyes away. "Why did you bring me here?"

"My horse insisted."

"You mock me."

"Do I? You had been wandering in the forest too long; your feet and hands are frozen. Perhaps you should be honored; I don't often have guests."

"I am honored, then," said Vasya. She could not think of anything else to say.

He studied her a moment more. "Are you hungry?"

Vasya heard the hesitation in his voice. "Did your horse suggest that as well?" she asked, before she could stop herself.

The man laughed, and she thought he looked a little surprised. "Yes, of course. She has had any number of foals. I yield to her judgment."

Suddenly he tilted his head. The blue eyes burned. "My servants will tend to you," he added abruptly. "I must be gone awhile." There was nothing human in his face, and for a moment, Vasya could not see the man at all, and instead saw only a wind lashing the limbs of ancient trees, howling in triumph as it rose. She blinked away the vision.

"Farewell," said the frost-demon, and was gone.

Vasya, taken aback by his departure, glanced cautiously about. The tapestries drew her. Vividly alive, the wolves and man and horses looked ready to leap to the floor in a swirl of cold air. She walked the room, examining them as she went. Eventually she fetched up in front of the oven and stretched out her frozen fingers.

The scrape of a hoof sent her whirling round. The white mare came toward her, bare of any harness. Her long mane foamed like a spring cascade. She seemed to have emerged from a door in the opposite wall, but it was closed. Vasya stared. The mare tossed her head. Vasya remembered her manners and bowed. "I thank you, lady. You saved my life."

The mare twitched an ear. *It was little enough.*

"Not to me," said Vasya, with a hint of asperity.

I did not mean that, said the mare. *I meant that you are a creature as we are, formed raw from the powers of the world. You would have saved yourself. You are not formed for convents, nor yet to live as the Bear's creature.*

"Would I have?" said Vasya, remembering the running, the terror, the footsteps in the dark. "I wasn't doing too well at it. But what do you mean, the powers of the world? We were all made by God."

I suppose this God taught you our speech?

"Of course not," said Vasya. "That was the vazila. I made him offerings."

The mare scraped a hoof against the floor. *I remember more and see more than you,* she said. *And will for a considerable time. We do not speak to many, and the spirit of horses does not reveal himself to anyone. There is magic in your bones. You must reckon with it.*

"Am I damned, then?" Vasya whispered, frightened.

I do not understand "damned." You are. And because you are, you can walk where you will, into peace, oblivion, or pits of fire, but you will always choose.

There was a pause. Vasya's face hurt, and her sight had begun to fracture. The snowy countryside tugged at the edges of her vision.

There is mead on the table, the mare said, seeing the girl's drooping shoulders. *You should drink, then rest again. There will be food when you awaken.*

Vasya had not eaten since suppertime, before she'd ventured into the forest. Her stomach took a moment, forcefully, to remind her. A wooden table stood on the other side of the oven, dark with age, rich with carving. The silver flagon upon it was garlanded with silver flowers. The cup was of hammered silver studded with fire-red gems. For a moment the girl forgot her hunger. She lifted the cup and tilted it in the light. It was beautiful. She looked a question at the mare.

He likes objects, she said, *though I do not understand why. And he is a great giver of gifts.*

The flagon indeed contained mead: thin and strong and somehow piercing, like winter sunshine. Drinking it, Vasya felt suddenly sleepy. Heavy-eyed, it was all she could do to put down the silver cup. She bowed in silence to the white mare and stumbled back to the great bed.

ALL THAT DAY, a storm tore across the frozen lands of northern Rus'. The country folk ran inside and barred their doors. Even the oven-fires in Dmitrii's wooden palace in Moscow danced and guttered. The old and the sick knew their time had come and slipped away on the crying wind. The living crossed themselves when they felt the shadow pass. But at nightfall the air quieted, and the sky filled with the promise of snow. Those who had resisted the summons smiled, for they knew that they would live.

A man with dark hair emerged from between two trees and raised his face to a cloud-torn sky. His eyes glowed an unearthly blue as he scanned the mounting shadows. His robe was of fur and midnight brocade, though he had come to the twilit borderlands where winter yielded to the promise of spring. The ground was thick with snowdrops.

A song pierced the newborn night, thin and soft and sweet. Even as he turned toward it, Morozko tasted the darker side of the magic he had set in motion, for the music reminded him of sorrow: of slow hours heavy with regret. This sorrow he had not felt—had not been able to feel—for a thousand years.

He walked on regardless, until he came to the tree where a nightingale sang in the dark.

"Little one, will you come back with me?" he said.

The tiny creature hopped to a lower branch and cocked its dull-brown head.

"To live, as your brothers and sisters have lived," said Morozko. "I have a companion for you."

The bird trilled, but softly.

"You will not come into your strength otherwise, and this one is generous and high-hearted. The old woman cannot gainsay it."

The bird cheeped and raised its brown wings.

"Yes, there is death in it, but not before joy, or glory. Will you stay here instead, and sing away eternity?"

The bird hesitated, then leaped from its branch with a cry. Morozko watched it go. "Follow, then," he said softly, as the wind rose again around him.

⸭

VASYA WAS STILL ASLEEP when the frost-demon returned. The mare was dozing near the oven.

"What think you?" he asked the horse, low-voiced.

The mare was about to reply, but a neigh and a clatter cut her off. A bay stallion with a star between his eyes burst into the room. He snorted and stamped, shaking snow off his black-dappled quarters.

The mare laid her ears back. *I think,* she said, *that my son has come where he should not.*

The stallion, though graceful as a stag, had yet a trace of long-legged colt about him. He eyed his mother warily. *I heard there was a champion here,* he said.

The mare switched her tail. *Who told you that?*

"I did," said Morozko. "I brought him back with me."

The mare stared at her rider with pricked ears and trembling nostrils. *You brought him for her?*

"I need that girl," said Morozko, giving the mare a hard look. "As well you know. If she is foolish enough to roam the Bear's forest at night, then she will need a companion."

He might have said more, but he was interrupted by a clatter. Vasya had awakened and tumbled out of bed, unused to bedding that was also a snowdrift.

The big horse, his dark bay coat glowing black in the firelight, minced over, ears pricked. Vasya, still only half-awake and rubbing a very sore shoulder, looked up to find herself nose to nose with a huge young stallion. She held still.

"Hello," she said.

The horse was pleased.

Hello, he answered. *You will ride me.*

Vasya clambered to her feet, much less thickheaded than at her last waking. But her cheek throbbed, and she had to marshal her tired eyes in order to see only the stallion, not the shadows like feathers that fluttered around him. Once her vision settled, she eyed his back, two hands above her head, with some skepticism.

"I would be honored to ride you," she answered politely, though Morozko heard the dry note in the girl's voice and bit his lip. "But perhaps I may defer it a moment; I should like some more clothes." She glanced around the room, but her cloak, boots, or mittens were nowhere to be seen. She wore nothing but her crumpled underdress, with Dunya's pendant lying cold against her breastbone. Her braid had raveled while she slept, and the thick red-black curtain of her hair tumbled loose to her waist. She brushed it from her face and, with a touch of bravado, made her way to the fire.

The white mare stood beside the oven with the frost-demon at her head. Vasya was struck by the similarity in their expressions: the man's eyes hooded and the mare's ears pricked. The bay stallion huffed warm breath into her hair. He was following so close that his nose bumped her shoulder. Without thinking, Vasya laid a hand on his neck. The horse's ears made a pleased little swivel, and she smiled.

There was plenty of space in front of the fire, despite the incongruous presence of two tall and well-built horses. Vasya frowned. The room had not seemed as large as that when she woke last.

The table was laid with two silver cups and a slender ewer. The scent of warm honey floated through the room. A loaf of black bread, smelling of rye and anise, lay beside a platter of fresh herbs. On one side stood a bowl of pears and on the other a bowl of apples. Beyond them all lay a basket of white flowers with modestly drooping heads. Podsnezhniki. Snowdrops.

Vasya stopped and stared.

"It is what you came for, is it not?" Morozko said.

"I didn't think I'd actually find any!"

"You are fortunate, then, to have done so."

Vasya looked at the flowers and said nothing.

"Come and eat," Morozko said. "We will talk later." Vasya opened her mouth to argue, but her empty stomach roared. She bit back curiosity and sat down. He sat on a stool across from her, leaning against the mare's shoulder. She surveyed the food, and his lips twitched at her expression. "It's not poison."

"I suppose not," said Vasya, dubious.

He twisted off a lump of bread and handed it to Solovey. The stallion seized it with enthusiasm. "Come," said Morozko, "or your horse will eat it all."

Cautiously, Vasya picked up an apple and bit down. Icy sweetness dazzled her tongue. She reached for the bread. Before she knew it, her bowl was empty, half the loaf was gone, and she sat replete, feeding bits of bread and fruit to the two horses. Morozko touched no food. After she had eaten, he poured the mead. Vasya drank from her silver-chased cup, savoring the taste of cold sunshine and winter flowers.

His cup was twin to hers, except that the stones along the rim were blue. Vasya did not speak while she drank. But at last she set her cup on the table and raised her eyes to his.

"What happens now?" she asked him.

"That depends on you, Vasilisa Petrovna."

"I must go home," she said. "My family is in danger."

"You are wounded," replied Morozko. "Worse than you know. You will stay until you are healed. Your family will be none the worse for it." More gently, he added, "You will go home at dawn of the night you left. I can promise it."

Vasya said nothing; it was a measure of her weariness that she did not argue. She looked again at the snowdrops. "Why did you bring me these?"

"Your choices were to bring your stepmother those flowers or to go to a convent." Vasya nodded. "Well, then, there you have them. You may do as you will."

Vasya reached out a hesitant forefinger to stroke one silky-damp petal. "Where did they come from?"

"The edge of my lands."

"And where is that?"

"At the thaw."

"But that is not a place."

"Is it not? It is many things. Just as you and I are many things, and my house is many things, and even that horse with his nose in your lap is many things. Your flowers are here. Be content."

The green eyes flared up to his again, mutinous instead of tentative. "I do not like half answers."

"Stop asking half questions, then," he said, and smiled with sudden charm. She flushed. The stallion thrust his great head closer. She winced when the horse lipped her injured fingers.

"Ah," Morozko said. "I forgot. Does it hurt?"

"Only a little." But she would not meet his eyes.

He made his way around the table and knelt so their faces were on a level. "May I?"

She swallowed. He took her chin in one hand and turned her face to the firelight. There were black marks on her cheek where he had touched her in the forest. The tips of her fingers and toes were white. He examined her hands, drew a fingertip along her frozen foot. "Don't move," he said.

"Why would—" But then he laid his palm flat against her jaw. His fingers were suddenly hot, impossibly hot, so that she expected to smell her own flesh scorching. She tried to pull away, but his other hand came up behind her head, digging into her hair, holding her. Her breath trembled and rasped in her throat. His hand slid down to her throat, and if anything the burning grew. She was too shocked to scream. Just when she thought she could not endure it another instant, he let go. She slumped against the bay stallion. The horse blew comfortingly into her hair.

"Forgive me," Morozko said. The air around him was cold, despite the heat in his hands. Vasya realized she was shivering. She touched her damaged skin. It was smooth and warm, unmarked.

"It doesn't hurt anymore." She forced her voice to calm.

"No," he said. "Some things I can heal. But I cannot heal gently."

She looked down at her toes, at her ruined fingertips. "Better than being crippled."

"As you say."

But when he touched her feet, she could not keep the tears from her eyes.

"Will you give me your hands?" he said. She hesitated. Her fingertips were frostbitten, and one hand was crudely wrapped in a length of linen to shield the ragged hole in the palm from the night the upyr had come for Konstantin. The memory of pain thundered at her. He did not wait for her to speak. It took all her strength, but she swallowed back her cry while the flesh of her fingertips grew warm and pink.

Last, he took up her left hand and began to unwind the linen.

"It was you who hurt me," said Vasya, trying to distract herself. "The night the upyr came."

"I did."

"Why?"

"So that you would see me," he said. "So that you would remember."

"I had seen you before. I had not forgotten."

His head was bent over his work. But she saw the curve of his mouth, wry and a little bitter. "But you doubted. You would not have believed your own senses after I had gone. I am little more than a shadow now, in the houses of men. Once I was a guest."

"Who is the one-eyed man?"

"My brother," he said shortly. "My enemy. But that is a long tale and not for tonight." He laid the linen bandage aside. Vasya fought the urge to curl her hand into a fist. "This will be harder to heal than frostbite."

"I kept reopening it," Vasya said. "It seemed to help ward the house."

"It would," said Morozko. "There is virtue in your blood." He touched the wounded place. Vasya flinched. "But only a little, for you are young. Vasya, I can heal this, but you will carry the mark."

"Do it, then," she said, failing to keep the tremor out of her voice.

"Very well." He reached to the floor and scooped up a handful of snow. Vasya was for a moment disoriented; she saw the fir-grove, the snow on the ground, blue with dusk, red with firelight. But then the house re-formed around her and Morozko pressed the snow into the wound on her palm. Her whole body went rigid, and then the pain came, worse than before. She bit back a scream and managed to keep still. The pain rose past bearing, so that she sobbed once before she could stop herself.

Abruptly it died away. He let go her hand, and she almost fell off her stool. The bay stallion saved her; she fell against his warm bulk and caught herself by seizing his mane. The stallion put his head around to lip at her trembling hand.

Vasya pushed him aside and looked. The wound was gone. There was only a cold, pale mark, perfectly round, in the middle of her palm. When she turned it in the firelight, it seemed to catch the light, as though a sliver of ice was buried under the skin. No, she was imagining things.

"Thank you." She pressed both hands into her lap to hide their trembling.

Morozko stood and drew away, looking down at her. "You'll heal," he said. "Rest. You are my guest. As for your questions—there will be answers. In time."

Vasya nodded, staring still at her hand. When she looked up again, he had disappeared.

24.

I HAVE SEEN YOUR
HEART'S DESIRE

"FIND HER!" KONSTANTIN SNAPPED. "BRING HER BACK!"

But the men would not go into the forest. They followed Vasya to the brink and balked, muttering of wolves and demons. Of the bitter cold.

"God will judge her now, Batyushka," said Timofei's father, and Oleg nodded in agreement. Konstantin hesitated, caught. The darkness beneath the trees seemed absolute.

"As you say, my children," he said heavily. "God will judge her. God be with you." He made the sign of the cross.

The men tramped away through the village muttering with their heads together. Konstantin went to his cold, bare cell. His dinner porridge lay heavy in his stomach. He lit a candle before the Mother of God, and a hundred shadows sprang furiously to life along the walls.

"Wicked servant," snarled the voice. "Why is the witch-girl free in the forest? When I told you she must be contained? That she must go to a convent? I am displeased, my servant. I am most displeased."

Konstantin fell to his knees, cowering. "We tried our best," he pleaded. "She is a demon."

"That demon is with my brother, and if he has the wit to see her strength . . ."

The candle guttered. The priest, huddled on the floor, went very still. "Your brother?" Konstantin whispered. "But you . . ." Then the candle went out, and there was only the breathing darkness. "Who are you?"

A long, slow silence, and then the voice laughed. Konstantin wasn't sure he heard it; he might only have seen it, in the quiver of the shadows on the wall.

"The bringer of storms," murmured the voice with a certain satisfaction. "For once you so summoned me. But long ago men called me the Bear—Medved."

"You are a devil!" whispered Konstantin, clenching his hands.

All the shadows laughed. "As you like. But what difference is there between me and the one you call God? I too revel in deeds done in my name. I can give you glory, if you will do my bidding."

"You," whispered Konstantin. "But I thought . . ." He had thought himself exalted, set apart. But he was only a poor dupe, and he had done a demon's bidding. *Vasya* . . . His throat closed. Somewhere in his soul, there was a proud girl riding a horse in the summer daylight. Laughing with her brother on her stool by the oven. "She will die." He pressed his fists to his eyes. "I did it in your service." Even as he spoke, he was thinking, *they must never know.*

"She ought to have gone to a convent. Or come to me," said the voice matter-of-factly, with just a faint seething undercurrent of anger. "But now she is with my brother. With Death, but not dead."

"With Death?" whispered Konstantin. "Not dead?" He wanted her to be dead. He wanted her alive. He wished he were dead himself. He would go mad if the voice kept speaking.

The silence stretched out, and when he could not stand it anymore, the voice came again. "What do you want above all, Konstantin Nikonovich?"

"Nothing," Konstantin said. "I want nothing. Go away."

"You are like a maid with the vapors," said the voice sourly. And then it softened. "No matter; I know what you want." And then, laughing, "would you have your soul cleansed, man of God? Would you have the innocent girl back? Well, know that I can take her from the hands of Death himself."

"Better she die and leave this world," croaked Konstantin.

"She will live in torment before she dies. I can save her, I alone."

"Prove it, then," said Konstantin. "Bring her back."

The shadow snorted. "So hasty, man of God."

"What do you want?" Konstantin choked on the words.

The shadow's voice ripened. "Oh, Konstantin Nikonovich, it is such a fine thing, when the children of men ask me what I want."

"Then what is it?" snapped Konstantin. *How can I be righteous with that voice in my ears? If he brings her back, I will be clean again.*

"A little thing," said the voice. "Only a little thing. Life must pay for life. You want the little witch returned; I must have a witch for myself. Bring me one, and I give you yours. And then I will leave you."

"What do you mean?"

"Bring a witch to the forest, to the border, to the oak-tree at dawn. You will know the place when you see it."

"And what will happen," said Konstantin—little more than a breath—"to this—witch that I bring you?"

"Well, she will not *die*," said the voice, and laughed. "What good is a death to me? Death is my brother, whom I hate."

"But there are no witches save Vasya."

"Witches must *see,* man of God. Is it only the little maiden who sees?"

Konstantin was silent. In his mind's eye, he saw a plump, shapeless figure kneeling at the foot of the icon-screen, seizing his hand in her moist one. Her voice sounded in his ears. *Batyushka, I see demons. Everywhere. All the time.*

"Think on it, Konstantin Nikonovich," said the voice. "But I must have her before sunrise."

"And how will I find you?" The words were softer than snowfall; a mortal man would not have heard them. But the shadow heard.

"Go into the woods," hissed the shadow. "Look for snowdrops. Then you will know. Give me a witch and take yours; give me a witch and be free."

25.

THE BIRD THAT
LOVED A MAIDEN

VASYA AWOKE TO THE TOUCH OF SUNLIGHT ON HER FACE. SHE
opened her eyes on a ceiling of thin blue—no, on a vault of open sky.
Her senses blurred, and she could not remember—then she did. *I am in
the house in the fir-grove.* A whiskery chin bumped hers. She opened her
eyes, and found, once again, that she was nose to nose with the bay stallion.

You sleep too much, said the horse.

"I thought you were a dream," said Vasya in some wonder. She had
forgotten how big the dream-horse was, and the fiery look in his dark
eyes. She pushed his nose away and sat up.

I am not, usually, replied the horse.

The previous night came back to Vasya in a rush. Snowdrops at
midwinter, bread and apples, mead heavy on her tongue. Long white
fingers on her face. Pain. She yanked her hand free of the blanket.
There was a pale mark in the center of her palm. "That was not a dream,
either," she murmured.

The horse was looking at her in some concern. *Better to believe that
everything is real,* he said, as if to a lunatic. *And I will tell you if you are
dreaming.*

Vasya laughed. "Done," she said. "I am awake now." She slid out of bed—less painfully than before. Her head was clearing. The house was still as a noonday forest, save the crackle and pop of a good fire. A little pot nestled steaming on the hearth. Suddenly ravenous, Vasya made her way to the fire and found luxury: porridge and milk and honey. She ate while the stallion hovered.

"What is your name?" she said to the horse, when she had done.

The stallion was busy finishing her bowl. He slanted an ear at her before replying. *I am called Solovey.*

Vasya smiled. "Nightingale. A little name for a great horse. How did you get it?"

I was foaled at twilight, he said gravely. *Or perhaps I was hatched; I cannot remember. It was long ago. Sometimes I run, and sometimes I remember to fly. And thus am I named.*

Vasya stared. "But you are not a bird."

You do not know what you are; can you know what I am? retorted the horse. *I am called Nightingale, and does it matter why?*

Vasya had no answer. Solovey had finished her porridge and put his head up to look at her. He was the loveliest horse she had ever seen. Mysh, Buran, Ogon, they were all like sparrows to his falcon. "Last night," Vasya said hesitantly, "last night, you said you would let me ride."

The stallion neighed. His hooves clattered on the floor. *My dam said I should be patient,* he said. *But I am not, usually. Come and ride. I have never been ridden before.*

Vasya was suddenly dubious, but she replaited her tangled hair and put on her jacket and cloak, mittens and boots, which she found lying near the fire. She followed the horse into the blinding day. The snow lay thick underfoot. Vasya eyed the stallion's tall bare back. She tried her limbs, and found them weak as water. The horse stood proudly and expectantly, a horse out of a fairy tale.

"I think," said Vasya, "that I am going to need a stump."

The pricked ears flattened. *A stump?*

"A stump," said Vasya firmly. She made her way to a convenient one, where a tree had cracked and fallen away. The horse poked along behind. He seemed to be reconsidering his choice of rider. But he stood alongside the stump, looking pained, and from there Vasya vaulted gently to his back.

All of his muscles went rigid, and he threw his head up. Vasya, who had ridden young horses before, was expecting something of the sort, and she sat still.

At last the great stallion blew out a breath. *Very well,* he said. *At least you are small.* But when he walked off, it was with a mincing, sideways gait. Every few seconds he turned his head to see the girl on his back.

※

THEY RODE ALL THAT DAY.

"No," Vasya said for the tenth time. Her night in the snowy forest had left her weaker than she had realized, and it was making a hard task harder. "You must put your head down and use your back. Right now, riding you is like riding a log. A large, slippery log."

The stallion put his head round to glare. *I know how to walk.*

"But not how to carry a person," Vasya retorted. "It is different."

You feel strange, the horse complained.

"I can only imagine," said Vasya. "You need not carry me if you do not wish to."

The horse said nothing, shaking his black mane. Then—*I will carry you. My dam says it grows easier in time.* He sounded skeptical. *Well, enough of this. Let us see what we can do.* And he bolted. Vasya, taken by surprise, threw her weight forward and wrapped her legs around his belly. The stallion careened between the trees. Vasya found herself whooping aloud. He was graceful as a hunting-cat and made about as much noise. At speed, they were one. The horse ran like water and all the white world was theirs.

"We must go back," said Vasya at length, flushed and panting and laughing. Solovey slowed to a trot, his head up, his nostrils showing red. He bucked with sheer high spirits, and Vasya, clinging, hoped he would not have her off. "I am tired."

The horse pointed an ear at her in a dissatisfied way. He was hardly winded. But he heaved a sigh and turned. In a surprisingly short time, the fir-grove lay before them. Vasya slid to the ground. Her feet struck the earth with a great jolt of pain, and she sank, gasping, to the snow. Her healed toes were numb, and some hours' ride had not improved her weakness. "But where is the house?" she said, gritting her teeth and heaving herself to her feet. All she saw was fir-trees. Day's end mantled the wood in starry violet.

It cannot be found by searching, said Solovey. *You must look away just a little.* Vasya did, and there, in a quick flash at the edge of her vision, was the hut among the trees. The horse walked beside her, and she was a little ashamed that she needed the support of his warm shoulder. He nudged her through the door.

Morozko had not come back. But there was food on the blazing hearth, laid by invisible hands, and something hot and spicy to drink. She dried Solovey with cloths, brushed his bay coat, and combed the long mane. He had never been groomed before, either.

Foolishness, said the horse, when she began. *You are tired. It makes not the slightest difference whether I am brushed or not.* But he looked vastly pleased with himself regardless, when she took extra care over his tail. He nuzzled her cheek when she had done, and he spent the whole meal inspecting her hair and face and dinner, as if suspecting she'd kept something back.

"Where do you come from?" Vasya asked, when she could hold no more and was feeding the insatiable horse bits of bread. "Where were you foaled?" Solovey did not reply. He stretched his neck out and crunched an apple in his yellow teeth. "Who is your sire?" Vasya persisted. Still Solovey said nothing. He stole the remainder of her bread and ambled away, chewing. Vasya sighed and gave up.

❧

VASYA AND SOLOVEY WENT out riding together every day for three days. Each day, the horse bore her more easily, and, slowly, Vasya's strength returned.

When they returned to the house on the third night, Morozko and the white mare were waiting for them. Vasya limped across the threshold, pleased that she could manage it on her own two feet, and stopped short, seeing them.

The mare stood by the fire, licking idly at a chunk of salt. Morozko sat on the other side of the blaze. Vasya slipped off her cloak and approached the oven. Solovey went to his accustomed place and stood expectantly. For a horse that had never been groomed, he adapted very fast.

"Good evening, Vasilisa Petrovna," said Morozko.

"Good evening," said Vasya. To her surprise, the frost-demon was holding a knife, whittling a block of fine-grained wood. Something like a wooden flower was taking shape under his deft fingers. He laid his knife aside, and the blue eyes touched her here and there. She wondered what he saw.

"Have my servants been kind to you?" said Morozko.

"Yes," said Vasya. "Very. I thank you for your hospitality."

"You are welcome."

He was silent while she groomed Solovey, though she felt him watching. She rubbed the horse down and combed the snarls from his mane. When she had washed her face and the table was laid, she tore into the food like a young wolf. The table groaned with good things: strange fruits and spiky nuts, cheese and bread and curds. When at last Vasya sat up and slowed down, she caught Morozko's sardonic look. "I was hungry," she said apologetically. "We do not eat so well at home."

"I can well believe it," came the reply. "You looked like a wraith at midwinter."

"Did I?" said Vasya, disgruntled.

"More or less."

Vasya was silent. The fire fell in on its core and the light in the room went from gold to red. "Where do you go when you are not here?" she asked.

"Where I like," he said. "It is winter in the world of men."

"Do you sleep?"

He shook his head. "Not as you would think of it, no."

Vasya glanced involuntarily at the great bed, with its black frame and blankets heaped like a snowdrift. She bit back the question, but Morozko caught her thought. He raised a delicate eyebrow.

Vasya blushed scarlet and took a great draught to hide her burning face. When she looked back at him, he was laughing.

"You need not make that prim face at me, Vasilisa Petrovna," he said. "That bed was made for you by my servants."

"And you—" Vasya began. She blushed harder. "You never . . ."

He had taken up his carving again. He flicked another chip off the wooden flower. "Often, when the world was young," he said mildly. "They would leave me maidens in the snow." Vasya shuddered. "Sometimes they died," he said. "Sometimes they were stubborn, or brave, and—they did not."

"What happened to them?" said Vasya.

"They went home with a king's ransom," said Morozko, drily. "Have you not heard the tales?"

Vasya, still blushing, opened her mouth and closed it again. Several dozen things she might say rushed through her brain.

"Why?" she managed. "Why did you save my life?"

"It amused me," said Morozko, though he did not look up from his carving. The flower was crudely finished; he laid aside his knife, picked up a bit of glass—or ice—and began to smooth it.

Vasya's hand stole up to her face where the frostbite had been. "Did it?"

He said nothing, but his eyes met hers beyond the fire. She swallowed.

"Why did you save my life and then try to kill me?"

"The brave live," replied Morozko. "The cowards die in the snow. I did not know which you were." He put down the flower and reached out a hand. His long fingers brushed the place where the wound had been, on her cheek and jaw. When his thumb found her mouth, the breath shivered in her throat. "Blood is one thing. The sight is another. But courage—that is rarest of all, Vasilisa Petrovna."

The blood flung itself out to Vasya's skin until she could feel every stirring in the air.

"You ask too many questions," said Morozko abruptly, and his hand dropped.

Vasya stared at him, huge-eyed in the firelight. "It was cruel," she said.

"You will walk a long road," said Morozko. "If you have not the courage to meet it, better—far better—for you to die quiet in the snow. Perhaps I meant you a kindness."

"Not quiet," said Vasya. "And not kind. You hurt me."

He shook his head. He had taken up the carving again. "That is because you fought," he said. "It does not have to hurt."

She turned away, leaning against Solovey. There was a long silence. Then he said, very low, "Forgive me, Vasya. Do not be afraid."

She met his eyes squarely. "I am not."

�❀�

ON THE FIFTH DAY, Vasya said to Solovey, "Tonight I am going to plait your mane."

The stallion did not exactly freeze, but she felt all his muscles go rigid. *It does not need plaiting,* he said, tossing the mane in question. The heavy black curtain waved like a woman's hair, and fell well past his neck. It was impractical and ridiculously beautiful.

"But you'll like it," Vasya coaxed. "Won't you like not having it in your eyes?"

No, said Solovey, very definitely.

The girl tried again. "You will look the prince of all horses. Your neck is so fine, it should not be hidden."

Solovey tossed his head at this question of looks. But he was a little vain; all stallions are. She felt him waver. She sighed and drooped on his back. "Please."

Oh, very well, said the horse.

That night, as soon as the horse was clean and combed, Vasya appropriated a stool and began to plait his mane. With a qualm for the stallion's outraged sensibilities, she abandoned plans for looping braids, curls, or fretworks. Instead she gathered his long mane into one great feathery plait along his crest, so that his neck seemed to arch more mightily than ever. She was delighted. Surreptitiously, she tried to take a few of the snowdrops that still stood, unwithered, on the table and braid them in. The stallion pinned his ears. *What are you doing?*

"Adding flowers," said Vasya, guiltily.

Solovey stamped. *No flowers.*

Vasya, after a struggle with herself, laid them aside with a sigh.

Tying off the last trailing end, she paused and stepped back. The braid emphasized the proud arch of the dark neck and the graceful bones of his head. Encouraged, Vasya hauled her stool around to start on the tail.

The horse heaved a forlorn sigh. *My tail, too?*

"You will look the lord of horses when I'm finished," Vasya promised.

Solovey peered about in a futile attempt to see what she was doing. *If you say so.* He seemed to be reconsidering the advantages of grooming. Vasya ignored him, humming to herself, and began to weave the shorter hairs over his tailbone.

Suddenly a cold breeze stirred the tapestries, and the fire leaped in the oven. Solovey pricked his ears. Vasya turned just as the door opened. Morozko passed the threshold, and the white mare nudged her way in after him. The warmth of the house struck steam from her coat. Solovey flicked his tail out of Vasya's grip, nodded in a dignified manner, and ignored his mother. She pointed her ears at his braided mane.

"Good evening, Vasilisa Petrovna," said Morozko.

"Good evening," said Vasya.

Morozko stripped off his blue outer robe. It slid off his fingertips and disappeared in a puff of powder. He took off his boots, which slid apart and left a damp patch on the floor. Barefoot, he went to the oven. The white mare followed. He picked up a twist of straw and began to rub her down. In the space of a blink, the twist of straw became a brush of boar's hair. The mare stood with her ears flopping, loose-lipped with enjoyment.

Vasya went nearer, fascinated. "Did you change the straw? Was that magic?"

"As you see." He went on with his grooming.

"Can you tell me how you do it?" She came up beside him and peered eagerly at the brush in his hand.

"You are too attached to things as they are," said Morozko, combing the mare's withers. He glanced down idly. "You must allow things to be what best suits your purpose. And then they will."

Vasya, puzzled, made no reply. Solovey snorted, not about to be left out. Vasya picked up her own straw and started on the horse's neck. No matter how hard she stared at it, though, it remained straw.

"You can't *change* it to a brush," said Morozko, seeing her. "Because that would be to believe it is now straw. Just allow it, now, to *be* a brush."

Disgruntled, Vasya glowered into Solovey's flank. "I don't understand."

"Nothing changes, Vasya. Things are, or they are not. Magic is forgetting that something ever was other than as you willed it."

"I *still* do not understand."

"That does not mean you cannot learn."

"I think you are making a game of me."

"As you like," said Morozko. But he smiled when he said it.

That night, when the food had gone and the fire burned red, Vasya said, "You once promised me a tale."

Morozko drank deep of his cup before replying. "Which tale, Vasilisa Petrovna? I know many."

"You know which. The tale of your brother and your enemy."

"I did promise you that tale," said Morozko, reluctantly.

"Twice I have seen the twisted oak-tree," said Vasya. "Four times since childhood have I seen the one-eyed man, and I have seen the dead walking. Did you think I'd ask for any other tale?"

"Drink, then, Vasilisa Petrovna." Morozko's soft voice slid through her veins with the wine. "And listen." He poured out the mead, and she drank. He looked older and stranger and very far away.

"I am Death," said Morozko slowly. "Now, as in the beginning. Long ago, I was born of the minds of men. But I was not born alone. When first I looked upon the stars, my brother stood beside me. My twin. And when first I saw the stars, so did he."

The quiet, crystalline words dropped into Vasya's mind and she saw the heavens making wheels of fire, in shapes she did not know, and a snowy plain that kissed a bitter horizon, blue on black. "I had the face of a man," said Morozko. "But my brother had the face of a bear, for to men a bear is very fearsome. That is my brother's part; he makes men afraid. He eats their fear, gorges himself, and sleeps until he hungers again. Disorder he loves above all; war and plague and fire in the night. But in the long-ago I bound him. I am Death, and guardian of the order of things. All passes before me; that is how it is."

"If you bound him, then how——?"

"I bound my brother," said Morozko, not raising his voice. "I am his warden, his guardian, his jailer. Sometimes he wakes and sometimes he sleeps. He is a bear, after all. But now he is awake, and stronger than he has ever been. So strong that he is breaking free. He cannot leave the forest. Not yet. But already he has left the shadow of the oak-tree, which he has not done for a hundred lives of men. Your people grew afraid; they abandoned the chyerti and now your house is unprotected.

Already he satisfies his hunger with you. He kills your people in the night. He makes the dead walk."

Vasya was silent a moment, absorbing this. "How may he be defeated?"

"By trickery sometimes," Morozko said. "Long ago I defeated him with strength, but I had others to help me then. Now I am alone, and I have faded." There was a small silence. "But he is not free yet. To break free entirely he needs lives—several lives—and the fear of the tormented dead. The lives of those who can see him are the strongest of all. If he had taken you in the woods the night we met, then he would have been free, though all the powers of the world were ranged against him."

"How may he be bound anew?" said Vasya with a touch of impatience.

Morozko half-smiled. "I have one last trick." Was it her imagination, or did his eyes linger on her face? Her talisman hung heavy on her throat. "I will bind him at midwinter, when I am strongest."

"I can help you."

"Can you?" Morozko said, with faint amusement. "A girl-child, half-blooded and untrained? You know nothing of lore, or battle, or magic. How exactly can you help me, Vasilisa Petrovna?"

"I kept the domovoi alive," Vasya protested. "I kept the upyry from my hearth."

"Well done," said Morozko. "One newborn upyr slain in daylight, one pallid little domovoi clinging to life, and a girl who fled like a fool into the snow."

Vasya swallowed. "I have a talisman," she said. "My nurse gave it to me. From my father. It helped on the nights the upyry came. It might help again." She lifted the sapphire from beneath her tunic. It was cold and heavy in her hand. When she turned it in the firelight, the silver-blue jewel blazed up with a six-pointed star.

Was it her imagination, or was his face a shade paler? His lips tightened and his eyes were deep and colorless as water. "A little talisman," said Morozko. "An old, frail magic, to shield a girl-child. A paltry thing to set before the Bear." But his glance lingered on it.

Vasya did not see. She let the necklace go. She leaned forward. "All my life," she said, "I have been told 'go' and 'come.' I am told how I will live, and I am told how I must die. I must be a man's servant and a mare for his pleasure, or I must hide myself behind walls and surrender my flesh to a cold, silent god. I would walk into the jaws of hell itself, if it were a path of my own choosing. I would rather die tomorrow in the forest than live a hundred years of the life appointed me. Please. *Please* let me help you."

For an instant, Morozko seemed to hesitate.

"Didn't you hear me?" he said at last. "If the Bear has your life, well, then he will be free, and there is nothing I can do. Better you stay far away from him. You are only a maiden. Go home where you are safe. That will help me; that is best. Wear your jewel. Do not go to a convent." She did not see the harshness about his mouth. "There will be a man to marry you. I will make sure of it. I will give you your dowry: a prince's ransom, as the tale prescribes. Will you like that? Gold on your wrists and throat, the finest dowry in all Rus'?"

Vasya suddenly stood, sending her stool crashing to the floor. She could not summon words; she ran out into the night, barefoot and bare-headed. Solovey glared at Morozko and followed.

The house was left in silence, except for the crackling of the fire.

That was ill done, said the mare.

"Was I wrong?" said Morozko. "She is better off at home. Her brother will protect her. The Bear will be bound. There will be a man to marry her, and she will live in safety. She must carry the jewel. She must live long and remember. I will not have her risk her life. You know what is at stake."

Then you deny what she is. She will wither.

"She is young. She will suit herself to it."

The mare said nothing.

❧

VASYA DID NOT KNOW how long she rode. Solovey had followed her into the snow, and blindly she clambered onto his back. She'd have ridden forever, but at length the horse returned her to the fir-grove. The house among the firs wavered in her sight.

Solovey shook his mane. *Get off*, he said. *There is fire there. You are cold, you are weary, you are frightened.*

"I am not frightened!" snapped Vasya, but she slid from the horse's back. She flinched when her feet struck the snow. Hobbling, she brushed between the firs and stumbled over the familiar threshold. The fire leaped high in the oven. Vasya stripped off her wet outer things, not noticing the silent servants that took them away. Somehow she made her way to the fire. She sank into her chair. Morozko and the white mare had gone.

At last, she drank a cup of mead and dozed off with her chilled toes near the oven.

The fire burned down, but the girl slept on. In the darkest part of the night, she dreamed.

She was in Konstantin's cell. The air reeked with earth and blood, and a monster crouched over the priest's thrashing body. When it raised its face, Vasya saw its lips and chin all covered in gore. She raised a hand to banish it, and it shrieked and sprang through the window and disappeared. Vasya knelt beside the bed, scrabbling at the torn blankets.

But the face between her hands was not that of Father Konstantin. Alyosha's dead gray eyes stared up at her.

Vasya heard a snarl and turned. The upyr had returned, and it was Dunya—Dunya dead, staggering, halfway through the window, her mouth a gaping hole, the bone showing in her finger-ends. Dunya who had been her mother. And then the shadows on the priest's wall became one shadow, a one-eyed shadow that laughed at her. "Weep," it said. "You are frightened. It is delicious."

All the icons in the corner came alive and screeched their approbation.

The shadow opened its mouth to laugh, too, and then it was not a shadow at all, but a bear—a great bear with famine between its teeth. It roared out flame—and then the wall was burning; her house was burning. Somewhere she heard Irina screaming.

A grinning face showed between the flames, mottled blue, with a great dark hole where an eye should have been. "Come," *it said.* "You will be with them, and you will live forever." *Her dead brother and sister stood beside this apparition and seemed to beckon from behind the flames.*

Something hard struck Vasya across the face, but she did not heed. *She reached out a hand.* "Alyosha," *she said.* "Lyoshka!"

But a quick pain came, sharper than before. Vasya was yanked out of the dream, strangling on a sound between a sob and a scream. Solovey was butting her anxiously with his nose; he had bitten her upper arm. She seized his warm mane. Her hands were like two lumps of ice; her teeth chattered. She buried her face in his coat. Her head was full of screaming, and that laughing voice. *Come, or you will never see them again.* Then she heard another voice, felt a rush of frigid air.

"Get back, you great ox." There was a squeal of indignation from Solovey, and then there were cold hands on Vasya's face. When she tried to look, all she could see was her father's house burning, and a one-eyed man that beckoned.

Forget him, said the one-eyed man. *Come here.*

Morozko struck her across the face. "Vasya," he said. "Vasilisa Petrovna, *look at me.*"

It was like dragging herself across a great distance, but his eyes came into focus at last. She could not see the house in the woods. All she saw were fir-trees, snow, horses, and the night sky. The air curled frigid about her. Vasya tried to quiet her panicked breaths.

Morozko hissed out something she did not understand. Then, "Here," he said. "Drink."

There was mead at her lips; she smelled the honey. She swallowed, choked, and drank. When she raised her head, the cup was empty and her breathing had slowed. She could see the walls of the house again, though they wavered at the edges. Solovey was thrusting his great head down to hers, lipping at her hair and face. She laughed weakly. "I'm all right," she began, but her laughter became tears, and she was seized with a storm of weeping. She covered her face.

Morozko watched her, narrow-eyed. She could still feel the imprint of his hands, and one cheek throbbed where he had struck her.

At length her tears slowed. "I had a nightmare," she said. She would not look at him. She hunched on her chair, cold and embarrassed, sticky with tears.

"Do not look so," Morozko said. "It was more than a nightmare; it was my own mistake." Seeing her shiver, he made a sound of impatience. "Come here to me, Vasya."

When she hesitated, he added shortly, "I will not hurt you, child, and it will quiet you. Come here."

Bewildered, she uncurled and stood, fighting back fresh tears. He put a cloak round her. She did not know where he had gotten it from— perhaps conjured from midair. He picked her up and sank onto the warm oven-bench with her in his arms. He was gentle. His breath was the winter wind, but his flesh was warm, and his heart beat under her hand. She wanted to pull away, to glare at him with all her pride, but she was cold and frightened. Her pulse throbbed in her ears. Clumsily she settled her head in the curve of his shoulder. He ran his fingers through her loosened hair. Slowly, her trembling eased. "I'm all right now," she said, after a time, a little unsteady. "What did you mean, your own mistake?"

She felt rather than heard him laugh. "Medved is a master of nightmares. Anger and fear are as meat and drink to him, and so he captures the minds of men. Forgive me, Vasya."

Vasya said nothing.

After a moment, he said, "Tell me your dream."

Vasya told him. She was shaking again when she had done, and he held her and was silent.

"You were right," said Vasya at length. "What do I know of ancient magic, or ancient rivalries, or anything else? But I must go home. I can protect my family, at least for a time. Father and Alyosha will understand when I have explained."

The image of her dead brother tore at her.

"Very well," said Morozko. She was not looking at him, and so she did not see his face grim.

"May I take Solovey with me?" said Vasya hesitantly. "If he wishes to come?"

Solovey heard and shook his mane. He put his head down to look at Vasya out of one eye. *Where you go, I go,* said the stallion.

"Thank you," Vasya whispered, and stroked his nose.

"Tomorrow you will go," Morozko broke in. "Sleep the rest of the night."

"Why?" said Vasya, pulling away to look at him. "If the Bear is waiting in my dreams, I certainly will not sleep."

Morozko smiled crookedly. "But I will be here this time. Even in your dreams, Medved would not have dared my house, if I had not been away."

"How did you know I was dreaming?" asked Vasya. "How did you come back in time?"

Morozko raised an eyebrow. "I knew. And I came back in time because there is nothing beneath these stars that runs faster than the white mare."

Vasya opened her mouth on another question, but exhaustion hit her like a wave. She yanked back from the brink of sleep, suddenly frightened. "No," she whispered. "Don't—I could not bear it again."

"He will not come back," returned Morozko. His voice was steady against her ear. She felt the years in him, and the strength. "All will be well."

"Don't go," she whispered.

Something crossed his face that she could not read. "I will not," he said. And then it did not matter. Sleep was a great dark wave, and it washed over her and through her. Her eyelids fluttered closed.

"Sleep is cousin to death, Vasya," he murmured over her head. "And both are mine."

※

HE WAS STILL THERE when she woke, as he had promised. She crawled from her bed and went to the fire. He sat very still, staring into the flames. It was as though he hadn't moved at all. If Vasya looked hard, she could see the forest around him, and he a great white silence, formless, in the middle. But then she sank onto her own stool, and he looked round and some of the remoteness left his face.

"Where did you go yesterday?" she asked him. "Where were you, when the Bear knew you were far away?"

"Here and there," replied Morozko. "I brought gifts for you."

A heap of bundles lay beside the fire. Vasya glanced at them. He lifted an eyebrow in invitation, and she was child enough to go immediately to the first bundle and pull it open, heart beating quickly. It contained a green dress trimmed in scarlet, and a sable-lined cloak. There were boots made of felt and fur, embroidered with crimson berries. There were headdresses for her hair, and jewels for her fingers: many jewels. Vasya hefted them in her hand. There was gold and silver, in saddlebags of heavy leather. There was cloth of silver and a rich soft cloth that she did not know.

Vasya looked them all over. *I am the girl in the story,* she thought. *This is the prince's ransom. Now he will take me back to my father's house, covered with gifts.*

She remembered his hands in the night, a few moments of gentleness.

No, that was nothing. That is not how the story goes. I am only the girl in the fairy tale, and he the wicked frost-demon. The maiden leaves the forest, marries a handsome man, and forgets all about magic.

Why did she feel this pain? She laid the cloth aside.

"Is this my dowry?" Her voice was soft. She did not know what showed on her face.

"You must have one," said Morozko.

"Not from you," whispered Vasya. She saw him taken aback. "I will bring your snowdrops to my stepmother. Solovey will come to Lesnaya Zemlya with me if he wishes. But I will have nothing else from you, Morozko."

"You will have nothing of me, Vasya?" said Morozko, and for once she heard a human voice.

Vasya stumbled backward, tripping on the prince's ransom scattered at her feet. "Nothing!" She knew he knew she was crying and she tried to speak reasonably. "Bind your brother and save us. I am going home."

Her cloak hung by the fire. She put on her boots and caught up the basket of snowdrops. Part of her wanted him to object, but he did not.

"You will cross the barrier of your village at dawn, then," said Morozko. He was on his feet. He paused. "Believe in me, Vasya. Do not forget me."

But she was already over the threshold and away.

26.

AT THE THAW

*S*HE IS ONLY ONE POOR MAD FOOL, THOUGHT KONSTANTIN NIKO-novich. *He said he will not kill her. I must get him to leave me. No one can know of this.*

Gray dawn and a red sun rising. *Where is the border he spoke of? In the forest. Snowdrops. The old oak before dawn.*

Konstantin crept to Anna's chamber and touched her shoulder. Her daughter slept beside her, but Irina did not stir. He put a hand to Anna's mouth to muffle her shriek. "Come with me now," he said. "God has called us." He caught her with his eyes. She lay still, her mouth gaping. He kissed her on the forehead. "Come," he said.

She stared up at him with wide eyes suddenly brimming with tears. "Yes," she said.

She followed him like a dog. He had been prepared to whisper, to speak foolishness, but all it took was one glance and she followed him. It was dark, but the eastern sky had lightened. It was very cold. He put her cloak round her and led her from the house. It was months since Anna had gone out-of-doors, even in daylight, but now she followed him with only a slight quickening of her ragged breaths as they crossed the barrier of the village.

They came to an old oak just a little way into the forest. Konstantin had never seen it before. All around them was winter, the shroud of bitter snow, the earth like iron, the river like blue marble. But beneath the oak the snow had melted, and—Konstantin stepped closer—the ground was thick with snowdrops. Anna clutched at his arm. "Father," she whispered. "Oh, Father, what are those there? It is still winter, too soon for snowdrops."

"The thaw," said Konstantin, weary, sick, and certain. "Come, Anna." She wound her hand in his. Her touch was like a child's. In the dawn light, he could see the black gaps between her teeth.

Konstantin drew her nearer the tree, with its carpet of untimely snowdrops. Nearer and nearer.

And suddenly they were in a clearing that neither of them had ever seen. The oak stood alone in the center, while the white flowers clustered about its hoary knees. The sky was white. The ground was slush, turning to muck.

"Well done," said the voice. It seemed to come from the air, from the water. Anna let out a sobbing scream. Konstantin saw a shadow on the snow, grown monstrously vast, flung out long and distorted, the blackest shadow that he had ever seen. But Anna looked not at the shadow, but at the air beyond. She pointed one trembling finger and screamed. She screamed and screamed.

Konstantin looked where Anna looked, but he saw nothing.

The shadow seemed to stretch out and quiver, like a dog at its master's stroking. Anna's screams split the blank air. The light was flat and dim.

"Well done, my servant," said the shadow. "She is all I could desire. She can see me, and she is afraid. Scream, vedma, scream."

Konstantin felt empty, strangely calm. He put Anna away from him, though she clawed and scrabbled. Her nails dug into his wool-clad arm.

"Now," said Konstantin. "Keep your promise. Leave me. Send the girl back."

The shadow went still, like the boar that hears the hunter's distant footfall. "Go home, man of God," it said. "Go back and wait. The girl will come to you. I swear it."

Anna's terrified screams grew even louder. She flung herself to the ground and kissed the priest's feet, wrapped her arms around him. "Batyushka," she begged. "Batyushka! No—please. Do not leave me, I beg. I beg! That is a devil. That is the devil!"

Konstantin was filled with a weary disgust. "Very well," he said to the shadow.

He pushed Anna aside. "I advise you to pray." She sobbed harder still.

"I am going," said Konstantin to the shadow. "I will wait. Do not forsake your word."

27.

THE WINTER BEAR

Vasya came back to Lesnaya Zemlya at first light of a clear winter dawn. Solovey carried her to the part of the palisade nearest the house. When she stood on his back she could reach the top of the spiked wall.

I will wait for you, Vasya, said the stallion. *If you need me, you have only to call.*

Vasya laid a hand on his neck. Then she vaulted the palisade and dropped into the snow.

She found Alyosha alone in the winter kitchen, armed and pacing, cloaked and booted. He saw her and stopped dead. Brother and sister stared at each other.

Then Alyosha took two strides, seized her and pulled her to him. "God, Vasya, you frightened me," he said into her hair. "I thought you were dead. Damn Anna Ivanovna and upyry both—I was going to go and look for you. What happened? You—you don't even look cold." He pushed her away a little. "You look different."

Vasya thought of the house in the woods, of the good food and rest and warmth. She thought of her endless rides through the snow, and she thought of Morozko, the way he watched her over the fire in the evening. "Perhaps I am different." She flung down the flowers.

Alyosha gaped. "Where?" he stammered. "How?"

Vasya smiled crookedly. "A gift," she said.

Alyosha reached out and touched a fragile stem. "It won't work, Vasya," he said, recovering. "Anna will not keep her promise. The village is already fearful. If word of these gets out . . ."

"We'll not tell them," said Vasya firmly. "It is enough I kept my half of the bargain. At midwinter, the dead will lie quiet again. Father will come home, and you and I will make him see sense. In the meantime, there is the house to guard."

She turned toward the oven.

At that moment, Irina came stumbling into the room. She gave a cry. "Vasochka! You are back. I was so afraid." She flung her arms around Vasya, and Vasya stroked her sister's hair. Irina pulled away. "But where is Mother?" she said. "She was not in bed, though usually she sleeps so long. I thought she would be in the kitchen."

A cold finger touched Vasya on the back of her neck, though she was not sure why. "Perhaps in the church, little bird," she said. "I will go and see. In the meantime, here are some flowers for you."

Irina seized the blossoms, pressed them to her lips. "So soon. Is it spring already, Vasochka?"

"No," replied Vasya. "They are a promise only. Keep them hidden. I must go find your mother."

There was no one in the church but Father Konstantin. Vasya walked soft in the stillness. The icons seemed to peer at her. "You," said Konstantin wearily. "He kept his promise." He did not look away from the icons.

Vasya stepped around him so that she stood between him and the icon-screen. A low fire burned in his sunken eyes. "I gave everything for you, Vasilisa Petrovna."

"Not everything," said Vasya. "Since clearly your pride is intact, as well as your illusions. Where is my stepmother, Batyushka?"

"No, I gave everything," said Konstantin. His voice rose; he seemed to speak despite himself. "I thought the voice was God, but it was not.

And I was left with my sin—that I wanted you. I listened to the devil to get you away from me. Now I will never be clean again."

"Batyushka," said Vasya. "What is this devil?"

"The voice in the dark," said Konstantin. "The bringer of storms. The shadow on the snow. But he told me . . ." Konstantin covered his face with his hands. His shoulders shook.

Vasya knelt and peeled the priest's hands from his face. "Batyushka, where is Anna Ivanovna?"

"In the woods," said Konstantin. He was staring into her face as though fascinated, much as Alyosha had. Vasya wondered what change the house in the woods had wrought in her. "With the shadow. The price of my sins."

"Batyushka," said Vasya, very carefully. "In these woods, did you see a great oak-tree, black and twisted?"

"Of course you would know the place," said Konstantin. "It is the haunt of demons."

Then he started. All the color had fled from Vasya's face. "What, girl?" he said with something of his old imperious manner. "You cannot mourn that mad old woman. She would have seen you dead."

But Vasya was gone already, up and running for the house. The door slammed shut behind her.

She had remembered her stepmother staring, bulging-eyed, at the domovoi.

He desires above all the lives of those who can see him.

The Bear had his witch, and it was dawn.

She put two fingers in her mouth and whistled shrilly. Already smoke trickled from chimneys. Her whistle split the morning like the arrows of raiders, and people spilled out of their houses. *Vasya!* she heard. *Vasilisa Petrovna!* But then they all fell silent, for Solovey had leaped the palisade. He galloped up to Vasya, and he did not break stride when she vaulted to his back. She heard cries of astonishment.

The horse skidded to a halt in the dvor. From the stable came the neighing of horses. Alyosha came running out of the house, naked sword in hand. Irina, behind him, hovered flinching in the doorway. They stopped and stared at Solovey.

"Lyoshka, come with me," said Vasya. "Now! There is no time."

Alyosha looked at his sister and the bay stallion. He looked at Irina and he looked at the people.

"Will you carry him as well?" said Vasya to Solovey.

Yes, said Solovey. *If you ask it of me. But where are we going, Vasya?*

"To the oak-tree. To the Bear's clearing," said Vasya. "As fast as you can run." Alyosha, without a word, sprang up behind her.

Solovey put his head up, a stallion scenting battle. But he said, *You cannot do it alone. Morozko is far away. He has said he must wait until midwinter.*

"Cannot?" said Vasya. "I *will* do it. Hurry."

৪◊३

ANNA IVANOVNA HAD NO more voice. The cords and muscles were all wrenched and broken. Still she tried to scream, though only a ruined rasp escaped her lips. The one-eyed man sat beside her where she lay on the earth and smiled. "Oh, my beauty," he said. "Scream again. It is beautiful. Your soul ripens as you scream."

He bent nearer. One instant she saw a man with twisted blue scars on his face. Next instant, arcing over her, she saw a grinning, one-eyed bear whose head and shoulders seemed to shatter the sky. Then he was nothing at all: a storm, a wind, a summer wildfire. A shadow. She cringed away, retching. She tried to stumble to her feet. But the creature grinned down at her and the strength went from her limbs. She lay there, breathing the stinking air.

"You are glorious," said the creature, bending nearer, slavering. He ran hard hands over her flesh. Crouched at his feet was another shape, white-wrapped, small. The face had shrunk to almost nothing, just close-set eyes and narrow temples and a mouth that gaped huge and ravenous. It crouched on the ground, head between its knees. Every now and then it looked at Anna, a light of hunger gleaming in the dark eyes.

"Dunya," said Anna, sobbing. For it was she, dressed as they'd buried her. "Dunya, please."

But Dunya said nothing. She opened her cavernous mouth.

"Die," said Medved with rapt tenderness, letting Anna go and stepping back. "Die and live forever."

The upyr lunged. Anna resisted only with feeble, scratching fingers.

But then from the other side of the clearing came the ringing cry of a stallion.

⁂

AS SOLOVEY GALLOPED, VASYA told Alyosha that a monster had their stepmother, and if it killed her, it would be free to burn up the countryside with terror.

"Vasya," said Alyosha, taking a moment to digest this. *"Where were you?"*

"I was the guest of the winter-king," said Vasya.

"Well, you should have brought back a prince's ransom," Alyosha said at once, and Vasya laughed.

Day was breaking. A strange smell, hot and rank, crept between the tree-trunks. Solovey raced along steadily, ears forward. He was a horse for a god's child to ride, but Vasya's hands were empty, and she did not know how to fight.

You must not be afraid, said Solovey, and she stroked the sleek neck.

Ahead loomed the great oak-tree. Behind her, Vasya felt Alyosha tense. The two riders passed the tree and found themselves in a clearing, a place that Vasya did not know. The sky was white, the air warm, so that she sweated under her clothes.

Solovey reared, bugling. Alyosha clutched Vasya around the middle.

A white thing lay prone on the muddy earth, while another shape lay heaving beneath it. A great pool of blood stood out around them.

Above them, waiting, grinning, was the Bear. But he was no longer a small man with scars on his skin. Now Vasya saw a bear in truth, but larger than any bear she had ever seen. His fur was patchy and lichen-colored; his black lips glistened around a vast, snarling mouth.

A little grin appeared on those black lips when he saw them, and the tongue showed red between. "Two of them!" he said. "All the better. I thought my brother had you already, girl, but I suppose he was too great a fool to keep you."

Out of the corner of her eye, Vasya saw the white mare step into the clearing.

"Ah, no, here he is," said the Bear. But his voice had hardened. "Hello, brother. Come to see me off?"

Morozko spared Vasya a quick, burning glance, and she felt an answering fire rising in her: power and freedom together. The great bay stallion was beneath her, the wild eyes of the frost-demon there, and between them the monster. She flung her head back and laughed, and as she did, she felt the jewel at her throat burn.

"Well," said Morozko to her, wryly, in a voice like the wind, "I did try to keep you safe."

A wind was rising. It was a small wind, light and quick and keen. A little of the white cloud blew away overhead, and Vasya could glimpse a pure dawn sky. She heard Morozko speaking, softly and clearly, but she did not understand the words. His eyes fixed on something Vasya could not see. The wind rose higher, keening.

"Do you think to frighten me, Karachun?" said Medved.

"I can buy time, Vasya," said the wind in Vasya's ear. "But I do not know how much. I would have been stronger at midwinter."

"There was not time. He has my stepmother," replied Vasya. "I had forgotten. She, too, can see."

Suddenly she realized that there were other faces in the wood, at the brink of the clearing. There was a naked woman with long wet hair, and there was a creature like an old man, with skin like the skin of a tree. There was the vodianoy, the river-king, with his great fish-eyes. The polevik was there, and the bolotnik. There were others—dozens. Creatures like ravens and creatures like rocks and mushrooms and heaps of snow. Many crept forward to where the white mare stood beside Vasya and Solovey, and clustered about their feet. Behind her, Alyosha gave a whistle of astonishment. "I can see them, Vasya."

But the Bear was speaking, too, in a voice like men screaming. And some of the chyerti went to him. The bolotnik, the wicked swamp creature. And—Vasya felt her heart stop—the rusalka, wildness, emptiness, and lust in her strange, lovely face.

The chyerti took sides, and Vasya saw all their faces intent. *Winterking. Medved. We will answer.* Vasya felt them all quivering on the cusp of battle; her blood boiled. She heard their many voices. And the white mare stepped forward, too, with Morozko on her back. Solovey reared and pawed the earth.

"Go, Vasya," said the wind with Morozko's voice. "Your stepmother must live. Tell your brother his sword will not bite the flesh of the dead. And—do not die."

The girl shifted her weight and Solovey took them forward at a flying gallop. The Bear roared and instantly the clearing fell into chaos. The rusalka sprang upon the vodianoy, her father, and tore into his warty shoulder. Vasya saw the leshy wounded, streaming something like sap from a gash in his trunk. Solovey galloped on. They came upon the great pool of blood and skidded to a halt.

The upyr looked up and hissed. Anna lay gray-faced beneath her, caked with mud, not moving. Dunya was covered in gore and filth, her face streaked with tears.

Anna breathed out one slow, gurgling sigh. Her throat was laid open. Behind them came a roar of triumph from the Bear. Dunya was crouched like a cat about to spring. Vasya locked eyes with her and slid off Solovey's back.

No, Vasya, said the stallion. *Get back up.*

"Lyoshka," said Vasya, not taking her eyes from Dunya. "Go fight with the others. Solovey will protect me."

Alyosha slid from Solovey's back. "As if I'd leave you," he said. Some of the Bear's creatures circled them. Alyosha cried a war cry and swung his sword. Solovey lowered his head, like a bull about to charge.

"Dunya," Vasya said. "Dunyashka." Dimly she heard her brother grunt as the edge of the battle found them. From somewhere, there came a howl like a wolf's, a cry like a woman's. But she and Dunya stood in a little core of silence. Solovey pawed the earth, ears flat to his skull. *That creature does not know you,* he said.

"She *does*. I know she does." The look of terror on the upyr's face warred now with avid hunger. "I will just tell her she need not be afraid. Dunya—Dunya, please. I know you are cold here, and you are frightened. But can't you remember me?"

Dunya panted, all the light of hell in her eyes.

Vasya drew her belt-knife and dragged it deeply across the veins of her wrist. The skin resisted before it gave, and then the blood raged out. Solovey shied back instinctively. "Vasya!" cried Alyosha, but she did not heed. Vasya took a long step forward. Her blood tumbled down, scarlet in the snow, on the mud and on the snowdrops. Behind her Solovey reared.

"Here, Dunyashka," said Vasya. "Here. You are hungry. You fed me often enough. Remember?" She held out her bleeding arm.

And then she had no more time to think. The creature seized her hand like a greedy child, fastened its mouth to her wrist, and drank.

Vasya stood still, trying desperately to stay on her feet.

The creature whimpered as it drank. More and more it whimpered, and then suddenly it flung her hand away and stumbled backward. Vasya staggered, light-headed, black flowers blooming at the edges of her vision. But Solovey was behind her, holding her up, nosing her anxiously.

Her wrist had been worried as though it were a bone. Gritting her teeth, Vasya tore a strip from her shirt and bound it tight. She heard the whistling of Alyosha's sword. The press of fighting swept up her brother and drew him away.

The upyr was looking at her with abject terror. Her nose and chin and cheeks were speckled and smeared with blood. The wood seemed to hold its breath. "Marina," said the vampire, and it was Dunya's voice.

There came a bellow of fury.

The hell-light faded from the vampire's eyes. The blood cracked and flaked on her face. "My own Marina, at last. It has been so long."

"Dunya," said Vasya. "I am glad to see you."

"Marina, Marushka, where am I? I am cold. I have been so frightened."

"It is all right," said Vasya, fighting tears. "It will be all right." She wrapped her arms around the death-smelling thing. "You need not be frightened now." From beyond there came another roar. Dunya jerked in Vasya's arms. "Hush," said Vasya, as to a child. "Don't look." She tasted salt on her lips.

Suddenly Morozko was beside her. He was breathing fast, and he had a wild look to match Solovey's. "You are a mad fool, Vasilisa Petrovna," he said. He caught up a handful of snow and pressed it to her bleeding arm. It froze solid, clotting the blood. When she brushed away the excess, she found the wound sheathed in a thin layer of ice.

"What has happened?" said Vasya.

"The chyerti stand," replied Morozko grimly. "But it will not last. Your stepmother is dead, and so the Bear is loose. He will break out now soon—soon."

The fighting had come back into the clearing. The wood-spirits were as children beside the Bear's bulk. He had grown; his shoulders seemed to split the sky. He seized the polevik in vast jaws and flung it away. The rusalka stood at his side, shrieking a wordless cry. The Bear threw back his great shaggy head. "Free!" he roared, snarling, laughing. He seized the leshy, and Vasya heard wood splintering.

"You must help them, then," snapped Vasya. "Why are you here?"

Morozko narrowed his eyes and said nothing. Vasya wondered, for a ridiculous instant, if he had come back to keep her from killing herself. The white mare laid her nose against Dunya's withered cheek. "I know you," the old lady whispered to the horse. "You are so beautiful." Then Dunya saw Morozko and a faint fear crept back into her eyes. "I know you, too," she said.

"You will not see me again, Avdotya Mikhailovna, I very much hope," said Morozko. But his voice was gentle.

"Take her," said Vasya quickly. "Let her die in truth now, so that she will not be afraid. Look, already she is forgetting."

It was true. The clarity had begun to fade from Dunya's face. "And you, Vasya?" Morozko said. "If I take her, I must leave this place."

Vasya thought of facing the Bear without him and she wavered. "How long will you be gone?"

"An instant. An hour. One cannot tell."

Behind them the Bear called out. Dunya shook at the summons. "I must go to him," she whispered. "I must—Marushka, *please.*"

Vasya gathered her resolve. "I have an idea," she said.

"It would be better—"

"No," snapped Vasya. "Take her away now. *Please.* She was my mother." She seized the frost-demon's arm with both hands. "The white mare said you were a giver of gifts. Do this for me now, Morozko. I beg you."

There was a long silence. Morozko looked at the battle beyond them. He looked back at her. For a flickering instant, his glance strayed into the trees. Vasya looked where he did and saw nothing. But suddenly the frost-demon smiled.

"Very well," Morozko said. Unexpectedly he reached out and drew her close and kissed her, quick and fierce. She looked up at him wide-eyed. "You must hold on, then," he said. "As long as you may. Be brave."

He stepped back. "Come, Avdotya Mikhailovna, and take the road with me."

Suddenly he and Dunya were astride the white horse, and only a crumpled, bloody, empty thing lay in the snow at Vasya's feet.

"Farewell," whispered Vasya, fighting the urge to call him back. Then they were gone, the white horse and her two riders.

Vasya took a deep breath. The Bear had thrown off the last of his attackers. Now he wore the scarred face of a man, but a tall, strong man, with cruel hands. He laughed. "Well done," he said. "I am always trying to get rid of him myself. He is a cold thing, devushka. *I* am the fire; I will warm you. Come here, little vedma, and live forever."

He beckoned. His eyes seemed to drag at her. His power flooded the clearing and the wounded chyerti shrank before him.

Vasya breathed in a frightened breath. But Solovey was at her side. She felt his sinewy neck under her hand and then, blindly, she clambered onto his back. "Better a thousand deaths," she said to the Bear.

The scarred lip lifted and she saw the gleam of his long teeth. "Come, then," he said coldly. "Slave or loyal servant, the choice is yours. But you are mine either way." He was growing as he spoke, and suddenly the man was a bear again, with jaws to swallow the world. He grinned at her. "Oh, you are afraid. They are always afraid at the end. But the fear of the brave—that is best."

Vasya thought her heart would beat its way out of her breast. But aloud she said, in a small, strangled voice, "I see the folk of the wood. But what of the domovoi, and the bannik, and the vazila? Come to me now, children of my people's hearths, for my need is very great." She ripped the skin of ice off the wound in her arm, so that her blood tumbled forth. The blue jewel was glowing beneath her clothes.

There was an instant of stillness in the clearing, broken by the chime of Alyosha's sword and the grunts of the chyerti who still fought. Her brother was surrounded by three of the Bear's people. Vasya saw his face intent, the gleam of blood on his arm and cheek.

"Come to me now," said Vasya, desperately. "As I ever loved you, and you loved me; remember the blood I shed, and the bread I gave."

Still there was silence. The Bear scraped the earth with his great forefeet. "And now you will despair," he said. "Despair is even better than fear." He put his tongue out like a snake, as though to taste the air.

Foolish girl, thought Vasya. *How could the household-spirits come? They are bound to our hearths.* She tasted blood, bitter and salty in her mouth.

"We can at least save my brother," Vasya said to Solovey, and the horse bugled defiance. One of the Bear's great paws flashed out, taking them by surprise, and the horse barely dodged. He backed, ears flat to his head, and the great paw drew back to strike again.

Suddenly all the domoviye, all the bathhouse-guardians and door-yard spirits from all the dwellings in Lesnaya Zemlya, were thronging at their feet. Solovey had to pick up his hooves to keep from stepping on them, and then the vazila sprang onto Solovey's withers. The little domovoi from her own house brandished a live coal in one sooty hand.

For the first time, the Bear looked uncertain. "Impossible," he muttered. "Impossible. They do not leave their houses."

The household-spirits roared out strange challenges and Solovey pawed the muddy earth.

But then Vasya's heart sprang into her throat and seemed to hang there, hammering. The rusalka had borne Alyosha to earth. Vasya saw his sword go flying; she saw him freeze, entranced, looking up at the naked woman. She saw her fingers go round his throat.

The Bear laughed. "Stay where you are, all of you. Or this one dies."

"Remember," Vasya called to the rusalka, desperately, across the clearing. "I threw flowers for you, and now I shed my blood. Remember!"

The rusalka froze, perfectly still except for the water running down her hair. Her hands around Alyosha's throat slackened.

Alyosha struck out, renewing the struggle, but the Bear was too near.

"Come on!" cried Vasya to Solovey, to all of her ragged army. "Go—he is my brother!"

But at that moment, a great bellow of rage came from the other end of the clearing.

Vasya glanced aside and saw her father standing there, his sword in his hand.

⸎

THE BEAR WAS TWICE and thrice the size of an ordinary bear. It had only one eye; half its face was a mass of scars. The good eye gleamed, the color of thin shadow on snow. It wasn't sleepy, like an ordinary bear, but alight with hunger and giddy malice.

Before the Bear was Vasya, unmistakable, tiny before the beast, riding a dark horse. But Alyosha, his son, lay almost beneath the beast's feet, and the great mouth reached down . . .

Pyotr bellowed, a cry of love and rage. The beast whipped his head around. "So many visitors," he said. "Silence for a thousand lives of men, and then the world descends upon me. Well, I will not object. One at a time, though. First the boy."

But at that moment, a naked woman, green-skinned, water glittering on her long hair, shrieked and sprang onto the Bear's back, clutching him with her hands and teeth. Next instant, Pyotr's daughter cried aloud and the great horse charged, striking out at the beast with its forefeet. With them came all manner of strange creatures, tall and thin, tiny and bearded, male and female. They threw themselves together upon the Bear, shrieking in their high, strange voices. The beast fell back beneath them.

Vasya half-tumbled from the horse's back, seized Alyosha, and dragged him away. Pyotr heard her sobbing. "Lyoshka," she cried. "Lyoshka."

The stallion struck out with his forefeet again and backed up, protecting the boy and girl on the ground. Alyosha blinked dazedly about them. "Get up, Lyoshka," pleaded Vasya. "Please, please."

The Bear shook himself and most of the strange creatures were flung off. He lashed out with one paw, and the great stallion barely evaded the blow. The naked woman fell to the snow, water flying from her hair. Vasya threw herself over her half-conscious brother. Monstrous teeth reached for her unprotected back.

Pyotr could not remember running. But suddenly he found himself standing, gasping, between his children and the beast. He was steady except for his pounding heart, and he held his broadsword two-handed. Vasya stared at him as at an apparition. He saw her lips move. *Father.*

The Bear skidded to a halt. "Get you gone," he snarled. He stretched out a clawed foot. Pyotr turned it with his sword and did not stir.

"My life is nothing," said Pyotr. "I am not afraid."

The Bear opened his mouth and roared. Vasya flinched. Still Pyotr did not move. "Stand aside," said the Bear. "I will have the old witch's children."

Pyotr stepped deliberately forward. "I know no witches. These are my children."

The Bear's teeth snapped an inch from his face, and still he did not move.

"Get out," said Pyotr. "You are nothing; you are only a story. Leave my lands in peace."

The Bear snorted. "These woods are mine now." But the eye rolled warily.

"What is your price?" said Pyotr. "I, too, have heard the old tales, and there is always a price."

"As you like. Give me your daughter, and you will have peace."

Pyotr glanced at Vasya. Their eyes met, and he saw her swallow hard. "That is my Marina's lastborn," he said. "That is my daughter. A man does not offer up another's life. Still less the life of his own child."

An instant of perfect silence.

"I offer you mine," said Pyotr. He dropped his sword.

"No!" Vasya screamed. "Father, no! No!"

The Bear squinted its good eye and hesitated.

Suddenly Pyotr flung himself, empty-handed, at the lichen-colored chest. The Bear acted on instinct; he batted the man aside. There was a horrible *crack*. Pyotr flew like a straw doll and landed facedown in the snow.

⚬⚬⚬

THE BEAR HOWLED AND LEAPED after him. But Vasya was on her feet, all her fear forgotten. She screamed aloud in wordless fury and the Bear whipped round again.

Vasya heaved herself onto Solovey's back. They charged the Bear. The girl was weeping; she had forgotten she held no weapon. The jewel at her breast burned cold, beating like another heart.

The Bear grinned broadly, tongue lolling doglike between its great teeth.

"Oh, yes," it said, "Come here, little vedma, come here, little witch. You aren't strong enough for me yet, and never will be. Come to me and join your poor father."

But even as he spoke he was dwindling. The Bear became a man, a little, cringing man that peered up at them through a watering gray eye.

A white figure appeared beside Solovey, and a white hand touched the stallion's straining neck. The horse put his head up and slowed. "No!" shouted Vasya. "No, Solovey, don't stop."

But the one-eyed man cringed down into the snow, and she felt Morozko's hand on hers. "Enough, Vasya," he said. "See? He is bound. It is over."

She stared at the little man, blinking, dazed. "How?"

"Such is the strength of men," said Morozko. He sounded strangely satisfied. "We who live forever can know no courage, nor do we love enough to give our lives. But your father could. His sacrifice bound the Bear. Pyotr Vladimirovich will die as he would have wished. It is over."

"No," said Vasya, pulling her hand away. "No . . ."

She pitched herself off Solovey. Medved cringed away, grumbling, but already she had forgotten him. She ran to her father's head. Alyosha had gotten there before her. He pulled aside his father's torn cloak. The blow had crushed Pyotr's ribs on one side, and blood bubbled up between his lips. Vasya pressed her hands to the wounded place. Warmth flared into her hands. Her tears fell onto her father's eyes. A hint of color tinged Pyotr's graying skin, and his eyes opened. They fell on Vasya and brightened.

"Marina," he croaked. "Marina."

The breath sighed out of him and he did not take another.

"No," Vasya whispered. *"No."* She dug her fingertips into her father's slack flesh. His chest heaved suddenly, like a bellows, but his eyes were fixed and staring. Vasya tasted blood where she'd bitten into her lip, and she fought the death as though it were her own, as though . . .

A cold long-fingered hand caught both of hers, leaching the warmth away. Vasya tried to wrench her hands free, but she could not. Morozko's voice wafted icy air across her cheek. "Leave it, Vasya. He chose this; you cannot undo it."

"Yes, I can," she hissed back, breath catching in her throat. "It should have been me. Let me go!" Then the hand was gone, and she spun round. Morozko had already drawn away. She looked up into his face, pale and indifferent, cruel and just a little kind.

"Too late," he said, and all around, the wind took up the words: *Too late, too late.*

And then the frost-demon had swung onto the white mare's back, up behind another figure, that Vasya could only see out of the corner of her eye. "No," she said, running after them. "Wait—*Father.*" But the white mare had already cantered off between the trees and disappeared into the darkness.

❦

THE STILLNESS WAS SUDDEN and absolute. The one-eyed man slunk off into the undergrowth, and the chyerti disappeared into the winter forest. The rusalka laid a dripping hand on Vasya's shoulder in passing. "Thank you, Vasilisa Petrovna," she said.

Vasya made no answer.

Solovey nuzzled her gently.

Vasya did not heed. She was staring at nothing, holding her father's hand while it slowly turned cold.

"Look," whispered Alyosha, hoarse and wet-eyed. "The snow-drops are dying."

It was true. The warm, sickly, death-smelling wind had chilled, sharpened, and the flowers wilted down onto the hard earth. It was not yet midwinter, and their hour was months away. There was no clearing, no muddy space beneath a gray sky. There was only a huge old oak-tree, its branches twisted together. The village lay beyond, now clearly visible, a stone's throw away. Day had broken and it was bitterly cold.

"Bound," said Vasya. "The monster is bound. Father did it." She reached out a stiff hand to pluck a drooping snowdrop.

"How came Father here?" said Alyosha in soft wonder. "He had— such a look about him. As if he knew what to do, and how, and why. He is with Mother now, by God's grace." Alyosha made the sign of the cross over his father's body, rose, went to Anna, and repeated the ges-ture.

But Vasya did not move, nor did she answer.

She put the flower in her father's hand. Then she laid her head against his chest and began, softly, to cry.

28.

AT THE END AND
AT THE BEGINNING

THEY KEPT A NIGHT'S VIGIL FOR PYOTR VLADIMIROVICH AND his wife. The two were buried together, with Pyotr between his first wife and his second. Though they mourned, the people did not despair. The miasma of death and defeat had gone from their fields and houses. Even the bedraggled remnants of half a burnt village, led past their gate by an exhausted Kolya, could not frighten them. The air bit gently, and the sun shone down, studding the snow with diamonds.

Vasya stood with her family, hooded and cloaked against the chill, and bore the people's whispers. *Vasilisa Petrovna disappeared. She returned on a winged horse. She should have been dead. Witch.* Vasya remembered the touch of rope on her wrists, the cold look in Oleg's eyes—a man she had known since childhood—and she made a decision.

When everyone else had gone, Vasya stood alone at her father's grave in the dusk. She felt old and grim and tired.

"Can you hear me, Morozko?" she said.

"Yes," he said, and then he was beside her.

She saw a subtle wariness in his face, and she laughed a laugh that was half a sob. "Afraid I will ask for my father back?"

"When I walked freely among men, the living would scream at me,"

Morozko replied evenly. "They would seize my hand, the mane of my horse. The mothers begged me to take them, when I took up their children."

"Well, I have had enough of the dead coming back." Vasya fought for a tone of icy detachment. But her voice wavered.

"I suppose you have," he replied. But the wariness had gone from his face. "I will remember his courage, Vasya," he said. "And yours."

Her mouth twisted. "Always? When I am like my father, clay in the cold earth? Well, that is something, to be remembered."

He said nothing. They looked at each other.

"What would you have of me, Vasilisa Petrovna?"

"Why did my father die?" she asked in a rush. "We need him. If anyone had to die, it should have been me."

"It was his choice, Vasya," replied Morozko. "It was his privilege. He would not have had it otherwise. He died for you."

Vasya shook her head and paced a restless circle. "How did Father even know? He came to the clearing. He *knew*. How could he find us?"

Morozko hesitated. Then he said slowly, "He came home before the others and found you and your brother gone. He went into the woods to search. That clearing is enchanted. Until the tree dies, it will do all in its power to keep the Bear contained. It knew what was needed, better even than I. It drew your father to you, once he entered the forest."

Vasya was silent a long moment. She looked at him narrow-eyed, and he met her gaze. At last she nodded.

Then, "There is something I must do," Vasya said abruptly. "I need your help."

※

IT HAD ALL GONE WRONG, thought Konstantin. Pyotr Vladimirovich was dead, killed by a wild beast on the threshold of his own village.

Anna Ivanovna, they said, had run out into the woods in a fit of madness. *Well, of course she did,* he told himself. *She was a madwoman and a fool; we all knew it.* But he could still see her frantic, bloodless face. It hung before his waking eyes.

Konstantin read the service for Pyotr Vladimirovich scarce knowing what he said, and he ate at the funeral feast hardly knowing what he did.

But in the twilight, there came a knock at the door of his cell.

When the door opened, his breath hissed out and he stumbled back. Vasya stood in the gap, the candlelight strong on her face. She was grown so beautiful, pale and remote, graceful and troubled. *Mine, she is mine. God has sent her back to me. This is his forgiveness.*

"Vasya," he said, and reached out to her.

But she was not alone. When she slipped through the door, a dark-cloaked figure unfolded from the shadows at her shoulder and glided in beside her. Konstantin could see nothing of the face, save that it was pale. The hands were very long and thin.

"Who is that, Vasya?" he said.

"I came back," Vasya returned. "But not alone, as you see."

Konstantin could not see the man's eyes, so sunk were they in his skull. The hands were of a skeletal thinness. The priest licked his lips. "Who is that, girl?"

Vasya smiled. "Death," she said. "He saved me in the forest. Or perhaps he did not, and I am a ghost. I feel a ghost tonight."

"You are mad," said Konstantin. "Stranger, who are you?"

The stranger said nothing.

"Alive or dead, I have come to tell you to leave this place," said Vasya. "Go back to Moscow, to Vladimir, to Tsargrad, or to hell, but you must be gone before the snowdrops bloom."

"My task—"

"Your task is done," said Vasya. She stepped forward. The dark man beside her seemed to grow; his head was a skull, and blue fires burned in the sockets of his sunken eyes. "You will go, Konstantin Nikonovich. Or you will die. And your death will not be easy."

"I will not." But he was pressed against the wall of his chamber. His teeth rattled together.

"You will," said Vasya. She advanced until she was near enough to touch. He could see the curve of her cheek, the implacable look in her eyes. "Or we will see to it that you are mad as my stepmother was, before the end."

"Demons," said Konstantin, panting. A cold sweat broke over his brow.

"Yes," said Vasya, and she smiled, the devil's own child. The dark figure beside her smiled, too, a slow skull's grin.

And then they were gone, silently as they had come.

Konstantin fell to his knees before the shadows on his wall. He stretched out supplicating hands. "Come back," begged the priest. He paused, listening. His hands shook. "Come back. You raised me up, but she scorned me. Come back."

He thought the shadows might have shifted just a little. But he heard only silence.

⚜

"HE WILL DO IT, I think," Vasya said.

"Very likely," said Morozko. He was laughing. "I have never done that at another's behest."

"And I suppose you frighten people all the time on your own account," said Vasya.

"I?" said Morozko. "I am only a story, Vasya."

And it was Vasya's turn to laugh. Then her laugh caught in her throat. "Thank you," she said.

Morozko inclined his head. And then the night seemed to reach out and catch him up, fold him inside itself, so that there was only the dark where he had been.

THE HOUSEHOLD HAD GONE to bed, and only Irina and Alyosha sat alone in the kitchen. Vasya glided in like a shadow. Irina had been crying; Alyosha held her. Wordless, Vasya sank onto the oven-bench beside them and wrapped her arms around them both.

They were all silent awhile.

"I cannot stay here," said Vasya, very low.

Alyosha looked at her, dull with sorrow and battle-weariness. "Are you still thinking of the convent?" he said. "Well, you needn't think of it again. Anna Ivanovna is dead, and so is Father. I will have my own land, my own inheritance. I will look after you."

"You must establish yourself as a lord among men," Vasya said. "Men will look less kindly upon you when it is known that you harbor your mad sister. You know that many will blame me for all this. I am the witch-woman. Has the priest not said so?"

"Never mind that," said Alyosha. "There is nowhere for you to go."

"Is there not?" said Vasya. A slow fire kindled in her face, easing the lines of grief. "Solovey will take me to the ends of the earth if I ask it. I am going into the world, Alyosha. I will be no one's bride, neither of man nor of God. I am going to Kiev and Sarai and Tsargrad, and I will look upon the sun on the sea."

Alyosha stared at his sister. "You *are* mad, Vasya."

She laughed, but the tears blurred her sight. "Entirely," she said. "But I will have my freedom, Alyosha. Do you doubt me? I brought snowdrops to my stepmother, when I ought to have died in the forest. Father is gone; there is no one to hinder. Tell me truly, what is there for me here but walls and cages? I will be free, and I will not count the cost."

Irina clung to her sister. "Don't go, Vasya, don't go. I will be good, I promise."

"Look at me, Irinka," said Vasya. "You are good. You are the best little girl I know. Much better than I am. But, little sister, you don't think I am a witch. Others do."

"That is true," said Alyosha. He had also seen the villagers' black stares, heard their whispers during the funeral.

Vasya said nothing.

"Unnatural thing," said her brother, but he was sad more than angry. "Can you not be content? Men will forget about all this in time, and what you call cages is the lot of women."

"It is not mine," said Vasya. "I love you, Lyoshka. I love you both. But I cannot."

Irina began to cry and clung closer.

"Don't cry, Irinka," added Alyosha. He was looking at his sister narrowly. "She will come back. Won't you, Vasya?"

She nodded once. "One day. I swear it."

"You will not be cold and hungry on the road, Vasya?"

Vasya thought of the house in the woods, of the treasures heaped there, waiting. Not a dowry now, but gems to barter, a cloak against the frost, boots . . . all she needed for journeying. "No," she said. "I do not think so."

Alyosha nodded reluctantly. Implacable purpose shone like wildfire in his sister's face.

"Do not forget us, Vasya. Here." He reached up and drew off a wooden object, hanging on a leather thong about his neck. He handed it to her. It was a little carven bird, with worn outspread wings.

"Father made it for mother," said Alyosha. "Wear it, little sister, and remember."

Vasya kissed them both. Her hand closed tight around the wooden thing. "I swear it," she said again.

"Go," said Alyosha. "Before I tie you to the oven and make you stay." But his eyes too were wet.

Vasya slipped outside. Just as she touched the threshold, there came her brother's voice again, "Go with God, little sister."

Even when the kitchen door swung shut behind her, it was not enough to muffle the sound of Irina's weeping.

⚜

SOLOVEY WAS WAITING FOR her just outside the palisade. "Come," Vasya said. "Will you bear me to the ends of the earth, if the road will take us so far?" She was crying as she spoke, but the horse nuzzled away her tears.

His nostrils flared to catch the evening wind. *Anywhere, Vasya. The world is wide, and the road will take us anywhere.*

She swung onto the stallion's back and he was away, swift and silent as a night-flying bird.

Soon enough, Vasya saw a fir-grove, and firelight glancing between the trees, spilling gold into the snow.

The door opened. "Come in, Vasya," Morozko said. "It is cold."

AUTHOR'S NOTE

STUDENTS AND SPEAKERS OF RUSSIAN WILL SURELY NOTE, AND possibly deplore, my wildly unsystematic approach to transliteration.

I can almost hear the hand-wringing of readers, who will be asking, for example, by what possible method could I have gotten *vodianoy* from the Russian водяной and then have turned around and gotten *domovoi* from the Russian домовой, a word with an identical ending?

The answer is that in transliterating, I had two aims.

First, I sought to render Russian words in such a way as to retain a bit of their exotic flavor. This is the reason I rendered Константин as Konstantin rather than the more familiar Constantine, and Дмитрий as Dmitrii rather than Dmitri.

Second, and more important, I wanted these Russian words to be reasonably pronounceable and aesthetically pleasing to speakers of English.

I like the way *vodianoy* looks on the page, just as I like the look of the name Aleksei (Алексей) but preferred to render the name Соловей as Solovey.

I dropped any attempt to indicate hard and soft signs, with apostrophes or otherwise, as these have absolutely no meaning for the average English-speaking reader. The only exception is in the word *Rus'*, where the extensive use of that spelling with the apostrophe in historiography has made it the most familiar of any to English-speaking readers.

To students of Russian history, I can say only that I have tried to be as faithful as possible to a poorly documented time period. When I have taken liberties with the historical record—for example, in making Prince Vladimir Andreevich older than Dmitrii Ivanovich (he was actually a few years younger) and marrying him to a girl named Olga Petrovna—it was for dramatic purposes, and I hope my readers will indulge me.

GLOSSARY

BABA YAGA~An old witch who appears in many Russian fairy tales. She rides around on a mortar, steering with a pestle and sweeping her tracks away with a broom of birch. She lives in a hut that spins round and round on chicken legs.

BANNIK~"Bathhouse dweller," the bathhouse guardian in Russian folklore.

BAST SHOES~Light shoes made of bast, the inner bark of a birch tree. They were easy to make, but not durable. Called *lapti*.

BATYUSHKA~Literally, "little father," used as a respectful mode of address for Orthodox ecclesiastics.

BOGATYR~A legendary Slavic warrior, something like a Western European knight-errant.

BOLOTNIK~Swamp-dweller, swamp-demon.

BOYAR~A member of the Kievan or, later, the Muscovite aristocracy, second in rank only to a *knyaz*, or prince.

BURAN~Snowstorm.

BUYAN~A mysterious island in the ocean, credited in Slavic mythology with the ability to appear and disappear. It figures in several Russian folktales.

DEVOCHKA~Little girl.

DEVUSHKA~Young woman, maiden.

DOCHKA~Daughter.

DOMOVOI~In Russian folklore, the guardian of the household, the household-spirit.

DURAK~Fool; feminine form *dura*.

DVOR~Yard, or dooryard.

DVOROVOI~In Russian folklore, the guardian of the *dvor*, or yard. Also, the janitor in modern usage.

ECUMENICAL PATRIARCH~The supreme head of the Eastern Orthodox Church, based in Constantinople (modern Istanbul).

GOSPODIN~Form of respectful address to a male, more formal than the English "mister." Might be translated as "lord."

GOSUDAR~A term of address akin to "Your Majesty" or "Sovereign."

GRAND PRINCE (VELIKIY KNYAZ) The title of a ruler of a major principality, for example, Moscow, Tver, or Smolensk, in medieval Russia. The title *tsar* did not come into use until Ivan the Terrible was crowned in 1547.

HOLY FOOL~A *yurodivy*, or Fool in Christ, was one who gave up his worldly possessions and devoted himself to an ascetic life. Their madness (real or feigned) was believed to be divinely inspired, and often they would speak truths that others dared not voice.

ICONOSTASIS (ICON-SCREEN)~A wall of icons with a specific layout that separates the nave from the sanctuary in an Eastern Orthodox church.

IZBA~A peasant's house, small and made of wood, often with carved embellishments. The plural is *izby*.

KASHA~Porridge. Can be made of buckwheat, wheat, rye, millet, or barley.

KOKOSHNIK~A Russian headdress. There are many styles of *kokoshniki*, depending on the locale and the era. Generally the word refers to the closed headdress worn by married women, though maidens also wore headdresses, open in back. The wearing of *kokoshniki* was limited to the nobility. The more common form of head covering for a medieval Russian woman was a headscarf or kerchief.

KREMLIN~A fortified complex at the center of a Russian city. Although modern English usage has adopted the word *kremlin* to refer solely to the most famous example, the Moscow Kremlin, there are actually kremlins to be found in most historic Russian cities.

KVAS~A fermented beverage made from rye bread.

LESHY~Also called the *lesovik,* the *leshy* was a woodland spirit in Slavic mythology, protector of forests and animals.

LESNAYA ZEMLYA~Literally, "Land of the Forest."

LITTLE BROTHER~English rendering of the Russian endearment *bratishka.* Can be applied to both older and younger siblings.

LITTLE SISTER~English rendering of the Russian endearment *sestryonka.* Can be applied to both older and younger siblings.

MEAD~Honey wine, made by fermenting a solution of honey and water.

METROPOLITAN~A high official in the Orthodox church. In the middle ages, the Metropolitan of the church of the Rus' was the highest Orthodox authority in Russia and was appointed by the Byzantine Patriarch.

MYSH~*Mysh',* mouse.

OGON~*Ogon',* fire.

OVEN~The Russian oven, or *pech',* is an enormous construction that came into wide use in the fifteenth century for both cooking and heating. A system of flues ensured even distribution of heat, and whole families would often sleep on top of the oven to keep warm during the winter.

PODSNEZHNIK~Snowdrop, a small white flower that blooms in early spring.

PYOS~Dog, cur.

RUS'~The Rus' were originally a Scandinavian people. In the ninth century C.E., at the invitation of warring Slavic and Finnic tribes, they established a ruling dynasty, the Rurikids, that eventually comprised a large swath of what is now Ukraine, Belarus, and Western Russia. The territory they ruled was eventually named after them, as were the people living under their dynasty. The word *Rus'* has lasted into the present day, as we can see in the names of Russia and Belarus.

RUSALKA~In Russian folklore, a female water nymph, something like a succubus.

RUSSIA~From the thirteenth through the fifteenth century, there was no unified polity called Russia. Instead, the Rus' lived under a disparate collection of rival princes (*knyazey*) who owed their ultimate allegiance to Mongol overlords. The word *Russia* did not come into common use until the seventeenth century. Thus, in the medieval context, one would not refer to "Russia," but rather to the "land of the Rus'," or simply "Rus'."

RUSSIAN~There are two adjectives in the Russian language, *russkiy* and *rossiyskiy,* that each translate to "Russian" in English. The first, *russkiy,* refers specifically to the Russian people and culture without distinction or boundaries. *Rossiyskiy* refers specifically to the modern Russian state. When the word *Russian* is used in the novel, I always intend the former meaning.

SARAFAN~A dress that looks something like a jumper or pinafore, with shoulder straps, worn over a long-sleeved blouse. This garment actually came into common use only in the early fifteenth century. I included it in the novel slightly before its time because of how strongly this manner of dress evokes fairy-tale Russia to the Western reader.

SOLOVEY~Nightingale.

STARIK~Old man.

SYNOK~An affectionate diminutive derived from the word *syn,* meaning "son."

TSAR~The word *Tsar* is derived from the Latin word *Caesar,* and originally was used to designate the Roman emperor (*imperator*), and later the Byzantine emperor, in Old Church Slavonic texts. In this novel, therefore, the word *Tsar* refers to the Byzantine emperor in Constantinople (or Tsargrad, literally "city of the tsar") and not to a Russian potentate. Ivan IV (Ivan the Terrible) was the first Russian Grand Prince to take the title Tsar of All the Russias, almost two hundred years following the fictional events of *The Bear and the Nightingale*. Russian rulers assumed the title of Tsar, because, following the fall of Constantinople to the Ottomans in 1453, they considered Moscow to be the "Third Rome," the heir of Constantinople's spiritual authority among Orthodox Christians.

TSARGRAD~"City of the tsar" Constantinople (see above).

UPYR~Vampire (pl. *upyry*).

VAZILA~In Russian folklore, the guardian of the stable and protector of livestock.

VEDMA~*Vyed'ma*, witch, wisewoman.

VERST~In Russian, *Versta* (верста). We take the English word from the Russian genitive plural. A unit of distance equal to roughly one kilometer, or two-thirds of a mile.

VODIANOY~In Russian folklore, a male water-spirit, often malicious.

ACKNOWLEDGMENTS

Writing a first novel is rather like tilting at a windmill, on the off chance that it might be a giant. I am more grateful than I can say to all those folks who were willing to play Sancho Panza on this long, strange charge.

In other words, thanks to everyone for believing. It's been a crazy ride.

To Dad and Beth, thank you for first reads, for many delicious dinners, and for being willing to harbor your very own madwoman in the attic. To Mom for keeping track of the fictitious shovel that literally no one else (including me) noticed. Carol Dawson for reading and liking and helping, long before anyone else not a parent did. Abhay Morrissey for dragging me into the sunshine when I threatened to stay at my laptop until I grew roots. Chris Johnson and R. J. Adler for films and songs respectively, and terrible vegan jokes from both of you. To Phyl Cast for raw chocolate and behind-the-scenes publishing info. To Kaitlin Maxfield for hoicking a pile of pages everywhere until she'd read something resembling a rough draft. To Erin Haywood for some really amazing hours spent making up stuff—if I'm ever stuck for an idea, I'm calling you. Robin Rice for crying at a Good Part and boosting my flagging confidence. Tatiana Smorodinskaya, Sergei Davydov, and the entire Russian Department at Middlebury College for an incredible education, which I hope I have not utterly disgraced. Carl Sieber, Konstantin, Anton, and all the folks at Carbon12 Creative for the most beautiful website a girl could ever have. Deverie Fernandez for being willing to take photos in the rain. Chris Archer for taking photos in the sunshine, and putting in the hours with mad Photoshop skills. Paula Hartman for kind words early on that got me through some tough spots. Ann Dubinet for delicious dinners and late-night advice. Sasha Melnikova for renaming a horse and not letting me get away with anything. Kim Ammons for winning ALL THE PRIZES in proofreading. Harrison Johnson for amazing critter art. Evan Johnson . . . because always. To all the people at Random House, starting with genius editor Jennifer Hershey, who has a knack for simple ideas that make a manuscript infinitely better. Thank you also to Anne Speyer, David Moench, Jess Bonet, Vincent La Scala, and Emily DeHuff. Thank you to everyone on the other side of the Great English Divide: Gillian Green for taking over my orphaned book; Tessa Henderson, Emily Yau, and Stephenie Naulls for so much kindness and hard work. To my amazing agent, Paul Lucas, who dragged me back into this game when I was on the verge of quitting and then went on to prove his confidence well-founded. I can't thank you enough. Thanks also to Dorothy Vincent, Brenna English-Loeb, Michael Steger, and everyone at Janklow and Nesbit.

To all of you, I am more grateful than I can say.

ABOUT THE AUTHOR

Born in Austin, Texas, KATHERINE ARDEN spent a year of high school in Rennes, France. Following her acceptance to Middlebury College in Vermont, she deferred enrollment for a year in order to live and study in Moscow. At Middlebury, she specialized in French and Russian literature. After receiving her BA, she moved to Maui, Hawaii, working every kind of odd job imaginable, from grant writing and making crêpes to guiding horse trips. Currently she lives in Vermont, but really, you never know.

katherinearden.com
Facebook.com/katherineardenauthor
@arden_katherine
Instagram.com/arden_katherine

sting of hypocrisy. After all, he was the one who filled my head with terrors: wild animals, thorns, sinkholes, bear traps, snakes, and monsters.

Monsters? I'd asked.

Especially monsters, he nodded. *Lynn, we never, ever go in the woods.*

Not even you?

Not even me, peanut.

I almost called out for him, but something about the way he walked with the men caused me to hesitate. Daddy was never in a hurry, his hands usually deep in his pockets, his boots lifting and falling in a routine rhythm. He now seemed to scurry along with the three men, deep into the foliage, all carrying lanterns despite the midafternoon sunlight.

When he had almost disappeared into the green, I threw open the door and followed. Mrs. Ross would have her head thrown back and would be deep into a snore by now anyway.

The rule about the woods was for both of us, Daddy.

Last fall, I brought home a balloon from the Davidson County fair, and the string had slipped from my grasp despite my taffy-coated fingers. I watched it float into the woods and become ensnared in a low-hanging cluster of branches. I could see the bobbing of the purple balloon not far from where I'd stood. I'd called for Daddy to fetch it for me. It couldn't have been more than a yard away. He'd just shook his head and took me by the hand into the house.

I told myself I'd watch him and the men from a distance, enough to know that he was all right. If something happened, I'd go for help. Pretending to be some sort of lookout helped temper the gnawing feeling in my stomach.

After a ten-minute walk, they stopped in a small clearing.

Daddy looked around and motioned to the man in the suit. He pointed to a corner of the grove, and the man hurried over and nodded in grim acknowledgment.

I hid behind the trunk of a maple tree that had squeezed itself into life among the oaks. Squinting, I could not only see what the man was looking at on the ground, but could read what was written upon it. My narrowed eyes widened.

On a count of three, the men lifted the glass canisters above their heads. The two wearing glasses clearly struggled, their doughy triceps trembling in short-sleeved shirts. The man in the suit held his own, as did Daddy. All began to walk, holding the lanterns, peering into the glass intently.

Inside, black spots began to sputter upwards, just as a batch of twigs beneath my uncomfortable shoes betrayed me.

At the sound of the snapping wood and the sight of my blue pleated skirt peeking out from behind the tree, the lantern fell from Daddy's hand, shattering to the forest floor.

I gasped, covering my mouth in a futile attempt to hide myself. I watched as small beetles began to crawl on the large pieces of broken glass now scattered between the men. Ladybugs drunkenly flew in unexpected escape, unsure of what to do with their newfound freedom.

I braced myself, as all children do when their parents' eyes simultaneously become too white and too pinched. Daddy reached me in seconds, his hands gripping my arms with unfamiliar fierceness. "What are you doing?"

He scooped me up and carried me back through the trees. Although my vision bobbed as Daddy's shoulder threatened to crash against my chin, I still saw the men gaping, straining their necks to watch as I was hustled away. Only when the man in the suit kneeled on the ground where Daddy had pointed did the other two tear their gaze from me. The last thing I saw was the man in the suit looking at the forest floor, covering his mouth in shock.

When we were once again on the lawn and free of the trees, Daddy set me down so abruptly I almost bit my tongue. I wanted to run away, frightened by this stranger suddenly embodied by my father.

He slapped me across the face. The same man who, as a single father, learned to paint my toenails, gave funny names to my earlobes, carried a curl of my hair in his wallet, and fluffed my pillow at night. I broke into tears, and I saw his hand tremble, threatening to strike again. Instead, his fingers curved, with only his index finger remaining, pointing up towards the greenhouse roof where, last summer, he had installed the bell that had once hung in the fire hall on Holly Street.

"Never, ever, ever again, do you step foot an inch beyond that bell. You go any further than that bell, Lynn Marie Stanson, and you're as good as dead."

"But you—"

"It doesn't matter what I do! You are never to enter those woods again!"

Tears pooled in my eyes. He leaned in closer, taking my chin roughly between his thumb and fingers. "Don't you know—you go in those woods again and you won't come back. Do you understand me? Do you?"

I nodded repeatedly in his grip, and he hissed at me to get inside the house. I ran and didn't look back.

Even now, decades later, if I stray too close to the woods, I seek out the bell. Even after Daddy died, and Tom and I added three thousand square feet to his house, painted it white and added a wraparound porch where I'd rocked each of my three daughters to sleep. Even after the girls grew up and started their own lives, and the glass from the greenhouse came down, the sign changing from "Bud's Greenhouse" to "The Rose Ped-dler," the bell remained. The contractor we hired to turn the greenhouse into a gardening shop had practically insisted it be removed. He declared the concept Daddy had implemented, of wiring the store phone to the bell so it would ring if a customer needed him while he was tending to his vegetable garden, was unnecessarily outdated. He suggested I have my business calls forwarded to my cell phone if someone was trying to reach me while I was watering the coneflowers and peonies that grew where Daddy's green beans and tomatoes once flourished. I had given my husband a look. "The bell stays," Tom had said to the contractor, with a wink. "My wife hates change."

The two had exchanged knowing glances. I let them be-lieve it.

It is not by chance that boxwoods stand as sentinels around the house, that roses and lilies fight for dominance in my for-mal garden, that hostas rest under four different willow trees, and that the front of the Peddler is flooded with coneflowers and daisies, yet I plant nothing remotely close to the tree line. The blot of red beneath the black shingles, on the verge of the trees, still holds sway.

I am a mother and grandmother, with my seventies on the near horizon. I should have let go of those fears long ago. But in all my life, I never entered the woods again. I may have been jarred that day Daddy hauled me out of the trees, but I know what that man in the wool suit had examined, then lifted from the ground of the clearing. I should have asked—and almost did, several times—but I never could find the courage to ask my father why the gravestone of a child was so deep into the woods.

TWO

The sound of Tom's sleeping kept me awake. It wasn't that he snores, or incoherently mumbles, or twitches under the covers. It was his even breathing, his bottom lip slightly jutted out, that made me want to shake him. Even if I had knocked over our dresser, he would just turn over. *How can you sleep after what you told us—?*

The first ring of the phone was like a jolt of black coffee. I quickly looked over at the clock. Almost midnight. My husband's soft breathing continued, even when it rang a second time. Despite having to make the biggest decision of his life, a decision that will impact generations of our family, and getting an ice-cold silent treatment from me, he proved yet again that he is a champion sleeper. Nothing rattled him, not the cry of a newborn daughter, not our veteran tomcat Voodoo scratching at the door, and obviously not the phone ringing in the middle of the night.

I, however, practically leapt for the phone. Any call this late is most certainly Washington with some sort of crisis. Either that or something was wrong with the girls. I snatched the phone and hit the answer button.

"Mama." Anne's voice was so thin I could hear her straining for oxygen. "We can't find William."

Ten minutes later, Tom and I were hurrying across the damp grass and past the pergola, our flashlights dancing off the pine and oak that lined the perimeter of the yard. Tom reached his hand back for me to take. Instead, I paused at the edge of the woods.

"OK, let's get this over with," he folded his arms across this chest. "Let me have it before we go a step farther."

"Let's not talk about that now."

"You don't want me to accept it, do you?"

"Please, Tom." I squinted, even though it was pitch black.

"William is probably curled up asleep on the dog's bed; the one obvious place neither Anne nor Chris have looked yet. We need to talk about this, Lynn. This would change our entire lives—"

Not our lives. My life. Your life is in Washington. My life is here, with our family, my shop, my house, my garden, and my friends. I don't want to leave any of that. I love my life. I don't love your life.

I sighed. "I'm still in shock about it. But right now, I'm worried about William."

I looked from the trees to the Rose Peddler on the other end of the property. Somewhere in the dark, at the pitch of the roof, the bell watched.

"I'm sure he's fine," Tom said. "But I know William is your favorite—"

"Stop that."

"And he's the one thing that could get you in these woods. We'll find him, and then you and I can have a long debate over waffles and coffee in the morning."

I was grateful when he took my arm. Together, we waded through the treacherous boundary of acorns the size of golf balls. I shined my flashlight on the soggy ground, forcing myself to keep walking despite my pounding heartbeat. *I'm sorry, Daddy.*

Tom held his arms up high to push back any branches. "Now, may I ask, why on earth would William be out here this late at night anyway during a thunderstorm?" he asked. "It poured hard after dinner for a minute"

"I told you, Chris let the older boys camp in the backyard when it looked like the weather might clear. William was upset he couldn't be with them. Anne thinks he opened the back door."

"How many times have I told them to install an alarm system?" he growled.

"Now, don't start on that, you'll only upset them more."

He snapped some twigs away. "I should have had a path put in between the houses a long time ago."

I would have never let you. It couldn't be more than a ten-minute walk through the trees to Anne's house, but no one, especially their boys, was allowed to use the forest as a short cut. Too much poison ivy and wild animals, I repeated to anyone who would listen. Even in the well-populated neighborhoods of west Nashville, swatches of dense forest were not uncommon. Tom occasionally kidded me about my fear of the forest, but stopped when he saw the shade in my glances.

"There, I see their flashlights."

As soon as Anne saw us she rushed over, her face ruddy with tears, speaking in a pitch usually reserved for theater majors. "We can't find him, Mom. We can't find him."

"Anne, are you sure you've checked the house thoroughly?" Tom asked wearily.

"Dad, I'm not overexaggerating!"

"He's here somewhere."

"He's not, he's not." Anne covered her mouth, looking around frantically.

"Where's Chris?" Tom asked.

"He headed off that way, there's his flashlight," Anne pointed. Tom nodded and walked in that direction.

"Explain to me again what happened," I asked.

Anne stifled a sob. "I don't know how William got out of the house, but he was so mad that he couldn't camp with his brothers. Chris has been promising Brian and Greg that they could camp all summer, and after we got back from your house tonight and the phone showed the rain had stopped for a minute, Chris set up their tent. You know he grew up camping, and he said a little rain wasn't going to hurt them. We explained to William that he wasn't old enough yet, and he threw such a fit that I thought he'd cried himself to sleep on the couch. I left him there; you know how he likes to sleep on the downstairs couch. Then Greg came to get me and said William had somehow gotten outside and wanted to get in their tent."

Anne cleared her throat. "Then there was something about them daring William to touch a tree in the forest, and if he did, they'd let him in, so he ran off. It started raining heavier, and when he didn't come right back, Brian followed him in."

"Who is watching the boys?"

"You remember our neighbor Ralph Swift? He's with Greg at the house. And Ralph's new wife, Peggy, is with Brian just over there."

"Brian is out here?" I asked, turning to where Anne motioned.

"He knows he's in big-time trouble, so he's not talking."

"Keep calling for William. Don't stop."

I hurried through the trees towards Brian, the top of his head illuminated by the screen of a phone.

"Thanks for coming, Peggy. I know it's late," I said, kneeling in front of Brian.

"It's no problem at all, Lynn. But I can't get Mr. Brian here to say a word."

Brian's freckled face was drained of color; it was obvious even in just the dim light from Peggy's phone. "Hey, buddy. You aren't in trouble with Nanna, Brian. You were just trying to find your brother. It's OK. Tell Nanna where you last saw William."

Brian said nothing, continuing to vacantly stare as if I, nor anyone else, existed in the world.

"Brian, look at Nanna."

He didn't move, didn't blink.

I looked to Peggy's concerned face and stood up. "Can you stay with him for another minute?"

"Of course," she said, placing her hand on Brian's shoulder.

"William!" I called out, hoping that the sound of my voice would cause William to stop, wherever he was, and call out to me. "William!"

The forest seemed ridiculously large, even though it couldn't be more than a mile in any direction. For heaven's sake, I thought, there was an Exxon not a half-mile away from where the trees ended.

That thought frightened me even more. What if William made it through the forest and to the road . . . ?

"Tom!"

I followed the sound of my husband's booming voice to find him shining a light under a fallen tree. "I'm worried William may have made it to the Harding Road. He's only seven, he could easily get turned around. I'm going to get in the car and drive, see if he's walking. Have you called the police?"

"Chief Stacks is coming with a few of his guys. They know to keep it off the scanners."

I felt a bit of anger flare, but I swallowed it as I hurried back towards the house. What Tom was saying was right. Once it hit the scanners that a boy was missing in Belle Meade in the middle of the night, the overnight photographers from the local stations would be jarred from where they napped in their news cars. Live-broadcast trucks would soon follow.

We'll find him long before that, I promised myself. Feeling my pants pocket, I pulled out the key fob to the Volvo, pushed the button, and saw the headlights flare to life.

I tried not to think about how relieved I felt stepping free of the trees.

When I drove back up the driveway a half hour later, two unmarked squad cars and an old Dodge pickup sat with their headlights on. I pulled up behind and hurried out. The beams from the vehicles shined on Anne frantically talking to one of the officers, who was taking notes and trying to calm her down. When she saw me, she once again burst into tears.

"We're gonna find him, we're gonna find him," I whispered as she collapsed into my arms.

"Ma'am, we're quietly calling in metro police to help comb these woods. If he's here, we'll find him," the officer said.

"If he's here? Of course he's here!" Anne cried out.

I petted her hair. "Shhh, Anne."

"Are you suggesting someone has him? Mom, what if someone was in the woods? What if he got to the road before you, and someone picked him up?" she asked.

"Excuse us, officer." I took Anne aside. "Honey, call your sisters. We need everyone's help. I'm going to get Brian and bring him into the house. He doesn't need to be standing out there."

"He won't talk to the officers, Mom. He won't talk at all. It's like he's in shock."

"Just call your sisters."

At the clearing, I was not surprised to see my daughter Kate had already arrived. She was pacing back and forth, talking on her cell phone in the same suit coat she had worn home from Washington. Tom and Belle Meade's police chief were kneeling in front of Brian, who looked exactly as he did when I left him forty minutes ago.

Kate reached out and gave my arm a squeeze, continuing to talk quietly on her cell. Tom spoke in a low voice at my approach.

"Brian's not speaking. Kate is on the phone with the feds."

He explained volumes in those two brief sentences. He believed Brian was in shock after experiencing something traumatic. And the fact that Kate, who along with being our daughter was the chief of staff in Tom's senatorial office, spoke intently on the phone with Washington meant she was talking to the FBI.

I headed straight for Brian. "I'm taking him to the house. He doesn't need to be out here anymore. Come on, baby."

I scooped him up, knowing he looked comically large in my arms.

"I'll carry him—" Tom began.

"Keep searching. William's here, we just haven't found him yet."

I could feel the heat from Brian's body as I whispered soothing words to him on our way out of the trees. Thankfully, as we reached the yard, I saw that the officer and Anne had returned to the woods. I didn't want her to see me carrying her son like a limp doll.

We entered the house, heading straight for the back rooms

where I kept spare pajamas for all my grandchildren. I quickly found his favorite: a pair of Avengers shorts and a T-shirt. I undressed him and slipped on the pajamas.

We went into the kitchen next, where I poured him a glass of cold milk and handed it to him with an Oreo cookie. He held the cup in one hand and the cookie in the other, continuing to stare, bringing neither to his mouth.

"Let's take them upstairs," I said, relieving him of both, knowing I was moving too fast, that I needed to calm down myself. But instead, I hurried us up the stairs to my bedroom, turning on one small lamp. I peeled back the quilt on my side of the bed and guided Brian inside, kissing his forehead, then rounded the bed, took off my shoes, and climbed onto Tom's rumpled side.

I took a deep breath and gently turned Brian's rigid body towards me, looking directly into his eyes, brushing his hair with my fingers.

"I love you, Brian bear. I want you to go to sleep. But we have to find William. Can you tell me where was the last place you saw him?"

He closed his eyes, and I rested my head on his pillow. His eyelids then slowly drifted open, only for a moment.

"The lights took him," he said softly.

THREE

My hands tested the strength of the ceramic mug as I watched the flashlights move in the trees. I'd come downstairs after Brian had rolled over and refused my repeated questions to explain what he meant about the lights. I'd covered his shoulders with the quilt, even though I was the one who was suddenly cold.

I almost wished to experience Anne's bold and unhinged panic, weeping and crying out William's name. Instead, my fear manifested differently, in horrible thoughts of my grandson, hurt, lying on the floor of the forest, unconscious from tripping, his bright red hair tangled with leaves, unable to alert even the police officer who stood unknowingly a few feet away. Or perhaps he was wandering in some nearby street having long since left the trees, his face flushed in tears, unaware of where home was and why no one had come to find him. In the darkest parts of my mind, I thought of William in the backseat of some stranger's car, a stranger who coaxed him through trees, loaded him into the car with promises of going to see his parents, and was driving him farther away with each passing minute.

I glanced at a sudden series of snaps from one of the outdoor lights on the porch. I expected to see a singed cicada, or perhaps a wounded moth, drifting to earth. Instead, the lantern was nearly covered in a mass of movement.

Ladybugs swarmed the light, popping like kernels in oil. I realized why all the lights were so dim on the porch: All the other lantern sconces were also covered in the beetles.

When I was a little girl, Daddy brought them to the property. Since the beetles were known to kill other plant-eating insects, he purchased hundreds of them through one of his mail-order catalogs. They'd been in the lanterns my father and those men had carried that day in the woods—

The coil on the screen door squeaked. Tom, Chief Jeff Stacks, and another officer walked out. I inhaled sharply at the sudden recognition. Paul Strombino was the metro detective I always saw on the news, with his fierce, full mustache and sunken eyes, the one who was always assigned to investigate the most disturbing crimes in the city.

"I can't get Brian to wake up," Tom said. "I'd forgotten what's it's like to try and rouse an eight-year-old when they're dead asleep. But he has to wake up, Lynnie; he's the last one to see William."

"What, again, did he say to you?" the police chief asked.

I cleared my throat, the words like thorns in my throat. "That the lights took William."

"Could be someone with a flashlight. Or the headlights of a car," the mustached detective said quietly.

"Lynn, this is detective Paul Strombino, with Metro PD," Chief Stacks motioned. "He's the best detective in town, maybe in the entire state."

"Not true, but thanks." The detective nodded in my direction. "I hope I can help, ma'am."

"Thank you for coming," Tom said. "I certainly hope you're not needed."

"I am not an alarmist, Senator. But I do not like the sound of this."

"He's got to be out there."

"I'm sure he is. We just haven't found him yet," the police chief said, his hands on his hips. "We have thirty men in the woods right now. Those trees aren't more than a square mile. We'll find him. And our patrol units are combing the neighborhood. We haven't issued an Amber Alert yet, but your grandson's photo is quietly being distributed throughout all police channels."

"Why would it be quietly sent out?" I asked. "Shouldn't we let as many people know as possible know that he's missing?"

Chief Stacks lowered his gaze and Tom squared his shoulders to me. "Because we have to be smart about this, Lynn. William is in those woods. Or he's wandered somewhere in the neighborhood. If we go sounding the alarm, and he's quickly found, never in harm's way, it will reflect badly upon Chris and Anne."

What you mean is it will reflect badly upon your political career—

A car came tearing up the driveway, squealing its tires as it came to an abrupt halt behind the police cruisers. Our youngest daughter leapt out of her Honda Accord, dropping her cell phone from her ear as she ran towards the house. Stella's hair, usually styled professionally for morning television, was pulled back in a hastily assembled ponytail. "Why didn't anyone call me sooner? Oh my God, Strombino? Why is he here?"

"It's OK, Stella. Detective Strombino is here as a precaution," Tom said.

"No sign of William?" she asked. "I couldn't reach Kate or Anne on their phones."

"They're in the woods with everyone else."

"Where is Greg?" Stella asked.

"Anne just checked on him. He's asleep at her house with the neighbor watching him."

"Oh my God, William," Stella bit her lip.

"Go, Stella, we're right behind you," I waved her on.

"Do I need to call the TV station? Get William's picture out?" she asked.

"No, not yet," Tom responded. "Go to your sisters, Stella."

Stella dashed across the lawn with the speed of the former track star she was in college.

"Let's all go," Tom took my hand. "We all need to keep searching."

"Brian shouldn't be up there alone."

"There's an officer stationed here," Chief Stacks motioned upstairs.

"Come on, Lynn." Tom tugged at my hand.

I swallowed, looking up at the bedroom window. I still wasn't convinced Brian was sleeping.

Once, when we were teenagers, my best friend, Roxy, stole some cigarettes. We snuck off towards the tree line with them when Daddy saw us from the nursery. "Lynn Stanson! Roxanne Garth! You take one more step and you'll wish the only trouble you were in was because of those smokes!"

I remember tilting my head, a rare flash, especially for me, of teenage defiance. But I saw Daddy approach with all the intensity of a bull, and I snatched Roxy's hand and dragged her back to the house. I'd glanced over my shoulder at Daddy, but he wasn't looking at us anymore. He was staring into the woods.

I should have asked you then. I should have made you tell me what happened that afternoon. Why those men wanted to go to that clearing with the gravestone. It was a gravestone—a child's grave-stone. I know what I saw. Why did they carry lanterns with ladybugs inside? There was so much I wanted to ask you, but I didn't learn to only fear the woods that day.

After Daddy died, and Tom and I moved into and remod-eled his house for our growing family, I made sure to read fairy tales to my girls of haunted forests where witches lived and children got lost. I routinely emphasized Lyme disease, and I sighed with relief when Anne declared she wasn't the nature type—and her younger siblings were thankfully in the throes of older sister worship.

But decades later, it was the grandkids who salivated for the woods. When Tom finally succumbed to years of whining, he tried to sneak them out back. I saw them through the dining-room window and came out blazing from the kitchen.

Poison ivy! Chiggers! Ticks! Underground caves! Old bear traps! I tried to remember every line my father used on me. I held back on telling them about the monsters. They would have laughed, and I would have lost ground. Instead, I got a lot of groans, but ultimately the sad parade marched back in the house, with my husband shaking his head.

But there was nothing I could do to keep Anne's boys from entering the woods from their own property. I knew Chris and Anne were wishing they had heeded my warnings, considered, up until this point, unwarranted. I had seen my son-in-law briefly in the last hour, and I wanted to grab his arm, tell him everything was going to be all right, that we would find his son. But Chris's face was so full of despair I let him go. His voice was already growing hoarse.

I tried to banish the thought of William unconscious, dirt smeared over his sweet face, lying on the ground. He's wan-dered off, I told myself. He's asleep on someone's screened-in porch. There are so many sprawling properties out here, mansions and estates filled with gardens and guesthouses and pergolas. Country-music executives, lawyers, doctors, and a few celebrities were our neighbors. There were so many places for William to go.

My phone began to vibrate again. Stella's name came up on the screen.

"Mom, my overnight assignment editor called. I let it go to voice mail. They know something is going on; the cops are everywhere. It's only a matter of time. I'm not returning the call. Dad needs to know it's started."

"I'll tell your dad. Keep looking."

"Mom." Stella's voice quieted. "Has Dad had the cops run the addresses of the registered sex offenders in the neighborhood?"

"Stella, there are no registered sex offenders around here."

"Mom, there are registered sex offenders in every zip code in the city. We have to think about these things. I'll find out myself if I have to."

"Keep looking, Stella."

I hung up and saw Chris's face among the flashing lights in the clearing, his fingers laced behind his head.

I hurried over. "Chris, where's Tom?"

"It's my fault, Lynn. I shouldn't have let them camp out tonight. Especially with rain still in the forecast. Will was so upset, he cried himself to sleep. I should have brought them all inside, if only to calm William down."

"Chris, I don't want to hear you say that again. No one is to blame. We will find him. Where is Tom?"

"I'm here," Tom said, walking up with Detective Strombino.

"Stella called. Her station knows something is happening.

She says she won't return their call. But they'll figure it out. They may already have cameras outside."

Tom whipped out his phone, turning his back to us.

I looked to the detective. "Has he told you yet?"

Strombino paused, and Tom looked back at me. He whispered a few more words and jammed the phone into his pocket. "Lynn, this isn't the time."

"Tom, these detectives need to know everything."

"Lynn, I will handle this."

Before I lowered my chin, I saw Strombino look at us, obviously uncomfortable in the simmering air.

"I'm not sure what the two of you are talking about, but I advise you to go public. The first twenty-four hours a child goes missing are crucial, and yours has already been gone for roughly two. I don't want to rattle off the statistics of how many children are actually found after that twenty-four-hour window closes—it ain't pretty. The longer this goes on, the more concerned I'm becoming about what your other grandson said. Lights don't take children—people holding flashlights or driving cars with headlights take children."

No, Detective. My throat was suddenly so tight I couldn't have spoken if I wanted to. *Not always.*

"I just ordered my staff to reach out to the TV stations, the papers and the radio stations, and to get it on social media. We need the most recent photo of William possible. But no news conference yet. Only that our grandson is lost in the woods," Tom said.

I almost didn't hear my husband; I was so alarmed by what Strombino had said about the lights.

It can't be. After all this time . . . it cannot be.

"Find a recent picture and send it out with the alert," Strombino suggested.

"We have the family picture on my dresser, but William was only a baby," Tom said. He then snapped his fingers. "Get the magazine cover. It has a huge picture of William."

"The boy was on the cover of a magazine?" Strombino asked, and then cleared his throat. "Get that photo out now."

AP NEWS ALERT—NASHVILLE, TENN.

The seven-year-old grandson of U.S. Senator Thomas Roseworth is missing and a massive search is underway in the woods directly behind the Tennessee lawmaker's home.

The metro police department confirmed the identity of the boy as William Thomas Chance, the youngest grandson of Roseworth.

Police said Chance was last seen Friday night entering the woods.

William Chance is the son of Roseworth's oldest daughter, Anne, who lives on the other side of the wooded area behind the Senator's home in Nashville.

The neighborhood is known for the estates of other prominent politicians, including Al Gore.

Chance was recently appeared on the cover of *Southern Living*, for an article profiling the home and garden shop of Roseworth's wife, Lynn.

Senator Roseworth is in Nashville to help in the search.

—*Copyright Associated Press*

"The lights took him."

I awoke to Brian's words, the last memory of a disturbing dream. I lay in a pool of morning sunlight, already hot from the August sun.

I slid out of bed, almost stumbling in my haste. I'd come up to check on Brian and found him tossing, so I sat down to pat his back as I had when he was a toddler with the croup. I'd lain down for only a moment.

How could I have done that, knowing William was out there somewhere? And if it was because of the magazine, it was all my fault.

I'd known, even then, the cover had been a terrible idea. A freelance writer for *Southern Living* had showed up early one morning in early spring, gushing about the store, my garden, and the house. I declined an interview and repeated over and over again that there was nothing special about any of it. Roxy, who managed the shop with me and had not had her coffee yet, wordlessly led the writer outside, took me by the hand out the front door, promptly went back inside herself, locked the doors to the building, told me through the glass to enjoy the early May heat wave, and to come back in the air conditioning when the interview was done.

After conferring with Tom, I consented. I had to admit, the end result had been a beautiful spread on the Peddler and the garden.

The writer thought the garden might make the cover, but none of us expected the photograph that was ultimately chosen. William had been corralled along with his brothers to the front lawn while the photographs were taken, but he had begged his mother for sweet tea after a while, and Anne had snuck him into the house. As they exited, the photographer cried out for silence (mainly directed towards Roxy), and snuck up on the little red-haired boy wearing only overalls carrying a glass of sugar-drenched tea, wandering through the garden. The end photograph was William looking back towards the camera, surrounded by calla lilies.

I should have been thrilled by all of it. But I could barely look at the magazine; horrified by the customers who asked me to sign it, inquiring if Tom knew how famous his wife was now.

With a quick glance at Brian to confirm he was still sleeping, I bolted across the bedroom and hurried down the stairs while hugging the rail like a car driving too fast on a curve.

The stairs led to a hallway off the kitchen, and the first person I saw was Tom, leaning on the counter and intently checking his phone.

"Was it all orchestrated?" I said, startled at the volume of my own voice.

I then saw the police officers crowded around maps on the kitchen table, with Kate in the center. By the refrigerator, two men in suits stopped their conversation with Detective Strombino.

Kate moved around the table quickly. Tom put away his phone. "Lynn—"

I waited till he was near enough for him to hear my whisper. "Your operatives, did they send that writer to the shop? Was that all part of some campaign?"

"What?"

"It's true, isn't it? The magazine cover. The profile of our family. It wasn't by chance that writer came. And now William is gone. How could you let me sleep?"

"It's only been an hour, Lynnie. Honestly, I didn't even know you were up there until about thirty minutes ago, when I couldn't find you—"

"I don't need to sleep. I need to know if that's how William ended up on that cover."

"What you need to do is calm down and not make a scene." He stepped in close.

"I have never made a scene in all my life."

Kate rubbed my arm. "Mom—"

"Where is Anne? I need to see her." I felt delirious from the swell of anger and exhaustion.

"Stella made her lie down in the back room. She's asleep, finally, and so is Stella, beside her. I think Stella strongly suggested she take a Xanax," Kate said.

"Then who's out searching?"

"Seems like half the police department," Kate looked out the window. "We came in to look at some of the geological maps in better light. We're all about to go out again. Roxy is here."

I walked past them and the police officers, heading out the screen door. I knew neither Tom nor Kate would follow.

I instantly heard Roxy's voice as I moved across the dewy grass that would soon become bone dry in the oppressive heat.

She was railing into her phone, which was barely visible amidst her mess of black hair streaked heavily with gray. She wore a white T-shirt with a Beethoven face, his eyes peering out from beneath her denim vest. There was some kind of embroidered flower on both the vest and her matching shorts. She slipped her feet in and out of her Birkenstock flip-flops.

"Get your ass over here, Rick. I'm calling the entire garden club. We're all going to help in the search. See you in a minute," Roxy said. She turned to see me walking across the grass.

"They can't find him."

"Don't start saying that." She pulled me close and patted the curls on the back of my head, just as she had done when Marty Throw broke up with me before the eighth-grade Sweetheart Banquet. Those same hands would later punch him in the gut in the alley behind the gym. "He's gonna turn up any second now."

"I wanted to call you, but I kept telling myself we would find him by now."

"You should have. I've already told the cops they need as many trusted volunteers as possible to comb the woods and the neighborhood. So I've already called the sewing group, the garden club, and the Roseworth Democrats, and they're all headed this way. I'm going to the shop to make coffee for everyone, then I told the cops I'd screen all the people showing up, to make sure no media types get in. No offense to Stella."

"I keep thinking about William, hurt out there or in some stranger's car—"

"Don't go there yet, Lynn."

"I have to get it together," I rubbed my face. "I tore into Tom about that damn magazine article."

"I doubt very much you tore into him. In fact, you haven't raised your voice to him in decades."

"If I wasn't so afraid, all I would be is angry. Let's just say we learned last night that the magazine was coinciding with a big announcement Tom would like to make."

Ever active in the Democratic Party, Roxy raised her eyebrows. But she quickly shook her head. "Go wash your face and change your clothes. Then get back out here. We'll find him, Lynn. Look at me. We'll find him."

I nodded once and turned back to the house. As soon as I began to hurry away, I heard Roxy once more on the phone. I could still hear her as I crossed the porch and entered the kitchen.

Kate and Tom were standing and talking to Detective Strombino, their arms identically crossed in front of their chests. The two men in suits were looking at a laptop computer and conferring with the police officers.

Kate approached me. "They're FBI."

"Strombino thinks he's been kidnapped, doesn't he?"

"He's not said that yet."

"That's what he thinks. That's why you've called in the FBI. Kate, you have to tell them about—"

A scream came from upstairs.

I scrambled up the stairs, everyone else in my wake. One of the officers said something about letting him go first, but I ignored him and pushed open the bedroom door.

Brian was sitting upright on the bed. Barely audible under his screaming was the sound of static coming from the television in the open armoire. I'd forgotten to turn off the alarm. The television was programmed to turn on automatically at 5:30 A.M. Instead of HGTV, all that buzzed was a grainy white-and-black screen.

"Baby, it's OK, it's OK," I swept him into my arms. "Tom, turn off the TV."

Tom scrambled for the remote. Brian continued screaming as I rocked him. Finally, Tom found the device and the TV went dark.

My grandson immediately stopped crying, but continued to stare at the screen.

"It's OK, it just scared him," I said. The cops and the FBI agents looked around the room to make sure. Tom came over to the bed and sat down, patting Brian's back.

"Hey buddy. You're OK. You got spooked."

"Must have been a power surge last night," Kate rubbed her eyes. "All the clocks in the house are blinking."

"He's asleep again," Tom noted.

I looked down to see Brian solidly passed out. I laid him down, brushing his hair from his forehead.

"We really need to talk to him," Detective Strombino said quietly from the hallway.

"Lynn, we have to wake him up."

"Not until one of his parents is here. Kate, go get Chris. Let Anne sleep."

I continued to stroke Brian's hair as the minutes dragged on. The clock in the room ticked irritatingly loud. Tom stood by the window and looked out at the large gathering of volunteers and police.

"You told them, didn't you?" I asked. "That's why the FBI is here. That's why you didn't tell me I was wrong about the article. They know, don't they?"

He kept staring. I buried my nose in Brian's hair.

"They know what?" Chris asked, wearily walking in, with Kate and Strombino behind him.

"About what I told everybody last night." Tom looked out the window. "The agents know what that means—"

Chris sat on the bed and put his arm under Brian, a little rougher than I would have liked. "Wake up, son. You've got to wake up."

I couldn't watch, hearing the frustration and desperation in his voice. I also feared that if he successfully woke Brian, the boy's only response would be a dense stare.

"You think this is all connected?" Chris asked.

My husband waited a moment before answering. "When you agree to run for vice president, you make a lot of enemies overnight."

FOUR

"Mom, are you with me?"

As my youngest daughter leaned in closer to apply a heavy coating of concealer under my eyes, I realized how haggard even she looked in the bright lights of the makeup mirror, although her face was void of wrinkles and age spots.

"If I can make myself look awake at four in the morning to read about car wrecks and shootings on TV, then I can surely make it seem like you haven't been awake for twenty-four hours," Stella said.

"I did sleep for a while. They shouldn't have let me sleep."

"Mom, you were probably asleep for fifteen minutes. You need to rest. You're going to bed right after the news conference—"

"I will not do it, Stella. I told your father that, and I told Kate that. I cannot do it. I am in no shape for it. The only reason I am sitting here now is because you practically strong-armed me. I should be out looking for him."

Stella put the makeup brush on the bathroom counter. "One thousand people, including members of the National Guard, combed over every foot of the woods. It's not that big of an area. Every house in the near vicinity has been searched. William is not in the woods. He is not in the neighborhood. You have to realize that. We have to reach a wider audience."

"I can't do it."

"Yes, you can. You've done a million election nights."

And I had hated every one. Sitting nervously in the room at the Hermitage Hotel watching the results come in, Tom pacing even though he knew he was a shoo-in every time. The Washington staff flown in for the election, complaining about the slow pace of the servers in the restaurants and checking their cell phones frantically.

"You have to do it, Mom. For Anne, Chris, for William. For Dad. It will be hard enough as it is for him to make the statement. All you have to do is stand beside him and hold that picture of William."

"I will start crying."

"You're not a big crier. You know that. I'm the same way. So is Kate. Anne got all the waterworks genes. You stand up there and know that what you're doing is getting William's picture out all over the country. It's urgent that we do this now. This news conference will be carried by every cable channel and will be in every paper in the morning. It will be the top story on every news website and will be all over social media— Twitter, Facebook. There is no place in the world that won't know he's missing. It will bring him home."

I looked down. "How much time do we have?"

"About ten minutes. But we should go down. All the stations in town will be taking the news conference live at the top of the six o'clock news. That's good, Mom. Most people will be home from work, if they work on Saturdays. And it's so hot tonight most people will be indoors. It's the best exposure you can get. And we need the exposure. Pretty soon, William will be missing for twenty-four hours. And you heard what Strombino said about that."

I looked back in the mirror, horrified at the yellow tint of my skin in comparison to my white shirt. My cheeks looked sunken, my eyes dark.

"Come on." Stella pulled on my hand softly.

I took my hand back gently to indicate I was fine to walk on my own. As soon as we walked down to the kitchen, I heard the screen door snap, and Kate was there, wearing a dark business suit. "Are you ready, Mom?"

I left the mug, thinking the caffeine might make me even more jittery. *If that were possible.*

The screen door exited to the north end of the wraparound porch. Tom, smoking a cigarette, paced beneath large Kimberly ferns. Another man and a woman, also smoking, stood nearby.

"Lynn, this is Tony and Deanna from the Washington office, they both just flew in." He quickly snuffed out the cigarette. "Tony, Deanna, this is my wife, Lynn, and my youngest daughter, Stella. You remember, Lynn, that Tony works with Kate in our press office. Deanna is kind of a surprise; I didn't know she was joining us. This is her first day. Some hell of a first day," Tom said, straightening his tie.

"I'm so sorry for all this," Deanna said, trying to hide the cigarette in her own hand.

Stella walked over and stopped her father's efforts, taking the tie into her own hands. He thanked her quietly.

Kate rounded the corner of the porch, motioning for us all to follow. Tom walked over and took my hand.

"My wife isn't a fan of the cameras. Or any attention, for that matter."

"I'll be fine," I replied, so softly only he could hear me.

"Oh Mom, wait." Stella rushed back into the house. She

appeared seconds later, holding a large framed photo of William's magazine cover.

"Oh my God, I almost forgot."

As we crossed across the porch, the woods beyond seemed to vibrate in the summer haze.

The lights took him, Brian had said.

You know you've heard it before.

My family called my mind a steel trap. I remember the ever-changing shoe sizes of my grandsons, how much aluminum to add or subtract in soil to change the color of a hydrangea, the names of quilt patterns. I am everybody's first choice on teams for Trivial Pursuit. Roxy commented she would give me psychedelic drugs if it meant I would stop recalling the time she admitted she found George W. Bush attractive.

How long can I pretend I haven't heard it?

Live-feed vans and satellite trucks, with tall masts and enormous dishes, lined the street in front of the house. I scanned the call letters on all the trucks, failing to recognize several of the stations, which had come from all over the state. Some of the larger trucks had no writing at all, which, I remembered from Tom's election nights, meant they were local production companies hired by the networks.

From the trucks rolled long black cables, stretching across the yard like snakes, leading to the sea of cameras standing in a row. It felt as if we were approaching a firing squad.

Tom gripped my hand and led us towards the microphone stand, a silver rod where more than a dozen mic flags were fastened, decorated with garish colors and numbers. Standing among the cameras were reporters, armed with notebooks. I could hear several of them talking, broadcasting live off the top of the six o'clock news.

". . . Marcus, Senator Roseworth is now approaching the microphone . . ."

". . . I can see his wife and two of his daughters with him . . ."

". . . One of them is Channel Four's own Stella Roseworth, who is obviously taking some time off to be with her family . . ."

". . . It doesn't appear the parents of the missing boy are here, and none of the other grandchildren are here, including the one we're told who last saw William Chance . . ."

". . . Let's listen in and see what the senator says."

Tom stopped before the microphones, squinting in the brilliant last light of day.

"On behalf of my wife, Lynn, our children, and our grandchildren, I want to thank you all for coming here tonight. And thank you to all the volunteers and police officers who have helped us try to find our William."

The lights took him.

Of course I remember. But I didn't even dare mention what I suspected; I just hoped we'd find him by now. We all just need to focus on alerting everyone to his disappearance—that's what matters now.

"As you all know, my youngest grandson disappeared in these woods late last evening. We have combed every inch of the area, spoken with all our neighbors, and there is simply no sign of him. We have no other choice but to assume he has somehow been taken."

The lights took him.

I can't tell them now. They'll think I'm hallucinating. Tom will rush me to the hospital, fearing I've had a stroke.

"We are asking everyone watching to take a good look at our boy. Our William. He is everything to us. His momma misses him, his daddy misses him, his brothers miss him, and his grandpa and nanna really miss him. He's our baby boy, our

Will, and we need all your help to find him and bring him home."

Like fireflies in evening shadows, the lights on top of the cameras started to glow. The sun had faded behind some powerful clouds, and the photographers scrambled to keep enough light on our family. The satellite truck operators turned on the large lights on stands that stood behind the row of cameras, to light both the press conference and the reporters who would soon turn back to the cameras to repeat what had just been stated. The lights bathed my family in white, causing my eyes to flare.

The lights took him.

With that, I admitted to myself what I'd worked so hard to bury. There was no use denying it.

William had been taken, just like all the others.

FIVE

I walked into the kitchen, pulled my sunglasses from the tangles in my hair, and glanced out the windows above our banquette. The purse that I intended to set on the counter slid off my shoulder and landed with a thud on the floor, and the keys I always carefully put in the drawer under the microwave crashed to the floor with it.

The window provided a wide view of the satellite trucks that had doubled, maybe tripled in number since I left that morning. The monstrous vehicles now appeared to line both sides of Evelyn Avenue. More photographers had arrived to stand on our side lawn, their lenses following investigators walking in and out of the woods. Heavy traffic prevented the trucks from parking on Harding Road, which is why I'd taken it when I'd returned a few minutes ago, fearing but not fully comprehending the chaos surrounding our home.

I should have known when I'd driven to Anne's before eight and found another crop of cameras waiting to document me hurrying into their house. I had never been so thankful that she drove a Subaru with tinted windows, so we could pull out of the garage and none of the cameras could get footage of Brian in the backseat.

I heard Tom's footsteps approach from the other room. He always scuffed his feet when he was anxious.

"Has Brian spoken yet?"

I wrinkled my nose. "Please don't smoke in the house."

"I was in the study with the door closed. And who the hell cares at this point, Lynn? How is Brian?"

"I care, Tom, because Ginger Roth from church died from lung cancer last year."

"Tell me about the doctor. Did he get Brian to talk?"

"No, Tom, he didn't. He wants Brian to come every day and do some experimental therapy to hopefully open him up to discuss what happened. But he thinks the same thing the police think: that whatever Brian saw stunned him into silence."

"Experimental therapy? My God, we don't have time for experiments. It's been almost twenty-four hours, Lynn. You heard what the detectives said. Every minute that passes means our chance of finding William diminishes. Brian needs to talk. He's the only one with answers. I should have gone."

His used that tone primarily when he was in Washington, with everyone from his staffers to Republican adversaries. It indicated that he knew everything about which he spoke. There was no room for debate.

"If you had gone, you would have ended up in a shouting match with the doctor. So no, Tom, you shouldn't have gone. I know you want this to end—"

"So I can get back to Washington and the VP offer? That's not true, Lynn."

"I didn't say that."

"But you were thinking it."

"This is my fault. I'm the one who allowed that photo-

grapher to take his picture and put it on the cover of that magazine. My God, what was I thinking? I just wished I'd known
the truth."

"If this magazine had anything to do with William's disappearance, I will live with that for the rest of my life. It's not
your fault. It's nobody's fault but my own. It was my idea. Even
Kate didn't know. I didn't think it would do any harm. I keep
saying it, over and over again. I know the agents are tired of
hearing me say it."

"But if you'd just told us about the formal offer to run for
vice president the night William disappeared, how could anyone else have known?"

"It's the worst-kept secret in Washington. And the FBI does
not hesitate to point out that you could fill a phone book with
the names of the people who hate me."

I actually sat in during the first meeting with the investigators from the government and local police, but became so upset
I had to leave in the middle of it. When the vice agents began to
talk about the desire of pedophiles, I couldn't hear anymore.

The likely culprit was someone who had staked out the
family, the investigators believed. It was no random act. Someone either had become fascinated with William from the article,
or wanted the deepest revenge possible on my husband.

"Could someone hate you that much?"

Tom's face took on a weary look. "Shall I begin stateside or
overseas?"

"I can't believe someone in the United States would do this
for political reasons."

"I never thought it was possible either, Lynn. I still can't
fathom it. But people are so angry now, they are so fired up by
the pundits on both sides . . . All it would take is one crazy
zealot who listened to one of the conservative commentators

call me an enemy of the state. The FBI played it back to me, a recording of what's-his-name, the bigheaded guy, looking at the screen, pointing. 'Take back your country. Do whatever you have to do stop Roseworth and his liberal agenda. Don't let him into the White House. Do whatever you have to do.' All it would take is one nut job to come up with the idea to hurt my family. Because that's about the only thing that would cause me to turn my back on politics forever. They know that."

"This certainly can't be an act of terrorism."

Tom twitched his lips. It meant he was craving a cigarette.

"Terrorism . . . do they really think . . . ?"

"It's been tense in DC. It's by design that I don't bring you or the kids there anymore. I have almost constant security now."

"Since when?"

"Since I started coming down hardcore on needing more ground troops in the Middle East. I knew it would be controversial when a Democrat called for it, but I didn't expect to become public enemy number one. ISIS obviously hasn't taken responsibility for William—that would have been plastered all over the internet. But domestic terrorism is a different story. We've seen what these extremists have done. It's all about seeking revenge. And there've been no calls, no letters, nothing demanding a ransom for William. I've had every theory thrown out to me by either the CIA or the FBI, and I get a real feeling they don't know a damn thing."

The lights. Tell him about the lights. What you heard, what you did all those years ago.

Instead, I nearly threw up, something I'd never done in my life, despite living through countless stomach flus with the girls. I hadn't even vomited with Anne, my only girl who had prompted late-term morning sickness. Anne's pregnancy had been so different than the others. . . .

"Lynn, listen to me." Tom placed his hands on my shoulders, leaning in close. "I need you. I need you to be the person you've always been for us. We need you to be solid, to be unwavering, to be calm. No more outbursts like the other morning, asking if the magazine spread was a setup. I can't have you acting like that. Anne and Chris need you to be supportive and encouraging. Brian and Greg need their grandmother to be loving, not frazzled. Greg especially is having a hard time. Being nine-years-old and having one brother missing and the other refusing to talk is weighing heavily on him. Kate and Stella are tough, but they need their mother too. And I . . . I need my rock. The person I can depend on for everything."

He pulled me into a tight embrace.

And with that, I decided to keep lying.

It was Roxy who broke me free. Leaving the house wasn't an option, with investigators and police still combing the woods, and Tom receiving hourly updates on no potential leads. All this meant there was no way to avoid the cameras, the calls from earnest-sounding producers from the *Today Show* and *Good Morning America*, the neighbors bringing food and insisting they were refusing all sorts of financial offers from the tabloids to gain access to a better view of our house.

Roxy showed up late in the evening. She scowled at the photographers who'd flicked on their lights to capture her arrival in her pickup truck, took one look at me pacing in the kitchen, and ushered me out the back door towards the Rose Peddler.

Our garden shop was already closed on Sunday anyway,

but she'd made a sign that read "Closed Indefinitely. This means you, *National Enquirer*."

As Roxy unlocked the door, the familiar smell of the lavender candles and fertilizer brought the first moment of peace I'd had since Anne's frantic phone call two days ago. I inhaled deeply as she led me out to the back to the small screened-in porch we added on a few years ago as a place for me to read magazines and for Roxy to drink margaritas after a long day.

"No one can see you here. No reporters, no investigators, no husband or children. Turn on Nina while I pour the tequila."

"My God, Roxy, I can't do this. What if the police find something, what if Anne needs me, and I certainly can't have alcohol—"

"Sister, that tequila is for me. I wouldn't waste it on you, you're drunk off half a glass of wine. And you know as well as I do that your phone is in your pocket set on the loudest ringtone possible. Tom saw me haul you out, he knows where you are. We need to talk, and we need to do it in private. And your house happens to be crawling with the FBI at this moment. Simone. Now."

I reached over and pushed play on the ancient, yellow CD player. The piano rift that began "I Want a Little Sugar In My Bowl" was barely audible above the cicadas outside. As Nina Simone began to sing about her heartbreaking longing, Roxy returned from the mini refrigerator with a margarita in a pouch, something she routinely stocked up on at the liquor store.

"Now." Roxy took a long swig. "Tell me everything."

"There's nothing to tell. No leads. No ransom notes. No threats. No homegrown terrorist taking credit. All the sex offenders in a twenty-mile radius have been questioned and their homes searched. Now—as Chief Stacks warned us—the attention is turning to us."

"To you?"

"To the family. You can't imagine how awful it is. Here are Chris and Anne, in the midst of the worst moment of their lives, having to answer the most awful questions. They asked Anne if Chris is abusing the boys. Not only physically, but sexually. She almost hyperventilated, especially when they said they'd tracked down her old fiancé from college, who claimed that Tom was mentally abusive to all of us."

"He said that because Tom told him at Thanksgiving dinner that he doubted the punk would ever make more than $12,000 a year." Roxy raised her index finger before taking a drink. "But regardless, how terrible."

"And they just circle the boys. They try to talk to Brian, who only sits in his chair and stares. I sat in when they interviewed Greg, and they asked him if he was ever afraid of his mom and dad. He looked at me and Tom in confusion and answered yes. You should have seen the FBI agent stiffen, and when they asked Greg why, he promptly told the story of when the dog pooped in the house, and he used the robot vacuum to try and pick it up, and it spread feces all over the upstairs carpets."

"He should have been afraid after that. That poor boy."

"And they know everything. All the times Chris has been sued by unhappy clients, when Brian was suspended from school for a day for bringing a pocketknife, what Anne posted on Facebook about her anger at people who complain about public breast-feeding. About that weirdo from Antioch who kept sending Stella those love letters at the TV station, demanding she friend him on Facebook. Anything—anything at all to indicate problems with our family, or who would hate us."

"Oh Sis, I'm so sorry. And it probably took them thirty

seconds to interview you. You have no enemies and you've never made anyone mad, except for me—those pastel garden hats we wore at my wedding were your idea. You may have put off a few of your fellow English students in college when you critiqued their awful short stories, but that's it. You're as noncontroversial as anyone could possibly be."

At that moment, I wanted to take the pouch from her and drain it dry. *You've been my best friend all my life, and even you don't know what happened.*

Roxy took another long drink. A wasp darted above us. Somewhere nearby, a lawnmower from one of the yard services roared to life.

"No family can survive this."

"Don't say that."

"We won't. We can't. Who could? We can't have Christmas. We can't have birthdays. How can you celebrate anything when you know he's out there? How will we ever recover? How can we go on without him?"

"You'll recover when William comes back. They will find him, Lynn."

"How? How can they find him? What if they don't know what they're doing? What they're even looking for?"

"Lynn, this is the FBI. That's what they do."

"What if they don't know? I'm so afraid they don't know."

"I know you are. We're all afraid. What do you think they don't know?"

I rocked instead of answering, and I knew Roxy understood what that meant, just like she knew what it signaled when I ate chocolate at midnight or crunched ice after watching Matthew Crawley on my DVD box set of *Downton Abbey*. When I rocked, it meant I was trying to work something out.

"Do you remember my father not allowing me to go into the woods?"

"Hmmm?" Roxy leaned back, folding her arms, a nap rapidly approaching. Ever since we were teenagers, it only took a little bit of alcohol to put her right to sleep.

"He absolutely forbid it when I was growing up. Once he told me that when you go into the woods, you don't come out."

"Your father was the sweetest and most overprotective man I ever knew. You were his only child. He raised you as a single father after your mom died so young. And let us not forget that he almost lost you too."

I reached up and let my fingers trace the back of my head, just behind my right ear. I was five when Daddy said the doctors discovered the brain tumor and insisted it be removed, even if the risks were great. My very first memory was waking up and seeing a man smiling at me. I asked who he was, and he barely could manage to say, "Your Daddy."

Some parents would have crumbled, but Daddy soldiered on and taught me everything about my life before the procedure, repeatedly showing me pictures of my mother to try and prompt me to remember her, which I never did. When I returned to school the next year, my friends (none of whom I remembered either) thought I'd moved away. Nashville was a lot smaller then. Daddy bragged to my teacher that I relearned to read in a week, and I was probably too advanced for kindergarten, but the school made me repeat the grade. Twelve years later, I graduated at the top of my class. In every picture from graduation, Daddy had tears in his eyes.

"He adored you. He didn't even want you riding in the car with me when I got my license, which, in retrospect, was a real concern. But honestly, do you think your dad could have foreseen this? Because that's impossible. I know you're running over every possibility in your mind. Don't torture yourself."

"Was that it, then? Him being overprotective?"

"Mmm hmmm." Roxy spoke in almost a hum.

"Maybe he was just being a helicopter dad. Remember when I came home from Illinois even though it was Tom's last semester in law school, because I was determined to have my first baby in Tennessee? Daddy never even told me how sick he was. When I was up north, he refused to let me come home and visit, saying that I needed to stay and support Tom in his last year. Even when I told him over the phone I was pregnant, he said I needed to start a new life there. I didn't even tell him I was coming home, and when I did, he had practically wasted away. He couldn't speak, write, or even eat on his own. All that time, he was protecting me from the truth about how sick he was."

I looked over to say more and saw Roxy's mouth was open enough for a soft snore to escape; her glasses had slipped down her nose. The tequila had kicked in.

"And do you know what else?" A hot wind blew through the trees, and I watched the leaves stir. "Do you know just before he died, he did speak to me? Only once. He said, 'Don't you raise that baby here, Lynnie. You go, and you never come back.' What did he mean by that?"

Roxy's chest rose and fell.

"I want to tell you." *I want to tell you everything. But once that door is opened, it can never be closed. And you would immediately begin to worry that I'd lost my mind.*

"What's that?" Roxy mumbled. "What . . . did you say?"

"Nothing." I took the pouch from her hand, placed it on the floor, and continued to rock. "I didn't say anything at all."

SIX

OCTOBER

I could feel the encroachment of night, even though daylight saving time hadn't officially ended. The only solace to the early dark was that I could go to bed a little earlier each evening, pull up the quilts, and close my eyes. On this night, though, sleep had other plans.

I thought of Kate talking in hushed tones on her cell phone in the corner of the kitchen, on the rare weekends she was home from Washington. She had twice now booked earlier flights to return to the capital.

Of Stella's resignation from the anchor desk and her agreement with her news director to take a pay cut to join the investigative unit. How she held the mic like a weapon on the six o'clock news tonight, thrusting it in the face of a minister who took money from his congregation then promptly closed the church and purchased two sports cars and a boat. "I need to nail some bad guys," Stella said quietly last week, over lunch.

Of Anne, who slept away much of the day. Of Chris's leave of absence from the law firm, spending his days poring over information on sex offenders in Nashville and pacing through the woods.

Of the alarm going off at 6:00 A.M., so I could be at Anne's house by 6:30 to get Greg ready for school. Of 3:15, when I picked him up, took him home, and peppered him with questions about school. *Don't you think you should rejoin scouts? Don't you think you should get back into flag football?* He preferred to sit in front of the Cartoon Network instead. I didn't mind. That programming was never interrupted with news updates, which occasionally pertained to our family.

Of Brian, vacant and wooden, staring out the window of the psychiatrist's office, refusing to engage with the doctor or anyone else. He was unresponsive at school, so Chris and Anne had to pull him out and hired a tutor to come to the house to try and work with him. Yet every day I brought Greg home, the tutor only shook her head. Chris had flown into a rage on Monday, screaming at Brian to tell them what he saw. Brian had gone into his room and laid on top of his bed. I hurried in, hoping to find him crying. His eyes were dry.

Of Tom's absence from the neighborhood Labor Day parade, which just last year he, Brian, Greg, and William had led, the boys tossing candy from Tom's 1990 soft-top Jeep Wrangler. How he disappeared into his library to stare at a photograph of the four of them, each holding a Jolly Rancher in their teeth and grinning like hyenas. He emerged smelling like smoke and whiskey.

Of our family's offer of $500,000 for any information that led to the safe return of our grandson. Of the hundreds of false leads that followed.

Of the flowers in the garden that I had abandoned at the end of the brutal summer. I felt like I had done the same to

William, in denying that I remembered where I had first heard the words.

The lights took him.

I have a difficult relationship with memories. I still remember how it felt to be five and know nothing. How I stiffened when Daddy went to hug me, until I was convinced he was, indeed, my father. My hesitantance to eat broccoli until I believed what Daddy had told me, that I did in fact love it cooked, but not raw. Forgetting memories is a task I have yet to master. Max Riddle lifting my skirt in front of the junior-high football team. What it was like to have three daughters, each with the stomach flu. The early morning call from Roxy about the cancer diagnosis for her husband.

Pushing aside memories, I have found, is easier. They're sneaky, though. When someone says to me they're so sorry about William, that they wish there was something they could do, memories start to sneak in. When Chris shares his latest research on his detailed spreadsheet of all the known sex offenders in the five surrounding zip codes, they try to dodge around the protective barrier I've put in place.

I've tried, I thought as I rolled over in the bed, seeking a cool spot on the pillow. I can't pretend anymore like I don't know.

The lights took him.

It seemed like it was always cold in the days I first heard those words.

The landscape had slowly altered outside the window of the Oldsmobile Cutlass, from the still-green trees in Nashville, to the relative lushness of Kentucky and Southern Illinois. *I will like it here*, I remember thinking. *It looks like home.* Three hours later we entered the cornfields of Central Illinois standing beneath the gray skies.

Tom, my husband of two weeks, had smiled sheepishly and kissed my cheek. "If I told you how terrible it is, you'd never have agreed to come."

We arrived in the town of Champaign-Urbana, the home of the University of Illinois. As picturesque as the university appeared, it still paled in comparison to my alma mater, Vanderbilt, which I'd only been able to attend thanks to a full academic scholarship. When we found our new apartment, I followed the landlord into the building and was nearly struck by the swinging door. It was the first time in my life a man had not held the door for me.

By Christmas, the snow piled high, along with our bills. My father never had much money, but I had never been this truly poor. It soon became apparent that Tom's life would have to become the law if he were to pass the bar. He was gone most of the day in class and was often away at night, studying at the law library. He wasn't on scholarship, and there wasn't time for a job. Tom's mother was dead, and he wasn't close to his father.

That meant I had to find a way to make money if we were going to eat. Stopping all attempts at writing my first novel, I took a job as a waitress at a late-night diner. I had a degree in English and graduated with honors, and I was serving up coffee.

When we returned to Nashville for Christmas, I went straight to Daddy, who took my face in his hands and told me that this was just part of marriage; that my home was in Illinois now and coming home wasn't an option; and that through the plant circuit, he knew a professor in the university's agriculture department who might be able to find me a job.

A few weeks later, I got a call from the university, thank-

ing me for my interest in an office-manager position and saying that I had been given a job. It was decent money that would
pay the bills, with a little left over for used books and cheap
wine. I wasn't thrilled, but it meant using my brain, and I was
proud that I was the sole breadwinner for my little family.
I was given directions to the building and instructed to start
work the following Monday.

At first, I thought I had the wrong building. But sure
enough, there was an office manager job not in agriculture
studies, but in the astronomy department, of all places. When I
reacted with surprise, the dean of the department said he could
certainly offer the job to someone else, but I quickly lied that
I had always been interested in the stars. Once I had even located the Big Dipper, even though I had no idea how to find it
again.

Yet the professors in the department didn't care. They were
thrilled that they now had a full-time office manager. At first, I
thought it was strange that a department with only five professors would even need such a position, but soon I came to understand why. There were, of course, the demands of students
and scheduling, but there was also need to proof articles for
industry publications, and near constant requests to book time
in the university's planetarium. I took all of the tasks in stride,
quietly enjoying being among the academics who seemed to
constantly push up their horn-rimmed glasses above the bridge
of their noses and thank me for completing even the smallest
task. They had long dealt with bored undergrads assigned to
man the front desk as part of their student work programs.

The only exception was Dr. Steven Richards. The young
professor never picked up his messages from his students,
never made eye contact with me as he walked briskly from his
classes, and always kept his office door closed, even when he

was inside. No one beside him ever entered. Sometimes, as he shut his door, I swore he lingered, staring at me while I typed.

And then there were the phone calls from nervous people anxious to speak with him. When he wasn't in, they insisted I write down bizarre messages to pass along to him. "Five stars on the horizon tonight," was a particular repeated message, and then their names and phone numbers. They called from all over the country—sometimes the world, based on the various accents. I started to think it was one big joke, and began to grow weary of the ridiculousness of it all.

While Dr. Richards always treated those messages with urgency, snatching them out of his mailbox and stuffing them quickly into the pocket of his tweed jacket, he would let messages from students pile up without responding.

Finally, when a student called for the fifth time, practically sobbing, saying she couldn't graduate unless she could talk to Dr. Richards about her final research paper, I'd had enough.

Granted, it had been a bad day. I'd broken the coffeepot at home, spilled ink on my white blouse, and the laundry Tom had promised to fold remained mounded up around the apartment. I took Dr. Richards's messages and marched to his office door. I knocked.

A soft response. "Who is it?"

"It's Lynn at the front desk. You have several students who need to speak with you, Dr. Richards."

"I'll get to them."

I turned the handle, expecting to open the door just enough to stick the messages in and then quickly close it. Instead, the knob turned easier than I thought and the door flew open.

"What are you doing?" Dr. Richards said.

"I am so sorry," I replied, my face flushed. I held out the messages. "I really feel like you should call them—"

I stopped in midsentence. The maps covering the walls all had red pins with connecting strings, making the room feel like a bizarre spider's web. Each of the pins seemed to have a note with some kind of furious writings. The maps continued all the way across the ceiling.

"Miss, you're going to have to leave. You're not allowed in here. And I will call those people back when I can."

"Those people?" I found myself firing back. *Stop talking! You need this job!* "They are your students! You don't even know my name, do you? I've worked here for four months."

It was clear he didn't. He ran his fingers through his hair, which was in desperate need of a cut. "I'm sorry, I'm very busy."

Be quiet! "Students are asking for their grades. Some are waiting to graduate."

"I will respond to them all today."

I nodded once and began to close the door when he spoke again. "You are Lynn Stanson, married name Lynn Roseworth. Vanderbilt graduate, English lit major, 4.0 grade point average, from Nashville, Tennessee."

I looked back at him in surprise, only to see that he was back to reading the papers in front of him. "I wouldn't let you take my messages if I didn't know who you were."

I turned to walk away and then stopped. "Why are those messages so strange? Is it some kind of joke? Are they friends of yours trying to be funny? Because they don't sound funny. They sound angry."

"They are colleagues of mine. Take down the messages and make sure you write them down exactly."

Get out of this office. "I'm the office manager, not just a secretary. The other professors even use me to proof their research papers. Dr. Long is sending me to the library now to do research for him. So I don't need to be told how to do simple tasks." *You are going to get fired, and Tom will have to drop out of school.* "I'll tell you what: From now on, if someone calls for you, I'll see if you are in. And if you are, you can take the call. If not, I'll ask them to call back later. That way, you'll never doubt that your messages were taken down correctly." *Thank you for the four months of employment.*

I had hoped the dean wouldn't call me immediately with the termination notice. I might have a day or two to find a new job—

"Mrs. Roseworth, do you think . . . you could do some work for me? Obviously, I'm a little disorganized. I don't mean to be aloof. It comes naturally."

When he smiled, it was almost childlike. He was clearly unaccustomed to it, like an awkward boy sitting for a school picture. Dr. Richards couldn't have been more than seven, maybe eight years older than me. *Shut up and thank him and agree to help.*

I stared over the rims of my own glasses. "Get those students straightened out, and I'll be happy to help you. What kind of work do you need me to do?"

"Just . . . keep taking the messages accurately for now. And I'll let you know when I need you for something more."

I closed the door, hoping he would never make the request. If my old babysitter, Mrs. Ross, had seen that mess of an office, she'd have said, "Bless his heart."

I'd gone back to the library and come back with so much research on solar flares for Dr. Long that he looked at me in astonishment. I wanted to explain that what I did two hours ago in Dr. Richards's office could have gotten me fired, so I needed to earn some goodwill among the other professors. Instead, I returned to my desk and prayed.

When I arrived the next day, two large boxes were stacked

on my chair. A note on top read: "Start with these. Organize by date. Only date.—Dr. Richards."

I put the boxes aside, thinking it would take me no time flat to organize the files by date, even though the boxes were quite heavy. I would do as Dr. Richards asked and politely thank him for the task. *Be sure to let me know if you need anything else,* I would say quietly.

The day had been busy with arranging meetings for students and the professors, fetching coffee, and copy editing an article about the gases around Saturn. The boxes stared at me like a hungry dog.

Before I prepared to leave, I peeked at a few of the files, knowing that my calendar tomorrow appeared freer, and I could tackle the project, maybe even finish it by late afternoon.

The first few pages in the file had most of the words blacked out. So many of the words were marked through I couldn't comprehend even what was typed or written on the pages. A quick glance through the files found them all to be the same.

Dr. Richards had to be in on this joke. My face grew hot. I strode down the hallway. Tom hadn't even thanked me for staying up late the previous night to prepare his lunch. He'd also washed my favorite blouse with a pair of his red basketball shorts.

I went to Dr. Richards's office and knocked on the door. When he didn't answer, I turned the handle.

He sat at his desk, several books stacked in front of him. He didn't look up. "Apparently, that lock is broken. I'll have to have maintenance come fix it. I didn't say enter."

"I saw you come in a few hours ago. You should respond when someone knocks on your door. So, is this a joke? There isn't a date on these, and they're all blacked out."

"There are dates. You won't find them in their usual locations. You have to look within the paragraphs."

"Why? What is this? Why is it all blacked out?"

He looked up, irritated. "When I feel like you can do this job, I'll explain more. If you can't do this job, then there's no need to explain."

I wanted to take his stupid boxes and stack them outside his door so when he opened it, he might trip on them. I flushed at the thought. "Yes Dr. Richards," I managed to say.

I returned to my chair, trying to ignore the boxes jeering at me. Tom would be working late. I had no interest in or desire to spend another night eating alone.

It was nearly seven o'clock when Dr. Richards left. As usual, he didn't acknowledge anyone or even note that I was still at my desk, hours after I was typically gone.

I immediately began pulling out the pages from the first box and began reading.

Two hours later, I was completely lost. At times, I could almost make out a few sentences, but even those made no sense. And what made it even more ridiculous was that none of it seemed to pertain at all to astronomy or his students' work.

Was he just crazy? Did he suffer from some kind of medical condition? I'd come across several dates that were not blacked out, but hundreds of other pages and letters had nothing to decipher.

I looked over at the picture of Daddy and me from graduation on my desk. Give a Stanson a job and we'll get it done, he always said.

This sudden attitude of mine could cost me this job. And I hated confrontation. Tom rarely became angry with me, and when he did, I quietly tried to even his temper to end the argument. I certainly never fought with Daddy. Perhaps it was that no one had ever totally dismissed me before or spoken to me like hired help.

I am wasting my time, I thought. I could be working on my writing. I leaned back in the chair, holding up two pages. *These are the last two. I'm dumping this all back outside his office and apologizing for my inability to finish the project.* I imagined sending all the students inquiring about him back to his office, and telling them to knock loudly because, despite being in his late twenties, Dr. Richards is a little deaf.

The fluorescent light above flickered. I sat forward and began to toss the papers into the box, when I stopped. I read the page again and found nothing. Then I leaned back and held up the pages.

The paper was so thin, I could easily see through to the blocked out words on the first page. I had encountered that problem myself before, when I tried to black out one of the professors' home addresses on a handbook that all the students would see, only to find the address could been seen when angled correctly in the light. But this time, it wasn't an angle that revealed what was marked through. When I held the two pages together, I could not only see the blacked out words, but also saw the words on the page behind it. The words from the second page fit the sentences from the first page perfectly.

I held the pages up to the desk lamp. I read them over and over again. The second page wasn't a second page at all.

I reread the sentence on the first page:

"I had noticed (blacked out) were blowing, so (blacked out) outside, and that's when I saw the (blacked out) and I (blacked out). The (blacked out) had (blacked out) him."

Dr. Richards—or someone, I guessed—took the time to type out a key for every single page. When I held the pages up to the light and matched up the paragraphs exactly, the words on the second page were, in fact, the words that had been blacked out on the first.

I had noticed (blacked out) were blowing.

The word behind the blacked out word was "trees."

I had noticed trees were blowing, it read. I smiled.

The words "trees," "ran," "streetlight," "panicked," "knew," "lights" and "taken" had all been blacked out on the first page and placed strategically on the second.

I snatched a pencil and wrote the words above the blacked-out smudges, and read the sentence in full:

I had noticed trees were blowing, so I ran outside, that's when I saw the streetlight and I panicked. The lights had taken him.

SEVEN

I had stayed until midnight the night I first unraveled the code of the files. It had not been dedication that had kept me glued to the pages.

The letters were not always written to Dr. Richards. Many were firsthand accounts, all had most words blacked out. I knew all I was supposed to be doing was finding the dates to figure out some kind of order, but I quickly realized it would be more complicated than that. While some were dated in the upper left-hand corner in standard letter format, the rest required full readings to find some mention of a day, a time, or even a month.

Soon, even if letters were clearly dated, I found myself reading them in their entirety. Several I read more than once. I had to put on my sweater due to the goose bumps on my arms.

When the clock hit 12:30, I grabbed my coat and hurried home, fearing Tom would be pacing in alarm. But he wasn't home either, which meant he was out with his law-school buddies, blowing off steam.

I made angry laps around the apartment. I'd never been a drinker, and while I didn't disapprove of alcohol, I certainly didn't like how it was contributing to my solitude. He hadn't even stopped by to leave me a note to say he was going out.

The next morning, I left without leaving him a note, making his lunch, or waking him, since had slept through his alarm.

I got to work early and waited. When Dr. Richards arrived, I practically blocked his entrance into his office, holding up one of the files.

"What is this?"

The professor's head was down as usually, but upon seeing the letters in my hand, he glanced at my face and told me to come in and close the door.

He sat down, folding his fingers behind his thick, dark-red hair, which was already streaked with silver, even though he wasn't yet thirty.

"You can read them?" he asked.

"Of course I can read them." I hoped the bags under my eyes didn't give away how long it had taken me. "I don't know how else to say this: It's disturbing. These are letters about people disappearing, being abducted, losing their loved ones. This has nothing to do with astronomy."

"It has everything to do with astronomy," he responded quietly.

I stood with my arms folded across my chest, waiting for him to continue. "I'll be honest with you, Miss Stanson—"

"It's *Mrs.* Roseworth."

"I suspected you were bright, but I actually didn't think you'd figure out the system this quickly."

"Well, you thought wrong. And I'm wondering if you should be giving this to police instead of to me to organize for you."

The professor reached deep into his pants pockets, and then fumbled in the interior of his coat, finally locating his keys.

He pivoted his chair around and unlocked an old file cabinet behind him, pulled out a drawer, took out a thick envelope, and slid it across the desk.

"Open it."

I picked it up and lifted the clasp. I expected to find more blacked-out papers, but instead saw what looked to be hundreds of photographs of varying sizes.

"What is this?"

"Those are the people we're trying to help. They've had someone disappear, or are missing themselves. I keep that envelope close by, and about once a day I open it, to remind myself why it's so important to keep all this so . . . shall we say . . . cryptic."

I once again looked around at the posters of space and maps of various states and countries, connected with pushpins, notes, and coordinates.

"What's going on here?"

Dr. Richards chewed on his lip.

"I will tell you one thing: The second I think you're up to something illegal, I'll go to the police."

"It's nothing like that. But you have permission to do so if I ever break a law. I suppose you could say that some people come to me when someone they love goes missing."

"Why would they come to you? You're an astronomy professor."

"Because they can't get answers from police. And they know something is wrong. I believe we have the ability to tell—to sense even—that something has happened beyond our understanding."

I raised my eyebrow.

"Has anything ever occurred in your life that you can't explain?"

"Honestly, no."

"Then you're lucky, and I hope, for your sake, that the rest of your life goes that way."

"I don't understand. Why would they come to you if someone is missing?"

"They don't just come to me. They come to all of us who are trying to find the truth."

"What truth?"

"That the government is aware of people disappearing and refuses to acknowledge it. I really shouldn't discuss this anymore until you agree to keep what we do silent. I had to see first if you could even decipher how we communicate—it can get complicated. Maybe I should have you sign something."

"Does the university know about this?"

"Oh, no. I'd be fired if they knew the amount of time I devote to this. They pay me to teach students about stars; students who actually don't care about stars and only want to fulfill their undergraduate demands."

Dr. Richards then added quickly, "I'll pay you to do this on the side."

I tried to not let on that at that very moment, I was ensnared. The student loans Tom would rack up by graduation seemed insurmountable.

"I won't do anything that's illegal, and I won't keep quiet if I even think you're doing something that harms someone."

"There's nothing harmful about anything we're doing. Honestly, most people would laugh if you told them what we do."

"And what is it, exactly, that you do?"

"Start organizing all those papers by date. You'll find the reference to a date on every other page. I'll pay you a $1.50 an hour."

I started doing the math in my head. It didn't even meet minimum wage standards for 1969, but it wouldn't be bad extra money. "I still don't know what this is about. Why are these people disappearing? Who is taking them?"

Dr. Richards stared hard at me, and then pointed up with one finger. I looked up at the ceiling covered in maps of the stars.

Like all children of the fifties, I'd seen the movies featuring the campy music, the flighty women, and cardboard-cutout heroes who fought against invaders from other worlds. When I had read over the documents from Dr. Richards's office, I tried not to think about those films. Because the people who documented the missing were real, and they were afraid. The letters, the bizarre phone calls, all came from very serious people.

I only told Tom that I was doing additional freelance copy editing work for a professor. It meant I would be staying later at the office. He certainly didn't object to the extra cash flow.

So I combed through the papers, leaving the neatly organized stacks in boxes outside the professor's office each evening. When I arrived the next day, the boxes would be gone.

One night, with the campus silent with snow, I had set a box outside Dr. Richards's door, surprised to see the light still on. I knocked. He looked up and motioned me in.

"You've been getting the checks in your mailbox?"

"Yes, thank you."

"No, thank you. It's unacceptable, the conditions of those files."

"Do they really think . . . ?"

He put down his pen and rubbed his eyes. "Think what?"

"That . . . aliens . . . took their loved ones?"

"You've read it all. What do you think?"

"I know they're afraid. They're really afraid. And I know

they're desperate to believe in something that explains what happened. But if you read the newspapers, you know that terrible things sometimes happen: drugs, alcohol, mental illness. I wonder if you're feeding them false hope."

Dr. Richards jutted out his jaw. "It's a fair criticism. Something I've wondered myself. But it's the commonality that keeps me up at night."

"Commonality?"

He leaned his chin on his right hand. "How can someone in Malvern, Arkansas, describe the same kind of being that someone in a remote village outside Kenya, Africa, says they saw as well? It's all the same, with some small variation. Look here."

He handed me two pieces of paper. "You know this family. The Gobels."

"How can you forget? It's terrible."

"Farm family. Outskirts of Cape Girardeau, Missouri. Wake up one morning to find their two-year-old daughter gone. Massive search, police, FBI, everything. No one finds anything. The mother, Sarah, is so distraught, she hires a hypnotist to force her to remember everything about that night. And when she's put under—what does Sarah see?"

"It's not what she sees. It's what she feels. Something probing her body. Large eyes. Wide forehead, gray skin. Then bright lights . . ." I paused, finding the words on the page, ". . . and her daughter going into them."

"The Semitacalous, from the Zakynthos Island in Greece." Dr. Richards slid me another folder. "You know their story too: Elderly couple. Go to bed one night. Anna wakes up the next morning, her husband, Georgios, is gone. But she doesn't need a hypnotist—she remembers everything. The probing, the wide head, the irregular eyes. The bright lights and her husband rising into them."

He placed the folders on top of each other. "The Gobels' daughter went missing on August 20, on the same night Georgios Semitacalou disappeared. Neither has ever been seen since."

He looked down, his pen scratching across the paper before him as if I had never interrupted him. "Now you tell me what to tell these families."

I looked out his small window. "I . . . hate it for them. How long can they keep looking? How long do you tell them to keep hoping?"

"Forever."

"Why? How can you even encourage them?"

"Because sometimes they come back," he said, continuing to write.

EIGHT

At first, I found the laminated cards that Dr. Richards gave to me to pass along to the families of the missing quaint and sweet. I had praised him for being compassionate enough to come up with the poem written on the front. His response had been an academic frown.

"It wasn't my idea. I honestly don't know why we hand them out. We started doing it about five years ago. I suppose it's supposed to be comforting, but I think it's a bit much. We're all instructed to do it, so it's become our calling card. Every family gets one."

I often sent them by mail, always with a handwritten note. I reread the poem each time I placed one in an envelope.

PRAYER FOR THE MISSING
You are not gone, as long as I remember.
You are not away, as long as I weep.
You have not vanished, as long as I can picture your face.
You are with me.
You are in the rain.

You are in my tears.
You are where the water falls.

Being an English major, I wasn't overly impressed with the poem, but it was a nice sentiment. And knowing Dr. Richards was atheist, handing out anything that resembled a prayer was a real stretch for him.

He told me to send one to Barbara Rush when she insisted on meeting with him.

"Her family is against our involvement," he said.

"She wants your help," I replied, flipping through her brother's case file.

Barbara was only eighteen, four years younger than me. Her twin brother, Don, had gone missing in a snowstorm in St. Joseph, Michigan, a small tourist town on a dramatic arch of Lake Michigan. Her parents had fallen apart after his disappearance, leaving the girl to search for her brother on her own. That led her to a missing-persons support groups, and ultimately to one of Dr. Richards's colleagues who attended such meetings to seek out questionable disappearances. When he heard her story, he encouraged her to call to the University of Illinois's astronomy department.

She had asked for Dr. Richards, and I took the call.

Don had casually smoked marijuana, Barbara explained, so the St. Joseph police thought he got stoned and wandered into the storm. Probably got too close to the lake, they surmised. His body will wash up soon with the ice balls, she heard one whisper to the other.

But she insisted that her brother—despite being a lifelong Michigander—hated the cold. Even high, he would have never gone out. And when she had awoken that night and found light streaming through her bedroom, she'd assumed a car was shining its headlights into her room—maybe one of Don's friends from the bowling alley had come to pick him up for a quick nip at the bar. She had parted the curtains and saw Don standing on the street, in the snow, looking up. Then the lights were gone, and so was Don.

"I told my parents," Barbara had said. "They thought I was sleepwalking. But I don't sleepwalk. Never have."

I had talked to her off and on for several weeks. But then her parents listened in on one of the calls and forbid her from calling "those whackos in Illinois" again. So she called from pay phones when she got off work at the restaurant around the corner from her house. I stayed late at work to accept her calls.

A month after her first call, Barbara showed up at the office.

"I took the bus all night. I had to see your face," she had said to my astonished expression. "You're as nice as I pictured."

Barbara sat and talked with Dr. Richards and me for hours, pleading with us to come to Michigan to help her search. The more she talked, the more she twisted a strand of hair on the back of her neck. "Nervous habit," she said, smiling sheepishly.

Dr. Richards had explained they didn't have a budget for traveling. She vowed to give them all her money. Steven shook his head. "I can get you in touch again with my colleague at the University of Michigan, who told you about us—"

"I don't want him. I want you. And Lynn. He talked about theories of missing people, including something called . . . Argentum? Am I saying that right?"

Dr. Richards frowned. "I'm sorry, Barbara. I can't help you, especially with that."

Even though I didn't have the money either, I had paid for her bus ticket back to Michigan. I gave her one of the laminated poems. She had cried at the bus terminal, and I cried along with her.

"That can never happen again," Dr. Richards later said. "Sometimes people expect us to drop everything and find their loved ones. Give them one of the cards and end it with that. It can't work any other way. We only gather information, take careful notes—"

"If all we're doing is gathering facts, how does this ever help anyone?"

"Because it might not now. Might not in ten years, twenty years. But one day, we'll have enough cases to show that this can't be ignored."

"Why was she asking about Argentum? Who is that? What is that?"

"I'm going to have a long talk with my esteemed colleague in Michigan about that. He knows better. It's a theory about extraterrestrials that we are all instructed to dismiss outright. I've heard some talk that it's about aliens inhabiting human form, or that it refers to interdimensional travel. It's our Loch Ness monster—everyone has heard of it, and no one has any proof." Dr. Richards didn't bother to hide his irritation.

"Perhaps I should refer her to some of the other organizations. I've read quite a bit about UFO theorists—"

"For God's sake, don't do that. Me and my . . . peers . . . we aren't like the others in those other groups. I mean, I appreciate the work APRO and NICAP are doing—"

"But you don't belong to them. The Aerial Phenomena Research Organization and the National Investigations Committee on Aerial Phenomena are quite open with their mission. Why not join them?"

When he raised his eyebrows, I shrugged. "I do research. I pay attention."

"Good organizations, good people, their focus is just different than ours."

"How?"

"We have a primary mission of trying to connect people who have gone missing to abductions. APRO and NICAP are doing admirable work on people who are returned quickly from abductions. My theory, and the theory that I share with my peers, is that unexplained disappearances of people all over the world can be tied to the abductions."

"Where's your proof, besides the stories told by people they leave behind?"

He chewed on the end of his pencil. "I wonder what you think . . ."

"What I think?"

He jotted down something on the paper in front of him. "You have a brilliant mind, Lynn." He looked once more, intently, at his writing.

I pulled my cardigan tighter around me.

I left work early, taking Barbara's file home with me. At home, I read through it five more times. Then I grabbed my coat. Tom had come home at that exact moment, and I told him I'd be back later. When he asked about dinner, I pretended I didn't hear.

Dr. Richards had already left his office, but he recently had given me a key, for emergencies. I figured this counted.

Three hours later, I found what I was looking for. I cleared off the battered couch in his office and lay down to read. At midnight, I'd meant to only close my eyes for a moment.

I awoke to Dr. Richards standing over me. "Your husband is banging on the doors outside the Curry Hall entrance. You better go."

"What time is it?"

"Seven A.M. Did you sleep here all night?"

"I have to tell you what I found."

"No, you have to go."

"It's the weather. That's the commonality. It's the weather."

"We can talk about this later. Go home. Take the day off and get some rest—"

"I have to tell you about this."

"Not a good time. Not only is your husband outside, but I have a faculty review today. I will have no time today."

"Then I will be here at the end of the day. Wait for me."

Tom and I had fought all day. I called him a stranger, he called me disconnected. I cried, he paced. I was grateful at dusk when he announced he needed to go out for a run. I lied about going to a coffee shop to work on my book.

I didn't even knock when I reached Dr. Richards's office. He put on his glasses as I sat down.

"You may not remember the Soothe case in Alaska; we don't have much on it," I began. "But something jogged my memory about the date. I realized why when I studied Barbara's case. A man went missing there, exactly two years to the day Barbara's brother went missing. In a snowstorm."

"There's always a snowstorm in Alaska in winter."

"His wife told police she saw lights in the snowstorm. You mentioned the abductions in Arkansas and on that Greek island. But you failed to mention it was during blistering nights of temperatures in the upper nineties—ninety-eight degrees to be precise—with scattered storms producing heavy down-pours that lasted mere minutes. Same dates, almost exact same weather pattern. What if that's what happens? If we started to piece together all those dates, and match them up with the weather . . ."

I then slowly shook my head in realization. "That's what

you've been having me do, isn't it? You're not putting them in some kind of chronological order. You're matching the dates of the missing and comparing the weather."

Dr. Richards slid back his chair and walked around the desk, clearly uncomfortable in his proximity to me. "I think they come on the same days, in different years, but in the same weather. And I think they return to the same places, too, over and over again. But the abductions can come years, even decades apart. I don't know why. But that's the key, I think. Lynn, it took me my whole life to figure this out. You put it together in a few months. I hoped you would help me get organized. But I never expected you'd become a colleague."

When I smiled, he did too. I was surprised at how his entire face lit up, his usual downtrodden eyes forming crescent moons.

I've found that life has no tolerance for dwelling in memories. I may have wanted to stay in bed, examining those thrilling and confusing times to seek clues that could help find William. But my recollection was ended by an exhausted sleep, and then the cat pawing at my face, ready to be fed. Since school hadn't let out for fall break yet, I had to rush to get Greg to school and check in on Brian, followed by a complete collapse by Anne, in which she sobbed on the couch for an hour, and then a call from Tom that we needed to have dinner together tonight to discuss some important things. I'd put some salmon in the oven, but when we sat down to dinner, I quickly lost my appetite over what my husband had to say.

As he started scraping his fork to gather the last remnants of the angel hair pasta, I rubbed my temples. When the base of his wineglass caught the edge of his plate and made a sharp clang, I scooted my chair back, walked over to the sink, and began to rinse the plates before putting them in the dishwasher.

"I guess you don't think we should do it," he muttered under his breath.

"Of course I think you should do it. *We* aren't doing it."

"It's Diane Sawyer, Lynn. She's giving us an hour in prime time."

"I know who she is, Tom. And I think it's the right decision. For you to do."

"Lynn, you need to take part in it. People are going to be more sympathetic to someone like you than some perceived beltway insider. You or Anne—"

"No," I laid the dishrag down on the countertop. "Not Anne. Not Chris. No one but you. This family is hanging on by a thread. I won't put Anne through it—"

The knock came at the door, and he checked his watch. "Deanna said she'd be here at seven. Listen to what she has to say, Lynn. She's a communications expert; she's been a valuable asset. And the FBI has already signed on to this."

I dried my hands, then put on too much lotion. The October air was already wreaking havoc on my skin. When I turned back around, Deanna Ruck, Tom's communication manager, who I'd met on the porch the day of the news conference, was setting down her briefcase.

"Hi Mrs. Roseworth. Nice to see you again."

"Hi Deanna. Can I offer you some coffee?"

"No, thank you, I've smoked too much for one evening, and I don't think my nervous system can handle caffeine too."

"Have a seat," Tom said quickly, knowing I refused to clean his clothes when he'd been smoking.

Deanna produced a thick folder. "So here are the talking

points, all approved by the FBI. ABC is giving you an hour, so they will need a lot; enough to keep the story line moving along until the last quarter hour—"

"Story line?" I winced.

"Lynn . . ." Tom gave me a weary glance. "She means we want to keep viewers tuned in until the end of the hour, when I reveal the increase in the reward."

"We're not a TV drama," I replied softly.

"Please go on," he said to Deanna.

"As we discussed, you'll take Diane and the crew through the woods. You'll provide all of the new photos of William approved by your daughter. ABC is asking again if Anne or Chris—"

"No," I insisted. "They will not be doing an interview. No other member of the family."

"Have you given any thought . . ." she began.

"I won't. I'm sorry, I can't."

She nodded. "Here's where we have to have a tough discussion. Senator, Mrs. Roseworth, forgive me, but I have to ask: Is there anything—anything at all—that could be considered controversial about your family that you haven't already disclosed? No pattern of runaway behavior by William? No affairs by Anne or her husband? Drug use? Nothing that would make the tabloids?"

"We've gone over this repeatedly with the FBI. We're terribly boring," Tom said.

"Because if there's one single bit of information that's outrageous, anything that casts doubt on the family or your sensibilities, you will lose the public's sympathy in a heartbeat. A sideshow will disrupt what really matters. I'm sorry to be so crass. The producers have made it clear: The information about Brian is a nonnegotiable."

"Nonnegotiable?" I asked.

"Lynn, they have to have something to tease," he said.

"Tease?" I was gripping the side of the table now.

"We have a daughter who works in television news, Lynn, who has spoken to us at length about this. Kate has spoken to you about this. The more the producers can tease that they have obtained new information, the more people will watch, and the more people will be on the lookout for William. I will discuss briefly that Brian may have witnessed it and has been in a traumatized state ever since. End of discussion, Lynn. Deanna, do we have a list of questions?"

I envisioned walking over to the cake plate, calmly taking the last piece of iced banana bread, and throwing it in Tom's direction. But instead I sat with my hands on the table.

"The network won't provide questions, but we know the ballpark. You need to be prepared. That's what's in the talking points—"

"I need to assume questions about the VP offer. And if William was a troubled kid; if we acted quickly enough in contacting police; domestic terrorism—"

"Does it have to go there?" I asked.

"It can go there and it will, Lynn." Tom was getting angry now. "You don't get it: ISIS is converting suburban high school kids into extremists and teaching them through social media to shoot up military institutions and attack the government any way they can. I've read the files. You couldn't stomach them. Of course, they could have staked out our family and waited for just the right moment. You think kidnapping a family member of the only Democratic senator who led the charge to increase military presence in Iran to bomb those fuckers is out of the question?"

"It could have been any of you, truly," Deanna said. "But after the magazine came out . . ."

I stood up and walked to the stairs.

"I'm sorry, but that question will certainly be asked." She sounded more irritated than apologetic.

Tom was on his feet. "Lynn! Come on, Lynn. God dammit!"

I hurried up the stairs, my hand on my mouth. I went through the bedroom and into the bathroom, closing the door. I ran the water to mask my sobbing.

Nothing outrageous, Deanna warned. Nothing salacious or controversial should come out about any of us.

I roughly wiped the tears from my face. The small amount of mascara I'd earlier applied streamed down my cheeks. I grabbed a Kleenex and leaned into the mirror.

I stopped. A flushed face with weepy eyes and smudges of black beneath reflected back.

The desire to smash the mirror was so strong that I actually began to step back, to contain myself. But instead, I leaned in closer, looking at every detail of my pathetic face.

I would burn that image in my memory to use as ammunition, should I begin to doubt what I had to do.

The bells above the door to the Peddler announced my arrival, and I could see Barry Manilow's face on the computer screen reflected in Roxy's glasses. She was obviously so engrossed in her online research into his denials of plastic surgeries that she only held up her finger. "Be with you in a minute."

"Don't keep the customers waiting too long," I responded.

"Well, good morning. What a nice surprise."

I rubbed my shoulders. "It's cold this morning. You've done a nice job with the Thanksgiving decorations. I can't thank you enough for tending to the shop during all this. And I've been such a terrible friend, I haven't even asked about how Ed was doing this month."

"A few more rounds of chemo and he's done for a while, I hope."

"I am so sorry, Roxy. I should be checking on him at least once a week."

"Ed's tough. He'll beat it, like he's beat it twice before. In fact, he practically shoves me out the door every day. Imagine if the two of us were pecking on him all the time—he barely survived being around us every day of high school. He doesn't even the let the boys do work around the house for him."

I bit my lip. "I hate to ask you this, but do you think that Ed is well enough for you to go visit your brother in Little Rock?"

"Excuse me? You know I hate my brother's wife."

"I was hoping you'd like to go. And that you'd insist I come with you."

Roxy tried to hide in the pity in her smile. "Honey, say the word and we'll be out the door in two shakes. Tom stopped by and told me about the interview with ABC tomorrow. I know you don't want to be here when they come. You need a break from all this. But I do think we should screw Little Rock, let's go to Tunica—"

I shook my head. "No one would believe that. Certainly not the girls. They have to believe I'm going to Little Rock. And you have to go—for a week, that's all. Then you can come back. We'll schedule it that we arrive back at the same time."

"You've lost me. I'm going to Little Rock . . . but you aren't coming with me?"

"I'm not done. I need you to rent a car for me. I don't want to use my debit card for Tom to see. Of course, I'll pay you back immediately. I also hope you can drive me to the Enterprise over on Charlotte Avenue. And then when we both get back, you can pick me up there. It will look like we've been together the entire time."

"Where are you actually going?"

"I need to go somewhere alone. And the girls would be too worried if they knew."

"If you're going to have me lie, which I only do under the most important of occasions—such as telling Ruth Boster last week that the bleach is really hiding the hair on her upper lip—then the tradeoff is that I'm going with you. I don't know where you're going or why, but I *will* be going. I lie, I travel. *Comprende?*"

I slowly opened the door to the room Brian had shared with William. Two twin beds were tucked into the corners, one with Spider-Man sheets and the other with Batman. The red sheets with webs had remained untouched since summer.

As he did each day, Brian sat in a chair facing a bay window overlooking his backyard. The books that Stephanie, the tutor, had read aloud, trying to get him to respond, were stacked near his ankles. I gave Stephanie two more weeks, tops.

"Brian bear, it's Nanna."

He continued to stare, motionless. Even his blinking seemed mechanical.

"Honey, Nanna has to take a trip. I really wish you would talk to me before I leave."

A strand of hair drifted across his eye. When he made no effort to remove it, I gently brushed it back. *I've never just come out and asked him. I have to do it.*

"Brian. Brian, honey, did William . . . disappear into lights? Lights from the sky?"

When Brian failed to respond, I closed my eyes. I might as well have been talking to a statue. I looked out the window at the trees beyond.

Not wanting to look again at his vacant face, I leaned down

and kissed his cheek, and started to walk out, when I stopped at the door.

I tasted his tear on my lips.

West Side Story took us from Tennessee to Paducah, Kentucky. *Camelot* blared as we blew through Southern Illinois. After a dramatic accompaniment to "If Ever I Would Leave You," Roxy frowned at the construction off Interstate 57 onto Route 13. "Glad we got to avoid that mess. I suppose you'll tell me when I actually need to get off the interstate?"

I nodded.

"Thinking about the girls?"

"Kate—and Tom, for that matter—seemed relieved I was leaving. They're both practical thinkers and know the TV shoot will go easier without me acting like an old guard dog. Stella was suspicious; she knows it's not like me to leave in a crisis. Anne looked so panicked when I told her I was going with you to Little Rock. I know she won't take part in the interview, but I feel like I'm abandoning her. It was like seeing her again at six years old, after I took her to the first day of kindergarten. I promised to call her twice a day, and I told her I would only be about five or six hours away, which really isn't that untrue."

"Ah-ha! At last, a clue. So we're going five hours away, then. Took us three and a half to get here, so . . ."

"You know we're going to Champaign, Roxy. You've known since I first told you I had to go to Illinois."

"Well, I guessed it, but I thought maybe you needed to go to Chicago. Or maybe Springfield. I still don't understand why, though."

I closed my eyes and leaned back. Roxy took a swig of her Diet Pepsi and pointed to the console. "If you're still going to be evasive you're going to have to listen to *Evita*. And not that Madonna crap, I'm talking Patti LuPone."

After *Evita* came *Phantom of the Opera*, and then *Chicago*. Roxy was about to launch into "All that Jazz" when she spied a Cracker Barrel and announced her bladder was full.

After lunch, as Roxy puttered around the souvenir shop, I sat in the booth and stared out at the leafless trees. We were nearing Mattoon now, which meant I was close to breaking the vow I'd made to myself all those years ago, whispering to the baby inside me, promising to never return to this desolate part of the world. It was spring then, and I felt with every mile the world was getting greener. I was escaping, I had my baby girl with me, and Tom could join us once he graduated. If I had had to walk home to Tennessee, I would have. More likely, I would have run.

"OK, I've overloaded myself with crap, including those peg puzzles no one can ever figure out but that still get passed on to grandchildren," Roxy announced as she returned to the table. "I bought one for each of your brood, they were on sale. Of course, my sons are depriving me of grandchildren, only giving me tattooed girlfriends. I've paid. Thelma, it's time to tell Louise what exactly we're doing."

I slid out from the booth and swept Roxy's hand. "Not yet."

When we at last arrived in Champaign, I repeatedly blinked; a bad habit that surfaced when I was surprised at something. Logic suggested that a college town I hadn't seen in forty years would of course look very different. But I had seen towns in Tennessee sit unaltered for longer than that.

As Roxy gassed up her pickup truck, I marveled at the sprawl of neighborhoods and gas stations, feeling a surprising twinge of fondness for the brick buildings. It was what I remembered the most about Champaign: the red brick, as if the founders of the university and the town knew that if the people were to survive the blistering winds and mounds of snow of winter, wooden structures weren't going to cut it. The buildings on campus were brick, the restaurants were brick, even many of the new gas stations were brick.

"OK, sister, where to now?" Roxy tapped on the window.

I gave the directions, relying mostly on Google Maps on my iPhone, which was one of only two apps I had mastered. I had no choice but to conquer texting or else Stella would have driven me insane, and Tom insisted I understand the map app in case I got lost in Atlanta or Savannah. Though the streets surrounding the university had multiplied and the campus expanded, I was able to rest the phone on my thigh as we entered the school and give directions by memory. When I directed Roxy into the parking lot of the mostly plain (brick) building, my throat started to tighten.

Roxy threw the truck into park. "Says I need a sticker to park here, but maybe the truck looks beat up enough that they'll assume I'm a student. Are we going in?"

I swallowed. "Give me a minute. Keep the truck running."

Roxy looked out the window. "Having done this now, I feel like a moron that I never came to visit you here. Six hours away in Illinois seemed like driving to Canada to me when I was twenty-two. Now, I know I should have gassed up that Chevy and headed up here all the time. It may have eased the pain."

"The pain?"

"It was the worst time in my life when you came here. We'd been together every day since the second grade. I felt like I'd lost you to the north, like some pining widow of the Confederacy. Do you remember how we cried when you moved? I think Tom had to pry us apart."

"The feeling was mutual."

"I don't remember much about all those years you were away. Did we not talk on the phone? Why do I have so few letters from you? Do I need to be taking gingko for memory loss?"

"I made a firm decision not to talk about my life here. It wasn't a happy time."

"Then why are we back here?"

I sighed and pivoted in the truck to face her. "Remember when I worked for the astronomy department here, while Tom was in school? I ended up doing extra work for a professor on a project. He was involved . . . in researching missing people. Now . . . I just want to see if maybe his research could help us."

"For God's sake, Lynnie. It's completely against your nature to do anything irrational, and I know that grief can cause a lot of smart people to do a lot of stupid things, but this isn't ridiculous at all. Why wouldn't you tell me from the beginning? And why would an astronomy professor do research into missing people?"

"Let's go in before I lose my nerve."

We walked across the lawn, brown grass crunching beneath our shoes. Roxie bemoaned her lack of scarf and hat. "Good God, this wind is so strong! And cold! Does it blow down all the way from Chicago? How can anyone stand this?"

"There's nothing to block the wind," I replied, turning up the collar on my coat.

While the astronomy building too had been remodeled over the decades, it still clung to its original boxy shape. I was so taken back by the familiar silence of the building, and the smells of coffee and old paper, that I stopped, my hands fidgeting.

"What time are they expecting you?" Roxy asked.

"I didn't make an appointment," I said, turning away from

what I knew would be a look of exasperation on her face. I led her down the main halls, past the grandiose photographs of the former deans of the department, to the office where I began my new life as a wife. The door was closed and a yellowed sign read, "Supply closet."

A female student passed by and I quietly asked where we could find the office manager for the professors. The girl shrugged and mentioned there was a student worker at the front desk, around the corner.

We headed in that direction and found a room with a long desk and a very bored-looking young woman checking her cell phone. She smiled at our approach and set the phone to vibrate. I appreciated the gesture.

"Hello. Are the professors' offices still that way?" I asked.

"I think so, but I've only had this job for a few days. Can I help you with something?"

"I wanted to see Dr. Steven Richards."

The girl's smile altered, and she looked quickly at her computer. "Uh, yes. He's actually unavailable right now."

"We should have called ahead—" Roxy began.

"I'm happy to take a message. I don't know how soon he'll be back."

"Will he be back today?"

The girl's face paled a bit. "I don't think so."

"That's all right. Thank you, though." I smiled pleasantly, took Roxy's arm, and walked away.

She could feel me trembling. "That's it? That's all we're doing?"

"I . . . thought he would be here."

"Did you ever think to even call and see if he was still teaching? That was forty years ago, Lynn. He's probably dead."

"He was only twenty-nine when I was here. That would

put him in his early seventies. And, the college's website stated that he was here. The course schedule online even showed him teaching three classes this fall."

"Well, clearly he's not here, and that student is acting a little spooky about it. Maybe she's failing his class. Maybe she has the hots for him. Was he good-looking? More importantly, what do you want to do now?"

"I want to go home. That's what I really want to do. But I can't just sit around that house, that big empty house, anymore. Every room feels empty. Everything feels empty without him."

"Maybe we should find this professor's office. See if maybe he's in there, and the student didn't see him come in."

I looked around. "If I still remember the layout of the building, and I doubt that's changed, he should be right around this corner—if he hasn't moved in forty years."

"Can't hurt to check."

We passed a row of nondescript doors with the names of the professors on the outside. I noted all the names had changed. All the professors I had worked for, except for Dr. Richards, were old when I was a young worker.

"He was handsome, in a messy kind of way," I murmured.

I turned another corner, not surprised in the least to see the last door on the hall still marked with the name "Dr. Steve Richards, Astronomy." He wouldn't have ever wanted to move all his belongings and maps.

What was a surprise, however, was the note on the door, signed in flourishing cursive with the name of the dean. The message was typed and concise: "This office is closed. Any questions, please see your guidance counselor."

"Strike two," Roxy said. "Well, shall we see the guidance counselor? Perhaps ask her about some continuing adult education for two old chicks while we're at it?"

I reached out and turned the door handle, but it was locked.

"Lynn, are you going to let yourself in?"

"I want to see his office."

"Why?"

"He kept his information on the missing people in that office. I can't have come all this way without seeing if any of my old work is still here. But what are we going to do? That girl won't let us in, and I don't think the dean will let us borrow a key."

Roxy looked up and down the hallway. "Move aside." She reached in her hand-quilted purse and dug around. She pulled out a hairpin. "When your hair is as ridiculous as mine, these things are a lifesaver."

"What are you doing?" I whispered. "You just scolded me for trying to get in."

"Yin and yang, kid. Only one of us is allowed to be the bad seed. If you do something wrong, the earth might break from its axis. Remember when we snuck into my dad's locked liquor cabinet? I sampled it all, and all you did was fret and watch for his car to pull into the drive. I haven't done this for years, but locks don't change."

After Roxy swore for a minute or two, I heard the click of the door, and the office opened. We shuffled inside and closed the door quickly.

"Jesus, Mary, and Joseph," Roxy said.

The campus street lamps were starting to come on outside, offering faint light to the rapidly darkening office. We didn't dare turn on the overhead lights for fear of drawing attention from anyone walking outside. Roxy did a lot of huffing and sighing as I combed through drawers and file cabinets.

"Again I ask: Do you care to give me an idea of what we're looking for?"

"Keep looking for anything that might explain where Dr. Richards might be. I went over his desk, and it's a typical man desk: coffee stains, no organization, and dry pens. His calendar is blank, so clearly he does everything on his computer. And, as I found, it's password protected, so I've come up with squat."

Roxy leaned back in his chair and stretched out her legs, only to bang them harshly against something under the desk. I sighed, closing another cabinet. Every file, every drawer was filled with articles and research. Clearly, he had moved all his private research to his computer, and that was inaccessible. I slowly looked up at the maps that still covered the ceiling and walls, practically untouched over the decades. Apparently, he still needed that kind of visual reference—

"Care to explain this?"

Roxy was holding up a photograph, black-and-white and badly faded, of two people sitting together at a table. They were not touching, but they leaned in towards each other. I walked over and stared at the picture of myself and Dr. Richards

"Where did you find that?"

"Stuck on top of the safe under this desk. Which is locked, I might add. But that's you, Lynn Roseworth. And I assume that's Dr. Richards. So the question is—why does he have a minisafe with your picture stuck on top?"

"Are you sure it won't open?"

"Yes, I'm sure, I tried it. And please answer my question."

I looked around. The light was fading rapidly, and I began to run my fingers over the maps on the walls. I looked up and grabbed a chair to stand on.

"What are you doing?"

"Try this," I gave her a key tied to a pushpin on the ceiling. She took it and knelt under the desk. "Did it open?"

"I think so."

"Can we lift it?"

Roxy peered out. "We're stealing now?"

"I have to see what's in it, and we're out of light."

"It's not heavy. It's made out of that plastic stuff that won't burn."

"Stick your head out the door, see if anyone is out there."

"Fine. But I want to know how you knew where that key was."

I pointed up.

"Yes, I see it, it's a star system. The fool has them all over this wacked-out office."

"See the red pushpin?"

"Yes."

"That's where the key was hanging."

"How did you guess it would be up there?"

"Because the pin marks my star."

"What?"

"He named a star after me," I said. "Let me carry the safe."

At our room at the Hilton Garden Inn, on a table usually reserved for brochures on Champaign's historic sites and loose change, sat takeout food from P.F. Chang's and the safe. Roxy devoured her General Tso's Chicken while I mostly played with my vegetable rice.

She at last put down her plastic fork. "Well, we've committed breaking and entering and burglary. If that's my last meal before jail, I'll be happy."

"We'll return all this tomorrow. No one will know."

"Are you sure he won't come back to his office tonight? Or first thing in the morning?"

"You saw the look on that girl's face. I don't think he'll be coming back anytime soon."

"What's in this safe, Lynn?"

"I don't know."

"I think you have your suspicions. Why was your picture taped to it?"

"Open it, Roxy. Tell me what's in it."

She stood up and slid the key into the safe. I continued to look out the window.

"Lynn."

At the tone in her voice, I closed my eyes, afraid to turn around.

"Lynn, look at this."

Roxy slowly slid a map out of a folder. It had yellowed and weathered, a relic now of a time before satellite mapping. The map was on a grid, with latitude and longitude markings. There were faded pencil marks, with arrows pointing to a forested area near a small square.

I recognized my home immediately.

Roxy was already sifting through dozens of newspaper clippings, all of which featured pictures of my family on election nights. The pile included the *Southern Living* magazine with William on the cover.

She reached out and took my trembling hand. "We need to go to the police with this."

"We can't."

"We most certainly are."

"I didn't come here . . . because I suspected he might have taken William. I came because of his research into missing people. He's spent his whole adult life dedicated to it. But when we showed up at that office and I saw that girl's expression, I knew something bad had happened. I had to get into his office to see if I could find his research—or, more importantly, my own. But when you found that picture, and now this . . . I'm afraid he's been gone from this university since William disappeared."

"How did this happen, Lynn? When did this happen? You have to go to the FBI."

"With what? A hunch? And destroy my marriage and what's left of my family?"

"Why would it destroy your marriage and your family? This guy is obsessed with you, obviously—but that's not your fault."

I placed the *Southern Living* cover on the old photo of Dr. Richards and me, covering up my face. Side by side, Dr. Richards and William had the same dimples, the thick hair, the soft chin.

"Because it is my fault," I said softly. "Dr. Richards is William's grandfather."

NINE

We sat in silence in the cab of Roxy's pickup, nursing coffee and fogging up the windows. The safe sat on the floor by my feet. Roxy turned on the defroster to once again clear the windshield, revealing the astronomy building in the blue morning light.

"I hate to ask again, but are you absolutely sure . . ."

I nodded. "I'd always hoped Anne was Tom's. But seeing that picture of Steven and that cover photo of William . . ."

"Lynn, I'm going to say it again: We should be taking that safe to the FBI, or at the very least the local police. I watch enough *Dateline*. And we should go now."

"We have no idea what we're doing, let's not pretend otherwise. How are we going to explain that we broke into his office and found it?"

"You had a hunch. And you proved to be right. And once the police see it, they'll agree. So we need to leave this parking lot. The professionals need to see it. We don't need to put it back."

"The police aren't going to buy this. Neither would the FBI."

"Are you nuts? This seems to me to be the most tangible evidence anyone has come upon since William went missing."

"But why? Why would he take William? It doesn't make sense. I know something is wrong, but I can't believe he would do it. Why he would do it? Steven researches missing people. He wouldn't do anything to put a family through this."

"Now we're calling him Steven? And that's the other thing," Roxy huffed. "I don't get how an astronomy professor is somehow this expert on missing people. If he taught criminal justice or something, I would get it."

"I had hoped at this point you would figure it out, so I wouldn't have to say it."

"Well I'm old and I'm tired, so my usual razor-sharp mind is dulled a bit. He has a map of your property, Lynn. He has pictures of you and your family. He has the magazine with William's picture. He's obsessed with missing people. And while it's hard for me to even say it, he's likely William's grandfather. But I get it; I get why you're afraid to go to police with this, because of the can of worms it's going to open—"

"You don't get it. The reason I feel like I need more proof is because if I go to the police now, they will roll their eyes. Because of what Steven does."

"He's a professor—"

"He investigates alien abductions."

Roxy choked on her coffee, then wiped her lips with the Starbucks napkin. "Pardon my French, but what the hell, Lynn."

"I thought the same thing too, at the beginning. I couldn't believe it. Who could believe it? Now do you understand? If I go to police and say, 'I had an affair with a guy forty years ago, who believes in aliens, and I stole a safe out of his office, and he happens to have a lot of articles about me and my family, and I think that's proof that he abducted my grandson,' then you can see the problem. Because I don't think he has my grandson, Roxy. But what if he knows . . . what happened to William?"

Roxy leaned back in her seat. "I should have gone to Little Rock."

"Do you know what I remember so vividly about all those cases of missing people? That sometimes there was a phrase repeated over and over again by the people who either claim to have witnessed the abductions, or were the last to see the missing people: 'The lights took them.' Or some variation of that. And you know that's the last thing Brian ever said. Yes, I know I'm desperate. Yes, I know this is hard to believe. It's still hard for me to believe all the stupid things I did in this town. But I have to do something. . . ." I inhaled sharply, to stifle the tears.

"Oh, sweet girl." Roxy reached over to place her hand on my knee. "I'm sorry for being such an ass. I know admitting all this has to be hard."

" 'It's the lies that undo us,' that's what I tell the girls, what I've always told the girls. And look what I've done. It all sounds so ridiculous, and I know it sounds crazy. But I thought if I came here and found Steven and begged him to tell me anything he'd uncovered in the last forty years about these missing people, maybe I could feel like I was doing something to help."

"Lynn," Roxy said, taking my hand. "Forty years ago you believed this junk—I mean this . . . research. And that's OK. Lots of people believe in dumb stuff when they're kids. Hell, until I was twenty-six, I believed that if I sent Elvis enough mental messages, that he would seek me out and find me on the strength of my love. May I ask, though, what in God's name were you doing having an affair with some nutty professor who believes in little green men? I mean, all those maps and files? About alien abductions? Come on, Lynn."

"This is why I wanted to come alone." I opened up the truck door. "Stay in the truck, I'll be back."

"Oh, for God's sake," Roxy muttered, lifting the hem of her denim dress and sliding out her door.

I carried the safe, with a sweater draped over it, into the building, Roxy shuffling behind. The hallway of the professors' offices was silent, and I set the safe down outside Steven's door. Roxy grumbled to herself as she once again picked the lock.

I went in and slid the safe under the desk. Roxy looked around with renewed disdain at the maps. "What do we do now?"

"I need to find out where he may have gone—"

"Excuse me, but how did you get in here?"

A young man stood in the door. He wore dark-rimmed glasses and a flannel with a Morrissey T-shirt underneath.

"We're housekeeping," Roxy said with a smile.

"This office is supposed to be locked."

"Perhaps you should mind your own business." She smiled wider.

"This is my business. I'm Professor Richards's graduate student. No one is supposed to be in here."

Roxy sighed. "It is too early to be this annoying—"

"I'm an old friend of Professor Richards," I said. "I'm trying to find him."

"He's not here."

"Do you know when you expect him back?"

"I think you read the sign on the door before you broke in. He's on leave."

"It's important that we find him. Does he have a cell phone? Or could you give me his address?"

"He keeps an unlisted number and doesn't give out his address."

"Are you his student or the head of his security detail?" Roxy asked.

"Could I give you my number? Perhaps you could pass it along to him?" I reached into my purse and quickly wrote it down on an old receipt.

"I suppose. But I need to know how you got in here."

"Oh, for God's sake," Roxy snatched the paper out of my hands and thumped it against the chest of the student. "Here, take it and stick it in your Velcro wallet. Come on, Lynnie."

I gave him a soft thanks as Roxy walked me down the hall. "We need to get the move on. Mr. Personality back there seems the type to call campus police. Tell me you didn't write your full name or phone number on that sheet."

"I most certainly did."

"Really, Lynn," she said, pressing her key fob to open the truck doors. "Why not give them all the proof they need to bust us for breaking in."

"I don't care at this point. I need to find Steven."

"The police can take care of that."

"I can't go to police with this yet. You know why now."

"Well, Google Agent Mulder, then. See where he lives. I'm going to that Shell station we passed to get us farther away from the scene of the crime."

As she drove down the street, I pulled out my iPhone and stared helplessly at its shining screen. "I know how to use Google, of course, but where's the symbol—"

"They're called apps. Jesus, Lynn." She took my phone. "Don't go getting all senior citizen on me."

"We are senior citizens. And thus, you cannot look at that phone and drive. There's the gas station."

Roxy parked, took off her glasses, and spent the next several minutes holding the phone a good one to two inches from her face, rapidly punching on the screen until she swore and put her glasses back on. "Well, nothing pops. Not in Google, not in whitepages.com. Mr. Keeper of the Gates back there was right about the unlisted address and all."

My phone vibrated with the ring tone of chimes. "It's Stella."

"You better answer. The texts you sent the girls were uncharacteristically brief."

I answered the call. "Hi, hon. Yes, I'm fine. We're having a nice time."

I responded with genuine interest to the mundane, adding here and there brief statements of where we were supposedly eating in Little Rock's River Market district.

"Tell Anne that I'll call her later—"

"Give me the phone for a minute." Roxy reached for the phone.

"Uh, well, Roxy wants to say hi." I gave her a warning glance.

"Hi, sweet girl. Listen, when you do all that snooping to find people for your stories, how do you find them? Uh-huh. Well, my brother's trashy ex-wife owes him some money, and we think she's invested it in a tanning booth franchise in Hot Springs, but she has an unlisted number. Uh-huh. Really? You have to pay for that? No, you don't have to do it." Roxy waved away my gesture to hang up. "Isn't there another way? Uh-huh. Uh-huh. Good tip! Property deeds. Public record. We'll try that. Thanks darlin', love you."

Roxy handed the phone back but covered up the speaker, "Wrap this up, sister."

•   •   •

"I'm going to say 1910," Roxy said, staring up at the Victorian. "See the columns? Gauging by those and that tired old foundation, I'd say early 1900s."

I hugged my arms, looking at the empty windows and the snow drifting on the stairs. A few neglected newspapers lay on the front porch, still in plastic bags. The county's home-ownership records indicated Steven lived here. Strange that I felt bold enough to waltz into his office, the very place where it all began, but I was hesitant to even approach the house.

"Well, shall we?" Roxy said, taking the cracked concrete pathway up to the stairs. I hovered behind.

She repeatedly knocked. No lights came on. No one peered through the blinds. "Let's try the back door."

I followed her from the porch and around the house. *What if he's here? What am I going to say?* I thought of the magazine with William's picture on the cover in the safe in Steven's office. My cheeks flushed in anger.

The door under a weary overhang in the back gently opened with the rapping of Roxy's knuckles.

"Well, someone isn't too concerned about the crime rate in Champaign-Urbana. You can't commit breaking and entering if the door is unlocked, right? Hello? Hello?"

"Roxy . . ." I cautioned as she walked inside.

The mudroom was dark. I blinked, waiting for my eyes to adjust, scanning the glass fronts of a stackable washing machine and dryer, seeing no clothes inside.

Roxy continued to call out as we moved down a hall into the kitchen. Vinyl floors first laid down three decades ago matched outdated appliances and countertops. Mismatched furniture and newspapers littered the house. In the living room, a vintage refrigerator for Coke bottles stood right next to a sixty-inch-screen television.

I looked for photographs, any indication that Steven had a family, maybe even grandchildren of his own. The bachelor-pad vibe was too overwhelming to think he did.

"Well, I'm going whole hog. I'm looking around," Roxy said. "He's clearly not here, but I want to see if there's any other fan mail waiting for you."

A quick walk-through of the first floor revealed empty drawers left open, paperless file cabinets, and bare closets.

"I would like to sit down, but you know Stanley Steemer has never cleaned that couch." Roxy pulled up one of the dining room chairs instead, watching me cover my lips with a balled-up fist.

"What are we doing, Lynnie? Do you think he's crazy? I mean, obsessive compulsive, bipolar, schizophrenic? I mean, he'd have to be—to a degree—to believe that alien stuff—"

"You don't know what you're talking about."

Her eyebrows rose.

"I'm sorry."

"Don't apologize, just explain this to me: In the last twenty four hours, I've learned my best friend, who I say affectionately is the most normal, least-controversial person on earth, had an affair forty years ago, and maybe a love child, with a UFO hunter. So give me a minute to let all this sink in."

"I believed him. I believed in what he was doing. I reviewed his research, I studied the cases, I talked to the families. I knew all about them, every one of them. I wasn't just the office manager, Roxy. I was one of them."

"One of whom?"

"They weren't the people you see on TV now, talking about alien sightings and conspiracies. Back then, they worked quietly, communicated between universities all over the world."

"So you're telling me you were a UFO researcher too? Come on, Lynn."

"I believed in it as much as I believed in anything."

"And yet when you came back to Nashville, you decided to never, not even once, share all this with me?"

"Things got bad at the end. The work got too . . . intense. And when I found out I was pregnant, I knew I didn't want that kind of life for my child. I knew I had to make a clean break. It's why I never even went back for Tom's graduation, why I've never come back here at all. Over time, with the kids and Tom's work and then his political career . . . it's been a long time, Roxy. I had no desire to go back to all that—"

My phone began to chime in my purse, and I sighed. "It's probably Tom, he's called three times." I dug it out, my eyes growing wide at the screen. "It's a 217 area code—I think that's Springfield. And Champaign."

"Well, answer it."

"Hello?"

"Yes, is this Lynn? Lynn Roseworth?"

"Yes."

"This is Doug Ellis. We met earlier today in Dr. Richards's office. I knew you looked familiar. You're married to Senator Roseworth. I also know you're Lynn Stanson, Steve's office manager from a long time ago."

That surprised me. "How do you . . . ?"

"I've been Dr. Richards's grad assistant for five years, and before that I was one of his students."

"It's very important that I find Steven. Can you please tell me what happened to him?"

"I had to give you the company line back there at school. I'm not sure if I can trust you."

"I promise you that you can."

He paused. "Can you meet to talk?"

"Of course. I have to find Steven. I thought he was still teaching, that's why I came all this way. I didn't even know he was gone until I arrived. We haven't spoken in decades."

"I'll have to talk to the others and see if they're willing to brief you about what they know. But I won't be able to reach them until tonight, and then they'll have to travel. How long are you in town?"

"Only for a few more days."

"Let me make some calls, but I think I can get everyone together tomorrow night. Can you meet at seven o'clock? I'll text you the address where to meet."

"Yes, I can meet you. Thank you, and please thank the others. If you need me before then, please call again."

He hung up without saying good-bye.

"What the hell was that, Lynn? Are we meeting Mr. McCreep? And who are the others?"

"I'm sure they're academics as well."

"Academics," Roxy grunted. "So we're going to stay in this Midwestern freak show for another day to meet more UFO hunters?"

"They're called Researchers," I said softly. "At least that's what we used to call ourselves. Let's go, OK?"

"Fine by me. All this tragic bachelorhoodness is making me crave a burger and a milk shake. Maybe I'll chase it with a Budweiser to complete the image."

As she walked out, I paused for a moment, looking around. The loneliness of the house was heavy, almost oppressive, as if it were waiting to sigh.

When I stepped out into the sun, my phone dinged. The text came from the 217 number Doug had called me from earlier. It simply read the address where to meet.

I put my phone in my purse, deciding not to tell Roxy yet that we would be returning to Steven's home.

Roxy was grumpy most of the next day. I let her stew as we flitted among antiques shops and bookstores. I texted with the girls and had a brief conversation with Tom, who said the interview had gone well, with no surprises. Roxy made little to no comment about anything, which meant she was about to blow. I'd learned over the years to give her space but remain close by when the clouds burst. We ate lunch and then dinner in a kind of understood silence, until she polished off her glass of red wine and narrowed her eyes at me. "So was this some kind of cult?"

"No."

"Because it sounds like a cult. And we're here for the reunion. And you said you were one of them? Really, Lynn, you believed in UFOs?"

I twisted my spaghetti with my fork. "I believed in Steven."

"You speak so calmly about it now. A day ago you nearly had a nervous breakdown even admitting it."

"It's freeing, in a way, to talk about it. It hung over me for a long time when I came back to Nashville, but then Anne came, and then Kate, and Tom and I got into a routine. Just as his political career was taking off we had Stella, and our lives were so hectic and full, it became easier and easier not to think about that time in my life. Now, speaking only to you, of course, I feel like I'm recalling some wild phase. Like when someone dyed her hair purple."

"That was not intentional, and it does haunt me to this day."

"It was like I was in on a secret, and all these really brilliant and strange and weird and daring people accepted me."

Roxy began to chew the last piece of garlic bread. "And Tom really doesn't know anything about it."

"No, he doesn't. He never had a clue. He was so wrapped up in his studies that I think he was happy that I had found something to occupy myself, and that brought in some extra money. But that's Tom; he never means to offend anyone when he's more interested in his work than he is in them, and I've come to accept that. I could blame the troubles in our marriage then on two young people who weren't ready to play house, but honestly, it was just a precursor to what would be the rest of our lives: him wrapped up in his career and satisfied if I appeared happy in whatever I was doing. It's only when he knows I'm frustrated or mad about something that he takes a break from whatever he's working on. If I'm happy, he's completely detached. I think after the girls were in college, he was more than ready for me to attempt, once more, to write a novel or start my own business. He couldn't be burdened with having to spend more time with his wife, who suddenly was without a purpose."

Roxy looked down at her plate.

"Please don't think I'm complaining," I said. "I'm certainly not. That's just how our marriage is, and most of the time I'm fine with it. In fact, I would have never come back here—ever—if William hadn't gone missing. Can you imagine if I revealed that I used to investigate missing people who we believed were abducted? Everyone would have thought I was having a nervous breakdown. No one would have believed me. And I would have created another problem for my family during the worst crisis of our lives. So I tried to push it aside. Now I can't seem to stop thinking about it."

"How could you have ever *not* thought of it?"

"I had to bury those years. That's the best way I can describe it. I had to smother them to make my marriage work, first of all. And when the girls came and Tom's career took off, I had to close the door on that feeling of . . . purpose? Is that the right word? First, I became a mother. Then a lawyer's wife. Then a state representative's wife, then a US senator's wife, and any ambitions I ever had to do something with my own life were gone. And once you've been given that taste of . . . professional acceptance, it's hard to douse. It took me years, Roxy, to get past it. But like all things, in time, I did."

Roxy took off her glasses. "I never knew. Here I am, your best friend, and I assumed you loved the whole mom-and-wife thing. That is, until we opened the shop."

"I do love it, don't get me wrong. But I got lost all those years ago, and it's reminded me that sometimes only by being lost do we find the path to who we are supposed to be. But . . . instead of staying on that path, I ran. I ran back home and away from everything here. So I never knew . . . what, or who, I could have been."

"Why did you run?" she asked quietly.

I looked out the window. "I was scared. I stood on the edge of a cliff to a wild and uncertain life and opted not to jump."

"And yet, here we are. Are you hoping to find out where this professor is, so you can track him down and make sure he's not involved with William's disappearance? Ask him why he had those maps of your property? Or do you honestly think . . . you'll find out something to explain where William has gone? If he has been . . . abducted . . . that these people will know how to call back the mother ship that took him?"

"I know sitting around Nashville putting Band-Aids on widely gaping wounds wasn't working. Maybe I'm doing it to convince myself I'm not useless. I can only explain what it feels like to have William missing. . . . It's like there's an elephant on my chest, and I can't breathe when I think about him being somewhere away from us. And being here, doing this, it's easier to breathe."

Roxy reached across the table and took my hand. "I promise to keep my mouth shut. Well, scratch that, we know that's not going to happen."

We took our leftovers, uncertain if they would ever be eaten, but knowing it was cold enough for them to remain in the backseat without going bad.

"So where are we having this Tupperware party?" Roxy asked as we slid into the truck.

I exhaled. "Steven's house."

"What? But he's not there and clearly hasn't been for a while. This is weird, Lynn."

"Maybe we were wrong. Maybe he actually lives somewhere else and he'll be there when we arrive. Maybe that's who Doug intended to be there all along."

"I'm biting my tongue, I'm biting my tongue," Roxy said, putting the truck in drive.

The old Victorian looked even drearier at night. No lights were on, but there were several cars parked outside.

"This is the part in the horror movie when the best friend advises the beautiful heroine not to go inside the haunted house. And do you know what happens to the friend in all those movies? She's the first to get her head cut off," Roxy said.

"Should we go around to the back again?" I asked, my heart in my throat.

"Nope. If no one answers at the front, we're not going in."

We approached the dark house and I knocked on the door. Within seconds, Doug opened the door, his cell phone illuminating his face.

"Come on in."

"Maybe you should turn on a few lights first," Roxy said, holding fast to the back of the sleeve of my coat.

"Everyone is downstairs," he said.

Roxy grunted. "There is no downstairs."

She rubbed her own forehead head as I turned to her in incredulity.

"I already knew you'd been here, I saw you on the security cameras." Doug motioned us in.

"You leave the back door open and you have hidden security cameras?" Roxy asked, still clinging to my sleeve. "And FYI, sir. I have 911 on speed dial."

"Just because a house looks like it has lousy security doesn't mean it actually does. Steven had to make it look like he left and never intended to return. And when he's out of town, he turns over the monitoring of his security to me."

"Is he here?" I asked.

Doug shook his head. "I wish he was, it would make this easier. Come on, I'll show you how to get downstairs."

He used the flashlight on his phone to lead us once more through the weary furniture towards the television. His light flashed over the monitor and then settled on the horizontal silver handle of the retro Coke-bottle refrigerator that had screamed bachelor pad to us when we first snuck in.

He pulled out his wallet and flashed what looked like a white credit card in front of the handle. We heard a soft beep, and he opened the door.

Instead of rows of Coke, there was nothing but faint light. Through the hollowed-out fridge was a staircase leading down.

"Clever. Creepy, but clever," Roxy noted.

"Steven had it custom built and the keyless entry added. We needed to have our meetings in private. I'd say ladies first, but I assume you want me to go down first."

"Sounds good to me," Roxy said, waving him on.

We followed him through the repurposed refrigerator and down the stairs that had clearly been reinforced over the years, for they failed to creak as we passed wood paneling dating back to the seventies.

We descended into an unfinished basement with enough patchwork to allow for gatherings for those unconcerned with comfort. Roxy said she felt like she was attending an AA meeting, but the looks on the faces of the people milling below kept her from saying anything more.

We slowed our descent as all the conversations stopped. Most of the people wore glasses and appeared to be roughly around our age. Several were in suits. Doug certainly stood out, and he beckoned for us to come all the way down.

"Let's everyone find a seat." He motioned to the scattered chairs and a battered couch, but everyone remained standing, staring at me.

"It really is you," one man said, taking a handkerchief out of his tweed jacket to clean his glasses. "I guess it's true: You believe in the little green men just like the rest of us. You look just like you do on TV."

I bristled at that. A woman walked forward, her long silver hair tied back in a braid. "Rupert, you prove yet again your impeccable skill for saying the wrong thing at the wrong time. It's been a long time, Lynn. You may not recognize the few of us who were here back in the day."

I cleared my throat. "I doubt you would have recognized me, or even remembered my name, if it hadn't been for my husband."

"Oh, I would have remembered," the woman said, smiling warmly. "I would remember the nice girl with the pretty blond curls who listened—didn't laugh at me, didn't judge—actually listened to me talk about my brother. Didn't think less of me when I twisted my hair like a little girl." She reached up and twirled a strand. "I still do it."

I tilted my head. "Barbara?"

The woman nodded. "And do you remember my brother's name?"

Don Rush. Of course I remember. But I don't know any of you. I could barely tell my best friend about my past. I'm not about to discuss my memories with strangers.

I forced a grimace. "I'm sorry, I don't."

"But I bet you remember his story."

"I remember wishing I could have helped you more."

"You did help." She reached out and laid a hand on my arm. "You made me feel like I wasn't crazy. You and Steven both. And you gave me this."

She handed me a small laminated card, frayed and yellowed over time. I smiled at one of the prayer cards Steven gave me to hand out to the families of the missing.

"Do you remember this? It got me through a lot of hard times. I whispered it like a prayer: 'You are with me. You are in the rain. You are in my tears. You are where the water falls,'" she recited.

I ran my fingers over the words, and Barbara closed my fingers around the card. "You keep it. Maybe it will bring you comfort now."

"How about me?" asked a morbidly obese man who was leaning on a chair. My heart skipped a beat as I instantly remembered him.

Marcus Burg. You were there for one of the most frightening moments of my life. "I'm sorry, it's been so long—"

"I wasn't this fat back then. I was fat, just not megasized. Marcus, the guy with the telescope? Ham radio operator? Trying to pick up the little green men on the radio? We met in a cornfield once."

"Oh yes, of course, Marcus."

"Again, let's everybody have a seat," Doug repeated. "We've got a lot to discuss."

A man in an expensive-looking Brooks Brothers suit frowned at Roxy. "No offense, ma'am, but this is highly sensitive information. I've never even seen you before. And I've only ever seen the politician's wife on television."

"Robert, at one time, this woman knew more about being a Researcher than you do," Barbara said.

"Prove it," the man insisted. "What's the Arthur Crowning incident?"

He disappeared while fishing after a rainstorm, his gear and lunchbox left inside the boat.

I shifted my eyes.

"What about the Doyle Robinson disappearance?"

Doyle Robinson went hiking on a trail in Giant City in downstate Illinois. Hiked the trail all his life. Was never seen again. But if I tell you everything I remember, you'll assume I'm still one of you. I have no idea what you intend to do with my memories.

I bit my lip. "I'm sorry, I don't remember."

"Those are only the most famous abduction cases in Illinois, and you don't remember them? So, again, we're here to make a deal with Steve's old girlfriend, and she doesn't even remember anything—"

"What about my brother Don?" Barbara asked quietly. "What do you remember about him?"

I will not, however, come off as a flake. "I remember he was your twin, and you were living in . . . Michigan. You awoke one night to lights in your bedroom. You went downstairs and found the door open, and you went to the window to see your brother standing out in a snowstorm. There were suddenly lights, and your brother was gone."

The room was silent. Barbara nodded slowly. "Yes, that's all true. You see, Robert, Lynn didn't investigate the Crowning or Robinson cases. But she did mine. And she cared, too."

I cared about all of them. I remember them all.

Doug cleared his throat. "We're here to talk about Steven."

"Yes," I said. "Why isn't he at the university?"

"The official word is that he was suspended for using university equipment, on university time, for personal use," he responded. "That's what Dean Fulton said. The only reason the dean even kept Steven around was because of his expertise. His articles about the gases on Mars alone have given this department a gold-star reputation in the academic world. But, as you may recall, Ms. Stanson—"

"It's Roseworth."

"Yes, as in Senator Roseworth, of course. You may recall, Mrs. Roseworth, that Steven is also terrible at playing the academic poker needed to stay ahead at this college. So I wasn't surprised when I showed up a few months ago and saw his office locked. I was surprised, however, that he left me no message. Nothing. All I had was the official word from the university's communications department that they severed ties with him, and that information was only supposed to be shared internally, not with anyone else."

"When did this happen?" I asked.

"End of the summer semester."

Roxy flashed me a look.

"Has there been no sign of him at all?" asked a woman in a long skirt, pulling her glasses up to rest on her crown of gray hair.

Barbara shook her head. "No, Mary."

"I don't understand," the woman continued. "Steven was so excited this summer. The last I talked to him, he felt like he was making some breakthroughs, especially on the Abel and Notish cases. And then, suddenly, he was gone. We still have no idea why, Doug?"

"As I've told you, I came to work to find that the dean had his office locked up. So I came here, and everything had been cleaned out, practically. And that's it."

"So he just skipped town? And no one has had any word from him? I know this drips with irony, but should you have filed a missing-persons report?" Mary asked.

The room grew quiet, and Doug shifted uncomfortably. "Can you imagine the questions police would have asked? Once I told them that the dean suspected he was using university equipment for personal reasons, and that all his belongings were gone, they would have assumed he was just lying low."

"Maybe he is," Robert said, loosening his expensive tie. "Listen, Steven is a great colleague. An even better Researcher. But there might be some truth to what the university suspects—"

"Bullshit," Doug interjected.

"—and Steven is trying to sort out his next move. But it's been three months. Even if he had a reason to disappear like this, we need to find him. Just to make sure he's OK."

"Which brings us to why we wanted to meet with you, Lynn," Doug said. "To see if we could help each other."

"I'm not sure how I could help. I came here for help myself."

Doug looked briefly to Robert. "We're willing to share everything with you. All of the records we've stored on thumb drives, or on the cloud, on every case. And, course, the video."

The room grew quiet and everyone looked at me, waiting.

"I'm sorry, what video?" I asked.

"Of course, you never saw it. It came to us years after you were gone," Barbara said. "Show her, Doug. Pull it up on your laptop."

Doug frowned. "Maybe we should finish talking about what we need her to do, first. I don't know about sharing—"

"Just show her, Doug," she insisted. "She was a Researcher long before you were even born."

In a move that was so dramatic that I knew Roxy was rolling her eyes, Doug reached into his shirt and pulled out a simple chain on which a thumb drive was attached. He slid a laptop out of a beat-up satchel alongside of his chair and opened it. After plugging in the memory stick, he huddled over the screen, keeping the keyboard close, so no one could see the passwords he was furiously typing.

After a few moments, he placed the laptop on a coffee table and swiveled it around towards me. "This is part of what we're prepared to share with you, if we can come to an agreement. But I must strongly warn you—"

"Doug, play it," Barbara said wearily. "And turn up the volume. It's hard to hear."

He reached over the screen to punch the volume key several times, and then hit the space bar. The blue video screen turned black, then the grayish-white image of a man sitting in a chair came into view.

Converted from film on which it was first recorded, the video occasionally flickered, showing the man dressed in all black, his hair slicked over, with the kind of hard part that was so popular when I was a little girl.

"I can't hear anything," Roxy said.

"It's coming, give it a second," Doug scowled.

"Are you comfortable?" the man in the video said, his voice

hollow, recorded on a microphone that was too far away from its subject.

The man leaned forward. "Can you tell me about what you saw?"

The film quality was so poor that I could barely make out that he was beginning to take notes.

"What do you remember about the ship in the sky?"

Doug reached over and snapped the computer closed. He stared at me, holding his chin high.

"What you've just seen is the first proof ever recorded of a government operative questioning someone who'd been abducted."

"*That's* your proof?" Roxy asked. "How does that prove anything—?"

"Where did that come from?" I asked softly.

"I wish I knew. Steven obtained it. But there's much more. And while we only have footage of the operative asking the questions, at the end, the camera moves a bit, and for a second you see whom he is talking to. I'm willing to show it to you, as well as all Steven's latest findings and research about the missing. It might help you too, because I know you think your grandson's been abducted too. There's one thing I'd ask for in return."

He leaned forward. "Go public. All out. Press conference and everything. Admit your past as a Researcher and how you feel your grandson has been abducted. Say that you're working with us to find him. The hope is that Steven will see it, wherever he is, and get back in touch with us. Or maybe even you."

I put my hand to my chest. "I can't . . . do that."

"Why?" Doug asked sharply.

"I can't."

"Then we tell you nothing." He waved his hand. "You once supported our efforts. You believed in it; Steven told me everything. Everything. Now your own grandson has gone missing, and you won't come forward with support for us? Do you care that much more about your husband's image than finding your grandson?"

I grabbed my purse. "It was a mistake coming here."

"Lynn," Barbara pleaded.

"I won't be forced into anything." I stood. Roxy joined me, chewing her cheek.

"Then you leave here with nothing."

"Doug!" Barbara said.

"Trust me, you want to see this entire film. But not without a guarantee."

"You are terrible people," I said, hurrying towards the stairs. Barbara stood, but Roxy held up a warning hand.

"You should be ashamed," Roxy scolded, wagging her finger. "Giving a grandmother false hope and all that. You're nut jobs, every last one of you. And don't think I won't call the cops on you all."

"You won't," Doug said. "Because it will all be traced back to Lynn, and apparently her public persona is more important than her grandson."

"Eat shit, you little punk," Roxy said, catching up with me at the top of the stairs as I stepped through the shell of the fridge.

We hustled through the house and out the door, Roxy's hand on the small of my back. I heard the truck unlock and practically ran around to get inside the cab.

My face was buried in my hands when she turned the key. "Oh, Lynnie."

"Drive, Roxy. Drive to the hotel and get our things, and then drive all the way home. Don't stop."

"Honey, let's think about this—"

"No, I want to go home."

"Of course."

I heard a rap at my window and turned to see Doug standing outside, shivering. He'd clearly run out after us, for he wasn't wearing a coat.

"Lynn, this isn't only about William." He was practically yelling.

"Back away from the car, you asshole," Roxy said.

"You'll never know. You'll never know the truth—"

Roxy threw the truck in reverse with such force that Doug stumbled back.

Outside, a bit of ice began to fall. It had been spring when I last left Champaign. It was fitting that it was winter now, and the air smelled like a snow. I was right to leave here and never come back. I prayed for the kind of whopper where snow covers the entire town. I could leave knowing everything here would be buried.

TEN

The silence in the truck was interrupted occasionally with my sharp intake of breath. When Roxy tried to comfort me, I shook my head. When we got into Nashville and neared the house, I proclaimed my stupidity for even suggesting the journey to Illinois. I insisted that I wouldn't put my family through any more agony, that we were never again to discuss what we had seen or learned. Roxy implored me to reconsider, said we should, at the very least, go to the police with the information that Steven had a map of the property and vanished at roughly the same time William disappeared.

"No," I said simply. "We'd be wasting their time."

Thus I perfected the art of denial.

The smells were my greatest ally. The earthy pine, the cinnamon candles, the burning of dry wood. Baking pumpkin bread, tangy oranges in bowls, and brewing flavored coffee were more powerful now than the things that once soothed the anxiety I routinely felt with the approach of the holidays. The idea of all those gifts to buy, all that wrapping, all that traffic, used to be balanced out by the white lights wrapping the trunks of the trees outside the house and Johnny Mathis holiday music. All those worries were petty and meaningless now, and no amount of music or decorations could lift my spirits.

So I relied on the scents of the season to smother my sadness. When I practically moved into the Rose Peddler, which we transitioned into its seasonal holiday phase, I inhaled deeply as I thoroughly checked each tree brought in from McMinnville for any traces of blight. When I was in the house, amidst the Christmas trees I couldn't bear to give more than a passing glance to, I put spices in a pot on the stove to simmer. My tall coffee mug was always in hand at the Green Hills mall, my nose kept close to the rim as I tried not to cry purchasing gifts for the grandkids, knowing who wouldn't be there on Christmas morning. When he was home on the weekends, Tom occasionally complained his allergies were kicking up because a candle seemed to be burning in every room.

Roxy kept the festive music at a lull in the store, but flooded the place with candies and freshly baked cookies to give to children as their parents fretted over finding the perfect tree. When Roxy caught me glazing over while looking at the small children, she rushed to the house and grabbed a bunch of buckeyes out of the fridge, returning as quickly as possible to fill the shop with peanut butter and chocolate.

I approached my daily tasks with a ferocity, finding if I baked twice as much gingerbread, vacuumed twice as often, the days passed instead of limping by. I sat in with Tom during the weekly updates with investigators, listening as he peppered them with questions, pretending to buy into their theories. My bottom lip developed a sore because I bit it so often.

When the second Friday of December arrived, and the discount prices on the Christmas trees began, I welcomed the crowd at the store as yet another blessed distraction.

It was nearly nine o'clock when the last family left and

Roxy declared it a night. We were sitting at the table behind the counter going over the receipts when Stella came in, her cheeks rosy from the chill. She'd come right from work to help with the Christmas crowds. "Mom, do you feel like one more customer? Some lady said you helped her out earlier, and she had a quick question for you."

"Sure, hon." I said, passing the receipts to Roxy.

"Oh, let me personally thank this woman for enabling me now to do all the closing by myself," Roxy said.

I patted her on the shoulder and grabbed my coat and scarf. The night was lit by rows of white lights strung above the trees. I slipped on my gloves and walked into the rows of pine, seeing no one.

"Hello?" I called out. "Did someone need help?"

Someone called out my name from the far end of the trees, and I hustled over. I peered out in the darkness beyond.

"Hello?" I said.

"Were there ladybugs swarming when your grandson disappeared?" a voice said from the trees.

I froze. A female shape stood between two trees, her long silver hair pulled back in a ponytail. She wore a long dark-blue overcoat, too thick and heavy for the southern winters.

"Barbara?"

It had only been a few weeks since I'd seen her, but she seemed thinner, even in her bulky winter coat.

"Did they, Lynn? Did they swarm?" Barbara asked.

I looked around for a moment before replying. "You know they did."

"It's been documented in so many cases. Sometimes the beetles cover entire walls, crawling like they've been driven insane. When I see ladybugs now, sweet as they are, it stops my heart."

She exhaled, her breath white in the icy night. "They have your grandson. They've taken him. Steven said he thinks he can help you find him. If your boy's been returned."

"Who has William? And where is Steven? I thought no one knew where he was."

"Steven is here now, Lynn. That's why I'm here tonight, to take you to him."

I looked past her to make sure neither Roxy nor Stella had come out to see where I was.

"How could you come here, after what happened?" I asked.

"I'm not happy about it either. Doug can be a first-class jerk, and can't see past his own ambition in order to do the right thing. The others think he's the Messiah, with his grand talk of taking all this public. He sees you as the key to do that, to finally get validation for all our work. And he is genuinely concerned about Steven. But he doesn't know how it feels to lose someone, like we do. You have to remember, Lynn, my brother was my twin. When he vanished, half of me vanished too. And you don't care if people believe you or not. You want to find him. My brother is long gone, but your grandson may not be. That's what Steven thinks. He thinks there's still a chance to find him."

A chill ran through me so severely that I tightened the scarf around my neck. "What do you expect me to do?"

"Come with me. Hear Steven out. That's all. You can walk away again if you want. It's just me and Steven this time, none of the others even know we're here."

"All this time, you've known where Steven has been? And you say he's here?"

"No. I hadn't spoken to him until he contacted me a few days ago. We only met here yesterday. I'll let him tell you where he's been; that's for him to say. I'm the only one who knows how to even contact him now. That was his decision when he decided to run."

"Run?"

"He can explain." Barbara looked back at the shop.

"He won't have to. I'm not going with you. I don't want anything to do with you or the others. Not after what happened. And I won't put my family through the scrutiny that Doug would require for this information."

"Doug isn't a part of this."

"I don't know that. For all I know, you could take me to him again. I'm sorry, but no. I can't do it. I won't do it."

"Steven thought you might feel that way." Barbara reached into her pocket. She brought out an envelope and offered it.

"What is that?"

"The names of two people Steven said for you to research. He said to look up their names at the local library, and you might change your mind."

I cautiously reached out and took the envelope. "I don't understand."

"Steven says you will, if you look into them. I'll give you all day tomorrow to inquire if you choose. Tomorrow night, if you want to see Steven, I'll wait for you at Chevron gas around the corner. I'll be there at nine o'clock. I'll wait thirty minutes. If you come, I'll take you to Steven. If you don't, then I'll take that as your decision. I won't fault you either way. I felt horrible about what happened, and I told Steven that you deserved better. That's why he came. That's why I'm here."

She buried her hands in her pockets. "It's colder here than I would have thought," she said, walking back once more into the pine trees.

.   .   .

I'd immediately gotten online after we'd closed the shop and Roxy and Stella had gone home, checking for anything about the two names typed on a single piece of white paper, along with corresponding dates. The fact that it wasn't written in Steven's all-caps handwriting seemed dubious, for anyone could have typed the names. But I looked anyway, and could find nothing about a Josh Stone, August 5, 1945, or an Amelia Shrank, August 2, 1934.

Amelia Shrank. I somehow knew the name. But like the answer to a Trivial Pursuit question that remained on the tip of your tongue and would not come until the other side of the card was read aloud, the explanation of how I recognized a name from the early 1930s would not surface.

I was at the downtown library as soon as it opened the next morning, and made my way to the microfilm room. It was as visually impressive as the rest of the library, with its light fixtures and paint colors straight out of Restoration Hardware, but it did not have the lure of the popular fiction section or the civil-rights collection. The emptiness of the room was disquieting; I feared any moment there would be some kind of whispered ambush from Doug in full entitled-Researcher mode, working alongside Barbara to get me alone to try and browbeat me into submission.

I cautiously sought out microfilm, peering down every aisle. I'd hoped the *Nashville Banner* published as far back as I needed to go. Before *The Tennessean* became the only newspaper in town, the *Banner* was its worthy competitor. Once I understood the catalog system, I found the archives of the paper for the entire year of 1934 and started sliding through the months.

The ancient technology still hummed as I remembered, but

I quickly grew frustrated with having to press the button to advance. I chastised myself, thinking of how I urged the grandkids to develop patience as they whined about a video taking too long to load on YouTube.

At last came August 2, and I immediately started reading the obituaries. It was the only way to search by name. When I finished the last obituary, and found no Amelia Shrank.

Was this just another way for Doug to try and wear me down? Was he watching from somewhere, maybe an adjoining room, to see how desperate I had become? Was he waiting, hoping I would break down in tears, when he would reveal himself, ready once again to make a deal? And what did he mean, that this wasn't only about William?

Barbara promised to take me to Steven, but if it were truly him, what would he want in return?

I thought of what Deanna, Tom's press secretary, had said: *Is there anything controversial about your family that we don't know about?*

Holding information for ransom wasn't the way of the Researchers I'd known. Intimidation, ultimatums, threats weren't how they operated. They were misfits, outsiders, even reclusive about what they knew, what they had seen. They wanted no attention.

In my time among them, I'd certainly learned they had reason to be afraid.

I leaned back and rubbed my eyes. A late night spent staring at a computer screen followed up by hours fixated on microfilm made my eyes as dry as the winter air. They'd felt that way so many times as I sat at my desk in the astronomy department, reading case after case, only finding relief when my tears moistened my bloodshot eyes.

•   •   •

I'd been so thrilled to escape that desk and all those tragic stories when Steven had come to me, almost in desperation, asking if I was able to meet one of his colleagues in a remote rural
area outside Springfield.

"It should be me going, but every spare second has to go
to my course review. I suppose I failed too many students last
semester. Dr. Roberts says it's something important and he
needs me to come tomorrow, and he doesn't come down from
Chicago very often."

"Dr. Roberts?"

"Mathematics professor at Loyola University. Chair of the
department. Rhodes Scholar. And one of us."

I had calmly, almost indifferently, agreed to go, but under
the desk clasped my hands together. I'd done my best to stay
aloof ever since Steven kneeled dangerously close to me in his
office the day I revealed the weather commonality of the disappearances. I didn't like how I left his office feeling flushed.

I told Tom the truth—at least the part that I had to go to
Springfield the next day for some research at the state capital.
When he had failed to even ask why an astronomy project
would require a trip to the home of the legislature, I knew he
wasn't paying attention and abruptly left the apartment.

I'd passed Decatur, rolling up the window at the smell of
the cornstarch plant, and headed down I-72, finally getting off
on exit 23. Cornfields flanked me on both sides as I traveled
down a paved road.

About twenty miles north of the interstate, I saw the lights
from police cars. Two squad cars were at the end of a dirt road,
and three more were parked around a white farmhouse tucked
on the edge of a tree line. An ambulance was rolling up to the
house. I'd slowed, and one of the officers waved me on past.
I'd hoped someone elderly hadn't died in the heat.

Five minutes later, on that same road, I found the address I was looking for. As Steven had explained, there was the heavily faded navy-blue stripe on the mailbox, the number thirty-five, and the dirt drive.

Yet as I stepped out of the car, I saw the house clearly hadn't been lived in for years. The windowpanes were cracked in several places and the roof sagged; it most likely was abandoned following one of the tornadoes that so plagued this area of the world.

"Mrs. Roseworth?"

I'd missed the pickup truck parked behind the house. A man leaned up against the bed. He was dressed in pressed pants and short-sleeved dress shirt.

"Dr. Roberts?

He walked out across the road, looking down in the direction I'd driven. His close-cropped white hair revealed skin splotchy with age spots, but he moved with a young person's urgency.

"So you're her," he extended his hand. "You're the one he talks so much about. Shall we be on our way?"

I was glad I wore a head scarf, or he would have seen that my ears flared an alarming shade of red.

"It's nice to meet you. I thought we were meeting in someone's house. . . ."

"That's the closest address that I could give to show Steven what I'd found. Apparently, no one lives there. Where we need to go is actually in the corn. You have on pretty shoes, but the ground is as dry as bone. They'll get dusty but not ruined. I'd pull your car back beside mine; we don't want to draw any attention from the road."

I did as he suggested and then joined him in the corn. Once

again, I was thankful for the scarf. I could already feel beads of sweat on my neck.

"Did you bring a camera?" he asked.

"A Hawkeye Instamatic."

"Good. Steven will need to see on the ground what I saw from the sky."

"Pardon?"

"I took some pictures from a friend's crop duster this morning. He's a photographer, too, and brought with him one of the photos we processed. But he can't print all of them in time for you to take with you tonight, so it's good you can snap some pictures while you're here. I'll send the aerial photo back with you, though."

"Photos of what?"

"We're almost there. I am surprised, though, that he sent a woman." He turned around with a sheepish grin. "Forgive me. There's not many of us of the female gender. But he obviously finds you capable, otherwise he wouldn't have sent you. I should have known he wouldn't have come."

"Why?"

"Because of the cornfield."

"I'm sorry, what's wrong with the cornfield?"

Dr. Roberts took out a handkerchief and wiped his forehead. "His sister, obviously. He still hasn't gotten over it."

He continued walking, and I hurried to catch up. "I don't understand what a cornfield and Steven's—I mean Dr. Richards's—sister, has anything to do with anything."

"You'll see."

We walked for another ten minutes, until the corn gave way to a clearing. The sunlight was blinding without the shade of the stalks. When I shielded my eyes, I realized it was no barren field.

Whoever farmed this land would soon come upon the bent stalks and ruined corn and most likely utter a litany of curses. The green stems and husks were pummeled to the ground for several yards in all directions. I knelt down, examining one of the stalks, seeing it was bent at a perfect ninety-degree angle.

"They're all like that."

I looked over to see a man sitting on an overturned bucket. The sight was almost comical, due to his immense size and how he somehow balanced himself on the pail.

"Lynn, this is Marcus Burg: pilot, ham-radio expert, and photographer. He's the one who first heard about the missing boy. He's also the one who found the circles."

"Circles?" I asked.

"Crop circles." Marcus held out his sagging arms. "You're in the middle of one now. Points right to where—"

"Let's let her look at the picture first, so she understands."

"Steven told me a two-year-old boy was missing, but that's all I know. How long ago did he disappear?"

"Two nights ago," Dr. Roberts answered.

"Two nights?" I looked out towards the police lights at the farmhouse. "He could still be alive, just not found yet. He went missing not far from here, correct? Why would you think he's been . . . ?"

Dr. Roberts gave me a pitying smile. "It took me a long time to say it out loud as well. And I'll admit, it's even strange to say it now. Abducted. By extraterrestrials. The longer you're at this, the easier it becomes to verbalize it. As you know, we typically don't get involved until much later, when the cops are gone and families get desperate. But when Marcus told me what he heard on the radio and what he saw from the sky, I came down. And summoned Steven here, figuring he wouldn't come. But I hoped, regardless."

"Why wouldn't he come?" I asked, frustrated at having to repeatedly ask for clarification of everything this man said.

"I probably shouldn't be the one telling you this, but if you're going to work with Steven, you need to know. Maybe sending you here is his way of letting you find out. He's strange, that one, but brilliant, and a good man."

"Steven's sister was abducted by aliens," Marcus said, rubbing his neck.

"Dr. Richards's sister is missing?"

"Abducted. It's the truth as he sees it, and it set him on this path, that's for certain," Dr. Roberts said. "I don't want to gloss over the details, and perhaps one day he will tell you all about it. He was eight, maybe nine. Steven, his parents, and younger sister, Elise, went to spend a weekend at their family farm in northern Iowa. I think it was his uncle's place. Anyway, there had been a terrible storm, and Elise and Steven were trapped in the house all day. When it let up a bit, they'd thrown on their boots to go play in the corn at dusk. Steven said his boots got stuck in the mud, and he was separated from Elise. He knew he would get in trouble for losing her, so he kept searching, until night. He was found by his parents, thanks to the farmers who saw his flashlight. A strong beam of light. Except that Steven wasn't carrying a flashlight."

Despite the heat, goose bumps rose on my arms. "His sister was never found," Dr. Roberts continued. "His mother later committed suicide, and his father blamed Steven for all of it. I don't know if Steven was a strange kid before that, but he certainly was afterwards, he even admits it. He became obsessed with trying to find Elise. It was only when he became a young man that he was able to get the police reports from that night. There was absolutely nothing to explain what happened. The assumption was that some kind of bobcat or something got her. The fields were even cleared to try and find her body. There was no sign of her. All the police report noted was that Steven's uncle didn't care if that particular stretch of land was cleared, because it was useless anyway. And it was useless, because something had flattened the crops in large circles."

Dr. Roberts motioned around them. "Obviously, no one took pictures back then, but when Marcus heard about the missing kid, and that the farmer of this land reported someone had ruined large swaths of his crops—"

"I took my plane up, and I saw the circles, but I couldn't take pictures while I had the controls. I had to get Max down here from Chicago, and when we went up, he took some pictures with my camera," Marcus said. "Want to see?"

When he didn't bother to stand, we walked over. He reached into the front of his bib overalls and took out a black-and-white photo and handed it to me. "I've only had time to print one of them."

The photo clearly showed a series of large circles—ten in all—in a single row among the corn. At closer inspection, I could see they varied in size, the first much larger, gradually diminishing to a tiny circle.

"We're standing in the middle of that row now," Dr. Roberts said. "You keep following the circles, and they end at the farmhouse where the boy is missing."

I looked closer at the photo. "It's like they're marking where they do it." Marcus pointed. "An arrow straight to their target—"

"That's my bucket."

The voice caused us to turn around. In the row we had walked now stood a thin man.

He was filthy, with tattered, dusty clothes and hair that clearly hadn't been washed for days. I couldn't tell if it was the angle of the sun or his complexion that enhanced the dark circles around his eyes, which had caused me to misjudge his age. He couldn't have been more than sixteen.

"Mama says we can take an ear or two," the teenager said. "I need my bucket."

"You live near here?" Dr. Roberts asked.

The boy flicked his thumb back down the row. "You done parked at my house. Why you'ins out here? You wit' the cops? They ain't gonna find that boy. Not them men in suits neither."

"Shit," Marcus said. "Max—"

"Why won't they find him?" Dr. Roberts took a step forward. "Where is the boy?"

"You got money to pay me to tell you what I seen? Them suits had money."

Dr. Roberts dug into his back pocket and pulled out a worn wallet. He slid out a few singles, handing them over.

The boy smiled, exposing rows of crooked teeth and squinting in the sunlight. "Mama says I'm lyin', but I seen it. I seem 'em get dragged right up into them clouds. He gone. Straight up to heaven. That's what I told them suits too."

"When did you talk to these men in suits?" Dr. Roberts demanded.

" 'Bout two hours ago."

"Shit!" Marcus said, looking around wildly. "Shit!"

"Go," Dr. Roberts ordered, motioning for me. "We've got to go."

"But I haven't taken a single picture," I said, watching Marcus practically bulldoze into the corn after brushing past the teen.

"It doesn't matter." Dr. Roberts took me by the arm. I looked back one last time at the boy, who stared after us with dull eyes.

"They could be anywhere!" Marcus cried out.

"For Christ sake, keep it down, Marcus!" Dr. Roberts whispered.

"What is going on?" I asked.

Dr. Roberts didn't answer. When we at last emerged at the house, Marcus was already in the truck, firing up the engine.

"Come on, Max!"

Dr. Roberts ushered me to my car. "Drive until you hit the interstate and don't stop. Drive the speed limit. If anyone in a black suit tries to pull you over or talk to you, remember my sexist comment about Steven sending a woman. If you can, don't stop, keep driving. Do you have enough gas to make it back to Champaign?"

"I filled up when I got off the interstate—"

"Then go. Right now. And take this," he said, giving me the photo.

"Max, let's go!" Marcus yelled.

"Give it to Steven, tell him what we saw." Dr. Roberts ran over to the truck. As he got in, he leaned over Marcus. "Hide that photo in your purse, Lynn! Go now!"

I'd slid the photo beside my wallet, turned the keys, pressed the gas, and the car lurched forward. The engine died immediately. Even with Marcus's truck gunning past and Dr. Roberts motioning at me wildly to drive on, I forced myself to calmly turn on the car once more, and drifted out onto the dirt drive.

I turned left, even used the blinker, and was once more on the road. In the rearview mirror, just as the corn hid the house from view, I saw the boy from the field point in my direction to a large woman with similar dark circles under her eyes who came out to stand on the dilapidated front porch.

As Dr. Roberts had instructed, I kept my speed at the limit. *What is it, exactly, we're running from?*

As my pulse started to slow, I saw the lights from the police cruisers. I tapped the brakes to go at an even more casual pace, even giving a friendly, gentle wave to one of the officers stationed at the perimeter of the missing boy's property. He tilted his hat.

I almost didn't see the man in the black suit until he was right in front of me.

He stepped out so casually from beside the squad car, it was as if he was perturbed that a car had chosen to drive in his path. I hit the brakes, but I was already going so slowly that the car only took a moment to stop. The man rounded the hood and came over to the window. I rolled it down slowly.

"Sorry if I startled you there, ma'am."

Everything on him, except for his crisp white shirt, was black. I imagined his eyes black as well, hidden beneath his dark sunglasses.

"I saw you drive down the road here a bit ago, I wanted to make sure you were all right," he said, leaning his arm on the door. "There's a boy missing around here."

I saw another shadow. Another man in a black suit was even more jarring, given the contrast to his white-blond hair. He leaned on the driver's side door, peering in.

"That's terrible." I felt the sweat on my upper lip. "I'm actually such a fool; I think I took the wrong turn to my aunt's house. I have to take the next exit on the interstate, apparently."

"You're quite a ways from the interstate," the blond-haired man's voice was muffled through the glass. "You've taken quite the wrong turn."

I knew they could see me sweating now. "How long has the boy been missing?" I blurted out. "His poor parents must be devastated—"

"They are," the first black suit said, looking out down the

road from which I came. "Not sure what happened to him. You didn't see anyone strange on your wrong turn, did you?"

"Nothing but a lot of corn." I attempted to laugh.

"Not much to take pictures of."

I glanced at the camera in the passenger seat.

"Because the last thing the boy's family needs is to make this situation worse, with anyone trying to document all this," he said, still looking down the road. His hand, however, had drifted into the car, his long fingertips brushing the handle of the purse I'd hurriedly sandwiched between my hip and the door. "Doesn't feel right . . . a woman by herself driving around with all this . . . strangeness going on. Maybe you should step out of the car."

The blond-haired man rapped on the window. "Why don't you step on out, ma'am."

If you encounter anyone in a black suit, remember my sexist comment about Steven sending a woman, Dr. Roberts had warned. I heard the door handle lift.

"Oh, you're right about that," I leaned back casually in the seat. "I do wish my husband was here to drive, he knows I can't find my way around anywhere except for my kitchen. And my sister can't even make pancakes to save her life! If I don't get there soon, my little niece Amy, who's turning three this month—I can't believe how big she's getting—won't even have a birthday cake! I don't understand why we couldn't have the party at my sister's house—"

"Just be careful," the man quickly withdrew his hand, continuing to walk across the road. The blond stared at me for a good minute before slowly walking away.

I lazily rolled up the window and gently eased the car forward.

When I finally approached the interstate entrance, I took off the head scarf and rolled down the window. The hot wind on my face was hardly refreshing, but I needed as much air as I could take. I wished desperately for some water or a Coke, something to quench my desperately dry throat.

The dark car pulled up on the shoulder of the road so quickly that I almost gasped in surprise. Theirs was a rolling stop, just enough time for me to see another man in a black suit and sunglasses at the wheel. I caught a glimpse of the teenager from the cornfield in the backseat, and a heavyset woman with her arm around him. Even though she had been far away when I saw her at the ruined house, I knew she was the teenager's mother. Were those tears on her cheeks?

When she slammed her hand against the glass and cried out something to me, and the car sped away up onto the entrance ramp towards Springfield, all I could do was watch in horror. I saw her turn around, and then the car was gone.

I was on the interstate a moment later, breathing in and out as if I had finished a marathon. Even though it had never happened to me, I knew I was close to hyperventilating. *Where were they taking them? If they'd looked at that photo, would I ever have been seen again? Should I call the police?*

I knew I wouldn't, and I hated myself a little bit more every mile I sped away. What could I do for them? I didn't even know why the black suits had them. *Of course you do. They took her because of what her son saw, and what he told her of how the missing boy went into the sky. The black suits paid her son money, and in return came and collected them all.*

I'd spent the next two hours in a fog, repeatedly replaying the entire encounter in my mind. I was surprised when the sign with the population of Champaign came into view, and how near my tank was to empty. I exited the highway, gassed up, and headed straight for the university.

I wanted to rush into Steven's office and breathlessly describe what had happened. But I knew there was no room in his world for anyone who couldn't emotionally handle the work. So I sat in the parking lot, collected myself, and reapplied my lipstick.

Steven answered the door to his office, and I did my best to walk in calmly. I sat, smoothed out the wrinkles in my skirt, and produced the photograph.

"Dr. Roberts and his friend explained to me the theory of the crop circles."

Steven had stared for a long time at the photograph without speaking.

"I'm very sorry to hear about your sister."

He looked up. "He told you?"

"You should have told me."

"Yes." He looked back at the photograph. "I should have."

"You know, if you shared your sister's story with more people, then all this," I motioned around the room, "wouldn't seem as . . ."

"You know I'm not a great communicator. Thank you, Lynn. I'll put in a call to Dr. Roberts tomorrow."

"Tell him I did encounter a man in a black suit. Actually two. But I got away without them realizing anything."

His astonished reaction was exactly what I'd hoped for. I crossed my legs.

"Jesus!" he said, dropping the photograph on his desk. "Lynn, what happened?"

"Who are they? The mention of these black suits by a boy in the field made both your colleagues run off like the corn was on fire. And then I saw the mother of that boy being driven away, and she looked terrified."

"Wait, what happened?" Steven kneeled before me. "Start from the beginning."

I'm certain he rubbed his forehead seventeen times before I finished.

"You . . . actually encountered men in a black suits? You're certain?" he said.

"I'm quite sure I know the color black."

"If I had any idea, I would have never sent you. I would never, ever have sent you." He then took my hand in his. "I'd never forgive myself if something had happened to you."

Somehow I remained calm, although I wanted to profess how terrified I was as well. "What would have happened to me? What happened to that mother and her son? Who are these men?"

Steven took off his glasses. "We aren't exactly sure. They show up sometimes when people go missing. The arrival of the men in black is a clear indication that an abduction has occurred. They are the reason we have to be so secretive about our files, our findings. We know . . . they know about us."

"How can you be certain?"

"Because when people vanish, sometimes our investigators go missing, too."

"Miss?"

I looked up from the microfilm machine to see a college-age girl with a Bettie Page haircut and a polka-dot shirt smiling at me. "Are you finding everything you need? I'm assigned to archives and a few other sections, and I didn't know anyone was in here."

"I'm fine, thank you."

"Most people don't even know how to operate these anymore," she said with a smile. "They think Google can find everything. One day, hopefully, we'll even have these old papers online."

"I used to do a lot of research." *I used to be brave, too.* "I'm a bit rusty on the microfilm, but it's slowly coming back."

"Holler if you need anything."

I smiled back and returned my attention to the glowing square screen. I read once more through the death notices of the day, the next day's obits, and then the day prior. As I prepared to fast forward to read the rest for the entire week, the black-and-white face of a girl whirled by.

I slowly rewound, finding the girl's photo on the front page of the August 2 issue. She was smiling, with a left front tooth missing and straight-cut bangs. It was obviously her family's picture, provided to the newspaper.

GIRL GOES MISSING IN MILLER'S WOODS
By Clark Bass Sr.

The search continues for a three-year-old West Nashville girl missing since early Friday morning.

The parents of Amelia Shrank report they fear she had somehow wandered out of the house.

"They think she went looking for the family's missing dog in the middle of the night," said detective Ralph Fulton.

Shrank is the daughter of Dr. and Mrs. Mark Shrank, who described their daughter as being three feet five inches, wearing a black-and-white nightgown and her hair in a long braid.

The Shranks' home backs up to the woods off Woodmont Avenue.

Woodmont Avenue was just a few streets away from my home. And just like that, I remembered how I knew Amelia Shrank.

I knew I was starting to sweat. I popped out the canister, making sure to keep it close by, and inserted August 5, 1945. Instead of going directly to the obituaries, I slid to the front page. But it was page three news that told of missing hunter, Josh Stone.

HUNTER PRESUMED DEAD IN CREEK
By William Buck

A 32-year-old father of twins is believed to be dead somewhere in Richland Creek, Nashville police report.

Josh Stone was last seen by his wife, Janet, heading out to squirrel hunt in the early morning hours Friday.

Janet Stone found her husband's shotgun several yards away from Richland Creek late yesterday evening, according to police.

"We can only surmise that he walked too close to the edge and fell into the creek," said Captain Kris Kemper.

Police said Stone wasn't a good swimmer, and are focusing on searching the waters for his body.

The location of the gun is well known to locals in that area, due to the grave marker placed there by the Shrank family ten years ago, to mark the last spot their daughter, Amelia, was seen.

"He may have stopped to pay his respects, and that's why he left the gun there—because he thought he'd be right back," Kemper said.

Police said they will resume their search of the banks of river Sunday morning.

"Because of all that rain we've been having, we've had a lot of erosion, and on top of that, the creek is fast-moving and swollen," Kemper said. *"If somebody who couldn't swim good fell in, it could be a real bad deal. It's been so hot this August, maybe he thought he could get a quick drink and the ground collapsed under him."*

Next to a photo of Stone and his wife was another picture of a child-sized gravestone with Amelia Shrank's name engraved upon it. A gravestone I had discovered as a child, when I followed my father and those strange men into the woods.

I sat forward. Amelia Shrank had disappeared in August, as had Josh Stone.

Eighty years later, in the same month, William would vanish from the same woods.

ELEVEN

I could see the yellow from the edge of the trees. In those first terrible weeks, the crime-scene tape, marking the spot where Chris found Brian in a state of shock, had been hidden by the dense foliage. Now, with the leaves fallen and the branches covered in a thin layer of snow, the garish yellow was easily seen.

The realization of what afforded me the view brought bile to the back of my throat. I stood under the bell on the back of the shop, and I could feel its weight bearing down on me like a wicked headache. It was here, nearly fifty-five years ago, that I watched my father and those men enter the woods. From here, the place where William disappeared was only a short walk away.

Moving through the burr oaks was easier now than in the summer; low hanging branches easily snapped away in the gray afternoon light. The winter winds, or perhaps a confused and panicked deer, had torn one section of the tape apart.

Chris could be out here. He was known to wander with everything from rakes to hoes, clawing at the ground, desperate to find some sign of his youngest son, something to indicate what had happened to him.

I'd also seen Detective Strombino a few times in the woods. Once, I had gone out to ask him for an update. He only shook his head.

I doubted either would be out here today, for the conditions were miserable. Sleet spit from the sky, and the thin layer of icy snow crunched beneath my feet. I felt confident no one would see what I was about to do.

I set the cloth grocery bag on a flat stone and lifted out the glass terrarium. I had several of them in the house and in the shop. Even in the deepest of winter, I could have moss and ferns growing inside with just a little water and maintenance. The empty terrarium I carried was my smallest, but what it contained needed little space.

Taking one more look around, I walked through the cordoned-off area, holding the terrarium over my head. I looked up through the bottom to see the ten or so ladybugs I'd collected from inside the house crawling erratically.

I'd fully understood, then, why Daddy had dropped his glass lantern when he saw that his little girl had discovered him and those other men. If anyone now came up on me suddenly, I would be unable to explain what I was doing. The glass container certainly would have slipped from my fingers as well.

You'd warned—no, threatened—me not to come in these woods. What did you know? Were those strange men some of the first Researchers, who had come to these trees investigating the disappearance of Amelia Shrank and Josh Stone? Had they needed your permission to come out here? Had they explained what they were doing with those ladybugs? You weren't a suspicious person, and you always wanted to help people. Did you think they were a bit eccentric? Why did you help them? What did you think you would find—

The popping sound came from above.

I lifted the terrarium even higher, and the beetles inside responded with even more ferocious swarming, slamming against the glass like little rocks, just as the ladybugs had done in the sconces on the front porch the night William disappeared.

I lowered the terrarium to my waist, and almost immediately, the ladybugs stopped their furious dance. I thought of Barbara's words the night before: *"That's what ladybugs do when they arrive. We don't know why. But it's been documented in so many cases. Sometimes the beetles cover entire walls, crawling, like they've been driven insane."*

The terrarium was out of my hands and smashed against the ground before I could even comprehend what I'd done. The sound of the shattering echoed for a moment through the lonely trees. The anger and the irrationality felt addictive and I wished for more things to break. I thought, for a wild moment, I might run into the house to gather more of the glass canisters and then return to break them all around the site, like a christening of a cursed ship.

I wanted to scream to the heavens, curse whatever crossed the skies to hover here, taking my William and leaving behind some kind of lingering force that enraged the beetles. A ruthless calling card that no one would ever understand. I imagined trying to explain it to the police, to the FBI, to my husband, to Anne and Chris. *You see, they obviously come close to the earth, and whatever they use to entrap people leaves behind an aura that also happens to aggravate beetles at a certain height, like a radio frequency that only insects can pick up. What's that? No, I don't take antipsychotics.*

Instead, I knelt and started to pick up the glass. What would happen if Chris came back out here and wondered why the glass was everywhere? He might call the police—

The police.

I ran then to the house, not caring at that moment if anyone found the glass. I rushed into house, rummaging through the utility drawer to find the business card.

I dialed, brought my cell to my ear, and listened to four rings before Detective Strombino answered.

"Mrs. Roseworth? Is everything all right?" he asked in his thick Boston accent.

"I'm really sorry to bother you. I have a quick question."

"Of course. I wish I had some new news for you."

I took a deep breath. "Detective, do you know if anything was found in the woods where William went missing?"

"No, ma'am. Nothing. As I've told you, there is no trace of who took him."

"I'm not talking about something someone left behind. I mean something on the ground."

His silence told me everything I suspected. "I'm not sure—"

"I want to know if you found a gravestone. A small marker for a girl named Amelia Shrank."

More silence until he cleared his throat. "Yes, Mrs. Roseworth, we did find that, but it was of no consequence—"

"Then why was it taken into evidence?" I asked.

"Ma'am, I would have certainly shared it with you if it had pertained at all to your grandson's disappearance—"

"A child's gravestone was found in the same location where my grandson went missing and you don't find that strange?"

"That girl disappeared almost eighty years ago, Mrs. Roseworth. There is no connection—"

"Thank you, Detective, that's all I needed to know," I managed to say before sinking down into a chair at the table as I disconnected the call. I could picture them, the detectives or police or even the FBI, finding the grave marker, wrapping it in protective plastic, and thinking they had been to first to find some bizarre remnant of history, like an ancient piece of crockery. They'd done the research into Amelia, of course, and dismissed it. A weird coincidence, nothing more.

They didn't know a grown man had vanished there as well.

The headlights from my Volvo flashed over the Honda Accord parked in the corner of the Chevron. Barbara's hair was momentarily illuminated, and she squinted. I pulled up next to her and lowered my passenger-side window.

"You're welcome to ride with me," Barbara offered.

"My friends and family use this gas station all the time, and if my car was left here unattended, it would raise some eyebrows."

Barbara nodded. "I'm not a fast driver, and I'm unfamiliar with these roads, so stay with me. We're going to the Holiday Inn in a town named Murfreesboro. Sound familiar?"

"It's right off the interstate not far from the square. I know where it is."

"If we get separated, I'll wait for you in the parking lot, and we can go in together."

"I won't lose you. In fact, why don't you follow me? The interstate's the quickest way, and we can pick it up a few miles down Harding."

Barbara appeared grateful. I took a deep breath and turned the wheel.

Anne seemed fine to watch the boys tonight, even if it meant she slouched with Greg on the couch while Brian sat in his room alone and Chris was in his study. No one would think it was strange I'd chosen to stay home alone on Saturday night. Tom would be in on the eleven o'clock flight, and a car would bring him home. As long as I was home by then, no questions would be asked.

It would take thirty minutes to get to the hotel, and thirty minutes to get back. I wouldn't have long to spend with Steven.

This is stupid to do alone. Roxy would throw a fit if she found out. But I'd already dragged her six hours away on a fruitless endeavor and then refused to even discuss what happened.

My cell rang as I got onto the interstate. I briefly looked to see that it was Tom calling, and I silenced the phone. I looked in the rearview mirror to make sure Barbara was still behind. The Accord was keeping up.

I thought of picking up the phone to call him back. *What would you say if you knew?* I pictured his jawline jutting out when he paced while on the phone with his staff, dealing with either a domestic or foreign crisis. *Or would you walk around for hours with your hands behind your head, as you did when Stella left for college or when Anne nearly married that set designer? Or, worse, would you stare off out the window with tears in your eyes that you could somehow keep from running down your cheeks, as you did all those nights when William first disappeared? What version of your heartbreak, your anger, would surface if you knew what I did then?*

The first time Steven kissed me, after I'd returned from the cornfield and the encounter with the men in the black suits, I was surprised at his intensity. Given that he often seemed nervous when we came in close physical contact, I expected soft brushes of lips. Instead, he was unbuttoning my shirt within seconds of our lips touching for the first time. Our clothes were soon tossed onto the floor of his office.

I should have felt incredible guilt afterwards. Instead, I lay in his arms on the couch and smiled as he pointed out the star on the map above us that he had secretly named after me.

From then on, he didn't give me assignments. The calls that came in often asked for me first, because I'd become the point person. *Lynn Roseworth, please*, they said.

Steven began to introduce me to the other Researchers who visited from universities in Illinois and other states such as Indiana and Missouri. The Researchers had potlucks, and some expected me to stay in the kitchen. Instead, I would sit next to them on the couch and point out there was no common shape of the ships as described, and that even though the descriptions of the beings were similar, that could just be the brain's reaction to such a traumatic experience.

I remembered how they cocked their heads at me, cleaning off their glasses, wondering how the young woman in the floral swing dress knew so much about the reported height differences in the aliens known as the Greys.

When Steven led their meetings, I didn't sit at his side and certainly didn't serve appetizers. Instead, I often leaned on the doorframe, clarifying the data. He would gesture to me in those rare moments of emotional expression. "That's right! Listen to her, fellas. Listen to her," he would say.

Sometimes I found them staring at me, and I chalked that up to the lack of exposure to the opposite sex. In time, they didn't just ask for my input—they bombarded me with questions. Did I think the aliens could communicate telepathically? What about inbreeding with humans? Did the creatures even have genders?

"OK, boys, that's enough," Steven would say, placing his hand on the small of my back. He was always touching me. At the end of the day, he rubbed my shoulders. As we sat at his desk in the office, with the door firmly locked, one hand would be writing and the other would rest on my knee. When we went to his apartment to make love on our lunch break, he wrapped his arms around me until the very last moment before we had to get dressed. I could see the pride in his eyes when he introduced me. My wedding ring felt heavy on my finger.

I awoke one fall afternoon in his bed and found Steven looking at me from where he lay on his pillow. I scrambled to get dressed, fumbling with the clock to see the time.

"It's only two-thirty," he said. "You fell asleep at one. It's OK. I have no classes, and it's Friday, so no one's in the office. Come back to bed."

I snuggled up to him, and he brushed a curl from my forehead.

"I've been thinking about something. Do you remember that once you told me that the missing come back?" I said. "I have yet to find a single case of that happening."

He brushed my cheek with his fingers. "I'd rather talk about you. I wonder, who do you more look like—your father or your mother?"

"I don't remember my mother, but from the pictures Daddy kept of her, she had curly blond hair like mine. Otherwise, I'm all Stanson."

"How old were you when she died?"

"Daddy says it was right before the discovery of my tumor that I've told you about. I can't imagine how my Dad handled it: the death of his wife and then a terrible diagnosis for his only child. He couldn't talk about her without tearing up."

"If you are anything like her, I can see why he was so devastated. It's awful to lose someone you love. But . . . to have someone you love vanish, without an explanation, never knowing what happened to them . . . that's a different kind of torture."

I kissed him again. He never discussed his sister. It was clearly too painful.

"Have you ever actually met one of the missing who returned? What did they remember? All those horrible stories about being probed and violated . . ."

His response was to pull me closer. It was the last time we made love.

It rained heavily the next day, and my passenger seat was stacked with files. I didn't know why Steven had insisted I bring them out of the office and to the motel on the outskirts of campus.

A fierce humidity forced me to constantly wipe the windshield with my hand. I saw Steven's car as I pulled into the parking lot. The red sheen of his hair stood out in the haze. A man with a beard stood near him, smoking. I pulled in quickly, behind a bread van.

I peered over the steering wheel, trying to identify the stranger. It wasn't Dr. Roberts, as I had hoped. I hadn't seen him, or Marcus, again, after that day in the cornfield. Steven explained that Marcus didn't play well with others, and Dr. Roberts's wife's cancer had advanced so he wasn't able to travel. I suspected it was actually something more, remembering that look of fear in both Marcus and Dr. Roberts's eyes. Maybe they'd had enough.

The man talking to Steven hadn't attended any of the Researchers meetings, and his face didn't look familiar from any of the scientific journals I'd reviewed at the bequest of the astronomy professors. I unconsciously reached over and put my hand on the files protectively. All Steven had said was to bring the files on the Allen, Bristoff, and Carson cases. I assumed we were meeting another out-of-town Researcher, and it wasn't strange he was staying at a discount motel. None of them was in it for the money.

I watched the man toss the butt of the cigarette aside as he and Steven stepped into the room, leaving the door ajar.

Not wanting to risk the files getting wet, and frankly feeling that I needed to know more about this man with whom we were sharing data, I opened my umbrella and dashed to the end of the overhang.

I didn't know if the water on my forehead was sweat or rain. Why was I acting so possessive? Why did I feel so off kilter? Yes, I worked hard on these cases, but it certainly wasn't only my work. It was Steven who helped me become a Researcher. He could show the files to anyone he pleased.

I thought for a moment of how it would look if, by some terrible coincidence, Tom drove by and saw his wife enter a motel room with two men. Usually, my resentment towards him helped justify my indiscretions, but at this moment, I felt ashamed. I tried to brush it off, hurrying past the other motel doors. The curtains were drawn in the room that Steven and the other Researcher had entered. Smoke was drifting from the room, explaining why the door remained open.

"These wingtips are killing me," I heard the stranger say.

"Pretty high end for someone in our circle," Steven said.

Just another professor. I reached to open the door. *Probably from Chicago—*

"What does she know?" the man asked. I withdrew my hand.

"More than I do, at times. She's whip smart."

They must be sitting just inside the door, maybe on the edge of the bed.

"I mean, how much does she know? About the weather? About the other theories? Even Argentum?"

I bit my lip, remembering Barbara asking for an explanation of Argentum, and how Steven refused to even discuss it with me.

"Why would I waste her time with that?" Steven replied. "We don't even know what it is. It's a glorified urban legend about aliens, without any details. We've all been told to dismiss it anyway. Why do we keep asking what it is if we don't even have a shred of information?"

"Is this smart, Steven? She's not even a scientist, or a professor."

"Not all of us are in academia. It does us good to have others."

"If we go underground, will she do it?"

"I think she would, especially if I decide to as well. She's seen a lot, enough to understand why this is so important."

"It's necessary, Steven. Not everyone agrees, but we have to become more militant about things."

"Militant isn't the word I would use. I think it's important for those of us in academia to continue gathering information from the families of the missing. I know you say that you've been contacted by some . . . parent organization over the Researchers. But come on. I've been doing this for nearly ten years, and I haven't heard of such a group."

"The Researchers aren't calling the shots. Don't you realize someone . . . something. . . . is driving all our work? Sure, we Researchers share information, but something is connecting us, beyond a shared passion. All I know is that the call I received came from someone with the Corcillium, which, if you remember from Latin class, derives from *corcillum*, meaning 'heart,' as in 'heart of the organization.' This is a chance, Steven, to join the true mission. To go so far under the radar that no one can find us, especially not the Suits. They say it's the only way we can move around the country without being recognized. And they said if you were interested, that you should come meet with them. I didn't anticipate you insisting that your girlfriend come too."

I shook off a surge of nausea, leaning into the door.

"You really think they're monitoring us? The Suits?"

"Of course they are." The man sounded weary. "They're not stupid. They know we're asking questions. They can dismiss us for only so long. This remote research is important, but it's only scratching the surface. We would live among these people, spend time in their communities. Understand the commonalities that we have theories about. Live in all these places for a while, spending weeks, maybe months, in the locations of the disappearances. You said she can cook? That might be helpful."

I was really fighting the urge to vomit. *What is wrong with me? Is today the thirtieth? It is. I should have started last week.*

I stepped back, my hand on my stomach. *It's been more than that. It's been two weeks. I'm two weeks late.*

"I'll have to think hard about it. How do we know this isn't a setup by the Suits? You think they may even have information . . . about what happened to my sister?"

"I think they've got information beyond anything we've ever known. Steven, they say there is more to the Argentum theory than what we know. But they made it clear over the phone: Once you're in, you don't get out. I'm ready for it."

"I'm not sure. I know I want to be with her, and I think she's more than ready to move on with her life."

Navigating what I would later realize was my first bout of morning sickness, I teetered back to my car in the rain, not bothering to even pick up the umbrella. Steven was carrying it when he returned to his apartment, where I had gathered the few belongings I had recklessly left there.

"I found your umbrella outside the hotel door," he said. "How much did you hear?"

Having already thrown up twice before his arrival, my tone was as cold as a January morning. I explained that no one would be taking me underground or anywhere away from my family and friends. I wasn't going to live my life skulking from one remote location to the next. And how dare he talk about me like some kind of trophy girlfriend? And I certainly wasn't going to cook for him or anyone in that underground world. This was goodbye.

He practically got down on his knees, begging for forgiveness; he said all he wanted to do was to protect me. That without me, he wouldn't join whatever this secret organization within the Researchers was.

I leaned in close and said I never needed anyone's protection in my life. From this moment on, he was no longer part of it. He'd helped me realize whom I needed to be with, and that was my husband.

He chased me down to my car, grabbing my arm and imploring me to listen. I snatched my arm away and slammed the door.

I drove away, and only allowed the tears to come when the sight of him standing in the rain and holding my unopened umbrella had vanished from my rearview mirror. *I just can't, Steven,* I remember thinking. *I just can't raise a child in that world.*

More than forty years later, I was coming back to him.

I flicked on my blinker in a startled realization that we had reached the exit. I swerved to make it, and saw with relief that Barbara was far enough behind that the sudden jerking of my car didn't throw her.

I followed the ramp and crossed over the interstate, looking for the glowing Holiday Inn logo.

The green-and-white sign with the cursive capital H beamed in the dark, and I pulled into the circle drive. My heart was beating faster than I would have liked.

Barbara parked and stepped out of her car, looking tired. "He already has a room. 404. He's waiting inside."

Glass doors opened at our approach. The smell of steam-cleaned carpet and soap wafted through the lobby and stayed with us in the elevator, up to the fourth floor, and down the hallway. I didn't have to ask if Barbara had a key.

A quick swipe, a beep, and Barbara motioned me in. "I'll be down in the lobby," she said, shutting the door. "I'll give the two of you some privacy."

I slowly walked in, past the bathroom and into the bedroom. The man sitting on the edge of the bed stood.

He wore a tan jacket of a style popular in the late 1990s, with a button-over collar and slightly too short sleeves. His jeans were from the same era as well, though his Reeboks were of this decade. His hair had gone completely gray, and he was shorter than I remembered. But he had become more handsome as he aged.

He pushed up his glasses from the side, not in the middle as he had done throughout our time together.

"Hello, Lynn."

I breathed through the slight purse of my lips. "Hello, Steven."

"You look good. Great, actually."

"What do you know about the disappearance of my grandson?" I clutched my purse in both hands.

Steven blinked. "He . . . has my hair, or the color, at least, which didn't last long after you left. And your oldest daughter looks just like my mother, from what I've seen in the papers and on TV—"

"My husband, Tom, is the father of my children and grandfather to our grandchildren."

"I never had a chance to be Anne's father."

"Is that what this is about? Because if I need to beg for forgiveness, I'll beg—if it means getting information about what happened to William." I hated that my voice was cracking. "I want him back."

"I wish I had him to give to you, Lynn. But I don't."

"Then why am I here?"

"Because I failed to keep a promise to your father, and now our grandson is gone because of it."

"What are you talking about? My father? You didn't know my father."

He reached inside his coat and pulled out a yellowed envelope. "I never met your father. But I did know him."

"You know nothing about my father."

"You think it was by chance that your father, this land-scaper, could pull strings at a university two states away and get you a job in the astronomy department, of all places? I got a call from a colleague in St. Louis who said he knew of a young woman looking for a job at the university, and that her father *supported our work*. What do you think that meant?"

"This is insane."

"Read this." He held out the envelope. "He only had one request of me, and I failed him. Please, Lynn."

He held up the envelope to show the handwriting on the front. In Daddy's bold, decisive letters, were Steven's name and the address of the astronomy building.

I took the envelope and slowly opened it. The pages inside were rigid with age and still smelled faintly of pipe smoke.

Dear Dr. Richards,

I want to thank you for bringing Lynn into your fold. I am not at all surprised to hear that she is exceeding all of your expectations. My girl has always been remarkable.

I also want to thank you for so readily taking my phone call all those months ago. I didn't know if you would, given that I had to limit my interactions with your peers for many years now.

I simply couldn't risk what happened to my wife happening to Lynn.

Daddy's words began to blur, and I blinked, holding the paper closer.

As I told you on the phone, Lynn doesn't know the truth, and I honestly hoped she never would know. Yet I've always been plagued with guilt that she doesn't know her own true story. When you become a father, all you ever want to do is protect your children. I thought that when she moved to Illinois, she would finally be safe. But I fear that one day she will return to our land, and I beg you, sir, to do everything in your power to keep that from happening. I am not a well man, and if it comes to it, you must explain to her why she must never move back. In order for her to understand why, you have to know what happened.

Lynn was five when they took her. There had been a wicked storm, and she and I were on the porch, watching the fireflies come out, late on an August evening. She wanted so desperately to chase them. I must have dozed off, and the next thing I knew, I awoke to a terrible light in the trees and ladybugs swarming everywhere. I couldn't find Lynn, and when I went to look in the woods, I found her shoe. My wife, Freda, and I looked through the night. You have to remember how remote our home was then—we barely have neighbors now, almost twenty years later. There was no one to call for help that late.

My wife and I didn't sleep, and I was preparing to head into town to find help the next morning when this man shows up. Dr. Rex Martin. He said he was a professor who lived in St. Louis and had received several reports from the area of power outages and lights coming from the heavens. I told him that all I cared about was finding my missing daughter. He calmly put his hand on my arm and said that my daughter was gone. But he thought he knew where she would be.

Those words would change my life. I would regain my daughter and lose my Freda.

What happened over the next six months is something that I still cannot fully comprehend. Where Dr. Martin led us, and what we found. Freda kept pushing us until we found Lynn. My brave, brave wife would never would stop. She sacrificed herself in the end so we could escape.

It is a story perhaps for another time. It's still too painful for me to think about. In the end, I returned home with only my little girl.

I had to concoct two stories: that Lynn had gotten sick with a brain tumor and we took her to have it removed in St. Louis, and that Freda died of a sudden heart attack and was buried in her home state of Missouri. Of course, there was no surgery; nothing was ever removed from Lynn, but it was all I could come up with to explain our absence and Lynn's lack of memory when we finally found her. And thanks to Dr. Martin, I was even able to produce forged medical records for Lynn and a death certificate for Freda. We were private country people with almost no family, so there weren't many who even knew us well enough to mourn.

By the Grace of God, Lynn finally began to accept me as her father and relearned everything. If you didn't know,

you'd have thought she had a normal life. I've done everything in my power to give her one.

Even when Dr. Martin and others in your profession
needed to come and study the woods and the location where
all the people have vanished, I was hesitant. I let them come
once and only once. I could not risk more. It cost Freda her
life having to enter your world of secrets and shadows.

And now, the most important person in my world is in
your care. I fear I will not live long enough to explain all this
to her, and it's why I felt better about deceiving her into
thinking she was getting a job in the agriculture department.
I need you to teach her what you know about the missing,
and if I don't survive, explain to her why she cannot return
to our home.

She will fight you on this. This is our land, and Lynn is a
homebody. She sees Illinois as a temporary location, but it
must become more than that. Dr. Martin believes the devils
come back from time to time, and I cannot risk the possibility that she could be taken again.

She will be stubborn. Her husband, Tom, is a good boy, but
he too will have difficulty believing all this, so you must start
with her. She is deeply rooted in reality, as am I. I wish I could
go back to the beliefs I had before this, where the only purpose
of the stars was to bring us light in the dark. Now I cannot look
too long into the heavens for fear of what I might see.

> Sincerely,
> *Bud Stanson*

I read the letter twice. I wanted to find a chair and collapse
into it.

*It couldn't be. Not me. That happened to all those other people
whose disappearances I'd researched.*

Not me.

But it explained the bell. The day he entered the woods with the strangers. Why he could never speak of my mother. His last words to me not to raise my children near the woods. I tried to fold the letter up and place it back in the envelope, but my hands were shaking too hard.

"How could you have kept this from me?"

"Because I was angry. You broke my heart. I realize now that I was a self-involved, self-important jerk. Your father wanted you to know about what happened to you on your own terms. I intended for you to learn it either from him or, in time, from me. And when you left me and I found out you returned home, I assumed your father would tell you, and you would come back to me. When you didn't, I thought you had made your choice."

"My choice?" I held up the letter. "My father couldn't speak when I moved back home. He couldn't explain this to me. I settled there. I raised my family there. And they were all in danger! You let this happen!"

"I know that." He took a step towards me. "It's all my fault. I even tried telling you, so many times. All those years ago, you asked me how we could keep encouraging families, telling them that sometimes the abducted come back. But how do you explain to the woman you love that of all the missing we were researching, she was the only one who ever did?"

"That's what I was, wasn't I? A test case," I said, my eyes narrowing. "The Researchers who constantly peppered me with questions—they just really wanted to ask if I remembered anything about being abducted. You all were studying me. I was a glorified test subject—"

"No. You were never that. We all had fallen in love with you—"

I placed Daddy's letter in my purse. "I should have never trusted you."

"It's why I had to go into hiding. *They* know that I know."

"I don't even care to know who *they* are."

"Your husband's employer."

He took off his glasses and rubbed between his eyes. "When I first heard that your—our—grandson had vanished, I immediately feared the worst. I knew if I suddenly showed up, after all these years, with a wild story of you being abducted as well, it would have made an already bad situation worse. But I had to do something. I started with downloading the maps of your property, so I could know where to start searching. That was my first mistake. Not two hours later, I was summoned to the office of our esteemed dean, who promptly fired me for using university equipment for personal use. An anonymous tipster, he said, had alerted him. I was escorted out and blocked from all my work. I rushed home to find FBI agents carrying all my belongings out of my house.

"It was no coincidence. I should have known they would be monitoring any outside internet searches. Especially from any-one who worked in astronomy. So I had to run, with only the shirt on my back. And when you're my age, that's not easy. I couldn't contact you or anyone. Even getting cash out of an ATM was out of the question, since they were monitoring that too."

"Steven, please—"

"It's vital that you know how far they'll go, Lynn, because of what I'm about to tell you. If it hadn't been for the Corcillium, I wouldn't have been able to even find out about the other miss-ing people from your property."

"Corcillium—?" I asked, and then stopped. I knew the

name. I'd heard it, all those years ago, when that Researcher had tried to convince Steven to take me deep into what he had called the underground.

"Consider them . . . a board, of sorts, that governs the Researchers' work. I knew someone was distributing information to us, but I never knew who. I was so destitute that I was living in a homeless shelter when they found me. They not only rescued me, but their resources allowed me to find out about the others abducted from your woods. It took me some time, but once I had the information, I immediately headed for Nashville. When I reached out to Barbara, she told me that you'd come searching for me first. As soon as I heard about William, I wanted to come to you. But you know the danger. There was a time when you came face-to-face with the Suits yourself."

"I don't live in that world anymore. I was young and naïve and, frankly, desperate for anything that would have saved me from my marriage at the time. You could have been doing research into chimpanzees and empowered me like you did, and I would have thrown myself into that too."

"I don't believe that. It took you a few months to figure out the climate patterns and the commonalities in these cases when it took me years to realize them. You could have done anything with your life."

"You know nothing about my life."

"Listen: I think I know where William is."

"He's still alive?" I asked, a twinge of hope swelling in my chest.

He nodded. "What I've learned from the Corcillium in just the past few months makes me believe we can find him. But Lynn, there are risks—"

"Steven, please. You owe it to my father to tell me. Tell me what you know—"

"We go together, then. I'll tell you everything when we get in the car," he responded, looking around the room. "I don't dare say much more here, as I've come to learn they have ways to monitor everything—"

"Tell me now. Right now."

"I'm not talking about losing a job and having all your property seized by the government. No one has returned alive from where we're going. But I want to find William too—"

The door suddenly beeped and Barbara pushed through. "Jesus, Steven, they're here! They're all wearing FBI jackets, coming up the stairs."

"What?" he asked, now angrily scanning the room. "Dammit, I knew it!"

"They're coming now!"

"Go out the back stairs and take your car, like we talked about. Take it and run. Now, Barbara!" Steven ordered.

"Come with me," she pleaded.

"I'll be right behind you,"

She gave us one last, fleeting look before running out.

"What's going on?"

Steven rummaged through his duffel bag and brought out a folded-over envelope. He leaned in close and whispered softly, "Put this in your purse."

"What is this?"

"Look for your star."

"What are you talking about? I don't understand—"

"Lynn, the Argentum theory—"

The door thudded. A second later, it smashed open, and

agents dressed in SWAT jackets swarmed in. Steven moved past me, holding up his hands.

"You got me, OK? You got me. Don't hurt her."

"We have no intention of hurting her," one of the agents said, seizing Steven and cuffing him.

"Dr. Richards, you are under arrest on a charge of domestic terrorism and kidnapping," declared another agent, her voice muffled under the full protective mask she and the others wore. "Where is William Chance?"

"This won't silence me," Steven grunted, grimacing in pain. "Don't believe them, Lynn!"

They turned him around, and he twisted back to me. "Remember what I told you!"

The agents forced him out the door and into the hall. He stumbled, and they yanked him around the corner.

I started to follow. "Please, don't—"

"Mrs. Roseworth, I'm so sorry," said the female agent, her ponytail now loose from where it was tucked into her shirt. "Are you all right?"

I nodded once. "I'm sorry it came to this. We had to follow you until Dr. Richards could be found. We knew he would, at some point, reach out to you. Senator Roseworth said you used to work for him."

"My husband knows?" I asked, dazed.

"He does as of tonight, when we told him we were moving in. I want you to know we're going to find that woman, his accomplice. We're tracking her now. She may know the location of your grandson. Let's go, your family is anxious to see you."

She took off her mask, and slipped a cigarette between her lips. I blinked in recognition.

"I know you don't like cigarette smoke."

"But you're Tom's press person," I stammered, thinking that it wasn't that long ago when she sat at my kitchen table. "Why are you wearing an FBI jacket?"

"Let's get you home," she said, sneaking a quick drag and gently taking my arm.

TWELVE

"I'm sure you are more than capable of driving," Deanna said, the red and blue lights of the police escort flickering on her face, "But after what you just went through, I thought it might be best for you to rest a bit. I know I've asked you already, but do you need anything? I have an extra water in my backpack."

"Where are you taking him?"

"Likely the Davidson County jail. He'll be booked there."

I kept watching the snow that was starting to fall. "May I ask your actual name?"

"It's Deanna. Deanna Ruck. I used my real name when I was assigned. There was no need to tell your husband otherwise. He thought I was a specialist in crisis communications."

"Why did you have to lie to him?"

She tapped on the steering wheel. "Your husband will understand. Sometimes the FBI does things in order to protect and serve important people in Washington."

"Why not come clean from the beginning that you were an agent assigned to him?"

"Because I wasn't assigned to him. I was assigned to you."

I looked at her. "What do you mean?"

"We identified Dr. Richards as a possible suspect pretty quickly. We've seen the map of your property he kept in his safe, along with the articles about your family. I know you've seen them too. We thought he might reach out to you."

"You followed me to Champaign?"

"We found William's jacket in the basement of Dr. Richards's house. We have a team there now, looking for any trace of him."

"Why would he leave William's jacket there?"

"Because he was on the run, Mrs. Roseworth. Our intelligence shows he's been involved in this antigovernment group linked to domestic terrorism. He obviously has some sort of obsession with you and your family, and he harbored some kind of vendetta towards your husband. He thought if he kidnapped William, he could hurt the senator."

"What you're saying doesn't make sense."

"It makes perfect sense." She looked at me briefly. "It needs to make sense."

I let that one sink in. "What does that mean?"

"No one has to know that you went in search of him. No one has to know about your relationship. It's really going to be in the best interest of everyone involved that you have a long talk with your friend Roxy and decide that keeping all this quiet will allow your family to move on. Questioning our investigation would only force us to disclose everything."

I sank back into the seat. "You all really think this is going to work?"

"What do you mean?"

"You get your suspect, and I get my family back? The problem is that it isn't true, and I'll never know what happened to my grandson."

"Dr. Richards kidnapped your grandson, Mrs. Roseworth.

We have William's jacket and enough evidence to convince any jury. If he starts to blather on about his alien abduction theories, everyone will think he's insane."

"William wasn't wearing a jacket."

"Did I say jacket? I meant pajama top."

I turned back towards the window, closing my eyes.

"I'm glad we could ride together, Mrs. Roseworth. Your family has already been briefed on all this: How one of Dr. Richards's operatives contacted you and insisted you come alone to get information on his whereabouts. How you bravely went, hoping to get information, and how we trailed you without your knowledge. You're a real heroine in all this. You might even get a profile in *People* magazine."

"I don't read that magazine."

"I know you'll do the right thing, Mrs. Roseworth. Your husband is home from Washington, and your entire family now knows. They'll be waiting for you. After you catch up with them, you'll encourage your friend Roxy to sit up with you until you fall asleep. The two of you can use that time to get on the same page."

"Or what?"

"It's not even pleasant to talk about that."

"You can really save the pleasantries at this point."

Deanna turned up the heat a bit. "It's a shame she isn't better about hiding all those plants her husband grows in their garden."

"He has cancer," I said quickly.

"And there's all those people to whom she sells the weed—"

"She doesn't sell. She gives it away, for medicinal purposes." My chest was now tight.

"Drug trafficking is serious business in Tennessee. She'll go to prison. Think about it, OK? Let's all get on the same page.

Plus we've been watching Dr. Richards for some time, and we have recording devices in that hotel room. You know what was said between you, and what a disaster that would be for your family to hear. You want to spare them that kind of embarrassment."

"He didn't tell me anything. You and your agents came just as he was about to tell me where he thought William was."

"He would have lied to you, Lynn, to keep you hoping, to throw you off his track."

I stared hard at the young woman's face. "Will you keep looking for William? Or did you ever really look?"

"We did the best we could. I'm fairly sure William . . . what we believe to be William . . . will be found in Dr. Richards's basement. It will be difficult to identify, but even badly burned . . . it will be enough to convict. What's important is that your family can move on, once and for all. Do this for them, Mrs. Roseworth. Close this sad chapter."

We sat in silence for the rest of the drive. As the police escort pulled onto our street, and I could see the girls' cars in the driveway alongside several others with government plates. The house beamed as if every light and lamp were turned on.

Deanna put the car in park. "Let me come around and help, it might have turned icy—"

"I'm fine," I said, opening the door and walking briskly through the cold.

Tom was waiting at the back door, and he embraced me with such fierceness it took the wind out of me for a moment. "You should have told me, Lynnie. You shouldn't have put yourself in any danger."

"I was never in any danger—"

"Mom." Stella pulled back Tom to hug me. "Jesus, Mom, what made you think this was a good idea?"

"Going off on your own, Mom?" Kate said, her hands raised. "We were worried sick—"

"Let's give your mom some breathing room," Deanna said, closing the door. She met my husband's disapproving gaze. "I'm sorry, Senator. I wish I could have been more upfront from the beginning."

"I have a lot to discuss with your boss. But for now, I want to know everything. And these fellas haven't told us much." He motioned to the men in suits standing uncomfortably, near the pie safe. He leaned in to me. "Is it true, Lynn? That this is all because of that professor? Steven Richards?"

"Mama?" Anne slowly crossed the room, her eyes bloodshot and her voice breaking. "What did this man do with William?"

"Where is my son," Chris demanded, his hands behind his head. "Who is Steven Richards?"

"Everyone, please, I know you have lots of questions," Deanna said. "Let me fill in the holes my partners here couldn't. Mrs. Roseworth, please have a seat."

"I don't need to sit," I said, but Stella sat me down at the kitchen table, squeezing my hand.

My ears starting to ring as Kate poured another cup of coffee. I watched her fumble with the coffee maker while vaguely hearing the words "obsessed with your mother," and "domestic terrorism."

I don't need to pay attention. I've already been given the presentation.

"Your mother led us right to him," Deanna said.

"Where is my boy?" Anne shrieked.

I started to stand, but Stella held me back. "Mom," she whispered, "She needs to hear this."

"We're combing Dr. Richards's house in Champaign right

now," Deanna said, and then exhaled. "Mrs. Chance, I'm sorry, but we've already found his pajama shirt."

The family eruption sounded hollow to me. I stared numbly at the wooden table, reaching out to run my finger over a carving, done either by a child, or a nick from a fork or knife.

"I'm going there right now," Chris said.

Deanna raised one hand. "Mr. Chance—"

"I don't care if you are with the FBI, lady, we're going there now," Chris said, striding from the room. Sobbing, Anne stood and stumbled after him, with Kate helping her to the door.

"Mama!" Anne stopped, looking back wildly.

"Go, Sis," Stella said. "We'll take care of the boys."

"Lynn." Tom knelt beside me. "I'm going too. I'll call you from the car. Are you OK? I'll stay here if you need me—"

"Just go," I said softly.

"Why would he do this, Lynn?" he asked.

I shook my head and closed my eyes. I could feel him looking at me, but when he heard the sounds of the cars engines turning on, he hurried out.

Deanna walked across the room to stand on the other side of the table. "I hope we're wrong about William, that he's still alive. Whatever happens, know your mother is pretty remarkable. It's amazing what she did for this family."

"Thank you, Agent," Stella said.

"We'll leave a team outside if you have any other questions, and we'll brief you on any new developments," she said. "Take care of your family, Mrs. Roseworth."

I did not look at her as she and the other agents walked out.

"Mom, don't worry about Brian and Greg. The neighbors are watching them, and I'll head over there later," Stella said.

Kate was already on her cell. "Trevor? I know it's late, but things are moving faster since our last briefing. Here's the deal:

Deanna Ruck is no longer working press for us, that's got to be you for a bit. It will be very clear quite soon. . . . I know you don't know what's going on, but have a bag ready, you might be going to Champaign, Illinois. I'll explain in a minute. I'm calling both the Nashville office and the Washington office with strict instructions: All network calls go to me, all local press calls go to you. But here's what you need to know: No one, I repeat, no member of the media is to approach my mother or my family. Repeat that in your head. . . ."

"Mama." Stella pulled up a chair, taking my hand. "You heard the agent. They could be wrong. William could still be alive—"

"It's a lie," I whispered.

"What?"

"Nothing." I pushed away from the table and walked to the sink. My hands were shaking so badly that I dropped the cup into the sink, where it clanged jarringly.

"Mom?" Kate asked, and briefly turned back to the phone. "Marcus, I'll need to call you back."

"What is a lie, Mom?" Stella asked, slowly standing.

"Everything!" I cried out, startling both my daughters. "Everything is a lie."

"I knew there was more," Stella said, pointing her finger towards me. "I could tell it the minute you came in here. Did that bastard do something to you? Did he, Mom?"

"He didn't do anything. He didn't do anything to me or to William."

"What is it, Mom?" Kate asked.

"Tell us, Mom. That's how you raised us. No lies. Not ever, even if it's ugly," Stella said. "What happened—?"

The back door came flying open and a red-faced Roxy strode in, her gray-streaked hair wet from the snow. "Why in the hell wasn't I called? Some FBI agent called about twenty minutes ago and told me to hightail it over here, something about you leading them to Steven Richards."

"You know about him too?" Kate asked.

"Um, not really, that's just what the agent said," Roxy replied.

"You're a terrible liar, Roxy." Stella flicked a hair from her forehead.

"Well, somebody tell me what's going on," Roxy said.

"The FBI said this Steven Richards, who Mom worked for back when Dad was in law school, is obsessed and kidnapped William. Has some kind of vendetta against Dad. Some woman contacted Mom and led her to a Murfreesboro motel where he was waiting. That's when the FBI nabbed him," Kate explained. "They think they've found William's pajama shirt at his house."

Roxy stormed across the room. "This was tonight? Lynn, why didn't you tell me? I would have gone with you! Does the FBI really think he kidnapped William? Do they know—?"

I raised my hand ever so slightly, and Roxy bit her lip. Stella saw it all. "I don't know what you two aren't telling, but you better spill it. Mom says this Richards character didn't hurt her or William. Mom, for the last time, what is going on?"

"Tell her, Lynnie," Roxy said.

"You don't know what they'll do, Roxy. I do. They made it very clear that we all have to play along. They'll come after you too."

"No one is coming after anyone," Kate insisted. "I can guarantee you that."

"You can't guarantee this, Kate," I said.

"I can tell you one thing, Lynn Roseworth . . ." Roxy leaned on the table. "I'm not afraid."

"Well, I am."

"Tell them, Lynn."

I looked from Roxy to my girls and sighed. "I don't even know where to start."

"Oh hell," Roxy said, sitting down at the table. "Start with the damn aliens."

THIRTEEN

Complete silence was so rare in the house that I was surprised by the noises that surfaced in the sudden stillness of the room. I'd never noticed, even in the deep of night in Tom's frequent absences, how the pantry door slightly tapped against its wood frame when the heat kicked on; how the holly bush outside the east kitchen window flicked against the pane; even how the energy-efficient bulbs that were now so dramatically expensive at Target hummed in the black chandelier above the dining-room table. But I heard it all in that moment. The air even seemed unsure what to do, as if no one was bothering to breathe.

It was in the silence that sprung from my daughters' astonishment, hearing me tell of my work with Steven Richards, that I knew I would not share everything. That would be for Tom and Tom alone.

"You . . . were a UFO researcher?" Kate asked at last.

"I told you, I wasn't a Researcher, at first. I was only an office manager."

"It's going to take me a minute," Stella said. "The guy who kidnapped William studies UFOs? And you used to be his assistant? And you went to his motel room tonight? What did he tell you?"

"He said . . . he was going to tell me what really happened to William. He doesn't have William." *And what happened to William happened to me, as well.*

"What do you mean 'What really happened'?" Kate asked. "That William . . . was abducted by aliens?"

When I didn't respond, Kate shook her head. "Mom, come on. Mom, are you kidding me?"

"Give your Mom a break, Kate," Roxy scolded. "She's been through a lot."

"I know Steven isn't responsible."

"How could you possibly know that, Mom?" Kate walked to the edge of the table. "And do you care to elaborate on why he has such an obsession with you and this family?"

"Watch that East Coast tone when you talk to your mother, Kate Elizabeth," Roxy warned.

"I know we're not getting the whole story, Mom," Kate said.

"I had to do whatever I could to try to find William."

"Are we talking about getting answers from UFO researchers?" Kate asked.

"What if it helps us find William? And I can't live with someone being punished for something he didn't do—"

"Jesus Christ, Mom," Kate said. "Why do you want to protect this man so much? Are you even listening to what you're saying?"

"I saw the reports once, I knew them inside out. I worked hard on those cases, I made the connections. I wasn't just some housewife—"

"Is that what this is all about? Trying to reclaim some past independence?" Kate said. "My God, Mom, you will ruin Dad. You will ruin this family—"

"I will *not* let this family be ruined." A sob caught in my throat. "Don't you see why I had to do this? Losing William, and Brian in the state he's in now, will hang over us forever."

"Mom, this is over." Kate circled the table and knelt, unsuccessfully trying to get me to look at her. "You have to get it together. William . . . could be dead. We have to prepare for that. Listen to what the police are saying. To what the FBI is saying. I know you don't want to let go of William, none of us do. They said they found his clothes. . . ."

"It's not the truth. It's not the truth even if Steven is charged. Even if he's convicted. It's not the truth."

"Fine, Mom, fine. Buy into their crazy shit—"

"Kate, back off," Stella said.

"I won't back off. Good God, Mom, you aren't even crying! William is dead—"

"He's not dead! Steven said he knows where he is—"

"Don't you dare say that to Anne or anyone else. I will not let your delusions give her irrational hope or make us the laughingstock of the country. Do you know what they'll say? 'Oh, that poor wife of Senator Roseworth, she's so distraught she's lost her mind.'"

"Jesus, are you always in PR mode? Have you ever known this woman to be delusional? Ever? For one moment in our entire lives?" Stella asked.

"Did you ever know that our Mom believes in aliens?" Kate motioned to me. "Or that she had an affair on Dad?"

"Kate Elizabeth!" Roxy stood.

"It's so obvious. I'm done here." Kate walked across the room and grabbed her purse. "But know for damned sure I'm not letting you do this, Mom. No fucking way." She walked out and slammed the door.

"Go after her, Stella," I said softly. "Let her smoke a bit, but don't let her drive. She's too upset."

"I'm going to tell her where she can shove those cigarettes." Stella lifted her coat from where it hung on a chair. "I have to be honest with you, Mom—this is really . . . hard to understand."

She obviously wanted to say more, but instead walked out the door.

I stood and looked out the window. Stella chased after Kate, her hands rubbing her arms. "Clash of the Titans, there. Daddy's girl versus momma's girl," Roxy said, coming to stand beside me. She put her hand on my shoulder. "Lynnie, you have to rest," she whispered.

"I can't—"

"It's not a suggestion. Time to take an Ambien, or maybe one of Anne's Xanax, if she left one lying around. I'm not kidding, Lynn. Tomorrow is going to be tough when word comes out about Steven. You are going to have to get some sleep."

"How can I sleep? How can I sleep knowing what's about to happen?"

"You don't know what's about to happen."

"I have to tell Tom. He has to know."

"In time you can tell him everything."

"There isn't time, Roxy. Don't you see? They're going to *plant evidence* in Steven's house, to try to prove William is dead. How can I live with that?"

"Plant evidence? Really? Oh Lynn, why would they do that—?"

"They'll arrest you for drug trafficking. They know about your basement."

"What?" Roxy said in astonishment. Seeing my horrified

look, she forced a smile. "So I'll become a folk hero in East Nashville, big deal."

"They'll send you to prison!"

"Oh Christ, Lynn, I'm nearly seventy. They won't prosecute me. Plus, even if they do, I'll be out in a few days anyway. Some Colorado attorney will swoop in and save me."

"I can't live with that!"

"Well, I can't live with you having a heart attack or a nervous breakdown, which is where you're headed if you don't get some rest. It's been a terrible night, and there's nothing you can do now. I'll stay with you—"

"No, go home. I'll call you in the morning."

"I suppose I better go home and destroy the evidence." Roxy rubbed her eyes. "I'll go play referee with the girls. You, take some good *legal* drugs and knock out. Understand?"

I nodded, watching Roxy pull on her gloves, point towards my bedroom and then step out the door.

I slowly ascended the stairs to the dark bedroom. On the edge of the bed, green eyes flashed. The cat had all but vanished in the commotion, but Voodoo decided it was safe to resurface. As I laid down, he approached in the darkness and nuzzled my hand. I softly scratched his neck.

After several minutes, I heard Roxy's pickup drive away. I didn't hear the door to the house open, which meant the girls were still at it.

My lower back ached. My favorite flannel nightgown was still on the chair by my bed. Voodoo's nuzzling was already making me drowsy. *My eyes won't feel so dry when I shut them.* Kate was right; this is over. I will offer support. I will be stable. I will pick up the pieces of our family and put us back together in time. I will move us away from this property and fulfill Daddy's last wish.

I closed my eyes, ready to let the darkness lull me away. But instead, all I could think of was a little boy. Not William, but Brian, lying in this very bed on the night William disappeared, after he had whispered the last words he would ever speak.

We lost two children that night.

I was on the stairs a moment later, hurrying to where my coat lay limp on the table. I quickly buttoned it up and looked out the window, seeing the embers from Kate's cigarette flashing in the spitting snow as she and Stella argued near the back porch.

Keys in hand, I walked through the dining room and into the formal living room, exiting through the rarely used front door. I quietly locked it behind me and slowly walked down the front stairs, then rushed to the Volvo. I slipped in, fired it up, and tore down the driveway, embarrassed by the gravel I was kicking up.

In my rearview mirror, I saw the girls waving and calling out my name frantically. I hated that I would cause them to worry, on top of the news of William's supposed death.

I reached over to silence the phone as the first call came in from Stella. I pressed the gas, knowing I would be long gone before either could get to their cars and hope to follow.

The late-night patrons at the Waffle House near downtown appeared even bleaker under fluorescent lights. It was nearly midnight, and the crowd from the honky-tonks on Lower Broadway wouldn't start filing in until closer to three or four. I sat stirring my tepid coffee across the aisle from two drunk sorority girls and a furiously texting man wearing a cowboy hat. You can always spot the tourists, Tom always said, because they're the only ones in town wearing Stetsons.

There was no chance anyone I knew would come across me here.

I glanced at my dark phone, long since powered off, knowing Tom would be trying to reach me once Kate reported that I'd driven away. *Are you on the road still, insisting on driving so Anne or Chris could sleep, even though neither will? Have you repeatedly called, now that you've had the time to piece together the fact that some man from our far-flung past will be charged with our grandson's murder? Are you wondering why he would come after us? Are you surprised that you didn't even remember his name?*

Or, even worse, would you lean into the phone and ask quietly, "Did you love him back?"

Steven had actually been quite brave, standing in front of me as the agents burst into the room. I should have reached out to him, reminded him he was old and so was I, and it was an unnecessary gesture. I cannot bear to think of an old man in a jail cell because of me.

And had the agents found Barbara? Was she still on the run too?

It was all my fault, all of it. What I did decades ago was slowly taking down one life at a time. If I did tell people, even the local police, what I suspected, the story would eventually unfold in the papers, online, on television. The looks of pity I would get from customers, from friends. *It isn't your fault, Lynn,* they would say. *He was crazy.*

I reached for my purse to open the envelope Steven had given to me, smoothing out the two pieces of paper tucked inside. One was an enlarged section of a map of Colorado from an atlas in the *National Geographic* magazine. The upper left-hand corner revealed a copyright of September 1960.

The other was a map of the stars.

I remembered what I learned during my time in the astronomy department, so I knew the placement of the constellations was comical. The Big Dipper was in the wrong place. So was Andromeda. Whoever did the map had skills in graphic design, but the artist knew nothing of the heavens.

There was only one true accuracy: my star, right where it should be.

"Look for your star," he had whispered, softly enough that the recording devices in the room from the FBI couldn't pick up his words.

And then, he had said something about Argentum.

Another ghost from the past. That theory that Steven dismissed when Barbara first mentioned it all those years ago. He'd said he didn't even know what it was, and it was not worth discussing. I'd heard that again outside the motel room, when Steven and the Researcher had discussed going into hiding. Steven referred to it as an urban legend about aliens, without a shred of proof. He'd clearly been annoyed with it.

A quick Google search on my phone revealed only two explanations: that *argentum* meant silver in Latin and that a senior-living association had adopted the name.

I scanned the enlarged section of Colorado, dotted with the names of towns and counties. I'd have to dig out my reading glasses to attempt look at them all.

Again I returned to the star map. My star wasn't the only one of a different hue. While most were a brilliant white, a few others were larger in scale and gold.

My fingertips were smudged from ink. Both documents had been recently printed.

I felt a flare of anger. I didn't have time for this. Too much was happening, too much was at stake, to sit here and try to unravel a riddle. Just like those files, all those years ago, with all the blacked-out words that so infuriated me—

I stood so quickly I almost banged my knees on the table. I walked briskly to the counter.

"Excuse me," I asked a ponytailed young man scraping burnt leftovers on the stovetop. "Do you have any tape?"

He laughed. "When your menus are this old, something has to hold them together." He rummaged around under the counter. "Aha!"

I thanked him and hurried back to my table. Taking a deep breath, I placed the Colorado map on top of the celestial map, taping them together at the top and bottom so they would align and not slip.

The two fit nearly perfectly on top of each other.

An encryption. Just like all the blacked-out documents. The stars were in the wrong place because Steven had made the celestial map not for accuracy, but as a key.

I slowly raised both towards the light. The smaller stars didn't show through the state map, but I could see the larger gold ones.

My star was harder to find because it was nearly lost in the Rocky Mountains. I squinted, seeing it match up at the base of the range. The star appeared to be in a gap in the mountains in the Colorado map.

I tore off the tape and separated the two pages, madly scrambled to find my glasses in my purse, and looked closely at where the star had rested in the state. That area was completely barren, void of anything except for the tiny name of one town, deep in the mountains.

The town's name was Argentum.

FOURTEEN

I balled up my scarf, the only spare piece of clothing I had besides my coat, and tried to use it as a pillow. The few other passengers quietly chose their seats. I turned to the window and looked out on the blackness of the tarmac.

There would be snow when we landed. I would have to buy not only boots, but days' worth of clothes and all my toiletries. I would have to rent a car, drive in a strange city, and navigate a mountain range. I almost wished I were going to Washington; at least I knew where to catch the taxi at the airport.

There's still time to get off the plane and get home before anyone notices—

"I don't suppose this seat is taken."

I didn't dare open my eyes. I couldn't have fallen asleep and dreamed this—

"Seriously, Lynn, move your purse. This stupid coat is going to take up a seat in itself."

"How are you here?" I asked.

Roxy struggled to take off her long overcoat and unwrap her scarf before unceremoniously plopping down. "We have about two seconds to get off this plane. But we're going to raise some eyebrows if I start dragging you down the aisle. So, I'm here to yank you home if—for the first time in your life—you're drunk. Or perhaps overly medicated. But most importantly, I am here to find out what the hell you're doing."

"I don't know what I'm doing. How are you even here?"

"Here are the Cliffs Notes, as the attendants are circling. You didn't make it easy, sister. Stella called me after midnight, pretty frantic, even though you texted her to say you were all right. I figured you were driving around, maybe even got a hotel room to get some peace. You never carry cash, and you lost your debit card last week—as you will recall—so that meant you used your credit card. And for shits and giggles, I checked the Peddler charge card—thanks for putting me on that account, by the way—and it showed you'd bought a ticket to Denver. So I booked myself a ticket too and hustled my fat ass over here. I stopped to kiss Ed and tell him to burn the stash and pop a few extras to numb the pain. I told him I could be back this morning. Or it might be a few days, if you needed to meet Tom in Champaign."

"You can't leave Ed, not if he's having pain—"

"For Christ sake, Lynn, he has stage-four colon cancer. He's gonna have pain. But he's fine. I filled him in on what happened with Steven's arrest. Well, not everything—for God's sake, I don't want the man to have a stroke as well as cancer. Now, Lynn, what are you doing?"

"I'm so glad you're here." The words barely came out of my throat. "I can barely breathe, I'm so nervous."

"Lynn, you need to tell me right now if whatever it is you're doing—you are doing it of a sound mind and body. Or if you've been threatened and are in danger of some kind."

"At this second, I am lucid. But my stomach is doing backflips."

"Well, there's a convenient puke bag right here if things go south. But let's avoid that if we can. Do I need to order you a drink?"

I shook my head, and Roxy waved over a tired-looking flight attendant. "Can we get a cup of water? Thanks." Roxy then dropped her voice. "Why are you going to Denver?"

"I'm not going to Denver. I'm going to a town called Argentum, somewhere in the Rocky Mountains."

"And why, pray tell, are you going there?"

The flight attendant brought over a small cup and reminded Roxy to fasten her seatbelt, as they were preparing to take off.

"Time's up, Lynn. This is when you tell me if you need me to get you off this plane, or if we're about to make a cross-country flight."

"You can't go with me."

"I most certainly can and will. Case closed. Now, why Colorado?"

I set the cup down in the console. "I think it's where Steven thinks they've taken William."

Roxy's eyebrows rose. "That little nugget of information was not shared during our wonderful experience with the girls. And just who is it that's taken William? I can't believe I continue to say this, but—the aliens?"

"I don't know. I don't know anything. And I could be completely wrong about all of this. All I know is I have to try, because if I don't . . ."

"Here's what we're going to do. We're going to use this flight as good long nap when we take off. But first, you're gonna spill it all, friend. Everything. Got it? Start with telling me everything about going down to Murfreesboro and seeing Dr. Richards. OK?"

I took a long drink.

Roxy nodded and bit her lip a few times to keep herself from interrupting. I couldn't bring myself to talk about Daddy's letter to Steven, so I finished with the discovery of the celestial map fitting onto the road atlas. "There wasn't time to ask him if that's what he intended me to figure out. And God, Roxy, I could be wrong. Steven could be insane, he could be trying to confuse me to keep the investigation off himself. The FBI could be completely right, and I'll be in Colorado when my family needs me the most."

He couldn't have faked my father's handwriting, though.

Roxy settled into the chair. "I need some time to think this through. Of course I brought nothing useful, as I had no time to pack anything, but I happen to carry my sleeping mask during Ed's chemo. So it's yours. It will be daylight soon, and you need sleep."

"I can cry myself to sleep and now no one will see."

"You're due some tears. Now lower that window shade."

We slept the entire trip, waking groggily to a ding alerting us that we had landed at Denver International Airport. After the plane came to a halt, we walked down the connector onto a red carpet, standing amongst the sea of people at the gate.

"Well, I've been wearing these clothes for two days now; shall we buy ourselves some nice 'I love Legal Marijuana' sweatshirts? Speaking of love, I'd kill for a shower. Can we get a room and sleep some more?"

I powered up my phone. "I can only imagine how many calls I've missed."

"What do you want to do, Lynn?"

"If we're going, we'll need clothes and a car. And I did get a new debit card after I lost mine, thank you very much, and I took out a bunch of cash before I headed to the airport, so there's no way for anyone to know where we are now."

"You don't watch *Dateline* as much as I do. If Tom starts to suspect you're not in Nashville, it will take the FBI two seconds to get access to all your credit cards, and they'll see our flights. And I know Tom never balances your checkbook, but if he looks at your account, he'll see the money you took out. And if they want to know where you are, all they have to do is track your phone to the closest cell tower. Wherever we're going, we better get there fast. Or seriously convince your family you need time alone to grieve. I also clearly watch too much *Dateline*."

I pressed my phone to my forehead. "I've missed fifteen calls and there are ten voice mails. I have twenty-five texts. I can't even look at them."

Roxy pointed to the rental-car signs. "We can get a car. It's now or never. We either book a flight back home or head to Enterprise."

I sat down in an empty row of chairs. "Tell me doing this isn't crazy."

"Lynn, we are nearing seventy." Roxy sat down beside me. "Women our age are dyeing wool and wandering through yard sales. Instead, we have gone to Illinois, broken into an office *and* a house, met with UFO researchers, and you just witnessed an FBI raid. So I think we're already far along on the crazy train. Flying to Colorado on a hint from someone who could be a lunatic seems pretty par for the course."

"He's not a lunatic."

"Listen, I'm not going to tell you this isn't crazy. The last six months have been horrible. You're desperate to find your grandson, and I don't blame you for that. And I know what you're thinking: It's not only William you're trying to find. You're trying to bring Brian back from whatever dark place he's in. But you have to be prepared for all of this to be a hoax, and the possibility that right now the man who kidnapped your grandson is in police custody and William is gone. I won't judge you, whatever you decide to do. I've told you that before. Even if I don't believe in these alien abductions, I have always believed in your instincts. So tell me, what does your gut say—?"

"You're her."

We both looked across the aisle at a teenager with floppy bangs hanging over a forehead of acne. He pulled out his ear-buds, the light from his iPad reflecting in his glasses. "You are. You're her," he said.

"I'm sorry?"

"You're the alien lady. The one who believes aliens took your grandson."

"What are you talking about?" Roxy demanded.

Taken aback by Roxy's tone, he pointed to his screen. "I just saw you online. Don't be offended. I agree with you. I think aliens are real—"

"Give me that." Roxy strode over and swooped up the iPad.

"Hey," he said, but her look froze him to his chair.

"Oh sweet Jesus," she said.

I hurried over. "What is it?"

Roxy scrolled up to the top of the NBC News home page, where a red headline screamed: "Professor arrested in U.S. Senator's grandson's disappearance."

Below the headline, a subhead read, "Video shows Senator's wife asking for help from UFO researchers."

I was suddenly so flush I thought I would break out in sweat. I wanted to sit down, but I forced myself to keep reading.

PROFESSOR ARRESTED IN U.S. SENATOR'S GRANDSON'S DISAPPEARANCE

VIDEO SHOWS SENATOR'S WIFE ASKING FOR HELP FROM UFO RESEARCHERS

By Dave Botcher

Champaign, Illinois—FBI agents raided the Champaign, Illinois, home of a former University of Illinois professor overnight and announced they have found clothing belonging to the missing grandson of U.S. Sen. Tom Roseworth, D-Tennessee.

Dr. Steven Richards was taken into custody late Thursday evening in Nashville, Tenn.

FBI spokesman Raymond Lewis said Richards had attempted to abduct Roseworth's wife, Lynn, at a hotel in Murfreesboro, Tenn.

Lewis said Richards lured Lynn Roseworth to the motel with the help of accomplice Barbara Rush, who is also now in custody.

"These two took advantage of a grieving grandmother in her most vulnerable moments to try and convince her of her grandson's whereabouts," Lewis said, "when all along it appears the boy's clothing had been in Richards' basement. We're searching the residence now."

Lewis would not elaborate as to the connection between Richards and the Roseworth family.

Hours after Richards' and Rush's arrest, a group of supporters of the professor released a video on YouTube, decrying the charges and posting video of what appears to be Lynn Roseworth meeting with Rush and others in a basement in Champaign late in October.

In the video, Doug Ellis, identified only as a researcher, talks about how Richards and Rush are innocent of any

*crimes and were only trying to assist Roseworth in finding
her grandson.*

*"The FBI has pushed our hand to release this video,"
Ellis said in the video. "But we have no choice but to show the
world that Lynn Roseworth herself met with us and acknowledged our work into the existence of extraterrestrials. Barbara sought to help her, nothing else. As did Steven Richards."*

*The video shows a brief interaction between Lynn Rose-
worth and Rush. Ellis can also be seen in the background.
You can watch the clip here:*

I raised a trembling finger and hit the link.

The video player that emerged showed a still frame of me
standing in the basement of Steven's house, surrounded by the
other Researchers.

"That bastard recorded us," Roxy said. "Little shit had one
of those GoPros or something set up."

I swallowed and hit the play button.

"It really is you," the researcher in the tweed jacket could
be heard saying. "I guess it's true: You believe in the little green
men like the rest of us. You look just like you do on TV."

Barbara could be seen walking up to me. "Rupert, you
prove yet again your impeccable skill for saying the wrong
thing at the wrong time. It's been a long time, Lynn. You may
not recognize the few of us who were here back in the day."

In the video, you could hear me clear my throat. "I doubt
you would have recognized me, or even remembered my name,
if it hadn't been for my husband."

The video then cut off, and Doug Ellis once again leaned
towards the camera. "Lynn Roseworth once was one of us and
came to us for help. To think Steven Richards or Barbara Rush
had anything to do with that boy's murder—"

I stepped away. "Put it away."

"Here." Roxy thrust the iPad back at the teenager.

"Can I take a selfie with you?" I could hear the teenage boy ask as I ran towards the nearest bathroom.

I barely made it to the toilet. Very little came up, as I'd eaten almost nothing in the last twenty-four hours. I wished for a heart attack or a stroke—any way I could die at that very moment.

Instead, I waited till my temperature dropped, sitting on the toilet. I then flushed and went out to wash my face and hands.

Roxy stood waiting for me. "Lynn, I'm so sorry."

I rinsed my shaking hands. "It's what the text messages and phone calls are about. It's everywhere now. Everyone has seen it."

"I'll go see about the latest flight back."

"No." I looked up at my haggard face. "Go buy me some sunglasses and a hat."

The four-wheel-drive Suburban was much too big for the meager clothing and basic toiletries that we carried in plastic bags from the shops in the airport, but when Roxy explained to the rental-car worker where we intended to go and that we needed a Mazda, he arched his eyebrows. "You realize it's December in Colorado. The mountain towns can easily be snowed in. That car won't make it."

Roxy asked for specific directions to Argentum. I stood behind her wearing dark circular sunglasses and a ridiculous sock hat. "I have to be honest with you, ma'am, I've never heard of it, and I'm from the mountains near Pueblo," the worker said.

I'd already worn out my phone's battery trying to find anything on a town named Argentum, but the search engines gave me nothing. Why the town showed up on the old road map but nowhere else was a nagging enigma.

I showed the guy behind the counter the page from the atlas Steven had given me. He raised his eyebrows.

"Huh. It would have to be San Juan or Hinsdale County. Pretty isolated. It's all national forest out there. I wonder if it's not even a town anymore. That map looks pretty old. Are you sure that's the right place? Do you plan to take a four-wheeler with you? 'Cause that's the only way you're going to get in. We've had a break from the snow for the last few days, but a whopper of a storm is coming. You'd have to take 160 and just ask around, as long as it stays open. But any roads leading off it won't be when the snow starts."

Roxy mumbled that she wouldn't be riding any four-wheeler, but she would be driving. When the worker explained that they only took credit cards, I mentioned how much he looked like my son, who was waiting tables in Fort Collins. I said that I always carry cash so I can tip people who work hard but don't make a lot of money. He accepted my cash, including the extra twenty dollars I counted out and gave him, and had me fill out paperwork, which I returned filled with blatant lies. I breathed a sigh of relief when we were safely in the SUV and on our way to the interstate.

From the airport we turned south on I-25. I nervously tapped my phone as it repeatedly dinged. "How easily can they track my cell signal?"

"Easily, but only if they ask the cops to look for you. And they're probably getting to that point. Say you're too upset to process what's happening and need some time alone."

"It just sounds so pathetic. The girls won't buy me disappearing like this. They know I wouldn't leave them under any circumstances. Tom won't believe it either. I have to convince them that I had to leave. No . . . *you* convinced me to leave."

"I have no problem being the bully."

"That's our story. I wanted to drive to Champaign. But I saw the YouTube video and am terribly embarrassed, and you said the last thing I needed was to show up there and have the attention focus on me. So you're driving me to a halfway point—let's say Paducah—and we will head to Champaign as soon as there's confirmation of anything."

Roxy nodded with appreciation.

"Give me your phone. The text is going to come from you."

"Throw in a few F-bombs to make it seem authentic," she suggested.

I sent a group text to Tom, Kate, and Stella.

It only took a minute for Roxy's phone to ring with my husband's number displayed in red.

"You have to answer it."

Roxy picked up the phone. "Hi, Tommy. Yes, we're fine. Yes, she's fine. She's right here with me. She's tired and scared and embarrassed and a little sick to her stomach. We're in Paducah. It was my call; it's a good place to wait. No, we're not going to Little Rock. No, we never went to Little Rock in the first place, but that's a conversation to have with your wife when she's feeling up to it."

I watched as Roxy listened for a while, her face finally wrinkling in annoyance. "Yes, we've seen the news. We had no idea we were being recorded in that basement. Lynn's taking it hard. Real hard. Uh-huh. Yes. Uh-huh. She wanted to come to Champaign this morning, but she doesn't need to be anywhere where there's going to be cameras. You tell Anne that her momma is close by and will be there in a heartbeat if you get confirmation— Yes, Tom, I am aware of how far Paducah is from Champaign, you're going to have to handle this until there comes a point when we need to get there. Uh-huh. She knows it, Tom. She hates to be away from Anne. Listen, I love you like a brother and I hate that this is happening, but you are getting on my nerves so I'm going to go."

Roxy hung up and sighed. "He is so used to everyone doing what he says, he can be a real pain."

"Did he buy it?"

"He actually said it was a good idea. He's used to you handling all the family drama stuff. He knows how to bark orders, not how to calm Anne when she's upset. So as long as there's no word on William, and Anne holds it together, we'll be OK."

"What did he say the FBI were doing?"

Roxy gave me a worried glance. "It's not pretty. The media is going nuts. That's why Tom thinks it's wise you're staying back for now. They caught the other woman, I can't remember her name. The one who brought you down to Murfreesboro."

"Barbara."

"She and Dr. Richards are being kept in complete isolation. His house in Illinois is blocked off with police tape, and the agents are scouring it. They're giving Tom and Chris and Anne hourly briefings, but they haven't come up with anything yet, besides the discovery of pajamas. Lynn, if they found what they think are William's clothes . . . ."

"They could be manufacturing all of it. You didn't ride in the car with the agent. She was very clear about how far they would go."

"But why, Lynn? Why do all this? What does the FBI gain? What does anyone gain by framing the wrong guy?"

"I don't know. I have no idea. Maybe they look bad because they haven't found the person responsible? Maybe . . . they're covering something up."

Roxy gave an exasperated sigh. "OK, sorry for that. But come on—"

"Let's not talk about it anymore." I leaned my head against the strap of the seatbelt while watching the bleak landscape rush by. "Look for Route 50 and take it west."

We expected the ease of the Smokies. Like many Tennesseans, we'd breezed past the goofy golf courses and Dollywood attractions of Gatlinburg in order to climb through the mountains to get to the Biltmore Estate on the other side. We'd laughed nervously when the air became crisper, and sighed with relief at the decline towards North Carolina, slightly embarrassed that we'd been anxious at all to travel through the mountain range.

The Rockies, however, were like arrogant giants, towering above in annoyance at the vehicles scurrying up the highways crisscrossing through the peaks, like ants crawling up their pants legs. I'd never seen such white, even having lived through the bitter winters of central Illinois and the occasional whiteouts in Tennessee. But here, everything was blanketed in it: the earth, the mountain peaks, the miles and miles of evergreens scouring the valleys. I was grateful for the sunglasses. If I didn't have them, even the deep crow's feet around my eyes would be weary from my squinting.

The further we drove, the whiter Roxy's knuckles became as she gripped the steering wheel, asking every five minutes if our exit was coming up. Even as we approached hour five, I didn't mind the repeated questions. I couldn't imagine making the harrowing drive alone.

I looked down at my phone, hovering my thumb back and forth over the voice mail icon. I finally touched it, and a row of messages appeared, most from Tom, several from Stella, and the most recent from Kate, from just a few moments ago. *I'll start with hers and work my way down.* I pressed the phone to my ear.

"Mom. We are all worried sick. Dad just told me that you were in Paducah with Roxy. Please just stay there for now. I'm really worried that you'll try to find those people. Those . . . Researchers, or whatever they're called.

"Mom, I hate to leave this on a voice message, but you *can- not* talk to them again. I know some part of you thinks they want to help you; that maybe this Steven Richards wants to help you. He does not. They do not. They are crazy. Steven Richards had maps of our property. The FBI says he hates Dad. Do not speak to these people. Do not promise them anything. We can handle the fallout from the video. We can say you were desperate. No one will judge you. But we have to make sure the story is about William from here on out. If you get in touch with these people again, all the public will ever hear about is how you believe in—I can't even say it. It's going to be plastered on every tabloid. It will be the top story on every website. But it's a twenty-four hour news cycle. The video story will pass as long as you never have anything to do with them again. Please, Mom. Whatever you've done, call me. Please, Mom, just call—"

I hit end and turned off the phone.

Roxy endured the silence for a few moments. "I keep tell- ing myself, 'It will be easier going down. It will be easier going down.' We have to be close now. Tell me again what I'm look- ing for?"

"The man at the counter said it is either in San Juan or Hinsdale county—"

"The least populated counties in Colorado, according to that charming fact from Google. It has the fewest roads, the fewest people. It sounds delightful."

"Look, San Juan County. That exit," I pointed.

Roxy exhaled loudly as we veered onto an exit ramp and were immediately surrounded by pine trees. The suburban started crunching over hundreds of fallen pinecones. The ramp rambled down to a road without a sign. One way led back onto the highway, the other curved into the trees.

"When is this snowstorm supposed to start?" she asked.

"I'm trying not to think about that."

"We're going five miles—tops—and if there's no sign of where we are, we're turning around."

We surpassed five miles, then ten, then fifteen. I hoped Roxy wasn't watching the odometer as closely as I was.

"Thank you, Jesus, there's a gas station," she said. "And don't think I don't know we're well past five miles."

We parked next to an ancient pump and stepped out to the smell of fried chicken coming from a building covered in badly faded cigarette and beer ads. The smell was both nauseating and comforting, a reminder that the southern favorite was a staple of gas station fryers all over the country.

"We don't have much gas," a man called out, sucking his teeth. "Trucks won't be coming up for another two weeks."

"We'll take what you've got," I said. "Is this the exit for Argentum?"

The man leaned on a post. "Never heard of it. I'm not from around here."

I once more brought out the old map and approached him. He took a close look and nodded. "Well, how about that."

"Any idea where it is?"

He shook his head.

"Can you direct me to the next closest town? They might have heard of it."

"Only unincorporated towns around here. Little pockets of people. Old mining towns scattered here and there. Impossible to know all the names."

"I'm guessing if there's a gas station here, there must be a town nearby. I didn't pass any on the way from the interstate. I'm assuming they're farther up the road?"

He nodded and again sucked his teeth.

"All I can get is five dollars out of this," Roxy said.

"I told you we were low."

"Thanks for your help," I gave him a small wave.

"Do you want some chicken for the road?"

I waved Roxy into the Suburban, knowing if the man made the noise again, there might be a brawl.

"Better hurry," he called out. "Feels like a storm's coming."

After sixty-five miles of nothing, Roxy started driving at a crawl, looking for any sign of life. We passed no towns, not even a side street. It became abundantly clear why the gas station was low on fuel; there couldn't be enough people to justify frequent deliveries.

"Hon, I don't even want to think about what we'd do if this SUV broke down."

"Someone has to be out here. Just a bit more."

We both pointed at the same time when the barn and a side road appeared. Hoping a house would be nearby, we turned onto the road, potholes and other precarious dips causing us to bounce in our seats. The closer we got to the barn, the more our hopes teetered. As we pulled up in front, it was clear the wood slats were beyond dilapidated. The doors had long since fallen away, revealing an empty interior.

I began to suggest we get back on the road when I caught a glimpse of a large letter *A* painted in faded white on the edge of the barn's eastern side.

"Can you drive around there?"

"Please keep an eye out for sinkholes."

Next to the painted *A* there was an empty space, and following it were a faded *G* and an *E*.

"Pull back a bit," I said.

Roxy looped around and then stopped. "Well, shut my mouth."

From that view, we could see that a long time ago, someone had painted a single word with a stream flowing underneath. Time had erased two of the letters; now it only read *"A GEN UM."*

"Argentum," I said softly. The painted stream ended in the tip of an arrow, pointing down the crumbling road.

Roxy applied the gas. "Well, here we go."

We drove down the road, navigating more potholes, a fallen limb, and a perilous rise, finally stopping on a ridge.

"Well, this is . . ." Roxy said.

"Quaint."

"I was going more for bleak. Does this town only have one street?"

"I bet it was a silver-mining town."

"It looks like a ghost town."

It would have been easy to dismiss the town as abandoned. The road leading into Argentum was ruined from endless cycles of snow and ice eating away at the aging infrastructure. The pine trees cleared enough to reveal a town that had taken on the colors of winter; the wood of the weary buildings was the same shade as the dirt-caked snow that clung like moss on a fallen tree.

Roxy pulled up to the first structure, a whitewashed

building with two strong wooden posts holding up a front porch. A sign read, "The Argentum Inn," and smoke drifted from the chimney.

"At least someone is alive in there," Roxy observed.

Wincing in the icy wind, we scurried up the front steps and opened the door. The front room was cozy, with overstuffed chairs and a crackling fire. I suddenly felt very tired.

"Well, hello there," said a young woman with deep red hair, who came from a back room to sit behind the counter. "I thought I knew everybody in town. I'm Sarah."

"Just visiting for the day," Roxy said.

"Visiting? I'm not sure we've ever had an actual visitor! But you know about the storm, right? Once it hits, we may be shut off from the hard road for a while. I don't mean to be crass, but are you lost?"

Roxy shook her head. "We're two old spinsters who like to visit all the mountain towns. Do you have any vacancies?"

"When exactly is the storm supposed to hit?" I asked.

"Tomorrow, the radio says," she answered, and then blinked. "Oh, we're not an inn, despite what the sign reads outside. We're more of a boarding house for the locals who like having their beds made and not having to shovel steps."

"Do you have rooms we can rent for just the night?"

"Come to think of it, we do. Just one, though. Mr. Peterson died over the summer and no one has claimed the room yet."

"Charming. We'll take it," Roxy said. "Tell me it has two beds, though."

"Sorry. One queen."

"That's fine. So tell me, what do we need to see? And more importantly, where do we eat? Are you a local?"

"I've lived here and there. It won't take you long to see the town. You may be ready to go home in an hour."

• • •

"All right," Roxy said as we slid back into the Suburban. "Even if we knocked on every door in this town, we'll probably be done in twenty minutes."

"Sarah said that off Main Street, there are a few more streets."

"What's your plan, Lynnie?" Roxy wiped off her sunglasses with her scarf. "I mean, we are, absolutely, in the middle of nowhere. There are probably two hundred people in this town, tops. I know we've talked about this, but why in the world would Dr. Richards tell you this is where William was taken?"

"I don't know." I looked at the empty storefronts in the street that made up the entire downtown.

"And Lynn, who exactly took him? The government? Homegrown terrorists who hate Tom? Maybe some even more wacked-out version of the Researchers from Illinois? There's never been a ransom note. No one has ever asked for money in exchange for returning William. Nothing legit has come from the reward. Do you think maybe Steven knew he was about to be arrested and needed to come up with something to try to make you believe he's not guilty?"

"All I know is that when I worked for Steven, the word 'Argentum' came up more than once. He didn't even know anything about it—he called it an urban legend about aliens. So for him now to direct me here . . ."

"OK. So all you know is that people—who believe in alien abductions—mentioned a theory about something called Argentum, but Dr. Richards had no idea what it was?"

"I remember his frustration about it. That it was an unproven theory. I took it to be almost like a code word for something. He even mentioned once that it was a theory about other dimensions or something. He said several times that he and his fellow Researchers were told to outright dismiss it. So imagine my surprise when he whispered it to me in the hotel room. That and . . . other revelations."

"For Christ sake, Lynn, you hadn't kept a secret from me in sixty years, I thought. Now you keep popping them out, one after another."

"I'm sorry. Everything has been a blur since Barbara waited for me outside the shop two nights ago."

"Wait, what? That Barbara woman came to the shop?"

"She waited for me in the Christmas trees."

I told her of the two names Barbara had given me to research, and how I went to the library and found that the girl, Amelia Shrank, had vanished in 1935, and that the hunter, Josh Stone, disappeared a decade later.

"And they both went missing in the woods behind my house. In the same month William disappeared."

"We're talking nearly three missing people in a century's time, Lynn, how can there possibly be a connection. I mean, don't get me wrong. It sounds strange."

"It gets even stranger." I took a deep breath, and told her about seeing my father and the men in the woods. Then, I reached into my purse and brought out the letter Daddy had written to Steven.

When she was done reading it, Roxy looked at me in astonishment. "Is this real?"

I nodded. "It's Daddy's handwriting."

"Lynn . . . your father believed you were abducted as well? From the woods?"

"I still have trouble accepting it. But this is my father's letter. And . . . I believe him. That he and Mama found me once. I can only hope I can do what they did."

"Did they find you here?"

"I don't know."

"I still can't believe any of it." Roxy looked out the windshield. "I need a moment to wrap my head around all this. As long as you have no more revelations for the moment, I suppose we need to figure out where the hell we go now."

"I have no idea."

"Well, I'm old and cranky and scared and need caffeine. I don't suppose they have a Publix out here anywhere, so that charming country store sign must indicate our only option."

We rolled down the street to stop at the end of the businesses. A sign hung from the porch; it depicted a man waving from atop a mountain, with the word "Climbers" underneath.

"I'll go in," I offered. "If there are any customers, I'm going to show them William's picture while I get you a drink. It can't hurt to ask."

"That depends. You realize that everyone in the country knows William's picture. And if they have a TV, or a radio, or wifi, they've seen the video and may be talking—at this very moment—about the alien-obsessed wife of the senator."

"Oh God, you're right."

"Let's stick with me asking about William. You can't see me in that video. And if anyone makes a joke about it, I'll give them a fat lip. Just keep that sock hat and your sunglasses on if you run into anyone. And be quick with that Diet Pepsi. I'm dragging."

I slid out of the car and walked across the wooden porch, entering the building that smelled like pipe tobacco and cardboard. Three rows of boxed goods, limited produce, and random medical supplies made up the entire shop.

"Can I help you?" asked an older man sitting at the front counter, a pipe in his mouth. He had hair that curled like duck-tails around his ears.

I almost asked for the sodas, but all I could think about was that video released online. How dare those people use William's disappearance to try to shame me into supporting them? They only made it harder for me to find him.

"Yes, I'm actually looking for someone."

"By the ring on your finger, I'm sad to say it's probably not me," the man said, smiling kindly.

I brought out the picture of William. "Do you happen to recognize him?"

The man squinted and looked closely, then shook his head. "Sorry. Never seen the handsome devil. And I know every-body in this town. Let me guess: custody dispute? You the grandma? Your daughter won't let you see your grandson or something?"

"No, nothing like that. It's a long story. He's my grandson, and I'm trying to find him."

"His parents hippies or something? Come up here to take a stab at the marijuana trade? Can't think of any other reason someone would bring a little boy this far out here. We don't have many kids. All the ones I know are locals."

"I wish it were that simple. Well, thank you. Oh, do you happen to have any sodas?"

"Got a few Diet Cokes and some Mountain Dew from my quarterly trip to civilization for supplies. Can't get any of the delivery trucks to come here."

"I'll take a Diet Coke."

The man reached under the counter, and I heard the faint whoosh of a small refrigerator door. The man placed the bottle on the smooth wooden surface. "On the house for the pretty lady."

"Thank you."

"I have to be honest with you: If there was a new kid in town, I'd know. We only have a few hundred people anyway."

"I understand. But I have to try."

"Good luck!" He added a small wave.

I opened the door of the Suburban to Roxy's scowl. "Jesus, I hate Diet Coke."

"You'll survive. Let's start at the bar."

"OK, I'll go there. I carry a flyer with William's picture on it wherever I go, so I have something to show."

"I'll wander up and down the main drag, see if I run into anyone."

Ten minutes later, having only seen abandoned stores and no people, I found Roxy sitting in the Suburban. "Sorry, Sis, no luck. In the laundromat, there was only a stoned couple—thanks for that, Colorado. Apparently, TV—and the internet for that matter—isn't big around here, so they hadn't seen him. Nor had the three people inside the bar, and their TV was set to SportsCenter. Let's leave this booming metropolis and just start driving."

We got in and drove for an hour, up and down the few quiet streets, seeing no one. "It's getting dark now. And I'm beat. Let's find somewhere to eat."

I nodded. "I think that Scotty's bar is all that's open."

At Scotty's, we took a booth and ordered two small salads and grilled chicken sandwiches.

"What if he's not here?" I asked.

"Honey, all you could do was check it out. And you did. You have done everything you could for William. And Brian.

And Anne. You were supposed to call her tonight. I'm actually surprised there haven't been any calls or texts. But I guess no news is good news."

We ate our meal in silence. After a short drive back to the inn, we climbed the stairs to our room. Roxy opened the door and a small piece of paper fluttered to the floor.

"They didn't wait long to stick us with the bill," Roxy said.

I picked it up, realizing it was no bill. The old postcard had an artist's rendering of the Argentum Inn back in its prime, perhaps the early twenties, surrounded by images of small waterfalls landing in creeks. Written in flourishing cursive were the words: "Stay at beautiful Argentum! Where the Water Falls."

My arm immediately tingled in pinpricks.

"Where the Water Falls."

The poem on the cards that I, and untold numbers of Researchers, had given so many times to the families of the missing came whispering in my mind.

You are with me.
You are in the rain.
You are in my tears.
You are where the water falls.

All those years ago, Steven had dismissed the poem. He grumbled that he didn't even know why we handed it out. He'd only said one of his colleagues started doing it and insisted all Researchers follow his lead.

Steven hadn't realized the poem wasn't intended to comfort families. Whoever that colleague was, he had meant it as a guide.

You are where the water falls.

"Sweet God," I whispered. I looked again at the picture and quickly turned it over to show to Roxy when I saw the writing on the back.

In all capital letters, someone had scrawled: "LEAVE BEFORE THE STORM."

FIFTEEN

The wood complained with every step as Roxy thudded down the stairs. I stood at the top of the staircase, holding the banister to keep from swaying. I looked down to see her reach the counter and repeatedly hit the small gold bell until Sarah came out from the back.

"Hello ma'am—"

"Who's been up in our room?"

"No one. Joan won't even come until eleven tomorrow to start cleaning—"

"Then who, do you suppose, slipped this into the door?" Roxy slid the postcard across the counter.

Sarah scanned the card. "I have no idea—"

"Someone clearly intended for this to spook us, and I'd like to know who. Right now."

"Ma'am, I have no idea. I've been in the back all night, and only locals live here—"

"Then which of those locals would have done this? Would you like me to complain to the owner?"

"I'm really sorry this upset you. I would move you to another room, but there aren't any left."

Roxy leaned on the counter. "I'd like to speak with the owner."

"Ma'am, please, I need this job. . . ."

"And he's going to can your butt if he hears someone has been harassing one of your customers while you were on duty."

Even from my vantage point from above, I could see Sarah nervously brush back a strand of her hair. "Please, I'm so sorry. . . ."

"You're from around here. Tell me who lives here."

"I'm not local."

"When we checked in, you said you knew everybody in town."

"I do know most people in town. Or, at least, I've learned their names and faces over the past six months or so."

Even though I couldn't see her face, I knew Roxy's eyebrows were rising. "Then I suggest you tell me which of these faces went by our room tonight. I'm a lot meaner than I look, and I'm aware, right now, with these dark circles under my eyes, I look pretty frightening."

"I need this job," Sarah blurted out.

"Well, I'd like to speak with your boss, Sarah . . . whatever your last name is."

When the girl burst into tears, Roxy shook her head. "Oh, for God's sake, here. . . ." She reached into her purse, bringing out some Kleenex. "Why are *you* so worked up—?"

"You don't understand . . . if you go to the owner and he fires me, I have nowhere to go." She wiped her eyes. "And I can't tell you my last name because I don't know what it is. Who's going to hire someone who doesn't know their last name?"

"Listen, I'm full up with drama, trust me. Clearly, this is

getting me nowhere. But I'm serious. I will find out who left this postcard, and if I get another one, I will track down this owner and seriously chew some ass. *Comprende?*"

The girl nodded, and Roxy gave her the rest of her Kleenex packet. "I don't suppose you have surveillance video of the hallways or who's come in the front door?"

The girl shook her head.

"What does it mean, 'Where the Water Falls'?"

The sound of my voice surprised both of them. I must have come down the stairs so quietly they didn't hear.

Sarah exhaled in an attempt to compose herself. "I asked the same thing of the old timers when I first saw it. When the first settlers came here, they said the creeks were so shiny they looked like argentum, which I've since learned is Latin for silver. And when the snow melted, there were so many little waterfalls leading into the creeks that it became a way to try and lure others to visit in the spring."

"And how many of these old postcards are conveniently lying around town?" Roxy waved it in the air.

"I haven't seen one in a while. Listen, I'm really sorry—"

"We'll figure it out." Roxy took me by the arm. "But I'm dead bolting our door tonight!"

Roxy muttered all the way up the stairs and loudly shut the door as we entered our room. I went to stand before the window.

"Well, don't know if you heard her say it, but that girl says she doesn't know who left this," Roxy said. "She said they don't keep surveillance."

I stared into the dark. "Ten minutes ago, I was wondering if I was wrong about everything."

"Just to play devil's advocate, couldn't it be somebody

worried about two old broads who could be stuck here in a snowstorm?"

"I don't think anybody in this town is concerned about our welfare."

I thought about telling her about the connection I thought I'd made to the Researcher's poem. But the idea of explaining to Roxy the theory, and thinking about how she would certainly respond with sarcasm, made me very tired.

"Should you call Tom?" she asked, digging through her bag for the nightgown we bought at the airport.

"I tried as we were coming up the stairs. Couldn't get a signal out. Can't send a text either. Might be why there's been no calls or texts. Oh God, I hope nothing's happened that has Anne panicked. If she can't reach me, and Tom can't, it may prompt him to ask police for help tracking me down."

"Lynn, I have to tell you, this scares me a little. I don't like this note. Should we call the police? Go make a report?"

"And tell them what exactly? Anyone who hears what we're doing would think we're the crazy ones. Especially if they've seen the news."

"I thought we were crazy too," Roxy said, holding out the postcard. "Until this."

I took the postcard from her. "Even if they can't get ahold of me, and they try to trace us, I don't care. I'm not leaving until I know if William is here."

"I would say I'm hormonal, but that ship sailed long ago, so I guess I'm just hankering for some guilty pleasures," Roxy said as the Suburban rolled down the street. "I'm going to need some Doritos,"

"It's 8:15 in the morning," I replied, wincing. It was still bright outside, even with the endless gray skies. I looked down at my phone. No calls or texts, either to my phone or Roxy's. Clearly there was no service here. There was no doubt Tom would start worrying. We were running out of time.

"I don't want to go back into that bar, even for decent food. So when you can't have scrambled eggs, you have Doritos, and I saw some in the window of that general store. Climbers, was it? Why don't you bat your eyes at that old man and get us a free bag to go with my free Diet Coke from yesterday?"

"That old man is probably younger than us."

"Look, we're already here. One perk of this town is you can be anywhere in two seconds."

I slid out, feeling a bit ridiculous that we drove instead of walking. But from here on out, we would be driving the rest of the day, trying to map out a plan. As I once again stepped in the store, the tobacco smell reminded me of Daddy. Had he been in this town as well? Looking for me?

"Well, this is my lucky week," the man said with a smile, still perched at the counter.

"Good morning. I hope you have coffee."

"That, my dear, I have plenty of."

"This isn't for me." I slid the bag of Doritos across the counter.

"Hey, whatever gets you through the day."

"Can you make it two cups?"

"Don't break my heart and say that you're here with your husband."

"Just here with an old friend."

"Still on the search?" he asked, pouring the coffee.

"Back at it today."

"Like I said—don't get your hopes up. If the wind blows in a different direction, I'm usually the first to know."

I studied the man's face. "I don't suppose you tried to warn me of the storm with a postcard stuck in my door last night?"

"Somebody warn you about the storm in a note? Around here, warning about snowstorms is as common a greeting as good morning and good night.'"

"Something like that."

"You staying up at the boarding house? Pretty nice folk up there, doubt they'd do anything to scare somebody. When we get storms, it's no sweet Georgia rain. The snow comes in and it pounds us. Generators keep us alive; sometimes we go days without power. I doubt you have to deal with that down south."

"The accent gives me away?" I paused before signing my name.

"It's a beautiful accent." He held up the receipt. "Nice to meet you, Lynn . . . Stanson."

"What's your name?"

"Joseph, but I go by Joe." He reached out and shook my hand. "Please let me know if I can be any assistance to you."

"The coffee helps a lot. Are you from here?"

"Wish I knew," he grinned. "Now, don't you start thinking I'm one of those old guys with Parkinson's or dementia. I can tell you the names of the starting lineups in the bullpens for the Rockies since the early nineties and every song on Johnny Cash's first album. But anything from my childhood or teenage years . . . nothing."

"Nothing?"

"Woke up in our little medical center on the edge of town with absolutely no idea who I was. Can you believe it? Memory never came back. I assume I was some messed-up kid. Maybe some drugs fried my brain, or I got into some hell of a bar fight. No one ever came looking for me, so I must not have been a real charmer. Anyhow, people in this town were really good to me, so I stuck around. Started stocking shelves here, got friendly with the owner, Mr. Climbers. When he got sick, he asked me to run the place till he got better. That was fifty years ago! So here I am. Just me and Moses."

"Moses?"

Joe pointed out the side window at what appeared to be one of the largest pickup trucks in the world.

"That's something else," I said.

"Instead of parting the Red Sea, I part the snow. My other job is helping to clear the streets when the snow comes in. I'll have a busy next couple of days, if what the radio says is true."

"So," I started hesitantly, "do you listen to the radio a lot? Aren't there more accurate warnings on TV or online?"

"Spend about five minutes in Argentum and you'll see we're a bit behind the times. Internet service is for shit up here, and no company is going to invest in fiber lines for a small town with less than five hundred people. Plus, most folks here like living off the grid, it's why they're here. Our major news source is pretty much AM radio. We don't even get the Denver TV stations."

At least there's one town in America that doesn't think I'm insane, I thought.

"It's been nice talking to you, Joe, but I really have to go."

"You be careful Miss Lynn. You run into any problems, you know where to find me. Especially if you get stuck!"

I waved as I walked out.

"Jesus, did you give him your number?" Roxy said as I climbed in. "Give me that coffee and those Doritos, in that order. So, what did Mr. Handsome have to say?"

"I didn't realize you were watching that closely through the window."

"That's a fine-looking man, Lynn, like you didn't notice. I may be postmenopausal, but I'm not dead. Maybe he's the one who left you the note."

"I flat-out asked him." I sipped at the coffee.

"Well, someone left her shyness back in Tennessee."

"What are we going to do if we get snowed in?"

"We best get a move on and do whatever it is we're going to do, and maybe drive back towards the interstate for a bit to try and get a signal to call Tom. Did Romeo in there have any suggestions as where to start?"

"Poor man, he doesn't even know if he's from here. He doesn't remember—"

"I'm sorry, what did you say?" Roxy put down her coffee.

"He said he can't remember anything from his childhood, had amnesia of some sort—"

"He really said that?"

"Yes. Why does that matter?"

"Because if you were eavesdropping properly last night, you would have heard young Sarah at the front desk say she doesn't remember her last name. And she doesn't remember where she's from either. That's why she freaked out when I demanded to know who owned the inn. She said she was afraid she'd lose her job if he found out, because who would hire a girl who didn't even know her last name."

Roxy placed her hand on my leg. "Lynn, my God. My God."

"What?"

"You always thought that brain tumor caused you to lose your memory as a kid. You always said your first memory was waking up and not recognizing your father. You had to relearn everything. But your father's letter stated you never had a brain tumor. What if, Lynn, you were just like them?"

I remembered Daddy's words from his letter to Steven:

I've always been plagued with guilt that she doesn't know her own true story.

I felt hot all over, regretting the coffee. I tapped the power window to allow a crack, letting the icy air brush my face. Daddy had concocted the story. Faked the medical records. All to cover up the fact that his daughter had no memory and couldn't explain why to anyone.

I lowered the window even more, taking several deep breaths, the air stinging my lungs.

"Lynn?"

"Let's just drive."

"I could be wrong. Let me turn down the heat—"

"I just need some more air. I promise to roll it up in a minute."

We drove down the same few streets, seeing no one. Finally, we found one woman walking her corgi. She shook her head sadly at William's picture. "He's a handsome boy. A few of the kids play up at the old ball field around the corner; you might find someone there who has seen him."

"You should have asked her if she knew her last name," Roxy said as we drove away.

We arrived at the park and found it to be as deserted and neglected as the rest of the town. A tiny yellow bus was parked nearby, and a few kids ran and screamed on a weary-looking playground.

"Hang around here. I know you said Mr. Hot Stuff back at the store got all his news from crappy radio, and so far no one has recognized you or William, but let me take it from here. Looks like there are a few houses around the baseball diamond down there. I'll look for signs of life. I'll be right back."

"I need to walk a bit. But I'll stay close."

We both exited the Suburban, and I watched as Roxy

walked away. I huddled in my coat, wishing I had bought thicker gloves. I'd gone from hot to bitter cold quickly, and I shuffled along to keep up the circulation.

I brought out my phone to power it up. Maybe I could get cell reception out here. I needed to call Anne—

A laugh in the distance caused me to almost drop the phone.

Four boys on the other side of the park were playing a game of touch football. One of them had dropped his hat, exposing his red hair.

The boy turned around. For a split second, I saw his face.

William pulled his hat over his ears and laughed.

SIXTEEN

"William?"

I started at a jog, not daring to take my eyes off the boy chasing the others. "William! William!"

He was giggling, holding his sides at whatever joke someone had said. I had heard that laughter a hundred times before, at SpongeBob on television, when Chris tossed him over his shoulder, as Tom pretended to gnaw off his fingers when ice cream dripped on his little hands.

"William! Baby, it's Nanna! William!" I was sobbing as I reached him. I grabbed the sides of his face, seeing replicas of Anne's eyes, my own freckles on his cheeks, his dimpled chin.

"Oh, thank you God, thank you," I pulled him close. "Oh baby. . . ."

I felt his small hands push away as he stammered back. "Miss Cliff," he said, looking around, his eyes wide with confusion.

I reached out and took off his hat, running my fingers through the hair that I had combed for two summers, when he would take a bath at my house before Anne came to take him home, knowing he would fall asleep on the two-minute drive. "Oh, baby. It's me, it's Nanna."

"Miss Cliff!" William practically screamed.

The boys that had gathered around us began to part, making way for a slow-moving woman whose face was lined with wrinkles.

"What's going on here?"

"This is my grandson." I smiled through tears. "I've been looking for him. Oh William, I can't believe it—"

"Miss, I think you have the wrong boy," the woman said, placing a weathered but protective hand on William, who moved in closer to her.

"You don't understand. William, it's Nanna."

"Miss Cliff," he said anxiously.

"Your birthday is June 26." I kneeled down, flinching as he stepped farther away. "You hate peas. You love dinosaurs. If you pull up your pants leg, you'll see the birthmark you have on the back of your right thigh—"

"Miss, you're scaring the children. Boys, take Alan and go to the bus."

"No!" I cried out as William and the boys turned and ran.

Miss Cliff shuffled in front of me, her ancient voice lowering to a whisper. "You need to go. Right now. Whoever you are, get out of here *now*."

"No." I tried to step around her.

"I warned you," Miss Cliff said, looking back to the bus. "Security! I mean, officer, can you please come here?"

"William!" I screamed, seeing him look back once more before hurrying on the bus.

I easily sidestepped the woman and ran, seeing a figure emerge from a car that I hadn't noticed was parked behind the bus. A man, wearing a dark blue jacket and matching pants, put out his arms.

"What's going on here?" he said.

"That's my grandson!" I cried out, pointing to the bus. At the door, the hunched-over figure of Miss Cliff was herding the other children on, pointing one curved and bony finger to hasten their step.

"Please calm down, ma'am, and tell me what's going on," the man said, blocking me.

"My name is Lynn Roseworth, my husband is Senator Tom Roseworth. We've gone on television to say our grandson is missing. And he's right there!"

"OK, OK, calm down."

"Lynn!" Roxy waved as she hurried over. "Lynn, what's happening?"

"He's on the bus! He's in there! William's in there!"

The doors to the bus closed and the engine fired up.

"Lynn, are you sure?" Roxy was almost out of breath.

"Ma'am, just relax," the officer said.

"It's leaving!" I said as the wheels of the bus shuddered and turned. "No! Stop that bus!"

"Ma'am, that's enough. You're going to have to calm down—"

"And who the hell are you?" Roxy demanded.

"I'm police—"

"If my friend says her missing grandson is on that bus, then you better stop that bus."

The man murmured into the speaker on his shoulder. "Five-ninety, please send a car to the north end of the park."

"No!" I watched the bus drive way. "Roxy, no. . . ."

"What the hell is wrong with you?" Roxy squared off with the man. "Stop that bus!"

"You both have caused quite the scene out here. That bus is only going up to the day care, and once you've calmed down, we'll see about going up there and checking this out. But I saw that little boy, ma'am, and he didn't know you from Adam."

A white car pulled up, its red light lazily spinning on the dashboard. I turned to Roxy with frantic eyes. "He didn't recognize me, Roxy. He didn't know it was me. He didn't *remember*."

Roxy's hand went to her mouth. She reached into her purse and began to dig around for her phone.

"What's going on?" another officer, also dressed in dark blue, asked as he approached, looking intently at Roxy as she tore into her purse.

"I'm going to call her husband right now, who happens to be a US senator."

"What we're all going to do is calm down," the first officer said. "Let's take a ride and go over all this."

"Let's go." The second officer took Roxy gently by the arm.

"Get your hands off." She tried to jerk away, until she looked closely at his face.

He sucked his teeth loudly. Even I could smell fried chicken from where I was standing.

"Jesus," Roxy said softly.

"You have a good memory," the man said, opening the door to the squad car.

The front hallway of the building the officers called their police station was sparsely decorated with historic photographs of Argentum in cheap frames, including one of an old barbershop in which a mural was painted with a waterfall spilling into a creek. *Where the Water Falls* was written in decorative letters in the stream.

That photograph melted into my blur of panic. I knew I'd been wild-eyed in my demands for my phone to call Tom, practically screaming at the officers as I kept looking out the back window of the squad car for any sign of the bus. Even when they ushered us into the building, I took another glance before the door shut, hoping to catch a glimpse, to even know the direction William was going.

I had him. And I let him go.

The men took us to a back room, telling Roxy to try and calm me down. She responded with a colorful tirade of curse words interspersed with idle threats. They shut the door and said through the glass that they were getting in touch with the FBI.

"Google her, you assholes!" Roxy shook the locked handle. "Lynn Roseworth! Wife of Senator Tom Roseworth! Her grandson's disappearance has been announced all over the world! What kind of rock have you been living underneath?"

I paced the room, my fingers entangled in my hair. "What the hell is going on, Lynn? What is wrong with this place? That officer was the gas station creepo yesterday, now he's a cop?"

"She didn't call them officers at first," I said, my eyes darting.

"What?"

"The woman with William and the other children. She told me I needed to leave, and then said she tried to warn me. She called 'security,' and then quickly referred to him as officer."

"My God, now that I think about it, they weren't wearing any badges. . . ."

"I shouldn't have let that bus go. How can I ever tell Anne that I had him, and I let him go?"

"You could have hung on to the back of that bus and it

wouldn't have made a difference," Roxy said, then she added quietly. "Are you sure, Lynn? Are you sure it was him?"

"It was him."

"Dammit," Roxy stood, wincing. She had run too fast from the other end of the park when she saw the commotion. "Why didn't we call Tom, or Ed, or anyone for that matter, to tell them where we are?"

"Because I know what they would have said. I could blame the cell service, which doesn't seem to exist here. But I could have called from the road. I knew the second I called, I would hear Anne plead for me to come to Champaign, or Tom would remind me how reckless this is and all the damage I've caused."

"Speaking of Tom, and I know you hate to hear this, but you're both public figures, and they can't keep you locked up in here. One search online and they'll see everything they need to know. We're going to get William, Lynn."

"He didn't recognize me. Is that what's happening here? People who are kidnapped are brought to this town? Joe at the general store woke up in the hospital in this town without his memory. Sarah at the inn doesn't remember anything of her life, either. Roxy, is this is where Daddy found *me*? I didn't have a memory either."

"Well, we know two things: that Dr. Richards was both right and wrong about William being here. Your boy ended up in this town, but obviously wasn't abducted by aliens and isn't soaring around the cosmos in a spaceship."

"So what, then? He was taken by someone, maybe some sort of group, and the people they abduct end up with memory loss?"

"And it doesn't explain how Dr. Richards knew he would be here. If I had my phone . . ."

"They're not going to give us our phones."

"Well, my patience has officially run out. We've done nothing wrong, they can't lock us up in here when we haven't committed any crime—"

The door handle turned and a small man stepped in, quietly closing the door behind him. His thinning hair was parted to cover a sizable bald spot, his skin color an ashen gray. He fumbled in his suit coat to bring out a pack of cigarettes. Every bit of clothing on him, from his head to his shoes, was black.

"We have a pretty bad storm approaching, ladies. It's best that you get out of here before it hits."

"I don't think so," Roxy said. "I don't know who you are, but we have come here to find my friend's grandson, who she just saw at a park in this town. And I'm happy to remind you again who she is married to—"

"We will be pleased to arrange for transportation out of here." The man fired up a cigarette. "We'll make sure you get out safely."

"I will not leave my grandson."

"We want to return you to your family, Mrs. Roseworth," the man said, taking a deep drag. "We understand you must be very desperate. In light of what's on the news websites now, I know it must be hard to admit he's gone. No one is sure, though, why you thought he would end up here—"

"Because she saw him," Roxy interjected.

The man ignored her and kept looking at me. "Your family has gone through a great loss. Please don't make them go through another."

"I will not leave him—"

"Lynn, I want to go home." Roxy reached out and touched my arm. "I can't do this anymore. I need to get home to Ed.

My back hurts, I can't go through a storm like that without my pain meds, and I'm out. Let's do this. Obviously you were wrong. If it were William, he would have recognized you. You must be delirious or something. We have to admit that now. Let's take this ride out of town. I'm done."

She squeezed a bit harder. "I'm too tired to do this anymore."

I looked at her, and under her weepy eyes, Roxy flared her nostrils.

"Thank you, we'll take that ride," I said.

"Good," the man said, already finishing off the cigarette. "I have a car pulled around. We'll take you by the inn to get your things."

"We'll need our purses," Roxy said.

"Of course. It's all waiting for you in the car."

"Thank you," she said, wincing as she stepped. As the man walked out, Roxy mouthed words to me: "Act old."

"What are we doing?" I mouthed back.

We walked out of the building as slowly as possible. The white unmarked car waited outside, with the red light still spinning beneath the windshield. "Is it OK if I sit in the front?" Roxy asked. "I can never get comfortable in the back."

"Of course," the man in the black suit said, nodding.

"Welcome, ladies," said the teeth sucker as we got into the car.

Roxy slid into the front seat. "Lynnie, is my purse back there? I need to see if I have any of my OxyContin left. My hip is killing me."

"It's here."

"I have a bum leg too," Teeth Sucker said, pulling the gear into drive. "Tough living with the pain."

I looked out the window, making eye contact briefly with

the man in the black suit. He lit a cigarette and watched us drive away.

Roxy dug around in her purse. "Can't barely move without my meds."

"If you're looking for your phone, it's in there, but damn it all if the batteries aren't dead. You must have left it on too long without charging it."

"Oh, that's fine." Roxy gave a careless wave. "I just need my medicine. Don't have anybody to call anyway."

Teeth Sucker began to hum as we drove. "You must be busy, working the gas station and being a police officer," Roxy commented.

He grinned. "We're all called to serve."

I looked out through the back window, seeing the downtown disappearing behind us. Soon the police building was gone over a hill. I couldn't see any of Argentum. The panic was rising to my throat.

I could see Teeth Sucker looking at my reflection in the rearview mirror. "Don't you worry. I have to make a quick stop at the hospital, it's just around the bend from here. After that, we'll head right back to the inn."

"My ass," Roxy said, pulling out the mace from her purse.

"Fuckin' fuck!" he cried out as she sprayed his face.

The car veered wildly. Roxy kept spraying as he reached out to block her. "Fucking bitch!" When the chemicals truly sunk in, he started to scream.

"Roxy!" I cried out, watching the car weave across the road and then take a violent turn towards a telephone pole.

The impact threw me back, but not before I saw Roxy crash into the dashboard. As Teeth Sucker frantically wiped his face, I sat stunned for a moment, my head spinning. I could hear a hissing sound from the engine, and I closed my eyes to try and stop the vertigo.

"Roxy! Are you OK—?"

She moaned and then flinched away as Teeth Sucker reached out for her angrily, his sausage fingers grabbing the hood of her coat.

My wallet, stuffed with Target receipts, credit cards I'd closed but forgot to throw away, and volumes of my grandchildren's photographs, was the first thing I threw at him. Maybe it was that I was so close behind him that my aim was so true. It struck him sharply on the back of his head. The metal clasp on the wallet must have hit him in a soft spot as the impact produced another yelp of pain as he continued to wail and wipe his eyes. I started throwing everything I could grasp in my purse: a compact, a small flashlight, pencils, mints. When an eyeliner pinged off his right temple, he reached back for me blindly.

I fell back into the backseat, smacking his hand with my purse. My eyes were starting to sting from the mace as well. I could hear Roxy fumble with the door handle and she practically fell out the door, her feet momentarily in the air.

Teeth Sucker lunged in the direction of the sound. He wrestled at his waist and pulled out a gun. Gunshots rang out in the car.

"Roxy!" I screamed, once again striking him with my purse. He pivoted the gun back towards me. As I bent down, I heard the gunfire and the back windshield shatter.

The door beside me jerked opened and Roxy outstretched her hand. She yanked me out as he fired again into the backseat. The cushions absorbed the zings of the flying bullets. "You fucking bitches!" he yelled.

"Sweet God," Roxy whispered, wiping at her own eyes. "That mace works. Even the residual hurts like the devil."

We hustled down the road, hearing Teeth Sucker curse among screams of pain as he realized he was out of bullets.

"Are you hurt? You're limping—"

"Here I pretend to be old for a minute, and now I actually feel like it."

I looked back at the crashed cruiser. Teeth Sucker had fallen out now, rubbing his eyes and screaming for us.

I took her arm as I hurried our pace. "We have to get away from here."

"Mr. Black back there didn't want to dirty his hands with actually having to kill a senator's wife, so he sent numb nuts back there to do it. I guess the first security guard or whatever he is from the park couldn't stomach it. Well, we aren't so old, are we, assholes? Good thing I bought that mace at the airport. Never leave home without it. There, go down that back street."

"Who are they? They clearly aren't police. That teacher tried to warn me. I know why now."

The street off the main road was lined with more vinyl-sided houses and empty driveways. "We have to keep heading towards town."

"Our only chance now is that Fried Chicken couldn't open his eyes enough to see where we went. But it's not going to be hard to find two old women stumbling around. Damn, does my ass hurt."

"We have to get to that hospital. If William has lost his memory, then maybe he's in treatment there. Maybe Joe is at the store. He said he was cared for at the hospital. I guarantee Sarah was a patient too. I'm also sure our Suburban has been seized now. We'll have to convince someone to take us there."

"We can't get far on foot, that's for sure," Roxy said, blinking in surprise at the wetness on her temple. "Jesus. Am I bleeding?"

I looked over, feeling the same on my face. "It's starting to snow."

SEVENTEEN

It became clear almost immediately why we'd heard so many repeated warnings; why everyone from the young man at the car rental to Sarah at the inn and even the man who just tried to kill us, had cautioned us about the storm. By the time we reached downtown Argentum, the snow fell not in sheets, but in buckets, camouflaging the storefronts in walls of white.

Roxy looked over her shoulder, seeing no sign of police lights. "Hope that scumbag gets frostbite to go with the pain in his eyes. If he has a phone, he's called his boss—or whomever the suit is—to tell what happened. If it wasn't snowing like this, we couldn't even walk this out in the open. Watch your step, the last thing either of need is to break a hip right now. Though mine hurts like the dickens."

"I knew what that man at the police station meant when he said he didn't want my family to endure another tragedy. I just didn't have a plan to get away. Thank God you did."

"I knew I had mace inside my purse, and that was the extent of my plan. We're lucky all they really wanted was our phones."

We could barely see the outlines of the mostly abandoned buildings, looming in the snow like gray sentinels.

"Looks like Joe's shop is closed. We have to get to a phone. In fact, we need to do that right now, before anything else."

"We'll stop in Scotty's, use theirs. It should be right here. . . ."

The "closed due to snow," sign on the door was laminated and worn from frequent use.

"You know it's bad when the bar closes." Roxy breathed into her hands.

"That inn is old. It must have a landline phone somewhere that still works in this weather. We aren't far."

We made to the end of the boardwalk and looked across the street. Even in the pummeling snow, we could see the lights of the police cars parked in front of the hotel.

"Fried Chicken must have radioed in," Roxy said.

"I didn't see anywhere else open."

"I saw a bunch of trash cans out behind the inn. Let's see if we can sneak in. If not, we'll find another plan. But right now, we have to get inside somewhere, and it's the only place open. That's our first priority. We'll freeze out here. We were stupid not to buy some kind of parkas at the airport; these coats we're wearing are made for football weather in Tennessee."

I took Roxy's arm again. We walked across the street and down an alley, the accumulation preventing us from moving as fast as I wanted. As we emerged behind the stores, we braced ourselves to walk directly into the snow, shielding our eyes the best we could.

There was already an inch of snow on the trashcans and on a maroon Voyager van parked behind the inn. In the ferocious winds, a screened door repeatedly slapped against its wood frame. My face hurting now, I held the screen door while Roxy slowly turned the handle of the main door.

The hallway inside was dark, and the doors to the other rooms were shut. We listened for sound of voices but heard nothing.

Roxy immediately tried to open the door to one of the rooms, finding it locked. As she moved on to the next, someone turned down the hallway. I held my breath as the person stopped, and then approached cautiously.

"What have you two done?" Sarah whispered. "Why are the police looking for you?"

"Listen, we just need a phone," Roxy said.

"The phones don't work in this weather." She looked back down the hallway while fumbling with the keys in her hands.

"Of course phones work when it snows. It only started falling a few minutes ago."

"That's not what happens here. Everything shuts down: phone, internet. That's why the man who rents this room hoofed it out before the storm for his girlfriend's house. He knows there's no contact after the weather gets bad. I see his van is still out back," she said, looking over her shoulder and opening the door to her right. "He won't even know somebody's been in his room. Come in here."

We followed her into a room where laundry sat in piles. "You have to stay in here; they've already been up in your room. They're still here, outside on the porch, smoking."

"Your landline phones must work," Roxy whispered.

She shook her head. "We got rid of the landline phones at the inn. No use for them anymore. I don't know anyone who has them."

"That ancient technology shouldn't have been abandoned

by your generation," Roxy scowled. "A good old-fashioned cord would save our asses right now."

"The officers won't even say why they want to find you. What did you do?"

"We didn't do anything. I'm here to find my grandson, and my friend is here to help me. And we found him. Today. In this town. But he didn't recognize me."

"Did you understand that?" Roxy leaned in to Sarah. "Her own grandson didn't recognize her, because he didn't remember her. He didn't even know his own name."

Her eyes darted back and forth.

"We have to get to him," I said, trying to stay calm. "I don't know anything about you, Sarah, but Roxy said you don't have much of a memory either. I don't know what's happening in this town, but my grandson is just like you. Could he be at the hospital here?"

"I don't know, but this is making me too nervous. Stay here, I have to go back up front. Don't come out. My boyfriend should be over soon. He might know what to do."

She slipped out, and Roxy shook her head. "Lynn, we have to get out of here. Now."

"I won't leave him. I can't, Roxy."

"The roads are going to be impassable soon, Lynn. There aren't any phones. Even if Tom were starting to look for you, there's no cell towers to trace our phones. We will be trapped here, and they already tried to off us once."

I hugged myself, rubbing my hands up and down my arms. Roxy walked over to the desk, rummaging around. She then moved over to the dresser.

"What are you doing?"

She slid a pair of keys out from behind an ashtray. "It can't be that easy."

"What are you talking about?"

"Our ride is here. At least I hope it is. The van parked out back. It's a Voyager, and Sarah mentioned that the guy who rents this room drove a van. Don't you pay attention to this stuff? And these look like van keys. We're giving it a shot. Let's go."

"You go. But I cannot—I will not—leave here without William."

"No one knows where we are, Lynn. We get out, we find a phone, and one call to Tom will have the FBI, the CIA, and maybe even the armed forces here. We know the hospital is here. William must be there. But we can't just bust in and try to find him, Lynn. It's too risky. If they find us again—"

"Please go, Roxy. Please. You're right. You have to get help. And the roads are going to get worse. Please, go. Go now." I took Roxy's hands. "You understand, right? You understand I can't go without him."

"We have to go. It doesn't make sense to stay here."

"It does. I will make Sarah tell me more. I'll find out the location of the hospital. By the time you get back with help, I'll have convinced her to spill it."

Roxy glared and pointed. "You stay hidden. Lock yourself in here if you have to. I'll find a phone, and I'll come back for you."

"I know you will. Please be careful. We don't get a lot of snow in Nashville."

"Hell, I drive a pickup with four-wheel drive. I don't even know if these are his keys. Stealing a car is a new one, even for me."

She gave me a quick, fierce hug and went to the door, opening it gently. "Stay in here," she said, and slipped out.

I hurried over to the window, parting the heavy curtains.

To my relief, I could still see the van through the blinding snow. I didn't dare breathe as Roxy's hunched-over form scurried through the snow and held out the keys. The van blinked its lights in recognition.

She clambered inside and fired up the engine. At first, she clearly gunned it too hard. It lurched and nearly knocked over the trashcans. Then it slowly backed up and quietly moved down the alley.

"Where's your friend?"

I flinched as Sarah stepped through the door. "She's trying to find a phone."

"She went out in this? I'm telling you, there's no phones that will work."

"She took our car."

"And left you here? The officers said you would be on foot."

"She knows I won't leave my grandson."

Sarah looked back at the door. "The police were gone when I went up front. I . . . want to talk to my husband about this. Just stay here."

She again slipped out, and I turned once more to the window. Thinking of Roxy navigating the unfamiliar streets, I made the sign of the cross. I then whispered the Hail Mary, picturing a boy standing somewhere in this town, maybe looking out at the snow too, wondering about the strange lady who hugged him so tight and called him William.

How long had my grandson been in this horrible town? How many other people without memories are here, their families oblivious to the fact that they're alive? Obviously one of the Researchers had enough information about this place to start writing that poem all those decades ago.

If it was meant was a guide, how it is Steven hadn't known that, all those years ago? Fast-forward forty years, and he was set to take

*me here from that hotel room, before the FBI burst in. He'd even
created that encrypted map, just in case we were separated.*

Anger churned in my chest. Either Steven was telling the
truth, that he'd just recently learned the truth about Argentum,
or there had been decades of lies—

I suddenly looked back at the door.

Sarah said she wanted to talk to her husband about this.
But she had referred to him as her boyfriend when we first
came into the room.

I should have caught on to that quicker. *You don't realize it
yet, but you're going to explain everything to me, young lady.*

I eased towards the door, slowly opening it to the dark
hallway. I could hear static of some kind, and then a clicking.
The unmistakable sound of radio communication came from
down the hall.

"I don't know, Mark. I know she's driving that maroon
Voyager. Over," Sarah said in a whisper.

"I can't hear you, Sarah, speak up. Over."

Reflected in the window, I could see Sarah leaning on the
counter, a two-way radio in her hand.

"I can't talk much louder. She's got to take Singer Street and
then Main Street. I gotta go."

When she put down the radio, I emerged, my eyes dazed
in anger. "How could you?"

She gasped. I shook my head. "How could you!"

"She shouldn't have stolen that van! I didn't have a choice!
They were going to find out, and then they'd know I knew! I
can't go to jail, I just started to have a life!"

"Don't you want to know? Don't you want to know what
happened to you? What happened to all of you?"

"It doesn't make sense, what you're saying!"

"I only want to find my grandson! Don't you wonder if someone ever came looking for you? And *this* is what you do?"

"Please. Stay here and talk to the police, they will help you—"

I turned and rushed down the hallway.

"Where are you going?" she cried out, stepping around the counter. "Miss, don't go out there!"

I reached the end of the hall and flew through the back door, the snow temporarily blinding me. Without hesitation, I plunged into the white.

EIGHTEEN

It took two steps to realize the insanity of what I had done.

The snow that had swirled and blurred before was nothing to the whiteout conditions that now pummeled the town. I could see nothing, not even the trash cans that Roxy had almost knocked down. I reached back to touch the wall of the inn as some kind of proof that the entire world wasn't lost in white. I used its wooden surface to navigate away from the door. If Sarah was still calling out my name, she was drowned out in the oppressive howl of the winds.

I reached the edge of the building. Were the security officers on their way? Were they tracking Roxy instead? Was she far enough away by now that they couldn't follow?

The temperature felt as if it had dropped ten degrees. I gauged the distance between the inn and the first building on the boardwalk as ten feet at best. But it may have well been a thousand yards away. If I lost my sense of direction, even for a moment, I could wander into the street and never find my way. But the alternative was to stay and wait for the officers to find me.

I forced myself to imagine William again, standing in front of a window, watching the snow.

My fingertips left the building, and I stepped one foot directly in front of the other, convincing myself that it was as simple as following a line. I reached out with my right hand, not unlike the way I had as a girl trying to swim from one side of the YMCA pool to the other. I hadn't been brave enough then to open my eyes, so I swam blindly, holding my breath as long as I could, aiming for the other end. More times than not, my lungs gave out and I surfaced, opening my eyes to realize I was only inches from the edge.

I'd walked fifteen feet, hadn't I? I should have reached the stores now. *My God, I'd gone off course.* I kept reaching, with both hands now. Even with my thick gloves, my fingers ached in the cold. *Just touch something—*

I felt it, then, a fleeting surface. I waved my hands wildly, striking the wood post with such force that I gasped in pain. With my other hand I clung to it like a life preserver, reaching out for the wall.

I leaned against the cold wood and took several deep breaths. I inched along the wall, at last coming to the corner. The blinding wind was just as fierce here. *How can it blow in more than one direction?*

I continued feeling along the wall, noting a jut-out of shutters. I felt a door handle at my waist and shook it frantically, finding it locked.

You are going to die here.

Keep moving. Don't stand still. Think of William.

I felt along the storefronts. Even the abandoned buildings' shutters were locked tight. I passed the empty laundromat and approached the general store. *Please let there be a light on, please let someone still be inside.*

I was met again with tightly closed shutters and a dead-bolted door. I leaned my forehead against the wood. This was it. Climbers was the last of the stores on the row. I didn't dare cross the street to the other businesses, all of which were already closed.

My skin started to hurt. The temperature must have dropped again. I wanted to sit down, huddle in my coat against the elements. But I knew I needed to keep moving, keep the blood circulating. How long before hypothermia would set in—?

The roar of an engine and two blaring lights momentarily shone through the snow at the end of the boardwalk. Gears shift loudly and ice crunched.

"Wait!" I cried out, daring to hurry alongside what remained of the wall. I slipped a bit and caught myself on the edge of a shutter. "Wait!"

The headlights began to diminish as the truck went in reverse. I stepped out away from the wall and waved my arms, scuffling a few inches along the wood floor.

I misjudged, and dropped off the edge.

Waves of pain shuddered through my kneecap as I landed. The headlights were now pointed in another direction, and I could barely make out the cab of the truck. I cried out as I forced myself to stand and shuffle through the foot of snow now on the ground over to the truck window, slamming my palm hard against the glass.

"Jesus Christ!" Said a muffled voice from within.

"Wait!" I whimpered.

"Good God, who's out there?"

The door opened and a man in a red-checked hat with flaps over his ears looked out at me, astonished, with ice-blue eyes under the rim of his hat.

"Joe!"

"Miss Lynn?" said the proprietor of Climbers, sliding out

of the truck. He helped me stay upright as I hissed in pain, holding my knee.

"What in God's name are you doing out here?" He put my arm around his shoulder and helped me limp around the plow of the truck and over to the passenger door. He practically lifted me into the seat, and hurried back around.

He got in and shut the door, turning up the heat. "What are you doing?"

My eyes closed in pain. "I had to see if any of the stores were open."

"Why? What in the world were you needing that badly that you had to come out in this storm?"

"I needed to find a phone."

"And you thought you'd take a stroll? That was a pretty damn stupid thing to do. I closed up hours ago, but left some propane tanks here that I needed. If I hadn't needed to come back so desperately, you would have been up shit creek, lady. Have you lost your mind?"

I slowly looked to him. "I found my grandson. My friend has gone to get help. I won't bother telling you everything that's happened, but I have to try to get to him."

"You found your boy?"

I nodded. Joe leaned his wrist on the steering wheel. "Well, where is he, then? Why isn't he with you?"

"Because he didn't remember me."

When he didn't respond, I cautiously turned back to him. He was staring out the windshield. "He didn't remember?"

"What's happening in this town? Why can't my grandson remember me? Why do you not have a memory? Why does Sarah up at the inn not have a memory? And why would the police go to such lengths to get us out of town?"

"The police?" The lines around his eyes creased.

"I found my grandson with other children at the park, and some woman boarded him on a bus and called for police. Some men showed up and took me and my friend Roxy into custody, and then we were told we needed to leave immediately. They clearly had other plans for us, and Roxy got us away. Now the police are looking for us."

"Argentum doesn't have a police department. We have one officer, Chief Max, but he's a good ten years older than me. And there's Milford, but he's not even full time. Was it those two old boys who took you into custody?"

I hugged myself, feeling suddenly colder. "The men I met were not old. These were young men, in dark uniforms."

Joe muttered a curse under his breath. "I've seen them before. Only once. I worried this might happen, when you showed up asking about your missing grandson. I tried to discourage you. I hoped you and your friend would leave. I guess you've probably figured out you're not the first who's come here looking for someone."

"It was you, wasn't it? Who left that warning note in my room."

He sighed. "Like I said, I tried to discourage you."

"Whoever came here looking before . . . did the police take them away too?"

He turned the wipers to a faster setting as the snow began to pile up on the windshield. "It was a while ago. I don't know what happened to them. They were a couple, I guess. Young. Glasses. Tried to act natural. Said they were new to town. Wanted to know if I knew other new arrivals, so they could join a 'newcomers' group. Once they warmed up to me, they started showing me pictures of some people they were looking for. Said they were some kind of researchers or something."

I swallowed. "You called the police?"

"No. I didn't recognize any of the people in their photographs, and they left. They made the rounds, like you did. Not four hours later, I saw them hauled out of Scotty's over there, by some cops I'd never seen before and two others wearing suits. I met up with some of the old boys at the bar later, and they said some officers just came in and seized them. The regulars at Scotty's thought they were out-of-town cops with some agents from the Colorado Bureau of Investigation, which explained the black suits."

If it were possible, I felt even colder. "What happened to them?"

He shook his head. "Don't know. Honestly, didn't think much about it until you came along. I got a bad feeling . . . you seemed so nice. Not like that couple, you could tell they were only a bunch of academics. They never even said why they were looking for those people, never said they were missing. But it started to add up a bit after you left that first time. I didn't want anything to happen to you."

"Are you afraid of these . . . officers . . . too?"

"I don't even know who they are. And even if I did, am I afraid enough to turn you over to them? The answer is no."

"Because Sarah up at the inn certainly is afraid. She called one of them to let them know my friend left town. I'm sure they're back at the inn now, looking for me."

"Good God, Sarah." He whistled. "Nice girl, but as nervous as a whore in church. Forgive the language. The medical center helped her find a good job, and I think she even dates some nurse at the hospital. She brought him into the store once. How the world would she even know those poser cops?"

"They didn't seem like posers to me. And I'm worried to death about my friend, who drove off to find help. And my grandson; I know he's here. Could it be that he's a patient at that the medical center you've mentioned, just like you were?"

Joe exhaled through his nose. "I saw a few kids when I was in the hospital. Not many, though. You said your grandson was put on the bus by a woman? Was she a lady who looked like she had at least twenty years on us? Miss Cliff her name?"

"Yes! That's what William called her. And before she called the police or security or whatever they are, she told me to leave now. Like she was afraid for me."

"Verna Cliff is not the friendliest of folks in town, and she's a closet alcoholic. But she's in charge of the small day care for the hospital kids. Even though she's got to be in her late eighties—shoot, maybe even nineties—she still lives on her own. She actually stays a few houses down from me."

"Joe," I began, "I already have risked my best friend's life. I cannot fathom the idea of getting someone else getting in trouble. I promise you, I will tell no one that you took me to her house. But I would be forever grateful if you would. She tried to warn me. I have to find out why."

His response was a downshift of the gears, and the truck glided into the snow, the plow slowly descending. "If it weren't this nasty outside, we'd be there in five minutes. I'll get us there in seven."

"I can't thank you enough."

"Given my ornery tendencies, I can only imagine I must have been quite the troublemaker in whatever young life I had before this one, so I really don't mind kicking up the dirt once in a while. Even though that couple was strange, I got a bad feeling when those cops arrested them. I don't like that it happened to you too, especially now knowing that you, and maybe those other two, came here to find somebody they loved. Maybe I'm just jealous, because no one ever came to find me."

"You don't remember anything? At all?"

"Blank as a clean chalkboard. Sometimes a word or a first name will sound somewhat familiar, but that's it."

"And your whole life it's been that way?"

"My whole life. I woke up in White Crest as a teenager, not knowing anything. That first year, they gave me the name Ethan. But it never felt right. Then one of the nurse's names was Joseph, and it just felt right to me, felt authentic—more so than Ethan. So I took that name, and forty some years later, I'm Joe the snowplow guy."

"I'm not sure how old you are, but I'm guessing you're about my age. You must have friends, family, somewhere."

"I assume I do, but where? No one ever came looking, and I have no memories before White Crest. The hospital said I was found by the side of the interstate, lying in a ditch. No injuries besides a knot on the back of my head. No car accident, nothing. Who can say? I don't match any missing-persons cases in Colorado or anywhere else that I could find. Seems like to me someone wanted to get rid of me, or I was involved in something bad and ended up dumped. Who knows? Good doctors up there at the medical center, though. They taught me everything to act like a human being again. It all came back quickly, and for that I'm grateful. I'm sure your boy's getting good treatment. How it is you knew he would be here?"

"It's a long story. Let's just say an old friend thought he might be in this town. But I'll be honest with you: I had no idea there was even a hospital here. And how can a hospital even exist in this remote of an area?"

"It's too small to be a true hospital. Amnesia is their specialty. Maybe I was a mean kid who got drunk and blacked out and conked my head. Again, who knows? I owe a lot to the good people up there. And I never had to pay a dime. I guess they assumed I didn't have health insurance, since I didn't even have a driver's license. Some of us need to even be retaught how to read, how to walk. I'm lucky, I guess; I picked up everything pretty quickly."

"That's where my grandson has to be. I have to find a way to get in. I should just bypass going to see the teacher. Could you just drive me to the medical center?"

"I'd take you right now, but you have to have a code to get in after hours, and the staff is mostly gone this time of night, especially in this weather. And they change the code from time to time; there's a lot of turnover. Miss Cliff has the current code, that's for sure. I've been gone from White Crest for a long time, and honestly, I'm in no hurry to go back. The loneliness, the confusion, the anger, you can't imagine what it's like to have no memory. And honestly—most of the patients don't leave. They can't. They can barely function. Can't comprehend light switches, microwaves, even straws. Sarah's the only one I've ever known in the past couple of years who could even hold a job."

"So it's not only memory problems the patients have?" I thought of how damaged William may be. *If I could relearn, so could he. . . .*

"Oh, it's memory problems, all right. They can't remember their past, and many of them can't remember what happened yesterday. It's like dementia, I think. It's awful."

"Why would my grandson be there? Be in this town?" I clenched my hands together. "How did he get here?"

"Can I ask what happened to him?"

"I don't know if you'd even believe me if I told you. The last time anyone saw my grandson—William is his name—was in the forest behind our house. He simply vanished. My husband . . . is a politician. We all feared he'd been kidnapped."

"Obviously, I never get to see the news. Now I wish I did. And where do you live again?"

"Tennessee. Nashville."

He whistled low. "William disappeared from Tennessee and now he's in the Rocky Mountains? My God . . ."

We drove in silence for a while through the growing snow-drifts. *You're wondering where you came from*, I thought as I glanced at Joe's puzzled face. Maybe somebody did want to find you.

Joe slowly applied the brakes. "Here we are."

He pulled up next to a row of houses covered in the falling snow. "That's Miss Cliff's house, with the light on. My house is only three down. I'll walk you up, introduce you."

"Joe, I'm so sorry, but I have another huge favor to ask you."

"Ask away."

"I'm very worried about my friend Roxy. I told you she drove off out of town to try and find a phone to call my husband. Would you mind looping back to see if she made it out OK? I wouldn't ask, but you seem quite capable of navigating the snow."

"I start the clearing on the main drag, so I have to go that way anyway," he said with a smirk. "But I have a feeling that you don't want me to be there when you talk to Verna."

"It will be easier to turn me away if I have an escort. She can't leave me outside in this."

"Well, she might. She's pretty tough. Even though those kids could blow on her and she'd fall over, I've seen her tear into them from time to time. Well, if she does kick you out, or she won't answer the door, go down three houses, mine is 333, the one with the dead plant out front. Keys underneath that. Snow's calming a bit, but it could pick up anytime. Don't you let her toss you out if the snow kicks back up; you could have died back there. Anyhow, I'll be back. I'll take the road all the way to the interstate to make sure your friend isn't in a ditch somewhere. If you're not at my house when I get back from my rounds, I'll snoop around and see if you made it into her house."

"God bless you, Joe," I said, opening the door.

"Three houses down, Miss Lynn!" he pointed.

I gave him a grateful wave and stepped down, realizing the snow was still fierce but not as blinding as before. Thankfully, there was a light on in the front room. Mustering up my most pathetic face, I reached out and rang the doorbell. When no one answered, I knocked on the glass. The hallway beyond remained dark.

I shivered, walking down the porch and crunching through the snow to approach a bay window. The curtains were parted, and I could see legs propped up in a recliner, a hand laying limp over the armrest.

I rapped on the glass. When the hand didn't even flinch, I pounded with my fist.

The teacher from the park sat up suddenly and looked around, disoriented. I knocked again, and the woman turned to the window, her wig slightly askew. She stared at me as I waved desperately. Miss Cliff's mouth gaped a little, and muttered a series of curse words that I could easily make out.

She pulled the wooden lever on the chair and slowly climbed out, glaring as she shuffled into the front hall. I hurried around to the porch once again and waited by the door. The light in the hall came on, and the curtains on the small window in the door parted.

"Are you insane?" she asked through the glass.

"Please, I need to speak with you."

"How in God's name did you end up here?" The woman's wizened eyes narrowed, blinking rapidly.

"Please, it's very cold."

"You need to get back in your car and drive away."

"I don't have a car. I have nowhere else to go." I forced a dramatic trembling of my lips.

"Jesus Christ."

I whispered a silent prayer of thanks as I heard the dead bolt turn.

"The only reason I'm even letting you in is because there's no earthly way anyone saw you come here. Get in here quickly. Jesus, you'd think the wife of a senator would know better than to come out in the middle of this mess."

I was so astonished, I stopped pulling back my hood midway. "You know who I am?"

"I didn't at first," she said groggily, the ice in her glass clinking as she moved across the runner lying across the wood floors in the front hall. As she entered the adjoining living room, she drew together the already small openings in the curtains.

She slowly turned around. "But you're her, aren't you. You're Roseworth's wife."

"You know who I am. You have to help me get to William. Please."

"I don't have to help you do anything, lady."

She went to a decanter on a side table and refilled her drink. Her hand shook a bit as she poured the bourbon to the rim. "And he goes by the name of Al . . . Alan . . . now."

My God, she's completely drunk. "I don't understand. If you know who I am, why did you put William on that bus?"

"I didn't know who were you were then," she said, moving

with the speed of a turtle over to a footstool covered in magazines. "And I tried to warn you. But when you were making
such a scene, you cooked your own goose. Had to call security.
Dammit!" Her foot caught the edge of the thick rug and she
teetered, careful not to spill a drop from her drink. I instinctively reached out, fearing one fall would mean the end of the
woman. But she righted herself, reached down, and messily
slid the magazines on the top to the floor. "There. That's how
I found out."

"The Senator's Nightmare," the cover of *People* magazine
shouted, featuring a picture of my husband and our family
from the news conference, with William's picture in a smaller
square beneath them.

"I always thought I had seen Alan—or William, as you call
him—before. When I came home today, I started going through
my magazines, and I do love *People*, even with their stupid
Kardashian covers—"

"Where is he?" I moved towards her. "Please take me to
him, Miss Cliff."

"It's Verna, calling me Miss Cliff doesn't make you any
younger, sweetheart," she said, easing herself into a maroon-
colored La-Z-Boy, taking another long drink. "He doesn't remember you. And he won't ever remember you."

"It doesn't matter. I have to get to him. I have to get him
home."

"You don't get it. He is home. The only home he knows.
He's just now starting to sleep through the night—"

"You know he's my grandson! Why didn't you tell
anyone?"

"I think you're aware we're in the middle of a blizzard and
our phones aren't working. Otherwise, you wouldn't be here.
And it's not like they're going to let him leave."

"Who's not going to let him leave?"

"The same people who sign your husband's paychecks. Listen, have a seat. Do you want a drink—?"

"I would love a drink," I lied. As she got out of her chair for the side table where several glasses surrounded a bourbon decanter, I sat on my hands to keep them from reaching out and shaking her. I thanked her when she handed me the glass, and pretended to sip. The smell was so intense I almost gagged.

"I know you want to help William, you've already done so much for him." I spoke slowly. "And he looked healthy at the park; I'm so thankful to you."

"I love all my kids."

"It's really obvious. You're a godsend to them. But please, Verna, please. I need for you to tell me where he is, how I can get to him—"

"Now you listen to me," she brandished her bent index finger as I'd seen her do to corral the children. "I'm taking a real chance even talking to you. Don't know how you got away from security, but since you're still here, it means you're on the run. And don't think for a moment they've contacted your husband. Plus, he doesn't mean shit out here. You don't understand the mistake you've made coming to Argentum. Your husband is nothing here. *You're* nothing here."

"It doesn't matter whom I'm married to. I could be married to a truck driver for that matter. All that really matters is he's my grandson—"

"All *they* care about is that Alan—I mean William—will never leave."

"Who? The people at the hospital?"

"Oh, for God's sake, Argentum doesn't really have a hospital, Mrs. Roseworth," she snapped, finishing off her bourbon and quickly filling up the glass again.

"Of course there's a hospital—"

"It's no town either," she waved her hand. She downed another glass, and refilled quickly.

At that moment, I was thankful I was sitting down. "It's an old silver-mining town—"

"That they made into a military base. Doesn't matter what I tell you, you'll never leave here. They won't let you. Even the townies, outside of myself, don't know this whole place is basically a military prison. And anyone who ends up at the section of the base that's used as a hospital never leaves."

As frustrated as I was dealing with a person who was just moments ago clearly passed out, and had drank three additional bourbons in the last five minutes, I was grateful for the liquor. She was talking, divulging more than she would have sober. At the park, Verna was rigid, protective. Obviously, anticipating being trapped inside her home for days meant there was no limit on how much she could drink.

"How do I get to him?"

"Honestly, I don't even know if he's still there." She polished off the glass, reaching again for the decanter.

"What do you mean?" I moved to the edge of the chair.

"They know you're here in the town somewhere. They'll want him out, shipped off to one of the other bases. You might be in luck, though. The storm might have kept him here. But I saw Alan—William—before I left for the night. His room was packed up. Poor thing."

"They would move him just to keep me from finding him?"

"Jesus, you are naïve. I can't blame you, I guess. I've been around for so long, I understand how things work. Hell, all I've ever known is this town. Thought it was a pretty great place growing up. Even if my old auntie wasn't the nicest of people, she still took good care of me. All I ever knew was

Auntie. Couldn't have been easy taking on some three-year-old who nobody wanted."

"Verna, please—"

"Auntie always said my mother must have been a real degenerate, dropping me off at the fire station like she did. Good thing Auntie had a thing for the fire chief and he liked her pancakes, 'cause she's the one who found me outside the fire hall door while delivering breakfast—"

"Your auntie showed the kind of kindness to you that you, in turn, showed to the kids here, and my William in particular. Your auntie took care of you. She would be so proud of you, of what you've done. All I want is to do the same for my grandson."

"It's always been my job to protect those kids, make them feel safe after what they've been through. I don't handle the adults, but those kids are *my* kids, and I take care of them."

"I can't thank you enough for taking care of him all this time," I said, knowing I was laying it on thick. "But Verna, I don't understand. What happened to William? How did he end up here? Why doesn't he remember me?"

"You wouldn't believe me if I told you." She threw back her head to shoot the rest of the drink.

This is more than a binge. This is how she copes. "I would believe you."

"I don't think so."

"Was he abducted?" I asked carefully, seeing the woman's eyebrows rise lazily. "By something that most people . . . don't even believe in?"

"But you do?" Verna asked quietly, refilling and taking another swig.

I swallowed. "I've seen a lot."

"Oh, you haven't seen anything. You haven't seen people

show up in a field, some wearing suits, some wearing jeans, some wearing hijabs. Kids, too. Your boy. All in a field behind White Crest."

"A field?" I asked, horrified at the thought of little William standing in the cold, lost and confused.

Verna was starting to drink slower now. "He's a sweet boy, that grandson of yours. All the kids love him, they just flock around him. Took to me real quick, too. Now I understand why. He has a maw maw who loves him. Never had kids of my own, so they're all my grandkids."

"Then you know how I feel. Of course you know."

"The docs always give the line—and I bought it for a long time—that the patients come here from all over the country to get help. And once they became functional, they'd return to their families. Except, they weren't coming from all over the country, it turns out, just from a field out back. And their families never came to get them; they just get driven away from the hospital. And I never see them again."

She sighed. "I never expected to do it my whole life. I felt so sorry for them, still do. But about ten years ago, I wanted to retire. At the beach. I was too old to drive in the snow anymore. That's when they told me I couldn't leave. *'No, Miss Cliff, we can't lose you. No, Miss Cliff, the kids need you.'* And they sat me down and showed me what was *really* happening. I didn't even have a choice. They even set up this new house for me so I could get to work easier. It became very clear I wasn't leaving. Hell, I'd been there longer than anybody else. Everyone else at that damn place leaves after a year or so, even the docs. They say they can't handle it, or they're too sick to work anymore. They won't even get close to the kids. But honestly, I couldn't leave my babies. Poor things don't even realize they don't have amnesia. None of them do. Or did."

"What's happened to them then?"

"Their memories are straight up gone when they come back. Blank as a slate, standing there in the field. But then, there are the special ones," she said, raising her wrinkled index finger. "Those are the ones who present a problem."

"Special ones?"

"They don't know why for sure. But unlike the adults, a few of the kids *remember*. I've heard the docs whisper—'cause they don't think I can hear—that it's a genetic thing that their memories are stronger than whatever those bastards in the cosmos do to them. And if those kids come back, well, the Suits have all kinds of good drugs to make those memories, and everything else, go away. Remember that drug that Michael Jackson OD'd on? They love that one, cleans out those memories real good. Can't risk those kids getting out and talking and causing a mass panic."

I was so horrified all I could do was watch her sip.

"All those families . . . they deserve to know what happened. What's been done to them," I finally said.

"They wouldn't want to know." Verna licked her lips. "They're vegetables, most of the grownups. Whatever they do to wipe out their memories, most adults can't handle. Only a few even learn to talk again. The kids, for some reason, are different. They can learn what they've forgotten. There are very few exceptions with the adults, like that young Sarah up at the inn, and, of course, Joe."

Verna scowled after a sizable slurp of her drink. "Is he the one who ratted me out? Is that how you got here? Caught the eye of that old fart, and he dumped you off?"

"I swear to you, I will tell no one that I was here."

"They'll kill me, you know," she said, her eyes bulging in her attempt to stay awake.

I leaned forward. "They wouldn't kill you."

"Why do you think they won't let me retire? They won't let me *leave*, Mrs. Roseworth. And they can't erase my memories because they need me to take care of the kids. You still don't get it? If word of this gets out—what will the world think? That those assholes in DC have known about the abductions for decades? Mass chaos, lady. It's why your boy won't leave. It's why *you* won't ever leave."

"You don't have to do anything more than what you've already done. I need to know how to get to the hospital."

"No need for much security. No one remembers anything, so they have nowhere to go. There's no way you'll get in. You do have to have a code to get in. And it changes every month."

"If I could just get that code . . . And just an idea of how to get to the hospital."

"Hell, you won't survive walking. It's below zero out there."

"Joe should be back soon. . . ."

"There may not be that much time." She looked out at the windows in the dining room. "The snow is letting up a bit. They're going to move him."

"Let me have your car. I beg you. I'll never find him again. You said you considered all them your kids. There's nothing more important than William getting home."

Verna took a long slurp. "What do you think will happen? Alan—I mean William—won't know his parents. He won't know you. You are jusht a shtranger to him. . . ."

Oh God, don't fall asleep. "Then I'll spend the rest of my life reminding him that he's ours, and we never stopped looking for him."

The teacher narrowed her eyes and then closed them, leaning back into the chair. "They'll find you," she said, her eyes closing. "And you'll be like the rest of them."

"May I take your car?"

"My car is under two feet of snow . . . you're shit out of luck. And you . . . you can't go my way . . . our way . . . you'll get lost . . ."

"What do you mean?"

"You'll never find him," she said, yawning. "I can't even remember the number of his room . . . they probably moved him to the second floor. You'll never find him. . . ."

"Tell me the code. How do you get to the hospital?"

"Hell, I don't remember the code." She wiped her mouth.

"How do you get in?" I wanted to shake her.

"First thing . . . I do . . . when I walk up . . . put it on the fridge. First thing . . . every time . . . I walk up."

"Walk up?"

"First . . . thing," she muttered.

I started to ask more, then held my breath. After a few moments, the woman's mouth opened a bit, and her chest began to rise and fall deeply.

I fought the urge to slap her. She was so far gone, even if I woke her, she'd be incoherent.

Make some coffee. Make her drink it.

I went to the hall, looking around frantically. The green lights from an ancient microwave revealed the kitchen to the right. I entered and turned on a light above the stove.

The light illuminated an olive-green fridge. On its door were a few magnets, including a small dry-erase board with a dangling marker attached. Scrawled hastily on the board were the numbers 16-0-19-8-25-30.

I found a pen in a junk drawer and wrote the numbers on the back of my hand. But what good would the numbers do if I couldn't even get to the hospital? I could wait for Joe to return, but that could be another hour. And if Verna was right, and they were preparing to move William when the storm broke, I had only a small window of time to find him.

Seeing no coffeemaker, I hurried out of the kitchen. Verna had said that when she came in tonight she had written down the code, which meant she had to have gotten here through the snow. I walked down to a back door, hoping that she had been lying, that there was a covered car park, or maybe even a garage. Instead, I could just make out a Buick with snow tires parked around back, its fading blue paint barely visible under the mounds of snow.

Did they shuttle the workers back and forth? Was there some kind of hospital bus service that operated even in this weather? And if there was, what was I going to do? Put on one of Verna's wigs, throw on her coat, and call for a pick up?

I went back into the living room where she now snored softly. I hated to do it, but I found a purse on the closed lid of a piano. A row of pictures sat on top of the piano, watching as I violated a woman's most private of belongings.

Her wallet was mostly empty except for some cash and an ID that read "Verna Cliff. White Crest: child care." Nothing was written on the back.

I scavenged through the rest of the purse and found only an empty miniature bottle of Bacardi at the bottom. I sighed, glancing at the photos witnessing my transgression.

It took me several moments to start breathing again.

In the center of the photos was one badly aged with time, yellowed on the edges, featuring a heavyset woman wearing an apron, with a small child on her lap. The woman appeared stern, clearly the auntie Verna had described. The girl on her lap had dark hair and a gap-toothed smile.

I had seen the girl before. Only a few days ago, sitting in the Nashville library, in an old photograph next to a newspaper article from August 5, 1934, about a girl who went missing from the woods behind my house.

That girl sat on Auntie's lap.

In the photos, Amelia Shrank turned eight, then ten, and finally became a teenager. But it was the photo of the Amelia as a young woman, probably in her midtwenties, smiling, leaning on a post, that bore a strong resemblance to Verna Cliff.

I covered my mouth with my hand while looking at Verna's slumbering body.

You don't know who you really are. That you once had a family so devastated by your disappearance that they made a grave for you in the woods where you vanished. That you, and me, and a hunter, and my grandson, and God knows how many others all vanished from the same clearing in those trees.

I doubt very much that you showed up on a firehouse stoop. I bet the military gave you to your auntie because they weren't equipped to deal with you. You weren't a baby—you were a three-year-old girl without a memory. I bet your auntie was the first in this town to start caring for a child who remembered nothing. And then so many kids and people started showing up, they had to build that hospital. . . .

I rushed back into the kitchen, scanning the refrigerator for phone numbers; anything to show how Verna got to the hospital in this weather. I searched the entire kitchen again. Nothing.

I started going through a utility drawer in desperation when I saw the boots by the pantry door. They'd clearly been tossed there and abandoned for the thick, plaid house shoes on Verna's feet. But there was no puddle, not even a drip of moisture on them.

I looked at the pantry door and saw it had a dead bolt.

I walked over, turned the bolt, and opened the door. Steps led down into the dark, barely illuminated by orange bulbs placed above a railing. The metal stairs went down far too deep to lead to just a basement.

The lights steadily increased in brightness. I could now make out the metal circular sconces holding the bulbs in place, and how, in a very clear, precise stamp, each was marked with the words, "Property of the U.S. Government."

NINETEEN

The tunnel at the bottom of the stairs extended in two directions, with metal casing on the floor, ceiling, and walls. My fears were no longer fluid, no longer intangible; they were rooted in this man-made tunnel buried underneath a town whose silver mine shafts had been remade into bunker-style passageways.

Roxy was probably far along on the interstate now, closing in on a gas station with a working phone. Whatever communication disruption occurred in the town when this kind of storm hit, it couldn't happen all throughout the mountains. Once Roxy reached Tom, nothing would stop him from getting here.

If Verna was right, my grandson would be gone when they arrived.

I had to find William, convince him to come with me, and find our way back to Verna's home. Even if she refused us, I would have to beg her to let us through so we could hide in Joe's house until the storm was over.

The tunnel stretched before me, with no indication which way would lead to the hospital. I was terrible with directions anyway, and I had no idea in which area of town the hospital stood. All Joe had said was that it was on the outskirts.

Stepping around the stair lift that was obviously put in place to allow Verna easy passage up and down the long staircase, I moved into the tunnel, looking for any markings, any pattern of the lights that would indicate which direction to take. There appeared to be nothing—no arrows, no signs— nothing. And how did Verna get to the hospital? At the pace she moved, it would take her a day just to walk a mile. It didn't make sense.

Just like in the snowstorm. One foot in front of the other.

I chose left and started walking. *What if I encounter another security guard? What would I possibly say to explain myself? Did the houses of other hospital workers lead into this tunnel?* I could feel heat, but I was still so chilled I kept my hood up and my hands in my gloves.

I passed another stairwell identical to Verna's. At least hers had the stair lift, so it was clear which one I would need to take when I returned with William. If I returned with William—

The dead end came up so suddenly, I actually held up my hand to stop myself from walking right into the wall. Angrily, I hurried back down the opposite direction. How much time had I wasted?

Fifteen minutes later, another tunnel opened up to my right, snaking into a long darkness, again lit only by orange lights. *How many tunnels were down here? Had the military used the same shafts of the miners? Or did they do all this as the town slowly declined into near abandonment, the locals unaware of what was being dug beneath them? There had to be questions as to why the workers at the hospital never left their homes but somehow got to work every day—*

Stop it. Stop trying to make sense. Just find William.

I had no choice but trial and error. I could only guess the new tunnel headed towards town and the hospital was farther out. But how far? Yards? Miles? It couldn't be; someone of Verna's age couldn't walk that distance every day.

I kept walking down the tunnel and noticed in the near distance how it began to expand quite dramatically, its walls receding into the darkness beyond the reach of the meager lights. The sound of my footsteps disappeared into the space without an echo. As the far end of the tunnel came into view, another metal staircase emerged, not off to the right or left, as had the others, but in the center. The answer as to how Verna arrived here each day was a golf cart parked to the side, right by another stair-lift chair. Verna didn't walk to work. Someone came to get her.

As I approached, I could see, at the top of the stairs, a door leading to an upper level, somewhere above ground. I hurried towards it, looking up at the now familiar orange lights above.

When I reached the first step, the sides of the hallway suddenly flared with fluorescent lights. I stumbled in surprise, seeing now how the orange lights at the top of the stairs were also glowing brightly. I'd triggered a sensor of some kind.

A passing glance at the white lights coming from the walls of the hall revealed the man staring at me.

The greenish pall of the fluorescents weren't coming from sconces on the walls, but from rooms with glass doors. I was so intent on reaching the stairs that I hadn't even noticed the dozens of doors stretching down the corridor, or the face of the man looking out.

He was lying down, his head resting on some kind of bed. I waited for him to react to me or speak. Instead, he blinked, yet his blank expression remained the same.

I left the stairs and hesitantly stepped closer. Approaching the door, I could see his eyes were unnaturally glassy, and that he wasn't alone. Dozens of rows—no, maybe hundreds of rows—of people on beds, all connected to tubing and machines, all dressed in white. All their eyes were open, faces either staring at the ceiling or turned to the side.

I stepped back to the middle of the tunnel, eyeing the doors, each with the same light. Did all of those doors lead to rooms full of comatose people?

I walked across the hall to a nearly identical sight, but this time, it was a young woman on the closest bed; beyond her were more rows of people. As she stared at the ceiling, I watched her chest rise and fall. An older man next to her appeared to be breathing as well. All had tubes going into their nostrils or mouths.

They're vegetables, Verna had slurred. They don't remember anything, Joe had said, not even how to tie their shoes.

William isn't like them. There's still time.

I propelled myself up the stairs, trying to ignore the pain in my knees. My heart was racing when I reached the top. This door had no window, no indicator of what lay beyond.

There was, however, a keypad.

I held up my hand to the orange light. My stomach sank as I saw how my hands had sweated in the gloves. The numbers were smudged a bit. I punched in 16-0-18-8-25-30.

The keypad flashed red.

I looked closer at my hand. Was that an 18 or 19? I tried it again. 16-0-19-8-25-30. No red flash, nothing. I looked closer at my hand, trying to recall the exact numeration—

The door unlocked and swung open an inch.

I pushed through it, momentarily relishing the familiar bright light of a hallway. Gone were the orange glow and the ghostly fluorescents, replaced with a stark white light illuminating well-traveled tile and undecorated walls.

I eased down the hall, looking all around for any signs of

life. Verna had said something about William being moved to the second floor. But he could be anywhere, and I had no idea how large the hospital was or even where I was in it.

If William had been taken from his usual room here, were the other children from the park still here? If I did find another child, could I, in good conscience, ask for help finding William and leave that child behind?

I came to a door with a black sign reading "Stairwell." I entered, cringing at the echo of my footsteps.

On the second floor, I peered out, seeing another empty hallway. I had no idea what time it was, but the storm must have emptied the place. The rooms here had no plates, only numbered plastic containers holding files and papers.

The windows in these doors were mostly dark, but as I walked, I saw one man sitting at a desk, his head resting on top of his arm. I stopped, wondering if I should knock. When he failed to move at all, I kept walking. Another window in another door revealed a woman standing directly in front of a wall, staring. I could feel the desolation without having to enter.

I started counting: twenty, forty, eighty rooms. I grew sadder with each step, as there were only first names on the folders; names likely assigned to them, like animals at the pound. I thought of Joe who, even without a memory, knew the name they'd first given him rang hollow.

William believes his name is Alan. Does that name sound wrong to him too?

I looked through each window, finding most rooms to be pitch black. If there was anyone inside, they were asleep. I kept moving. Room after room down the hall, no sign of anyone else awake. I prayed to Mother Mary, for soon I would have to start venturing into the darkness of each room, blindly looking for my grandson.

A faint light came from room 212. The lamp was bright enough, however, to show the red in the sheen of a boy's hair, sitting at the edge of the bed, wearing navy-blue pajamas, his knees pulled up tight.

I whispered a thanks to Mary, forcing my hands to stop shaking and reaching deep in my coat pocket, finding the one thing I couldn't bear to throw at the security officer who tried to kill us a few hours ago.

William turned when I opened the door and flinched when he saw me emerge. "Don't be afraid, William." I smiled, forcing back tears of relief. "Miss Cliff told me you'd be here."

William didn't move, looking so much like his mother that I found it difficult to speak. As I took a step closer, he slid a bit farther away on the bed.

"Honey, you don't have anything to be afraid of—"

"My name is Alan. Miss Cliff told me not to pay any attention to you. She said you were crazy."

"That's before she knew who I was. Now she knows, and she told me where you would be. That's how I found you. I'd like to show you who I am. Is that OK?"

He eyed me warily. I briefly glanced around the room, finding it completely empty. Two small bags were packed by end of his bed.

I took out the thin plastic photograph holder from my now-lost wallet and removed a single picture. "This is me and my husband, Tom. We live in a place called Nashville, Tennessee."

William looked at it briefly, and I put it away, bringing out another. "This is an old picture of my daughters. That's my youngest, Stella, there's Kate, and my oldest, Anne. Want to see my whole family?"

The boy shrugged, and I took out another picture. "Look at how many of us there are! Do you see all the boys?"

With that, William leaned in closer. "I only have grand-sons. They are bigger now, including the baby. Do you want to see what the baby looks like, the one sitting in his Aunt Stella's arms?"

I swallowed and took out a final photograph. "This was taken last summer on the Fourth of July. That's Anne's family—that's her husband, Chris, and her sons Greg, Brian, and William."

William stared for a moment and then slowly reached out. I gave him the photo, letting him look closely. "That's you, my sweet boy. I know they call you Alan here. But your real name is William. William Grant Chance. You are seven and will turn eight this summer. And we've been looking for you for a long time."

"But I don't know you," he said, still looking at the picture.

"I know you don't, and that's OK," I eased onto the bed. "Maybe you will remember us one day. Your mom, your dad, your brothers, your aunts, and especially your grandpa, they all want you to come home. I'd like to take you there."

"I'm not supposed to leave my room. Plus, they told me I'm moving. They said I was leaving first thing in the morning. They said I'll like it where I'm going. They said it's warm."

"Well, where I live is really warm. We have a new minor-league baseball stadium, and even have two different water parks because it gets so hot in the summer."

"Two water parks?" William's eyes lit up, but then nar-rowed. "Miss Cliff said not to go anywhere."

"Maybe we can go see her right now, and while we're walk-ing to her, I'll tell you more about your family."

His eyes softened. "You really are my grandma?"

I couldn't stop the tears from glistening in my eyes. "I am. And I have missed you every day."

"Can I keep the picture?"

"Of course. You can have all of them if you want."

"I just want this one. My shoes are by my suitcase and my coat is in the closet. Are we going outside?"

"I hope not. It's so cold!" I forced a smile, trying to appear casual. I opened the closet door and found the jacket. I knelt on the floor and opened the suitcase, finding a heavy sweater on top.

"I want to wear my jeans," he said, still staring at the photo.

I grabbed a collared shirt, jeans, a pair of socks, and a long-sleeved T-shirt.

"Do you have gloves?"

"On the hook by the door," he said, throwing off his pajama top and putting on his shirt. "Will I get to say goodbye to Miss Cliff?"

"I hope so. I know she'd like to see you before you go."

"Is Tennessee close to the mountains? I'll miss my friends. Especially Todd, he's funny. He wears red-high tops. I didn't want to move, but they said it was for my own good."

"I promise you, I will do everything I can for you to see any of your friends here again. But right now, I want to get you home."

"What if they don't want me, once they find out I don't re-member them?" he asked, slipping on his boots.

I wanted so badly to rush over and pull him into my arms. "Hon, we've all been waiting to see you for so long, it doesn't matter what you do or don't remember."

"Then why am I here? How did I get here? All everybody says here is that we don't have memories and they don't know where we came from. But somebody has to know. Why did it take you so long to find me?"

I reached out and touched his arm. "I didn't know where you were. Nobody did. And your parents would be here too, but I just figured it out first."

"Figured out what?" he asked, his sweater now over his head.

"Let's talk about all that when we get out of here. Can we go now?"

William clearly picked up on my nervousness. "I'm not supposed to leave my room, you know."

"Well, Miss Cliff told me where you would be. She knew I had to get to you. Should we go see her?" I asked, hating the lie.

"Sure," he shrugged.

"Let's go quietly." I put my hand on his back and carefully opened the door.

I led him out and we began to walk down the hall. With each door we passed, I fought the urge to grab him and run. He was coming willingly; I couldn't do anything to spook him. I didn't even dare hold his hand, although I wanted to desperately. I could see the sign for the staircase. We could be down to the first floor and out the door to the tunnel in a few minutes' time. *Roxy must have made the call by now, and Tom knows that William is here.* I did put my hand on his back, hoping the gesture would move his little legs faster. All we had to do was make it down—

"Mrs. Roseworth."

I closed my eyes. William quickly turned around, but I didn't need to. I recognized the voice.

TWENTY

The woman who I thought was my husband's press secretary, who once sat in my own kitchen giving us political advice, who then showed up in the FBI's raid of Steven's hotel room, was now wearing a black suit.

Deanna Ruck had her hair pulled back in a ponytail, just as she had when she drove me from the Murfreesboro motel back to Nashville. Walking up briskly behind her were two men dressed in white scrubs.

"Please let us go," I whispered, placing my hands on William's shoulders.

"I wish I could, Mrs. Roseworth," she said. "Hi Alan. We haven't met. But you know Josh and Rick. Josh is going to take you back to your room."

"But this lady says she's my grandma." He looked up at me. "She showed me pictures of my family. She says my name is William."

"I understand it's confusing," Deanna said with a sympathetic smile. "Tell you what: I need to talk to Mrs. Roseworth first, and then when we're done, we'll try to come to see you. OK?"

"Just let us go." I pulled William close. "I swear to you, I won't say anything."

"Mrs. Roseworth, you're only making this more difficult."

"She said my name is William," he grumbled with a sullen tone, pressing up against me.

It was that movement that made me grab William's hand and run for the door. As I seized the door handle, a strong grip clamped down on my arm. I tried to pull away, but the man held tight, closing the door with his other hand. The other tore William from my grasp.

"William!" I cried out, trying to yank my arm free, knowing the strength of the man would leave bruises.

"I'll come for you!" I struck out, trying to peel away from his grip. "Let me go!"

As I struggled, I saw William lift his hand towards me, his eyes wide with confusion, as he was carried back into his room.

"Right in there." Deanna motioned to a door across the hall. With a good one hundred pounds on me, the man led me with ease, despite my attempts to wrestle away. He opened the door and sat me down in a swivel chair resting by a row of file cabinets. Shelves lined the walls, filled with thick plastic binders.

"Give us a few minutes," she said, following us in. The man at last let go, giving me a stern look as he walked out.

"How can you be doing this?" I exploded, rubbing my wrist. "You know William's alive! You know he's my grandson! I thought you were an FBI agent! You're supposed to be protecting people like us—"

"That's exactly what I am doing, ma'am. There's only one person responsible for this situation, and it's you. I told you back in Tennessee to let this go. I told you what could happen. When we'd learned you and your friend suddenly decided to

skip town in the midst of your family's worst tragedy, I knew you'd disregarded my counsel.

"I suppose I should be grateful to that teenager in the airport terminal who tweeted out that he saw you. We've been monitoring all social media for you. He took one photo of you walking away, but failed to earn even a single retweet from his seven followers, or everyone would know you're here. That tweet, by the way, no longer exists anywhere, in case you thought someone in your family might find it. We had to fly a helicopter through that storm to get to you. Do you know how dangerous that was? Just to come and find you? I don't know how much Dr. Richards told you about Argentum, but you really made a mistake coming here."

"Made a mistake? What kind of person are you? You have seen yourself what this has done to my family. And you're telling me it was a mistake to come find him?"

"It was a mistake because what your family will now have to go through."

"And what does that mean?"

She pulled up another swivel chair and sat down, leaning forward. "Because you can't go home now, Mrs. Roseworth. I wish you could, believe me. I don't want to see your family suffer any more. I don't know ultimately what my superiors will decide, but I do know with certainty that some sort of story will have to be arranged—"

"I promise you, I will say nothing about what I've seen."

Her lips pursed in a frown. "Really? You'll just show up with your grandson and not explain where you found him? And you just won't ever explain why he doesn't have a memory? This is why we go to extraordinary lengths, such as keeping this facility secluded in this godforsaken corner of the world and

blocking it from Google maps and internet searches; to avoid exactly the kind of situation we are in now."

Deanna reached down and pulled out a laptop from the satchel she'd been carrying. She tapped on the rectangle below the keyboard and turned the screen to face me. She touched the play button and frantic green pulses raced across the screen.

"Please listen."

She turned up the volume, and at first all I could hear was rustling. Then, my own voice. "You know nothing about my life."

"Listen," came Steven's voice. "I think I know where William is."

"You think he's still alive?" I heard myself respond. Then, a pause. "Steven, please. You owe it to my father to tell me. Tell me what you know—"

Deanna hit the pause button. "You know this is coming from that hotel in Tennessee. Obviously, we had the room bugged. You need to know that this audio—along with photographs of Steven Richards being forced out of the hotel room by FBI agents, and you and I leaving afterwards—is compiled in a file that can be sent, with the click of a button, to FOX News and *The Washington Post*. Can you imagine what they'd do with this after what's already been released about you in that basement with Richards's supporters? What it would do to your family? Because this is where we're at now, Mrs. Roseworth. You either agree to go quietly into obscurity, or we release this. It will show you in a hotel room with your former lover. Agreeing to do anything he asks. Is this the last memory you want your family to have of you? For your husband to have of you?"

I heard it then, a slight tapping, coming from the corners of the room. As I glanced over, Deanna snapped her fingers. "Stay with me, Mrs. Roseworth. I need to know you understand. If you will agree to vanish—with our assistance—the recording never goes anywhere. It's also imperative that you tell me how it is you found this town. We didn't hear the two of you discuss Argentum in the hotel room. How did Steven Richards tell you about it?"

The tapping sounds grew louder now. They came from the corner of the room, directly behind where Deanna sat. Over her shoulder, I could see a tall pneumatic tube stretching from floor to ceiling. Something tiny was inside, popping.

"They have a right to know," I said softly, looking at the glass tube, then back to her. "Families all over the world spend their whole lives dying a little more every day wondering what happened to their loved ones, and you've had them all the time. And if anyone tries to find them and tracks them here or to any of the other bases, you have no qualms about murdering them, too."

"It's not that simple, Mrs. Roseworth. Surely you must realize that. We're in the containment business, not the killing business. Back to my earlier question. We need to know how you got here. The more open you are with us, the more we can be lenient in letting you see your grandson before . . ."

"Before what? The man ordered to kill us obviously failed. My husband will soon know where I am—"

"I hate to be the one to tell you this, but your friend didn't make it. And it's no one's fault but your own."

I paused. "I don't believe you."

"A tragic accident, from what I'm told. She drove off the road, crashed the van. She wouldn't have been driving in this horrible weather if you hadn't directed her to leave—"

"You're lying."

She sighed, took out her phone, punched with her finger

and then held it out for me to see. "One of our officers came upon her wrecked vehicle."

I leaned in and could see the van sunk in a snowbank. Even on the small screen, it was easy to see that the shattered back window was riddled with bullet holes.

"My God," I whispered.

"No one wants any more tragic accidents involving anyone else you love."

"You wouldn't hurt William—"

"You need to start explaining how it is you came to find Argentum," she said, having to raise her voice over the now-frantic popping sound. She turned around to the tube as the entire building shook for a moment.

In response, the long canister began to fill up, as if some sort of film was suddenly coating the glass from the inside. The building rattled again, and Deanna had to steady herself against the wall. When the shaking stopped, she began to type briskly on the computer.

"What's happening?" I asked.

"Nothing you need to concern yourself with."

The door opened and a man in camouflage stuck his head in, a long-range rifle over his shoulder.

"Ms. Ruck, you need to come. Right now."

"I'm debriefing—"

The building shuddered. The wheels under my chair began to roll.

"Right now," the soldier insisted.

Deanna held on to the wall. "You might have noticed, Captain, that I am not in your military, and I don't take orders from you. And the tremors aren't unusual. Gather them up—"

"Ma'am, there are *two* ships. And they're sending them down."

"They always come down."

"No. Not people. *They're* coming down."

Deanna stood up. She stole one more glance at the tube and grabbed the door. "You'll have to stay here, Mrs. Roseworth. I should be right back. Use this time to think about what we've talked about. You know what you need to do."

As she hurried out, a series of beeps came from outside and another tremor rippled through the building. I went to the door. The handle refused to even move.

I covered my mouth with my fingertips.

Roxy.

My oldest friend, my constant companion for so many years, dead because she wouldn't let me come here alone. My girls, my grandsons, Tom, all lost. The military would take Roxy's truck and my Volvo from the Nashville airport, crash hers off some rural road in Paducah, and have mine crushed. If they had gone so far as to frame Steven for the death of William, they could certainly go to extraordinary lengths to hide the truth about what happened to us—

No. I will not. I began to pace, keeping my hand on the wall. *I will not let it all be in vain.*

The glass tube was now emitting a low humming sound. I approached it and knew why the sound was so familiar. My throat tightened in realization.

It wasn't humming. It was vibrating.

Inside, thousands of ladybugs swarmed, frantically smashing against the glass and climbing on top of each other. The bottom of the tube was difficult to see, making it unclear where the bugs originated.

There was no doubt why the medical center kept a tube like this in the room.

The soldier said *they* were coming down.

The room shuddered violently and the lights dimmed as pads of paper and clipboards slid off the shelves and slapped onto the floor. I instinctively reached out to balance the tube, but found it firmly set into the concrete. William's room had been empty, right? I didn't remember seeing breakable things up high, heavy things, that could have fallen on him. Was he still in the room? What if they had already taken him some-where else—?

The lights went out. I held tight to a table as darkness swallowed the room. I eased alongside the table, brushing up against a chair. I looked for the door, but the window in the door was nowhere to be seen, as the lights out in the hallway were also extinguished. I fumbled to where I thought the door was and slid up against the wall.

In the pitch blackness of the room, I saw it: the blinking light of the battery of Deanna's laptop where it had fallen to the floor. Maybe there was wifi, maybe there was a way I could send an email or something to the outside world.

I felt through the darkness. But once I opened the laptop's brilliant screen, my hopes were dashed. The internet signal was gray, with no bars.

I could still use it as a light source, try to find something to break through the door. But even if I happened upon a circular saw or a sledge hammer, I realized, I still couldn't get through the electronically locked door.

The screen glared at me. The laptop belonged to a woman who had to be one of the top officials amongst the black suits. Maybe she had the pass codes to the doors in one of the folders.

Each file appeared administrative: budget, addresses, PowerPoint presentations, research models. I continued to read the headers: overlays, contact points, spreadsheets, survivors' interviews, satellite coordinates—

I stopped scrolling down to instead use the track pad to move the arrow over to the second to the last folder in the row.

Survivors' interviews.

I clicked on it to find several internal folders. Each was marked with a code: JFAZ206, HTNY85, RJIL72, EKOK11 . . .

Get back to the main screen, keeping looking for anything that could contain pass codes.

I could barely navigate Microsoft Word on my computer, how could I possibly understand what these folders meant?

CJCA82, TRPA72, TDIL73, KVIL73, LSTN51—

Those letters and numbers . . . LSTN51 . . .

I held my breath. LSTN51. LS, my initials with my maiden name. TN for Tennessee. 51. The year I was born.

I opened up the folder. Three QuickTime movies were inside, each with their own label: subject camera, interviewer camera, and combined cameras.

The room rumbled slightly. I clicked on the first movie. After the color wheel spun for a few seconds, a screen opened up. *When the video clip proves to be nothing, I'll go back to searching the rest of the computer.*

As the video began to play, my hand raised to my chest.

A little girl sat in a chair in front of a table. Despite the grainy footage that was obviously taken from a filmstrip, it was easy to tell she was exhausted. Even though it was in black-and-white, even though the clip had several jumps from when the old film flickered, even though the camera was several feet away, I knew her.

It was me, at five years old.

"Yes," I heard myself say softly.

At the sound of the voice of an adult, I watched the much younger version of myself squirm at bit, looking around for the words. "I saw the people. The people I told you about. They change colors."

I know this. My God, I know this.

I stopped the clip and moved the arrow directly to the "interviewer" video clip. Only after the video played for a few moments did I finally begin to breathe.

I had first seen the man in the video on Doug's computer in the basement of Steven's home. I remembered Doug had clamped the laptop shut, saying he would show me the rest of the video if I promised to go public. The first known interview of an abductee, he had said.

After I'd left, he'd followed us to the street, standing outside my window. *"You'll never know. You'll never know the truth—"*

I didn't need to go to the end of the clip to see what it would reveal. But I did anyway, fast-forwarding to the end, as the man took off his glasses and rubbed his forehead.

The camera panned for a moment from the man to where my five-year-old self sat at the other end of the table.

Though the camera was on me, I heard the man whisper, his mic still picking up his words. "I'm not getting anything here. Get the Propofol ready." The film stopped rolling.

My breath caught in my throat. Every card-carrying member of AARP knew that Propofol is used before major surgeries, but can also cause memory loss. My God—

I doubled clicked on the video labeled "combined cameras." It began as the second video had—with the man in the horn-rimmed glasses and the fierce part in his hair.

"Are you comfortable?" the man asked.

The video then cut to show five-year-old me sitting at the table, looking out the window beside me. "Yes," I said, squinting in the sunlight streaming through. When the camera adjusted to the lens flare from the sun, I could see endless waves of water stretching out from a long beach.

The edited video featuring both cameras continued with the man leaning forward. "Can you tell me about what you saw?"

"I saw the people. The people I told you about. The people in the sky change colors," I heard myself reply.

"What do you remember about the ship in the sky?"

My little eyes looked back to him. It looked like I started trembling. "Mama and Daddy took me to St. Louis once, it was bigger than that. It changes colors too. Especially when they caused it to rain."

"Rain?"

I watched myself nod. "When we came back down . . . everything was clear . . . then it got stormy. All around us. Bad clouds. Big winds. They did it. They brought the storm . . . when they came down."

The man furiously scribbled and then tapped his forehead with his pencil.

"I know you've been through a lot. I need you to explain this to me. You told me before that you never actually talked to the . . . people in the sky. That you . . . understood them—like you spoke with your thoughts."

"We shared."

"You shared?"

I nodded. "Some of mine, some of theirs."

"This is very, very important, Lynn. Is this how they communicated with you? Was it like a conversation?"

"Back and forth. Back and forth. I showed them the cornfield by my house, they showed me how they fly over cornfields. But then . . . it was not nice. They . . . wanted more. Like when they wanted to see if I get sick. I showed them when I got chicken pox that one time and Mama made me take a bath in all that white stuff. And then . . . I saw how they want to make other people get sick, and eat food that's bad, and get hurt. In all kinds of ways."

"How are they going to hurt people?"

I watched as my younger self reached up behind my head and winced. "There's something . . . in me. And in the other people they bring back. They want to see . . . if everyone around us . . . gets hurt by what this does. I don't want it in my head—"

"Get hurt by what?"

"What's in here," I saw myself motion to the base of my skull. "Can I see my mama and daddy now?"

"That's all for now. Thank you, Lynn. I know it's been difficult. You're a strong, special girl—"

I stopped the video with a sharp tap.

Special ones, Verna had said. *They don't know why for sure. But unlike the adults, a few of the kids actually remember. I've heard the docs whisper—'cause they don't think I can hear—that it's a genetic thing that their memories are stronger than whatever those bastards in the cosmos do to them. And if those kids come back, well, the Suits have all kinds of good drugs to make those memories, and everything else, go away—*

No, no, no, I thought, exiting out of the folder and frantically scanning the others. *A genetic thing . . .*

The government gave me drugs—certainly the Propofol—and took everything I knew about my parents away.

WCTN11, WCTN11, WCTN11–

Oh, no.

The very last folder was WCTN11.

WC, William Chance. TN, Tennessee. 11. He was born in 2011. I clicked on it. Again, three movies. I frantically opened the third.

The video was incredibly clear, obviously recorded in high definition, and this time it was a younger man sitting in a stark white room. He adjusted his black tie and smiled with the warmth of an ice rink.

"Hello, William. Are you OK?"

My grandson sat in a chair, his short legs dangling. "I want to see my mommy and daddy."

I blinked back angry tears. *He remembered us.*

"You will, son, but I need to ask you a few questions—"

"Want to see my mommy and daddy and my nanna."

"Sure you do. But I need to talk to you first. About what you saw. And what you drew for us."

"I already told the other man. They're mad. I wanna go home."

"They're mad?"

"Really mad. I wanna go home. Don't let them take me back up there."

"You're safe now, William. You told my colleague Dr. Cody that the people in the stars who took you—"

"They aren't people. Please, can I call my mommy?"

"Why are they mad, William?"

"I already showed you."

The man opened the folder in front of him and drew out a few pieces of paper. He looked directly into the camera and indicated to the photographer to zoom in. The lens focused, and the picture came into closer view.

"William, can you confirm that you drew these?" He slid the pictures over to William.

"Uh-huh."

"Tell me what you've drawn. We know how they share memories, so you don't have to explain that. All we need to know is what you saw from them."

I heard William sigh. I leaned in closer to the screen,

seeing on the top sheet several stick figures inside a building. "Those . . . are the people they sent back. But . . . you trapped them here."

The man pointed to another group of stick figures walking on a hill. "Then who are these other people?"

"That's what all the people they brought back are supposed to be doing. Moving around. Not stuck here and in the other places you keep them."

"You mean everyone . . . with the bump like yours?"

William nodded. "Will it go away? It hurts."

"In time, it goes away. Back to the people who are supposed to be walking around, why do you have those lines around their heads?"

As the camera zoomed in closer, I saw what appeared to be waves coming from the heads of the figures. "That's what some of us are supposed to be doing."

"Some of you? But not all of you? Why?"

"Because . . . they haven't flipped the switch on everybody yet."

"What does that mean?"

William waited a moment and then took the man's pen from where it lay and added waves around all the heads. "They're almost ready for everyone to start together. But they had to be spread out. So they went to see where everybody was, and found out . . . that you stopped them."

"Stopped them from what?"

William reached over and touched the bottom of the picture, where a few stick figures lay on the ground, their eyes marked with Xs instead of dots.

"William, listen to me. I know this is hard to understand. Do the people in the stars know why we're containing the people they've returned—in hospitals?"

"Do I get to leave the hospital? I wanna go home."

"Of course."

"The monsters showed me how you trapped the people here and in all the other places like this. But the people they send back are not supposed to be trapped—they're supposed to go everywhere and cause trouble, with what the monsters put in here," William said, gently touching the back of his head and then reaching out for the rest of his drawings.

The camera moved in, showing more of William's stick figures. People emitting the waves were standing under dark clouds from which tornadoes were descending.

"Some of them make bad storms."

He turned the page. More stick figures, but this time standing with crudely drawn cows cut in half among what I thought at first was weeds, but then realized were plants with yellowed seeds in the ground.

"Some of them make our food so it's bad for us to eat."

The next picture was especially disturbing to know my grandson had drawn. One stick figure stood on a hill while people below were shooting at each other. A red crayon had been used to draw the blood.

"Some of them . . . just make other people so mad they fight and hurt each other. And then the rest . . . make people get sick. Just to see how well it all works. And when the tests are done, they'll flip the switch, and they'll all do it at the same time."

"But we've seen time and time again it doesn't happen to everyone," the man said, clearly thinking out loud in exasperation. "Why? Why only trigger some people and not all? What's the tactic?"

William waved his little hand across the picture. "Some get turned on now. Some get turned on at the end, when everyone is in place. They're supposed to be all over the world; that was their plan. The ones that get triggered now . . . the monsters wanted to see what each one of them could do on their own, how far . . . uh . . . their . . ."

"Range?"

"Range would reach." William snapped his fingers. "That's the plan. The monsters pick us up, put the bump in our heads, drop us back off, and then go back to the stars for a while. But this time, when they returned to see where everyone was, they found out you messed up their tests. They're so mad."

He then pulled out the last picture. Another stick figure, this time of a man shaking, his mouth shaped like an *O* and his eyes forced shut. Arrows rained down in a single line from the stars to the man's head, all while he held his hands over his ears in obvious pain. Once again, a red crayon indicated blood, this time seeping between the man's fingers.

"I don't want them to flip my switch. They showed me how it hurts your head, how your ears bleed. How the sound is so loud in your head, you can't hear anything else. Have you seen it happen to the people here?"

"We have, to some of them. We try to keep them away from everyone when it starts. We want to find a way to stop it, or maybe even prevent it."

"That will only make them madder if you do that."

The man rubbed his face. "You keep saying that. How do you know they're so mad?"

William finally looked up. "Because they're coming back for us."

The room rocked again.

I rushed to my feet, carrying the open computer to use as a light source. *I have to get him. I have to get him out.*

I shone the computer light along the wall to the corner, and then over the door frame. I found the handle. *I might have to get under it to see if there's some way to loosen it—*

When I yanked down on the handle, the door immediately opened. When the power went out, all the automatic locks had been shut off as well.

Good God, Lynn! Wanting to throw the computer in frustration with myself for not thinking of that earlier, I instead set it down and shoved the door open, stepping out to strange, multicolored lights beginning to flicker through sparse windows. I inhaled sharply, seeing the hallway jammed with people all wearing the same gray pajamas, wandering or standing still.

I rushed through them, nearly colliding with a man who was pacing, a look of utter confusion on his face. I thought of the dozens of rooms I'd passed before finding William; people without memories, already unable to remember how to do anything, now completely confused as to what was happening.

I edged along the wall. 216, 215, 214, 213, 212—

I seized the handle and pushed open the door. "William?"

"Yes?" a small voice came from the blackness.

"Honey, it's your nanna. I'm here in the door. Can you come to me?"

I expected him to hesitate, but in a moment be was right in front of me.

"My sweet boy." I knelt down to hug him.

"Why did they take me away from you? Josh said that we were going to play UNO until it was time for bed, but then everything started shaking and he ran out and the doors locked. I hate it when the doors lock at night. Why are all the lights out? Why is everything shaking?"

"I don't know, honey, but I really want to go. Let's go find Miss Cliff."

"What if they find us again? Will they take me away from you? Hey, those other boys in that picture you gave me, do they like Transformers?"

"They love Transformers. And they have dozens of them, and you can play with all of them as much as you want. But we have to go."

He let me take his hand and step out into the hall.

"Why is everyone out of their rooms?" he asked. "I wonder if my friends are out too. They're in a different building. My room used to be there until they moved me over here tonight."

I can't go for them too, I thought in despair. *All those children whose parents don't know they're still alive.*

The lights dimly came back on, and the doors down the hallway started to beep again. *Down to the first floor, then the tunnel.* I reached the staircase door and turned the handle.

A panel underneath the "Staircase" sign flashed red. I yanked the handle again, and the red flash repeated. *They lock them in, all of them on this floor. The staff can come in, but no one goes out without the code.*

"What's wrong?" William asked.

I looked at my hand, my writing now completely smudged.

"Honey, is there another way out of this hallway? Another staircase?"

William shrugged. "I think so. I remember seeing it once. Don't know where, though."

I moved us down the hallway. Most of the patients didn't appear to even notice us. I checked the sign next to every door, hoping one might to lead to a staircase, anything to lead us out.

Five doors down from us, there was a long beep, and three men in white scrubs emerged from a room. I swept William into the crowd of patients.

"Jesus, they're all out!" said the first man. "Round them up and hurry, before the power goes out again. Tony, go right to room 220, make sure she's still in there—"

The building shook and the lights dimmed, but the power stayed on. I guided William slowly towards the wall, thankful for the slow-moving, clogged group around us. I watched as one of the workers stuck his clipboard in the door to keep it from closing and then hurried down to the other end of the hall, followed by the two others, who began to usher the patients into rooms.

I lifted William into my arms. *Please don't turn around, please don't see us.*

I reached the door, caught it with my foot and held the clipboard. I quietly slipped through the door and put the clipboard back in place. Through the slight gap, I heard one of the men call out from down the hall, "She's not in the room!"

I ignored my throbbing knee and hurried down the hallway. This wing was just as stark, but with no windows and no patients wandering about. I frantically scanned each of the nameplates.

The building rocked, and William cried out as the lights went off. *We'll never know which door leads to a staircase now.*

He began to cry, and I held him close, my arm beginning to ache with his weight. "Don't you worry, I'm with you," I whispered in his ear. "Won't you walk with me? Hold my hand?"

Keep moving. Put as much distance between you and those men as you can.

The hall was almost pitch black. I took William's right hand and used my other hand to feel along the wall. I reached one door, opened it and could tell immediately from the smell of cleaning supplies it was a closet. I moved on, opening the next, and again could sense it wasn't open enough for a stairwell. I slid my hand along the wall and came to a sharp turn. *Oh God, another hallway, we'll never find our way—*

I almost fell on the first step, and yanked William back.

There's no door. There must be no patients on this wing.

I lifted him again. "Nanna's going to carry you, baby, down the stairs."

"I'm not a baby," he grumbled.

"No, you're Nanna's big boy, but I don't want you to fall," I said, feeling out with each footstep.

After several stairs, the floor stopped dropping, and I followed the railing to another landing and another flight. I knew if we moved too fast, we would tumble into the dark.

When the railing ended, I reached out with my foot and felt no more decline. I set William down and reached out for the wall, following it to an angle and then a slight crevice. Finally, I reached a cold door handle.

"Don't go out there," whispered a voice from the dark.

I whirled around, a protective hand holding William back.

"Don't do it," said the voice again, originating from under the stairs. The light from the screen of a phone flashed briefly across the face of Deanna Ruck.

"What are you doing?" I whispered back.

"They're out there. They're in the hospital." The panic in her voice was so thick that I squeezed William's shoulder.

"What do you mean?"

I heard it then, the click of a safety going off on a handgun. In the light of the phone, I saw her pointing her gun directly at us.

"Stay away from us," I said.

I hear her cock the pistol. "Don't go out there!" she begged.

I opened the door and rushed William through.

"Why is she hiding under the stairs?" he asked.

I began to hush him when I nearly tripped, reaching out to steady myself on the wall. In dim, pulsing lights coming from down the hall, I could make out a shape on the floor. A long semiautomatic weapon lay just beyond the motionless body of the soldier who had come into the room to summon Deanna.

To the left of the body was another soldier, bent in an unnatural way, his face turned towards us, eyes open but not blinking. Crouched over that second soldier, something turned towards us.

At first, I thought it held the tip of another rifle, for something long extended from its arm. Then it twitched—too long and too curved to be a barrel. Several other membranes then moved alongside it.

William started to scream.

It rose to its full size, about a foot shorter than me. If it had a color, I couldn't recognize it, for it seemed to constantly change. For one moment, it was the camouflage of the soldier's uniforms; for the briefest of seconds, it bore the face of the dead man sprawled before it.

"*The people in the sky change color,*" my five-year-old self had said in the video.

Then, that face was gone, morphing into almond eyes under a large, smooth forehead. It lacked a nose, had only a tiny lipless mouth above a pointed chin.

It was a face I had seen drawn by people all over the world.

Its head tilted sharply, its eyes without pupils, and for a moment, William's terrified face reflected in its inky eyes. Then it turned to me, made a clicking sound, and it gave me the same stare.

I began to feel it. A numbing in the back of my head. It was an almost calming feeling, all of the anxiety I had felt for days starting to drain away. William wasn't screaming anymore, either. My shoulders relaxed, and my fingers let go of his hand—

I immediately reached back down and snatched his fingers, shaking my head, trying to clear my suddenly cloudy thoughts.

I felt the numbness again, this time stronger than before. The creature had moved closer to us now, making the clicking sound more intensely.

A kind of comfort I hadn't felt since childhood swept over me, and the hallway around me vanished in a wash of white light.

From the light came Daddy.

He held my left hand so firmly that I could feel the calluses on his skin. In my other hand, I carried a purple balloon that danced above us. I could taste the cotton candy, smell the diesel fuel from the rides, hear the laughter from the crowd

"I knew you'd love the fair," Daddy said.

I tugged at him to leave the midway, pointing towards the livestock tent. He happily obliged, laughing as I wrinkled my nose at the scent of hay and manure. I shooed away the goat that chewed on the hem of my dress, and grinned at the baby pigs squealing and running in circles around their slumbering mother. We wandered over to the cows, and I reached over the divider to pet the coarse, white hair—

In a flash of light, a cow was on its side, split open. Not the cow from the tent, but a different one, lying on a vast sea of grass. In its open mouth, I could see its tongue had been removed. Other incisions riddled its body.

I wanted to scream, but realized I wasn't there.

I was the inside the alien's memory.

It stood over the mutilated animal, observing an angular box with strange writing hovering over the animal. With a motion of the creature's hand, a searing red light from the box continued to slice into the cow's abdomen, precisely removing the skin to expose the small intestine.

When the incision was finished, a rapid series of flashing lights penetrated the wound. I desperately wanted to look away but my gaze was fixed, horribly tied to the alien's examination of the animal's organs—

A searing shot of white light, and Daddy helped me into the car.

"Don't let go of my balloon," I said.

Daddy had eased it into the backseat, making sure it and the string were safely inside before he shut the door.

I leaned back against the seat, looking at the carnival lights through the window. I was stuffed with funnel cake and French fries, and was beginning to feel drowsy. As my eyelids drooped, my eyes adjusted, and I could see my own face reflected in the window. On my rounded cheek, was a dab of ketchup from that delicious hotdog—

From the blast of light, came a face so similar to mine that there was no doubt he was my grandson.

The creature stood above William as he lay on the triangular table, a webbing of sorts covering his body. Lights pulsated behind the boy's head.

The creature leaned him over and clicked. Once more, I shared its memory.

Each has a role, it thought as it studied William's face. *Summon the storm, bring the disease, damage the food, start the war. But not you. You are different. You are the center. You are the nerve system. You are our conduit. You will unite them all. You are the final stage—*

A softer white light, but still just as jarring, showed Daddy opening the door for me. "Did you fall asleep, sweet girl?"

"Uh huh," I muttered from the backseat.

"Come on, let's get your pajamas on," he said, lifting me.

I snuggled into the collar of his shirt, smelling pipe smoke, fried fair food, and aftershave. I held him tight, and he squeezed me in return. With Mama gone, he was my whole world.

It had been such a fun night. I didn't get a stuffed animal, but I did get—

"My balloon!" I cried out.

He turned and I lifted my head, seeing the balloon, starting to already lose some of its helium, drift into the trees.

"Daddy, we have to get it," I whined.

He paused for a moment. "No, Lynn. It's just a balloon."

"It's not!" I reached for it. "Daddy, you won me that balloon."

"No, Lynnie," Daddy pulled back so our faces were just an inch apart. "We never, ever go into the woods."

Never go in the woods.

I jerked my head back, breaking the creature's hold. The hallway in the hospital came into clear view, along with a clarity that nearly brought me to my knees.

Summon the storm, bring the disease, damage the food, start the war.

The creature stood just a foot away. On seeing my dazed expression, it began to click again.

I knew what it wanted. From me, from all the returned.

It began to click faster, its head tilting. It stepped forward to where there was only a few inches between us.

All it needed was a few memories more, to determine what they'd put in me. What they sent me back to do.

What weapon I carried within me.

"No!" I cried out. "Stay away!"

I stumbled back, trying to steady myself. I awkwardly

swept up William and blundered down the other side of the hallway, ignoring the screaming pain in my knee. The further I moved away, the sharper my thoughts became.

We're their weapons. Whatever they put in us, whatever we carry in us, they activate and watch the chaos unfold.

William's drawings flashed through my head like videos on the evening news. The unexplained rise in hurricanes, tornadoes, cancer, and even deadly allergies to food—science struggled to understand why.

It was all by design. Our world is where they test these weapons.

And whatever they planned to do in the end, it said William was the final stage.

They cannot have him. Whatever happens, I have to get him out.

The frantic, strobelike lights made me feel as if I could go crashing into a wall at any moment, but I kept running. The lights were growing brighter now, coming through wide glass windows of the room beyond.

The hallway led into a lobby. Several men in heavy camouflage coats, their rifles pulled up to their shoulders, ran past the windows outside. The light fell on the drifting snow, making it look like it was raining confetti.

William was still entranced. I carried him to the glass entrance doors and waited a moment for them to open.

The power's out, they won't open.

I set William down and tried to pry the doors open at the seam. "Come on," I pleaded.

Through the glass I saw a man, standing a yard or so away. He wore a heavy coat and a sock hat and stared up at where the light originated, transfixed by whatever he saw.

"Joe!" I cried out, banging on the glass. "Joe!"

I even saw his massive truck parked nearby, its plow

covered with a layer of snow. "Joe!" I said, striking the glass repeatedly.

He continued to stare, his eyes wide, the lights spilling over his face. *He isn't even blinking.*

The lights in the lobby came roaring back on. I hurried to stand before the doors.

The glass didn't part. I looked around, seeing another key-pad flashing beside the door. *Of course there would be a code here, they wouldn't just let anyone in. Or out.*

I heard the sound of William's feet scuffling.

I whirled around, seeing him beginning to walk back to where we came from. At the far end of the hall, I could see several shapes emerging.

I ran and seized William, rushing back to the door. I smashed my fist on the glass, screaming for Joe. I scanned the lobby for anything I could use to try and break the glass, but the only thing I could see was a computer monitor on the front desk, and it wouldn't have made a dent.

I could feel the numbness growing on the back of my head. I kept pounding. The memory of Daddy's warning about the woods broke me free of the creature's control before, but I didn't know if I could snap out of it again.

I looked out to see the interior light come on in the cab of Joe's truck. The door opened slightly, and someone peered out.

Despite my staggering panic, I gasped. Roxy's face was so bruised, so swollen from the ugly gash down her forehead, that I almost didn't recognize her at first. I cried out her name, waving my arms wildly. I saw her limp out of the truck towards Joe. She looked up in the sky, her hand covering her mouth in astonishment. She looked back at the truck, and then briefly towards the medical center.

I screamed her name, striking the glass. She did a double

take, and I could see her yell out my name. She moved towards Joe, pointing in my direction. Roxy shook him, but he continued to stare upwards.

I watched her give a frightened look in the direction in which Joe stared, and then she painfully moved towards us.

"Come on!" she motioned to me.

"The door won't open! We can't get out!"

Roxy went back to Joe, this time hitting him in the arm. When he didn't respond, she gave me a frantic look, made an obscene gesture at Joe and limped back towards the truck. She was practically dragging her right foot. I watched her open the driver's side door and haul herself in.

The lights went out again, and as soon as I turned back to the lobby, the numbness was back. All I wanted to do was relax. The feeling was so refreshing, such a relief, the euphoria almost too much to fight.

There were five, six, no . . . *ten*. They were like tall children, some walking, others . . . arranging themselves, twitching in rickety sections, angling and reaching out like a scurrying insect.

None of this was alarming. It was such a delightful feeling. I wasn't even worried that William was a few feet ahead of me, walking—

I heard the roar of engine. I groggily turned back to look outside, seeing Joe's truck move in reverse and make a sharp turn towards the lobby. The light in the cab came on briefly, and Roxy was motioning wildly at me from behind the wheel.

"Get back!" I could see her yell.

The headlights of the truck shone out over the plow as it barreled towards the doors.

I rushed forward and grabbed William, stumbling away, closing my eyes as the glass exploded behind us.

As the plow smashed through the doors, I heard them scream. The sound, metallic and feline, made me want to cry out myself. The numbing feeling was immediately gone.

The truck tore back in reverse. I seized William and carried him over the shattered glass, wincing as an icy blast hit us both.

"What the hell?" I heard Joe call out, now turned in our direction. "What are you doing?"

"What are *you* doing, you moron!" Roxy hollered while she rolled down the window. "Took me driving through a building to get you to pay attention! Lynn, get in the backseat! Joe, get the hell in here! I had to use my bad foot to hit the gas, and it's hurting like a son of a bitch!"

I opened the door and lifted William inside, looking back towards the lobby. "Go! Get away from here as fast as you can!"

"What the hell is going on out there?" Joe said, climbing in to take the wheel, rubbing the back of his head.

"Holy Mary Mother of God! William, is that really you?" Roxy reached out to brush his knee, and then winced in pain at the effort. "Lynn, you found him, you found him. . . ."

"Roxy," I said, my heart in my throat. "What happened to you?"

She leaned back. "Joe, get us the hell out of here."

Joe sat, still dazed. "I . . . froze. I just can't believe it. My whole head felt like I was doped up. What are those things? I mean, it can't be—"

"Shut up and drive."

The comment came from what I first thought was a pile of snowsuits on the other side of the bench. Instead, the groggy and wizened face of Verna Cliff revealed itself from within the hood of a long maroon coat. After scowling at Joe, she reached over and touched William's shoulder. "Sweet boy. Your grandma found you."

"How are you here . . . ?" I stammered.

"Cover his eyes, Grandma." Verna leaned forward. "Or he'll be as useless as Joe was out there. Hard not to be; even I couldn't look away."

I realized that William hadn't stirred. He was sitting on the edge of the seat, staring out the windshield.

I followed his gaze and immediately felt the numbing again. Beams of light spilled down from the snowing sky. Dozens of columns, white and gold, amid a flurry of colorful pulsating lights high in the gray night sky. As I looked beyond, I could see even more of the light beams behind the hospital.

Walking into the lights were people.

Even in the heavy snow, I could tell there were hundreds. They stood within each pillar of light, each wearing a hospital gown, looking up.

I knew with certainty that the basement to the hospital was now empty, and all those comatose people had risen for the first time. The power was out, so the door to the stairs was open. They had streamed out, a mindless mass, responding to the call.

I understood why. The closer we could all get to those lights, the better we would feel.

I reached over for the door handle when a large group of men in camouflage flooded past us, running to the hospital. I saw one point and sharply direct a few of his subordinates towards us.

Three soldiers broke off and ran to the driver's side of the truck, pointing their rifles at us. As soon I focused on them, the calm feeling was gone.

"Oh shit," Joe said.

"Put your hands where I can see them!" one of the men shouted.

One of the soldiers leaned into the glass and quickly spoke into the radio on his shoulder. "The boy and the old lady are in there. Do you copy? We've have them. They're here."

Drive, Joe! I wanted to scream.

"All of you, get out of the truck. Keep your hands up," the first soldier ordered.

"Tell him his buddy made me too sore to move," Roxy grumbled, her hands barely raised.

The soldier tapped the edge of his rifle on the glass. "Ma'am, we don't have time for this! Do you hear me? Get out—"

Four beams of light shot down before the now-shattered entrance to White Crest. One beam was so close to the truck that Joe cried out. The soldiers turned, blinded by the searing light.

Seconds later, more shapes began to emerge from the hospital. All in the same stark hospital garb, all their faces calm and serene, walking towards the lights.

The feeling was so strong to join them that I opened the truck door, and heard Joe's door ding, signaling he was feeling the same. William was already sliding across my lap to jump out.

"What the hell is wrong with you people?" Roxy cried out. "Drive, Joe! Dammit! And close the damn doors!"

"Shit," Joe said, wiping his eyes.

"Don't look at it!" I covered my own eyes. "Just drive Joe!"

Joe slammed on the gas. The pickup truck bolted forward, heading directly for the emerging masses.

"Turn!" Roxy yelled. The people in the light made no attempt to get out of the truck's way. Joe spun the wheel and barely cleared a man and a small woman. Joe made another wild turn and drove directly towards two armored cars.

Again Joe turned, this time too late. Despite its snow tires, the truck slid into the front end of one of the military vehicles. We were all momentarily thrown forward, but Joe gave us no time to recover. He immediately took off again, driving down the row of vehicles and hanging right on the wrong way of a circle drive. He headed down a long road leading away from the medical center.

"Everybody OK?" Joe asked, out of breath.

"I'm gonna puke if you keep driving like this!" Verna said.

"Serves you right," Roxy muttered.

"Whatever happens," I said to Joe, "do not—I repeat—do not look into the lights."

"What's happening to us?" he asked, looking at me with genuine terror in his eyes, reaching out to touch the back of his head.

Knowing I couldn't explain at this moment, I scooted to the edge of my seat. "Roxy, what happened to you? They showed me a picture of the van, they told me you'd been killed—"

A rifle shot suddenly sounded, and the back window of the quad cab cracked. I covered William's head.

"Dammit," Joe said, looking at his rearview mirror.

I turned to see three Humvees now following in the distance, their headlights beaming through the snow.

"Come on, Moses." Joe pushed hard on the gas as houses started to appear. "Why are they shooting at us?"

"You think the government wants to you cruise on out of town to tell the world about this shit show?" Verna said.

"Aw, hell." Joe took a sharp left down a side street. I was thankful for the chains I'd noticed on his tires. Otherwise, even on the recently cleared roads, we could have hit an icy spot and gone crashing into a building. Then another right, and another left, knocking down several snow-covered trash cans in an alley.

We heard another gunshot. "Can we get out of town?" I asked, feeling waves of carsickness.

Joe then swung another left and tore down the main drag, where he had earlier made the first pass in trying to clear the streets. Large mounds of snow lined the curb in front of the stores, making the street a single lane.

"They'll chase you to the ends of the earth. They won't let any of you leave," Verna said.

I saw Joe's jaw clench as he took a rough left turn. "Please don't have locked the shop. Please don't have locked it."

"We're going to your store?" Verna asked.

"Not my shop," Joe grunted as he turned in an alley. "Ron's place. When he's slow on business, he lets me park the truck there if it's gonna snow and I have to work late. I hope he's not working on anything."

The truck came to a sudden stop and Joe jumped out, leaving the truck running. "Roxanne, you'll have to take off if they come. Got it?"

"Yep." Roxy winced, touching her leg.

I held my breath, waiting to hear the engines of the Humvees as they tore down the alley. Instead, there was the small squeak of worn hinges as Joe opened two huge, metal double doors. Once he opened them as far as he could, he slid back into the truck.

He quietly pulled into the mechanic's shop and turned the engine off, running back to close the doors behind us.

We sat in silence, looking back to see Joe peering out a rectangular window to the alley. We waited for military vehicles, expecting angry pounding on the door.

After several minutes of nothing, Joe crept over and leaned in the cab. "Stay in the truck," he whispered. "Ron's got the heat way down low. Don't dare turn the lights on. You'll stay warmer in there. I'll keep watch out the window." He shut the door.

I turned back to Roxy. "Tell me what happened."

"It's not as important as what happened to you. William, I can't believe it. You're here. You're really here," Roxy said, touching his head.

"It matters to me," I whispered. "I thought you'd been killed. Did you crash?"

Roxy shook her head. "These bruises are courtesy of one of this town's finest after I got the van stuck. He was on me as soon as I slid off the road, like he knew where I would be. He didn't like my response when he asked for my ID and proof of insurance. I knew I was a goner at that point. Things got ugly fast, and it became clear very quickly I was not supposed to walk away from that encounter. But he didn't know how mean I can be. I even got his gun, can you believe it? But I've got terrible aim, and I shot up more of the van than him."

I almost laughed in relief, then, thinking of the picture Deanna had shown me on her phone. It had been Roxy shooting, not the other way around.

"He got the gun back fast, but it was out of bullets. He was a sick son of a bitch too—started taking pictures of me laying in the snow, and the van, I guess someone wanted proof. I was in a real bad way when Joe rolled up and saw the guy using me as a punching bag. He underestimated Joe too. For an old guy, Joe used that crowbar in the bed of his truck and showed him who was boss—"

"Are you OK?" I reached over to Roxy's swollen cheek.

"I hurt everywhere. My foot and face are the worst. But I insisted Joe get me back to you, and when we got to Miss Congeniality's house, she was so bombed she could barely make it to the door. Joe thought some sudden exposure to this wonder-

ful Colorado weather might perk her up, so we went for a ride—"

"Kidnapped, more like it," Verna grumbled.

"Didn't have a choice," Roxy said with a glare. "Joe said we needed that damn code of yours from the kitchen to get in. If Armageddon hadn't started when we showed up, I would have personally forced your butt through that hospital till we found Lynn and William."

"Didn't you want to come get me?" William asked quietly, looking at his teacher.

I watched whatever was left of her binge seep from the old woman's face. She reached out and gently squeezed his arm. "Miss Cliff was just tired, honey. And I'll admit it," she sighed, "I was a little afraid of the sky tonight."

"Afraid?" I whispered. "You knew . . . this . . . those ships, those . . . things, were coming?"

"Things?" Verna asked.

William curled up closer to me, burying his face in my side.

"Oh God, you actually saw them? I don't know if anyone here ever has. When I saw what kind of storm was brewing, I knew the ships would come. They always do when the weather gets this bad. And when all the phones and computers stopped working, I knew it for sure. But it didn't happen . . . like it usually does. They aren't dropping off people. They're taking them back. Everyone who's been marked. All those people, all my kids . . ."

She looked out the window, her eyes glinting with tears.

"You know . . . about the markings?" I asked in a hush, knowing I should cover William's ears.

Verna ran her fingers over the back of William's hair. "Honey, do you still have that bump on the back of your head

from when you fell off the bed that night? The one that hurts sometimes?"

"Yep," William yawned. "Are we gonna be here for a while?"

"Close your eyes honey," Verna said, looking at me. "That bump, it's always hurting him. The other kids complain about it too, but it goes away in time. It's under his hairline, you'd never see it. You have to *know* it's there."

"I don't know what you're talking about," Roxy whispered from the front seat, "Why does the military stand there and let those . . . ships . . . take those people?"

Verna smiled with traces of anger. "Because the government can't stop them. Believe me, they've tried. It hasn't been pretty. The military has tried to communicate with them, but they're not interested. It's like pigs trying to negotiate with a butcher. They've always just dropped off the ones they've abducted. I don't know why they're taking them back."

I do, I thought. You don't want to know.

I understood then that Verna's drinking wasn't to momentarily escape the sadness of what she'd seen. It was how she survived all those long years, watching the doctors and staff leave after working at the hospital for just a year or so—

I quickly looked to her, remembering her own words: *They say they can't handle it or they're too sick to work anymore. Won't even get close to the kids.*

Those doctors found out, too late, what happens if they're around the returned who have been activated. How not long after the patients scream in pain, their ears ringing and bleeding, the doctors themselves start dying.

Only Verna remains unaffected, and she doesn't even realize why. Even though she said she was mesmerized by the lights from the ships, she doesn't even realize she's one of us too—

"Lynn Roseworth," came a loud voice from a megaphone.

William sat up whining, and I looked around in panic. The voice came from outside the shop.

Joe ran from the garage window to the front of the building as the voice continued. "Lynn Roseworth, please come out. We know you are inside. Do not make us open fire. We do not want to harm you or your grandson. Come out, now."

Joe hurried back from where he peered out the small window facing the street. He slid into the front seat. "They're sitting there at the intersection, looking all around. They must not know where we are other than downtown somewhere."

"Don't doubt them. They will start shooting," Verna said.

"This is a mechanic shop, can we hide somewhere? Down in a pit or something?" Roxy asked.

"Where's the bathroom in this place?" Verna asked.

"Are you kidding me?" Joe hissed.

"Listen, I've drank enough tonight to put all of you under the table. When you're this old, and you gotta go, you gotta go, or you go on the spot," Verna said, sliding out. "I'll find it myself."

"Joe, what about Roxy's idea of the pit?" I asked.

"We're on top of it, and it's covered. I'd have to move the truck and pull off the metal cover—"

"Give me your coats," Verna commanded from outside the truck. We looked to see her standing by the light switch, her finger prepared to flick it up.

"Jesus, what is wrong with you?" Joe whispered.

"I will turn on these lights and they'll know in a second where you are. Give me Lynn and William's coats. Now."

"God damn you, woman," he said. "You're gonna go hunch down in the bathroom under all those coats and wait this out—"

"I'm counting down. Starting now: five, four—"

"Shit!" Joe yanked off William's coat and took mine as I shrugged it off.

"Miss Cliff," William said groggily. "Are you leaving us?"

"Sorry kid. I'm done with all this. I know what they're capable of doing. And your coat, too, gimpy. And that stupid sock hat of yours too, Joe. It will be cold in that bathroom."

"I hope when they start shooting, they aim for the bathroom." Roxy winced as she took off her coat.

Joe threw the coats out. As Verna slowly gathered them and walked towards the bathroom, the voice came again from the street. "Lynn Roseworth, you have one minute to come out. Please don't make us harm your family."

"Jesus, what are we going to do? We have to go," Roxy said. "Just gun it out of here, Joe. We'll have to take our chances."

"They'll be on our asses in two seconds, they're right outside. They missed before, but now they're at close range."

"There has to be another place we can hide," I said. Hearing the panic in my voice, William started to cry.

"Joe," Verna's voice came from the door. "Give me twenty seconds and then follow the alley down to where Janice Stoney had that crappy secondhand store. You can follow Sugarhill Street out."

"What are you talking about . . . ?" Joe said, watching Verna shuffle to the front of the building towards a door. Instead of her long coat, she now wore mine, and had the hood up. We could see she'd stuffed Roxy's coat into William's with the hood sticking out, and had placed Joe's sock hat in the hood.

To complete the image, she'd tied her own coat around the waist of the makeshift boy, to cover his legs from the cold.

"What is she doing?" Joe demanded.

"Verna!" I whispered, covering my mouth.

She couldn't have heard, but she did turn around and look

at me. "Tell him," she mouthed the words. "Tell him what I did. And *get him out*."

Verna unlocked a door and stepped out of the building onto the main street, closing the door behind her, holding the crudely assembled dummy in her arms. "I'm here! Don't shoot!" she cried out.

"Put the child down, Mrs. Roseworth!" the voice boomed.

"No!" Verna yelled out. "I won't let you have him! I want a phone!"

"We have to go," Joe said, jumping out of the truck and gingerly opening the doors to the alley.

"Mrs. Roseworth, put the child down. Walk over to us with both your hands in the air."

"I'm not coming a step closer until you get my husband on the phone! He's a US senator!"

Joe slid back into the truck. "What's going on?" William asked. "We can't leave Miss Cliff—"

"Now, Mrs. Roseworth!" the soldier on the megaphone ordered.

"No! I want my husband on the phone—"

There was no order to open fire, only the sound of automatic weapons unloading. Joe threw it in reverse. I covered William's face as we slid out of the garage and into the alley.

The shooting continued for several seconds more, masking our noise enough for us to make a sharp turn and approach another street.

"Jesus," Roxy's voice was tight. "Oh my God. . . ."

"God love you, Verna," Joe murmured quietly.

I made the sign of the cross across my aching chest.

"What happened?" William asked.

I held him close. "Miss Cliff wanted to save you."

"Shouldn't we go back and get her?"

I kissed his forehead and told him to close his eyes and try to rest.

Joe drove at a slow pace, unable to use his headlights. For the first time since arriving in Argentum, I was grateful for the fact that this was a small, isolated town. There were no street-lights on the side streets, which allowed us to creep along without being seen.

"Do you even know where you're going?" Roxy whispered.

"You could blindfold me and I could still make it around town. At least, I hope so."

"Once they . . . look closer at the coats, they'll know. They'll start looking for us," Roxy said.

"If we can get up and over the rise . . . ," he said.

"Well, I sure couldn't," Roxy said. "It's complete ice and snow. You better have a plan B."

"It's the only way out of town." He leaned in to the wind-shield.

The lights of Main Street were still in view off to our right. Joe drove as far on the side street as he could before it dead-ended. Then he had no choice but turn towards the town's main thoroughfare.

When we reached Main Street, he edged out just enough to look. We all leaned forward, seeing the Humvees along the boardwalk start separating. One disappeared down the alley where we'd gone to reach the mechanic shop, and the others turned towards the medical center before splintering off onto side streets.

"Hold on," Joe said, turning left. Almost immediately, we began to climb the incline that had stranded Roxy only hours before. I whispered a silent prayer for the sharpness of Joe's snow tires. We passed the crashed van and the police cruiser, its lights still flashing.

"Looks like my dancing partner survived after all," Roxy said bitterly. "He was lying by the car when we ran off. Someone must have come to get his sorry ass."

As we crested the hill, I looked back, certain we were being pursued.

My eyes lingered on the empty street for a moment before they were drawn to the heavens. Even the snow was unable to block out the two massive shapes hovering miles above the far edge of town. Their color was difficult to determine, but the thousands, maybe millions of lights, outlining their diameters and edges were clear. Comprehending their size brought on a wave of fear, like a child seeing a whale for the first time. I could only gauge they were the size of cruise liners, maybe even the battleships I'd seen on TV. I felt nauseous at the thought of William in one of them and looked away, but felt compelled to return my gaze, to make myself believe I'd really seen them.

Of course I had. I'd been in one too.

As we went over the hill, the last thing I saw was another beam of light shoot to the earth below.

Joe then stopped the truck, switched gears, and began to back up while turning the wheel.

"What are you doing?" Roxy demanded.

Joe ignored her, and pulled down the stick shift. The plow on the front of the truck slowly lowered.

Roxy's hands flailed. "Joe, just keep driving—"

"Woman, I'm telling you what," he said, waiting for the plow to crunch against the earth. He then drove off the road, the snow immediately piling up before him.

"They can't chase us if they can't get through," he muttered.

Joe continued to drive a half circle and promptly dumped

a huge amount of snow and ice on the road. He backed up and took another scoop, piling it behind the first.

"Now, we go," he said, slowly advancing onto the road.

I glanced back to see lights coming up over the hill from the town. A Humvee was over the rise a moment later.

"Joe!" I cried out.

He swore and gunned the gas, and we started to slide. I looked back out the window and saw that the driver of the Humvee apparently had the same notion when he saw us. I watched the army vehicle race down the road and weave as he tried to avoid the mound of snow and ice. But instead, the Humvee crashed into it head on, the snow falling onto its hood and covering the window.

"Drive, dammit!" Roxy yelled. Despite the heavily falling snow, I could see the headlights of the Humvee rock back and forth as the driver tried to steer it free.

"Eat that, asshole," Joe said, driving down the road as fast as he could while still controlling the truck on the ice. I saw one soldier get out of the Humvee with a long rifle and try to aim in our direction, but then we were off the road and onto the state route.

We crunched along, and Roxy patted Joe's arm. "You did good."

"Keep looking back," he said. "They'll be radioing in for anyone else to follow. It will be even more treacherous on these mountain roads. And it's night. I'll go as fast as I can, but the last thing we need is to end up in a ditch."

"Been there," Roxy said, holding up a finger, her eyes closed.

We drove in silence, the wipers pushing aside the snow that continued to fall, the pine trees rushing by in the dark.

"Joe, I'm so sorry," I said quietly. "I'm sorry you're caught up in this."

"Miss Lynn, looks like I've been part of this for a long, long time, even if I didn't realize it. I . . . can't believe it. . . ."

"How are we on gas?"

"I keep reserves in the wintertime, so I filled up before I started clearing the streets this afternoon. I have a reserve tank too. We'll be fine to get to Denver."

"What's to keep them from following us from above? Helicopters? Planes?"

"Would be hard to follow from the air in this blizzard. It is the government, however. They're probably tracking us by satellite at this very moment, following my cell signal."

"Do you have one? In the truck?"

"In the glove compartment."

Roxy opened the latch and pulled out the phone, handing it back to me. I powered it up and found it had no service. I shook my head and looked over to Roxy, who was clenching her eyes in pain.

"We'll get you to a hospital as soon as we get into the city."

"No," she said. "We're going straight to the airport, getting you and little man on a plane."

"They'll expect that. They'll have people waiting for us there. I have to be able to make a call. Just one call."

I knew Joe was doing the best he could in the conditions, but it felt like we were moving at a crawl. I kept looking back, expecting to see glaring headlights, or hear the thumping whirl of helicopters above.

We drove on, the snow pelting the windshield, the wind rushing against the glass. Roxy sat with her eyes closed, and

Joe kept whispering to himself, shaking his head. I held tight to William, and constantly looked in the rearview mirror.

It seemed like an hour later, but we finally reached the highway. "Honey," I whispered to William.

The boy had curled up deep under my arm, dead asleep. Delicately, I touched the camera app on the phone and took a quick photo, hoping the flash wouldn't wake him. As I looked at the sweet image of the sleeping boy's face, my heart leapt at the three strong bars of service.

I quickly dialed, and held my breath as it rang.

"Hello?" Tom answered immediately.

"Tom," I turned to face the window, speaking softly.

"Lynn? Jesus, are you OK? Where are you?"

"Listen to me. I can't speak loudly. I have William. Do you understand? I have William."

"What?"

"I am in Colorado approaching Denver. I am going to send you a picture you must immediately share with Anne and Chris. Roxy is banged up bad and we're heading for a hospital. Tom, William is alive."

"Lynn, honey, I don't know what you're talking about. Just tell me where you are—"

"I love you, Tom, but I'm hanging up. Look for a text from this number. I have many calls to make, then I'll call you back."

"Wait, who are you calling—?"

"I love you," I said, and hung up.

The phone immediately rang with Tom's number appearing. I ended the incoming call, touched the picture of the photo, and texted it to his number. He called again, and the phone made a swishing sound as the text went through.

A few seconds after the text went out, the phone stopped ringing.

I pulled up Safari and quickly typed, pulling up a number of different websites.

"You finally learned to use another app," Roxy observed, with a pained voice.

I touched one of the numbers that appeared, and I held up the phone to my ear. The phone rang three times before someone answered, "KUSA-TV, can I help you?"

"Is this the NBC station? Do I have the newsroom? My name is Lynn Roseworth, I am the wife of Senator Tom Roseworth of Tennessee. My grandson William has been missing for several months. Are you familiar with the story? Good. I am calling to tell you that I have located my grandson here in Colorado, and we are driving to the Denver Emergency Center, where I will be bringing him in to be evaluated. That's right, my grandson. The one who is missing. I am calling every television station in town, as I intend to make a brief statement after we arrive. I will also be sending you a photo of my grandson for verification purposes. I will call again as we approach the hospital. You can call my husband's press secretary within the hour to confirm that I have spoken with him. I hope you'll be there. I can be reached at this phone number as we drive into Denver, but if I don't answer, it's because I'm calling your competitors. I hope to see your crew there. What is a good phone number to text you this picture?"

When I hung up and began to search online again, Roxy painfully leaned forward. "What in God's name are you doing?"

"It's our only protection. If every TV station and newspaper sees that William is alive with me, they can't try to take him from us. It's the only way."

"What exactly are you going to tell them when we arrive?" Joe asked quietly.

I put the phone up to my cheek. "Are you the ABC station? Good. My name is Lynn Roseworth."

Two hours later, when we at last reached Interstate 25, the cell phone was hot from constant use. If it hadn't been for the phone charger Joe thankfully kept in the glove compartment, the phone would have died long ago.

Tom had called several times, as had Kate, Anne, and Stella. I hadn't answered, only texted them the picture. I felt so tired after talking to all the journalists, knowing they were all wondering what the crazy alien lady would say at the hospital. It was only a taste of what was to come.

Roxy knew it too. "You need to call Anne."

"I will, in a minute. I need to get my head together."

Roxy reached back across William and took my hand.

I squeezed. Tom was no doubt on a plane, probably having called in a favor to a wealthy donor to get on a private jet. He would bring Anne and Chris. Stella would probably muscle herself on board. Kate too. There would be so many questions, but I would insist that word of William's discovery be sent to Nashville's metro police immediately. Steven had to be released. And Barbara as well—

I quickly turned to Joe, who was whistling softly. For the first time, I noticed the silver swirl of his hair that lay over the back of his collar, and how he was twirling it, round and round.

The angle of his jaw. The sharpness of his nose. The light shade of his blue eyes. None of it registered then, but it did now.

It can't be.

When Barbara was a teenager and had come to ask for our help all those years ago, she had twirled her hair. She did it again in that basement in Champaign as well. Barbara Rush, silver hair, soft chin, sharp nose, brilliant blue eyes. Barbara, who never stopped looking for her brother Don.

Twins, from St. Joseph, Michigan.

"Joe," I asked. "You don't remember anything of your past?

"Nope."

"So you don't even know . . . if you had . . . maybe a sister?"

"Not a thing. My God, all that time . . . was I . . . taken?"

"So you don't remember anyone named Barbara?"

"Barbara? You know, funny you should ask," Joe said, a sad smile coming to his face. "Remember when I told you that some names sound kind of familiar? Like how I chose Joseph? Well, of all the names of women I've heard, Barbara has always been my favorite."

EPILOGUE

I rested the tip of the pen on the blank square of the question, tapping it repeatedly. The capitol of Maine. Seven letters.

I swear it's Bangor. But the "b" doesn't fit, and it's not long enough. I know this. I know this.

I looked out across the garden, laying the crossword puzzle on the arm of the Adirondack. The chair was by the lavender bush for a reason: Daddy always said the scent had calming effects. I breathed in and closed my eyes, trying to slow my racing heartbeat, looking down at my watch for the thousandth time in the last fifteen minutes.

I tried to focus on the billowing hydrangea bush in its myriad blues and pinks, taking long breaths to slow my heartbeat. The garden has come back after so much neglect—isn't it remarkable?

We agreed to meet at three o'clock.

Yes, I'd lost some finicky gardenias, and my pots all had to be replanted, but they had been filled with annuals anyway.

I won't have much time with him, but there's so much that has to be said.

The hydrangeas are suffering, and they'd be wilting right now in the early evening heat, even if I hadn't abandoned them late last summer.

I have so much to ask him.

Augusta. Augusta, Maine. I wrote down the word. Now move on to the next, stop thinking about what could be within us—

All those terrible diseases. Horrible storms. People getting sick after eating meat—

"Miss Lynn?"

I looked over, across the fence. It needed its yearly painting, but I planned on having that done in the fall, when the temperatures were bearable. The man just beyond the fence stopped and wiped his brow with a handkerchief, setting down the wheelbarrow full of mulch he pushed. "Do you want me to take the mulch up to the garden by the shop, or dump it here?"

"I'll use it for the rose bed by the Peddler's front door. You can dump it there."

"Uh, no, you cannot."

Roxy huffed from the other side of the garden. I could hear the keys jingling in the front of her overalls, indicating she'd just closed up the shop. She walked with a cane, and would for the rest of her days, Dr. Burcham said. He had suggested plastic surgery for the deep gash on her forehead that required a series of ugly stitches and had left a wicked scar, but she said at her age, she wasn't concerned about smooth skin. "Jesus, Lynn, are we running a trailer park here? No, you can't dump that mulch there, Don. Wheel it around back and we'll get to it tomorrow."

"Yes, Miss Roxy." Don winked at me.

"Don, you really don't have to do that," I said, fanning myself with the newspaper.

It's the heat. That's why I'm sweating. My nerves can't be this bad already.

"Trying to earn my keep," he said with a grin. "Any foxes in the garden today?"

"Oh, I think I saw one a while ago," I said, looking around.

"Not too hot for foxes, I hear. I've found the more I expose myself to this Tennessee heat, the more I become used to it."

Just like you got used to everyone calling you Don. Just like you got used to your sister hovering around you constantly. It didn't take you long to see how your mannerisms are exactly the same, and how you both have the exact same color of silver in your hair. You knew it as soon as you met. And now . . . how your eyes light up when she comes to visit you, driving down from Illinois every other weekend.

Has Don told you, Barbara? About our pact, our promise to each other? That, if suddenly, we have blinding pain in our heads, our ears begin to bleed, and we hear a terrible ringing, we know what's happening. We know they've activated us, and God knows what we could do to you and to everyone around us.

Don said that from time to time he saw it happen to patients, when he was being treated in the hospital. He said the doctors whisked them away, and he never saw them again. He says it never happened to him, and I know it has never happened to me.

But if it does, Don and I agree to leave and disappear. Despite the pain I know all too well of having a loved one suddenly disappear, I would vanish in a heartbeat, jump in the closest car and keep driving away, if it meant protecting my family.

And William. What did those monsters mean that he was the conduit? That he wouldn't harm people when he was activated, but instead, he was the final stage—

"Looks pretty busy in the kitchen right now." Don motioned with his chin to the house. "I think I'll break into the back of the shop and get some water. Clean up a bit."

"Clean up a lot, please," Roxy muttered.

"I'm just happy to have a job with you, Miss Roxy!" he called out.

"The man thinks because he rents my back room that I like him," she said, carefully navigating the paving stones through the grass. "Husband enjoys his company, though. Two peas in a pod, those two, pickin' at guitars, thinking they're Johnny and Waylon. Ed may have advanced cancer, but he's healthy enough to stay up and smoke cigarettes with Don. Good thing you've found room for him on the payroll, or else all they'd do is play guitar and drink beer. I guess Don's not planning on going back to Colorado."

I knew Roxy saw me purse my lips and what that meant. She came to sit down next to me. "Crossword puzzle. The vacuum must be broken. What's got you all riled up—?"

"Nanna!"

The screen door screeched open, and Brian stuck his head out. "Where's the Nutella?"

"Pantry, second shelf. Next to the microwave popcorn."

"I didn't see it!"

"Jesus, boy, are you hoping the neighbors will be able to help you find it?" Roxy asked.

"Sorry Roxy! Brian waved.

You yell all you want. I could listen to you yell every minute of every day for the rest of my life. From the moment you saw William and said his name, I swear I cried for two days straight.

"Will! Mom says to come inside soon!" Brian yelled, and then slammed the screen door.

"Don't want to."

We both turned to the boy crouching down next to a turtle statue, barely visible under a rose bush.

"There's that redheaded fox we've been looking for!" Roxy smiled.

"I know Don saw me," William said, his hand in his pocket. "And you're wrong, Nanna, about the turtle."

I loved his jutted-out bottom lip so much. "No, I'm not, William. You will. I promise."

"I won't," he said glumly, walking over to the chair. I reached out and rubbed his head, careful not to irritate the bump of his head. Already, I'd noticed it was starting to diminish, but he still winced when anyone even came near it. I didn't dare mention to anyone what that bump could indicate.

"I won't ever remember."

"It was your favorite statue, and it will be a memory one day."

"I don't remember anything," he pouted. "I don't remember that stupid turtle. I don't remember you, I don't remember Mommy or Daddy or Roxy or Grandpa or anyone."

I leaned in towards him. "Here's what I promise you: One day, when you're all grown up, you will remember that turtle and how I told you that when you were a really little boy, you loved it. I tell you that every day, so it will become a *new* memory for you one day."

You will relearn, as I did.

"But I want to remember it *now*."

"I know," I said, looking down at my watch. Three o'clock.

"William, why don't you show Roxy where we found that frog yesterday by the fountain? That foxglove is really spreading behind the Peddler, and I may want to make a bed there. I might have Don put the mulch back there."

I quickly walked towards the shop, as Roxy's raised

eyebrow was like a stick poking me in the back. She knew I hated foxglove.

"Nanna, how long will you be gone?"

"Not long," I said, giving him a wave without looking back.

I left the garden, pausing only to pick a few daylilies. The red bell jeered at me from the pitch of the roof of the Peddler. *Look what happened to your life once you disregarded your father's warning.*

I glared back. I would have it removed this week. I certainly didn't need it anymore.

Even though it was in deep summer and the trees were heavy with leaves, I could see the iron fence that now lined my property. It had been a massive expense; jaw dropping to get the final bill. But to install an entire eleven-foot tall fence, with extending upper rows of wicked barbed wire, around the entire perimeter of the woods, was an expensive project. And pricier still when I demanded the keyless entry.

I looked back to see Roxy and William deep in discussion near the fountain in the garden. I stepped past the first tree and reached into my pocket for the tiny remote. I'd practiced the code many times, for I was the only one who possessed it. Though my memory was legendary in my family, I still forced myself to recount the code every morning, to make sure it was set in my mind. I didn't dare write it down. No one would ever be able to enter the woods again.

I had already activated the gate earlier that afternoon. As long as I was within a mile of it, the remote prompted it to unlock. So I had casually stepped outside, punched in the code, and went back inside.

Exactly an hour later, I was now standing directly in front of the gate. You couldn't tell where the fence would open; there was no visible gate, at my request. The ironworkers who made it had looked at me with confusion at my request, but ultimately worked with a locksmith to design the hidden mechanics.

The remote looked like a small calculator in my hand. Once I touched the right combination, I heard a buzz, a click, and one section of fence opened.

I quickly seized it, for it was also manufactured to close within five seconds. I stepped inside and shut it behind me, making sure it locked.

The woods were bustling with a crush of squirrels, buzzing in the branches above. I was careful where I stepped. I was grateful for the way the woods were stubbornly territorial, trying to cover as much of the earth as possible with tangling underbrush and fallen limbs, preventing encroachment of the outside world. The fence was my contribution to the effort.

It should have been difficult to locate the clearing, with the crime-scene tape long removed and the evidence of hundreds of searchers now covered in decaying leaves under a new growth of weeds. But he still found it, as I knew he would. He'd come just as I'd opened the gate remotely and slipped in.

"Hello, Lynn."

Steven stood in the center of the grassy area. Perhaps it had been the unflattering light of the hotel lamps the last time I saw him, in that frantic meeting before the government agents stormed in, but his skin seemed healthier now, his tan showcased nicely against his closely cropped white beard.

"Thank you for agreeing to meet with me," he said.

I nodded. As he slipped his hands into the pockets of his jeans, I walked to the far end of the clearing. A few butterflies flew drunkenly before me. In the shadows of the tree line, I knelt down in front of the gray headstone I'd had delivered before the fence was finished. I laid the lilies before the stone.

Amelia Shrank, 1931–2018. Beloved Daughter, Friend to Children.

I traced my finger across her name, and then turned to Steven. "I'm here because I am indebted. Especially to you. To say a proper thank you for leading me to William. And also . . . to say I'm truly sorry for what all of this has cost you."

"It wasn't your fault. The government forced my hand when they planted the trumped-up investigation and then labeled me a child murderer. Even after the charges were dropped, I knew the damage was done. I should have left academia a long time ago and devoted all my time to investigating the disappearances. Not that I've had much of a choice, but I've chosen to go underground."

"With this group you mentioned in the hotel? The Corcillium?"

"They've shown me so much, Lynn. The Researchers are just the front lines. The Corcillium guides it all. The Researchers are necessary to gather the intelligence, but the Corcillium is truly the heart of the effort. Through them, I finally learned the truth about Argentum."

"So all that time, when you said Argentum was just a debunked theory . . . you truly didn't know?"

He nodded. "Not even what it meant. The Corcillium wanted it that way. To protect all the Researchers."

"I don't understand."

"You will. It all started when one of the members of the Corcillium came in contact with, of all things, a janitor," Steven said, and then chuckled sadly. "A janitor in love, who fell for a woman with no memory. Helped her escape some sort of hospital in a remote town in Colorado."

Despite the summer heat, I rubbed my arms.

Steven continued. "Of course, that colleague took extensive notes of his discussion with this janitor and his girlfriend. But not a day later, the two were killed. Tragic accident. Their car exploded. Brand-new car, too. Then that member of the Corcillium went to Argentum himself, to confirm what he'd been told . . . and was killed in a skiing accident. Strange, don't you think? And when the Corcillium sent others to try and verify, they all disappeared. It became simply too dangerous. They knew what the janitor said—about people with no memories appearing in shafts of lights from the heavens—but could never prove it. And anyone who tried to find out never returned."

I remembered what Don said about the academic couple who came to Argentum and were seized by the police and never seen again. And, of course, what almost happened to Roxy and myself.

"The janitor and his girlfriend had no proof, and when they died, their stories died with them. All the Corcillium had were the notes from the interviews with the janitor. To honor their sacrifice, they developed the idea of the poem to send to all the families of the missing. The idea was to give the families part of the key, and if the day came when we could prove the abducted were returned to Argentum, then the answer was there. In the last line of the poem. But I, and all the other Researchers, never knew."

"The Corcillium did that to protect you."

His mouth formed a straight line. "They assumed in our web of research, someone might come across a mention of Argentum. They couldn't risk any of us losing our lives pursuing it. So they purposely disseminated what came to be called the Argentum theory. It was one of the first pieces of information a Researcher learned: never to believe anything that mentioned 'Argentum.' It was part of our vernacular. We debated it endlessly. I still remember getting my first piece of encrypted information, containing what avenues not to explore. The Argentum theory was at the top of the list. We all learned to dismiss it."

I exhaled. "When I was in Argentum, I was told of a couple—academics—who came to Argentum. They were seized by who the locals thought were police."

"Dr. Adam Abraham and Dr. Nancy Little. Two members of the Corcillium. They were never seen again. It was only when the Corcillium rescued me, and I acknowledged that it was my own grandson who was abducted, that they told me. And warned me I would likely never return. But I was willing to risk it. I knew you would risk it as well. Of course, in the end, you were the only one to ever come back."

"Steven—" I took a deep breath. "I need to know . . . if this Corcillium has determined . . . what we carry inside us."

Steven rubbed the back of his neck in response.

"Then you know about it," I said. "I am hoping you have uncovered more. I'm deeply worried about my family and their safety."

He shook his head. "I wish I could tell you more, Lynn. But there's a lot that I have yet to learn. Even though the Corcillium has investigated this, I know there's no physical evidence. There's never been any device or implant ever discovered in someone who claims to have been abducted. Now, we've never had someone like you or William—"

"There will be no inspection of my grandson."

"But, there is . . . you."

I smiled sadly. "Observing me all those years ago wasn't enough, was it? Do you want to dissect me now?"

"Of course not. But . . . we have to try to determine what may be within you. You're the only one, Lynn. The Corcillium understands allowing them to run tests on you would be . . . taxing. That's why they're offering up your father's letters. About your mother."

I blinked. "There are more letters?"

"I was shown the first just before I came. There are several, I'm told. They explain how your parents found you. And honestly, it led to a great discovery. It's incredible where they found you—"

"That I wasn't returned to Argentum but to one of the other bases the government set up to contain us?"

His eyes widened as I continued. "Obviously you've seen the brief footage of me at the end of that interrogation film. I'm looking out a window, and beyond that window are a beach and an ocean. At my last recollection, there is no ocean in Colorado."

"You're as sharp as ever, Lynn. You see a brief flash of something in an old film, and you connect the dots."

"I've also seen the entire film, including my responses to the government agent's questions. I know what I described aboard that ship. I know what William saw too, because there's a recorded interview of him as well. And . . . I saw *them*."

I could see that Steven had stopped breathing. "You saw one of them? What did it say?"

"I want those letters, Steven. I want to know what happened to my mother."

"And you should have them. You must have them. We asked Barbara to give you my message asking to meet here for two reasons. One—we need access to this site to study. There are so few places in the world that we know of where multiple abductions have occurred. It's vital we try to understand why. And two, because . . . because they want you to come join us."

I brushed an unruly curl from my face. "I risked everything to keep my family together, Steven. There's nothing that could convince me to leave them now. Or ever."

"I'm not asking you to leave them forever. But Lynn . . . what you've seen . . . the fact that you had some sort of communication . . . it's essential we learn from you. And you from us. What the Corcillium has uncovered. What they know about the abductions—"

"I'm not leaving my family. Ever again."

"If those letters were mine to give, you'd have them right now. But I don't. Only the Corcillium has them."

I breathed out slowly through my nose. "I get it. They entice me with the letters, show you just enough to whet my appetite, as a way to draw me in. Well, you will remind them that this is my land, and neither you nor any of your peers will ever step foot here again without my permission. So here are my terms: If you want to come to this site to study, you will only be given access when and if I deem it possible. I don't know what you hope to find, but whatever you do, you will then report to me and answer my questions. *All* of my questions. You will share every single shred of information, regardless of how minute, about what may be implanted within us. And as a token of your appreciation, you will deliver all the letters from my father. It's that simple. If you agree, you can pass your requests to come here through Barbara and I will reply with the appropriate times. There's no negotiating on this."

Steven managed a smile. "You still hold all the cards, Lynn. It's why the government and the entire world is waiting on you to explain how you found William. What is it you said when you gave that statement to the reporters in Denver? 'There is a vast government conspiracy, and I'm working to uncover the truth.' No wonder the government still has Argentum shut down and closed off for 'homeland security' reasons. And all those people with missing loved ones are still rallying outside, protesting, demanding to know if the person they've been searching for is in there."

My face softened. "I wish I could tell you that I saw your

sister, even though I wouldn't have begun to know what she looked like. The people who have called me, written me, asking if I saw their missing friend or relative—I can't bear to tell them the truth."

Steven hesitated. "The truth?"

"That if their loved one was once abducted and then returned, only to be contained in the government bases, they're gone now. All those people were taken back into the ships that arrived above Argentum. What they intend to do with the people, I don't know. But there is another stage, something else is coming. If your Corcillium has any information about what's happened or may happen, I must be told."

"I have to warn you, Lynn, that the Corcillium closely guards what it discovers. Of course, they want to share everything with the world, once they have all the proof they need. But they have concerns . . . about Tom. They can't risk this information being leaked. All Tom has ever said publically is that he believes you, just before he withdrew from consideration for vice president. Would you intend to share everything with him? They don't feel they can trust someone who still very much serves the government."

"I trust my husband completely–" I paused and cocked my head slightly. "Your Corcillium doesn't want some simple grandmother exposing the truth. *They* want to do it. *They* want the credit. You can tell them that I started discovering their secrets forty years ago. Sitting at that desk at midnight, unraveling how to read documents with so many words blacked out. You can remind them how quickly I figured out the rest."

My hands joined at my waist. "Those are my terms, Steven. Tell your Corcillium that I am eager to learn of their findings. Ten minutes from now, I will remotely open the gate, and it will be your only moment to slip out."

I nodded to him once and headed back to the gate.

"I know you've seen it, Lynn," Steven called out after me. "The book that's coming out. *The Senator's Wife*, they're calling it. It doesn't seem fair to you. You shouldn't be known as just a politician's wife."

There was half a mile of woods between the clearing and my house. The leaves obscured the view so entirely that I could see nothing. But I knew that beyond the trees, Brian, Greg, and Anne were inside, sitting around the kitchen table, waiting for me to start making a promised chocolate cake. That soon, Chris and Stella would arrive hungry for Friday night dinner. That Tom and Kate would be on the five o'clock flight from DC. That a little redheaded boy was leaning on the fence, waiting anxiously for his grandmother to return.

"It doesn't matter what they call me," I said, feeling the scattering of sunlight falling on my face as I walked towards my home. "I know who I am."

ACKNOWLEDGMENTS

You hold in your hands a dream thirty-four years in the making, and these are the people who made it happen: My agent at Donald Maass, Paul Stevens, whose editorial insight and constant support makes him a hero to me and to other aspiring writers. I am indebted to the incredible team at St. Martin's Press: Pete Wolverton, who fought for this book, found the answers when I couldn't, and ripped the Band-Aid off when necessary; Jennifer Donovan, whose attention to detail saved the day; Jen Enderlin, who was right all along about the title; Sophia Dembling, a copyediting savior; Ervin Serrano, who plucked an idea from my head and designed a cover I've waited my whole life for; Janna Dokos, Meryl Gross, Paul Hochman, Joe Brosnan, Kris Kam, and Omar Chapa, thank you for leaving your imprints on this book.

This is a book about the love of family: My mother-in-law, Linda Howerton, who inadvertently gave me the idea for this book, but truly inspired it based on her unwavering support for her family; my mother, Pam Finley, who would cross the stars for her sons and granddaughters; my brother Jason, for helping me talk through the specifics of alien technology; my late father,

Dr. John Finley, and my father-in-law, Robert Howerton, whose actions allowed me to write about heroic grandfathers. A reader once asked me how I knew so much about the love of grandmothers, and the answer is the women who were mine: the late Freda Finley Stephens and Christine "Teeny" Blondi.

To my wife, Rebecca, who endured seventeen years of late night and early morning typing and was the first to put my name on the spine of a book. Because of you, because of Eve and Charlotte, I am able to write about unconditional love.

To my earliest supporters and readers: Karyn Esbrook, Bill Applegate, Janet Smith, Jayme Robinson, Anna Beth McKeown, Amy Goodhart Koepsell, and Michelle and Mary Ann Gaffney. Thanks for believing. To my literature and English teachers, from elementary school to college, for opening the door.

While this is a work of fiction, I relied heavily on the research of people who are seeking the truth about the mysteries around us: The Mutual UFO Network, The National Investigations Committee on Aerial Phenomena, and the Aerial Phenomena Research Organization. And to Whitley Strieber and Carl Sagan, for paving the way.

My heroes have always been writers, and I could fill a book with my gratitude to them. J. T. Ellison resides at the very top. If there is a patron saint of aspiring thriller writers, you are he.

To the person who is both friend and family, Todd Doughty, who never, ever, gave up, even when I threatened to. I am forever grateful.